A WHITE WOLF REDISCOVERY TRIO

# T H R E E   I N   T I M E

THE WINDS OF TIME
BY CHAD OLIVER

THE YEAR OF THE QUIET SUN
BY WILSON TUCKER

THERE WILL BE TIME
BY POUL ANDERSON

FOREWORD BY ARTHUR C. CLARKE

JACK DANN, PAMELA SARGENT, GEORGE ZEBROWSKI SERIES EDITORS

Borealis is an imprint of White Wolf Publishing.

White Wolf Publishing
780 Park North Boulevard, Suite 100
Clarkston, GA 30021

World Wide Web Page: www.white-wolf.com

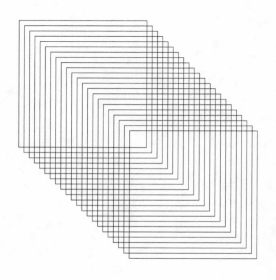

# CONTENTS

## ABOUT THIS SERIES:

The word "rediscovery" is almost a contradiction; you can only discover something once. But we all know what it means: people have forgotten and need to be reminded. Also, there are new readers, for whom discovery is still a possibility, even if the book was published a long time ago and forgotten. A book you haven't read is just as good as a new one published this year. The literature of science fiction has grown so incredibly rich and varied in this century that any group of reprints will inevitably fall short of what could be done to keep important works in print. White Wolf has undertaken to set this right, to the best of its resources. Future White Wolf Rediscovery Trios will include the themes of SPACE TRAVEL, POST APOCALYPSE FUTURES, and others. If you have suggestions, please make your views known by writing to the editors, and by supporting the series.

JACK DANN

PAMELA SARGENT

GEORGE ZEBROWSKI

SERIES EDITORS

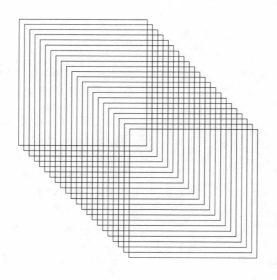

# FOREWORD

BY ARTHUR C. CLARKE

It has been said (I believe by Ted Sturgeon) that the Golden Age of Science Fiction is around 15. This locates me fairly accurately at the birth of *Astounding Stories*, and I have just been browsing through Mike Ashley's invaluable *The Complete Index to Astounding/Analog* to see what titles still ring a bell after more than sixty years.

A surprising number: how many, I wonder, of today's readers ever heard of Ray Cummings' "Beyond the Vanishing Point," "Phantoms of Reality," "Brigands of the Moon," and "Jetta of the Lowlands;" S.P. Meek's "Cold Light" and "Beyond the Heaviside Layer;" Charles W. Diffin's "The Power and the Glory" and "The Finding of Haldgren;" Arthur J. Burk's "Earth, the Marauder;" Murray Leinster's "The Fifth Dimension Catapult;" Paul Ernst's "World Behind the Moon" and "The Raid on the Termites;" Edmond Hamilton's "The Sargasso of Space;" Robert Wilson's "Out Round Rigel"…pardon me while I wipe away a manly tear and misquote Wordsworth: "Sweet in that dawn it was to be alive, But to be an S.F. fan was very heaven."

And though I have not looked at any of these tales for more than half a century, I am quite sure that many of them merit rereading—if only for historic interest, and as a reminder of the astonishing scientific progress we have been privileged to see in a single lifetime. "Beyond the Heaviside Layer"—I still recall a thrill that title once gave me! When I was a boy, such a locale seemed as remote and mysterious as Mars, or the other side of the Moon. Yet today, as I write these words, there are a dozen astronauts up there, probably complaining to NASA that the zero-gee toilet is giving problems once again.

I therefore welcome this new series, and the efforts of Jack Dann, Pamela Sargent and George Zebrowski to recover works that have been unjustly forgotten. I doubt if they comprise even 10% of the canon (Sturgeon again: "It's said that 90% of science fiction is crud—but then so is 90% of everything"). Well—would you believe 5% of noncrud?

The writers in these Trios have contributed disproportionately to that worthwhile 5%, and I am happy to see that most of them are still with us. And so, incredibly, is the writer whose 1930s tales epitomise the best of the era, and who is still going strong—Jack Williamson (born 1908). Perhaps today's retired Professor of English may be embarrassed if I remind him of his early works and of course much of their science is hopelessly dated—but across the decades I am still moved by the poignant ending of "The Moon

Era." It is indeed amazing how many ideas that are now tools of the trade originated with Jack—"terraforming" (he coined the very word), "ceetee" (contraterrene matter, created for the first time in late 1995 in the CERN Low Energy Antiproton Ring), parallel universes...and, perhaps most far-sighted of all, the danger that might be posed by benevolent robots whose prime directive was to serve Man. (Not, as in Damon Knight's little classic, broiled or fried.)

Another giant from that period was John Taine (Eric Temple Bell), whose "The Time Stream" also made an indelible impact on me. (Recently I was happy to assist his biographer Constance Reid to locate a long-lost branch of his family in Sri Lanka: see "The Search for E.T. Bell": *Mathematical Association of America*, 1993.) I still have the Buffalo Book Company edition of his masterpiece—the first hard-cover s.f. I ever bought (on 25th November 1946!), and even now the hair rises on the back of my neck when I read the opening paragraph:

We have explored to its remotest wildernesses a region that all but a few hold to be inaccessible to the human mind...a trivial accident precipitated events which time had been holding in suspension for ages.

If "The Time Stream" is out of print, I hope this deplorable omission is soon rectified.

Yet, when one considers that several science fiction (not to mention fantasy) novels are published *every day*, can such excavations from the genre's Early Bronze Age be justified? I hope so: to quote from my sadly missed friend Isaac Asimov's Foreword to this series' precursor: "Naturally, the revival of these classics will benefit the publisher, the editors, and the writers, but almost by the way. The real beneficiaries will be the readers, among whom the older are likely to taste again delicacies they had all but forgotten, while the younger will encounter delights of whose existence they were unaware."

Hear, hear...

Arthur C. Clarke
Columbo, Sri Lanka
1996 January 14

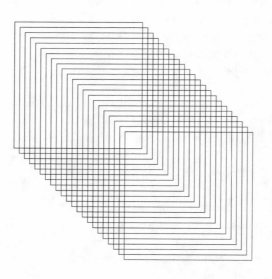

INTRODUCED BY GEORGE ZEBROWSKI

AFTERWORD BY WILLIAM F. NOLAN

# THE WINDS OF TIME

## BY CHAD OLIVER

# INTRODUCTION

In 1962, a student sat in the lunchroom of DeWitt Clinton High School (called "The Governor's Mansion" by the boys of the Bronx, New York). He was reading a paperback copy of this novel. He read somewhat skeptically, I recall, for he was growing fast, swallowing as many minds as he could; and he had been reading science fiction since 1958—a whole five years! Prove something to me, he was saying to this novel, because he hungered for more ambitious fare these days, and would need even better as time went on, I remember clearly.

"Hey, this is good!" a voice shouted inside him. He tried to control his enthusiasm; but as the chapters went by, the novel got even better. Its central situation of humanlike aliens stranded on Earth fifteen thousand years ago, unable to go home or anywhere else, except into time, was inspired. The boy was held by the emotions. He was moved, and felt grown up.

Today, a writer himself, what has survived of the boy reread this novel as one of the editors of this series. Would it hold up? Rereading was the honest thing to do if the book was to be reprinted. Hold your breath.

And the novel is just as good as it was! And so many other writers seem to have borrowed from it, the grown-up boy included. The writer marveled anew over the wonder of the central situation, which got even more intriguing when it invaded the daily life of an unhappy man from the twentieth century. Together, the young boy and the grownup again climbed inside the characters in unexpected ways. They found moody, poetic words as good as Bradbury, Simak, Clarke, and Heinlein; and time travel as it might actually happen!

❊

Chad Oliver belongs to that small, distinguished group of science fiction writers who are also scientists. The list includes Isaac Asimov, Arthur C. Clarke, Fred Hoyle, Gregory Benford, and others; but Chad Oliver was, and remains, the only anthropologist in the group. As such, he brought anthropology into science fiction. His training permeated all his novels and short fiction, in which he also achieved a compelling, graceful style of poetic, vigorous storytelling.

Science fiction's best and brightest gave Oliver's works an enthusiastic reception. Damon Knight, Frederik Pohl, Anthony Boucher, and Harlan Ellison, among others, all saw him as a major figure, the equal of Isaac Asimov, Arthur C. Clarke, or Robert A. Heinlein. Today, writers like Michael Bishop, Howard Waldrop, and Gregory Benford hold Oliver's work in high regard. Yet he never won an award for his science fiction, and publishers routinely mishandled his infrequent novels.

These began with *Mists of Dawn* (1952), a time travel story that helped set the standard for Winston's SF series for young readers. The novel presents a very sympathetic view of early humankind. The time travel adventure is thrillingly written, and even today it's a novel many readers finish in one sitting, as I did. It was one of the first SF novels I read.

*Shadows in the Sun* came out in 1954. J. Francis McComas, writing in the New York Times, called it "the best novel of the year." P. Schuyler Miller, writing in John W. Campbell's *Astounding Science*

*Fiction* for May 1955, named it the "best science fiction novel with an anthropological theme that I have seen." When the novel was reissued in the mid 1980s, Harlan Ellison wrote: "I have been an enthusiastic admirer of *Shadows in the Sun* since it was originally published. Among other virtues, it was one of the first genuine New Wave novels, and that long before there was a New Wave. Chad Oliver is among the most underrated writers in science fiction."

The New Wave appellation is a plausible one, because of Oliver's deep focus on character and place, on daily reality and emotional undercurrents. These are a feature of all of Oliver's fiction. He has the ability, in Damon Knight's observation, "to touch the heart of the human problem." But the science is just as real, and so the novel also belongs to the realm of genuine science fiction, even to the "hard SF" school, despite the fact that this description is too often unfairly claimed for science fiction based on physics, chemistry, biology, and astronomy. So-called "hard SF" too often fails to combine writerly virtues with genuine science fictional concerns, and the challenge to do so still faces most SF writers. Chad Oliver met it from the start.

*Shadows in the Sun* is thematically linked to two other novels about human-alien first contact. These are *Unearthly Neighbors* (1960) and *The Shore of Another Sea* (1971), in which the theme is carried forward, first to the idea that culture may be even more alien than biology, and finally to a confrontation with a "genuine other," an alien both biologically and culturally alien. These three novels make a trilogy about human-alien contact, and deserve to be read together. About *Unearthly Neighbors*, Frederik Pohl wrote: "Other science fiction writers have invented more 'alien' aliens than these for us to make contact with. Few, though, have been as able as Oliver to convince us that this is the way first contact is going to be." And more recently, Gregory Benford acknowledged that *The Shore of Another Sea* is "probably the best anthropological SF novel ever written—powerful, convincing, and dramatic."

But before completing his "aliens trilogy," Oliver published his third novel, *The Winds of Time* (1957), which also deals with human-alien contact; it also confronts the reader with the repetitious failure of human history, with time travel, and the human protagonist with difficult personal choices. It does not properly belong to the progression of the "aliens trilogy," which moves from understandable aliens to genuine others. In *Winds* we have a more Swiftian lament about humanity. We are presented with a Galaxy-wide problem for intelligent life: civilizations tend to destroy themselves when they reach their first romance with technology. The alien explorers have seen this again and again, and by the time they are stranded on Earth, they are beginning to wonder if our culture is also on its way out. Then, still hopeful, they think that perhaps they have arrived too early....

The novel received mixed but respectful reviews that admired its qualities but claimed that the whole did not measure up to the parts. Anthony Boucher, writing in *The Magazine of Fantasy and Science Fiction*, confessed to liking the novel more than he thought he should. After rereading the novel for this edition, I looked at some of these reviews and concluded that although I could see what they were getting at, they also showed a marked blindness to the novel's style, to its bitter but compassionate criticism of human failure, both personal and historical, against which Oliver pits a heroic hope for the future.

Throughout Oliver's career, no one seemed to notice how good a writer of prose he was. The influence of Hemingway is always clear— not the Hemingway of machismo and public posturing, but the Hemingway of sparely presented tenderness toward his characters' hopes, fears, and failures. Few commented on Oliver's elegance of line, the beauty of his emblematic SF imagery (a spaceship standing on the northern Asian steppe fifteen thousand years ago), or the thoughtfulness of the anthropologist writing with a sense of the puzzle of human history; and an anthropologist willing to consider that an alien culture might seem to be primitive, but might be in fact superior to the one making the judgment.

Humankind, for Chad Oliver, is an open problem of vast proportions, an unfinished project run by an only intermittently enlightened artisan, humanity itself. Either we will learn enough to help ourselves mature as a culture (we do this better as individuals at this point) or we will remain on a kind of historical treadmill (if we don't destroy ourselves). Oliver's novels combine this critical approach with anthropological insights, with a writer's careful attention to his own individual experience, and the result is a searching, probing science fiction in which "the science is as accurately absorbing as the fiction is richly human," in Anthony Boucher's words. This is the kind of writing that deserves the term *science fiction* because it delivers on its full, genuine meaning. It delivers a mature fiction that shows us the human impact of possible future changes. By depicting possible meetings between human and alien, Oliver asks what is a human being—and the answer is a form of intelligent life with a specific biological history and culture superimposed on the biology. The line between human and alien blurs. Intelligent life is the focus

Anthropologist Paul Ellery in *Shadows in the Sun* decides to stay on Earth rather than be educated by aliens, not because he wouldn't like to go, but *because it would be bad anthropology for him to go*; he would be exchanging one set of cultural problems for another, for ones that he would have to understand from scratch. Character, plot, and science move dramatically toward the novel's conclusion at the same time, with feeling and poetry, sparking implications left and right in the reader's mind. Compare this with Richard Dreyfuss donning a red suit and rushing to board a flying saucer in the film *Close Encounters* (a work that has more than a few echoes of Oliver's work in it, but less of his sophistication; a film that is sophisticated and Oliverlike is *Cocoon*). The final, moving validity of Paul Ellery's decision to remain on Earth in order to study himself and his own kind, is the kind of profound anthropological commitment that Chad Oliver found as a scientist and teacher. Suddenly we see, through Paul Ellery, and through Wes Chase in *The Winds of Time*, that cultures are angular views of the universe, and that their unique cultural perspectives are of vital importance, a reservoir from which others will have to draw in order to grow and survive and avoid stagnation. Paul Ellery chooses his humanity, knowing that at his moment of decision progress cannot be imported; to be real it must be won from within, in endless ways, just as understanding must be built up afresh in each individual. For Wes Chase, in *Winds*, he has come to the end of his personal life, to the end of his dealings with his own kind, and decides to voyage forward in time with the alien visitors, into a better future.

Howard Waldrop recently pointed out that Chad Oliver "mined just about all the first and second alien contact anthropological concerns that were or could be. When other writers stumbled over them, they found that Chad had been there first." This is true of the novels and also of his many short stories, novelettes, and novellas. *The Winds of Time* is not only about first contact, but a story in which time travel is a solution for the protagonist and a way out of the predicament of the alien visitors. Here we see real time travel, as it might be done, through biotiming. It is a sign of the novel's maturity that it is about the characters' "hard, hard choices and time travel the hard way."

*The Winds of Time* is an emotionally charged, magnificently written novel to which a new generation of readers will now have a chance to respond, and with which readers who know Oliver's work can make a new acquaintance. In my experience, Oliver's novels and stories are immensely rereadable, startling in the new responses, both emotional and intellectual, that they evoke, in addition to the sheer pleasure of their beauty. I have learned that if I have read an Oliver novel once, then I have not really read it. Come to think of it, what good is a novel one can only read once, a piece of music one can only hear once?

Unhappily, Chad Oliver never won an award as a science fiction writer. His two awards are for his historical novels, *The Wolf Is My Brother* (1967) and *Broken Eagle* (1989). His last novel, also historical, was *Cannibal Owl* (1994), and like *Broken Eagle*, it was shamefully neglected by its publisher. These books are of a piece with Oliver's science fiction, revealing the same anthropologist's sensibility and writerly concerns. If someone were to put a gun to my head and ask me what the bottom line about Oliver was to be, on pain of death, I would say, "He was just as good as Hemingway. Not better. Just as good. At least as good as Hemingway in *The Sun Also Rises*. Truly."

And as a science fiction writer there was no other like him.

George Zebrowski
May 4, 1996
Delmar, New York

# THE WINDS OF TIME

## BY CHAD OLIVER

TO CHUCK BEAUMONT AND BILL NOLAN
BECAUSE THE WORLD IS LIKE A FALCON

The cabin was a neat compromise. For the man, fed up to the gills with the stinks of the city and afflicted with the annual back-to-nature bug, it had yellow pine walls with prominent rustic knotholes. For the woman, resigned to another season of losing her husband to a series of glassy-eyed trout, it offered an electric refrigerator, moderately efficient gas stove, a shower with hot water, and inner-spring mattresses on the beds.

Weston Chase, pleasantly fueled with ham and eggs and three cups of coffee, had only one immediate aim in life: to get out of the cabin. He sat on the unmade bed and tied the laces of his old tennis shoes, then clapped a stained mouse-colored felt hat on his head and shrugged into a supposedly waterproof jacket. He stuffed chocolate bars and cigarettes into his pockets and picked up his tubular rod case and his trout basket.

Now, if only—

"Will you be long, hon?"

Too late, he thought. Now came the Dialogue. He knew what he would say, and he knew what his wife Joan would say. The whole thing had the massive inevitability of Fate.

"I'll be back as soon as I can, Jo."

"Where are you going?"

"Up the Gunnison, I think. Pretty rough going that way. Sure you wouldn't like to go?"

"Wes, there's nothing to *do* up there."

Weston Chase edged toward the cabin door.

Joan sighed audibly, shoved back her fourth cup of black coffee, and put down the paper with a flourish. (It was the Los Angeles *Times*, which caught up with them two days late.)

"Run along, hon," she said. "Mustn't keep the trout waiting."

He hesitated, smothering his guilt feelings. It *was* sort of a dirty deal for Jo, he supposed. He looked at her. With her blond hair uncombed and without her make-up on, she was beginning to show the years a little. She had refused to have any children, so she still had her figure, but her good looks were blurring a bit around the edges.

"I'll be back early," he said. "Tonight maybe we can go see Carter and Helen, play poker or bridge or something."

"Okay," Joan said. It was a neutral noise; she was Being a Good Wife, but not pretending to be ecstatic about it.

Wes kissed her briefly. Her mouth tasted of sleep and coffee.

He opened the door, stepped outside, and was a free man.

The thin air was clean and cold, and it hit him like a tonic. It was still early, with the Colorado sun wrestling with the gray morning clouds, and the deep breaths he took tasted of the night and stars and silence. He got the engine of his car running on the third try—the carburetor wasn't adjusted for mountain driving yet—and then switched the heater on.

He pulled out of the Pine Motel drive, vaguely annoyed by the two wagon wheels at the entrance, and drove back through Lake City. Lake City wasn't much to look at but, as always, it filled him with a nameless longing, a half conscious summer wish to get away from the smog and the traffic and settle down in a place where the world was fresh. His eyes told him the truth: Lake City was not precisely a ghost town, but the coffin was ready and the hole was dug. It was just a pale collection of wooden stores and houses at the foot of Slumgullion

Pass, kept more or less alive by tourists now that the silver mines were gone. The sign on the road outside of town claimed almost a thousand residents, but most of them must have been of the invisible variety.

But he watched the curls of blue smoke rising in the air and sensed the warmth behind the glass windows of the Chuck Wagon, where a tired girl was putting plates of ham and eggs on an old scarred counter. He saw three oldsters already swapping lies in front of the ramshackle post office, and he was honest enough to envy them their life.

His car hummed out of town, crossed the bridge, and sped into the morning along the Gunnison River. The Gunnison was blue and inviting, framed by snow-capped mountains and bordered by dense green brush and reddish strips of gravel. He opened the window and could hear the icy water chuckling and gurgling by the road. He knew the Gunnison, though; it was swift and deep and rugged. Wes cut off from the main road a mile outside of Lake City and drove over a dirt trail until he came to a small winding creek that tumbled down out of the mountains. He took the car as far as he could, and then parked it in the brush. He opened the door and climbed out.

There was only one sign that a man had ever been in this spot before—an empty, dirt-streaked jar that had held salmon eggs lying by a rock. He had tossed it there himself a week ago.

He smiled, feeling the years fall away like discarded clothing. He felt his heart eager in his chest, and his mind filled with warm, faraway images: a boy shooting tin cans on the Little Miami River in Ohio, building rock-and-clay dams on backyard creeks, snagging a sleepy catfish from a green river island…

He locked the car, gathered up his gear, and hit the path with a long, springy stride. He grinned at a jay squawking across the sky, caught just a glimpse of a doe fading into the brush ahead of him. The path angled upward through a valley of green and gold, choked with grass and flowers, and then climbed along the white-flecked stream into the mountains.

The trail was rough and little used, but he stuck with it. For the most part, he kept the stream on his right, but he had to cross it twice when the rocks and brush cut him off. The water was glacially cold and his tennis shoes squished when he walked. He knew there were trout in the creek, fanning their fins in the ripples and hovering in the black, shaded pools. There were enough of them so that he could count on getting seven or eight if he spent the day at it, and probably two of them would be pretty good rainbows. But today he wanted to do better than that. There was a tiny lake, fed by melting ice, up above timber line, and there the golden native trout were sleek and hungry, far from the hatcheries and the bewildered fish that were dumped into the more accessible streams and caught before they knew where they were.

The lake was almost fourteen thousand feet up, so most of the boys with the fancy equipment left it alone.

Wes climbed steadily, knowing he would be dog-tired before he got back down again, and not caring. His doctor's mind told him his body was in good shape, and he was reassured. The sun was still playing tag with grayish streaks of cloud, but he could feel his face burning a little in the thin air.

Around him, he was aware of magnificent scenery without looking at it directly: cool pines and stands of graceful aspens, their slender white trunks like cream in the sun. A miniature jungle of ferns and hidden insects, and a soft wind rustling through the trees. Once, the mournful cry of a wolf far above him.

If only a man could come here and live, he thought. If only he could forget his security and the string of runny noses that were his patients.

And then the trapping whisper of reason: *You'd freeze in the winter, Jo would hate it, where would your kids go to school if you had any kids....?*

It was eleven o'clock when he got above the timber line, and even the stately spruces were behind him. The path twisted through rocks and dark clumps of brush with startling green leaves. The stream was only some three feet across here, but fast and cold as it rushed with a sibilant *shhhhhhh* down from the lake.

The lake itself, when he finally reached it at twenty minutes past eleven, was nothing much to look at, unless you happened to be a fisherman. It was a flat pond, almost circular, perhaps one hundred and fifty feet across. The sun was almost directly overhead, and the water appeared dark green; the few spots that were rock-shadowed looked black. There was still ice on the peak that rose behind the pool, blinding in the sunlight.

It was as silent as though the world had just been created, fresh and clean and new.

Wes sat down on a rock, shivering a little. He wished the clouds would disperse for good, even though the fishing would be better if the sun weren't too bright. He wasn't tired—that would come later—but he was hungry. He wolfed down two chocolate bars, getting an almond fragment stuck in his teeth as usual, and drank some cold water from the stream where it ran out of the pond.

He slipped his brown fly rod out of its case and stuck it together firmly. He took the black reel from his trout basket and clipped it into place. He squinted at the leader, decided it was okay, and tied on two coachman flies. Probably the salmon eggs would do better in the deep water, but there was plenty of time.

He stood up, lit a cigarette, and maneuvered himself into position: shielded on one side by rocks, but with a clear space behind him for casting.

The world held its breath.

He flicked the flies with an easy wrist motion and they patted the water to his right, only five feet from shore. He left them a moment, two specks of brown and red resting on the green surface of the water. There was a slight wind ripple on the pond; otherwise, all was still.

He tried again, letting out more line and casting straight out in front of him. Nothing. He drew the line back, wiggling the flies in the water—

Strike!

A flash of flame-colored fins, a heavy shadow beneath the surface, and the flies disappeared. The line tautened, the fly rod bent double and jerked with a life of its own.

Wes excitedly muttered a crackling string of choice swear words, directed at nothing in particular, and backed away from the lake. A bad spot to use the net, just toss him out on the rocks—

There! The trout broke water and tried to snag the line on a boulder. Wes kept the line tight, waited until the trout relaxed just a trifle, and heaved.

He had him. The trout flopped on the rocks, the fly worked out of his mouth—

Wes snatched off his hat with his left hand and dived for the fish, clapping the hat over him like a basket. Carefully he reached under the hat, grabbed the trout, and broke its neck with one quick jerk.

He sat on the rocks, grinning idiotically, admiring his catch. It was a nice one—a good fourteen inches, and heavy with firm flesh. Wes popped him in the basket, fastened the buckle, and shook out his line.

"Won't get skunked today," he said, exhilarated out of all proportion to what had happened. What was it about a fish, anyhow, that made him feel like a kid again? The thought died in birth; he didn't care why it made him happy. It *did*, and that was enough.

He advanced on the pond again with a sure instinct that today was his day to shine. He forgot everything: food, rest, promises to Jo. Every atom of his being was concentrated on the trout in the pool. Every fish he caught stimulated him to want more.

For Wes Chase time ceased to exist.

The trout basket grew heavy against his hip.

His wet feet ached, but he didn't feel them.

He noticed the gray clouds that filled up the sky around the mountain peak only because the fishing was even better now that the water was shadowed and restless.

At four o'clock in the afternoon the storm hit with a paralyzing suddenness. He was taken utterly by surprise as the pond before him was instantly transformed into a pitted black mass of excited water. He felt a numbness in his wrist where something icy rested. He looked around, trying to adjust himself to a change that had caught him thoroughly flat-footed.

Hail.

It wasn't rain, but hail—round pelting chunks of ice that seemed to materialize on all sides, blanketing the rocks and plunking into the water. It was very still; there was no wind.

At first he wasn't afraid. He was annoyed, and that was all. He picked his way back to where he had left his rod case, took the rod apart, and put it in the tube. The hail got under his collar, melted, and trickled down his back.

He noticed two things: it was darker than it should have been, and he was cold. His first thought was of shelter, but the unhappy fact was that there wasn't any. He was above the timber line, and there wasn't even a tree to break the hail.

He stood up straight, trying to make as small a target as possible. He wished fervently that his hat had a wider brim on it; he could hear the hail pocking into the felt, and the crown was already getting soggy.

He remembered an abandoned miner's cabin back down the trail. Its roof had collapsed, but the four walls were more or less intact, unless his memory was tricking him. No matter—the cabin was a good two miles away, and the hail was so thick he could hardly see the trail.

The storm got worse.

A cutting wind came up, sweeping out of the north, slashing the hail against his face. He stuck his red, numbed hands in his pockets and held the rod case under his arm. He raised his head and looked around almost desperately.

There was nothing. The slick rocks were blanketed with hail, and the world that had seemed so inviting a few hours earlier now presented a bleak aspect indeed. He checked his watch. Four-twenty. It would take him two hours to make the car under the best of conditions, and he wasn't anxious to try that path in the dark. He waited, shivering, but in ten minutes the hail showed no sign at all of letting up.

He turned his back to the wind and managed to get a cigarette going on the fifth match. Then he squinted his eyes and fumbled his way to the path that led along the rushing stream, back down the mountain. He was decidedly miserable, and more than willing to concede that civilization wasn't so bad after all.

If he could just *get* to it.

The hail rattled down with a vengeance, and Wes began to worry about his glasses. If they broke, he would be in a bad fix for following a mountain trail. He tried to keep his head down, but that exposed his neck.

He tried to increase his pace, and promptly slipped on the hailstones and fell on his back. He got up, unhurt but touched by panic.

*Slow down*, he thought. *Take it easy.*

It was hard to see. He couldn't just follow the stream because the rocks and brush barred his way. If he could remember which side of the stream the path was on—

He couldn't. He floundered along what he had thought was the trail, and it just stopped against a rock wall. The wind was whistling now, the hail the worst he had ever seen. He looked at his watch.

A quarter to five.

It would be dark in an hour unless the clouds lifted.

He tried to retrace his steps and fell again, landing in a clump of wiry brush that scratched his face.

*Wouldn't do to bust a leg. No one knows where I am.*

He stopped, shielded his eyes, tried to spot something, anything.

There.

Above him.

Was that a rock shelter, that shadow beneath the ledge?

He put down his rod case and trout basket and scrambled up the rocks. He ripped his trouser leg, but he couldn't feel a thing. The stinging hail was right in his face and he lost his hat. He flopped over a ledge—like a fish, he thought wildly—and scrambled into the hollow made by a rock overhang.

The wind still cut at him. He bent over double and squeezed his way toward the back of the rock shelter. He saw an opening—not a big one, but large enough to admit his body.

A cave?

He didn't care what it was.

He took a deep breath, felt ahead to make sure there wasn't a drop, and squirmed inside.

CHAPTER

It was too dark for him to see clearly, but it was dry. He fumbled in his shirt pocket under the jacket, took out a match, and struck it. He held it above his head, trying to make out where he was.

The tiny light didn't do much good. He must be in a cavern of some sort, he reasoned; he could see only one side of it, although the ceiling was within easy reach. Something gleamed with a metallic reflection about fifteen feet behind him—a vein of ore, probably.

The match went out.

He listened, ready to translate the slightest scrabble or scratch into wolves, snakes, or other charming companions. He heard nothing. There was only a hard, dust-covered silence in the cave. He thought: *I may be the first man in the world who has ever been in here.*

Ordinarily, the notion would have given him considerable pleasure; as it was, he was too miserable to be impressed. He was wet, cold, and tired. There was nothing he could make a fire with. Outside, a scant two yards from his head, the storm was cutting loose with an icy, persistent ferocity.

And it was getting dark.

*Why didn't I bring a flashlight?* He thought of those cheerful cartoon ads in which deep-sea divers, bear hunters, and dauntless young executives were inevitably saved by good reliable flashlight batteries. Suppose you didn't *have* a flashlight? Could you throw the batteries at the enemy?

He laughed, felt a little better, and lit a cigarette. The smoke, at least, was warm. His patients were always asking him about lung cancer, and he always answered them solemnly. Just the same, he stuck to his tobacco.

He made plans, shifting his position to get a sharp rock out of his side. He would stay here all night if he had to; the storm couldn't go on forever. Then get back to the car, drive to the cabin, and tell Jo what had happened. Then a hot shower, breakfast with steaming-hot coffee, and a round of antibiotics from his bag. He had plenty of free samples, fortunately. The drugstore in Lake City was probably still in the blackstrap molasses and yogurt era.

Was his throat already getting raw, or was that imagination?

*Physician, heal thyself.*

Two cigarettes later and it was six o'clock. Night had fallen outside in the storm, and a deeper blackness crawled inside the cave around him. There was a change in the sound of the storm; he heard a hissing and a gurgling that must mean that the hail had turned to rain. A hard, driving rain. He knew from past experience that the water would be gushing down the mountain trail two or three inches deep. It would make for treacherous going at best. He would never make it at night without a broken fibula or so, and that would be a pretty picnic.

He peeled the paper from a candy bar and ate the chocolate slowly. He decided to save the remaining two for breakfast before he started down the mountain in the morning.

He was already stiff and sore, and he knew that a night on the rock floor of the cavern would do nothing to loosen him up. But he *was* tired. Maybe if he could doze a little the time would pass more quickly.

He twisted around on the rocks to find a more comfortable position and discovered that there *were* no comfortable positions. He wadded up his handkerchief for a pillow and closed his eyes.

The storm roared wetly outside, but it was a steady sound, almost soothing…

He slept.

He tossed fitfully on the hard floor of the cave, asleep and yet somehow aware that time was passing. He held on to sleep almost consciously, as though a part of him knew that it was easier than waking up in the cold.

And then, quite suddenly, he was fully, intensely awake.

Something had awakened him.

What?

He lay very still, listening. The rain had stopped, and the world outside was hushed and dripping. Pale moonlight filtered into the cavern, touching it with ghostly silver.

He checked his watch. Two o'clock.

*There.* A sound: a muffled click, like a metal latch.

It was inside the cave with him.

He held his breath, his aches and pains forgotten. His eyes searched the cave, seeking—

Another sound. A rasping scratch, like a fingernail on a blackboard. From behind him, where the cavern wall glinted a little with a metallic sheen.

An animal?

His eyes tried to pierce the gloom. He could *almost* see in the half-light, but details were fuzzy. He was filled with a nameless, irrational dread. All at once there was no civilization, no science, no knowledge. There was only himself, alone, and a primeval darkness choked with horror.

He rolled over as quietly as he could. He got up on all fours and crawled toward the cave entrance. He put one hand outside, grasping for a hold on the damp rock.

Then he heard it.

It was something *opening.*

He looked back.

Someone—something—was walking out of a hole in the cavern behind him. It was tall—it had to bend over to keep from hitting the roof of the cave. It had a cadaverous face, pasty white. It had eyes—

It saw him.

It came after him.

Wes Chase couldn't think; his mind was paralyzed. But his muscles could act, and did. He threw himself out the cave opening, scrambled down the rock shelter. He listened for the stream, swollen with rain, and ran for it.

He found the stream, almost black in the silver blue of the moonlight. He spotted the trail, a deeper darkness in the rocks. He plunged down it as fast as he could go. He slipped, almost fell, caught himself on some tough strands of brush.

*Slow down*, he thought. *You'll kill yourself.*

He looked back over his shoulder. He saw only a pale lunar world. He heard nothing but falling water and long, long silences. He turned his attention to the trail again, picking his way as carefully as he could.

*Get down in the trees, at least. Hide.*

A shiver trembled over him uncontrollably. He had *seen* that face, there was no question about that. He hadn't been dreaming, and he wasn't crazy. He didn't bother pinching himself; he was sore enough without that.

He kept moving as fast as he dared. He had to cross the stream, and it was high and turbulent. The icy water soaked him up to his hips. His tennis shoes squished on the rocks.

*Get hold of yourself, boy.*

He picked up a sharp rock and kept it in his hand. What had that thing *been*? He wasn't superstitious, at least ordinarily, and he had seen enough corpses to be assured that they didn't do much strolling around. Okay. The thing looked like a man, so it must *be* a man. But what was it—he still couldn't think of it as he—doing there? Another fisherman? Surely he would have seen him, or heard him. A hermit? Ridiculous—he couldn't survive long in this country, not without a house and wood for a fire.

Wes began to get mad. He had left a basket full of golden trout up there, to say nothing of his rod and his hat. But he wasn't about to turn around and go back. The man had been big, perhaps a lunatic of some kind. Get some help, maybe, and then go up there in the daylight and see what was going on....

He heard a noise to his right.

The stream?

Some animal?

He increased his pace, holding the rock tightly in his hand. It was faster going down than coming up. He should reach the timber line in a minute or two. Should he keep going, try for the car? He was warming up now, feeling a little better, but it would be cold when he stopped, and more than three hours until sunrise.

He decided on the car.

He settled into a steady, loose-jointed walk, almost a trot. His feet squished and slipped, but he kept his balance. Time was healing the shock a little now.

*Must be some natural explanation. An airplane crash? Maybe I should have said something, tried to help....*

But he kept moving.

Trees began to loom up around him, and he caught the lush smell of wet pines. The moonlight was filtered now, and shadows tricked him on the path. He forded the stream again, kept going.

The path twisted sharply to the right.

Wes took the curve almost at a run, then stopped as though he had slammed full-tilt into a brick wall.

The same man was waiting for him on the trail.

He stood there, not moving, only half revealed by the chilled radiance of the moonlight. His face was as dead white as it had seemed in the cave. He was tall, taller than Wes, and thin. His eyes were living shadows in the pallor of his face.

"Who are you?" Wes called. His voice was higher than he had intended. "What do you want?"

The man said nothing. The brook gurgled in the night.

"Talk, damn you! What the hell're you trying to pull?"

No answer.

Wes steadied himself, gripped the rock in his hand. He was not going to run back up the mountain again. "Get out of my way," he said.

The man—if such he was—did not move.

Wes had been a reasonably creditable halfback in his high school days, and he had run over bigger men than this. He took his glasses off, put them in his trouser pocket, where they wouldn't be hit directly. Then he squinted, took a deep breath, and rushed the man standing in the trail, his rock ready to swing.

Quite calmly the man raised his arm. He had something in his hand. The something gave a soft *choog* and Wes Chase found himself flat on the ground, his face actually touching one of the man's shoes. He had never seen a shoe like it before.

He seemed to be fully conscious, but he could not move. He heard his heart thudding in his chest. He could not feel the ground under him. He was suddenly peaceful, peaceful beyond all reason. It was the peace of a dream, where nothing mattered, for soon you would wake up and it would all go away…

It didn't go away.

The man—it *must* be a man—did not speak. He picked Wes up and tossed him onto his shoulder, not urgently, but with a singular lack of concern. *Like a sack of potatoes,* Wes thought.

The man began to climb back up the mountain. *I weigh almost two hundred pounds, he can't possibly lug me all the way to the top.*

But he was doing it. He gasped for breath and set Wes down every few hundred yards while he rested, but he kept going. Wes watched the trees fade out and the rocks begin, and he saw the moon, alone and cold and remote in the night.

Slowly, determinedly, they climbed toward the glacial lake. They turned off toward the rock shelter. Wes saw his trout basket still lying where he had dropped it, and irrelevantly thought that the fish would still be good because it had been so cold. He saw his rod case, too, but his hat, wherever it had fallen, was outside his field of vision.

The man went into the cave first and pulled Wes in after him. Then he dragged him some fifteen feet across the cave floor, to where Wes had first seen the metallic reflection he had thought was a vein of ore.

*Not ore. Door.*

The man opened a concealed port that looked like the hatch of a submarine. Pale radiance, not unlike the moonlight outside, spilled into the cavern. The man went through the port and pulled Wes after him.

Then he shut the port. Wes heard the distinct click as it locked.

The man dragged him into a semblance of a sitting position against one wall and then backed off. Wes tried to move, but failed. He had no sensation of pressure where he sat or where he leaned against the wall. He was dead from the neck down.

But his eyes worked. He looked around as best he could.

He was in a large rock vault, perhaps forty yards across at its deepest point. It was apparently a natural cave of some sort, although it had been cleared of all debris until it was rather featureless.

And, of course, it had been sealed off from the world by that curious entry port.

It was utterly silent except for the sound of breathing—his own and the man's.

The vault was not empty. That was the worst part. Wes knew that his normal reactions had been somehow inhibited, but he felt a tendril of apprehension at what he saw in the far wall.

There were niches cut into the rock.

Five of them.

The light was not good in the chamber, coming as it did from tubes like flashlights, but he could see that there were bodies in four of the slots. The fifth one was empty, but it was no great feat of mental gymnastics to figure out who had been there before.

Forget about an airplane crash, then.

Forget about hermits.

Forget about fishermen.

The man looked at him, his white face expressionless. He glanced at the figures in the niches, as though checking.

Then the man moved toward Wes, his eyes very bright, and stretched out his hands.

Wes Chase could not move.

The moment was intolerable, and it would not end. The cave, the niches, the hands—all were razor-sharp in his mind. He had seen many men die, and had often wondered, rather casually, how death would come to him. His life did not flash through his brain. Instead, a moment out of time was pinpointed and a line he had read in college shouted at him, insanely, over and over:

*This is the way the world ends, this is the way the world ends, this is the way—*

But it wasn't.

Incredibly, the man's hands touched him and were gentle; there was no malice in them. Wes looked into the man's eyes. They were a clear gray, and he could read nothing in them. The face was a human face—there was a human skull under that flesh. Wes ticked them off: mandible, maxilla, zygomatic arch, nasal cavity, orbits, frontal bone…

And yet the face was a face unlike any other he had ever seen. It was pasty in its skin texture, but that wasn't the important thing. The proportions were odd in a way he could not define. And the *expression*. Eyes bright, skin taut, thin lips open, breathing fast—

Hate?

Hunger?

Hope?

The hands went over him lightly. His pockets were emptied. His watch was taken from his wrist. The gold wedding ring on his finger was examined, then left where it was. The man was looking for something, Wes was certain of that. But what?

The loot was something less than sensational. A brown billfold Jo had given him for Christmas a year ago. Some loose change—a quarter, two nickels, four pennies. A black comb, not too clean and with one tooth missing; Wes had been meaning to get a new one at the drugstore. A key ring with three keys on it. One was for his car, one for his home on Beverly Glen off Sunset, and one for his Westwood office. Two packs of cigarettes, one of them crumpled and almost empty. A folder of paper matches, also pretty well shot. Two chocolate bars wrapped in shiny paper. A couple of trout flies and a stray, faded salmon egg. No handkerchief—Wes remembered that he had used that for a pillow; it was probably still over there on the rocks.

The man sat down on the cave floor and examined the things intently. Intently? It was more than that. He studied them with an eagerness that bordered on desperation.

The watch seemed to interest him the most. He held it to his ear and listened to it tick. He fiddled with it uncertainly, then wound it a little and moved the hands. He shook his head as though he were disappointed.

*It's a good watch. What's wrong with it?*

The man turned his attention to the billfold next. He took four dollar bills out of it and studied them. He rubbed them with his fingers. He hesitated, then placed the bills in a pile with the coins. He rifled the rest of the billfold carefully, frowning at the assortment of cards, licenses, and the like. There was one photograph, in color, of Jo. Wes remembered the picture well—it had been taken three years ago, on her birthday. Jo had been wearing a tweed skirt and a brown cashmere sweater; she looked fresh and clean and young. A pang of regret stabbed through Wes, cutting through the haze of the drug. But it passed, he couldn't hold it. Dimly he recognized that it was just as well.

The man took a cigarette out of the pack that was already open, sniffed it, tore the paper off, and looked at the tobacco. He tasted it, frowned, and rubbed it off his tongue with his wrist. He picked up the matches, nodded to himself, and struck one on the first try. He watched it burn down almost to his fingers, then blew it out.

He looked at the keys, tossed them into a pile with the dollar bills and the coins. Then he picked up one of the candy bars and scratched it experimentally with a fingernail. His eyes brightened. With a feverish excitement he ripped the paper off and stared at the brown chocolate with the almond lumps. He hesitated, clearly fighting with himself about something.

The man got up, paced the rock floor, fingering the chocolate bar nervously. Twice he made motions as though he were going to eat it, but each time he hesitated, caught himself, stopped.

*He doesn't know whether or not it's edible. Where can he be from if he's never seen a chocolate bar before?*

The man came to some decision. He broke off two squares of chocolate, knelt down by Wes, and gently opened the doctor's mouth. Then he crumbled the chocolate between his fingers, threw an almond away, and placed the shredded chocolate on Wes's tongue, a little at a time. Wes started to gag, and was unable to chew. But he could swallow, if he took it easy, and he got the chocolate down.

*Guinea pig,* he thought. He remembered the little test animals in their cages on the top floor of the hospital. He remembered, too, one of the daughters of old Doc Stuart—Louise, her name had been—and how shocked she was when she found out that the guinea pigs were injected with disease strains to see what would happen....

The chocolate was good, anyway.

The man sat down and made an obvious effort at self-discipline. He sat quietly, watching and waiting. Several hours must have gone by, but it was difficult now for Wes to keep track of the time.

The man got up finally, felt Wes's forehead, looked at his eyes and his tongue. And he smiled. The effect was startling, as though a movie monster had paused momentarily in his dimwitted pursuit of the dim-witted heroine and tossed off a minstrel joke or two.

Then the man ate the chocolate bars.

Ate them?

He *demolished* them, swallowing convulsively, as a man trapped in a desert might hurl himself into a stream, desperate for water.

The man smiled again and rubbed his hands together in a curiously out-of-place gesture of satisfaction. A little color appeared in his pale cheeks. Even his black and rather lank hair seemed to lose some of its lifelessness.

Evidently encouraged by his new-found energy, the man went to work with a will. He put Wes down on the rock floor and carefully undressed him, taking mental note of every button, buckle, and zipper. He covered Wes up with his own clothing, and then struggled to dress himself in his new clothes. He managed it, though not without a few muttered sounds that might very well have been swearing of some sort. Wes was surprised to see that his clothes were not a bad fit at all; apparently the man was not as tall as he looked.

The man stuffed his pockets, paying special attention to the money, and slipped the watch over his wrist. He seemed nervous again, but determined.

*He's going to Lake City,* Wes thought, and was suddenly warm with hope. *He's done his best, but he still doesn't look like the All-American Boy. Somebody's bound to notice him. Somebody's bound to recognize those clothes. Jo will have called the police by now, they'll be watching...*

The man opened the port and went out into the cave. The port clicked shut behind him.

Wes still could not move. He lay on his back, covered by the man's clothing, and out of the corner of his eye he could just see the niches in the far wall, where the four silent bodies slept.

He hoped *they* didn't wake up.

Even through the fog of the drug doubts assailed him. Would the man actually *get* to Lake City? It would be a pretty fair walk if he didn't spot the car. Could he drive? If he had never seen a chocolate bar, had he ever seen an automobile?

Suppose he made it to Lake City. The police would be looking for Wes, not for a man they had never seen. Would they spot his clothes? After all, they were just the standard fisherman's rig. The trousers were torn a little, but there was nothing very unusual about that. And the hat was missing, unless the man picked it up on the way. The car was the best bet, the car with the California plates. If he took it—

How odd would a man have to look before a merchant would call the police? If Wes were running a drugstore and that man came in, what would he think? Probably just write him off as a weirdie and let it go at that. Remember, during the war, the two guys in Nazi uniforms who strolled through Times Square, or wherever it was…

Time seemed to be passing rapidly. Wes was not quite asleep, but not completely awake either. It was as though he had a slight fever, dozing in bed, waiting for a cold to go away.

He knew what the man was after in town, or thought he did. He was obviously starving. If Wes had been in that position, he would have tried to buy some food, and it seemed reasonable to suppose that the man would think along the same lines. But there were only four dollars in that billfold. If the man was figuring on stocking up on provisions, he was in for a rude surprise.

Wes felt suddenly cold. It was not so very far from here, back in the old days, where a miner had gotten snowed in for the winter with three companions, without enough food to go around. When spring came, the miner came out of the cabin alone, sleek and well fed. The story was that he had died in the penitentiary, a confirmed vegetarian....

If the man couldn't get enough supplies in town, then what?

Wes tried to turn his thoughts to more pleasant subjects.

That turned out to be not so easy, however. No matter where he started, his thoughts always came back to the man, to say nothing of his four snoozing companions. Who were they? Where could they have come from?

And what did they *want*?

In spite of himself Wes had to admire the man. Looked at through his own eyes, he was doing a brave and remarkable thing—even a fantastic thing. He seemed to be utterly alien, completely unfamiliar with even such a common article as a chocolate bar. He either did not know English or refused to speak it. Presumably Wes looked just as strange to him as he did to Wes. And yet he was willing to put on another man's clothes and try to find his way to a town where he could buy food he had never seen before with money he couldn't possibly understand.

The man was having his troubles too.

Somehow that made Wes feel a little better.

He dozed off, fell into an uneasy sleep.

He was awakened by the click of the port when it opened. The man hurried through and closed the port behind him. He looked utterly exhausted, and he was trembling violently. Wes tried to get up, and still couldn't move.

The man looked at Wes—how? Angrily? Hopelessly? He put down a cardboard box he was carrying and unpacked it. It was pitiful, even to Wes. Four loaves of bread. Two cans of asparagus. And about fifty assorted candy bars.

Looking very pale again, the man stretched out on the rocks next to Wes, sighed a little, and went to sleep. He snored.

There was nothing to look at. Wes felt that by now he had memorized every detail of the vault, from the dark shapes in the niches to the cracks on the rocks that hemmed him in. He was no longer tired, and he thought his mind was somewhat clearer. Oddly, his terror had left him. He was still afraid, still uncertain, but the whole affair had taken on a remote dreamlike quality, in which nothing was played for keeps and everything would somehow be all right in the end.

He recognized the symptoms of shock in himself.

*That means the stuff is wearing off. If I can just get hold of myself before he wakes up—*

He waited. There was nothing else to do.

He thought of the sleeping man next to him. He had made it to Lake City, evidently. Had he walked or taken the car? He had bought some things, and that must have involved some experimentation with the money. Surely, *surely*, he had created a stir in Lake City. Sooner or later someone would make the connection with Wes, if he hadn't done so already. And then—

Could they find him?

And what would they find? A living man—or something else?

The time passed very slowly. Wes thought he was coming out of it a little, but not fast enough. And when the man at his side woke up, Wes could still do no more than move his head a trifle from side to side.

*Here we go again.*

The man got up and looked closely at Wes. Wes lay very still, almost holding his breath. The man smiled a little and touched his shoulder in what Wes interpreted as a reassuring gesture.

*Or is he just picking out a haunch?*

The man stretched and ate two candy bars, not with any very obvious relish. Then he walked over to the niches and examined the forms that still slept in them. He watched them for a long time, touched one of them gently.

There was no response.

Wes was glad of it.

He didn't know *what* would come out of that niche, and he was in absolutely no hurry to find out.

The man took out the gun, the same one he had used on Wes. He checked it carefully, reset a dial on the butt end of it.

He licked his lips.

Wes suddenly got very cold, but recovered himself promptly.

*Stop thinking about it! You're making it worse!*

In a somewhat more objective frame of mind Wes realized what the man was going to do. It was obvious enough. No matter how alien the man looked, his thought processes were not by any means impossible to follow. If he couldn't buy enough food for a decent meal, he had to get it some other way.

Therefore he was going hunting.

The man went out again through the portal, taking his gun with him.

Wes was decidedly curious despite his position. If the man were just after food, and if he could really use that gun for hunting, why go all the way to Lake City in the first place? There was plenty of game in these mountains, especially if you weren't overly particular what you were eating. Wouldn't it have been simpler just to bag a deer or something right off the bat?

*But I don't think he knew how far away Lake City was. And maybe he was after something more important than food.*

What?

Information, of course.

*He's trying to find out something about us. I'm positive he's never seen a man like me before. He's looking for something.*

What? And why?

The man was gone a long time. When he came back he had fresh meat with him, already skinned and cleaned. It looked like a wolf. He had also carried back some dead wood and twigs, so he must have been down below timber line.

He built a fire very carefully, using bark for paper. He lit it with one of the matches he had taken from Wes, and it caught at once. It was just a small blaze, but Wes could feel its warmth. He noticed that the smoke was carried out through the top of the vault; there must be an air duct of some sort up there.

The man sliced off four steaks with a knife Wes had not seen before, and began to roast them on the end of sticks. Juices dropped into the fire and sizzled.

Wes could smell the meat cooking. His mouth literally watered, and he was suddenly desperately hungry.

When the steaks were done, the man went to work on one. There was nothing now of the gulping haste he had shown with the first candy bars. He took his time, chewing each piece thoroughly, savoring every bit of it. The pallor in his face was much less marked now than when Wes had first seen him.

He got up and took the metallic gun from the pocket of the jacket he had borrowed from Wes. Once more he reset the dial on the butt.

He aimed it at Wes's shoulder.

The gun made a whispered *choog*.

Wes tried to brace himself, but felt nothing.

The man waited.

And then, slowly, incredibly, feeling flowed back into Wes's body. It felt like ice water. His skin prickled and itched. He tried to move his arm, and the effort was agony, as though his arm had been asleep and he had suddenly smacked it against a door.

He began to shake violently.

He was coming out of it.

The man watched, and waited, and said nothing at all.

CHAPTER

It was like being born again.

Weston Chase could feel the life coming back to him, and life was a million icy needles in his veins. Sometimes it was better to be only half alive. When you were sick enough you didn't feel the pain. When you got well enough to hurt and to remember, things got tough.

He lay on the cave floor and wanted to scream. Perhaps he did; he couldn't be sure. He was sick and miserable and empty. His mouth tasted like stale tobacco smoke. His skull ached as though there were a knife in it. His body was so sore he couldn't even crawl.

But that was only physical.

He could take that.

But the *other* things—

He was in a cave with a maniac, or worse. And Jo didn't know where he was, *nobody* knew where he was. How long had he been here? What was Jo thinking? Surely she would know he hadn't just run out on her—or would she?

Images blinked on and off like slides in his brain. Jo with her swimming pool he had been so sarcastic about. The kid next door who had fallen off his bicycle, the blood on his head, and Jo helping him fix the boy up. A nice boy, the son he had always wanted. And Jo that night in her house, the year before they were married—

Jo.

He groaned, he wanted to cry like a baby. God, this was fantastic, a nightmare, it couldn't happen—

A pale hand slipped under him.

He was pulled into a sitting position. The white, strange face was next to his.

*Dracula,* Wes thought hysterically. *I'm in a damn silly vampire movie. Garlic! Where's the garlic?*

He laughed. When he heard himself he stopped.

The pale man hooked something over Wes's ears. Glasses. His glasses. Then he opened Wes's mouth and put something in it. Wes choked, started to chew. His jaws didn't work properly, but rich juices trickled down his throat, warming him. Meat. Tough, but sweet and clean.

The man fed him, and Wes ate. He swallowed one steak and half of another before he was through, telling himself he should take it easy but being too hungry to care. Then the man gave him some cold water from a skin bag.

"Thanks," Wes said. His voice was a croak.

The man nodded, but said nothing. He went back to work on his own meal, chewing slowly and thoughtfully, as though making up for lost time. Wes lay on the floor, feeling a drowsy strength flow back into him. Now was his chance, he thought. Get up, slug that man, get out somehow—

Before he could frame much of a plan he was asleep. He did not dream. He had no way of telling how long he slept, but he awoke refreshed. He opened one eye.

The man was watching him, smiling a little. The man took his arm, helped him up. Wes was dizzy, but he could stand. The man took him step by step over to the circular port that was the only exit to the vault. He stood him against it, then backed off and sat down on the floor.

*Free. I'm free. He's letting me go.*

Desperately Wes fumbled at the projections on the port. He pulled them, pushed them, twisted them, hit at them with his fists. Nothing happened. He put his shoulder against the port and pushed. The circular door did not move. He backed off, ran at it blindly.

It was, literally, like running into a stone wall.

He collapsed, sobbing.

The man picked him up, gave him another drink of water. Then he looked at Wes and shook his head. The meaning was clear enough. Wes couldn't get out unless the man let him out.

And Wes suspected it would be a sub-arctic afternoon in hell before *that* happened.

The man sat down and gave Wes a cold piece of steak. Wes ate it without thinking. His mind was a perfect blank, holding the terror out.

Then the man leaned forward. He pointed at himself. "Arvon," he said slowly and distinctly. His voice was low and calm.

Wes hesitated. Then he nodded, pointed at himself. "Wes," he said. "Wes Chase."

The man smiled eagerly.

In a way that was the real beginning.

Wes Chase didn't know a phoneme from a hole in the ground, and if he had ever heard of a lexicon he would have vaguely associated it with a Roman lawgiver. Linguistics hadn't exactly been all the rage of the campus when Wes was taking pre-med at Ohio State, and the medical school at the University of Cincinnati had emphasized practical subjects.

Of course, a man never knew what was going to be practical and what wasn't. This wasn't the first time that Wes had regretted the pressures of a busy life, a life that nibbled you to death with schedules and telephones and appointments and runny noses. If only there were time to find out a few things, to read, to listen…

But it was a little late now.

Wes *did* know, from his agonizing battle with Latin and the damnable tripartite division of Gaul, that learning a language was apt to be a losing proposition even under the best of circumstances. When a man had to learn a language from scratch, without the medium of a common language to explain things in, it should take a spell.

It did.

Nevertheless, Arvon learned with incredible rapidity. He made no attempt to teach Wes his own language, whatever *that* might have been, but concentrated on mastering English. He started with nouns, things that could be pointed to: cave, shirt, shoes, meat, candy. He kept a list of words, writing them down on a curious sort of tablet, and Wes soon caught on to the fact that Arvon was not so much after the words themselves as he was interested in the significant sounds that went into them. He used recording symbols Wes had never seen before, but he assumed that they were phonetic marks of some type. He started with hundreds, marking every tone and pause and inflection, but rapidly whittled his alphabet down to a realistic series of marks as he discovered what counted in English and what didn't. Then he went on to the structure of the language, the way the word units were strung together. When he got the hang of the agent-verb-object series, his progress was rapid.

Still, it took time.

There was time to be bored, even in this uncanny, impossible vault in the rock of a Colorado mountain. There was time to eat fresh meat and fish until he was sick of them. There was time to be impatient, and worry, and be afraid.

There was too much time to remember the life he had cherished so little—the life that waited for him now at the foot of a winding trail, where an icy trout stream chuckled out into a valley of green and gold. A valley in the sun. He had not seen the sun for—how long?

He could see every detail of his life in the sun: the clear warmth of morning before the smog rolled in, the carbon trails down the Hollywood Freeway, the dark sparkling green of dichondra under the sprinklers, the damp red banks of geraniums, the bright flowered shirts by the sea in Santa Monica....

He could see it.

And Jo—where was Jo? Was she lonely in that empty house that they had shared? Or was she—the thought would not go away—was she just a little glad that he was gone? She had failed him in many ways, but what kind of a life had *he* given her, really?

There was time for too many memories, not all of them pleasant.

But Arvon stuck with it, with a steady patience that still could not hide the light in his eyes. He cracked the language barrier, imperfectly at first, and then the vault was a little less lonely, a little less alien.

Wes was caught in a situation he could not control; he recognized that and tried to adjust himself to it. He was as nearly helpless as a man could be, but some of his fear was gone now.

He even managed to forget the bodies in the niches, at least most of the time.

He began to feel a charge of excitement, a thrill of being close to something utterly beyond his understanding. It was a sensation he had had once before in his life, when he had started out to do endocrine research soon after leaving medical school. He had given that up little by little; he had never really known why.

Well, he couldn't give *this* up.

Almost, he was glad that he couldn't.

He made himself as comfortable as he could, and he knew that he was sitting on a story that would make the first atomic bomb seem like a back-page gossip item for a movie columnist. It was not an altogether unpleasant sensation.

He talked, and listened, and tried to do the hardest thing of all.

He tried to understand.

Wes had developed, over the years, a rule-of-thumb psychology that all doctors had to have. Medicine was not all midnight jaunts with the accelerator floored and crises in the operating room, particularly if you happened to be an eye, ear, nose, and throat man. A great deal of his practice was routine, and a lot of it was a crashing bore. He played a game with himself during the long office afternoons, trying to size up new patients as Miss Hill showed them through the door. Were they really sick, or after drugs on one pretext or another? Were they the nervous type who caught pneumonia every time they sneezed, or were they actually in bad shape? What did they do for a living? More importantly, sometimes, what did they *want* to do for a living?

Wes was pretty good at it. He could often peg a person within two minutes, and be close enough to be of some aid in the diagnosis. But how did you evaluate the personality of a man with whom you had *nothing* in common? How much of what he thought of as personality was just a cut of clothes, a way of speaking, a choice of familiar pastimes, a taste for Toynbee or funny books?

He was no fool. There was nothing to be gained by panic and hysteria, but the plain fact was that Arvon was a man utterly outside the frame of his experience. Wherever he had come from, whatever he was, he was *different*. How could you tell what his motives were? They might be anything. How could you tell whether he meant you harm or was just defending himself? Defending—against what threat? How could you tell whether he told you the truth or lies? How could you tell what he wanted information *for*?

And yet Wes felt a sort of trust, almost a kinship. If it hadn't been for Jo and the discomfort—

"Look," Arvon said. "Paintings."

He handed Wes a packet of colored prints.

"Photographs," Wes corrected him.

He stared at them. Many were of rolling plains, knee-deep in grasses. Some were of snow and ice. Several showed strange men in skins. They looked a little like Eskimos. Wes tried to recall the Disney short on Eskimos, but couldn't remember the details. In any event, they weren't *quite* Eskimos, he was certain of that. There were shots of animals he had never seen—a great shaggy beast like an elephant, a thing like an overgrown buffalo.

Mostly there were fields, and grasses, and ice.

"Your—ummm—world?" Wes asked, feeling a little foolish.

Arvon looked blank.

Wes borrowed the man's tablet and the writing instrument. *Let's see now*, he thought. *How do they do it in the movies?*

He started with the sun, drawing a circle in the center of the page. So far, so good. But what came between the sun and the Earth? Wes had never had time to bother with a course in astronomy, and he was neither more nor less ignorant of such matters than the bulk of his fellow citizens.

Well, eliminate some of the outer planets. Pluto, that was the little one way out on the edge; throw that one away. But what else? How many planets were there, anyhow? Eight? Nine? Ten? He shook his head. Mars was the one he was after; that was where aliens always came from in the movies, so there must be *some* reason behind the choice. But which side of the Earth was Mars on? Toward the sun or in the direction of Pluto?

"Hell," he said.

He drew ten planets in a straight line out from the sun and handed the tablet to Arvon. Arvon looked at it with blank incomprehension. After all, it was just a series of circles on a piece of paper. Arvon studied it solemnly, and finally folded it up and put it in his pocket.

So much for *that*.

Time passes slowly in a confined space. Wes got his watch back so he could keep track of the hours, but he still had no idea how long he had been in the vault before he was able to read the dial on his watch again. Quite possibly it was autumn outside, with winter on the way. It would be cold in the mountains, and snow would make the trail a tough one, if he ever saw it again.

It took him two days of concentrated effort to get across to Arvon the idea that he wanted to write Jo a letter—just a note saying that he was okay, that he loved her, that he would explain everything to her someday. He even wrote such a letter, explained about addresses, and spent a miserable few hours trying to get across the concept of stamps.

Arvon took the note and read it. He read it not once, but many times. He took it apart and put it back together again. And then he shook his head sadly.

"But why? It can't hurt you—can't *hurt* you. Small thing to ask—"

Arvon refused firmly. "Desire to help," he said slowly. "Desire to help, but must *not* help." He groped for words. "Risk. Danger. Big chance."

Wes felt his unnatural calmness desert him. "But you have no right to keep me here like this! You have explained nothing, done nothing, said nothing. What the devil kind of a man are you?"

Arvon frowned, puzzled.

*Oh God, this is impossible!*

Then, unexpectedly, Arvon tried to answer him. "*Right*," he said. "Hard word. Very hard word. Right for you or right for me?"

"Both," Wes almost shouted. "Right's right."

Arvon smiled and shook his head. "I try to explain," he said. He stopped, unsatisfied. "I *will* try to explain," he corrected himself. "You try to understand. I—we—mean no harm to you. I—we—do what we must. *Understand.*"

Wes waited.

The man's strange gray eyes grew distant, lost. His tongue groped with words that were not his words. He tried to tell a story that was beyond telling, across a gulf that could not be bridged.

And Weston Chase sat in the bare rock vault, where a tiny fire threw ghostly shadows across the dark forms who slept as only the dead may sleep, and the still air was hushed with long, long silences. He sat, and he listened, and he tried to understand.

The man talked on and on and on, and the fire grew low, and the pale radiance in the cavern was like the frozen silver of the moon....

CHAPTER

The ship was alone.

She was moving, and moving fast, but there was nothing around her to show her speed. She seemed suspended in a featureless universe of gray, transfixed in an empty fog, beyond space, beyond time, beyond understanding.

There were no stars, no planets, no far galaxies like milky jewels against the shadowed velvet of space.

There was the ship, and the grayness, and that was all.

Inside the ship a plump, balding man named Nlesine jerked a stubby thumb toward the blue metal wall that sealed them from the desolation Outside. "In my humble opinion," he said, "that is the ideal home for humanity out there. We got off on the wrong foot right at the start, as any idiot should be able to see—even you, Tsriga. Man is slime, an infection in the cosmos. Why should he live on green planets under blue skies? If ever there were an organism that had earned an isolated place in Nowhere, man is it."

The high, irritating hum of the atomics powering the distortion

CHAD OLIVER

field filled the ship. The sensation was precisely that of listening to a bomb falling toward you, a bomb that never hit.

Tsriga, his rather flashy clothes startling in the subdued green room, was bitingly conscious of his youth, but determined to cover it up at all costs. He knew that Nlesine was baiting him; very well, he would go him one better. "You've understated the case," he said. "You're too optimistic, as usual. I think that even Nowhere is too fine a place for us. What we need is Somewhere more gruesome than Nowhere."

Nlesine laughed. He laughed considerably more than the joke warranted. He laughed until the tears ran out of his eyes. "You're a card, Tsriga," he said. "You should insure that priceless sense of humor for a billion credits, so that you may always be a little ray of sunshine in our lives."

"Go to hell," Tsriga said, and moved away.

Nlesine stopped laughing and turned to Arvon, who was seated across from him reading a novel. "What do you think, handsome?"

Arvon lowered the book reluctantly. "I think you ride the kid too much."

Nlesine made an impolite noise. "He's got to grow up sometime."

"Don't we all?"

Nlesine snorted. "A great line. Sounds like one of my own novels. You read too many books, Arvon. You're turning into an Intellectual. You should get out on the farm, sniff the barnyard smells, learn to *live.*"

Arvon smiled a little, his tall body relaxed in his chair, his book balanced easily in his strong hand. His gray eyes were more puzzled than amused, however. "I've never understood why you work so hard to be the Great Cynic, Nlesine."

"Meaning that I'm obnoxious enough without trying?"

"Meaning that it must get a bit tiresome, even for you."

"Why don't you preach to me about Golden Humanity, like Kolraq does? Explain about the unity of life, the harmony of the spheres, the cuddly qualities of the little furry creatures—"

"No, thanks," Arvon said, raising his book like a shield. "I'd rather read."

The ship shuddered slightly; the high hum increased its pitch to an uncomfortable whine.

A door slid open and Hafij, the navigator, stepped into the cabin. He was erect and calm, his strange black eyes sweeping the others with something that was more unconcern than contempt. "We're going to come out of it in a minute," he said. "Better strap yourselves in."

"The field still acting up?" Arvon asked.

"Some, yes."

"There won't be any—trouble—will there?" Tsriga wiped his hands on an overly fancy handkerchief.

The navigator shrugged.

Nlesine rose to the occasion. "It looks bad to Nlesine," he muttered, employing his favorite phrase. "We'll have to sleep our way home, if we ever come out of the distortion field at all. Is the emergency stuff all set up, Hafij?"

"It's ready," Hafij said, and didn't laugh.

"Hold on," Nlesine said, sitting up straighter. "You mean there's really going to be—"

"Better strap yourselves in," the navigator said, and went back to the control room.

The three men stared at each other, suddenly closer than they had been in the four years they had been together.

"It looks bad to Nlesine," Nlesine said wryly.

"It even looks bad to Arvon," Arvon muttered.

Tsriga, very young and very afraid, strapped himself in his chair and closed his eyes.

The ship shuddered again. Somewhere in the walls a cable began to spark hissingly.

The gray emptiness around them seemed very near, pressing in on them, suffocating them—

"Here goes nothing,'" Arvon said.

The lights dimmed.

They waited.

The ship came out of it.

When it happened, it happened all at once. There was no transition. The ship blinked out of nothingness, back into normal space, back into a dark sea where the stars were gleaming islands and no winds ever blew. It was a friendlier place, somehow, than what they had left behind them. Vast it was, this ocean where worlds were dust, and yet it was familiar, too, for it was the universe that had given birth to man; it could be understood, however dimly.

The ship swam through the deeps at close to the speed of light, but there was no sensation of movement, and the stars maintained their chill remoteness.

The ship still had a long way to go.

"Looks like we made it," Arvon said, unstrapping himself.

"We haven't landed yet," Nlesine reminded him.

"That *was* a rough pull-out," Tsriga said, the color coming back into his cheeks. "Nobody can tell me we weren't in trouble that time."

The sound of the atomics dwindled to a steady, throbbing hum—smooth, comforting, precise.

The control room door slid open again and Hafij stuck his head in. "Derryoc in here?" asked the navigator.

"Yeah," said Nlesine. "He's hiding under my chair."

"Probably back in the library," Arvon said. "You want him?"

"We should touch down in another twelve hours. Seyehi wants to get the computers set up for the first scan, and he says he doesn't want to have to do it all over again when Derryoc quits pounding his ear long enough to think up objections."

"I'll get him," Arvon said.

He got up and went back along the main corridor to the library. As he had expected, Derryoc was there, seated at a long table, squinting into a viewer. The anthropologist had films scattered all over the place, and had managed to accumulate a fair-sized collection of empty glasses, a few of which still had liquor in them.

Probably, Arvon thought, the man hadn't even noticed the rough passage when they had pulled out of the distortion field. Not because he was drunk, of course—Arvon had never seen Derryoc drunk despite the amount of drink he stowed away. But when he got immersed in one of his problems, the rest of the world might as well not exist. It was a habit of mind that Arvon recognized but found impossible to understand.

"Derryoc," he said.

The anthropologist waved a hand irritably. "Minute," he said.

Arvon gave him his minute, then tried again. "We're landing in twelve hours. Seyehi wants to get set up for a scan."

The anthropologist looked up. There were dark circles under his eyes, and his hair hadn't been combed in a week. He was a big man, running a little to fat, but he had an air of competence about him. Arvon had always rather liked Derryoc, but the anthropologist kept his distance. Derryoc tended to feel that anyone who wasn't a scientist of some sort really wasn't worth fooling with; Arvon knew he was just a playboy to him despite the zoology he had learned to qualify for the trip.

"Twelve hours?"

"Yes. We're out in normal space again."

"I wondered what was wrong with the damn lights." He pushed the viewer back, stood up, and stretched.

"Think we'll find anything this time?" Arvon asked.

The anthropologist looked at him. "No. Do you?"

Arvon shook his head. "No, but I hope we do."

"Hope's tricky. Don't rely on it. You know how many planets we've checked, counting all the ships that have ever gone out?"

"Around a thousand, I'd guess."

"One thousand two hundred and one, counting *our* last stop. So the odds are one thousand two hundred and one to one that we'll find what we always find."

"Statistics can be misleading."

"Not like hopes, Arvon. Always bet with the odds and you come out ahead."

"Mind if I come along to the control room with you?"

"Not at all." Derryoc smiled. "What's the matter—Nlesine wearing your hopes down?"

"Something like that," Arvon admitted.

The two men walked out of the library, into the corridor. They walked slowly toward the control room, and as they walked the ship around them floated through the great night, toward a new sun and new worlds—and, perhaps, a new answer to the problem that faced them all, the problem that had to be solved.

Inside the control room the atmosphere of the ship was subtly different. It was not a physical change; no gauge or meter could have registered the tension in that air. It was a question of personality. It was there, and you responded to it, but it was not easy to pin down.

Partly it was the room itself. At sea the man at the wheel is the man who feels the waves and the currents and the dark depths below, and it is not otherwise with the ships that sail that mightier sea of space.

Partly it was Hafij. The navigator was a man at home in space as other men never were; his thin body and his black eyes, remote as the stars themselves, *belonged* in this room, and were a part of it. It would not be true to say that he loved the dark recesses between the worlds, but he was drawn to them as a man is drawn to his woman, and to them he always returned.

Partly it was Seyehi: not much to look at, unobtrusive, he blended with the equipment in the room. More precisely, he was an extension of the computers he ran. The others called him Feedback, and he always smiled at the name, as though it were a compliment. He knew his machines, and he lived with them, and it might have been true to say that he loved them.

But mostly it was Wyik.

Wyik was the Captain to all of them; it was impossible to think of him as anything else. He must have had a life before he went into space, before he began the search that he pursued with a granite hardness that none of the others could match. He must have been born, been raised in a family, lived, laughed, loved. He must have had such a life, but none of them had ever seen it. This was his fourth trip, and twenty years in space is a long time for any man. The Captain was short, wiry, tough. He rarely smiled, not even when he got drunk, which was seldom. He was ablaze with energy. Even standing still, eyes staring into the plates, he seemed charged with electricity, tense, ready for sudden movement.

The control room was different. In the rest of the ship men might joke about the thing that had taken them light-years from their home, the thing that mocked them on every world they visited. In the rest of the ship men might relax, and even forget, for a while.

You didn't relax here, and you didn't forget.

Arvon kept out of the way. He was a stranger here; this was not his part of the ship, no matter how much he might have wished it to be.

"Get on with it, Derryoc," the Captain said. His voice was controlled, but vibrantly alive. "We'll be in position for you within eleven hours."

Derryoc looked at Seyehi. "The usual approach?"

The computer man nodded. "We'll make a circuit around the most favorable planet, five miles up. We're set up to scan for everything we can detect at that height: population concentrations, radio waves, energy emissions of any sort at all. We'll make one circuit at the equator first, then cross over the poles. I've got the computers set to make a level analysis of anything we pick up."

"I'll want maps," the anthropologist said.

"You'll have them. Anything else?"

The anthropologist clasped his hands behind his back. "Well, after your computers report that the planet is uninhabited by any so-called intelligent life—"

"You mean *if*, not *after*, Derryoc," the Captain interrupted.

Derryoc shrugged. "*If*, then," he corrected without conviction. "If the inevitable happens, I want Hafij to take her down as close as he can, where I can see for myself. There's always a mathematical chance for a low-energy culture, and I'll want to look at it before we go barging in on it."

"That all?"

"That's all for now." Derryoc turned to the Captain. "You'll have the screens up, Wyik?"

"I won't be taking any chances."

"Right. Come on, Arvon—let's have a drink before we go to work."

They left the control room and went back to the bar, which was little more than a cubicle set into the wall. Derryoc broke out a bottle and two glasses, and the two men drank.

Arvon felt the liquor warming him, and he was glad to have it. He tried not to anticipate the despair that was coming, but the hopelessness piled up with the years—it was not difficult to understand Nlesine's dark outlook, no matter how trying it became.

If only all the planets *were* uninhabited by men.

That wouldn't have been so bad.

"Why did you come out here, anyway?" Derryoc asked suddenly, pouring his second drink. "Didn't you have a deal at home?"

Arvon smiled, remembering. The big home in the country, the tapestries, the books, the warmth. And the cities, the plays, the women...

"I had too much of a deal," he said.

Derryoc downed half the drink at a gulp. "I don't understand you," he said honestly.

"That makes us even,'" said Arvon.

"We'll never find it, you know," the anthropologist said.

"We've got to find it," Arvon replied. "That's all there is to it."

"More hoping, Arvon?"

"A man can do worse."

The ship plunged on. Framed by stars, she lanced through darkness unimaginable, toward light.

Toward a yellow sun, flanked by two other suns, one near, one far away.

The system of Alpha Centauri, over four light-years from a world called Earth.

Kolraq sat alone, his thoughts making the silent journey down to the world below the ship. He did not like to be alone at a time like this, but Hafij was occupied, and the navigator was the only man aboard with whom he felt completely at ease.

*Something about the stars*, he had often thought of Hafij. *He has looked long at the stars, and that is the beginning of wisdom.*

Well, he could not share his thoughts with Hafij now.

Kolraq reflected, not for the first time, that a spaceship was a strange place for a priest. Most of the others, when they thought about him at all, dismissed him as a mystic and let it go at that. It was not a term of condemnation with them; when they stuck the mystic label on him they simply proved to their own satisfaction that he was no part of their world—he became a man to be treated with courtesy, but not a man to take very seriously.

Well, it was an odd business, this being a priest in this day and age. There had been a time on Lortas when the Church had been powerful, but the last century had seen it divided and weak; it was hardly more than a philosophy at best in these days, and at worst—

If only man had never gone into space! If only he had never found what he did find! But no, that was spineless thinking. Surely, a true God was not destroyed by the truth, no matter where it was found. There must be an answer, some other answer than the one men had been finding over and over again, the answer that mocked them on every habitable world in all the abyss of space....

Centaurus Four, now!

There was a chance, there was always a chance. If there was a unity to all life, as he had been taught, as he tried to believe with his heart and soul, then there had to be another answer than the one men had found.

Had to be, *had* to be!

"Ah, Kolraq!" a voice cut in on his thoughts. "What's new in the crystal ball department?"

Lajor, of course. Why couldn't the newsman leave him alone at a time like this? Would the man chatter on the brink of eternity itself? *But these are not charitable thoughts, Kolraq. If you cannot find charity in yourself, why expect it in others?*

"The crystal ball is cloudy, I'm afraid."

Lajor seated himself. He was a sloppy man, sloppy in his dress, in his work, perhaps in his thoughts. True, thought Kolraq, his travel books were more popular than the novels of Nlesine, but they would be sooner forgotten. *Charity, charity!*

Lajor scribbled on a pad. "Centaurus Four, open the door!" He chuckled, and Kolraq dredged up a faint smile. "Big scoop coming up, you know it! We'll go flipping around the old rock pile, with Seyehi's computers buzzing and clacking, and then we'll zoom down and let Derryoc squint at his eternal problems. Then down goes the *Good Hope*, splat! We all get out and scrabble around, and what do I get out of it? Another little old chapter, same as all the rest. Centaurus Four, you're a bore!"

"There's a chance," the priest said. *Was there, was there?*

"Sure, sure." Lajor screwed up his face into a fair imitation of Nlesine's plump features. "But it looks bad to Nlesine!"

"Nlesine has been wrong before," Kolraq said patiently.

"You bet he has, you just bet he has. Why, I remember the time—

back before we left old Lortas and set sail into the old sunrise—Nlesine was sounding off about…"

Kolraq shut his ears with an effort; the voice at his side became a drone, an irritant, nothing more. *Lord, Lord, are we no better than the rest? Must we bicker and pick at each other, even here, even now, in the Shadow?*

Far below the ship the brown world that was the fourth planet of Alpha Centauri spun through space, orbited around her flaming primary.

In the control room of the *Good Hope*, Derryoc looked up from the computer tapes and shook his head.

"Take her down," he said to the Captain.

Already the ship had eased down out of the endless night of space through a high, thin blue. She had settled through a rolling sea of white clouds, flashed into sunshine and winds and horizons.

Now she went down to where snow-tipped mountains almost ripped her belly. She roared and thundered, this gleaming titan; she ripped through winds and rains, and the air rushed in behind her with a thunder of its own.

She blasted over continents, across tossing seas. She threw her snake shadow over lonely islands and sent birds rising fearfully from forest trees. She flashed across yellow desert sands and left new dunes in her wake.

Derryoc stayed at his viewer-scope, not moving save to make rapid notes on a pad.

After six hours he stood up wearily. "It is the same," he said to Wyik.

The Captain stood steadily. There was no change of expression on his face. His muscles tensed a little more, and that was all. "Would you care to suggest a likely spot for the field investigation?"

The anthropologist consulted his pad. He nodded, gave Hafij the coordinates of the best site he had seen.

There was despair in the control room now, an old despair, unvoiced and unheeded. *The same, the same. It was always the same.*

The ship thundered back to the position Derryoc had given. She stood on her tail and rode a boiling column of flame out of the sky, down to the desert sands that waited for her with an ageless patience.

She landed, settled, stopped.

There was silence.

The air was tested, found unbreathable. Since the copter was such a nuisance to assemble, they decided to walk to the site— it was very close anyway. Derryoc, Tsriga, Nlesine, Lajor, and Arvon put on face masks. The others stayed with the ship.

The great airlock port sealed behind them. The outer door hissed open. Derryoc went out first, and down the ladder. Arvon was right behind him.

Arvon shivered, although it was not cold. His boots sunk into the yellow sand, and he stood a moment, listening. The sounds he heard were strange after the mechanical hums of the ship.

The sounds of wind, sighing across the desert, wind that had known ocean seas, and would know them again. The sounds of sand, rustling, sliding, shifting.

The sound was the sound of rain, but the sky above them was a cloudless blue, the visible sun warm and peaceful. Their shadows moved before them, sharply etched on the rippled sand.

Yes, and the sounds were the sounds of death, the dry whispers that spoke of life that had once been, and was no more.

*Death*, thought Arvon. *Hello, old friend.*

"Come on," called Derryoc, crunching across the desert floor. "Come on, we don't want to get caught out by nightfall."

Arvon fell into line, and single file they made their way across the sand, feeling it trickle into their boots, drift inside their shirts.

*A bath will feel good tonight*, Arvon thought, and smiled at the utter irrelevance of the notion.

Behind them the ship towered in a land of desolation.

Ahead of them, naked and gaping in the driven sand, waited the thing that had once been a city, the thing that men had once called home.

How do you describe the sadness of centuries? What epitaph do you inscribe on the tombstone of man?

Arvon looked at Nlesine and at Lajor. What lines would they scribble in their notebooks, what words could they find to tell what they were seeing here, on a world that was less than a name back home?

All the words had already been used so many times.

And he looked, too, at Derryoc, at the plump figure plodding through ruin. How could he see only problems here, in this city where even the dead had gone away? How could he see only house types and power sources, city plans and technological levels? What sort of eyes did it take so that you saw no ghosts? What kind of ears did a man need not to hear the whispers, the grief, the music lost and faraway?

Even as they were walking now, other men had walked, down this very street. No sand then, no jagged concrete ruptures, no decay and collapse and fire scar. Trees, perhaps. Green grass. A buzz of commerce. A blur of faces: happy, sad, handsome, ugly. A news screen: words and pictures from around the world. What had been news to them, so near the end? What could they have been thinking about, talking about, joking about?

*The weather tomorrow will be fair and cloudy, with light rain in the afternoon.... The Greens won the Silver Trophy today, on a sensational play by— A man went berserk on his way home from the office; he knifed three dogs before he was apprehended, and explained to police that barking kept him awake at night.... The situation in Oceania appears to be more serious than at first supposed, but the Council says there is no cause for alarm.... We repeat that the weather tomorrow will be fair and cloudy, with light rain in the afternoon....*

Voices, faces, laughter.

Arvon stepped around a fallen wall and followed Derryoc toward the center of the ruin. Oh yes, he was imagining things, imagining the phantoms that walked by his side, imagining the shadows that passed behind gaping holes that once were windows. But the ghosts were real, ghosts were always real in these graveyards of civilizations, as real as the men and women he had known at home on Lortas, and as unseeing—

*Cry for them, for they can sorrow no more. Cry for them, for they laughed and loved, and are gone.*

"Here's the library," called Derryoc.

"What's left of it," said Nlesine.

"What a mess," said Tsriga.

Lajor snapped a picture. "Chapter Umpteen," he muttered. "For summary see Chapter One."

They climbed inside, their flashlight beams sending little tunnels of pale light into the gloom. Their footsteps echoed down silent corridors. Sand was everywhere, and dust rose before them in puffs and clouds.

"No sign of fire here," Derryoc said, pleased. "Look for periodicals; they may have survived if it's been this dry for long. What do you think, Tsriga?"

Tsriga shrugged. "Not much sign of moisture. Probably dry since the blast."

"A good haul," Derryoc said. "Never mind the novels—see if you can find history books; check by the pictures. We'll just have to take tapes at random."

"Me, I'll take novels," Nlesine said. "Who knows, some poor guy probably thought his stuff would live forever."

For the first time Arvon felt some warmth for Nlesine.

What should you take from one library from one city from one more world of the dead? What words should you select for the linguists to analyze, for the computers to buzz over, for the newspapers to sensationalize? What lines could you find that would add up to one more footnote in one more history of man?

Arvon picked more or less as fancy dictated from the vacuum-sealed cases that preserved the old books. He had some knowledge of linguistics, enough to estimate what he looked at. Some of his guesses would be wrong, but anything he saved would be unique. Poetry, certainly. Novels, of course. And history, science, political tracts, and autobiographies, most definitely autobiographies....

"Let's go," Derryoc said after what seemed only a few minutes but had actually been hours. "We've got time for some close-ups before we start back. Did you see that statue out in the square? Almost untouched, if we could just find the head."

"Probably buried in the sand," Nlesine said. "I don't blame him."

They went about their task while the warm sun blazed down the arc of afternoon. It was a good sun, and it did its job as it had always done it, unconcerned that its rays no longer lighted a living world.

They already had maps of the city, photographed from the ship, so they spent most of their remaining time inside the ruins of houses, preserving what little they could on film.

When they were through they returned as they had come, back through the littered streets, out again into the sand sculptures of the yellow desert. The wind moaned in their faces, blowing into the city, whining around jagged buildings and through black holes that had once been windows.

Into the airlock quickly, for night was falling.

The outside port hissed shut. The dry air of Centaurus Four was pumped out, given back to a world that no longer needed it. The clean, slightly damp air of the ship came in. The inner port opened, and they were back in the ship.

Shake the sand from your boots, wash the sand from your body.

Put on clean clothes, clothes that do not smell of the dust and the centuries.

"That does it," Derryoc said. "Another world in the can."

"Little men, what know?" asked Nlesine.

It was difficult to joke, hard not to remember. It was always hard after a field party came back. What were the odds now, the odds against their own survival?

A million to one?

A billion to one?

*Try not to think about it. Do your job. Cry if you must. Laugh if you can.*

"I don't wish to conceal anything from you," the Captain said. He looked at each of them in turn. "We had trouble coming out of the field for this landing. We may have trouble again."

No one said anything.

"We'll have to start home soon, regardless," the Captain said. "The only question is, do we quit now or do we try once more?"

Silence.

"You decide, Captain," Hafij said finally.

"Is that agreeable to all of you?"

Whether or not it was agreeable, no one spoke out against it.

"Very well," the Captain said. His short, taut body turned back to the control panel. "We'll try again. Hafij, stand by to lift ship. Seyehi, compute our course for the nearest G sequence star. We blast in thirty minutes."

They were slow minutes.

The ship that had brought life briefly again to Centaurus Four stood poised in the desert sands, folded in a warm summer night. A city that had lost its dreams was only a deeper darkness beneath the stars.

The wind whined across the dunes, calling, calling.

A thrust of white flame, boiling.

A crash of thunder, shattering the silence, then hushed to a rumble that receded toward the stars.

The long silence came again.

The ship was gone.

CHAPTER

Far out in space the stars disappeared, and the night winked out as though it had never existed. The ship made the wrenching transition into the distortion field without apparent difficulty; the high hum again filled the ship, and the gray desolation of not-space surrounded it.

Even within the field, which had the effect of lessening the distance between two points in normal space by means of "folding" space around the ship, it took time to travel over four light-years.

Time enough to think.

The men in the ship—with the exception of the priest they always referred to it as simply the Bucket, never the *Good Hope*—went about the business of being themselves, presenting their social personalities to each other like so many suits of armor. But there was no man among them, no matter how flip his words, who did not carry a knot of ice deep within him, a chill that no thermostat could regulate, and no sun warm.

For the ship was searching, searching a galaxy as other ships had searched before her, and would search after her.

She was searching for hope, and there was no hope. Man had found many things in space: new worlds, new loneliness, new marvels.

But he had found no hope there, not on all the worlds of all the suns that sprinkled a summer night as stars.

It would not have been so bad, Arvon thought, if they had found no other men like themselves in the universe they knew. If they had sailed their ships out of Lortas and had encountered only rocks and empty seas and boiling lava—that would not have hurt them, that would only have meant that they were, after all, alone.

Or if they had but found the cardboard horrors pasted together by a generation and more of the innocents who happily constructed space thrillers for the young at heart—how wonderful that would have been, how gay, how exciting! Arvon would have welcomed that colorful fiction parade with open arms: reptilian monsters slathering after ripe young cuties, mutants who had no emotions coldly plotting the obliteration of the Good Guys with the Sense of Humor, hungry planets that were just overgrown digestive systems, waiting for spaceships as a starving man might await a tin can—

Better still, if only they had encountered the noble princes and beautiful princesses and nasty old prime ministers of Other Worlds, or even a galactic civilization of swell old geniuses, waiting to take the brash young people of Lortas by the hand, and eager to lead their immature steps into a Promised Land of togas and fountains and bubbles and Big Clean Thoughts…

But the ships had gone out, and space was no longer a dream.

Dreams could be fun, even nightmares.

Reality was different, and it hurt.

When the distortion field had been perfected, making possible interstellar flight in a matter of months instead of generations, the first exploring ships had gone out eagerly, confidently. Sure, they were armed to the teeth, ready for the monsters their myths had prepared them for, but they were ready, too, for men of their own kind. They were drilled, trained, disciplined. There would be no awkward incidents, no sophomoric misunderstandings that might lead to disaster. They were looking for friends, not enemies. Somewhere out there, they argued, somewhere in that vast starry universe that was their home, there would be other men, other intelligences, other civilizations.

The people of Lortas were not fools. They knew, even at the start, that one world alone was only a tiny fraction of the worlds that must exist. Just as an isolated island, completely cut off from contact with other islands and other continents, must develop a less complex culture than those areas situated at the crossroads of the world, so must a planet alone amount to far less than a planet that was a part of something bigger.

Cultures grow through contact with other cultures.

No great civilization ever grew in just one sealed area, with only its own ideas to keep it going.

Fresh viewpoints, new ideas, different historical traditions—these were the ingredients that made for greatness. Here a people learned to smelt metal, there a culture hit upon electricity, somewhere else a boy found a light wood and played with a glider, still elsewhere a tinkerer built an internal combustion engine. Separate, apart, they were gadgets. Together, combined, they were aircraft that freed man from the rocks and the land, gave him the sky for his own.

Alone, a planet could go so far, and no further. There is a point at which a culture exhausts itself, no matter how rich and varied it may be. There is a time when it—stops.

Not dies, perhaps.

But life is a process. It means change, development, challenge. When it merely repeats itself, when it only survives, it becomes at best insignificant, and sooner or later the effort is too much, and it is extinct.

There comes a time, too, in the history of civilizations when technology is not enough, when gadgets no longer satisfy. There comes a time when science itself can be seen in perspective, a method, a technique, that cannot supply *all* the answers.

And man is not only the animal with language.

He is the animal who asks questions constantly, incessantly. He asks questions as soon as he can speak, he asks questions as long as he lives. When men no longer question, when they are complacent enough to believe that they *know*, they are through. They may eat, work, sleep, go through the routine. But they are through.

The people of Lortas were still asking questions, but they were tougher questions than they had asked when Lortas was a young world. They knew there were no ultimate, final answers, but they were alive enough to want to keep trying.

Questions sent the men of Lortas out to the stars.

Not rare metals, not national defense, not even science in the strict sense of the word.

Questions.

Old questions, in a way, though asked in a new form. Old longings, old hopes, old dreams. What lies over yonder, behind the mountains? What lands may be found on the other side of the sea, beyond the edge of the world? Does the sun shine there, and do warm breezes blow? Would we be happy there, see new things, dream new dreams?

So the men of Lortas locked their bodies in shining cylinders and flamed and thundered outward into the great night. Not all of them, of course. Most people anywhere are content with whatever they have; change is too much trouble. But many of them went, at first, with a calm efficiency that could not hide the hope in their eyes.

They went out, and they looked, and many of them came back.

That was the end of the dream.

That was the beginning of horror.

They found other men, men like themselves.

*There must be some mistake*, said the people back home when the reports began coming in. *They can't be men, not men like us!*

But the anatomists said: They are men.

The biologists said: They are men.

The psychologists said: They are men.

There were minor differences from world to world, but the differences were for the most part not important: a variation in blood type, in body temperature, in skin color, in the number of vertebrae.

Man was not a rare animal in the universe, and it was the height of egotism to imagine that he was. All isolated peoples believe that they are the only human beings in the world, and when a planet thinks itself alone, before the ships go out into space, it is difficult for the people on that planet to conceive of other human beings elsewhere among the stars.

*Why, man evolved here!* they told each other on a million worlds, nodding sagely at their own wisdom. *He is amazingly complex, the line that led to him was a long shot, an accident, he could never happen twice.* And they thought, if they did not say: *We are wonderful, we can be found only here on this wonderful world of ours. This planet we live on has been singled out by Creation as the one, the only, and the original home of Great Big Adorable Us.*

Some just knew this to be true; others fiddled with statistics. They all ignored the supreme fact: they were taking a sample of one, their own speck of dust, and generalizing from it to the entire universe. Moreover, they were generalizing in an asinine way, for the one planet they had in their sample *had* evolved human life, and that made it unanimous, as far as they actually knew.

It was not that man was foreordained, built in from the beginning. It was simply that the evolution of intelligence, of the ability to develop culturally, necessarily proceeded along the road of trial and error, change and modification. A culture-bearing animal had to be warm-blooded, for he needed the energy, he had to be big-brained, he had to have free hands and specialized feet. A manlike form was the mechanical answer to one trend of evolution, and if conditions permitted he came along sooner or later.

So there were men, men like the men of Lortas.

*Yes,* thought Arvon, *and what had happened to these men?*

The reports came in, brought home by ships across the light years. For a short time, a very short time, there seemed to be little consistency to the reports. Then the pattern emerged, and was only repeated, as the number of reports grew to a hundred, to five hundred, to a thousand.

The pattern?

Well, stripped of its technical language, it boiled down to something elementary, something frightful in its very simplicity. The ships had discovered three kinds of planets that had developed men. On one type the men had not yet advanced to a state of technological development that gave them a chance to destroy themselves. On a second type, above the primitive level but not yet to the level of space flight, men were organized into groups, busily hacking away at each other with whatever weapons they could muster. On these worlds the visitors from Lortas were received with suspicion, with hostility, with fear. Their ships were impounded, their knowledge was used to fight in wars that were utterly meaningless to them. Crews that landed on these worlds seldom got home again.

And there was a third type, of which Centaurus Four was a good example. On these worlds man had evolved, he had developed weapons powerful enough to do the job, and he was extinct. The methods varied: germs, crop blights, cobalt bombs, gas. The result was the same: extinction.

*In all the universe they could reach, this was what had become of man. As soon as he was able to do it he destroyed himself.*

Ho, friend and neighbor!

Many thanks for the inspiring example you have set for us!

*And us, what of us? Are we not men, the same as they were?*

That, indeed, was the catch. The civilization of Lortas was an old civilization, and thought of itself as sophisticated. It had weathered many a storm and it had survived. The people had always felt a certain pride in this, and suddenly they had evidence to show them how right—or how foolish—this pride was.

*For Lortas, alone of all the worlds in the known universe, had spawned man, watched him develop a mighty technology, and lived to tell the tale.*

At first, even for a sophisticated people, this was a boost for the ego. They, and they alone, had mastered the art of living with each other in peace, and even in friendship.

We're different!

We've succeeded!

We're better than they are, smarter, wiser!

There was a religious revival, a time of thanksgiving. The inevitable cults appeared, the inexorable political philosophies: Let's pull in our horns, stay at home, live our own lives. Let's rejoice in our own goodness, keep away from other men, cultivate our own garden. Why?

Because we're different, unique, better!

Aren't we?

*Aren't we?*

The initial unthinking smugness could not last. It was a frail balloon at best, easily punctured by factual needles. And the facts were not pleasant. When all due allowances were made, when logic had been twisted until it could bend no more, the truth was still there.

Out of a thousand and more worlds of men, *all* had perished as soon as they were capable of it. There were no exceptions. And the men were the same everywhere, the same in the things that counted.

The men of Lortas were *not* different.

True, they had survived. They had survived for three hundred years after they had controlled their first atomic reactor. They had patched up their differences, there had been no wars. They *knew* that wars were obsolete when the first atomic bomb became possible, they *knew* that wars, ultimately, meant suicide.

But other peoples had known it too.

The books taken from shattered libraries on lifeless planets were full of it.

*They* had known, and they were gone.

Question: Is three hundred years long enough to let us relax?

Question: Is man of necessity self-destructive?

Question: If we go on living alone, never find another civilization to build with, what will become of us?

These questions were too tough for individual minds, but they were not too tough for computers. The data were fed in, the questions asked. The answers?

Other peoples had lasted three hundred years after harnessing the atom, but they had gone under eventually.

The odds were that man would always destroy himself. There was a chance that this was not true, but it was a slim one.

If Lortas built a figurative wall around itself, buried its head in the sand, its civilization would endure for a long time. It had gained that much by living past its first great crisis period. It might go on for thirty thousand years, but it would gradually slow, lose its vitality, stop.

One day it would be gone.

*What can we do?*

The analysis of the data showed one possibility. No human culture on record had ever succeeded in finding and establishing friendly relations with another human culture on a different planet. If a world could be found where men were sane, if contacts could be built up between them, if ideas and hopes and dreams could flow from one to the other—

Then perhaps man might someday be more than just another animal who lost his way. He might be more than just another extinct animal who couldn't change when the times changed. Then perhaps man could play a fuller role in the ebb and flow that was life in the universe.

*If* a world could be found—

The ships kept going out. But they had to go farther now, into parts of the galaxy so remote that the suns were no more than numbers in the great catalogues of the stars. They had to go farther, and they found nothing, and worse than nothing.

The world they needed was well hidden, if indeed it existed at all.

And it was all very well to speak of a *world* that was in trouble, a *world* that sent out ships, a *world* that was afraid. But most people are not afraid. More than that, they don't care.

*Thirty thousand years? My God, don't we have enough on our minds without dragging that up? Let 'em worry about it when the time comes!*

Of course, then it would be too late.

It wasn't going to fade away like a mirage.

So ships kept flaming outward, but their numbers dwindled. And their crews dwindled, too. A ship had to stay out five years in order to cover any area at all, and who wanted to go into space for five years?

Arvon thought of them.

Hafij, the navigator, was here because he belonged here. Seyehi would go anywhere he could be with his computers. And the Captain? The Captain was a driven man, Arvon was certain of that. But driven by what, and to what? Few men are motivated by vague principles and distant problems—it took something personal to get under your hide.

Derryoc? Well, this was his job; this was where his problems were. Tsriga? A boy, running away from an unhappy love affair, doing something romantic and exciting. Kolraq? His faith was tottering, he needed lumber to shore it up. Lajor? There must be more to the newsman than met the eye, and this was a long way to come for a travel book. And what made a man want to write a book, anyway? Nlesine? Who could understand Nlesine?

And himself, Arvon? Did he really know why he was here, why he had come?

No matter.

They were here.

And when the ship tried to come out of the distortion field, when it shivered and screamed and the lights went out, Arvon knew that they were in trouble.

The darkness was a terrible thing.

Arvon suddenly found himself without eyes, without a mind. He could hear a whine and screech of metal that ripped along his nerves. He could feel the sweat on his hands and forehead. He could sense his heart thudding against his chest.

But he could not think.

And he could not *see*.

In an instant he was a boy again, in a strange house. He was in bed, hidden beneath the covers. There is a wind, sighing through the trees outside the window. There is no light. There is silence, but a silence filled with sounds. There! What was that? A slither, a slide—a door opening? *His* door? Look out from under the covers, look toward the door! The noise again, but you can't see. There is blackness all around you. You hold your breath, close your eyes, and listen and wait—

And then he was back, no longer a boy. He felt the shrieking metal coffin of the ship around him, felt it jerking under his feet. He could see, but not with his eyes. He saw midnight around the ship, an ocean of midnight, an abyss of ice-flecked darkness, a black cavern with no beginning and no ending. He saw space lapping at the ship, trying to suck him out, set him adrift.

Space was very close.

A man forgot how close it was until his ship failed him. Then he remembered. He shuddered in the midnight of his mind, stripped of everything, even his personality. He was just a spark of life, flickering, trying not to go out forever—

The lights came on again, dimly at first, then with an unnatural white brilliance. The ship steadied. The chaos of screaming sound died away. The atomics settled down to an uneasy whine, far different from their usual comfortable throb in normal space.

*If* they had made it into normal space.

Arvon lay on the floor and felt life flow back into him again. He forced himself to lie quietly until he stopped trembling, and then he pulled himself to his feet. There was something the matter with the artificial gravity field; his feet felt as if they were encased in lead blocks.

Nlesine stumbled into the room, looking pale and wild-eyed in the naked light. "What happened?"

Arvon shrugged. "Don't know. We were coming out of the field—"

"The Captain said there might be trouble."

"I don't think he expected *that*, though."

"Come on," Nlesine said. "Let's see if there's anyone alive in the control room. Do you think we could run this buggy alone?"

Arvon laughed shortly.

Inside the control room the men were at their posts moving with a calmness that could not hide the tension in the air. Their faces were all curiously pale in the white light, and Wyik had a gash in his forehead that was leaving a thin trail of scarlet wherever the Captain moved.

Hafij was moving slowly from control panel to control panel, calling out a series of figures to Seyehi, who was punching them into his computer. The navigator's tall, thin body seemed crushed by the abnormal pull of the gravity field, and his black eyes were more concerned than Arvon had ever seen them.

Arvon checked the viewscreens with a quick glance and felt an unreasonable relief rush through him. The screens showed the black sea of normal space, which meant that they had gotten out of the distortion field, at least. He saw stars, friendly points of light despite their distance, and not far away a yellow sun burned in the screen.

The others filed into the control room and stood in a nervous huddle, trying to keep out of the way and yet needing, somehow, to be there, where they could see what was going on.

The strange hum of the atomics did nothing to ease their nervous systems.

The Captain hovered over Seyehi's shoulder watching the data come out of the computer. "Well?" he said. "How much time have we got?"

"Maybe twelve hours," Seyehi said carefully. "Maybe less."

Wyik turned to Hafij. "Set a course for the third planet, Hafij. We'll have to take it at full acceleration."

Hafij raised his eyebrows, but said nothing.

"Derryoc," the Captain said.

"I know," the anthropologist said. "Get set up for the standard approach."

"We *hope* it's a standard approach, friend. But there may only be time for a high-altitude circuit before we set her down."

Derryoc whistled. "That bad, is it?"

"Worse," the Captain said. He turned to the others. He stood there in his control room—short, powerful, unsmiling. His eyes were bright. Arvon would have almost argued that the man was enjoying himself.

"How much worse?" asked Tsriga nervously.

"Well, if you ever see home again it's going to be after a good long nap."

Tsriga paled, his young face suddenly very vulnerable. "You mean the field—"

The Captain nodded. "We got out of it by the skin of our teeth. We won't get back into it again."

"Are we okay otherwise?"

"You've got ears," the Captain said. "Listen."

The whine of the atomics shivered through the ship. It was a weird sound, rising and falling, dying away almost to a mutter and then swelling to a scream that cut through you like a knife.

"Can we land if we make it to the third planet?" Arvon asked.

"We'll get down all right. The question is whether we'll still be in one piece or not."

The heavy gravity pulled at all of them, giving their faces a faintly grotesque appearance.

"It looks bad to Nlesine," Nlesine said. He said it without his usual glum enthusiasm, as though it were expected of him and he didn't want to disappoint anybody.

"I don't know much about that planet down there," the Captain said. "It looks like the best bet from here. I'm gambling on it because I have to gamble. If we get in close and find it won't do we'll try the fourth one instead. But it had *better* be a world we can live on, because it looks like it's going to be home for a spell. I think we can land. I'm not sure we can take off again unless we find a civilization down there that's able to help us out."

"You won't find it," Derryoc said.

"We don't need a technology that's actually managed space travel, remember. If it's just far enough along to manufacture some parts we may be able to sleep our way home."

Derryoc shook his head doubtfully.

Kolraq said quietly, "I'll pray for it."

For once no one laughed.

Derryoc went into a huddle with Seyehi as they got set up to scan for population concentrations and energy radiations. Hafij checked and rechecked his charts. The Captain stood still, arms folded, staring into the screen.

The bright, pale light cast a pallor on all their faces.

*Like dead men*, Arvon thought. *This ship is our coffin, and we're going to be buried in it.*

"Well, this is something," Lajor said, his voice a shade too high for comfort. "A shipwreck in space! Man, if they thought I was corny before, what'll they think now?"

"They'll think you were corny before," Blesine told him.

"Okay, okay. Maybe we should have a drink on it."

"Just a little one," Nlesine agreed. "One for the road, you might say."

"That's not funny," Tsriga objected.

"It'll seem more amusing after six or eight quick ones," Nlesine assured him. "Let's go."

Avron followed them out of the control room, more because he felt in the way there than from any desire for a drink. They sat in the comfortable green room, sinking farther into the seats than usual, and kept up a fog of conversation as though, somehow, it might serve them as a barrier against what waited for them Outside.

They had a few, but nobody got even faintly drunk.

The ship moved on, swimming through the star-flecked seas of space. A flaming yellow sun floated ahead of her, with scarlet gas prominences puffing out from its equator and then raining back into the photoshere.

The ship was a tiny thing, lost in the immensity of the universe. It was a speck of dust, and less than that. And yet it was not insignificant, even here. If the flare of the ship's atomics was only a dot of light against the furnace of the sun, she still carried life and hope and fear. The silent challenge she threw at the abyss of not-life around her was a comic thing, and yet in its way it outshone the splendor of the stars.

The hours passed.

The ship picked her way toward the third planet, intersecting its orbit as it swung about its sun. Outwardly the ship showed no sign that it was in trouble; it moved gracefully and serenely, a canoe in quiet waters.

Inside the ship it was different.

The third planet hung hugely in the viewscreens, a globe of blue and green that blotted out the stars. White clouds banded the world, looking astonishingly like breakers in a choppy sea. There was a glint at the poles that hinted of ice, and lots of it.

The ship screamed down into atmosphere, and the noise inside the control room turned it into a bedlam of sound. The atomics gave out their piercing whine, the computers chattered, the very metal of the ship itself groaned in protest.

"Four miles," called the Captain. "We'll cut across the equator, and then circle the poles."

Derryoc hung on to a chair that was bolted to the floor. His face was flushed, giving it an odd dark look under the white lights. "Get those maps. We'll need 'em."

Seyehi said nothing, hunched over his computers, his usually sure fingers clumsy in the unsteady ship.

The planet flashed by under them, a mosaic of continents and clouds and seas. The Captain stared at the control panels and found with something like scorn that he was holding his breath.

"Got it," said Seyehi after an interminable time.

The ship gave a perceptible buck, shuddered, and seemed to settle under them.

The lights dimmed, faltered, came up again brighter than before.

"No time to fool with it now," the Captain said, trying to speak calmly and at the same time having to yell to make himself heard.

"Can we go down and take a look from close up?" asked Derryoc.

"I don't know. Hafij?"

The navigator shrugged his thin shoulders. "We can try. It's taking an awful chance, Wyik."

Derryoc tried to examine the computer tapes, but it was impossible. "I say try it if there's any chance at all. It may be rough, but it won't be as rough as trying to walk around this damned planet to find out what's on it."

"If we can still walk after we get down," Hafij said.

"If we *get* down," Seyehi added.

The Captain made his decision. "We'll try. Hafij, I want to be able to count snow crystals on the mountain peaks and see the fish in those oceans. Skin her close."

Amazingly, Hafij grinned. "Hang on," he said.

The ship roared and slashed her way down, blasting through the high clouds with her hot metal sides hissing. She flattened out over the land, jetting like a river of flame through a cold blue sky.

She hurtled around the planet at a reckless speed, flashing over seas and islands and ice and vast green and brown plains. She roared from high noon into midnight and out once more into the golden sparkle of a morning sun.

Then she faltered and shook.

The drive broke off into a staccato series of blasts. The ship began to vibrate and swing sickeningly from side to side.

"No more time," yelled the Captain. "Strap in!"

With a thunder that made mountains tremble, the ship that had come so far stood on her tail and rushed down a geyser of flame toward her last landing.

Toward a green world, third from its sun.

Toward Earth.

CHAPTER

The ship came down, shattering the silence. Below her a marshy rolling plain of tough grass and wiry shrubs and amazingly vivid wild flowers disappeared in a scorching cloud of smoke and steam.

The ship was coming fast, too fast. The braking jets were firing furiously but not accurately. The tongue of searing flame below the ship grew shorter and shorter, like a telescope slipping into itself. The noise was incredible, a blast of overpowering, crashing sound that rushed out and smacked into the plains like a granite fist.

For just a moment the ship stood poised, a scant few feet above the ground. Then she dropped with a sudden jerk, slammed tail first into the soft earth with a wet, shuddering concussion. She seemed to balance for just a second or two, and then she buckled and collapsed on her side. There was a muffled explosion, a flicker of intense white flame. Then sprays spurted out from the sides of the ship, sprays of liquid that threw puddles out in a circle a hundred yards around the ship.

The fires hissed out.

The ship settled, a broken, twisted thing dying far from the stars she had known.

Silence came back to the plain. Warm yellow sunlight flowed down from a blue morning sky, touching the reds and blues and golds of the flowers scattered through the clumps of grass. A shocked peace returned to the land, a hush unbroken by the song of a bird or the snort of an animal.

The ship was down, and inside it was very dark. After the whining roar of the atomics the quiet was a tangible thing, a hollow emptiness that was eerie and cold.

Inside the control room, sounds. A scratching, a cough of heavy breathing as someone pulled himself to his feet. A monotonous moaning, a continuous low cry of pain. A dripping of something liquid that patted on the twisted metal wall.

A light. A narrow white beam playing through the room, shaking a little in someone's unsteady hand.

A voice, low and choked.

"Where are you? Who's hurt?" The Captain's voice.

A shadowy figure struggled up, trembling. "Hafij here," the navigator said. "I think I'm all right."

The beam of light picked out a dark form slumped in a corner. The form did not move, and made no sound. The Captain made his way to the figure, shoving junk out of his way as he did so, and gently turned it over. He flashed the light into a man's face, then moved the light quickly.

"It's Seyehi," he said. "He didn't make it."

The moans could still be heard, helpless sounds made by an unconscious man. The light beam followed the sounds and spotted a body sprawled near the door that led from the control room. Hafij beat the Captain there.

"Lots of blood," he said.

The Captain studied Derryoc as best he could in the narrow circle of white light. The anthropologist's big frame looked somehow collapsed, and there was blood trickling from the corners of his open mouth. His weak cries were the sounds of an animal in unendurable pain.

"Derryoc. It's Wyik. Can you hear me?"

Derryoc did not move, and his eyes stayed closed.

"Hafij, take the light and see if you can get some painkiller from the dispensary. We don't want him hysterical when he wakes up."

"He's *got* to live," Hafij whispered. "Otherwise—"

"Here. Take the light. Get Kolraq up here, if anyone's still with us back there. Better keep the rest out until we figure out where we can put Derryoc."

"Should I tell them—how bad it is?"

Without thinking about it, Wyik and Hafij felt themselves as belonging together, with the others forming a separate group. Now that Seyehi was gone, they were the only ones left from the control room nucleus that really ran the ship. They regarded themselves as spacemen and tended to lump the others in the passenger category. In the old days the others would never have been aboard a ship at all.

"Better tell them," the Captain said. "They'll have to know sooner or later anyway. Tell Arvon to keep an eye on Lajor, in case he gets hysterical. I think the kid will be all right; this may be the making of him."

"If he's still alive."

"Of course."

"If only our two key men hadn't—"

"Derryoc's still alive, Hafij. Get the medicine. Can you tell from the controls whether or not the pile's dampened properly?"

"I threw the rods before we hit. I don't *think* we'll have a blowup."

"Tell the others you're *sure* we won't have one. The atomic jitters we can get along without just now."

"Right." Hafij took the light and fumbled his way out of the control room. It wasn't easy, since the ship was on her side and the door seemed to be jammed. He managed to kick it open and crawled through on his stomach. Wyik could hear him heaving something out of the way, and he thought he heard low voices.

Somebody was still alive back there, then.

He squatted in the darkness, his hand on Derryoc's wet shoulder, and sensed the hulk of the ruined ship around him. Somewhere out there past those twisted metal walls was a world, and they were stuck on it. He didn't even know whether or not the air was breathable, and he had no hope that the planet would be of any use to them now; the odds were overwhelmingly against it.

It had been his decision. He stared into the darkness around him and knew that he should never have tried for one more planet, one more sun. He had taken a calculated risk and he had lost. He had known the drive was risky but he had gone ahead regardless.

Why?

The Captain knew why he had done it. He knew that it had not been a rational decision. If only he could have forgotten what had driven him out in space in the beginning—

"Damn," he said.

It was too late now.

He heard sounds from beyond the door. Hafij was coming back, and he had someone with him.

"Well?"

"Good news," Hafij said. "We must have taken the toughest jolt up here—they're all alive back in the cabin. Just bruised up some, nothing serious at all. Nlesine hurt his left arm, but it isn't broken."

The Captain smiled.

"One more thing," Hafij went on. "The Bucket has sprung a leak back there—fresh air is coming in and it seems to be breathable."

"It *has* to be breathable. We haven't got any power, and our air won't last long without purification. Hafij, it almost looks as if our luck is changing!"

Kolraq moved forward into the pale circle of light. "I have an injection ready," he said. "If you're through congratulating each other, maybe we can help Derryoc."

"Sorry," the Captain said, and moved out of the way. "Hold the light on him, Hafij—I'll try to rustle up another one in the supply room."

The priest examined Derryoc with his short, surprisingly sensitive fingers. He bared the anthropologist's arm, swabbed it, and injected a sedative from a hypodermic syringe. Derryoc still did not move. Kolraq wiped some blood away from his mouth and stood up.

Wyik maneuvered back into the control room with two more lights, one of which he gave to Kolraq. "What do you think?"

"We'd better not try to move him. He's hemorrhaging inside, and dragging him around won't help any. There's some stuff in the sedative that will keep down the infection, and that's about all we can do."

Derryoc continued to moan with grating regularity.

"Will he live?"

Kolraq shrugged. "That's out of our hands."

Wyik leaned forward intently. "Will he come to at all?"

"Perhaps. It's hard to say."

"He's tough," Hafij said. "He'll come out of it, Captain—I've seen them like this before."

Wyik nodded. "Come on. We'll have to get every scrap of data that came out of the computers before we hit. Didn't Derryoc take some notes?"

"I think so. He had a tablet—"

"Find it. Get everything set up. Kolraq, have we got something that will keep him free of pain if he comes to, but something that won't make him fuzzy?"

"We can try," the priest said. "But he should rest. You can't work him right away—that's inhuman."

"We need his brain," Wyik said simply. "He's the only one who can tell us what we've got to know about this planet. If we work blind we'll never get out of this—none of us, including Derryoc. That's all there is to it."

Kolraq hesitated, then wormed his way out through the control room door to see what he could find.

Wyik and Hafij settled down to watch and wait. Neither man spoke, but each was grateful for the other's company.

It was a strange scene, and Wyik knew it. The two lights threw silver rods across the jumbled control room, touching broken machines that loomed darkly around them. What had been the floor now formed one wall, giving the whole room a grotesque wrongness that no amount of logic could correct. Derryoc stopped moaning, but gave no sign of recovering consciousness.

*This was my ship,* Wyik thought. *We took many journeys together, and now the end of the line is a world without a name.*

Outside the darkness of the dead ship was a greater darkness, the darkness of ignorance. A land far from home, filled with the mystery and challenge of the unknown. Walk out of the ship, and you stood on alien land. Breathe the air if you could, and look about you. Blue skies, perhaps, and green fields. A river not far away, rolling cleanly down its gravel bed to the sea. And from that sea, if this world was similar to other worlds of its type, life had come. Tiny one-celled organisms and fish and amphibians and reptiles and mammals and, possibly, man.

What kind of man?

Wyik felt the darkness pressing him in. He had seen much of men, and it was not easy to find hope in the history he had found on many lonely worlds.

If men survived long enough, Wyik thought, they built ships that lifted them toward the stars. That was a fact. But what led one individual man to ride one of those ships? What path did he walk that carried him out into the sea between the stars?

And how many men aboard this ship could guess at the secret that he, Wyik, carried within him?

The long hours passed, and still Derryoc did not move. He was breathing regularly, and there was no blood on his face. But—what if he didn't wake up, ever?

They had to take shifts, finally. Arvon and Tsriga threw together a cold and unappetizing meal from the synthetics, and Kolraq supervised a blood transfusion for Derryoc.

There was no panic. They moved through the dark cave of the ship with that heightened intensity of feeling that disaster brings in its wake. They talked quietly of Seyehi, and remembered that they had always called him Feedback. They found little to laugh at, but Nlesine kept up a constant stream of gloomy predictions that, surprisingly, made them feel a little better. Nothing could be as bad as Nlesine said it was, which was optimism of a sort.

No one left the ship. Without power the screens did not work, and they could not see the land around them. But presumably there was sunlight, warm sunlight, and then nightfall. They had seen a satellite coming in, so there would be a moon up there, floating against a backdrop of stars.

But inside the ship there were only shadows and pale light beams burning through the wreckage.

After many hours Derryoc stirred, whitened, and opened his eyes.

Arvon was at his side, waiting.

"Don't try to move, Derryoc," he said, touching his shoulder. "Just take it easy."

The anthropologist closed his eyes, then opened them again. His mouth was a thin, tight line. His breathing was shallow and choked, as though he had something in his throat.

"We're down," Arvon said. "It's all over. You got a sock on the head, but you'll be okay. Just don't move. Understand?"

Derryoc nodded weakly.

Wyik climbed into the control room, with Kolraq behind him.

Derryoc spotted the priest and managed a faint smile. "Am I ready for you?" he asked.

Kolraq hesitated. "I'm here as a doctor," he said finally.

Derryoc grimaced. "Don't feel so good, Doc," he said. "Stomach upset—like I was going to be sick or something—" He broke off, and his eyes clouded.

"Derryoc," the Captain said, "try to hold on a minute. We need you badly."

The anthropologist got his eyes back in focus. "Feel sick. Hard to think. Can it wait?"

"I don't know," Wyik said.

Derryoc looked at the priest. "How bad am I, Doc? Really?"

"You've got a chance," Kolraq said. "It depends."

Derryoc shut his eyes. "What do you need, Wyik?"

"The ship smacked down hard. It's not going anywhere again unless we can get help. We're down on a planet we don't know anything about. We don't know what we're up against, and we won't know if you can't tell us. Can you?"

"Big job," Derryoc whispered. "Sleepy."

Kolraq pulled the Captain back. "He can't do it, not now. What do you want to do—murder him?"

Wyik looked into Kolraq's eyes. His face turned very pale, and his breathing came fast. "Do you think that, Kolraq?"

"No. Of course not. I just meant—"

The Captain turned back to Derryoc. "Get some sleep, Derryoc," he said softly. "We'll try again when you feel a little better."

The anthropologist gave no sign that he had heard, but he seemed more comfortable.

"I'll stay with him," Kolraq volunteered. "I'll call you, Wyik."

"No. We'll stay together. All right?"

The priest nodded.

"The rest of you try to get some rest," Wyik said. "You'll be needing it."

The three of them were left alone in the wreck of the control room. They turned out the lights and sat in darkness.

Derryoc's labored breathing filled the silence.

"I hope he wakes up," Kolraq whispered finally. "I hope I did the right thing."

"You'd better pray harder," the Captain said.

CHAPTER

The anthropologist slept for eight hours. It was growing cold in the ship, and Kolraq had arranged a blanket over him, with a second blanket wadded up for a pillow. Derryoc made no more sounds of pain. Indeed, save for the shallow, rapid breathing that lifted and lowered his chest, he might have passed for dead.

After the eighth hour they fed him intravenously. The sugar solution dripped down the rubber tubing, and Derryoc seemed to take it well enough. At any rate, his internal bleeding appeared to be checked.

But he did not wake up.

It became necessary to dispose of Seyehi's body, since they had no way of refrigerating it. Arvon and Hafij put on face masks, even though they were by now reasonably sure that the air would not harm them, and went outside. There they dug a shallow grave and lowered Seyehi's body into it.

Nlesine offered to stay with Derryoc. Kolraq and the Captain went out to say the words men say when death comes among them.

THE   WINDS   OF   TIME

It was night, but after the gloom of the ship the vault of stars seemed brilliant and alive and compassionate. A silver half-moon swung over their heads and bathed the world around them in shadowed gray. They stood on level ground, as far as they could see, and the night wind was bitingly cold.

They saw nothing and heard nothing that lived.

Kolraq read the burial service in a steady voice, but his words were thin in the miles of moonlight. Wyik said what he could, and then the dirt covered Seyehi forever.

"He came a long way to die," Arvon said.

Now that he was gone, really gone, invisible under the earth, his loss struck home to them. The shock of the crash had worn off, and they were all suddenly aware that they stood very close to death and were far from the skies and the friends they had known.

It was strange to think that Seyehi would never again be a part of a control room scene, never again work with the computers he loved, never again smile gently when someone called him Feedback.

They went back into the ship and closed the lock as best they could against the cold.

"He's stirring a little," Nlesine called.

Wyik and Kolraq took their lights and hurried forward. Both of them tried not to think about the grave they had seen. But a second grave nudged icily against their minds....

The anthropologist moved one leg suddenly. His eyes opened, and he strained as though he were trying to sit up.

Kolraq caught him, held him down. "Easy, old friend. Don't move if you can help it."

Derryoc was awake now, and awareness came back. "I must be half dead if I'm your old friend," he whispered. "You never called me that before."

"I—"

"Don't apologize. Thanks. I appreciated it. Could I have a drink?"

"Water?" suggested Wyik.

Derryoc frowned, a little color coming into his pale face. "I guess it'll have to be water. Never thought I'd come to it, though."

The Captain laughed. Maybe he was getting better, maybe he would even get well!

Nlesine brought some water, and Derryoc sipped it gratefully. But he stopped after perhaps two ounces. His face whitened again. He coughed convulsively, his body straining under the blanket. Flecks of red appeared at the corners of his mouth.

The spasm subsided, just as Kolraq was getting the needle ready.

"Better not try *that* again," Derryoc said, and smiled weakly.

No one spoke. Wyik was afraid to suggest anything, and Kolraq was desperately trying to think of something that would help Derryoc, even though it was becoming clear that the man was beyond his help.

Derryoc himself broke the silence. "If we're going to work, we'd better get to it."

"Do you feel well enough?" the Captain asked.

Derryoc looked at him steadily. "I won't ever feel any better, will I, Wyik?"

Wyik didn't answer. Instead, he carefully propped Derryoc up on the blanket so that his head was in a position where he could read without straining. Then he fixed three lights above and behind Derryoc, and slid a magnetized panel into place to hold the computer tapes and notes.

Hafij squirmed around until he was able to hold items up for inspection without cutting off the light.

"This is going to be very much of an impressionistic job," the anthropologist warned them. "Don't trust it too far."

"Your guess will be better than anything we could work out on our own," Wyik said. "How long will you need before you can answer questions?"

"I *need* about a week to do the job right. I figure I've *got* maybe four hours before I conk out again. Do I have that long, Doc?"

"I think so," Kolraq said.

"Shoot some more stuff into me if you have to. All things considered, I think I'd better give you a preliminary reading before I go back to sleep—just in case. Let's say three hours on these tapes, and then I'll tell you what I can. Let's see that equatorial survey first, Hafij—it'll be coded A 14, I think. There, that's the one...."

Derryoc's eyes were clear and bright, although his color was not good and his breathing was irregular. He showed no sign of pain, and seemed almost to be enjoying himself. He lost himself in his work.

Evidently his powers of concentration were undimmed; it was quite obvious that the other people in the control room had ceased to exist as far as he was concerned.

The long minutes ticked by and became hours. Derryoc absorbed material rather than studied it; he could fix his eyes on a sheet for a few moments, then motion Hafij to replace it with a new one. He could not have explained the picture that was building up in his mind, a picture developed out of half hints and subtle clues that might have been meaningless to someone else. The configurations of continents and seas went into his calculations, as well as an occasional lucky bit of concrete information picked up by the camera scanners. Mostly he was guided by a lifetime of study about the processes of culture growth; he supplied data that were not actually before him on the basis of what *had* to be there.

After precisely three hours he nodded his head. "I'm ready. Can you cut those lights down?"

Wyik turned two of them around, producing a more indirect illumination, and turned the other up so that the beam passed over Derryoc's head.

"Do you feel strong enough to talk?"

"No. But let's not waste time being polite. You won't like what I've got to say, but you'd better hear it."

The others pressed closer, listening. This was no longer an abstract problem to them—it was a matter of life or death.

"First," said Wyik, forcing himself to ask the questions, "can we get help anywhere on this planet? Anyone we can go to and throw this ship together again?"

"No," said Derryoc. "There's no doubt on this point, Wyik. If you're looking for an advanced technology you've drawn a fat lemon."

"You mean there are no men? I thought—"

"Oh, men, sure. There are men here, although they're not very numerous yet. The trouble is that you're a bit too early. I may be a little off, but I'd say that there's not a single culture on this planet that's even developed agriculture yet. Helpful, eh?" Derryoc smiled a little.

"In other words—"

"In other words, you're in the middle of a Stone Age world. The men are mostly scattered in smallish groups, living by hunting wild animals and gathering wild plant foods—roots, berries, stuff like that. If you want to know how to fix a broken spear point you've come to the right place. If you want to know how to repair a spaceship you'll have to wait twenty thousand years or so and then ask somebody— except that somebody will have probably blown himself up by then."

There was a long silence.

"We're stuck, then," Wyik said finally. "We can't repair this ship, even for normal drive. As for a distortion field that might get us home again—"

"It's out of the question," Derryoc finished. "You haven't got the tools to make the machines to make the other machines that might fix your ship. You're not going to put this baby back together with a monkey wrench, you know."

"Looks like this is going to be home, whether we like it or not," Nlesine said. "There's nothing we can do."

"*Almost* nothing," the anthropologist corrected him.

"I don't follow you," Wyik said, frowning.

Derryoc paused, gathering his strength. Then his eyes became active and alert. He was clearly interested in the situation just as a problem, apart from any role he himself might play in it.

"What's the normal procedure for getting home if your distortion field breaks down and you can't repair it?" he asked.

Wyik watched him closely. "Compute the ship's course through normal space, set the controls on automatic, and sleep it out. But we happen not to have a ship, and no computers either."

"But you *have* got the sleeping equipment, right?"

There was a pause.

"We've got the stuff, yes," Wyik said. "It's nothing very complicated: an extract from the lymphoid tissue of hibernating mammals, coupled with an absorbent of vitamin D; a little insulin and some common drug derivatives that have been known for centuries."

The lights burned steadily in the ruined control room.

"It's powerful stuff, no matter how simple it is," Derryoc went on. "And why would you use it if you were suddenly deprived of your distortion field?"

"Simple enough," Wyik said, puzzled. "The ship can't exceed the speed of light in normal space—or in the distortion field either, for that matter. But the field has the effect of 'curving' space to bring two objects closer together; it's a kind of short cut, as you know."

"I didn't ask you for a lecture on elementary space navigation," Derryoc said testily. "I asked you why you would use the drug."

"It's an emergency device. It's the long way home if you can't get there any other way. Distances in normal space are enormously long, of course. You may be a hundred light-years or more from home when the distortion field conks out. At normal acceleration in normal space it may take you better than a hundred years to get home, and by that time you'll be dead. But the drug makes it possible for you to go into a sort of suspended animation; your bodily processes slow down until there is hardly a spark to keep you alive. When you get home you wake up—and even if hundreds of years have passed on the ship you're only a week or so older as far as wear and tear on your body is concerned. Of course, all your friends will be dead, you'll have to begin your life all over again."

"But you'll be home," the anthropologist interrupted. "Don't be so long-winded, Wyik; there's no time for that."

"I still don't get it," Hafij said. "We haven't got any ship, and the people here are still in the Stone Age."

"Sure, sure," Derryoc said impatiently. "They're in the Stone Age *now* and so they can't help you. But suppose you had landed here fifteen or twenty thousand years *later?* What then?"

Wyik hesitated. "Probably this would have been a dead planet. As soon as they got atomic energy, they'd go the way the rest of them went."

"*We* didn't destroy ourselves," Kolraq put in, with more fire in his voice than had been heard in the control room for many days. "We set out on this voyage in the hope of finding someone else who might survive, someone we could talk to. How do we know—*maybe those savages out there will be the ones we were looking for.* It would be a lovely, terrible irony...."

"The odds are against it," Wyik said flatly.

Derryoc coughed slightly, blinked his eyes, and went on. "For once, gentlemen, I'm with Kolraq. You speak of odds, Wyik, but you're not *thinking*. What chance do you have to get help from any other world but the one you're on?"

"No chance," Wyik admitted.

"Very well. Your *only* hope is with those people out there, those crude-seeming men hunting wild animals and starving half the time. Either they help you, or no one does. They can't help you now. Therefore you've got to wait until they *can* help you. Since you aren't likely to live fifteen thousand years or so you've got to use the drug— use most all of it—and sleep just as long as you possibly can. Then, maybe, you can go home in one of *their* ships."

"How do we know we'll even have a home to go to after all those years?"

"You don't. And you don't know, either, that these people will refrain from blowing themselves up until after they've developed space travel. But you're not going to throw a spaceship together out of mud and trees, I can promise you that. And you'll never have a chance to get home any other way. So there it is. Take it or leave it."

"Take it," Kolraq said instantly. "Take it!"

"I don't know," Wyik said. "It's a long, long chance—"

Derryoc coughed again, and this time there was blood on his lips. "Argue about it later. Hold up that map, Hafij—the big one."

Hafij held it up awkwardly where the light could fall on it.

"Listen closely," Derryoc said, speaking very fast. His voice was thin now, and hard to hear. "I may be wrong—I'm guessing from faulty data—but I've got some more advice."

"Yes?" Wyik moved still closer, looking worriedly at the anthropologist.

"The ship crashed *here,*" Derryoc said, his finger reaching up to the map. He touched a spot high in what would one day be called Northeast Asia. "I don't think you should stay here if you can avoid it."

"Why not?"

"Too complicated to explain, Wyik. It's a peripheral area, for one thing—it's out on the fringes. That means the odds are against its developing as rapidly as some other places. There are parts of our own world where they've never seen a spaceship—you don't want to wake up in one of those."

"True enough. But—"

"*Look at the map.* Quickly, now."

"I'm looking."

"The most intensive development of culture on this planet seems to be *here*," Derryoc said. His finger touched a part of what would in time be named France. "But there are people scattered all through this region, and down into this big continent here." He indicated Africa. "When agriculture develops, in my estimation, it should come first somewhere between these two major areas, at a sort of ideational crossroads. Perhaps along in here, near this body of water." He pointed to the Mediterranean.

"You think we should try to get to that sea?"

"*No.* That's where the population will be concentrated over a long span of time. Too great a risk of being found. What you need is an area that will be sparsely settled for many, many years—but an area that will blossom suddenly when new ideas hit it."

"I see that," Wyik said tensely. "But where is there such an area?"

"I can't be sure. I'm sorry, but I don't have all the facts I need. But this huge island *here* would not be a good bet—it seems to be mostly desert." His finger touched the island men would one day name Australia. His hand then swept over a number of Pacific islands. "These are too small, and impossible to get to unless you want to risk it in a boat you might make. But look at this."

Derryoc's finger traced the outline of the continental mass that would, thousands of years later, challenge the imagination of men as the New World.

"Is it inhabited?" asked Wyik.

"I don't know. It seems obvious that man did not evolve there on this planet, and there is certainly no great population there at present. I didn't *see* any men there on the tapes—but some few may have arrived. But look what's going to happen!"

The others looked, and saw nothing.

"Ah," said Derryoc in exasperation. "No time to explain. But some men are bound to get into that area—it's rich in land, well watered, enormous in extent. The men will come in from around where we are now—see, across here, down along here." His finger traced a path across the Bering Strait, down the corridor of Alaska. "In all probability, they are already filtering in now. They'll have a good part of this planet ahead of them—a paradise for hunters. But they'll be a long, long way from the cultural center of this world, which is away back here." He pointed again to Europe. "One day, when ships get good enough, men with a fairly complex culture will cross this ocean here, or possibly the other one; it doesn't matter. They'll find a virtually untouched land, and they'll take it from its original settlers. *Then* that area will boom, and that's where you'll want to be. You can stay hidden for thousands of years, and yet when you wake up you'll have what you need within easy reach."

The others stood silently in the gloom of the control room.

"Well, boys," Nlesine said after many minutes, "I guess we'd better slip into our old walking shoes."

The effort had been too much for Derryoc; it had eaten up his last ounce of strength. While the other men still stood around him, trying to understand the words he had spoken, he drifted into an exhausted sleep.

Wrapped in soft darkness, Derryoc dreamed. Kolraq might have called them visions, but the tiny spark of awareness that continued to burn in the anthropologist rejected the idea firmly. He even smiled slightly in his sleep, so that those watching him wondered what he could possibly be dreaming that could seem funny at a time like this.

At first his dreams were touched with vanity, and he was annoyed with them. He saw himself through a child's eyes: badly hurt in a crash and yet saving his companions by the wisdom he had stored up through the years. In the fog of what was now a coma, the notion pleased Derryoc. He had never been a really big man in his profession, and he knew that the others thought him cold. It was good to be appreciated, to be liked....

The picture faded. Equations danced through his mind, coupled with scenes from many lands and many worlds. He saw this curious animal called man as though in a many-sided mirror, everywhere a little different, everywhere the same. There was a flaw in the mirror, and he thought if he could only reach out, touch it, feel it…

Then he got better. The weariness evaporated, and strength flowed back into his veins. His mind cleared, and he saw everything around him with crystal sharpness. He was happy, very happy, for he had thought, he had been certain, that he was going to die. He was glad when they left the ship but he tried to show no emotion. What was he, a novelist or a priest, to rejoice in living winds and the smells of green grasses?

Still, it was good. The sun was a good sun, and warm, and it touched him with gold. It healed him as only the sun could heal. And then they saw smoke on the horizon, and the next day they heard sounds: cries, laughter, shouts. His pulse quickened. Men! He wanted to go to them, make friends with them, try to understand them. Oh, he would talk about data and statistics, but they came later, they were the rationale. For now there were only people, and fire shadows, and fresh meat and something to drink, something with a kick to it.

And perhaps here, too, he might find a man or a woman who would call him friend, who would make him feel just for a little while that he belonged. It had been so many years since she had died, the one who never should have died, the one who was going to live forever.

He was happy, as happy as he had ever been. The drink was good drink, it made his head spin, it was wet and warm and he could taste it in his mouth….

Within two hours after he had slipped into an exhausted sleep Derryoc was having convulsions.

In three hours he was dead.

It was a dirty, messy death, with no touch of romance about it. There were no last-minute curtain speeches. There was not even dignity.

Arvon and Kolraq carried his body outside, and they buried him in a grave next to Seyehi. All of them felt somehow futile and lost when Derryoc was gone. There were words they might have said, little things they might have done for a living man.

For the dead there is only silence.

For Derryoc there was only the night wind under the stars, the night wind blowing always across a world he would never know.

The sun was high in the sky.

Arvon sat on a flat rock, his tall body comfortably slouched, his chin resting in his cupped hands. The slight breeze that rustled through the grasses had a keen edge to it, but the sunlight was warm on his back. There were patches of white cloud in the sky, and whenever one of them drifted across the face of the sun it grew decidedly chilly.

He looked around and discovered somewhat to his own amazement that he felt better than he had in years. The ship, a hundred yards away in the middle of a circle of scarred vegetation and scorched earth, was crumpled but harmless; in a few years, he supposed, it would be only a shell, and within a century it wouldn't exist. There would be only the plains, the gleaming-tipped mountains, the winds.

Maybe that would be a good thing.

He felt a curious joy just in being outside, where he could breathe clean air and hear the long, living silences that washed in from far away. He rejoiced even in the bugs that plodded dutifully through the grass, bound on pressing bug business. He was more than *ready* for whatever might come—he was actually *eager* for it, even impatient for it.

A man was not born to live in a tube of steel. A man was a part of the land and the sky; his body knew that even when his mind reached out across the light-years, into star fields and challenge and desolation....

He was lonely for his home world of Lortas, and the loneliness was accentuated by the fact that this planet was so much like it in many ways, even though separated from it by a gulf of years as well as miles. But he was not desperately lonely; Lortas could wait, would *have* to wait. He was not proud of the life he had left behind him there—it had been too easy for him, and it had come too fast. Too many pleasures, too many women, too many nights that were so similar he could never tell them apart. Even high living can get monotonous, he knew; the rut of the idle is a deep rut indeed. If his father had given him less, worked him more—but it was childish to blame it on *him*.

He thought, surprised: *There are places on Lortas very little different from this world I see around me. There are open fields under our sun, and clean winds, and patient stone. Does a man have to come so far just to find himself?*

"Fine thing," a voice said unexpectedly. "Here we are splattered on an alien planet, and you're asleep at the switch."

Arvon jerked back to the present and looked up to see Nlesine standing in front of him. The novelist's balding head was already pinkish from the sun, and his eyes had a sparkle in them.

Nlesine sat down on a handy rock, found it unsuitable, and settled on another. "Wyik wants to see us, whenever you're finished daydreaming. Big council of war or something. What're you brooding about?"

"Things. But I wasn't brooding."

"I know." Nlesine smiled—an odd smile, at once cynical and understanding. "You've been acting like we're better off now than before we crashed."

"Aren't we?"

"It'll pass," Nlesine assured him. "You're so glad to be alive you're suffering from euphoria. Very dangerous disease. Wait'll it freezes up around here—you'll stub one of your bare toes and it'll break off like a rotten twig." He snapped his fingers cheerfully.

Arvon nodded. "Funny, though—I'd never have thought I'd enjoy anything like this, even for a little while."

"Keep your eyes open, son. You can tell a lot about a man by the way he reacts to something like this. Take Lajor, now—he's the only one who's scared silly. He'll be trouble—you watch. Wyik is the same everywhere. Hafij is lost, I think. He was the only one of us who really belonged in space—Seyehi liked it wherever his computers were, but Hafij *likes* it out there. He'll get back, if anyone does."

"And the others? Tsriga? Kolraq?"

"I'm still working on them. You tell me."

Arvon shook his head. "Kolraq seems older than the rest of us, and Tsriga younger. I wouldn't push it further than that."

"It's the extremes that are sometimes the hardest to predict," Nlesine said half to himself. He stood up then, briskly, and dusted himself off. "Come on. It's time for Momentous Words from Our Noble Captain."

Side by side they walked back through the early afternoon sunlight toward the wreck of the ship.

They sat in a circle on the sunward side of the ship, out of the cold wind. They were very close to the two raw graves, and it took very little imagination to see Derryoc or Seyehi among them.

Even seated on the ground, Wyik dominated the group. He was by no means a big man, but he was the man you watched if only because of his tightly controlled energy; he was a coiled spring, ready to go at the slightest touch. He was their leader in fact as well as in theory, and he led because he was *hard*—not blind or stupid or in any way sadistic, but simply tough from the core out.

Wyik did the talking. "You all heard Derryoc, you know what he said. He was the man best qualified to judge, and he advised us not to stay here. His reasons seemed to me to be good reasons at the time; they still do. But there are several questions that should be raised."

He paused, collected his thoughts.

"The first is this: Was Derryoc really in possession of all the facts he needed to arrive at a correct decision? It was a rush job, of necessity, and there were no computers to check him. He *may* have been wrong."

"His guess is still better than ours, Wyik," Nlesine said. "Mind you, a thousand-mile walk does not particularly strike my fancy."

Wyik smiled briefly. "I agree that his estimate of the situation is the best we have. If we ever want a chance to get home again, he's given us a blueprint that may work. There's really no other solution; there won't be another exploration ship out this way in a million years, and they'd never spot us if they came. Are we agreed on that?"

There were no objections.

"All right. Our problem is very simple, then. Do we stay where we are or do we set sail for that relatively uninhabited continent of Derryoc's? I'm sure that the point of this hasn't escaped you. We all know that the odds are overwhelmingly against this world ever attaining space travel, even in its most rudimentary form. The civilization here must be built by men, and we have seen, on world after world, that man characteristically destroys himself when he has the power. Those are the facts, and we can't ignore them. If we *do* make it to this other part of the world, and if we *do* survive a sleep of many thousands of years, there's a good chance we may wake up to a radioactive desert. If we do, that'll be that. There's a *chance* this may be the planet we've been looking for, the planet that will give us some company in this rather forbidding universe of ours. But it's an awfully slim chance. Is it worth taking?"

The youngster, Tsriga, spoke first. "You know, we wouldn't *have* to sleep that long, would we? I mean, we could just go under for maybe five or ten thousand years—however long it would take—and then wake up in a civilization of sorts, but one still without atomic energy. We wouldn't get home, but we could *make* a home for ourselves." His eyes brightened with enthusiasm. "It would almost be like going back in time, on Lortas I mean, seeing all the things you only read about in history books—"

"I'll take the history books," Nlesine said.

"Your idea is worth considering, Tsriga," Wyik said, ignoring Nlesine. "And, of course, there's more to it than that—"

"Sure!" Lajor interrupted with sudden enthusiasm. "Why didn't I think of that? *We could just stay here.* We know what we've got now, don't we? It's not so bad, is it? I mean, it's nothing like some of the worlds we've seen *after* they began busting up the old atoms—it's green, you can drink the water, you can swallow air without searing your lungs out. We'll never get home anyway, so why try? We could build ourselves a little settlement, plant some crops, live out our lives. What's wrong with that?"

"No women," Nlesine said bluntly.

Lajor laughed. "There are natives, aren't there? What's wrong with them? We could go into the god business!"

"A god without guts wouldn't appeal to them," Nlesine said, smiling with one side of his mouth.

"What do you mean by that?" Lajor half rose to his feet. "Nlesine, I've had about all I'm going to take from you—"

Nlesine didn't even look at him. "Fearless Reporter Socks Effete Novelist," he murmured.

"That's enough of that," Wyik said. He did not raise his voice, but Lajor sat down again. "Let's not accuse one another; we've got enough problems without that. The fact is, Lajor put his finger on exactly what I was thinking. Mind you, that wouldn't be *my* choice, but let's be realistic. I'm not the Captain any more; I'm just Wyik. I can't order you around, and I would be silly to try. The unhappy fact is that Lajor is right. If we just figure the odds, and if we believe that our only duty now is to ourselves, then we'd be better off staying right here. I think we'd survive. We might even have a good time."

"Vegetables don't have fun," Arvon said.

"How do you know?" asked Nlesine.

Arvon didn't answer him.

Kolraq, who had been silent throughout the discussion, got slowly to his feet and shielded his eyes with his hand. "Before we make too many plans about living with the natives," he said, "perhaps we'd better ask them what they think about the idea."

The others leaped up.

There, coming across the plains from the south, were dark figures. They were silent, but moving fast.

Men.

Instinctively they moved toward the dark port of the ship. Wherever he was found, whatever else could be said about him, man was dangerous. He was the supreme killer animal, and even his own kind faced him at their peril.

"Hold it," Wyik snapped. "There are only four of them. Nlesine, go inside and get some stun guns. The rest of you stay where you are."

Lajor moved a little closer to the port. He seemed about to challenge Wyik's authority, but he could sense that he would be a minority of one. "I think we should get inside the ship," he said. "We'd be safer there."

"But we couldn't *see*," Arvon pointed out. "What are we going to do—run and hide every time a hunting party comes our way?"

"Depends on what they're hunting," Tsriga said, smiling. "Stone Age men are often cannibals, aren't they?"

"The point is," Wyik said, "that we don't know anything about them. We've got to find out. I can't see any great danger—the range of our guns will be better than anything they've got."

"I hope you're not going to just open up on them," Kolraq said. "They may mean no harm."

"No one will fire unless we are attacked," Wyik stated evenly, looking at Lajor. "Ah—thanks, Nlesine."

Nlesine distributed the small hand guns.

They waited.

The four men who were walking across the plains were as silent as the wind. But they had a dog with them, and the dog barked a warning as he caught the alien scent.

Arvon watched the natives with a curious sense of awe. The figures moved closer, walking steadily and with no effort at concealment. He could almost make out details, but not quite. It was like looking into the past, staring into that vast and shadowed fog that was the cradle of man on many worlds. Here were men who had never known cities or agriculture or writing, men of the dawn, men only beginning the long climb that might one day lead to the stars—or to oblivion.

The contrast between their experience and his gave to the natives a kind of innocence. They would know fears and selfishness and perhaps horror, but they had yet to discover the evil that was within themselves.

They came on, walking out of youth, out of time. They stopped some thirty yards away, and Arvon could see them now.

They stood in a line, silent and unafraid. The dog that was half wolf put his belly in the grass and whined, his pink tongue dripping with saliva.

The reality, as usual, was something of an anticlimax when you saw it up close. And yet it had its own drama about it, the drama of sweat and hopes and smells.

The natives were not tall; there was not a man among them who approached six feet. Their hair was long, straight, and black. Their eyes were narrow and dark. Their skin was a yellowish bronze in color, and they were dressed in crude sewn hides.

The men were proud. They stood quite still and did not fidget. They eyed the strangers with a frank curiosity, but with an assumed superiority that waited for them to make the first move. They were armed—two of them carried stone-tipped spears, and two carried a kind of throwing stick armed with wicked-looking darts.

Arvon caught a whiff of them on the breeze, and had to smile. For phantoms these men had a certain solidity about them.

"Kolraq," Wyik whispered.

"Yes?"

"Go in the ship and get four sharp knives from the mess. Then we'll go out there and see if we can make some friends."

The priest ducked into the ship as the natives watched silently. What did they make of the ship, how could they explain it to each other? Arvon tried to see it through their eyes. They would know it was not a natural object, but would they connect it with the thunder that had shattered their world a few days ago?

Kolraq came back with the knives.

"Let's go," said Wyik.

The two men walked slowly toward the natives.

The dog leaped up, bristled.

The natives lifted their spears.

Wyik held a knife in each hand, gripping them by their points so that the handles were pointed toward the natives. Kolraq did the same. To the natives the intent must have been obvious, for the two strangers were helpless before their spears.

"*Nanhaades!*" one of the natives called, raising his spear to the throwing position. "*Nanhaades!*"

The dog growled deep in his throat.

"Put 'em on the grass," Wyik said. "Then back off."

They put the knives down, being careful to make no sudden movements. They essayed smiles that were perhaps not remarkably successful, which wasn't too surprising under the circumstances. Then they backed away from the knives, pointing first to the natives and then to the knives.

The dark-eyed men were not stupid. The one who had spoken stepped forward, scooped up the knives, and stared at them. He tested the edge of one against the skin of his arm, and seemed startled when it drew blood. He held the metal up to the sun, watching it gleam as it caught the light. He grinned delightedly.

The others moved up to him, looking and chattering as though gags had suddenly been yanked out of their mouths. The one with the knives backed away from them, trying to balance four knives and a spear in his hands. The three natives without knives followed him, talking rapidly. Obviously the leader was disposed to keep the knives for himself—and equally obviously the others weren't too keen on the idea.

A first-rate wrangle promptly developed, and stopped only when the man with the knives, after trying in vain to decide which one was the best, divided them up. Then they all got to laughing and reflecting sunlight into each other's eyes with the shining metal blades.

It was good fun, and Arvon found himself enjoying it hugely from a distance. He sneaked a look around him, and saw that even Wyik had a smile on his face.

Nlesine caught his eye and winked. "It looks good to Nlesine," he said.

And then, incredibly, the four natives simply turned their backs on the ship and walked away, with the dog bounding on ahead of them. They didn't look back at all, and appeared utterly unconcerned.

Soon they were only shadows again, and then they were lost from view.

"Well, I'll be damned," Nlesine said, grinning wryly. "What do they think this is—a supply dump?"

"I guess we're not as important as we thought we were," Kolraq said. "We've just had a lesson in ego deflation."

Wyik shook his head. "They'll be back."

"How do you know?" asked Kolraq.

Wyik suddenly looked older, as though a fraction of his tremendous energy had momentarily deserted him. "They always come back," he said, "one way or another."

They slept inside the ship that night, and it was like sleeping in a tomb. The silence there was the silence that waits under the earth, and even the dreams were dark.

They posted no guard: once the air lock was shut nothing could get at them. But the ship had changed—in only a few days, it had grown old, it belonged to the past. There was not a man in it that night who did not think of that closed air lock with a feeling of unreasonable fear, as though he were sealed off forever from the sun.

Arvon and Nlesine had stretched out side by side, and they were both uncomfortable; the ship was pitched at an awkward angle. They stayed awake for hours, although they spoke only once.

"How about the scouting copter?" Arvon whispered. "Couldn't we take it instead of walking?"

"Maybe. I'm not sure just what the range of that thing is. It runs on power storage units, you know—too small for a bulky atomic engine."

"I don't understand why Wyik hasn't mentioned it. It's almost as though he's avoiding the subject, but we've all seen that copter."

Nlesine laughed shortly. "Mathematics," he said.

"Mathematics?"

"Well, call it arithmetic. How many men will that copter hold?"

Arvon considered. "Two, normally. But we could get more than that in if we had to."

"More, yes—but there's a limit. A quart bottle just holds a quart, no matter what. We might be able to cram four of us in that cabin—I think it would fly, but not well. Four isn't seven."

"I think it would carry five."

"Maybe—but what if it did? What about the other two?"

"Couldn't we make two trips?"

"Hardly. I know there's not that much stored energy in those units. It might be possible to just go halfway in the copter, but I have a feeling it wouldn't be too smart to split up at this stage. This isn't going to be any stroll through the park, remember."

Arvon yawned. "We'll work it out."

"Your optimism is a little sickening, my friend. I'll bet you actually believe we'll get home again someday. I'll bet you really think this is the world we've been looking for. It's too neat, Arvon. Life doesn't work that way."

"Sometimes it does," Arvon said stubbornly.

Nlesine chuckled. "Good night," he said.

"Good night."

The silence came again, a silence that blanketed the ship in cold breathlessness. As Arvon drifted into sleep, he thought: *It's quieter here than in the deeps of space.*

It was not a pleasant idea.

The natives came with the sun.

There was something almost supernatural about their appearance. One minute the plains were empty of human life, and the next minute men were there, as though they had simply materialized out of the grass and rocks and morning wetness. No, not supernatural, Arvon corrected himself—it was rather that they were *supremely* natural, a part of the land itself.

The natives brought meat with them, and there was nothing supernatural about that. They built a fire on the sheltered side of the ship, using what looked like dried dung chips for fuel, and roasted great chunks of red meat in the flames. The meat sizzled and dripped, and it was superb after too long a time on synthetics.

"A trifle raw," as Nlesine put it, "but what's a little blood between friends?"

They threw a piece to the dog, who wolfed it down gratefully, belched, and settled down to a sensible nap in the sunlight.

The natives did not seem concerned by the fact that they could not understand the language of the men who lived in the strange tower. Evidently they had come across groups of men before who spoke tongues different from their own, and it was surprising how well they could make themselves clear just by smiles and gestures. They certainly seemed friendly enough, although it was always possible that they were just impressed by the knives and wanted more of them.

Looking at the rippling muscles in their arms and legs, and the jagged points on their spears, Arvon preferred to hope they were merely congenial—and would stay that way.

When breakfast was over, the leader stood up, stretched, and pointed toward the south. There, across the plain, the land grew more rolling and a low chain of hills was visible, rising out of a purple haze. He pointed again to the hills, then to Arvon and the rest, and then back to the hills.

"He wants us to go with him," Wyik said.

"Probably got the old stewpot bubbling," Nlesine observed. "I vote we offer Lajor as a sacrifice."

"Cut it out," Lajor said nervously.

"Well, do we go?" Hafij asked. "Should we leave the ship?"

The four natives drew back slightly as they talked. They were not smiling now.

"I don't think it would be smart to refuse their hospitality," Kolraq said. "They mean no harm."

"How do *you* know?" asked Nlesine. "Have a vision?"

"I'm for going," Arvon said. "I agree with Kolraq—the more friends we have the better. We can close the port on the ship; no one could get in."

Wyik nodded. "We'll go. Take your guns, and let's gather up a supply of gifts—go easy on the knives, though. Maybe some clothes, a flashlight, things like that. All right?"

They got ready, clambering through the ship with an odd sense of sadness. Of course, they would be back, and the ship was a ruin. Still, it gave a man a funny feeling to leave his last tie with home.

The natives watched with expressionless dark eyes. They saw the men climb in and out of the black tunnel in the gleaming wall, but made no attempt to follow them inside.

When they had loaded themselves up and put on warm clothes against the chill in the air, Wyik nodded and pointed toward the hills.

The natives grinned, as though pleased, and set off across the plains. The dog was up in an instant and led the way. He didn't bark now, and kept his black muzzle to the ground.

The land was not as level as it looked, Arvon found. The grass seemed to cluster in clumps, and the black soil was rocky in between. There were hidden depressions that caught at your ankle and thorny bushes that scraped at your hands as you went by. Some of the bushes had brilliant red berries on them, and he wondered whether or not they were good eating. There were many flowers, poking delicate wet heads up out of the grasses. The air was crisp, clean, and cold.

The natives chattered among themselves and kept up a brisk pace. Nlesine was soon puffing visibly, and it was hard on all of them. The men from the ship were not used to walking, and Arvon found that he was developing a prize blister on his left heel.

"Trying to walk us to death," Nlesine panted.

"Don't look so weary," Wyik said. "We don't want them to think we're softies."

"We *are* softies," Nlesine objected.

Once they glimpsed a herd of animals ahead of them. They were beauties, large and delicately poised, with lovely brown coloring and tossing antlers. But they were downwind from the men, and caught the scent long before they were in range of the dart throwers of the natives. They milled a bit, then a stag shook his antlers decisively, snorted, and set out at a trot toward the west. The herd followed him, not really running, but moving right along.

The leader of the natives pointed at them, said a word that Arvon didn't catch, and called back the dog that had started out in eager pursuit.

They walked for hours, and the men from the ship were playing out rapidly. Soon it would be no joke; they would *have* to stop. Arvon found that his mouth was so dry he could not swallow, and his chest was stabbing him when he breathed.

"Hail the conquering heroes from outer space," he muttered, and concentrated on putting one foot in front of the other.

The land began to rise, and they were suddenly on a definite path that wound into the hills. The hills, seen close up, were fairly formidable, and the rocks were worn and treacherously smooth, as though something heavy had ground them down.

They kept walking.

Behind them and to the west black clouds began to pile up in the sky and the wind moaned down across the plains. The grasses undulated in the wind like waves, and far off in the distance there was the rumble of thunder.

The natives kept chattering happily.

The men from space stuck their heads down and kept with it.

Even Nlesine, for once, had nothing to say.

Within an hour it was raining hard.

You don't notice scenery in the rain.

The water whirs and drums all around you, splashing on the rocks and digging tiny holes in the wet black earth. Your hair is plastered down on your forehead, and water drips from it and slides across your slick, shining face. Rain gets in your eyes, and you blink, and they get red and stingy.

Your clothes hang on your body like heavy felt sacks, and your own sweat makes you clammy and hot. There is water in your shoes, gallons of it, and every time you take a step you feel your toes squishing in your own private river.

The ground under you is slippery, and occasionally you fall down. You grab out for a tree or a limb to support yourself, but there are no trees. Soon your face is cut a little, and it stings where the rain hits against it.

No, you don't have much time for scenery.

Arvon didn't know where he was, and didn't care. He was wrapped in a tight cloak of misery, splashing along and half wishing he were dead. A good many of his romantic views on primitive life he left behind him in the mud.

Then, incredibly, it was over.

One of the natives ahead of him cried out, and a woman's voice hollered something in return. Arvon got his eyes to working again, and picked out a blur of warm yellow light in the gray haze. He squinted and saw some roundish humps rising up out of some sheltered high ground at the head of a small valley. They seemed too short to hold a man, but the party was making straight for them.

He stumbled on, and someone caught his arm and steered him toward a light. He was guided through an opening, and almost fell as his foot missed a short flight of steps inside. *Sunken living room,* he thought vaguely.

But it was light, and warm!

A fire. He clumped over to it, shook his hair out of his eyes, and held out his hands to the blaze. He was conscious of figures around him in the little pit house, and he heard some laughter. A small boy, he noticed, was staring at him with frank curiosity.

Arvon was quite close to collapse, and knew it. They must have walked a good twenty miles over a tough trail, and the plain fact was that none of them was used to that kind of work. Already, after only a moment or two by the fire, he could feel the tiny ache in his legs that meant stiffness within a few hours.

Still, a man had his self-respect.

Arvon dug around and found a smile somewhere. He used it on the dark-eyed, round-faced boy. The boy considered it dubiously, but finally gave him a broad grin in return.

"Ho for the outdoor life," a voice muttered brightly. "Hooray for open trails and the symphony of the rain."

"Hello, Nlesine. I see you survived."

"There are two schools of thought on that. Where's the hospital?"

Arvon shrugged.

The two of them stood side by side and dripped. The pit house wasn't big enough to hold the entire party; Arvon supposed that Wyik and the rest were grouped around other fires. It occurred to him that all of them would be duck soup for the natives if they proved hostile.

"I guess we're not as clever as we thought we were," Nlesine said, thinking along the same lines. "It's hard to remember, sometimes, that we're not on a spaceship any more and the rules have changed."

"Let 'em carve me up if they've a mind to," Arvon said. "All I want is a place to lie down."

At that moment the native who had led the party from the ship stepped into the room. He had on dry skins, though even these were spotted by rain, and he carried his new knife stuck in a kind of sash around his waist.

The native smiled and made chewing motions with his mouth. Then he pointed at Arvon and Nlesine.

"The import of your message is frantically plain," Nlesine announced as the native watched him blankly. "We are happy that you consider us edible, but must respectfully decline your recent invitation."

Arvon pulled out his gun. "Nobody's going to eat *me*," he said, forgetting his sentiments of a few moments before.

Then a decidedly haggard Wyik stuck his head in through the entrance flap. He saw the gun in Arvon's hand and his eyes widened in astonishment.

"What in the world are you doing?" he snapped. "Put that thing away—you want to get us all killed?"

"This joker wants to eat us," Nlesine said. Oddly, the words sounded a bit lame.

"*Eat* you?" Wyik stared and then doubled up with laughter. He clutched at his middle and got red in the face and short of breath. Tears ran down his wet face. Some of it was undoubtedly hysteria induced by weariness, but Arvon had never seen the Captain laugh like that before.

"I don't get it," Nlesine said, looking faintly hurt. "Arvon and I may not be the rarest of all delicacies, but I daresay any stewpot would be honored by our presence."

Wyik got himself under control. "Our friend here doesn't want to eat you," he explained. "He wants *you* to *eat*. In other words, he's inviting all of us to a feast."

Arvon put his gun away. He felt like an utter idiot, but he was too tired to care. "No," he said. "I'm out on my feet."

"No," Nlesine echoed. "Negative. Not going. Forget it."

The native grinned some more and chewed.

"We've *got* to go," Wyik said. He was weaving slightly as he talked. "This is no time to insult our hosts."

"A feast," Nlesine said with an absolute lack of enthusiasm. "Boy!"

"Maybe it'll last all night," Arvon offered grimly.

"Come on," said Wyik. "Time to kick up our heels and be gay."

One after the other, with the native leading the way, they went out of the pit house into the night and the rain. They sloshed along toward a larger structure, from which yellow light spilled out in long, warm splashes.

Someone was singing, and there was much laughter.

Arvon took a deep breath and determined to work on Having a Good Time.

Amazingly, it wasn't bad at all—at first.

As soon as he got inside the hot, steaming, hide-lined building, he saw a young girl who was sensibly dressed in virtually nothing at all. She came up to him, smiled, and handed him a somewhat squishy bucketlike affair that had liquid in it. Arvon, his mind reeling with exhaustion and the closeness of the air, felt that he had nothing to lose. He took a healthy swallow of the liquid. As he had expected, it wasn't water, and it burned.

Just the same, he felt better.

Even while a corner of his brain whispered that this whole thing was incredible and outrageous, he took another drink, and felt still better.

"Easy there, boy," Nlesine said. "It's going to be a long night."

Arvon nodded. He was sweating profusely in his wet clothes and wondering how many of them he might discard with propriety. Another drink, he felt sure, would settle the problem nicely.

With an astounding abruptness he saw things with that sudden tricky clarity that alcohol sometimes brings. They had all been cooped up too long in that ship, they had all been *serious* for too long. They needed a break, needed it desperately. They needed to forget, just for a little while. Yes, and they needed to *remember*, too—remember that being human wasn't all long thoughts and sad faces.

Arvon winked at the girl in what he hoped was a universal

language, and it seemed to him that the years peeled away from him like leaves from an autumn tree. It was fun to be young, to forget....

He knew that he was going to make a fool of himself, and he was glad of it.

The party was on!

Arvon went through the whole thing in something of a haze. It seemed to go on forever; event piled on event, and yet when he bothered to check he found that only minutes had gone by.

There was food, and plenty of it. Great slabs of dripping meat were roasted in the fire and served skewered with sticks. There was a kind of paste that was passed around in a wooden trough; Arvon wasn't sure, but it tasted as if it had a wild root of some sort as a base. There were berries mixed with animal fat and pounded into a tough, dry cake. It made you thirsty to chew on it, and that called for more of the warming home brew.

The fire threw great twisting shadows on the skin walls. Thin, tight things like tambourines with bone rattles were shaken and drummed on with fingers. Wild, joyous chants rocked the roof, and there was dancing that left you excited and exhausted.

Arvon was dizzy with drink and heat, and he was bone-tired. But he kept going on nervous energy alone, with that tense exhilaration that seems to carry you on forever. He felt a glow of good fellowship that made him everybody's friend and he was, in fact, having one hell of a good time.

Cannibals were very far away indeed.

He was aware of the others without actually watching them. Wyik was drinking politely, but his mind was clearly on sleep. He kept smiling, neither liking the party nor disliking it. He didn't seem in any way *superior* to it; it was just that it was nothing but an interlude for him, marking time.

Hafij had promptly taken on more than he could handle, had crawled outside to be sick in the mud, and was now comfortably oblivious by the fire.

Lajor wasn't having any, period. The newsman sat back in a corner, as far from the center of activity as he could get, and surveyed the scene with poorly disguised contempt. He drank as a man drinks to be sociable, which meant that he stuck out like a miserable sore thumb.

Tsriga was high and sailing with the wind. He was pouring out the story of his great shattered love to a middle-aged woman who couldn't understand a word he said, but who kept passing him the hide joy dispenser whenever he paused for breath.

Kolraq, oddly, seemed to be enjoying himself hugely in a quiet sort of way. He had cornered the local shaman and appeared to be trying to learn the native language. That was curious, Arvon thought vaguely—why bother with the language when tomorrow you'd be back at the ship?

Nlesine was in his element. Quite sober, despite the amount of lightly fermented juice he had swallowed, he was putting first things first. He had cornered a youngish, wide-eyed female, and he was talking to her in an improvised sign language that was a model of simplicity and clarity.

All in all, it was a fine party. The tambourines rattled and the dancers danced. Gradually the fire died down, and Arvon thought he saw the gray light of early morning come filtering into the hide house. By then he was more than a little fuzzy, however, and it was hard to tell.

He didn't quite pass out. A girl helped him back to the pit house he shared with Nlesine, and it seemed to him that it had stopped raining. The earth was spinning under him then, and someone was tucking a fur blanket around him.

He did not sleep alone, but when he finally woke up the girl was gone, and he never did remember who she was or what had happened.

As a matter of fact, he remembered hardly anything when he came to and saw the sunlight streaming through the door flap. He had a thumping headache and he felt too weak to move.

He just agonized.

He heard Nlesine moaning something about a planet-sized hang-over, but it was too much effort to turn his head and look at him. He lay quite still and wondered if he was going to die. After a while he slept again, and when he woke up he was shaky but hungry.

He stood up, blinked his eyes, and decided he was alive. He was also alone, and he went outside to see where everybody was.

Judging by the position of the sun, it must have been late in the afternoon. Long shadows filled the valley, and he heard birds chirping.

The village itself was soaking up the sun, and only a few puddles dotted the rocks to remind him of the rain. He took a deep breath of the cool, crisp air and headed for the biggest house in sight.

Inside it was dark; the fire had dwindled away to a heap of orange coals, and there were no windows. When his eyes adjusted to the gloom, he found Nlesine and Tsriga sprawled on the floor, awake but not eager for action. Two old native women were padding about, and one of them brought him a chunk of meat and a hide pouch full of clean, cold water.

"Wyik and Hafij are out hunting with the men," Tsriga said. "I guess we should have gone along, but I don't think I could even defend myself from the birds today, let alone wild animals."

"Kolraq's still talking to the witch doctor," Nlesine said. "He seems determined to learn the language; I can't figure out why."

"Maybe he likes it here," Arvon suggested, drinking the icy water gratefully.

"Maybe he's got a point," Nlesine conceded. "As a noble ancestor of mine once phrased it, this is no bad deal at all."

"It's worth thinking about," Tsriga said earnestly. "After all, we've got everything to lose and probably nothing to gain by following Derryoc's advice. This way we could at least live out our lives. If we take the long nap, chances are we'll wake up in one of those deserts where even the rats are poisoned."

"Better take a longer look around, pal," said Nlesine. "I'm sure it isn't *all* dancing and singing around here. Probably starve to death in the winter. Anyhow, Wyik won't stay—you know that. Duty calls, and all that."

"Well," Arvon observed, biting into a chunk of meat, "we won't go back to the ship today, anyhow—it's too late in the afternoon."

They didn't go back that day, and they didn't go back the next.

The natives were friendly, hospitable, and intelligent.

It began to look as though they would *never* go back.

Arvon felt the tension drain out of him, and the color came back to his skin. He was even getting a tan, despite the chill in the air. He was happy and relaxed and contented.

For the present he was more than willing to leave it at that.

CHAPTER

When they had been there a week, Wyik called a meeting.

They all sat in a half circle on the rocks, facing him. They knew what he was going to say as well as he did, and yet the gathering was more than just a formality.

It was a turning point.

It seemed to be growing colder, and the men shivered in the thin sunlight. Below them, down in the valley, a small stream trickled along to nowhere, and it glinted like ice as it flowed. The few trees were evergreens, but they were dark now, almost black, and waiting for the winter's cold.

Wyik got down to business without any fussing around.

He stood up, composed but not calm. He could never be calm, not with his nervous system. He was always wound up, as though he might explode at a touch. He was not a tall man and yet, curiously, he seemed the biggest man there.

"Well, gentlemen," he said, "the holiday's over." His voice was not loud—you had to strain to hear it, but you listened. "I couldn't give you orders if I wanted to, and I don't want to. The fact remains that I didn't leave Lortas and spend years in space in order to go live with some tribe on a planet I never heard of before. I came here to find something, and I'm not quitting until I *do* find it—or until I'm dead. Our home is far away from us now, and maybe it's easy for you to believe it doesn't exist. It *does* exist. Some of us have children there, and there will be other children. I like these people here, don't you?"

The others murmured assent.

"Maybe—just maybe—*this* is the planet we have to find. Maybe this is the world that will make it, that will get into space without destroying itself first. If it does make it, thousands of years in the future, *Lortas must know.* A civilization cannot endure in isolation; we know that. If this world gets into space, and if we're not there to direct those ships to Lortas—the odds are that they will never find each other. You have all given up many things, and it is not for me to remind you of your duty. *I'm* going back to the ship, and I'm going to carry out Derryoc's plans even if I have to go alone. I hope you'll decide to come with me, but that's up to you."

He turned and walked away from them, alone. It seemed to Arvon that the Captain was always alone.

The others sat in the failing sunlight and talked. Some argued one way, some another. But they spoke without much conviction; they were going through the motions. Kolraq excused himself early and went off to find Wyik.

Arvon listened to the men around him and knew they would go with the Captain.

They went.


It was cold and overcast the day they left the native village. The wind whistled down through the hills, and the women and children came out to smile and wave good-by, and then hustled back inside their warm houses.

Arvon felt that he could always come back to this small spot, lost in time, and be among friends. Sure, they had distributed a lot of presents, and they hadn't hurt anything. But you could not buy these people, and they apparently really liked most of the men from the ship. Perhaps that was a good sign, but he could just hear old Derryoc snorting at the sheer wishfulness of the notion.

The same four natives led the way.

It wasn't as bad a trip as it had been the first time. Once they got out of the valley they had a downgrade most of the way, and it wasn't raining. They weren't uncomfortably cold as long as they kept moving, and they never stopped for long.

From some of the high ground they could see far out over the plains, where the tall grasses and the flowers stretched out in cold green waves, like a vast inland sea. It looked cold and forbidding when the wind rippled it, and it wasn't hard to see it sheeted with drifting snow, with animals starving and the sun only a pale disc in a wintry sky....

They could even see the ship, a shadow lying in a dark charred circle. It was miles away, but the clear air made distances deceptive. And, far to the north, they could see just a glint of ice clothing the mountains in chill white silk.

Glaciers, probably. A scant century ago might have seen them more widespread, although the sea of grass did not look as if it had ever been glaciated.

They kept a steady pace, and soon they were out of the hills, walking across the uneven land. Rocks bruised their feet and thorny bushes caught at their clothes. They could no longer see the ship, and there was no path.

Nevertheless, the natives never faltered, and the wolf dog padded through the grass with unerring instinct. It was very quiet, except for the rustle of the wind. It was warmer, though, once they left the hills.

They walked, and Arvon was pleased to find that he wasn't as tired as he had been the first time. It still wasn't easy, however, and he envied the natives their smooth strides and even, relaxed breathing.

He thought: *It's all very well to talk about walking halfway around the world, but we'd never make it. We aren't trained for it, we aren't tough enough for it. Not one of us would come through alive. It's got to be the copter, but the copter won't carry all of us. Wyik must know that.*

He watched the short, wiry figure of the Captain ahead of him and wondered. Did he know something that the rest of them didn't know?

The sun was sinking on the horizon before the ship finally loomed up ahead of them, and you could see faint stars in the sky. It was growing very cold. They would have to rip up some brush to build a fire; the wood was damp and probably wouldn't catch well....

"Home again!" sang out Nlesine gloomily. The ship *did* look cold, like a tomb waiting for them.

It was at that precise instant, just as Wyik stepped forward to open the air lock, that a shriek split the air.

Suddenly the charred grass around them erupted dark figures.

Something burned at Arvon's shoulder. He looked back and was startled to see that there was an arrow stuck in his upper left arm. Warm, red fluid dripped down into his hand, and he recognized with a shock that it was his own blood.

One of the natives dropped, choking, with a shaft through his throat.

Wyik frantically manipulated the air lock open and fell inside. He twisted around, yanking out his gun, and yelled, "Get down! Hit the dirt! Damn it, Arvon, get *down*, man!"

Stupidly Arvon discovered that he was still standing bolt upright, as though paralyzed. He dived for the ground, wincing as the arrow shaft tore out of his shoulder. As though in a dream, he fumbled out his gun and looked for something to shoot at.

There wasn't anything. All he could see was grass. He shuddered. If someone knew where he was, there wasn't enough cover to protect a flea. He gripped the gun and tried to look in all directions at once.

He never heard a sound. But suddenly there was a figure over him, a stone knife plunging at his chest. He twisted out of the way and hit the firing stud on his gun. He heard the *choog* of the weapon, and then a body smashed against his face.

He struggled desperately, and then stopped quickly as he sensed that the body was a dead weight. He lay very still, hardly breathing, listening to the drip of his own blood. The body of his attacker was heavy, and it stank.

He heard cries and shouts, and once a scream of agony. *Can't lie here*, he thought. *They might need me. But if I stick my head up—*

Arvon squared his shoulders on the ground, ignoring the lance of pain from the arrow point still lodged in his shoulder. He got the body of the paralyzed man on top of him, and then carefully hoisted the head up until it cleared the grass.

*Whack!*

A spear cracked into it, and Arvon cried with horror as something wet splattered into his face. He dropped the body, slid out from under it.

Wait, one of their friends must have thrown that spear, and that meant—

"Hold it!" he yelled. Then he stopped. The native couldn't understand him! He shivered, then tried again, louder, "Nlesine!"

"Ho!" came Nlesine's voice. "Stay down—don't move!"

Arvon stayed down.

The harsh, convulsive sounds of combat faded. Voices filled the air again with friendly tones. Arvon got his head up, gave a quick look around, and then climbed to his feet. He felt pretty good, considering. It had all happened so fast that he was more keyed up than afraid.

He *looked* terrible, though. His shoulder had bled a dark stream down his side, and he was smeared with the blood of the dead native next to him.

Kolraq ran up and threw an arm around him for support.

"I'm all right," Arvon said. "Better than I look, at least. Anybody hurt? What happened? Where'd they go?"

The priest smiled. "Nothing wrong with your curiosity, anyway. One of our natives—his name was Nanyavik—is dead. Wyik was hit in the leg, but not seriously. Two of *them* are dead."

"Who were they? What did they want?"

Kolraq shrugged. "I understand that there's much raiding between different groups in this area—it's the way a man gets prestige in his tribe. Our friends weren't the only ones who saw the ship come down, apparently."

Arvon could feel the stone point grating against the bone in his shoulder. "Just a little good, clean fun, is that it?"

Kolraq looked away, his eyes sad. "In their eyes, Arvon, it was something like that. They are men, after all. Our own ancestors on Lortas did much the same thing, and with as little reason, a few thousand years ago. The test is whether or not men know when to stop."

"Can you get this rock out of my shoulder?"

"Yes. No trouble there, I think. We can give you low-order paralysis, then dig the point out with a knife and sew you back up again. It'll be stiff for a while, but I don't think the arrow severed a muscle."

They started for the ship. It was dark now, but the natives were building a fire and there was already a pale glow of artificial light from a tube inside the ship.

It was cold, and Arvon shivered.

"I'm glad you'll be with us, Kolraq," Arvon said.

Kolraq smiled faintly. "I'm not going," he said.

Arvon looked sharply at him, but the priest said nothing more.

They patched up Arvon's shoulder and bandaged Wyik's leg. Then they buried their dead—three more bodies in graves by the silent, broken ship.

"This place is jinxed," Nlesine said. "At this rate none of us will live out the year."

The next day—cloudless but cold—Wyik told them what they had been waiting to hear.

"You men know that we cannot walk to that other continent that Derryoc showed us on his map. We're not strong enough. The natives say that other men have passed this way, heading north and east after the game animals, but never in winter. Isn't that right, Kolraq?"

The priest nodded.

"I think the longer we delay the less chance we have of making it," the Captain said. "I may be wrong, but that's my decision. So there's only one way to try it—in the copter. I'm not sure how far we'll get, or how well the copter will fly in a bad storm—it's only intended for short survey work, as you know. But I plan to go as far as I can in it, setting it down at night when we see a place to land. The copter won't carry all of us, and that's that. I think it will handle four of us safely, and five in a pinch. This is a pinch."

He paused, looking at them.

"Kolraq and Lajor are staying here," he said.

Nlesine frowned. "Hold on, Captain. You can't give an order like that." He moved forward, his face pale, breathing fast. "It's not for you to decide who's to go and who's to stay."

"I didn't decide," Wyik said slowly. "They did."

Kolraq nodded. "I saw this coming as soon as Derryoc spoke to us. When we got to the native village, I set about learning the language. It's no sacrifice for me, Nlesine. These people are close to the things I believe in—a unity of life, a oneness with nature. I sometimes think we have forgotten too many things, we civilized men. I want to stay and try to learn some of them back again."

There was silence.

"And Lajor?" Nlesine asked. "Don't tell me *he's* got religion."

Wyik looked at the newsman, who shook his head. "Lajor doesn't have to give his reasons," Wyik said. "It's his decision—and, frankly, Nlesine, it's none of your business."

Arvon looked at Lajor: sloppy, loudmouthed, friendless. *How little we can ever know a man*, he thought. *It's one thing to talk about staying here with all the others as a lark. It's something else again to do it for the rest of your life with only one other man of your own kind.*

"We're taking off tomorrow if we can get the copter assembled by then," Wyik said. "We need to pack the sleep drug *very* carefully, and some preservatives as well. Aside from that we'll need the maps and some food capsules. We'll take our guns. There won't be room for anything else—it's for Kolraq and Lajor, and the tribe." He paused. "Any questions?"

There were no questions.

They got to work.

It was a dark and dreary day, with shapeless gray clouds blotting out the sky from horizon to horizon. The wind was cold and even, but didn't pack much force behind it.

The little gleaming copter perched on the ground beside the wreck of the spaceship, looking very much like an odd minnow hatched from an egg carried by a giant defeated mother.

They shook hands all around, with Kolraq and Lajor and the natives who had befriended them. No one had much to say, and hopes were far from high. Somewhere above them Lortas waited, and a thousand other worlds, hidden beyond a blanket of gray. Somewhere ahead of them was—what?

They crowded into the copter and sealed the port. The thing had a complicated lock on it, necessary in any craft that was used for exploration work. Hafij took the controls, and Wyik sat next to him. The others squeezed into the back.

"As long as nobody puts on weight, we'll do fine," Nlesine said.

The engine whined and kicked over as the natives outside watched in amazement. It roared, belched, growled. The copter blades sizzled over their heads, a circle of silver against the gray.

Hafij kicked in the boosters.

They were air-borne. The craft wobbled as a gust of wind hit it, but evened out and began to grab for altitude.

Arvon looked down. It was as though he stared into a well of time. There were the natives, skin-clad figures against the green of the grass. A dog, already ignoring them, nose to the ground. Kolraq and Lajor waving. Only shadows now, shadows on a rolling plain: brave and beyond time and forever lost.

Soon even the bulk of the wrecked ship was lost from view.

The copter climbed above the wind and came around toward the northeast. They saw a world below them, checkered green and brown and white.

Hafij set their course. The copter arrowed on, almost eagerly, toward a hope that was beyond hope, and toward an unknown land that men would one day name America.

CHAPTER

The copter was a fragile insect, drawn to the sun. It hummed along a rugged coastline that bordered a cold blue sea. It was almost alone in the sky, but several times birds paced it for a few miles before falling behind.

The scene below them was one of wild desolation. Great mountains of ice floated in the sea, their peaks rearing up and glittering in the sun, their bases eerie dark shadows below the surface of the water. The coast was rocky and deserted except for nesting birds.

They saw no men, and there were no ships on the sea.

They flew for days and saw no animals.

It was a cold planet of the dead, and worse than that. Death implies life, and it was hard to imagine life in those rocks, or in the depths of that icy blue sea.

They spoke little. They just endured.

When evening shadows painted black fingers across the world, they set the copter down in sheltered coves and tried to sleep. But the driftwood made poor fires, and the frost bit at their hands and feet. Inside the copter it was too crowded to sleep.

They ate synthetics, when they ate.

The coast curved toward the east, a tongue of barren land licked at the choppy sea....

There.

One great continent stopped, and another one began. Between them was a narrow band of shallow water—they could see the rocks on the ocean floor. It looked as though it were really one land mass and a playful giant had splashed a few buckets of water into a trough to cut them apart.

The water was perhaps sixty miles across, and was broken in the middle by some tiny forsaken islands. It was not a formidable barrier; there were undoubtedly times when a man could walk from one continent to the other on a bridge of ice.

The copter hummed over the water, and in doing so it moved from Siberia to Alaska over the Bering Strait, from the Old World into the New.

The copter turned and headed south.

There was plenty of snow, but most of the area was unglaciated. In fact, it looked very much like the country they had crashed in: essentially tundra, with great rolling belts of black earth, carpeted with grass and sturdy bushes.

They discovered something else. The mountain chains ran along a north-south axis, which meant that they did not constitute much of a barrier to land travel along their flanks.

"A funny feeling," Tsriga said, looking down over Arvon's shoulder.

"What?" asked Arvon, though he knew what the boy meant.

Tsriga gestured vaguely. "All that down there. If Derryoc was right, this part of the world is practically uninhabited by human beings. Just think: millions of square miles that have never seen a man."

"Yeah," said Nlesine. "We call them lucky miles."

Tsriga ignored him. "I mean, here we are, actually flying over the route that men will take someday—or are taking *right now*. I wonder who they are, what they're like? Arvon, do you think we'll *see* any of them?"

Arvon felt a thrill despite himself. The eyes of youth were better eyes than his, and they saw more deeply. "I don't know. Maybe. But I expect man is still a rare animal down there. We'd probably be lucky to see him."

"I hate to step out of character as a cynic," Nlesine said suddenly, "but what's that down by that lake? Over there, on your right?"

The copter buzzed toward a glassy lake. It was cloudy and hard to see, but there *were* dark figures in the grass, and they seemed to be in some sort of formation. They were drawn up in a circle, and several of them had formed a line as though to do battle.

"Wyik,"

"I see them. Hafij, can you drop her down a bit?"

The copter lost altitude, skimmed over the lake.

They saw the things more clearly now, and they were not men. They were shaggy four-footed beasts with horns. They stood in a circle, the calves out of danger, while the bulls tossed their heads and pawed at the wet ground.

A pack of smaller animals were howling away impotently, eyeing the calves. The smaller animals looked rather like the wolf dog they had seen before.

Very few of the animals took any notice of the strange silver insect buzzing over their heads. They were intent on their own business.

Tsriga took a picture, as he had been taking pictures ever since the ship crashed. It was developed right in the camera, and he grinned at the print, holding it up for the others to see.

The copter climbed back up the ladder of the sky. The little lake disappeared, along with the animals. They were soon replaced by other lakes and other animals.

It was a vast panorama below them, a world of water and earth and grass. The sky was a clean, cold blue, with a golden sun. The land was a patchwork of brown and black and green, ribboned with streams of glass and dotted with ponds that were blue mirrors reflecting the sky.

It was almost as if they were following a trail of grass into the south. What animals had followed that trail before them, and what animals would follow it in the centuries yet to come?

Darkness came early, and they had to land.

The copter touched the soft earth, the blades slowed and stopped.

They got out, listening.

At first, silence.

Sounds, then: the sounds of life in the wilderness, the sounds of a world men had not yet spoiled. Water chuckling over rocks, a snort from nostrils they could not see, a cold bracing wind that blew in from far, far away....

Night was coming, but there was a moon.

Arvon stretched his cramped muscles and felt an unreasoning joy run through him.

"Damn it," he said. "I'm going fishing."

A pause. "I'll go with you," said Nlesine.

They rustled up some line, a cake of stuff to use for bait.

Then they set off, side by side, the copter forgotten, into the night, into the pale radiance of the moon, into the beginning and the ending of time.

Southward the copter flew, a dot in a lonely and cloud-streaked sky. And now the character of the land beneath the whirling blades began to change.

The barren lands of the tundra, broken only by lakes and stands of dark trees along the river valleys, gave way to a forest of stately conifers. The copter sailed over a sea of green, a cool forest that invited them with soft shade and damp mosses.

It was a hunter's paradise, teeming with game: caribou, deer, wild turkey. If you hovered in the blue sky over a forest pond you could hear the *slap* of a beaver's flat tail smacking the water.

And always the living silences of the big woods, a vibrant hush that was not emptiness but an amalgam of bird song and whispering pines and the pad, pad, pad of cunning feet....

There was plenty to eat now. They simply spotted their prey from the air, shot it from the copter, and stopped for the night with their meat ready and waiting for them.

Once they thought they saw a man, dark eyes staring out of a green thicket. When they investigated, he was gone, and they found no tracks.

Once they spotted a curl of smoke from the air, but when they reached the fire only silence greeted them.

They flew on, into the south, and the country below them changed yet again. High plains rolled away from the mountain flanks, plains rich with grass and flowers, plains that undulated like the sea.

They saw animals in profusion now: lumbering elephants, a few wild horses, fantastic herds of big bison that blackened the plains for miles.

And they saw men, dark figures that hunted in packs like the wolves, stalking the herds with spears at the ready. Once they flew over a camp at evening, a rude skin shelter, a woman patiently scraping away at a hide with a stone tool, a child watching her solemnly.

Arvon stared at them, imprinting them forever on his mind. *You there!* he thought. *You, tired hunter, hungry child, working woman! Do you know you have conquered a world? Do you know that men like you will live and die for centuries, and then be replaced by men with guns from the other side of oceans you have yet to see? Do you know you have won a continent, and that one day it will be taken from you? Eat your meat, hunter, and laugh while you can! Tomorrow will be long, and a great night creeps from the depths of the sea....*

The copter hummed through the skies, over the sea of grass. The plains continued into what would eventually be the eastern part of the state of Colorado.

Then they headed westward, into the mountains. The copter slowed, an eagle searching for a nest.

Their power units were almost exhausted.

They landed high in the mountains by a tiny glacial lake.

One journey had ended.

The first night was cold, and the blanket of stars was remote and uncaring. They slept in the shelter of the copter since there were no trees.

Arvon lay on his back looking up at the stars. The air was crystal-clear, and he could see them plainly. There a blue one, there a red one, there one that seemed to pulsate as he watched.

He had gone through much of his life like other men, taking it for granted. Even the search through space had often not touched his soul with awe. And yet how strange life was, all of it! That sea of stars, those diamonds in chill black water. He had sailed that sea, and he knew that those stars were mighty suns, and around many of them drifted planets like his own, or like the world on which he found himself. Somewhere out there, in that infinite ocean, was there a man looking this way at a star in the night?

*Hello, friend! Good luck to you!*

He listened for a long time to the night sounds around him, the sounds of an alien planet far from home.

It was late when he slept.

In the morning, when the sun had climbed over the mountains, they fanned out over the area, looking for a suitably concealed spot for the long sleep that was coming. They worked down along the stream until they were well below timber line in a stately forest of pines and aspens, but they did not find what they needed.

Well, there was no hurry. The fact was that they all subconsciously welcomed a chalice to delay the injection of the drug. They fished and lazed around in the sun, breathing the fresh air, trying not to see the dead planet that all this might become....

But they kept looking.

It was Arvon who first stumbled on the rock shelter. He had followed a little cut up from the mountain stream, and the dark shadowy slit of the scooped-out place in the rock wall stood out like black paint on white paper. He crawled inside and was delighted to find that there was a small opening in the back of the shelter.

He hurried down to the copter to get a tubelight, and he and Nlesine came back for a closer look.

The cave was nothing much—merely a hollow room in the rock of the mountain. There was a slow drip of water trickling down one side, and the place was damp and uninviting.

White bones gleamed on the floor; some animal had crawled in to die. Or had it been killed by something that lived in the cavern, something that would be back?

"I guess this is it," Arvon said. His voice seemed very loud in the silence.

"Swell," said Nlesine. "A granite bedchamber, complete with hot and cold running bones. Just what I always wanted. Know any good bedtime stories, Arvon?"

"A few, but they're not for children."

"Thanks very much."

They called the others, and after that it was simply a question of two weeks of hard work.

They stripped the vault of everything they could move to protect themselves against quakes. For the same reason they took tools out of the copter and carved themselves niches in the back wall of the rock chamber.

They arranged the tubelights, which would last virtually forever, around the room.

They took the preservative that all ships carried and applied it to everything they thought they would need: their clothes, their weapons, their notes.

They rigged a portal to seal the vault off from the rock chamber by using the gimmicked door of the copter.

They spent two days outside, doing things that were not strictly necessary. No man among them was anxious to crawl into one of those stone beds to sleep while the centuries whispered into dust....

Finally, they could find no more excuses.

They went into the vault.

The last thing Arvon saw was the silver copter that had carried them so far. It stood outside the rock shelter now, its blades stilled, its cabin empty.

When next that portal opened, that copter would be dust.

The portal closed.

The men took their places for the long sleep.

Wyik sterilized the syringe. He opened the self-refrigerating duraglass container, which kept the drug sealed at a temperature close to absolute zero. When it was ready, he filled the syringe.

"I'll have to use it all," he said. "We'll go as far as we can."

"How far? How long?" The voice was Tsriga's.

"About fifteen thousand years." Wyik's tone was matter-of-fact.

*Fifteen thousand years.*

"Get on with it," Arvon said. "I don't want to think." *Don't want to think that no one has ever had to sleep so long to get home, think that this world may be radioactive dust when I wake up, think that I am afraid, afraid...*

The gleaming needle went to work.

Tsriga first, his lonely eyes frightened, then closing, closing…

Hafij, his fingers crossed in the niche where he thought no one could see them.

Nlesine. He said it: "It looks bad to Nlesine."

Arvon. He was rigid. He fought it.

He saw Wyik inject himself. There was still a drop or two in the duraglass container—not enough to do them any good, not enough to put them to sleep for five years. He saw Wyik smile bitterly, reseal the useless thing, toss it on the floor, where it, too, grew colder and colder, refrigerating itself toward absolute zero….

Arvon tried to scream, but it was too late now.

CHAPTER

The fire had been replenished many times, but now it was only a heap of glowing coals. The rock walls of the vault pressed inward, muffling sounds, somehow creating an atmosphere of cozy comfort despite the barrenness of the cave.

They were all awake now, gathered about him, watching him.

The niches were empty in the walls.

Weston Chase shook his head, adjusted his glasses, and said, "My God, Arvon, I never heard of anything like it."

"It's true," Arvon said.

"Yes, I know it is. That's what makes it so hard."

Wes felt a sense of shock swelling within him; he couldn't shake it off. It wasn't easy to have your feelings, your beliefs, the very structure of your world, yanked out of their sockets, uprooted, twisted around so that nothing was what it had seemed.

There was no more horror left in Wes Chase.

Instead, he was close to tears.

"I think I understand," he said to Arvon—and to the others,

although they could not speak his language. "It's—well, it's incredible."

Arvon frowned. "You don't believe me? You think—"

"No, no." Wes waved his hand helplessly. "It's just staggering, that's all. Not just the story, but *you*. You've changed, all of you."

How could he express it to them? How could he make them see, as he was seeing, with new eyes?

They were all so *different* from what they had seemed. He knew what it was like. That first year of medical school, at the University of Cincinnati. He had gone down from Ohio State, and he had hardly known a soul. He had looked around him in those first classes, and he had seen only strangers—cold, aloof, frightening. And then, years later when he left to serve his internship at Christ Hospital, he could barely remember how it had been, those first few days. Why, they were all his friends, or at least his acquaintances. He had studied with them, rigged skeletons with them, gotten drunk with them. They were no longer a sea of hostile faces—they were Bill and Sam and Mikowta and Holden. He knew them, he *belonged* with them.

And now, here in this strange vault in the Colorado mountains, it was the same.

The white-faced figure from hell that had chilled his blood that night so long ago was just Arvon—a man with a different background from his own, but a man he understood for all that. As far as that went, he knew Arvon better than he knew most of the people he saw every day in Los Angeles—and liked him better, too.

And the others, the ones who had awakened while Arvon talked, the ones who had wolfed down the food Arvon had gathered, the ones who stared at him curiously with those odd expressions of hope and fear and desperation?

He needed no introductions.

There, that man watching him with the deceptively sarcastic half-smile on his face. Nlesine, of course. He was balder than Wes had pictured him, and thinner. He must have lost some weight since the crash of the ship, Wes decided. Lord, had that been fifteen thousand years ago? He noticed Nlesine's eyes: shrewd and green, with just a hint of buried warmth in them.

And that tall, skinny fellow with the strange black eyes—that would be Hafij, the navigator of the Bucket. Yes, he saw what Arvon had been driving at about Hafij. The man had a caged look about him; he was not of the land or the sea or the friendly blue skies. His heart was out in the star-shredded deeps, his home was in steel and darkness. Wes disliked him at sight, but he admired him.

Tsriga. Wes almost smiled. He *was* young, hardly more than a boy. His clothes, subtly, were more garish than the ones the others wore. He was tall, gangling, knobby-boned. He was probably more nervous than Wes at this point. Wes felt a pang of regret—Tsriga was too close to the son he had wanted, but never had.

And the Captain. There was no ignoring *him*. Wyik dominated the vault without ever saying a word. He paced the floor with short, jerky steps. He reminded Wes of a boxer in the ring, waiting for his opponent to come out of his corner. He was taut, wound up, dangerous. He was more than just alive—the man blazed with energy. He didn't smile, not once. Short? Yes, but you didn't notice that. The overwhelming impression you got of Wyik was that he was *hard*, granite-hard, unyielding. There was a mystery about the man; he carried it with him like an aura. He was restless, driven, at war with himself. Wes watched him, and thought: *Watch your step, Wes. That man would destroy you in a second if he thought it necessary.*

Wes took out a cigarette and lit it. Ten eyes watched him do it. The smoke was stale in his mouth.

How could he tell them? He had journeyed with them between the stars, braced himself for the crash when the spaceship hit, laughed at the feast in the hide-covered pit house, stared down with them on a green and unknown land below the copter blades....

It had been an odyssey that surpassed imagination, an odyssey that wound out of space and out of time, only to end here, in a rock cave in Colorado.

Only to end in failure.

He looked at them. Aliens? How stupid the word seemed now! A thing was not alien when you understood it. He almost wished that he had never gotten to know them, never shared their adventures.

Wes could not keep the sadness out of his eyes.

"Arvon," he said slowly, "there's something I must tell you, right now. It isn't easy for me to say, but you must believe that it's the truth. Arvon, it *was all for nothing.*"

Arvon stared at him, uncomprehending.

"We haven't got space travel yet," Wes said, hating the words. "I don't know whether we're going to blow ourselves up or not; I wouldn't take any bets on it either way. But we haven't got any spaceships, that's for sure. Arvon, you're stuck—all of you are stuck. It was a one-way trip."

Arvon stood up slowly. Stunned, he shook his head. He said something to the others in their own language.

There was a shocked silence.

"To come so far," Arvon whispered finally. "To take the chance, to wake up and find the world still alive, to hope, and then—"

He stopped.

Wes felt an icy shiver run through his body.

Wyik was walking toward him, and he had death in his eyes.

Wes backed away, his fists clenched. He knew desperation when he saw it, and he didn't propose to be murdered if he could help himself. Something had snapped in Wyik; he would kill blindly if he got the chance—

Nlesine stepped out, caught the Captain's arm. Wyik shook him off, but by then Arvon blocked his way.

They talked rapidly, persuasively.

Wyik cooled off, his eyes cleared. He shook his head, disgusted with himself. He looked over at Wes and managed a smile of apology. Wes smiled back without notable enthusiasm.

"He's sorry," Arvon explained. "It is very hard for him—harder than for the rest of us, perhaps."

Wyik said something to Arvon earnestly.

"Are you sure of what you told me?" Arvon asked Wes. "I do not think you would lie to me—but are you *sure?*"

Wes tried to relax, but the strain of his imprisonment in the vault was beginning to tell on his nervous system. "You went to the town down there at the foot of the mountain, you looked around. Did Lake City look like a spaceport to you?"

"That means nothing. There are villages on Lortas that look the same way—sleepy, backward, forgotten. Surely, in your cities—"

Wes sat down, keeping an eye on Wyik, who was pacing up and down irritably. "We're close," he admitted, "but just not close enough. We used an atomic bomb in a war—oh, that was more than ten years ago now." He caught the look in Arvon's eyes and flushed. "We've done some work on rockets, I think—guided missiles and things like that." He flushed again, and then, annoyed at his own reaction, rushed on: "We *have* announced plans for an artificial moon of some sort, a little one they're going to shoot up into space. You could call it a spaceship if you wanted to, but I don't think you're going to ride home in it."

Arvon translated Wes's remarks to the others. There was a flurry of conversation. Wes noticed Nlesine's wry smile. If it had looked bad to Nlesine, his glum prediction had indeed been verified by time.

"These rockets," Arvon persisted. "You mean liquid-fuel arrangements? Powder? What?"

Wes shrugged. "I'm a doctor, not a space cadet." Arvon looked blank, so Wes amended his statement. "I don't know much about rockets. We have jet aircraft; I think they all use liquid fuels. No atomic jobs, as far as I know."

Arvon nodded dispiritedly.

"Wait a minute!" Wes snapped his fingers, and Wyik started like a cat. "We *do* have engineers, factories, designers. Why couldn't you tell them what you want—tell them how to do it— and have them build a ship for you? With your knowledge you ought to be able to cut centuries off the time it would take us to build a star ship under normal conditions!"

Arvon laughed. It was a short, staccato noise, utterly unlike him. He spread his hands helplessly. "You don't see the problem," he said. "It is difficult for me to make examples—no, that isn't the word I want." He paused, searching his memory. "It is hard for me to take *analogies* from your experience. But I can guess at some of the stages through which you must have passed. You have ships, large ships, for ocean travel?"

"Yes. We call them ocean liners."

"Well, then. Suppose you are the captain of an ocean liner and you suddenly find yourself on foot several centuries in the past. That date would be?"

"Around 1700, I suppose," Wes supplied.

"Yes, around 1700. As captain of a liner, you search out a shipbuilder and tell him what you want. Perhaps you even draw him a picture. Can he make an ocean liner for you?"

Wes shook his head, beginning to get a glimmer of the problem.

"Of course he can't. Now, with a spaceship equipped with an interstellar drive, the problem is magnified many times. Such a ship is built by specialists, with specialized knowledge. We did not build the ship any more than one of your jet pilots throws his plane together before he flies it. Wyik was our Captain, but he couldn't design the atomic drive that powered the Bucket. Hafij was our navigator, but he couldn't give you more than a general description of how a distortion field works. If we had the ship now, we could take your engineers to it and *show* them some things; that would help. But our ship is dust now. The things we know might save a little time—cut out a few blind alleys—but that's all. If you have given us accurate information, your people are more than a century away from interstellar flight. The Moon will come sooner, of course, but it won't do us any good. We won't live a century more, Wes—particularly not after the effects of that sleep we had to take."

Wes waited, but Arvon seemed to have retired into thought.

"It doesn't look good," Wes said finally.

"You sound like Nlesine." Nlesine looked up at the sound of his name and bowed gravely. "But you're right. It doesn't look good for us—and it doesn't look good for you. This world you call Earth seems like a good bet to survive—it may even attain interstellar flight, as we have done. But then you can see what will happen."

"We'll go out into space," Wes said slowly, "and we'll find the same things you found. We'll feed the results to our computers—and then it will be our problem."

"Exactly. The odds against your ever finding Lortas are prodigious; it was only a lucky accident that we found you. Of course, I don't know that the Earth will survive; I don't know that much about it. What do you think, Wes?"

Wes remembered the paper he had read the night before he had gone fishing. He remembered the headlines, he remembered the talk he had heard at parties, in bars, in his office.

He remembered Hiroshima, and Nagasaki.

He remembered Hitler, and all the rest.

"I don't know, Arvon," he said. "I just don't know."

Arvon looked around him, at the bare walls, at the glow from the lights salvaged from the wreck of the ship. He was silent, and Wes knew he was seeing far beyond those rock walls, back into the gray mists of time....

"A century!" Arvon exclaimed, overcome by the irony of it. "To sleep for fifteen thousand years—and to fail because of a hundred more!"

He turned, gestured toward the others. He spoke rapidly to them and showed them the notes he had made. He talked for a long time, and Wes caught some English words.

Arvon was teaching the others English.

Wes felt a hollow ache in the pit of his stomach. He was suddenly back in the present with a vengeance, and the effect of the story Arvon had told was wearing off.

Damn it, he was still a prisoner in this hole!

"Arvon."

The man looked up at him.

"You have no right to go on holding me here like this. My wife will be worried half to death."

Arvon hesitated. "We do what we must," he said reluctantly.

"You mean you still won't let me go?"

Arvon came over and stood before him. "I like you, Wes, believe that. But you are a man, after all. We know nothing about you except what you've told us. We've risked too much, come too far, to take chances now. You might lead an army to us, might drop atomic bombs on us, might capture us and pen us up like wild beasts. Such things have happened to men from Lortas on other worlds, with other men. We have not decided what to do with you yet. I promise you this: we will not kill you unless it becomes absolutely necessary."

He turned away and began explaining something to Wyik.

Wes tried to control a sudden fury. The arrogance of the man! Here he, Wes, had believed *his* story without question, fantastic as it had seemed. And now Arvon wasn't sure about Wes!

"Hell," he said quite distinctly.

And then he thought: *Suppose I were one of them, fighting an impossible fight on an alien planet. Suppose I caught one of the natives snooping around my hide-out. Would I let that native get away, go back to his tribe, tell all the others?*

But reason could not help him now.

He was desperately homesick.

He thought of Jo, remembering her before she had been his wife, and after. Her hair, like delicate silk when she pulled off her bathing cap after a dip in the pool, her eyes that sparkled when she'd had too much to drink, her laugh that he had not heard in so long. He saw his house on Beverly Glen: rock and redwood, and geraniums in the gardens. And green dichondra glinting under the sprinkler spray....

Jo. He couldn't keep his thoughts away from her, and not all the thoughts were pleasant. God, how long had he been here? What had she thought? What was she doing, now, this very minute? Did she still love him, really? Had Norman—

No, don't think that. It isn't fair.

Is it?

He made no sound, but buried his head in his hands. He felt the beard on his face with surprise. He closed his eyes, and he was sick with loneliness.

His life was far away, and that life had not been all that he had once dreamed it might be.

Somehow that hurt more than all the problems of all the other men who had ever lived, or ever would live.

He slept, and dreamed, and cried out from the darkness within him.

The hours passed slowly and rolled up into days.

Arvon was working hard, teaching the others English. The atmosphere in the cave was one of utter gloom. Occasionally Arvon asked Wes for help with a word or phrase. Sometimes Wes cooperated, sometimes he sulked and refused to say anything.

Alternately Wes was fascinated by the situation in which he found himself and indignant at being held a captive. It must be at least October, he figured, and perhaps even later. When the vault door was opened, gusts of cold air blew into the chamber, and he caught the crisp, metallic smell of snow.

It was a long way down to timber line, and the tiny fire didn't really keep them warm.

They were, in fact, miserable—all of them.

Twice they felt the ripping vibrations of jets in the air over the mountains. Each time the men from Lortas ran out of the cave and stared into the sky. They could tell that the jets were outdistancing their sound trails. But they could also see the stubbed wings.

For his part, Wes felt oddly displaced, as though he had been changed in some subtle fashion. He looked down at himself, at the old tennis shoes, the torn pants, the supposedly waterproof jacket with the rust stains on it. He felt the mouse-colored hat, which he had recovered, somewhat the worse for wear. He listened to the ticking of his watch, fingered the three keys on his key ring, felt the lump of his billfold in his pocket.

Many times he slipped the photograph out of its plastic holder and looked at it: at Jo.

She stood there, in her tweed skirt and brown cashmere sweater, looking at him, smiling a little.

Jo.

It hurt to think about her.

He came back to himself, wondering. Could this really be Wes Chase—a moderately successful eye, ear, nose, and throat man? A guy who liked to go fishing in old tennis shoes and a battered felt hat? A guy who liked to get tight once in a while? Could this be the Wes he had always known listening to talk about interstellar ships and sleeps that lasted fifteen thousand years?

The isolation of cultures, the destiny of man—

Surely, these things weren't part of *his* life?

Surely, spaceships and all that were things that intelligent people laughed at, like flying saucers. Fun to give you the creeps at a movie, maybe, but not part of the *real* world.

He shivered suddenly, almost seeing life as these other men in the cave saw it. Why, up there, beyond the rock, beyond the blue of the sky, there were other worlds, other men, other fears and laughter—and yet they were all the same, everywhere.

God, how ignorant he was! How ignorant they all were, here on Earth. How—what was the word?

*Provincial.*

They were hicks, country boys who thought the city was a myth, the world was flat, evil was a dream.

He shook himself, literally. It was hard to grow up.

The really surprising thing about Arvon and Nlesine and Wyik and Hafij and Tsriga—yes, and about Kolraq and Seyehi and Lajor and Derryoc—was how familiar they seemed. Aliens? He knew men like them, like every one of them, in Ohio or Colorado or California. Supermen? Nonsense. They were just men, and he could understand them.

Understanding, he put himself in their shoes. Here they were, stuck on Earth. Here they were, and after years of searching they had perhaps found the one world in all the universe that could help them—but they had come too early. The ship had yet to be built that could carry them home again, and could do more than that.

A ship that could fuse the two great civilizations—a ship that could fertilize two great cultures, keep them going, give birth to a new, varied way of life that might carry man—how far?

But a ship that did not exist.

He knew what they were thinking; the same thing he would be thinking if their positions had been reversed.

*Suppose he's lying? Suppose he's like too many other men we've known? Suppose he's tricking us, trying to catch us off guard? Suppose his people really have conquered space and he doesn't want us to know?*

Or, more kindly: *Perhaps he means well but doesn't have the facts. He's just a doctor, they wouldn't tell him everything. Maybe there's some political reason why they don't tell their citizens what goes on. Maybe there's a war brewing....*

Castles in the air, of course. But what else could they build?

Sure enough, in time, Wyik went to work on him.

"Your home, Wes. Where is it?" His voice was smooth, controlled, but there was a harsh undertone to it he could not quite conceal.

"They call it Los Angeles—that's Spanish, really, not English. It's a city in a place called California."

"How far from here?"

"Hundreds of miles. Too far to walk."

"It's a big city?"

"One of the biggest."

"They have many things there, Wes? Factories, technicians, scientists?"

"Sure. All that and Marilyn Monroe, too."

"Marilyn Monroe?"

"She's a kind of goddess who lives in Hollywood—that's a part of Los Angeles where they make dreams out of celluloid."

"She would be important to see?"

"She'd be worth a look, yes. Take your mind off your troubles."

Wyik frowned uncertainly. "Wes, we need your help. I know we have no right to ask it after keeping you here so long. But we—some of us—must go to this city of yours. Can you get us there without calling any attention to yourself? We want to trust you." He smiled. "But we can't, of course."

Wes thrilled, and color came into his face.

*Here's your chance. You can get out! You can go home!* "It won't be easy," he said.

"I know that. We have discussed it thoroughly. It seems to us that the basic requirement is money. Can you get some?"

Wes nodded.

"Without communicating with anyone unless one of us is present?"

Wes hesitated. That *did* raise some problems.

"Think it over," Wyik said. "We'll give you until tomorrow. And think carefully, Wes. Don't make any foolish mistakes."

Wes looked into the Captain's cold, hard eyes.

"I won't make any mistakes," he said evenly.


The next day he went through the circular port, out into the rock shelter. Behind him was the bare vault with the five niches cut into the wall, five rock beds where five men had slept for fifteen thousand years....

Ahead of him—

Light.

White, blazing, blinding light.

Sun and snow, and the outward thrill of immensity.

He was free. True, Arvon and Nlesine were with him, and both were armed. But this was his world, and he knew it better than they could ever hope to know it. His freedom was his to take, when and if he wanted it.

*If* he wanted it?

*Damn fool! Of course you want it!*

Nevertheless, he turned and waved at the rock shelter: waved at Tsriga, trying to be brave; and at Hafij and Wyik, withdrawn and silent.

They all waved back.

"I know the way," Arvon said. "I'll go first, then you, Wes, and then Nlesine. Be careful—the trail is slippery in spots."

"So this is civilization," Nlesine muttered, his balding head pink in the bright, reflected sunlight. He picked his way over some rocks. "Kolraq had the right idea after all."

The stream was still running, chuckling blackly between banks of snow. Above them was the glacial lake, probably iced over in part, and below them, at the foot of an invisible trail, was Lake City, Colorado.

They set off at a good clip. For the most part the snow was thin and dry. They had to wade the stream several times, and their feet grew numb with cold. Wes was not in very good shape, and he puffed quickly in the thin air, but his excitement kept him going without tiring him too much.

Timber line, and black trees like burned stumps resting in the snow. Spruce and pine and aspen, patient trees, waiting out the winter. The air was cold, but it smelled wonderful, and as long as they kept moving they were warm.

It was late afternoon when they passed through the valley in the mountain foothills—the valley that had been choked with green and gold the last time Wes had seen it. Now it was barren and empty, with black rocks and clumps of brush like ink splotches in the snow. The stream deepened and slowed after its tumble from the heights, and it glided like oil over the comparatively level land.

There—that was where he had left his car. There was no sign of it now. It had undoubtedly been found within a day or two. He supposed that Jo had it—she had a key in her purse, he remembered. How many times had he locked his own key in the car and phoned Jo to come open the door for him?

*Phone Jo. If only—*

Well, they were still roughly two miles from Lake City. It was unlikely that they would see anyone, but there was a chance. A few hundred people lived there all year round, and there would be hunting parties as well.

"Better wait until after dark," Arvon said. He searched out a rock and sat down behind it, out of the wind. Wes and Nlesine joined him.

"I expect to freeze to death," Nlesine said. He sighed. "It would all make a dandy novel, but who would ever believe it? And old Wes here is too middle class for a good villain."

Wes shivered, and flexed his numb toes in his tennis shoes. It wouldn't be any fun to get frostbitten. He wasn't certain he cared for Nlesine's remark. "You've got things turned around, friend," he said. "If nothing else, you're guilty of kidnapping—and that carries the death penalty."

Nlesine raised his eyebrows, interested and not in the least alarmed. "You still have the death penalty? I wouldn't have expected it at this level."

"We've got it," Wes assured him.

Arvon shrugged. "We've nothing to lose. You're a funny guy, Wes— bringing that up at a time like this. Maybe we have a crazy man for an informant."

His smile took the sting out of his words.

Wes tried not to think; it was easier that way. The big problem, of course, was clothes. The odd dress of Nlesine and Arvon could hardly go unremarked, especially in Lake City. If they were seen there would be talk. And then, regardless of their intentions, the men from Lortas might be crowded into a corner where they would have to fight.

In which case the outlook for Wes would not be bright.

No, he wanted no trouble while he was still in their hands.

But to get clothes he had to have money. Sure, they could steal some, probably successfully, but then what? Everyone would be looking for them, and there would be no chance at all of keeping things quiet.

"It's an odd situation," Nlesine said, idly packing a snowball. "Here we are, and we mean no harm to anyone. And yet there's no one we can go to for help. This culture simply isn't ready for our story. There *aren't* any men from space, as far as they're concerned. And even if someone believed us, what could he do? We'd get all balled up in local politics and spend the rest of our lives trying to convince the experts that we don't know how to make a death ray or a fleet of spaceships. These things have happened before, Wes."

"You *could* tell your story and show them where Lortas is on a star map," Wes said. "Then, someday, maybe they'd get there."

Arvon laughed. "You're suggesting we're not quite the disinterested altruists we claim to be? You mean we're worried about Arvon and Nlesine as well as mankind?"

"Damn right we are," Nlesine said. "I want to get home myself. I have no desire to be a statue—I've carted too many of 'em off too many dead worlds."

"Still, if you can't get back—"

"We'll do what we can," Arvon said. "But we haven't given up yet."

The sun drifted down the sky, and shadows lengthened over the snow. The breeze died away, fortunately, but it was cold—well below freezing.

When they could see the first cold stars they got to their feet. They were stiff and sore, and they stamped around to get their blood circulating again.

Then they hoofed it toward Lake City.

They kept off the road when they reached the highway and ducked behind rocks when they saw headlights coming. They could see the Gunnison River on their right, gleaming icily in the starshine.

At first Lake City was only a cluster of warm yellow lights, an island of warmth in the night.

Then it was dark buildings, wood houses, the bulk of a summer riding stable. Voices, the thud of feet hurrying along the sidewalk. Music: a jukebox in the Chuck Wagon, muffled by the walls.

Wood smoke curling fragrantly in the night air.

Wes felt his palms sweating. *God, I'm glad to be back*, he thought. And then: *But I'm scared stiff.*

Arvon and Nlesine stuck close by his side.

They crept up through shadows, between two wagon wheels....

"Easy does it," whispered Arvon.

"Yeah," said Wes nervously. "Easy does it."

CHAPTER

He got them through it somehow.

First there was the meeting with Jim Walls, the salty manager of the Pine Motel. He wasn't ever likely to forget Jim's look of utter astonishment at the sight of Doc Chase: a bearded, skinny, bedraggled wreck of a man. Jim stared at him as though he were Rip Van Winkle, then he insisted on feeding him and giving him a drink—which Wes used to good advantage.

Wes had been stopping with Jim for a number of years, and knew him well enough to fend off his questions. Jim accepted his check for five hundred dollars and obviously felt that Wes had run off with some girl and gotten her into what was locally referred to as motel trouble. He promised not to phone Jo, and Wes took him at his word.

He was acutely aware of Nlesine watching him through the window.

Next day he bought some simple clothes for Arvon and Nlesine, and found a man with a 1938 Ford he was willing to sell for three hundred dollars cash.

And so it was that on the sixteenth of November, with a cold sun staring out of a blue-white sky, they ground up the twisted road across Slumgullion Pass in an old Ford. Arvon and Nlesine crowded in beside him in the front seat, their faces worried and drawn.

*It's like a dream to me,* Wes thought, *but how strange it all must be to them! An alien world, an alien time, an alien city at the end of the road. And Lortas, not even a light in the sky, spinning toward death, waiting for a visit that would never come.*

But for him—

Jo, and home.

He tried to coax more speed out of the car, without success. He had to keep it in second for a long time, and Lake City was gone, and on either side the world dropped away into pinemarked canyons of sugary snow.

It was a curiously prosaic trip.

Wes settled down into the routine of driving, and even found himself worrying because the car used so much oil. He was involved in an immense problem, he knew that. One day historians might say that the destiny of the human race rode with them in this old car, and it could very well be true. If they ever made a movie of it, Wes was certain that he and Nlesine and Arvon would speak grandiloquent lines about Man and Civilization and Stars. Every police car they saw would be a threat, eyes would regard them suspiciously as they drove.

In actuality, their main problem was where to find a decent meal. They picked up 66 at Gallup, and although New Mexico and Arizona had many charms, good food was not among them. They endured a series of grease-bound cheeseburgers, they drank gallons of coffee that was indistinguishable from the battery acid in the car, and they stared without fascination at the fungoid growths of "trading posts" that dotted the desert, offering real-for-sure Indian tom-toms for only a dollar apiece.

Nlesine ventured the observation that perhaps this was a primitive part of the planet and Wes a savage who just hadn't heard about the spaceships and what not on the other side of the pond.

In their khaki shirts and jeans and light jackets, Nlesine and Arvon looked less alien than ever. And, like Wes, they seemed to live mainly for the shower at the end of the day.

It was hard to remember the impersonal forces at work in the universe around them, forces that would touch Earth as well as Lortas if Earth didn't blow herself up before then. The world of the present, of stale candy bars and filter-tip cigarettes and soft drinks in gas stations, was too immediate.

Wes was worried about money. He was not a rich man, and five hundred bucks would put a very perceptible dent in his checking account. How could these men ever pay him back?

He laughed aloud.

Five hundred dollars. Would he give that much to save his world? Would he, voluntarily?

Well, five hundred dollars was a lot of money.

It was easier to let someone else do the worrying. What was the future to him?

*Maybe,* he thought, *maybe. Maybe that's why man becomes an extinct animal.*

They went through Needles.

"So this is California," Nlesine said, unimpressed. "It looks just like Arizona."

"It gets different," Wes assured him.

They drove on.


Los Angeles sprawls out like an octopus, extending tentacles of gaudy hamburger stands and fuming automobiles for miles toward the north, the south, and the east. Westward lies the sea, and one has the decided feeling that in time that, too, will be straddled by floating housing units and department stores built like pyramids.

There is no abrupt transition from desert to city. It is only that the towns get closer and closer together—Welcome to West Orange Orchard and Gracious Living You Can Afford—and then they are all one big city, and that is Los Angeles.

At one point the road goes over a rise, and you can look down into the basin that holds the bulk of Los Angeles. You can't actually *see* the city, of course: all you see is a gray pall of fog, mist, smoke, and that special urban effluvium called smog.

"You mean people live in that without face masks?" asked Nlesine in genuine astonishment.

"I'm afraid so. It isn't so obvious when you're right down in it; you have to get above it to get the full visual appeal."

"Incredible," Arvon said, taking out his pocket handkerchief and holding it over his mouth with what he hoped was a casual manner.

Wes tooled the car along without thinking very much about it. The traffic was heavy, but nothing compared to what it was on a Sunday. He sensed the admiration of his companions, both of whom clearly expected to die at any moment, and he responded to it by driving with an elaborate casualness.

He took them in by way of Union Station, where they picked up the Hollywood Freeway. He edged out into a river of cars and kept to the far right lane because his old automobile couldn't compete in the eternal speed and endurance contests in the center speed tracks. They hurtled out of downtown Los Angeles—that gray jungle left behind to rot when the city exploded toward the Valley and Santa Monica and a myriad of other destinations—and rode the bedlam toward Hollywood.

In a surprisingly short time he cut over to Sunset Boulevard and drove down the wide, curving street in the general direction of Westwood. The character of the place changed drastically now. Mainly it smelled of money.

It was a typical Los Angeles day: cool but not cold, moist and yet not exactly humid. The sun was vaguely visible through the haze, and everywhere you looked there were huge yards choked with brilliant green foliage and dotted with clumps of bright red flowers. The houses, set back at varying distances from the road depending on how much money the owner had, tended toward white Spanish castles and long, low ranch buildings.

There were old ladies seated at booths along the road selling maps that would direct the young at heart and infantile in mind to genuine homes which belonged to real live movie stars—or had belonged to them last week when the current map had been printed.

There were more cars than they had seen on the highway from Colorado to Arizona. All kinds of cars: sedate old black sedans driven by Retired Couples, junk heaps piloted defiantly by the very young or the very poor, brand-new gleaming vehicles with brand-new gleaming Successful Men at the wheels, buglike foreign sports cars weaving in and out of traffic, their goggled drivers ignoring mere stock cars with a vast superiority.

There.

Wes's hands tightened on the wheel.

He stopped at the light on Beverly Glen. If he turned right, toward the Valley, he would be home in five minutes.

*Jo.*

"Keep going straight ahead, Wes," Arvon said quietly.

The light changed. Grimly Wes stayed on Sunset.

"Where to, gentlemen?" he asked, his voice tight.

"Tourist court," Nlesine said. "Easy does it, Wes—as soon as we find out what we have to know, you can go home and forget all about us. That's a promise."

Arvon looked at Nlesine sharply, then smiled a little.

"Does Wyik know about that?" Wes asked.

Nlesine shrugged. "You escaped."

Wes felt a glow of warmth. Again his mind seethed with contradictions. These men had held him prisoner—and yet, damn it, he was on their side.

The trouble was, he saw suddenly, that he was between two worlds. He was not a part of the mission that had brought the men from Lortas to Earth. And, oddly, he was not quite a part of this world around him either, although he had spent years of his life here.

Somehow *he* had become the alien—and it was not a pleasant feeling.

They passed the black and white sign that pointed toward the University of California at Los Angeles. Turn left there and he would wind up in Westwood Village, where his office was. God, he probably didn't have a patient left any more. If he walked in the door, would Miss Hill still be there, as always?

He stayed on Sunset, stopped again for a light at Sepulveda. He looked around him, at the cars, the houses, the trees, the hustle. There was a newspaper—the *Mirror-News*, not the *Times*—in an orange serve-yourself stand on the corner. He could read the big black headline: RUSSIA SAYS MAYBE. Maybe what? He could even see a photo of some blonde in the left-hand corner. Married? Divorced? Murdered?

The light changed.

He went on, up the hill.

And suddenly the city around him seemed to change. The green lawns and trees became sand, the buildings collapsed and were only steel skeletons fingering the sky. Sand drifted everywhere, tough weeds grew out of sidewalks, the street pavement was cracked and concrete slabs stuck up like dominoes.

Silence, emptiness.

Wind and sand.

Death.

Oh, he knew what he was seeing. It was the world of Centaurus Four, seen through Arvon's eyes. Yes, and hundreds of other worlds that he had never heard of. Worlds of men that had once lived and laughed and brawled as this city blared thoughtlessly around him now.

Wes shivered and came back from reality. Not to reality—*from* reality.

He looked at Arvon and Nlesine beside him, and knew that they, too, were seeing Los Angeles as it would one day be. They, too, knew that today was just an early scene in the first act of the tragedy of man.

Why, why had they come too early?

Wes's own problems faded away, a drop in a bucket to be poured into the ocean. He *knew* somehow that this world, this Earth, would survive to master space. And then Earth would find only death around her in the universe, and Earth would count herself unique, and in time Earth would stagnate and die, an isolated island, unable to find her counterpart on Lortas that could give her life forever....

"Turn in there," Arvon said quietly.

Wes started, reached for the lever to turn on his left taillight, then remembered where he was. He stuck out his arm for a turn and pulled into the driveway of a plush motel just off Sunset, still a half mile or so from the Pacific.

The car stopped.

They spent two weeks at the motel, and Wes was never alone.

Arvon and Nlesine took turns going out; sometimes they took Wes along, but not often, for there was always the chance that he would be recognized.

Somewhere Nlesine got some money. He didn't say how he had gotten it, and Wes never asked him. Nlesine blossomed out in a neat charcoal suit, while Arvon merely looked uncomfortable in a moderately clashing sport coat and slacks.

One motel room is much like another. They are fine for spending the night, and there had been a time, with Jo, when Wes had enjoyed them. But two weeks is a long time. He studied the three trite paintings—a rose, a boy examining a bandage, a pallid sunset—and memorized the pattern in the bedspreads. After that he fed the TV set with quarters, and he was not amused.

He supposed that the people on Centaurus Four might have watched such programs just before the world went bang.

There was nothing particularly mysterious about what Arvon and Nlesine were doing. They went to various libraries and looked things up. They bought magazines, particularly news magazines. They made appointments by hook or crook with various technical men, and talked to them guardedly. They made notes.

Nlesine discovered a lending library in a drugstore. He checked out novels and leafed through them rapidly. He was not reassured by an endless series of stories about sadists, supermen, and crafty business executives.

"Is your world *really* like this?" he asked.

Wes shrugged. "Some of it. Not all of it, I hope."

There was nothing at all dramatic about it. They ate three meals a day, got enough sleep, and worked steadily. They made a mountain of notes.

But, gradually, the inevitable became the obvious.

Arvon had dark circles under his eyes.

Nlesine got more and more sarcastic.

On the second day of December, Arvon threw a book at the wall.

"I give up," he said.

"It looks bad to Nlesine."

Wes sat on the bed and stared at his hands. "I tried to tell you."

Arvon paced the floor. "There aren't any magic outs. This world hasn't got manned spaceships, and won't have for a hundred years. It may be two centuries before they hit on an interstellar drive. We're whipped."

Nlesine turned to Wes. "I think you're on our side, Wes. I don't think you'll turn us in for kidnapping, or whatever you want to call it. I promised you we'd turn you loose if we couldn't find anything. We've found nothing, in spades. The only thing we're gambling with now is our lives." He grinned wryly. "Hell, man, why don't you go see your family?"

Wes trembled, got himself under control. "How about you?"

Nlesine shrugged. "We're licked, friend. Any way you cut it, we're not going back to Lortas. I don't believe anyone will listen to us, but I suppose Wyik will try to tell people here about our world and what brought us here. They'll laugh—it'll be great material for comedians. But if we get enough publicity, perhaps someone will remember, someday—when they find out what's waiting for them above the sky." He paused. "Me, I guess I'll find myself some comely wench and see if I can write a novel about the future. It'll stink, of course—a man has to have roots, and mine aren't here. Silly to worry about that now, isn't it?"

Suddenly Wes didn't care. Jo filled his mind, Jo and home and things he understood. He was hungry for them, and he wanted to forget all about space and doom and all the rest of it.

He hardly remembered saying good-bye.

He just walked out, climbed in the car, and headed back up Sunset Boulevard.

It was that simple.

He didn't think, he just drove.

And the city was a song around him: *Jo, Jo, Jo...*

CHAPTER

Beverly Glen is a curious, contradictory street, and yet it is typical of Los Angeles. From Pico to Wilshire it is a fairly featureless patchwork of identical apartment houses. From Wilshire to Sunset it anticipates Bel-Air Road by featuring spacious lawns, banks of flowers complete with Japanese gardeners, and expensive, dull houses. After the jog at Sunset its character changes sharply.

Coming from the direction of the ocean, Wes turned left on Beverly Glen, joining the steady stream of cars that wound up the hill toward the Valley.

From the moment that he turned, he was home. He smiled, responding to the street he had selected for the arena of his life. Jo had never liked it, and he could see why—it was a crazy street.

But it was his kind of a place.

There wasn't a great deal of money on this part of Beverly Glen, but there was a lot of imagination. More than that, there was variety, the missing ingredient in Los Angeles, where Wes had observed everyone trying so hard to be different that they all wound up looking exactly alike.

There were weird balconies sticking out over the narrow road, there were garages fixed up as studio apartments, there was a modest wood house with a rock castle tower. There were modern all-glass-and-redwood homes, where people seemed to live in shower baths and sometimes pulled the curtain and sometimes didn't, and there were dumps rented to college kids for seventy-five dollars a month.

It was the *feel* of the place that Wes liked. It was shady and reasonably quiet, and there was a surprising amount of open hillside, still beautiful because the landscape experts hadn't gotten to it yet. Wes often had deer come into his back yard, and rabbits and wonderful greenish hummingbirds that buzzed through the sprinkler sprays. And there were always friendly California lizards scrabbling around in the leaves.

He could have driven it with his eyes shut, even in the old Ford. He had a strange feeling that he had never been away, that he had just gone to the office as usual and was coming home for dinner.

There were no spaceships on Beverly Glen.

He passed a sign painted in the middle of the street in big red letters. It said: BILL REMEMBER JIMMY'S BICYCLE.

He grinned, wondered who Bill was, and could almost see him snapping his fingers, turning around, and rushing back somewhere for Jimmy's bike.

It was a good street.

He turned off on one of those streets that seem to go straight up the side of the mountain, ground along in second for two minutes, and turned right into a driveway half hidden by a brilliant green hedge.

He was home.

Wes felt tears in his eyes and damned himself for a sentimental fool. He stopped the car. He got out, smelling the green, wet air as though it had been created for him alone. There—he saw his own car in the carport. And the rock and redwood house—nothing sensational, maybe, but it was his, or would be with a few more payments.

He listened, heard nothing but a dog yapping down below.

Jo was alone.

He ran across the dichondra to the front door, slipped his key in the lock, pushed it open.

He glanced quickly through the kitchen, the living room, the semi-enclosed brick patio. Then he hurried down the hall, excited as a kid, and opened the bedroom door.

"Jo," he said.

And stopped.

Norman Scott got up off the edge of the bed, his face whiter than the sheets.

"Wes," whispered Jo. "Oh my God, *Wes.*"

She covered herself, hid her face in the pillow, sobbing.

"Look here, old man," Norman said, talking very fast. "Look here, old man." He ran out of gas, stopped.

Wes stood absolutely still. His stomach tied itself into knots and his head was spinning. He couldn't see. He felt nothing, nothing at all.

"I—we thought you were dead," Norman whispered. "No word, no nothing. What were we to think? We didn't know, couldn't know."

"Shut up," Wes said. He said it softly, without anger. He didn't want to hear Norm's voice. That was all.

Jo didn't look at him.

"I'd better be going," Norm said inanely.

"Yes. You'd better go."

He didn't see him leave, but he was alone with his wife.

He touched her bare shoulder, not ungently. It felt cold, like marble. "Shut up," he said.

Jo choked into silence. She lay there trembling. She still didn't look at him.

"You love him?" Wes asked. It was an empty question; he didn't care.

"Yes. No. I don't know." Jo's voice was so muffled he could hardly understand her.

Wes fumbled out a cigarette, lit it. His hands were steady. He looked around. The bed—he remembered how they had shopped for a mattress that wouldn't sag with his weight, yet wasn't too hard for her.

Pale blue wallpaper. Closet with his clothes in it, her dresses. A slip hanging on the bathroom doorknob.

He heard her voice from a long way off: "Where did you go? I was frantic. What could I do? He was so nice to me, so kind. Wes, why did you leave me?" Her voice hardened. "I *told* you never to go off and leave me sitting in that miserable cabin! Was I supposed to wait all winter?" She began sobbing again. "Oh, Wes—my God—"

Wes wasn't listening.

He looked at her. She had lost a little weight, her blond hair was gold on the pillow.

"Stiff upper lip and all that," he heard himself saying.

"What?"

"Nothing. Adults. Be civilized, sophisticated."

She looked at him now.

"No, I'm not crazy." He smiled without humor, wondering what she would think if he told her where he had been, what had happened. Then he shrugged.

It didn't matter now.

He was a stranger here. This was not his home, this was not the woman he had married. Like all the rest of his life, this too had been taken from him.

He was alone in the room, with a stranger.

Jo climbed out of bed, shivered into a robe, pushed back her hair. "Give me a cigarette, Wes."

He didn't even hear her.

"I ought to beat the hell out of you or something, but it isn't worth the effort."

"Please give me a cigarette."

"You'll be taken care of. You haven't a thing to worry about."

"Wes, I don't understand you."

"Never mind."

"Wes, I'm going to call Horace. You need a doctor. You look—awful. Look, can't we talk this over? This isn't the Middle Ages. We're sensible men and women."

Wes turned and walked out the door.

"*Wes!*"

He walked out of an alien house into alien sunshine.

He felt nothing, saw nothing.

He got in the old Ford, backed into the street, and drove into nowhere.

When he came back to himself, he was driving on Olympic Boulevard and he was sobbing. He had a cigarette in his mouth and it had burned down too far; it seared his lip. He spat it out the window without touching it with his fingers.

He watched an intersection go by. Vermont Avenue. Practically downtown. He had no idea how he had gotten there and didn't care. He made three right turns and then a left, and he was headed the other way, toward Santa Monica.

He stopped at a liquor store and bought three fifths of White Horse Scotch.

"Gonna have a party?" the man asked.

"Yeah. My debut."

Back in the car. To Beverly Glen again, and over to Sunset. Down Sunset in a crush of cars.

The motel.

He got out, knocked on the door of the cabin.

No answer.

He knocked again.

"It's Wes," he said. "Open the door, damn it."

The door opened slowly, and there was Nlesine with a gun in his hand.

"Paralyze me," he said. "Please."

Nlesine eyed him, looked up and down for policemen, and let him in.

"I was afraid you'd be gone," Wes said.

"You took our car, pal." Then Nlesine noticed his face. "Wes. What's wrong, man?"

"The world just ended ahead of schedule. I hope you would like to get drunk, because I hate to drink alone."

Then Wes ran out of words. He fell on the bed. He couldn't even cry.

Arvon closed the door carefully.

He touched Wes's shoulder.

He spoke in his own language, but what he said could be understood anywhere, in any tongue.

"Come on," Nlesine said when the silence was too much to bear. "Open the bottle, Arvon."

Wes's glasses had fallen off, but he didn't need them for what he was seeing.

The scotch went down like warm oil, but he was cold, cold as the emptiness between the worlds.

They went after the first bottle with a certain steady determination, but it was evening before they polished it off.

From that point their course was clear before them.

They started in on the second bottle.

Wes told them what had happened. He tried to be very hard-boiled and unconcerned about it, but he wasn't fooling anyone, least of all himself.

While he talked, he thought: *I wonder what happened to Arvon and Nlesine back on Lortas. This is what drives a man outside himself, even to the stars. It isn't high-minded, it isn't abstract. This is what it is: fear and loneliness that can never be forgotten, no matter how far you go, no matter how long you travel....*

"A toast, gentlemen," Nlesine said. "To the rescuers of the Universe, the heroes of the Cosmos!"

They had one on that.

They similarly honored the girls on Lortas (no finer brand on any planet), Happy Wyik, and red-blooded American boys.

They got on famously, and Wes began to feel slightly better. But then the inevitable happened: Arvon and Nlesine began to reminisce about old times. Soon they were laughing hysterically, slapping each other on the back, lost in long-ago events in which Wes had no part.

He was alone again.

He was also sobering up. The scotch just made him sick at his stomach. He sat on the bed and listened and stared at the wall.

He looked at his life.

He didn't like it.

He was not a fool. He knew that he had built up too rosy a picture of Jo while he was lying in that cave. Jo hadn't been like that, not for many years. But a man had to believe in something, had to have a home....

Sure, it had been his fault, too. He had been crazy about Jo, he'd had to have her. He had known she didn't want his kind of life, but he hadn't cared—then.

*Oh, you're a great man, Wes. Three cheers for you.*

He remembered Cincinnati, himself as a boy. Winter snow and sliding down those crazy hills, dodging the trees, coming up *smack* against black logs. Going back to the house, fighting to get his wet shoes off, the way his numb feet tingled in the warmth. Summer nights, hot and muggy, and you let the fan blow on your sweat and listened to the train whistles over in Norwood, it seemed a million miles away, and a million years....

Spring and baseball, every afternoon, playing until it was too dark to see the ball down in the empty lot at the end of the street. Woods and secret green trails, swinging on vines over the creek, catching crawdads under the rocks. September and football and knowing you were good, knowing the girls were watching you, the wonderful fearful mysterious girls, and dreaming that somehow, someday, you would marry one of those girls and then, of course, it would be an orgy every night and life would be swell forever.

It all seemed pale after that. College was a gray blur of coffee and greasy eggs and dreary singsong teachers. He remembered one old duffer reading a poem by Sandburg, then mumbling, "Is that a poem? If that's a poem, I'm Hercules!" And Tom was going to dress up in a leopard skin and come to class and leap up and say, "It is a poem, and I am Hercules!" Only he never had.

Med school was better, and the research had caught his interest. The lab had excited him—God, he used to work all night. But Jo wanted money, and that had meant the runny noses and the office, the millions and billions of runny noses, the endless afternoons....

Was he different? Was he unique? Or did this happen to all American men? He tried to think of men he knew who were happy, really happy. It seemed that as soon as you got to know a man well you discovered that he hated his work, or tolerated it, and wanted to get away—where?

And then Colorado, and the fantastic weeks in the vault where five men had slept for fifteen thousand years. And the story, the wonderful story of a ship that had touched the stars, searching, searching....

It had been the most interesting thing that had ever happened to him. And now even that had ended in failure, and that failure was a personal thing, and here they were, three bums in a motel slugging down the booze.

Nlesine almost finished the second bottle and smacked his lips. There was still a drop or two in it, but hardly enough to bother about. He put the cap back on tightly, though. "Save it for later," he muttered, and opened the third fifth.

Wes suddenly got up off the bed.

He stared at the two men with him and he was cold-sober.

And hopeful.

Maybe—

"Wait a minute," he whispered. *"Wait a minute."*

# 20

There was black coffee, argument, and more black coffee.

There was restless, nervous sleep.

And then, after a morning tug of war with fried eggs and bacon and still more black coffee, there was only one thing to do. They had to get back to Colorado, and fast.

That same afternoon they drove out Sepulveda to the International Airport and caught a twin-engined plane for Denver. It was a choppy flight, and did their stomachs no good. At Denver they rented a car and drove to Lake City, coming into it behind Slumgullion Pass, which was pretty well iced over.

It was a tough climb up the mountain along the black, icy stream, but they hardly noticed the snow and the wind and the bitter cold. Numb and red-faced and excited, they clambered into the rock shelter and rapped on the port.

There was no answer.

"It's us, damn it!" Nlesine hollered out in Lortan. "Spring is here, and we knew you'd want to go pick wild flowers. Come on out, you crusty old men!"

The port opened slowly, and there were Wyik and Hafij and Tsriga, guns ready.

"Fine welcome," Nlesine observed, moving into the vault. "Your joy at our return touches us deeply."

Wyik caught his shoulder. "Don't play with us, man! What did you find out? Quick!"

"We can't build a ship," Arvon said. "It's impossible."

Wyik's face fell.

Tsriga sat down on the floor.

Hafij didn't bat an eye.

"Hold off awhile on the suicides, though," Nlesine said quietly. "I think we've got a chance—and we can thank Wes for thinking of something we all stupidly overlooked." He grinned. "Yeah, the alien nobody would trust. *Him.*"

Wyik turned to Wes. "But what—"

"Wait." Arvon hurried over to the five niches cut into the rock wall. He fell to his knees, pawing through the pebbles and dirt and twigs that had accumulated.

"I don't see it," he whispered.

"Fine housekeepers," Nlesine muttered, and joined him.

"It's *got* to be—"

"Hold it. Here it is."

Nlesine held it up, and it was just as they had known it would be.

They sat and talked and hoped and ate a whopping meal of venison; the newcomers relished the venison more than the three men who had been eating it for weeks.

Then they slept the sleep of the exhausted.

Next morning Wes and Arvon and Nlesine went back down the mountain trail, their prize wrapped in a handkerchief and pinned in Nlesine's coat pocket.

Two days later they were back in Los Angeles.

That was where Wes got down to business.

The arrangements were not easy, but Wes Chase was almost happy as he worked. For once he had come up with something he could be proud of, and for once he was doing something that really interested him.

Not by himself, of course—but it was his brain that set it in motion.

For a while he forgot about Jo, forgot about everything but the problem at hand. This was his kind of a problem—and it could be licked.

It took them the better part of two years.

Wes had friends from his endocrine research days who were now strategically spotted in the big labs. They helped carry the ball, and the whole thing was virtually a routine performance for a trained team of researchers.

It cost Wes money, of course, but he didn't care. He cashed in his pile of stocks and bonds with something like relish.

The steps were the usual ones:

First, a detailed qualitative analysis.

Second, a delicate quantitative one.

Finally, a lengthy process of purification, repeated tests with drug derivatives, experiments on white mice and rhesus monkeys.

It was tough going, but no miracles were required.

It boiled down to this: *It was impossible for today's technology to manufacture a spaceship out of vague mental blueprints. Even had the ship still existed, many problems would have been almost insoluble—and the ship was dust and less than dust after fifteen thousand years. But the substance that had put the men from Lortas to sleep in the first place was a relatively simple compound. As Arvon had told Wes, the injection that produced suspended animation was an extract from the lymphoid tissue of hibernating mammals, like the woodchucks, in combination with an absorbent of vitamin D and insulin and some common drug derivatives. If the labs had a sample to go by, no matter how small, the stuff could be synthesized. And Wyik had not used quite all of the drug. He had resealed a few drops in the self-refrigerating duraglass container and dropped it on the floor. There it had stayed, preserved at a temperature close to absolute zero, while centuries marched by....*

The wonder was that none of them had thought of the possibility until Wes had seen Nlesine recap the scotch bottle with a few drops still left in it. After that, with Wes's own earlier experience in endocrine research as a trigger, the result was almost a foregone conclusion. The seasonal changes in the functioning of the pituitary glands of hibernating animals were well known to him, and offered a ready-made excuse when he went to the labs with his problem.

In less than two years they had it.

"You'd better be careful with this stuff, Wes," Garvin Berry, in charge of the project, said when they were through. "It knocks our lab animals out like a light."

"We'll watch our step, Garv," Wes assured him.

It was as simple as that.

The three of them had taken a somewhat uninspired apartment in Santa Monica, but Wes did not go directly back to Arvon and Nlesine. He had something he had to do first.

The priceless drug, sealed in a thick glass bottle, was on the front seat next to him as he drove. It looked oddly commonplace, even to Wes—with a little imagination it became only a bottle of milk; he had picked it up at a Westwood grocery, and now he was bringing it home to Jo...

But it was a bottle of milk that had set him back many thousands of dollars.

And there was no more Jo.

And no more home.

He had gotten used to it, he supposed. There was no more pain, only a hollow emptiness somewhere inside of him where his life used to be. He did not blame Jo, or Norm. He had made a fizzle out of his life without any help from them.

If he had only been man enough to do what he wanted to do instead of what Jo thought she wanted him to do.

If he had insisted on children.

If he had taken charge of his own life while there was still time.

If, if, if.

The hell with it. His hands tightened on the steering wheel. At least he had not failed in this. He had done one thing in his life that was worth doing. And he wasn't through yet.

Half unconsciously he began the pilgrimage.

He drove through a summer haze out along the coast highway. The road was crawling with cars. The sandy beaches were littered with people soaking up the sun. The hamburger and hot-dog stands were doing a roaring business. And the private cottages that lined the ocean, the cottages that all winter were so brown and damp and desolate, had their windows open and cars in their garages.

He pulled in at the Point and went inside.

"Doc!" One of the waiters hurried over to him, smiling. "Haven't seen you in years. How's Mrs. Chase?"

"Fine, fine." How strange to be called Doc again! Were the pieces of his life still scattered here, waiting to be picked up? "Bring me a scotch and soda out on the balcony, would you please?"

"Right away, Doc. Good to have you back."

He went out on the balcony and seated himself in the shade there. He could hear the water below him, hissing and murmuring as it curled in on the beach and sucked around the black rocks. He looked out over the ocean, blue and sparkling under a clear sky. There were fishing boats out there, black dots in the sunshine, but mostly there was loneliness, and peace.

He watched the gulls wheeling over the shallows, nosing down after fish. Along the shore line some pipers were earnestly examining the wet sand, then skittering back to avoid the breakers when they folded in.

He took off his glasses and closed his eyes, nursing his drink. The murmur of the sea was infinitely soothing. He and Jo had come here many times in that other life, had gotten tight, laughed, done crazy things. If only a man could go back, he thought—back to childhood springs, back to light hearts and carefree nights that would last forever....

*If.*

He put his glasses back on and stared, almost hypnotized, at the sea. *We're all aliens here on the land,* he thought. *We're fish out of water, Flopping on the rocks.*

"Wes old boy," he said aloud, "you are one cheerful bastard."

He paid for his drink and left a much bigger tip than necessary.

He climbed in his car and drove back along the beach, up the hill to Santa Monica, then out Wilshire to Westwood. He found an empty parking space near his office, put two pennies in the meter, and just sat in his car looking. He had let Miss Hill go, of course, but some obscure impulse had led him to keep up the office rent. He could read the black and gold sign outside the building: WESTON J. CHASE, M.D.

His middle name was Jasper, and he hated it. He remembered when Jo had had a fake sign made up once as a gag: W. JASPER CHASE, M.D. He smiled. God, that was a long time ago.

He didn't know how long he stayed there, but he noticed with a start that the meter was red. He drove off: down Olympic to Beverly Glen.

*The boundaries of my life.*

He made the jog at Sunset, where Bel-Air started, and drove along through the quiet shade of Beverly Glen. He looked for the sign that had reminded Bill to remember Jimmy's bicycle, but it was gone, of course. He turned up his hill, angled off into what had been his driveway.

He stopped the car, got out. He stood half-hidden by his hedge. He could have been seen from the house if anyone had been looking. He didn't move, neither calling attention to his presence nor concealing it.

He wondered whether he wanted to be seen.

The air was wet and green, and the dichondra was as smooth as a golf course. Jo was keeping the yard in good shape. The rock and redwood house was peaceful in the afternoon shadows.

Was she there?

He had seen her several times in the past two years, but only with their lawyer. She was well taken care of, and she had seemed happy.

*Glad to be rid of me, probably.*

No, that was unjust. He knew Jo. She would never admit that she had been hurt, even as he had been hurt. She would have given no sign to him.

He saw himself walking up to the door. She answered it, not looking her best. She brushed back her blond hair, wished she had remembered to put on lipstick.

"Wes."

"Jo, I've been thinking—about lots of things. Could I come in for a while?"

She hesitated, only a moment.

"You're alone, Jo?"

"Of course, silly. Come on in, Wes."

He would go in and then—what?

Would she take him back? Did he want her back? Oh, the attraction was still there, and he hadn't been with her for two years. Just walk up to the door….

Could they begin again?

Wes knew the answer to that one. They could begin again—you could always begin again. But how would it end?

He knew the answer to that one, too. He was what he was, and she was what she was. It hadn't worked, not really, and it never would.

He stood there by the hedge, unmoving. *You fool*, he thought. *You're waiting for her to come out to you.*

If she saw him, she gave no sign.

He didn't go in.

The shadows lengthened and it was night. He saw stars sprinkled in the sky above him.

"Good-bye, old girl," he said.

He got back in the car and drove away.

This time when he got to Santa Monica he went to the apartment where Arvon and Nlesine were waiting for him.

"Ho!" said Nlesine, tossing down a novel he was reading. "Did you get ambushed or something?"

"Or something," Wes admitted.

Arvon took the heavy glass bottle and gave it a smacking kiss. "You got it!"

"It's ready. Garv says it's an exact duplicate of the stuff we gave him to work on. I hope he's right."

"He's *got* to be right," Arvon said.

"The incurable optimist," Nlesine muttered, rubbing his balding head. "It's probably not as good as Nembutal."

They fixed themselves a dinner, with Nlesine showing off his new-found skill with spaghetti. It was good, and so was the wine, but they were all unusually subdued.

This was the end of the road.

"It's a crazy business," Arvon said finally. "We woke up after fifteen thousand years in a rock vault in Colorado, just when you happened to crawl into that shelter to get out of the storm. There probably hadn't been another human being in there since we went to sleep. And I had to grab you and scare you half to death and foul up your life for you."

"I did that for myself," Wes put in.

"Maybe. But there we were—and after fifteen thousand years we were still too early! I'm convinced now that Earth is the world we've been seeking—you are so much like us, Wes, that only almost identical cultural strains could have produced our two peoples. But we had failed until you came up with your bright idea. It looks like you saved us, Wes—and saved far more than that. But—" He paused.

"But you still get the short end of the stick," Nlesine finished.

"I think you're giving me credit for more altruism than I have," Wes said slowly. "I didn't do all this just out of the goodness of my heart. I didn't do it for that neat abstraction called the world, either. I'm a selfish animal, gentlemen."

"Ah. You have a price." Nlesine grinned as though reassured.

"Yes."

They waited.

Wes took a deep breath. "I'm going with you," he said.

There was no hurry now, so they drove through the Southwest to Colorado. They traveled at night in Arizona and New Mexico, and stopped in air-conditioned tourist courts by day.

Lake City was enjoying its annual rush season as the trout fishermen came in, and in truth the place *did* have a far livelier air about it than it had in the winter.

They left the car at the Pine Motel, with a note to Jim Walls, who had cashed Wes's check when he had first come back down the mountain. Then they hoofed it through the delightful Colorado sunshine, beside the blue waters of the swift-flowing Gunnison. The mountains loomed around them, inviting them with the enchantment of distance and the clean green of pine stands.

They turned off the main road at the creek, followed the tiny path into the brush. There were no cars parked along the stream, and that was good.

Up through the valley of green and gold, with the water chuckling and gurgling on their right. Even as they scrambled up the mountain trail, Wes caught himself eyeing one or two pools of dark water and imagining the trout that lurked in them fanning their fins....

They climbed on, past the cool pines and slender aspens, their boots treading on jungles of fern and flower. Then they left the spruces behind them and there was no more timber.

By the time they turned off at the shelter, they were good and tired, and Wes was worried. What would Wyik say?

Up into the rock shelter.

The port opened to receive them.

They were back in the vault.

Nlesine held up the thick glass bottle triumphantly. "We're in!" he said.

"We have Wes to thank for it," Arvon said.

Tsriga and even Hafij were smiling oddly secretive smiles.

Wes cleared his throat. "I came back with them," he said, and then stopped. *That's obvious enough, you idiot.* "I came back because I—because I hoped that you wouldn't mind if—"

"Shut up," Wyik said, not unkindly.

"What?"

"Are you blind, Wes?"

Wes looked around him, bewildered. Everything looked about the same. The untidy floor, the wood for the fireplace, the odds and ends, the niches cut into the far wall—

*Wait a minute.*

There had only been five niches before: Wyik, Arvon, Nlesine, Tsriga, Hafij.

Now there were six.

Wyik grabbed his hand, and the Captain's face relaxed into a rare smile. "We hoped you'd come along, Wes," he said. "After all, you're one of us now."

Wes found it hard to speak.

It wasn't the niche itself, it wasn't even the great adventure that the niche implied. No, it was more than that.

He was wanted. *God,* he thought, *somebody likes me, somebody wants to have me around.*

It was a good feeling.

*Damn it, I am NOT going to cry like a baby!*

CHAD OLIVER

"Thanks," he said. "Thanks very much."

Then he walked away, out of the vault toward the glacial lake that glinted in the pale sun, because this was a good time for a man to be alone with his thoughts.

The night before they started, Wes was sitting out under the stars, shivering a little in the high, thin wind, listening to some animal snort through the brush below him.

Arvon climbed out of the rock shelter and joined him.

"We used to sit out under the stars like this on Lortas," he said. "It's hard to think that all the girls you used to know have been dead for fifteen thousand years."

Wes nodded, although it was still hard for him to get used to the idea. "Funny, but I always think of all of you as going *home*, back to the world you left—but that's not the way it will be, is it?"

Arvon picked up a pebble and skipped it down toward the invisible animal, which responded with a flurry of movement. "Lortas will still be there unless all the predictions were wrong. But it won't be *our* Lortas—not after fifteen thousand years or so. It's almost as though you had left the Earth at the end of the Stone Age and come back to it today—but it's not quite that bad, actually. Things had slowed down on Lortas before we left, just as they will slow down here after another few hundred years."

"But you'll be strangers, just the same."

"We'll all be in the same boat, Wes."

Wes kept talking. He recognized the nervousness in himself, he needed reassurance, needed it badly. *We might never wake up*, he was thinking. *We might wake up and find the Earth a radioactive desert. The odds, the fantastic odds....*

"I think you're missing the point," Arvon said finally. "Sure, we keep talking about odds and statistics and all that. Sure, we were scared the first time—scared that this world would be like the others, all the others scattered through the skies. But, Wes, you *haven't* blown yourselves to bits—and you've had the technology to do it, and the provocation, too. The really incredible thing to me is how much, how very much, this world is like our own. Hell, I'm no more an alien here than you are now—a little different physically, maybe, but not so much that I couldn't walk through the streets of Los Angeles without anyone looking at me twice."

Wes smiled to himself. For all his claims, there were a few things Arvon still didn't know about Earth. "No offense intended," he said, "but I'm afraid most anything could live in Los Angeles unnoticed."

Arvon shrugged. "Okay, true enough. But it's no accident we are as similar as we are, Wes. This world, basically, is Lortas as Lortas was a long time ago. There are differences, important differences, of course. It's those differences that will make a new life possible for both worlds one day, if we can ever get them together. But it's the *similarities* that are important to us now. I *know* that Earth will not destroy herself. I *know* she will develop space travel. I *know* we're not going to fail now."

Wes lit a cigarette. "We have a custom called whistling in the graveyard," he said. "But, thanks, even if it was a whistle."

The two men sat in silence then under the glory of the stars.

Wes looked up at them out into the sea of night. *Sometime I may be out there, out with the suns and the darkness and the silence—*

It was late when they returned to the vault.

Wes remembered that other time, when Arvon had carried him into the shelter, when Arvon had been a creature out of a nightmare. It seemed a million years ago.

He did not look back, although he knew he would never see the world that waited at the foot of the mountain path again.

He heard Nlesine snoring lustily as he stretched out on the hard floor.

*How strange, how strange that we want a good night's sleep before we sleep for five hundred years....*

He slept.


The morning was filled with tense jokes.

They had always been careful to conceal any traces of their presence on the outside, so that was all attended to. They ate a good big breakfast, all of them eating more than they really wanted. After all, lunch was five hundred years away.

They sealed off the vault.

Wes got his hypodermic needle out and cleaned it in alcohol.

He was nervous, but his hands were steady.

"All right, Wes," Wyik said. "Let's get on it. Make absolutely certain that you give us all *exactly* the same dose. And be sure you lie down in the niche before you inject yourself—it hits fast."

Rather self-consciously they all shook hands.

Nobody said, and everyone thought, *What if it doesn't work, what if the lab made a mistake, what if this is the end...?*

Wyik slid into his niche, settled himself.

"All right, Wes," he said again.

Wes cleaned a spot on his arm with cotton dipped in alcohol, opened the heavy glass container, filled the hypo with precisely one cubic centimeter of the drug. The stuff compounded its effect as the dosage was increased, he had to be careful....

He inserted the hypo expertly, pressed the plunger.

Wyik's haunted, desperate eyes clouded, closed, and he slept. Wes stared at him. He didn't seem to be alive, he could see no chest movement. He took his wrist. Yes, there was the pulse, but fading, fading....

"Next," said Nlesine.

Very carefully, forcing himself to concentrate on the job and nothing else, Wes made the rounds.

A corner of his mind refused to be silent.

*All of you, all of you,* he thought. *You, Wyik, and Nlesine, and Arvon, and Tsriga, and Hafij. You have all lost something, even as I have lost something. What happened in your lives on Lortas that sent you here? A man can be driven only by the springs inside himself. You, Nlesine—were you a good novelist? Were you good enough? You, Arvon—if your life was empty, did you seek to fill it here? Tsriga, you were a boy when you came here, but you will be a man when you return. I hope the next woman will be worthy of you. Hafij, what loneliness made you seek the stars for your home? And, Wyik, strange Wyik, are you too running away? What made the black unrest in your soul?*

It was done.

Wes turned out the tubelights, all except one that he held in his hand. He filled the needle for the last time. Then, smiling a little, he carefully recapped the heavy glass container.

He crawled into his rock cubicle.

The vault was dark and empty around him, the solid rock above him seemed the weight of centuries.

And yet he was not alone. The men who slept in the darkness around him understood. They, too, had lost something, everything, and they, too, were searching....

He injected himself, switched off the light.

Darkness, shadows—

And a greater, softer oblivion.

Sound.

That came first.

It curled into his mind like smoke, blue smoke, wood smoke, and it was a voice, talking, whispering ...

A language he didn't know. Strange. What was it?

Ah! Lortan. He recognized it.

Wyik's voice.

Suddenly, shatteringly, he opened his eyes. Light. It hurt. He blinked, kept them open. He felt the rock under his body, he felt the squeezing heart in his chest, the liquid sluggish in his veins.

"I'm awake." He said it aloud, his voice a croak. "I'm not dead. I'm *awake.*"

A hand on his shoulder. Wyik's. "Easy," said the Captain. "Take it slow. There's no hurry. You're all right."

Wes lay still, gathering his strength. He was cold. He felt his chest, and scraps of rotted cloth fell away. *Naked,* he thought. *Me, a nudist.*

He managed a smile.

After a while he crawled out of the niche, stood up. He was lightheaded and thought he was falling, but he recovered himself in time. *Skinny, God, I'm skinny.* Wyik, too, was thin and pale, his eyes feverish in his head.

*Hungry.*

"Outside," he said. "Have you looked?"

"No. I listened, couldn't hear anything. I was waiting."

One of the others stirred, groaned. Tsriga.

"Let's wait until we can all go," Wyik said.

Wes sat down on the floor, shivering. It was hard to think, hard to come back from the dead. He wondered how Arvon had come out of it so fast that time long ago—how long ago now?

But he was *alive*.

They waited, and when they were all ready Wyik cautiously opened the port.

Light, light and silence.

They went into the rock shelter, looked out.

Nothing had changed. Sky, rocks, brush, stream—

Wes felt despair clutch him in an icy fist.

"What's happened? It's all the same. God, didn't the stuff *work?*"

Arvon shook his head. "It was like this before," he said. "A spot like this, high in the mountains—why would it change?"

Whistling in the dark?

They saw no human figure. They heard no animals—no sound at all save a sighing wind.

*Dead. The place is dead. Earth, too...*

"Wait."

He heard it. They all heard it.

A rumble, as of thunder, far away.

Coming closer.

A blasting roar, a hurricane of sound—

They saw it.

Above them.

A ship, a prodigious ship, a mountain of metal and glass that blotted out the sun. Its shadow crossed them. The thing was immense, so high in the sky, so beautiful—

And it was gone.

Only the thunder remained, rolling over the mountains.

Hafij was crying. "A ship, a spaceship." He said it over and over again, tasting the words on his tongue.

"We made it," Arvon said.

*We made it, we made it.*

He remembered, they all remembered: *No human culture on record had ever succeeded in finding and establishing friendly relations with another human culture on a different planet. If a world could be found where men were sane, if contacts could be built up between them, if ideas and hopes and dreams could flow from one to the other—*

*Then perhaps man might someday be more than just another animal who lost his way....*

They paused long enough to drink the cold, clean water from the glacial lake. They laughed and joked and cried, not daring to believe, but having to believe.

They started down the path, the swift mountain stream at their side, running, running—

Past the spruces, the whispering pines, the slender aspens.

Into a warm summer valley, all green and gold, alive with color and the songs of birds.

Toward a new world, a new hope.

Derryoc went with them, and Seyehi, and Lajor, and Kolraq, a smile on his face. Wes felt tears in his eyes. Jo was there too—Jo and the life that had almost been, and never was.

The sunlight was life, and promise.

Wes wasn't thinking about the world, or two worlds, or the universe.

*I'm only forty. That's not so old. There is still time for me, time for children and happiness and life. Only forty, only forty, there is still time for me....*

They were all moving into the unknown.

No one of them had a home.

But they knew now that the winds of time are patient and blow forever.

This was not the end.

This was the beginning.

# AFTERWORD

## REMEMBERING BIG CHAD
## BY WILLIAM F. NOLAN

Big Chad. That's what we called him, and he *was*—big in every respect: in heart, in talent, and in physical stature. He dedicated this book to me and to Charles Beaumont (our good friend, now long deceased), based on Chuck's and my stubborn contention that "the world is like a fountain." (After all these years I cannot, for the life of me, recall what we meant by this!) Just to be contrary, Chad would say: "No, the world is like a *falcon*!" Over the phone, reading his dedication to us, he chortled about having "the last printed word" on this mysterious subject. Chad's book dedication, however, had a solid subtext.

Love.

In the two and a half years that he and his wonderful wife, Beje, lived in the Los Angeles area (1953 into 1955), we had all formed a tightly knit group—me, Chad and Beje, Chuck and Helen Beaumont, and Richard and Ruth Matheson. We saw each other often and spent many warmly memorable evenings together. Chad meant a great deal to each of us, as we did to him, and his book dedication reflected this deep friendship and affection.

Chad and I were born in the same month of the same year, March of 1928—me in Kansas City, Missouri, and Chad (as Symmes Chadwick Oliver) in Cincinnati, Ohio. He was married in November of 1952 to Betty Jane Jenkins ("Beje") in Los Angeles, and we met, via Chuck Beaumont, early the following year, when Chad was a teaching assistant at UCLA, working toward his doctorate in anthropology. The Olivers became, and steadfastly remained, among my dearest friends. His death, at age 65, in August of 1993, was like a physical blow. I'm still not over it. A world without Big Chad? Impossible.

No one will ever replace him.

Before I write more about Chad, I'm going to let him speak for himself, through letters and interviews, as he outlined his early life, before I met him:

> My father, Symmes Francis Oliver, was a surgeon. My mother's name was Winona Newman, and she was from Lima, Ohio. The Olivers were from Cincinnati. Mom met Dad when she was a nurse in that city. My mother had the business sense and ran the household. She later became a painter of some distinction. My parents were both omnivorous readers, and our house was always full of books. My father was a gentle man, a dreamer, an avid sports fan and an expert fisherman. In fact, I caught my first trout with him in Maine, when I was seven. [Chad became a passionate trout fisherman from that point forward.]

In this novel, *The Winds of Time*, Chad incorporated many boyhood memories:

> …baseball every afternoon, playing until it was too dark to see the ball down in the empty lot at the end of the street. Woods and secret green trails, swinging on vines over the creek, catching crawdads under rocks…winter snow and sliding down those crazy hills…going back to the house, fighting to get my wet shoes off…summer nights, hot and muggy…listening to the train whistles over in Norwood.

Young Oliver was very active in sports until he contracted rheumatic fever at the age of twelve; he nearly died of it. ("I might very well have, if Dad had not been a doctor.") He was bedridden for seven months and reading became his salvation. Jules Verne, H.G. Wells, and Edgar Rice Burroughs fed his burgeoning imagination. He began subscribing to a wide variety of science fiction pulps, zestfully contributing to their "Readers' Department." Chad's letters, by the dozen, began appearing regularly in *Planet Stories*, *Thrilling Wonder*, *Startling*, and *Super Science*. But the Ohio years were ending...

> During the war [World War II], my Dad enlisted, and they sent him to Crystal City, Texas, as the Medical Officer in charge of a camp there. That's when our family moved to Texas, when I was fifteen...and that's when I really became a Texan. Just fell in love with the place, the country, the rivers, all of it...I've never wanted to live anywhere else. Then, after I graduated from high school in 1945, where I was heavily involved in football, I began attending the University of Texas, in Austin, and that was the start of everything....

His abiding interest in anthropology was ignited at the university. It was, indeed, "the start of everything."

> The whole problem of other cultures and of "contact" between different cultural systems had always fascinated me in science fiction. Therefore, I was already into the basics of anthropology. I took two courses in it during my freshman year, but I was not yet fully converted to the field. I was also drawn strongly to English, and took a lot of literature courses. Of course, I'd been sending out stories since the Ohio days. But my fiction sales were still a ways ahead of me.

The University of Texas occupied much of Oliver's life as he began his long association with this institution. He received his B.A. degree there in 1951, and his M.A. in 1952. After his stint in Los Angeles, he returned to teach at the university in 1955. He was promoted to Assistant Professor of Anthropology in 1959, and earned his Ph.D. from UCLA in 1961. He was promoted to Associate Professor in 1963, and to full Professor in 1968, the same year his only son, Glen Chadwick Oliver, was born. (His only daughter, Kimerley Frances Oliver, had been born in 1955.)

During these years he also worked as a Research Anthropologist in

Kenya and, East Africa, while he wrote books and articles on this subject. He later served as Chairman of the Anthropology Department at the university; he was still teaching there shortly before his death, having won (among many other honors) the Presidential Award for Teaching Excellence.

Throughout his life, Chad was a split personality: half teacher, half fiction writer. He very much enjoyed teaching, but he also yearned to write fiction on a full-time basis. He had determined to settle into full-time writing after his retirement, but his fatal illness, in 1993, cut short his plans.

Even so, in his severely limited career as a fictioneer, Chad turned out nine novels and some seventy shorter tales—the majority being science fiction, although he also won well-deserved awards for his superb historical westerns.

The word "love" always comes to mind when I think of Chad. He deeply loved his wife, his two children, and his many friends. Love was the keynote of his life, and it was returned to him in full measure. Chad Oliver was, truly, both loving and beloved.

This book, *The Winds of Time*, was first published in April of 1957, and is his third novel (after *Mists of Dawn* and *Shadows in the Sun*). Chad broke into pro fiction when he was twenty-two, in early 1950, and soon gained a solid reputation as one of the finest writers in the SF genre. *The Winds of Time* shows us why.

It's a terrific novel by my dear friend, Chad Oliver. No more need be said.

I hope you enjoyed it.

Chad would like that.

William F. Nolan
West Hills, California
February, 1996

**WILLIAM F. NOLAN** is best known for *Logan: A Trilogy*. Part one of the trilogy, *Logan's Run* (written with George Clayton Johnson), was made into a major motion picutore in 1976 and later became a television series. Nolan's more than fifty books include science fiction, fanasy, mysteries, and anthologies. He has been a full-time writer since 1956.

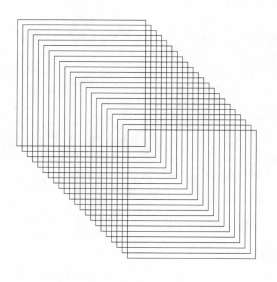

INTRODUCED BY

PAMELA SARGENT

# THE YEAR OF THE QUIET SUN

BY WILSON TUCKER

# INTRODUCTION

It was my good fortune to finally meet Wilson Tucker in 1995, at a science fiction convention in Detroit, Michigan. I was already well aware of how popular and legendary a figure he was in science fiction circles, and had heard about "Bob" Tucker for years—about his wit, his skill as a raconteur, his knowledge of science fiction's early history, and his friendships with many of the editors, writers, and fans who were involved in science fiction during the Thirties and Forties. Tucker is especially famed (or notorious) for using the names of other writers and fans as those of characters in his works (an additional treat for those in the know that does not impede the enjoyment of readers unacquainted with these people), a practice that became known as "Tuckerization."

His accomplishments as a writer merit much praise. He published *The Year of the Quiet Sun* when I was just beginning as a writer; I found much to admire in the novel, and knew that I could learn something by paying close attention to other works by its author. Yet Wilson Tucker, to many in the science fiction world today, is much better known as a fan than as a writer, more renowned as an entertaining toastmaster and popular speaker at public gatherings than for his published work. There are many who, having started out as fans of the genre—writing letters to the editors of favorite magazines, going to meetings of groups who shared their interest in science fiction, attending conventions, and publishing amateur magazines (or "fanzines") devoted to the field—later went on to great fame as writers and editors. Some of them have made a lasting impression on science fiction; among these former fans are such major figures as Isaac

Asimov, Donald A. Wollheim, Frederik Pohl, Judith Merril, Robert Silverberg, Harlan Ellison, Gregory Benford, and many others too numerous to mention. It's fair to say that most of the people who have heard of these writers and editors know little or nothing of their earlier lives as fans. Almost the opposite is true of Tucker; I met people in Detroit who had known him for years, and who had enjoyed his appearances at several conventions, who were barely aware of his published work; a few were surprised to find out that he had published over twenty novels. Tucker's editors have included the likes of noted British writer Clemence Dane, as well as science fiction editor Terry Carr, who discovered and published first novels or early work by Ursula K. Le Guin, William Gibson, Joanna Russ, Kim Stanley Robinson, and Lucius Shepard, yet a number of science fiction readers remain unaware of Tucker's literary contributions.

How did this happen? Some of this ignorance is undoubtedly caused by the vagaries of publishing; Tucker has not published a new book of fiction since 1982, and many publishers are increasingly reluctant to keep older works by a writer in print when no new work is forthcoming. In a field where many writers publish two or more books a year, Tucker's output, substantial as it is, can also seem small to those who expect SF writers to be excessively prolific. Tucker has admitted that he is past the point of feeling that there are stories or books that he *has* to write. As the noted writer James Blish once put it, part of being a good writer lies in knowing when to stop writing—at least for publication.

But Wilson Tucker is also a modest man who does not trumpet his accomplishments, much as they deserve attention and praise. Illustrious colleagues and critics, James Gunn and A. E. van Vogt among them, have asserted that Tucker has produced a body of work more distinguished than that of most science fiction writers, yet Tucker himself regards his own writing with characteristic constraint. As he wrote in a statement for the *St. James Guide to Science Fiction Writers* (Fourth Edition, 1996): "I write to entertain an editor, his readers, and myself, in that order. If I fail to entertain the editor, there will be no readers; if I fail to entertain the readers, my own livelihood will be reduced accordingly. Some critics have said that my books may paint a bleak picture for humanity but that I always offer hope and sunshine for the future. That's news to me. I had always believed that I was writing adventure and offering entertainment, nothing more."

Tucker's modesty may have helped make him the craftsmanlike writer he is. His prose is clean, clear, and economical; he doesn't lard his books with unessential digressions or call attention to his writing with pyrotechnics. His books are also as entertaining and enthralling as he intended them to be. But he is far too modest in his assessment of his writing; his novels are considerably more than entertainments, and *The Year of the Quiet Sun* has justifiably been hailed as one of his finest works.

※

Wilson Tucker was born in Illinois in 1914 and still lives in that part of the United States. He is a self-educated man who has pursued a deep and abiding interest in history and archaeology, which may account for the fact that one of his favorite themes is time travel. Until he retired in 1972, he worked as a stage electrician and as a movie projectionist, and the medium of film has clearly influenced his writing. In a recent essay about Tucker's work, Sandra Miesel wrote: "Wilson Tucker's stories have the modesty of realistic black-and-white films. His casts are small, his scale intimate, and his settings familiar. He develops his plots and characters using human actions and reactions. He prefers concrete imagery to abstract verbiage: he tells by showing."

Tucker's first four published novels were mysteries, beginning with *The Chinese Doll* (1946), followed by *To Keep or Kill* (1947), *The Dove* (1948), and *The Stalking Man* (1950); all were published by Rinehart in the U.S. and Cassell in Britain. In 1951, when his fifth mystery, *Red Herring*, came out, he published his first science fiction novel, *The City in the Sea*. To date, he is the author of twelve science fiction books, including two collections of short fiction, and eleven mysteries. Tucker's mystery novels seem to have had an influence on his science fiction writing. "One of his major contributions to SF has been his graphic realism," James Gunn notes, "perhaps a carryover from his mystery writing." Combined with the elegance of a cinematic style, this realism makes for books that are immensely readable and accessible even to readers who are unfamiliar with science fiction.

Tucker's second science fiction novel, *The Long Loud Silence* (1952), is a gritty tale of a post-holocaust world and is numbered among his best works. His novels *The Time Masters* (1953) and *Time Bomb* (1955) are two suspenseful and loosely connected stories of time travel. This characteristic Tucker theme is beautifully realized in *The Lincoln Hunters* (1958), in which a team of men from a repressive future U.S.A. go back in time to record a lost speech of Abraham Lincoln's; here, Tucker combines his love of history and of his home state of Illinois with a masterful use of the problem of time travel paradoxes to create tension. Other science fiction novels by Tucker are *Wild Talent* (1954), brought out in 1955 in England by the distinguished publishing house of Michael Joseph, and *To the Tombough Station* (1960). But it is *The Year of the Quiet Sun* that is widely considered his finest novel.

*The Year of the Quiet Sun* was published in 1970, and was a finalist for the Nebula and Hugo Awards, the two greatest honors the science fiction world can bestow. The novel also has the distinction of being the only book honored retrospectively with the John W. Campbell Memorial Award. This prize, named for the influential editor of *Astounding* (later *Analog*) *Magazine*, was given to Wilson Tucker in 1976; the jury for the award reasoned that since the Campbell Award had not been created until 1972, and no other novel published in 1975 measured up to *The Year of the Quiet Sun* in their opinion, that Tucker should be the recipient. Indeed, the well-known British writer and critic Brian Aldiss, one of the members of that jury, called *The Year of the Quiet Sun* "one of the most striking time travel novels since Wells."

Praise came from other quarters as well. P. Schuyler Miller, reviewing the book in *Analog*, said that the novel "shows that, good as Tucker was in the past...he is even better now...It's grim, but it's real—too real—and there are no concessions to formula." Harry Harrison has said about this novel: "In *The Year of the Quiet Sun* Wilson Tucker brings satisfaction to the most exacting reader...What I particularly enjoyed about this novel was the author's ability to get inside his characters. To make them realistic and believable and different. Characterization is never easy; in fact it is quite hard work.

But the successful author disguises that fact so that the reader is never aware of the effort that has gone into it."

One characteristic feature of Tucker's work is his subtlety, a quality that is present here. His books require close attention if important clues aren't to be missed, and rereading them in the light of what has been learned the first time around is even more rewarding. Another distinguishing characteristic of Tucker's is his ability to reveal much in a few words or a brief scene. In *The Year of the Quiet Sun*, clues to what has happened in the outside world are revealed by glimpses of a swimming pool at different times. Tucker, with his emblematic modesty, comments on what one commentator found in this novel and on what he intended:

> Some years ago an academic author published a long essay on *The Year of the Quiet Sun* and managed to startle me again and again by finding dozens, perhaps scores, of signs and symbols and hidden meanings to the novel. I had inserted a few symbols for story-telling purposes to be sure, but she said nothing of those and concentrated instead on the many signs and symbols she appeared to find in the novel. I was pleased, of course, as well as being startled because her findings and her commentary made me look like a genius and a superb if subtle novelist.
>
> One of her major points was my use of water, the water in a swimming pool. She said that I was using the waters of life to tell my story. I believed that I was using the pool only to show the passage of time. That pool was filled with clean waters and scores of people in the warm summer months when the immediate neighborhood was well populated; it was empty the following winter; when the neighborhood was abandoned in the following years the pool became a trash heap for unwanted debris and small dead animals. I truly believed that I was only showing the passage of time and the nearly empty neighborhood. The academic author liked my keen use of the waters of life as they reflected the human condition and she managed many hundreds of words on that symbol. I think she is marvelous.

A primitive people of a few thousand years ago would never recognize an airplane but in their oral descriptions and their myths it would likely become a sky-dragon, spewing dirt and destruction from overhead; it would eventually be banished by a hero standing on a mountain top scrubbing the dirty skies. Eventually again, that story would be put to ink and linen, rolled into a scroll and tucked away in some jar in a desert cave. I'm not really a genius—but I suspected that chain of events could really happen.

The story begins with Brian Chaney, demographer and Biblical scholar; against his will, he is pushed into becoming part of a time-travel project run by the U.S. government. The project's stated objective is to learn about the near future and its problems, and to use whatever knowledge is gained to further future political stability and the welfare of the citizenry. Matters turn out quite differently, as Chaney moves from a time in which his heritage, at least on the surface, is a matter of indifference to those around him to a time where it matters more than anything else in the world. The ancient manuscript translated by Chaney is an integral part of this compelling novel.

In the years since *The Year of the Quiet Sun* was published, I occasionally thought that Tucker might have been too pessimistic in his imagined future, that we might get past some of the prejudices that divide us. I am no longer so sure of that. In an age of armed militias talking of apocalypse, anger and bitterness among both poor inner-city residents and prosperous African-Americans, and a de facto segregation that still exists in too many walks of life, the future glimpsed in *The Year of the Quiet Sun* may be even more plausible than it was when the novel was written. Let us hope not; some prophecies, as Wilson Tucker demonstrates, can be self-fulfilling.

Prepare yourself for a compulsively readable book, a work that now stands as one of the classic stories of time travel.

Pamela Sargent
Albany, New York
May 15, 1996

# THE YEAR OF THE QUIET SUN

BY WILSON TUCKER

# 1

THE KIND OF PROPHET THESE PEOPLE
WANT IS A WINDBAG AND A LIAR,
PROPHESYING A FUTURE OF WINE
AND SPIRITS.

—THE BOOK OF MICAH

The leggy girl was both alpha and omega: the two embodied in the same compact bundle. The operation began when she confronted him on a Florida beach, breaking his euphoria; it ended when he found her sign on a grave marker, hard by a Nabataean cistern. The leap between those two points was enormous.

Brian Chaney was aware of only a third symbol when he discovered her: she was wearing a hip-length summer blouse over delta pants. No more than that—and a faint expression of disapproval—was evident.

Chaney intended to make short work of her.

When he realized the girl was coming at him, coming for him, he felt dismay and wished he'd had time to run for it. When he saw the object she carried—and its bright red dustjacket couldn't be missed— he was tempted to jump from the beach chair and run anyway. She was another tormentor. The furies had been hounding him since he left Tel Aviv—since the book was published—hounding him and crying heresy in voices hoarse with indignation. String up the traitor! they cried. Burn the infidel!

He watched the approach, already resenting her.

He had been idling in the sun, half dozing and half watching a mail Jeep make box deliveries along the beach road when she suddenly appeared in his line of sight. The beach had been deserted except for himself, the Jeep, and the hungry gulls; the inland tourists with their loud transistor radios wouldn't be along for another several weeks. The girl walked purposefully along the shoulder of the road until she was nearly opposite him, then quickly wheeled and stepped across a narrow band of weedy grass onto the sand. She paused only long enough to pull off her shoes, then came across the beach at him.

When she was near, he threw away his earlier supposition: she was a leggy, disapproving woman, not a girl. He guessed her age at twenty-five because she looked twenty; she wasn't very tall nor very solid— no more than a hundred pounds. A troublesome woman.

Chaney deliberately turned in his chair to watch the raging surf, hoping the woman would about-face. She carried the red-jacketed book clutched in hand as though it were a purse, and tried unsuccessfully to hide her disapprobation. She might be a scout from one of those damned TV shows.

He liked the sea. The tide was coming in and there had been a storm on the water the night before; now the whitecaps boomed in to break on the beach only a dozen feet away, hurling spray into his face. He liked that; he liked the feel of stinging spray on his skin. He liked being outdoors under a hot sun, after too many months at desk and bench. Israel had a lovely climate but it did nothing for a man working indoors. If these intruders would only let him alone, if they would allow him another week or two on the beach, he'd be willing to end his holiday and go back to work in the tank—the dusty, fussy tank with its quota of dusty, fussy wizards making jokes about sunburns and back tans.

The leggy woman halted beside him.

"Mr. Brian Chaney."

He said: "No. Now run along."

"Mr. Chaney, my name is Kathryn van Hise. Forgive the intrusion. I am with the Bureau of Standards."

Chaney blinked his surprise at the novelty and turned away from the whitecaps. He stared at her legs, at the form-fitting delta pants, at the tease-transparent blouse wriggling in an off-shore breeze, and looked up finally at her face against the sunshine-hot Florida sky. Her nearness revealed more. She was small in stature—size eight, at a guess—and light of weight, giving the impression of being both quick and alert. Her skin was well tanned, telling her good use of the early summer sun, and it nicely complimented her eyes and hair. The eyes were one attractive shade of brown and the hair was another. Her face bore only a hint of cosmetics. There were no rings on her fingers.

He said skeptically: "*That's* a novel approach."

"I beg your pardon?"

"Usually, you're from the Chicago *Daily News*, or the Denver *Post*, or the Bloomington *Bulletin*. Sometimes you're from a TV talk show. You want a statement, or a denial, or an apology. I like your imagination, but you don't get one."

"I am not a newspaper person, Mr. Chaney. I am a research supervisor with the Bureau of Standards, and I am here for a definite purpose. A serious purpose."

"No statement, no denial, and certainly not an apology. What purpose?"

"To offer you a position in a new program."

"I have a job. New programs every day. Sometimes we have new programs running out of our ears."

"The Bureau is quite serious, Mr. Chaney."

"The Bureau of Standards," he mused. "The *government* Bureau of Standards, of course—the one in Washington, cluttered with top-heavy bureaucrats speaking strange dialects. That would be a fate worse than death. I worked for them once and I don't want to again, ever." But the wind-whipped blouse was an eye-puller.

She said: "You completed a study for the Bureau three years ago, before taking leave to write."

"Does the Bureau have a complaint about my book? Short weight? Pages missing? Too much fat in the text? Have I defrauded the consumers? Are they going to sue? Now *that* would cap everything."

"Please be serious, Mr. Chaney."

"No—not today, not tomorrow, not this week and maybe not the next. I've been run through the mill but now I'm on vacation. I earned it. Go away, please."

The woman stubbornly held ground.

After a while, Chaney's attention drifted back from a prolonged study of the racing whitecaps and settled on the bare feet firmly embedded in the sand near his chair. A fragrant perfume was worn somewhere beneath the blouse. He searched for the precise source, for the spot where it had kissed her skin. It was difficult to ignore his visitor when she stood so close. Her legs and the delta pants earned one more inspection. She certainly wore her skin and that tantalizing clothing well.

Chaney squinted up at her face against the sky. The brown eyes were direct, penetrating, attractive.

"Dress like yours is prohibited in Israel—did you know that? Most of the women are in uniform and the high command worries about male morale. Delta lost." Chaney conveyed his regret with a gesture. "Are you serious?"

"Yes, sir."

"The Bureau wants a biblical translator?"

"No, sir. The Bureau wants a demographer, one who is experienced in both lab and field work." She paused. "And certain other prerequisites, of course."

"A demographer!"

"Yes, sir. *You.*"

"But the woods are full of demographers."

"Not quite, Mr. Chaney. You were selected."

"Why? Why me? What other prerequisites?"

"You have a background of stability, of constancy and resolution; you have demonstrated your ability to withstand pressures. You are well adjusted mentally and your physical stamina is beyond question. Other than your biblical research, you have specialized in socio-political studies and have earned a reputation as an extrapolative statistician. You *are* the definition of the term, futurist. You authored that lengthy study for the Bureau. You have a security clearance. You were selected."

Chaney turned with astonishment and stared. "Does the Bureau know I also chase women? Of all colors?"

"Yes, sir. That fact was noted in your dossier, but it wasn't considered a detriment."

"Please thank the good gray Bureau for me. I do appreciate the paternal indulgence."

"There is no need to be sarcastic, Mr. Chaney. You have a well-balanced computer profile. Mr. Seabrooke has described you as an ideal futurist."

"I'm *ever* so grateful. Who is Seabrooke?"

"Gilbert Seabrooke is our Director of Operations. He personally selected you from a narrow field of candidates."

"I'm not a candidate; I volunteered for nothing."

"This is a top secret project of some importance, sir. The candidates were not consulted in advance."

"That's why we're all so happy about it." Chaney indicated the book in her hand. "You're *not* interested in my hobby? In that? The Bureau doesn't expect me to deny my translation of the Revelations scroll?"

The faint expression of disapproval again crossed her face but was thrust aside. "No, sir. The Bureau *is* unhappy with your work, with the resultant notoriety, and Mr. Seabrooke wishes you *hadn't* published it—but he believes the public will have forgotten by the time you have surfaced again."

Emphatically: "*I'm* not going underground."

"Sir?"

"Tell Mr. Seabrooke I'm not interested. I do very well without him and his Bureau. I have a job."

"Yes, sir. With the new project."

"No, sir, with the Indiana Corporation. It's called Indic, for short, and it's a think-tank. I'm a genius—does your computer know that, Miss van Hise? Indic has a hundred or so captive geniuses like me sitting around solving problems for know-nothings. It's a living."

"I am familiar with the Indiana Corporation."

"You should be. We did that job for your people three years ago and scared the hell out of them—and then we submitted a bill which unbalanced their budget. We've done work for State, for Agriculture, for the Pentagon. I *hate* Pentagon work. Those people are in a hell of a rut. I wish they'd climb off the Chinese back and find some other enemy to study and outwit." He dropped back into the beach chair and returned his attention to the surf. "I have a job waiting; I rather like it. I'm going back to it when I get tired of sitting here doing nothing—tired of loafing. Find yourself another demographer."

"No, sir. Indic has assigned you to the Bureau."

Chaney came out of the chair like a rocket. He towered over the diminutive woman.

"They have not!"

"They have, Mr. Chaney."

"They wouldn't do that without my consent."

"I'm sorry, but they have."

Insistently: "They *can't*. I have a contract."

"The Bureau has purchased your contract, sir."

Chaney was dumbfounded. He gaped at the woman.

She removed a folded letter from the pages of the book and handed it to him to read. The letter was couched in stiff corporate language, it was signed, and it bore the great seal of the Indiana Corporation. It transferred the balance of term of employment of Brian Chaney from the private corporation to the public agency, then generously arranged to share with him on an equal basis the financial consideration paid for the transfer. It wished him well. It politely mentioned his book. It was very final.

The waiting woman did not understand the single Aramaic word hurled down the Florida beach.

The waves were crashing around his knees, spraying his chest and face. Brian Chaney turned in the surf and looked back at the woman standing on the beach.

He said: "There are only two buses a day. You'll miss the last one if you don't hurry."

"I have not completed my instructions, Mr. Chaney."

"I'd be pleased to give you certain instructions."

Kathryn van Hise stood her ground without answer. The gulls came swooping back, only to take flight again.

Chaney shouted his frustration. "*Why?*"

"The special project needs your special skills."

"*Why?*"

"To survey and map the future; you are a futurist."

"I'm not a surveyor—I'm not a cartographer."

"Those were figures of speech, sir."

"I don't *have* to honor that contract. I can break it, I can turn black-leg and go to work for the Chinese. What will the Pentagon do *then*, Miss van Hise?"

"Your computer profile indicated that you would honor it, sir. It also indicated your present annoyance. The Pentagon knows nothing of this project."

"Annoyance! I can also give that computer explicit instructions, but they would be as hard to obey as yours. Why don't you go home? Tell them I refused. Rebelled."

"When I have finished, sir."

"Then finish up, damn it, and get along!"

"Yes, sir." She moved closer to him to avoid raising her voice and permitting the gulls to overhear top secret information. "The first phase of the operation began shortly after Indic submitted its report three years ago, and continued all the while you were studying in Israel. As the author of that report, you were considered one of the most likely persons to participate in the next phase, the field implementations. Expertise. The Bureau is now ready to move into the field, and has recruited a select team to conduct field operations. You will be a member of that team, and then participate in the final report. Mr. Seabrooke expects to submit it to the White House; he is counting on your enthusiastic support."

"Bully for Seabrooke; he shanghais me and then expects my enthusiastic support. What implementations?"

"A survey of the future."

"We've already done that. Read the Indic report."

"A physical survey of the future."

Brian Chaney looked at her for a long moment with unconcealed amusement and then turned back to the sea. A red and white sail was beating across the Gulf in the middle distance and the tacking fascinated him.

He said: "I suppose some nutty genius somewhere has really invented a tachyon generator, eh? A generator and deflector and optical train that works? The genius can peer through a little telescope and observe the future?"

The woman spoke quietly. "The engineers at Westinghouse have built a TDV, sir. It is undergoing tests at the present time."

"Never heard of it." Chaney shaded his eyes against the sun the better to watch the bright sail. "*V* is for vehicle, I suppose? Well— that's better than a little telescope. What is the *TD?*"

"Time Displacement. An engineering term." There was a peculiar note of satisfaction in her voice.

Brian Chaney dropped his hand and turned all the way around in the water to stare down at the woman. He felt as if he'd been hit.

"*Time* Displacement Vehicle?"

"Yes, sir." The satisfaction became triumph.

"It can't work!"

"The vehicle is in test operation."

"I don't believe it."

"You may see it for yourself, sir."

"It's *there?* It's sitting there in your lab?"

"Yes, sir."

"Operating?"

"Yes, sir."

"I'll be damned. What are you going to do with it?"

"Implement our new program, Mr. Chaney. The Indic report has become an integral part of the program in that it offered several hard guidelines for a survey of the future. We are now ready to initiate the second phase, the field explorations. Do you see the possibilities, sir?"

"You're going to get *in* that thing, that vehicle, and go somewhere? Go into the future?"

"No, sir. *You* are; the team will."

Chaney was shocked. "Don't be an idiot! The team can do what they damned please, but I'm not going anywhere. I didn't volunteer for your program; I wasn't a willing candidate; I oppose peonage on humanitarian grounds."

He quit the surf and stalked back to the beach chair, not caring if the woman followed him. Gulls shrieked their annoyance at his passage. Chaney dropped into the chair with another muttered imprecation of stiff-necked bureaucrats, a scurrilous declaration couched in Hebraic terms the woman wouldn't understand. It commented on her employer's relations with jackasses and Philistines.

TDV. A furious stimulant to the imagination.

The gulls, the tide, the salt spray, the descending sun were all ignored while his racing imagination toyed with the information she had given him. He saw the possibilities—some of them—and began to appreciate the interest his Indic report had aroused in those people possessing the vehicle. A man could peer forward—no, leap forward into the future and check out his theories, his projections of events to come. A man could see for himself the validity of a forewarning, the eventual result of a prefiguration, the final course of a trend. Would sixteen-year-olds marry and vote? Would city and county governments be abolished, relinquishing authority to local state districts? Would the Eastern seaboard complex break down and fail to support life?

TDV. A vehicle to determine answers.

Chaney said aloud: "I'm not interested. Find another demographer, Miss van Hise. I object to being ambushed and sold across the river."

A man could inspect—personally inspect—the Great Lakes to determine if they had been saved or if the Lake Reconstruction program had come too late. A man could study the census figures for a hundred years to come and then compare them to the present tables and projections to find the honesty of those projections. A man could discover if the recently inaugurated trial marriage program was a success or failure—and learn first-hand what effect it was having on the birth rate, if any. It would be good to know the validity of earlier predictions concerning the population shifts and the expected concentration of human mass along the central waterways. A man could—

Chaney said aloud: "Give the team my regards, Miss van Hise. And tell them to watch out for traffic cops. I'll read about their adventures in the newspapers."

Kathryn van Hise had left him.

He saw her tracks in the sand, glanced up and saw her putting on the shoes near the weedy border of the beach. The delta pants stretched with her as she bent over. The mail Jeep was again visible in the distance, now coming toward him and servicing the boxes on the other side of the beach road. The interview had been completed in less than an hour.

Chaney felt the weight of the book in his lap. He hadn't been aware of the woman placing it there.

The legend on the red dustjacket was as familiar as the back of his hand. *From the Qumran Caves: Past, Present, and Future.* The line of type next below omitted the word *by* and read only: *Dr. Brian Chaney.* The bright jacket was an abomination created by the sales department over the inert body of a conservative editor; it was designed to appeal to the lunatic fringe. He detested it. Despite his careful explanations, despite his scholarly translation of a suspect scroll, the book had stirred up twice the storm he'd expected and aroused the ire of righteous citizens everywhere. String up the blasphemer!

A small card protruded from the middle pages.

Chaney opened the volume with curiosity and found a calling card with her name imprinted on one side, and the address of a government laboratory in Illinois written on the other. He supposed that the ten fifty-dollar bills tucked between the pages represented travel money. Or a shameless bribe added to the blouse, the pants, and the perfume worn on her breast.

"I'm not going!" he shouted after the woman. "The computer lied— I'm a charlatan. The Bureau can go play with its weights!"

She didn't turn around, didn't look back.

"That woman is too damned sure of herself."

# 2

ELWOOD NATIONAL RESEARCH STATION
JOLIET, ILLINOIS
12 JUNE 1978

A HAIR PERHAPS DIVIDES THE FALSE AND TRUE;
YES, AND A SINGLE ALIF WERE THE CLUE
(COULD YOU BUT FIND IT) TO THE TREASURE-HOUSE,
AND PERADVENTURE TO THE MASTER TOO.
—OMAR KHAYYAM

Two steps ahead, the military policeman who had escorted him from the front gate opened a door and said: "This is your briefing room, sir."

Brian Chaney thanked him and went through the door.

He found the young woman critically eyeing him, assessing him, expecting him. Two men in the room were playing cards. An oversized steel table—the standard government issue—was positioned in the center of the room under bright lights. Three bulky brown envelopes were stacked on the table near the woman, while the men and their time-killing game occupied the far end of it. Kathryn van Hise had been watching the door as it opened, anticipating him, but only now did the players glance up from their game to look at the newcomer.

He nodded to the men and said: "My name is Chaney. I've been—"

The hurtful sound stopped him, cut off his words.

The sound was something like a massive rubber band snapped against his eardrums, something like a hammer or a mallet smashing into a block of compressed air. It made a noise of impact, followed by a reluctant sigh as if the hammer was rebounding in slow motion through an oily fluid. The sound hurt. The lights dimmed.

The three people in the briefing room were staring at something behind him, above him.

Chaney spun around but found nothing more than a wall clock above the door. They were watching the red sweep hand. He turned back to the trio with a question on his lips, but the woman made a little motion to silence him. She and her male companions continued to watch the clock with a fixed intensity.

The newcomer waited them out.

He saw nothing in the room to cause the sound, nothing to explain their concentrated interest; there was only the usual furniture of a government-appointed briefing room and the four people who now occupied it. The walls were bare of maps, and that was a bit unusual; there were three telephones of different colors on a stand near the door, and that was a bit unusual; but otherwise it was no more than a windowless, guarded briefing room located on an equally well-guarded military reservation forty-five minutes by armored train from Chicago.

He had entered through the customary guarded gate of a restricted installation encompassing about five square miles, had been examined and identified with the customary thoroughness of military personnel, and had been escorted to the room with no explanation and little delay. Massive outer doors on a structure that appeared earthquake-proof stirred his wonder. There were several widely scattered buildings on the tract—but none as substantial as *this* one—which led him to believe it had once been a munitions factory. Now, the presence of a number of people of both sexes moving about the grounds suggested a less hazardous installation. No outward hint or sign indicated the present activity, and Chaney wondered if knowledge of the vehicle was shared with station personnel.

He held his silence, again studying the woman. She was sitting down, and he mentally speculated on the length of the skirt she was wearing today, as compared to the delta pants of the beach.

The younger of the two men suddenly pointed to the clock. "Hold onto your hat, mister!"

Chaney glanced at the clock then back to the speaker. He judged the fellow at about thirty, only a few years younger than himself, but having the same lanky height. He was sandy haired, muscular, and something about the set of his eyes suggested a seafarer; the skin was deeply bronzed, as opposed to the girl's new tan, and now his open mouth revealed a silver filling in a front tooth. Like his companions, he was dressed in casual summer clothing, his sportshirt half unbuttoned down the front. His finger pointed at the clock dropped, as if in signal.

The reluctant sigh of the hammer or the mallet plowing sluggishly through a fluid filled the room, and Chaney wanted to cover his ears. Again the unseen hammer smashed into compressed air, the rubber band struck his eardrums, and there was a final, anticlimactic pop.

"There you are," the younger man said. "The same old sixty-one." He glanced at Chaney and added what appeared to be an explanation. "Sixty-one seconds, mister."

"Is that good?"

"That's the best we'll ever have."

"Bully. What's going on?"

"Testing. Testing, testing, testing, over and over again. Even the monkeys are getting tired of it." He shot a quick glance at Kathryn van Hise, as if to ask: *Does he know?*

The other card player studied Chaney with some reserve, wanting to fit him into some convenient slot. He was an older man. "Your name is Chaney," he repeated dourly. "And you've been—what?"

"Drafted," Chaney replied, and saw the man wince.

The young woman said quickly: "Mr. Chaney?"

He turned and found her standing. "Miss van Hise."

"We expected you earlier, Mr. Chaney."

"You expected too much. I had to wait for a few days for sleeper reservations, and I laid over in Chicago to visit old friends. I wasn't eager to leave the beach, Miss van Hise."

"Sleeper?" the older man demanded. "The *railroad*? Why didn't you fly in?"

Chaney felt embarrassed. "I'm afraid of planes."

The sandy-haired man exploded in howling laughter and pointed an explanatory finger at his dour companion. "Air Force," he said to Chaney. "Born in the air and flies by the seat of his pants." He slapped the table and the cards jumped, but no one shared his high humor. "You're off to a fine start, mister!"

"Must I hold a candle to my shame?" Chaney asked.

The woman said again: "Mr. Chaney, please."

He gave her his attention, and she introduced him to the card players.

Major William Theodore Moresby was the disapproving Air Force career man, now in his middle forties, whose receding hairline accented his rather large and penetrating gray-green eyes. The ridge of his nose was sharp, bony, and had once been broken. There was the suspicion of a double chin, and another suspicion of a building paunch beneath the summer shirt he wore outside his trousers. Major Moresby had no humor, and he shook hands with the tardy newcomer with the air of a man shaking hands with a draft dodger newly returned from Canada.

The younger man with the bronzed muscular frame and the prominent dental work was Lieutenant Commander Arthur Saltus. He congratulated Chaney on having the good sense of being reluctant to leave the sea, and said he'd been Navy since he was fifteen years old. Lied about his age, and furnished forged papers to underscore the lie. Even in the windowless room his eyes were set against the bright sunlight on the water. He was likable.

"A civilian?" Major Moresby asked gravely.

"Someone has to stay home and pay the taxes," Chaney responded in the same tone.

The young woman broke in quickly, diplomatically. "Official policy, Major. Our directive was to establish a balanced team." She glanced apologetically at Chaney. "Some people in the Senate were unhappy with the early NASA policy of selecting only military personnel for the orbital missions, and so we were directed to recruit a more balanced crew to—to avert a possible future inquiry. The Bureau is mindful of Congressional judgments."

Saltus: "Translation: we've got to keep those funds rolling in."

Moresby: "Damn it! Is politics into this thing?"

"Yes, sir, I'm afraid so. The Senate subcommittee overseeing our project has posted an agent here to maintain liaison. It is to be regretted, sir, but some few of them profess to see a parallel to the old Manhattan project, and so they insisted on continuous liaison."

"You mean surveillance," Moresby groused.

"Oh, cheer up, William." Arthur Saltus had picked up the scattered cards and was noisily shuffling the deck. "This one civilian won't hurt us; we outnumber him two to one, and look at the rank he *hasn't* got. Tail-end of the team, last man in the bucket, and we'll make him do the writing." He turned back to the civilian. "What do you do, Chaney? Astronomer? Cartographer? Something?"

"Something," Chaney answered easily. "Researcher, translator, statistician, a little of this and that."

Kathryn van Hise said: "Mr. Chaney authored the Indic report."

"Ah," Saltus nodded. "*That* Chaney."

"Mr. Chaney authored a book on the Qumran scrolls."

Major Moresby reacted. "*That* Chaney?"

Brian Chaney said: "Mr. Chaney will walk out of here in high pique and blow up the building. He objects to being the bug under the microscope."

Arthur Saltus stared at him with round eyes. "I've heard about you, mister! William has your book. They want to hang you up by your thumbs."

Chaney said amiably: "That happens every now and then. St. Jerome upset the Church with *his* radical translation in the fifth century, and they were intent on stretching more than his thumbs before somebody quieted them down. He produced a new Latin translation of the Old Testament, but his critics didn't exactly cheer him. No matter—his work outlived them. Their names are forgotten."

"Good for him. Was it successful?"

"It was. You may know the Vulgate."

Saltus seemed vaguely familiar with the name, but the Major was reddened and fuming.

"Chaney! You aren't comparing this poppycock of yours to the Vulgate?"

"No, sir," Chaney said softly to placate the man. He now knew the Major's religion, and knew the man had read his book with loose attention. "I'm pointing out that after fifteen centuries the radical is accepted as the norm. My translation of the Revelations only seems radical now. I may have the same luck, but I don't expect to be canonized."

Kathryn van Hise said insistently: "*Gentlemen.*"

Three heads turned to look at her.

"Please sit down, gentlemen. We really should get started on this work."

"Now?" Saltus asked. "Today?"

"We have already lost too much time. Sit down."

When they were seated, the irrepressible Arthur Saltus turned in his chair. "She's a hard taskmaster, mister. A martinet, a despot—but she's trim for all of that. A really shipshape civilian, not an ordinary government girl. We call her Katrina—she's Dutch, you know."

"Agreed," Chaney said. He remembered the transparent blouse and the delta pants, and nodded to her in a manner that might be the beginning of a bow. "I treasure a daily beauty in my life." The young woman colored.

"To the point!" Saltus declared. "I'm beginning to have ideas about you, civilian researcher. I thought I recognized that first one you pulled, that candle thing."

"Bartlett is a good man to know."

"Look, now, about your book, about those scrolls you translated. How did you ever get them declassified?"

"They were never classified."

Saltus showed his disbelief. "Oh, they had to be! The government over there wouldn't want them out."

"Not so. There was no secrecy involved; the documents were there to read. The Israeli government kept ownership of them, of course, and now the scrolls have been sent to another place for safekeeping for the duration of the war, but that's the extent of it." He glanced covertly at the Major. The man was listening in sullen silence. "It would be a tragedy if they were destroyed by the shelling."

"I'll bet you know where they are."

"Yes, but that's the only secret concerning them. When the war is over they'll be brought out and put on display again."

"Hey—do you think the Arabs will crack Israel?"

"No, not now. Ten, twenty years ago, they may have, but not now. I've seen their munitions plants."

Saltus leaned forward. "*Have* they got the H-bomb?

"Yes."

Saltus whistled. Moresby muttered: "Armageddon."

"Gentlemen! May I have your attention *now?*"

Kathryn van Hise was sitting straight in her chair, her hands resting on the brown envelopes. Her fingers were interlaced and the thumbs rose to make a pointed steeple.

Saltus laughed. "You always have it, Katrina."

Her responding frown was a quick and fleeting thing. "I am your briefing officer. My task is to prepare you for a mission which has no precedent in history, but one that is very near culmination. It is desirable that the project now go forward with all reasonable speed. I must insist that we begin preparations at once."

Chaney asked: "Are *we* working for NASA?"

"No, sir. You are directly employed by the Bureau of Standards and will not be identified with any other agency or department. The nature of the work will not be made public, of course. The White House insists on that."

He knew a measure of relief when she answered the next question, but it was of short duration. "You're not going to put us into orbit? We won't have to do this work on the moon, or somewhere?"

"No, sir."

"That's a relief. I won't have to fly?"

She said carefully: "I cannot reassure you on that point, sir. If we fail to attain our primary objective, the secondary targets may involve flying."

"That's bad. There *are* alternatives?"

"Yes, sir. Two alternatives have been planned, if for any reason we cannot accomplish the first objective."

Major Moresby chuckled at his discomfiture.

Chaney asked: "Do we just sit here and wait for something to happen—wait for that vehicle to work?"

"No, sir. I will help you to prepare yourself, on the assurance that something *will* happen. The testing is nearly completed and we expect the conclusion at any time. When it *is* completed, all of you will then acquaint yourselves with vehicle operation; and when *that* is done a field trial will be arranged. Following a successful field trial, the actual survey will get underway. We are most optimistic that each phase of the operation will be concluded in good order and in the shortest possible time." She paused to lend emphasis to her next statement. "The first objective will be a broad political and demographic survey of the near future; we wish to learn the political stability of that future and the well-being of the general populace. We may be able to contribute to both by having advance knowledge of their problems. Toward that end you will study and map the central United States at the turn of the century, at about the year 2000."

Saltus: "Hot damn!"

Chaney felt a recurrence of the initial shock he'd known on the beach; this wasn't to be an academic study.

"We're going up there? That far?"

"I thought I had made that clear, Mr. Chaney."

"Not *that* clear," he said with some embarrassment and confusion. "The wind was blowing on the beach—my mind was on other things." Hasty side glances at Saltus and the Major offered little comfort: one was grinning at him and the other was contemptuous. "I had supposed my role was to be a passive one: laying out the guidelines, preparing the surveys and the like. I had supposed you were using instruments for the actual probe—" But he realized how lame that sounded.

"No, sir. Each of you will go forward to conduct the survey. You *will* employ certain instruments in the field, but the human element is necessary."

Moresby may have thought to needle him. "Seniority will apply, after all. We will move up in the proper order. Myself first, then Art, and then you."

"We expect to launch the survey within three weeks, given the completion of the testing schedule." Her voice may have held a trace of amusement at his expense. "It may be sooner if your training program can be completed sooner. A physical examination is scheduled for later this afternoon, Mr. Chaney; the others have already had theirs. The examinations will continue at the rate of two per week until the survey vehicle is actually launched."

"Why?"

"For your protection and ours, sir. If a serious defect exists we must know it now."

He said weakly: "I have the heart of a chicken."

"But I understood you were under fire in Israel?"

"That's different. I couldn't stop the shelling and the work had to be done."

"You could have quit the country."

"No, I couldn't do that—not until the work was done, not until the translation was finished and the book ready."

Kathryn van Hise tapped her fingers together and only looked at him. She thought that was answer enough.

Chaney recalled something she had said on the beach, something she had quoted or inferred from his dossier. Or perhaps it was that damned computer profile rattling off his supposed resolution and stability. He had a quick suspicion.

"Did you read my dossier? All of it?"

"Yes, sir."

"*Ouch.* Did it contain information—ah, gossip about an incident on the far side of the New Allenby Bridge?"

"I believe the Jordanian government contributed a certain amount of information on the incident, sir. It was obtained through the Swiss Legation in Amman, of course. I understand you suffered a rather severe beating."

Saltus eagerly: "Hey—what's this?"

Chaney said: "Don't believe everything you read. I was damned near shot for a spy in Jordan, but that Moslem woman wasn't wearing a veil. Mark that—no veil. It's supposed to make all the difference in the world."

Saltus: "But what has the woman to do with a spy?"

"They thought I was a Zionist spy," Chaney explained. "The woman without a veil was only a pleasant interlude—well, she was supposed to be a pleasant interlude. But it didn't turn out that way."

"And they nabbed you? Almost shot you?"

"And beat the hell out of me. Arabs don't play by the same rules we do. They use garrotes and daggers."

Saltus: "But what happened to the woman?"

"Nothing. No time. She got away."

"Too *bad*," Saltus exclaimed.

Kathryn van Hise asked: "May we continue, please?"

Chaney thought he detected a touch of color in her cheeks. "We're going up," he said with finality.

"Yes, sir."

He wished he were back on the beach. "Is it safe?"

Arthur Saltus broke in again before the woman could respond. "The monkeys haven't complained—you shouldn't."

"Monkeys?"

"The test monkeys, civilian. The critters have been riding that damned machine for weeks, up, back, sideways. But they haven't filed any complaints—not in writing."

"But supposing they did?"

Airily: "Oh, in that event, William and I would wave our seniority rights to you. *You* could go riding off somewhere to investigate their complaints, find out the trouble. The taxpayers deserve *some* breaks."

Kathryn van Hise said: "Once again, *please*."

"Sure, Katrina," Saltus said easily. "But I think you should tell this civilian what he's in for."

Moresby caught his meaning and laughed.

Chaney was wary. "What am I in for?"

"You're going up naked." Saltus lifted his shirt to slap a bare chest. "We're all going up naked."

Chaney stared at him, searching for the point of the joke, and belatedly realized it was no joke. He turned on the woman and found the flush had returned to her face.

She said: "It's a matter of weight, Mr. Chaney. The machine must propel itself and you into the future, which is an operation requiring a tremendous amount of electrical energy. The engineers have advised us that total weight is a critical matter, that nothing but the passenger must be put forward or returned. They insist upon minimum weight."

"Naked? All the way naked?"

Saltus: "Naked as a jaybird, civilian. We'll save ten, fifteen, twenty pounds of excess weight. They demand it. You wouldn't want to upset those engineers, would you? Not with your life riding in their hands? They're sensitive chaps, you know—we have to humor them."

Chaney struggled to retain his sense of humor. "What happens when we reach the future, when we reach 2000?"

Again the woman attempted a reply but again Saltus cut her off. "Oh, Katrina has thought of everything. Your old Indic report said future people will wear less clothing, so Katrina will supply us with the proper papers. We're going up there as licensed nudists."

**3**

Brian Chaney said: "I wish I knew what was going on here." His voice carried an undertone of complaint.

"I have been trying to tell you for the past hour, Mr. Chaney."

"Try once more," he begged.

Kathryn van Hise studied him. "I said on the beach that Westinghouse engineers have built a TDV. The vehicle was built here, in this building, under a research contract with the Bureau of Standards. The work has gone forward in utmost secrecy, of course, with a Congressional group—a Subcommittee—supplying direct funds and maintaining a close supervision over the project. We operate with the full knowledge of, and responsibility to the White House. The President will make the final choice of objectives."

"*Him?* A committee will have to make up his mind for him."

Her expression was one of pronounced disapproval and he guessed that he'd touched a sore spot—guessed that her loyalty to the man was motivated by political choice as much as by present occupation.

"The President is *always* kept informed of our daily progress, Mr.

Chaney. As was his predecessor." The woman seemed belligerent. "His predecessor created this project by an Executive order three years ago, and we continue to operate today only with the consent and approval of the new President. I am sure you are aware of the political facts of life."

Ruefully: "Oh, I'm aware. The Indic report failed to anticipate a weak President. It was written and submitted during the administration of a strong one, and was based on the assumption that man would continue in office for two full terms. Our mistake; we didn't anticipate his death. But this new man has to be nudged off the dime—every dime, every day. He lacks initiative, lacks drive." A side glance told Chaney that the Major had agreed with him on one point. Moresby was absently nodding concurrence.

Kathryn van Hise cleared her throat.

"To proceed. An experimental laboratory is located in another part of this building, beneath us, and the testing of the vehicle has been underway for some time. When the testing had reached a stage which indicated eventual success, the survey field team was recruited. Major Moresby, Commander Saltus, and you were each the first choices in your respective fields, and the only ones contacted. As yet there is no back-up team."

Chaney said: "That's uncharacteristic of them. The military always buys two of everything, just in case."

"This is *not* a military operation, and their superiors were *not* informed why Major Moresby and Commander Saltus were transferred to this station. But I would think a back-up team will be recruited in time, and perhaps the military establishment will be informed of our operations." She folded her hands, regaining composure. "The engineers will explain the vehicle and its operation to you; I am not well enough informed to offer a lucid explanation. I understand only that an intense vacuum is created when the vehicle is operated, and the sound you heard was the result of an implosion of air into that vacuum."

"They're making sixty-one second tests?"

"No, sir. The tests may be of any duration; the longest to date has probed twelve months into the past, and the shortest only one day. Those sixty-one seconds represent a necessary margin of safety for the passenger; the passenger may not return to his exact moment of departure, but will instead return sixty-one seconds after his departure regardless of the amount of elapsed time spent in the field." But she seemed troubled by something not put into words.

Brian Chaney was certain she held something back.

She said: "At the present time, the laboratory is employing monkeys and mice as test passengers. When that phase is completed, each of you will embark on a test to familiarize yourself with the vehicle. You will depart singly, of course, because of the smallness of the vehicle. The engineers will explain the problems of mass and volume being propelled by means of a vacuum."

Chaney said: "I see the point. I wouldn't like it very well if I came back from a survey and landed on top of myself. But why sixty-one?"

"That figure is something of a laboratory fluke. The engineers were intent on a minimum of sixty seconds, but when the vehicle returned at sixty-one on two successive tests they locked it down there, so to speak."

"All the tests were successful?"

She hesitated, then said: "Yes, sir."

"You haven't lost a monkey? Not one?"

"No, sir."

But his suspicions were not quieted. "What would happen if the tests weren't successful? What if one should still fail, after all this?"

"In that event, the project would be canceled and each of you will be returned to your stations. *You* would be free to return to Indiana, if you chose."

"I'll be fired!" Arthur Saltus declared. "Back to that bucket in the South China Sea: diesel oil and brine."

"Back to the Florida beach," Chaney told him. "And beauteous maidens in delicious undress."

"You're a cad, civilian. You ripped off that veil."

"But the maidens make that unnecessary."

"Gentlemen, *please*."

Saltus wouldn't be stopped. "And think of our poor Katrina—back to a bureaucrat's desk. Congress will cut off our slush funds: *chop*. You know how they are."

"Tightfisted, except for their pet rivers and harbors. So I suppose we must carry on for her sake, naked and shivering, up to the brink of 2000." Chaney was bemused. "What will the coming generation think of us?"

"*Please!*"

Chaney folded his arms and looked at her. "I still think someone has made a mistake, Miss van Hise. I have no military skills and I'm seldom able to distinguish a nut from a bolt; I can't imagine why you would want me for a field survey—despite what you say—but you'll find me a fairly complacent draftee if you promise no more jolts. Are you holding back anything else?"

Her brown eyes locked with his, showing a first hint of anger. Chaney grinned, hoping to erase that. Her glance abruptly dropped away, and she slid the bulky envelopes across the table to the three men.

"Now?" Saltus asked.

"You may open them now. This is our primary target area, together with all necessary data to enter the field."

Brian Chaney undid the clasp and pulled out a thick sheaf of mimeographed papers and several folded maps. His glance went back to the face of the envelope. A code name was typed there, under the ubiquitous *Top Secret* rubber stamp. He read it a second time and looked up.

"Project Donaghadee?"

"Yes, sir. Mr. Donaghadee is the Director of the Bureau of Standards."

"Of course. The monument is the man."

Chaney opened the map on the top of the pile and turned it about so that north was at the top, to read the name of the first city to catch his eye: Joliet. It was a map of the north central section of the United States with Chicago placed precisely in the center, and showing great chunks of those states surrounding the metropolitan area: Illinois, Indiana, Michigan, Wisconsin, and the eastern tip of Iowa. Elwood Station was indicated by a red box just south of Joliet. He noted that the map had been prepared by Army cartographers and was stamped Top Secret. Except for the red box it was identical to gasoline station maps.

The second map was a large one of Illinois alone and now the extra size revealed Elwood Station to be about eight miles south of Joliet, adjacent to an old route marked Alternate 66. The third map was equally large: a detailed plan of Will County with Joliet located nearly in the center of it. On this map, Elwood Station was a great red box of about five square miles, with several individual houses and buildings identified by a numbered key. The station had two private service roads opening onto the highway. The main line of the Chicago & Mobile Southern Railroad passed within hailing distance of the military reservation, and a spur of that railroad branched off to enter the enclosure.

The Major looked up from his scrutiny of the maps. "Katrina. The field trials will be here on station?"

"Only in part, sir. If you find the station normal when you surface, you will proceed to Joliet in transportation which will be provided. Always keep your safety in mind."

Moresby seemed disappointed. "Joliet."

"That city will be the limit of the trials, sir. The risk must not be underestimated. However, the actual survey will be conducted in Chicago and its suburbs if the field trials prove satisfactory. Please study the maps carefully and memorize at least two escape routes; you may be forced to walk in the event of a motor breakdown."

Saltus: "Walk? With cars everywhere?"

The woman frowned. "Do *not* attempt to steal an automobile. It may be difficult, perhaps impossible, to free you from jail. It simply wouldn't do, Commander."

"Naked and forlorn in a Joliet jail," Chaney mumbled. "I believe there is a state penitentiary there."

She eyed him narrowly. "I think that little joke has gone far enough, Mr. Chaney. You will be clothed in the field, of course; you will dress for the field trial and later for the full survey, but each time you must disrobe before returning in the vehicle. You will find an adequate supply of clothing, tools, and instruments awaiting you at each point of arrival. And the laboratory will be continuously manned, of course; engineers will always be expecting your arrival and will assist in the transits."

"I thought he was pulling my leg," Chaney admitted. "But how will you manage the clothing and the engineers—how will you have it and them up there waiting for us?"

"That has already been arranged, sir. A fallout shelter and storage depot is located below us, adjacent to the laboratory. It is stocked with everything you may possibly need for any season of the year, together with weapons and provisions. Our program requires that the laboratory and the vehicle be continuously manned for an indefinite period; a hundred or more years, if necessary. All times of arrival in the future will be known to those future engineers, of course. It has been arranged."

"Unless they've walked out on strike."

"Sir?"

"Your long-range planning is subject to the same uncertainties as my projections—one fluke, one chance event may knock everything askew. The Indic report failed to allow for a weak Administration replacing a strong one, and if that report was placed before me today I wouldn't sign it; the variable casts doubt on the validity of the whole. We can only hope the engineers will still be on the job tomorrow, and will still be using standard time."

"Mr. Chaney, the Bureau's long-range planning is more thorough than that. It is solidly grounded and has been designed for permanency. I would remind you that the primary target area is only twenty-two years distant."

"I have this feeling that I'll come out—come to the surface—a thousand years older."

"I am sure you will make do, sir. Our team is notable for individual self-reliance."

"Which properly puts me in my place, Miss van Hise."

Moresby interrupted. "What about those stores?"

"Yes, sir. The shelter is stocked with necessities: motion picture cameras, tape recorders, radios, weapons and weapons detectors, hand radar, and so forth. There is money and gems and medical supplies. Materials such as film, tape, ammunition and clothing will be restocked at intervals to insure fresh or modern supplies."

Major Moresby said: "I'll be damned!" and fell silent for a moment of admiration. "It makes good sense, after all. We'll draw what we need from the stores to cover the target, and replace the remainder before coming back."

"Yes, sir. No part of the supplies may be carried back with you, except tapes and film exposed in the field. The engineers will instruct you on how to compensate for that small extra weight. Do not bring back the recorders and cameras, and you are expressly forbidden to bring back any personal souvenir such as coins or currency. But you may photograph the money if you wish."

"Those engineers have an answer for everything," Chaney observed. "They must work around the clock."

"Our project has been working around the clock for the past three years, sir."

"Who pays the electric bill?"

"A nuclear power station is located on the post."

He was quickly interested. "Their own reactor? How much power does it generate?"

"I don't know, sir."

"I know," Saltus said. "Commonwealth-Edison has a new one up near Chicago putting out eight hundred thousand kilowatts. Big thing—I've seen it, and I've seen ours. They look like steel light bulbs turned upside down."

Chaney was still curious. "Does the TDV *need* that much power?"

"I couldn't say, sir." She changed the subject by calling attention to the sheaf of mimeographed papers taken from the envelopes. "We have time this afternoon to begin on these reports."

The first sheet bore the stylized imprint of the Indiana Corporation, and Chaney quickly recognized his own work. He gave the woman an amused glance but she avoided his eyes; another glance down the table revealed his companions staring at the massive report with anticipated boredom.

The next page plunged immediately into the subject matter by offering long columns of statistics underscored by footnotes: the first few columns were solidly rooted in the census figures of 1970, while the following columns on the following pages were his projections going forward to 2050. Chaney recalled the fun and the sweat that had gone into the work—and the very shaky limb on which he perched as he worked toward the farthest date.

*Births*: legitimate and otherwise, predicted annually by race and by geographical area (down sharply along the Atlantic seaboard below Boston, and the southern states except Florida; figures did not include unpredictable number of laboratory-hospital births by artificial means; figures did not include unpredictable number of abnormal births in Nevada and Utah due to accumulation of radioactive fallout).

*Deaths*: with separate figures for murders and known suicides, projected annually by age groups (suicides increasing at predictable rate below age thirty; females outliving males by twelve point three years by year 2000; anticipated life-expectancy increased one point nine years by year 2050; figures did not include infant mortalities in Nevada-Utah fallout area; figures did not include infant mortalities in laboratory-hospital artificial births).

*Marriages and trial marriages*: with subsequent divorces and annulments forecast on an annual basis after 1980, first full year of trial marriage decree (trial marriages not appreciably contributing to the birth rate except in Alabama and Mississippi, but tending to increase the murder and suicide rate, and contributing to the slow decline of long-term marriages). *Footnote*: renewable term trial marriage recommended; i.e., a second year of trial be granted upon application by both parties.

*Incidence of crime*: detailed projections in twenty categories, separated by states having and not having the death penalty (murder and robbery up sharply, but rape down by a significant percentage due to trial marriages and lowered legal age of all marriages).

*Probable voter registrations and profiles*: gradual emergence of enduring three-party system after 1980 (with registrations divided unevenly among three major and one minor party; black voters concentrated in one major and the minor party; pronounced swing to the conservative right in two white major parties during the next decade, with conservative Administrations probable until year 2000, plus or minus four years).

*Total population by the turn of the century*: based upon the foregoing, three hundred and forty million people in the forty-eight contiguous states and an additional ten million in the three remaining states (the northern tier of plains states projected as consistent annual losers but with Alaska up significantly; Manhattan Island reaching point of saturation within two years, California by 1990, Florida by 2010). *Footnote*: recommended that immigration to Manhattan Island, California, and Florida be forbidden by law, and that monetary inducements be offered to relocate in middle states having low densities of population.

Brian Chaney felt a certain unease about some of his conclusions.

Trial marriages could be expected to increase at a phenomenal rate once their popularity caught on, but with the trial term limited to one year he fully expected both the murder and suicide rates to climb; the murders were apt to be crimes of passion committed by the female because of the probability of losing her short-term husband to another short-term wife, while the suicides were predicted for the same reason. The recommended two-year renewable term would tend to dampen the possibility of either violent act.

A certain amount of joy-riding was to be expected in trial marriages, but he was gambling they would contribute almost nothing to the birth rate. Nor did he believe that another pill—the new pill—would affect his projections. Chaney held a low opinion of the recently introduced KH3-B pill, and refused to believe it had any restorative powers; he clung to the belief that man was allotted a normal three score and fifteen, and the projected increase of one point nine years by 2050 would be attributed to the eradication of diseases—not to pills and nostrums purportedly having the power to restore mental and physical vigor to the aged. The patients *might* live six months longer than their normal spans because they were buoyed by euphoria, but six months would not affect a mass of statistics.

Great population shifts had been earlier predicted and borne out, with the emphasis of change along the natural waterways. The greater densities of population—by 2050—would lie along five clearly defined areas: the Atlantic seaboard, the Pacific seaboard, the Gulf Coast from Tampa to Brownsville, the southern shores of all the Great Lakes, and the full lengths of the Ohio and Mississippi rivers. But he knew serious misgivings about those Lakes belts. The water levels in the Lakes had been rising steadily since the beginning of the twentieth century, and the coming flooding and erosion—combined with heavier populations—would create problems of catastrophic proportions in those areas.

Major Moresby broke the silence. "We will be expected to confirm all this, after all."

"Yes, sir. Careful observations are desired for each of the three target dates, but the greater amount of work will fall upon Mr. Chaney. His projections will need to be verified or modified."

Chaney, with surprise: "Three? Aren't we going up together? Going to the same target?"

"No, sir, that would be wasteful. The schedule calls for three individual surveys on carefully separated dates, each at least a year apart to obtain a better overall view. You will each travel separately to your predetermined date."

"The people up there will sneer at our clothes."

"The people up there should be too preoccupied to notice you, unless you call attention to yourself."

"Oh? What will preoccupy them?"

"They will be preoccupied with themselves and their problems. You haven't spent much time in American cities of late, have you, Mr. Chaney? Didn't you notice that the trains you rode into and out of Chicago were armored trains?"

"Yes, I noticed that. The Israeli newspapers did publish *some* American news. I read about the curfews. The people of the future won't notice our cameras and recorders?"

"We sincerely hope not. All would be undone if the present demand for privacy is projected into the turn of the century, if that present demand is intensified."

Chaney said: "I'm on their side; I enjoy privacy."

The woman continued. "And of course, we don't know what status your instruments may have at that future date, we don't know if cameras and recorders will be permissible in public, nor can we guess at the efficiency of the police. You may be handicapped." She glanced at Saltus. "The Commander will teach you to work surreptitiously."

Saltus: "I will?"

"Yes, sir. You must devise a technique for completing that part of the assignment without discovery. The cameras are very small, but you must find a way to conceal them and still operate them properly."

"Katrina, do you really think it'll be illegal to take a picture of a pretty girl on a street corner?"

"We do not know the future, Commander; the survey will inform us what is and is not legal. But whatever the technique, you must photograph a number of objects and persons for a period of time without others being aware of what you are doing."

"For how long a period of time?"

"For as long as possible; for as long as you are in the field and your supply of film lasts. The emphasis is on depth, Commander. A survey in depth, to determine the accuracy of the Indic projections. Ideally, you would be in the field several days and expose every roll of film and every reel of tape you are carrying; you would record every object of major interest you might see, and as many lesser objects as time allowed. You would penetrate the field safely, accomplish all objectives, and withdraw without haste at a time of your choosing." A shadow of a smile. "But more realistically, the ideal is seldom attained. Therefore you will go in, record all you are able, and retreat when it becomes necessary. We will hope for the maximum and have to be content with the minimum."

Chaney turned in the chair. "You make this sound like a dangerous thing."

"It could be dangerous, Mr. Chaney. What you will be doing has never before been done. We can offer you no firm guidelines for procedure, field technique, or your own safety. We will equip you as best we can, brief you to the fullest extent of our present knowledge, and send you in on your own."

"We're to report *everything* we find up there?"

"Yes, sir."

"I only hope Seabrooke has anticipated public reaction. He's headed for a rift within the lute."

"Sir?"

"I suspect he's headed for trouble. A large part of the public will raise unholy hell when they find out about the TDV—when they find out what lies twenty years ahead of them. There's something in that Indic report to scare everybody."

Kathryn van Hise shook her head. "The public will not be informed, Mr. Chaney. This project and our future programs are and will remain secret; the tapes and films will be restricted and the missions will not be publicized. Please remember that all of you have security clearances and are under oath and penalty. Keep silent. President Meeks has ruled that knowledge of this operation is not in the public interest."

Chaney said: "Secret, and self-contained, and solitary as an oyster."

Saltus opened his mouth to laugh when the engineers pushed their rig into a vacuum. The lights dimmed.

The massive rubber band snapped painfully against their eardrums; or it may have been a mallet, or a hammer, driven under cruel pressure into a block of compressed air. The thing made a noise of impact, then sighed as if it rebounded in slow motion through thick liquid. The sound hurt. Three faces turned together to watch the clock.

Chaney contented himself with watching their faces rather than the clock. He guessed another monkey was riding the vehicle into somewhere, somewhen. Perhaps the animal bore a label: *Restricted* and was under orders not to talk. The President had ruled his trip was not in the public interest.

Brian Chaney awoke with the guilty feeling that he was tardy again. The Major would never forgive him.

He sat on the side of the bed and listened carefully for tell-tale sounds within the building, but none were audible. The station seemed unusually quiet. His room was a small one, a single unit sparsely furnished, in a double row of identical rooms fitted into a former army barracks. The partitions were thin and appeared to have been cheaply and hastily erected; the ceiling was less than three feet above his head—and he was a tall man. Larger common rooms at either end of the only corridor contained the showers and toilets. The place bore an unmistakable military stamp, as though troops had moved out the day before he moved in.

Perhaps they had done just that; perhaps troops were now riding those armored trains serving Chicago and Saint Louis. Without armored siding, a passenger train seldom could traverse Chicago's south side without every window in every car being broken by stones or gunfire.

Chaney opened his door and peered into the corridor. It was empty, but recognizable sounds from the two rooms opposite his brought a measure of relief. In one of the rooms someone was opening and closing bureau drawers in frustrated search of something; in the other room the occupant was snoring. Chaney picked up a towel and his shaving kit and went to the showers. The snoring was audible all the way down the corridor.

The cold water was *cold* but the hot water was only a few degrees warmer—barely enough to feel a difference. Chaney came out of the shower, wrapped a towel about his middle and began rubbing lather on his face.

"Stop!" Arthur Saltus was in the doorway, pointing an accusatory finger. "Put down the razor, civilian."

Startled, Chaney dropped the razor into the bowl of tepid water. "Good morning, Commander." He recovered his wits and the razor to begin the shave. "Why?"

"Secret orders came in the middle of the night," Saltus declared. "All the people of the future wear long beards, like old Abe Lincoln. We must be in character."

"Nudists with bushy beards," Chaney commented. "That must be quite a sight." He kept on shaving.

"Well, you bit hard yesterday, civilian." Saltus put an exploratory hand under the shower and turned on the water. He had anticipated the result. "This hasn't changed since boot camp," he told Chaney. "Every barracks is allotted ten gallons of hot water. The first man in uses it all."

"I *thought* this was a barracks."

"This building? It must have been at one time or another, but the station wasn't always a military post. I spotted that coming in. Katrina said it was built as an ordnance plant in 1941—you know, during *that* war." He stepped under the shower. "That was—what? Thirty-seven years ago? Time flies and the mice have been at work."

"That other building is new."

"The lab building is brand new. Katrina said it was built to house that noisy machine—built to last forever. Reinforced concrete all the way down; a basement, and a sub-basement, and other things. The vehicle is down there somewhere hauling monkeys back and forth."

"I'd like to *see* that damned thing."

"You and me together, civilian. You and me and the Major." His head popped out of the shower and his voice dropped to a stage whisper. "But I've got it figured."

"You have? What?"

"Promise you won't tell Katrina? You won't tell the man in the White House I broke security?"

"Cross my heart, spit at the moon and everything."

"All right: all this is a plot, a trick to be ahead of everybody else. Katrina has been misleading us. We're not going up to the turn of the century—we're going back down, back into history!"

"Back? Why?"

"We're going back two thousand years, civilian. To grab those old scrolls of yours, pirate them, as if they *were* classified or something. We're going to sneak in there some dark night, find a batch of them in some cave or other and copy them. Photograph them. *That's* why we're using cameras. And meanwhile, you'll be using a recorder, making tapes of the location and the like. Maybe you could unroll a parchment or two and read off the titles, so we'll know if we have anything important."

"But they seldom have titles."

Saltus was stopped. "Why not?"

"Titles just weren't important at the time."

"Well—no matter; we'll make do, we'll just copy everything we can find and sort them out later. And when we're finished we'll put everything back the way we found it and make our escape." Saltus snapped his fingers to indicate a job well done and went back into the shower.

"Is that all?"

"That's enough for us—we've scooped the world! And a long time afterward—you know, whatever year it was—some shepherd will stumble into the cave and find them in the usual way. Nobody but us will be the wiser."

Chaney wiped his face dry. "How do we get into the Palestine of two thousand years ago? Cross the Atlantic in a canoe?"

"No, no, we don't ride backwards *first*, civilian—not here, not in Illinois. If we did that we'd have to fight our way though Indians! Look, now: the Bureau of Standards will ship the vehicle over there in a couple of weeks, after we've had our field trials. They'll pack it in a box marked *Agricultural Machinery*, or some such thing, and smuggle it in like everybody else does. How do you think the Egyptians got that baby bomb into Israel? By sending it parcel post?"

Chaney said: "Fantastic."

A face emerged from the shower. "Are you being disagreeable, civilian?"

"I'm being skeptical, sailor."

"Spoil-sport!"

"Why would we want to copy the scrolls?"

"To be first."

"Why that?"

Saltus stepped all the way out of the shower.

"Well—to be *first*, that's all. We like to be first in everything. Where's your patriotism, civilian?"

"I carry it in my pocket. How do we copy the scrolls in the dark, in a cave?"

"Now that's my department! Infra-red equipment, of course. Don't fret about the technical end, mister. I'm an old cameraman, you know."

"I didn't know."

"Well, I *was* a cameraman, a working cameraman, when I was an EM. Do you remember the Gemini flights about thirteen or fourteen years ago?"

"I remember."

"I was right there on deck, mister. Photographer's apprentice, stationed on the *Wasp* when the flights began; I manned the deck cameras on some of those early flights in 1964, but when the last one splashed down in 1966, I was riding the choppers out to meet them." A disparaging wave of the hand. "Now, would you believe it, I'm riding a desk. Operations officer." His face mirrored his dissatisfaction. "I'd rather be behind the camera; the enlisted men have the fun with that job."

Chaney said: "I've learned something new."

"What's that?"

"Why you and I were brought in here. I map and structure the future; you will film it. What's the Major's specialty?"

"Air Intelligence. I thought you knew."

"I didn't. Espionage?"

"No, no—he's another desk man, and he hates it as much as I do. Old William is a brain: interrogation and interpretation. He briefs the pilots before they fly out, tells them where to find the targets, what is concealing them, and what is defending them; and then he quizzes the hell out of them when they come back to learn what they saw, where they saw it, how it behaved, how it smelled, and what was new firing at them."

"Air Intelligence," Chaney mused. "A sharpie?"

"You can bet your last tax dollar, civilian. Do you remember those maps Katrina gave us yesterday?"

"I'm not likely to forget them. Top secret."

"Read that literally for the Major: he memorized them. Mister, if you could show him another map today with one small Illinois town shifted a quarter of an inch away from yesterday's location, old William would put his long finger on the spot and say, 'This town has moved.' He's *good*." Saltus was grinning with high humor. "The enemy can't hide a water tank or a missile launcher or an ammo bunker from him—not from *him*."

Chaney nodded his wonder. "Do you see what kind of team Katrina is putting together? What kind the mystery man Seabrooke has recruited? I wish I knew what they really expect us to find up there."

Arthur Saltus left his room and crossed the corridor to stand at Chaney's door, dressed for a summer day.

"Hey—how do you like our Katrina?"

Chaney said: "Let us consider beauty a sufficient end."

"Mister, did you swallow a copy of Bartlett?"

A grin. "I like to prowl through old cultures, old times. Bartlett and Haakon are my favorites; each in his way offers a rich storehouse, a treasury."

"Haakon? Who is Haakon?"

"A latter-day Viking; he was born too late. Haakon wrote *Pax Abrahamitica*, a history of the desert tribes. I would say it was more of a treasury than a history: maps, photographs, and text telling one everything he would want to know about the tribes five to seven thousand years ago."

"Photographs five thousand years ago?"

"No; photographs of the remains of tribal life five thousand years ago: Byzantine dams, Nabataean wells, old Negev water courses still holding water, still serving the people who live there today. The Nabataeans built things to *last*. Their wells are water-tight today; they're still used by the Bedouin. Several good photographs of them."

"I'd like to see that. May I borrow the book?"

Chaney nodded. "I have it with me." He stared at a closed door and listened to the snores. "Wake him up?"

"No! Not if we have to live in the same room with him all day. He's a bear when he's routed out of his cave before he's ready—and he doesn't eat breakfast. He says he thinks and fights well on an empty stomach."

Chaney said: "The company is Spartan; see all their wounds on the front."

"I give up! Let's go to breakfast."

They quit the converted barracks and struck off along the narrow concrete sidewalk, walking north toward the commissary. A jeep and a staff car moved along the street, while in the middle distance a cluster of civilian cars were parked about a large building housing the commissary. They were the only ones who walked.

Chaney asked: "This is swimming weather. Is there a pool here?"

"There has to be—Katrina didn't get that beautiful tan under a sun lamp. I think it's over that way—over on E Street, near the Officers' Club. Want to try it this afternoon?"

"If she will permit it. We may have to study."

"I'm already tired of that! I don't *care* how many million voters with plastic stomachs affiliated with Party A will be living in Chicago twenty years from now. Mister, how can you spend years playing with numbers?"

"I'm fascinated by them—numbers and people. The relief of a plastic stomach may cause a citizen to switch from the activist A to the more conservative B; his vote may alter the outcome of an election, and a conservative administration—local, state, or national—may stall or do nothing about a problem that needed solving yesterday. The Great Lakes problem *is* a problem because of just that."

Saltus said: "Excuse me. What problem?"

"You've been away. The Lakes are at their highest levels in history; they're flooding out ten thousand miles of shoreline. The average annual precipitation in the Lakes watersheds has been steadily increasing for the past eighty years and the high water is causing damage. Those summer houses have been toppling into the Lakes for years as the water eroded the bluffs; in a very short while more than summer houses will topple in. Beaches are gone, private docks are going, low land is becoming marshes. Sad thing, Commander."

"Hey—when we go into Chicago on the survey, maybe we should look to see if Michigan Avenue is underwater."

"That's no joke. It may be."

"Oh, doom, doom, doom!" Saltus declared. "Your books and tables are always crying doom."

"I've published only one book. There was no doom."

"William said it was poppycock. I haven't read it, I'm not much of a reader, mister, but he looked down his nose. And Katrina said the newspapers gave you hell."

"You've been talking about me. Idle gossiping!"

"Hey—you were two or three days late coming in, remember? We had to talk about something, so we talked about you, mostly—curiosity about one tame civilian on a military team. Katrina knew all about you; I guess she read your dossier forward and backward. She said you were in trouble—trouble with your company, with reviewers and scholars and churches and—oh, everybody." Saltus gave his walking companion a slanted glance. "Old William said you were bent on destroying the foundations of Christianity. You must have done *something*, mister. Did you chip away at the foundation?"

Chaney answered with a single word.

Saltus was interested. "I don't know that."

"It's Aramaic. You know it in English."

"Say it again—slowly—and tell me what it is."

Chaney repeated it, and Saltus turned it on his tongue, delighted with the sound and the fresh delivery of an old transitive verb. "Hey—I like that!" He walked on, repeating the word just above his breath.

After a space: "What about those foundations?"

"I translated two scrolls into English and caused them to be published," Chaney said with resignation. "I could have saved my time, or spent my holiday digging up buried cities. One man in ten read the book slowly and carefully and understood what I had done— the other nine began yapping before they finished the first half."

His companion was ready with a quick grin. "William yapped, and Katrina seemed scandalized, but I guess Gilbert Seabrooke read it slowly: Katrina said the Bureau was embarrassed, but Seabrooke stood up for you. Now *me*, I haven't read it and I probably won't, so where does that put me?"

"An honest neutral, subject to intimidation."

"All right, mister: intimidate this honest neutral."

Chaney looked down at the commissary, guessing at the remaining distance. He intended to be short; the subject was painful since a university press had published the book and a misunderstanding public had taken it up.

"I don't want you yapping at me, Commander, so you need first to understand one word: *midrash*."

"*Midrash*. Is that another Aramaic word?"

"No—it's Hebraic, and it means fiction, religious fiction. Compare it to whatever modern parallel you like: historical fiction, soap opera, detective stories, fantasy; the ancient Hebrews liked their *midrash*. It was their favorite kind of fantasy; they liked to use biblical events and personages in their fiction—call it bible-opera if you like. Scholars have long been aware of that; they know *midrash* when they find it, but the general public hardly seems to know it exists. The public tends to believe that everything written two thousand years ago was sacred, the work of one saint or another."

"I guess nobody told them," Saltus said. "All right, I'll go along with that."

"Thank you. The public should be as generous."

"Didn't you tell them about *midrash*?"

"Certainly. I spent twelve pages of the introduction explaining the term and its general background; I pointed out that it was a commonplace thing, that the old Hebrews frequently employed religious or heroic fiction as a means of putting across the message. Times were hard, the land was almost always under the heel of an oppressor, and they desperately wanted freedom—they wanted the messiah that had been promised for the past several hundred years."

"Ah—there's your mistake, civilian! Who wants to waste twelve pages gnawing on the bone to get at the marrow?" He glanced around at Chaney and saw his pained expression. "Excuse me, mister. I'm not much of a reader—and I guess they weren't either."

Chaney said: "Both my scrolls were *midrash*, and both used variations of that same theme: some heroic figure was coming to rid the land of the oppressor, to free the people from their ills and starvations, to show them the door to a brand new life and happy times forever after. The first scroll was the longer of the two with greater detail and more explicit promises; it foretold wars and pestilence, of signs in the heavens, of invaders from foreign lands, of widespread death, and finally of the coming of the messiah who would bring eternal peace to the world. I thought it was a great work."

Saltus was puzzled. "Well—what's the trouble?"

"Haven't you read the Bible?"

"No."

"Nor the Book of Revelations?"

"I'm not much of a reader, civilian."

"The first scroll was an original copy of the Book of Revelations— original, in that it was written at least a hundred years earlier than the book included in the Bible. And it was presented as fiction. That's why Major Moresby is angry with me. Moresby—and people like him—don't *want* the book to be a hundred years older than believed; they don't *want* it to be revealed as fiction. They can't accept the idea that the story was first written by some Qumran priest or scribe, and circulated around the country to entertain or inspire the populace. Major Moresby doesn't *want* the book to be *midrash*."

Saltus whistled. "I should think not! He takes all that seriously, mister. He believes in prophecies."

"I don't," Chaney said. "I'm skeptical, but I'm quite willing to let others believe if they so choose. I said nothing in the book to undermine their beliefs; I offered no opinions of my own. But I *did* show that the first Revelations scroll was written at the Qumran school, and that it was buried in a cave a hundred years or more before the present book was written—or copied—and included in the Bible. I offered indisputable proof that the book in the Christian Bible was not only a later copy, but that it had been altered from the original.

The two versions didn't match; the seams showed. Whoever wrote the second version deleted several passages from the first and inserted new chapters more in keeping with *his* times. In short, he modernized it and made it more acceptable to his priest, his king, his people. His only failing was that he was a poor editor—or a poor seamstress—and his seams were visible. He did a poor job of rewriting."

Saltus said: "And old William went up in smoke. He blamed you for everything."

"Almost everyone did. A newspaper reviewer in Saint Louis questioned my patriotism; another in Minneapolis hinted that I was the anti-Christ, and a communist tool to boot. A newspaper in Rome skewered me with the unkindest cut of all: it printed the phrase *Traduttore Traditore* over the review—the Translator is a Traitor." Despite himself a trace of bitterness was evident. "On my *next* holiday I'll confine myself to something safe. I'll dig up a ten-thousand-year-old city in the Negev, or go out and rediscover Atlantis."

They walked in silence for a space. A car sped by them toward the busy commissary.

Chaney asked: "A personal question, Commander?"

"Fire away, mister."

"How did you manage your rank so young?"

Saltus laughed. "You haven't been in service?"

"No."

"Blame it on *our* damned war—the wits are calling it our Thirty Years War. Promotions come faster in wartime because men and ships are lost at an accelerated rate—and they come faster to men in the line than to men on the beach. I've always been in the line. When the Viet Nam war passed the first five years, I started moving up; when it passed ten years without softening, I moved up faster. And when it passed fifteen years—after that phony peace, that truce—I went up like a skyrocket." He looked at Chaney with sober expression. "We lost a lot of men and a lot of ships in those waters when the Chinese began shooting at us."

Chaney nodded. "I've heard the rumors, the stories. The Israeli papers were filled with Israeli troubles, but now and then outside news was given some space."

"You'll hear the truth someday; it will jolt you. Washington hasn't released the figures, but when they do you'll get a stiff jolt in the belly. A lot of things are kept undercover in undeclared wars. Some of the things work their way into the open after a while, but others never do." Another sidelong glance, measuring Chaney. "Do you remember when the Chinese lobbed that missile on the port city we were working? That port below Saigon?"

"No one can forget that."

"Well, mister, our side retaliated in kind, and the Chinese lost two railroad towns that same week—Keiyang and Yungning. Two holes in the ground, and several hundred square miles of radioactive cropland. Their missile was packing a low-yield A, it was all they could manage at the time, but we hit *them* with two Harrys. You will please keep that under your hat until you read about it in the papers— if you ever do."

Chaney digested the information with some alarm. "What did they do, to retaliate for *that?*"

"Nothing—yet. But they will, mister, they will! As soon as they think we're asleep, they'll clobber us with something. And hard."

Chaney had to agree. "I suppose you've had more than one tour of duty in the South China Sea?"

"More than one," Saltus told him. "On my last tour, I had two good ships torpedoed under me. Not one, but two, and Chinese subs were responsible both times. Those bastards can really shoot, mister— they're good."

"A Lieutenant Commander is equal to what?"

"A Major. Old William and me are buddies under the skin. But don't be impressed. If it wasn't for this war I'd be just another junior grade Lieutenant."

The desire for further conversation fell away and they walked in pensive silence to the commissary. Chaney recalled with distaste his contributions to Pentagon papers concerning the coming capabilities of the Chinese. Saltus seemed to have confirmed a part of it.

Chaney went first through the serving line but paused for a moment at the end of it, balancing the tray to avoid spilling coffee. He searched the room.

"Hey—there's Katrina!"

WILSON TUCKER

"Where?"

"Over there, by that far window."

"I don't believe in waiting for an invitation."

"Push on, push on, I'm right behind you!"

Chaney discovered that he *had* spilled his coffee by the time they reached her table. He had tried to move too fast, but still lost out.

Arthur Saltus was there first. He promptly sat down in the chair nearest the young woman and transferred his breakfast dishes from the tray to the table. Saltus put his elbows on the table, peered closely at Katrina, then half turned to Chaney.

"Isn't she lovely this morning! What would your friend Bartlett say about this?"

Chaney noted the tiny line of disapproval above her eyes. "Her very frowns are fairer far, than the smiles of other maidens are."

"Hear! Hear!" Saltus clapped his hands in approval, and stared back impudently at nearby diners who had turned to look. "Nosy peasants," was his loud whisper.

Kathryn van Hise struggled to maintain her reserve. "Good morning, gentlemen. Where is the Major?"

"Snoring," Arthur Saltus retorted. "We sneaked out to have breakfast alone with you."

"*And* these other two hundred characters." Chaney waved a hand at the crowded mess hall. "This is romantic."

"These peasants aren't romantic," Saltus disagreed. "They lack color and Old World charm." He stared bleakly at the room. "Hey—mister, we could practice on *them*. Let's run a survey on *them*, let's find out how many of them are Republicans eating fried eggs." Snap of fingers. "Better yet—let's find out how many Republican stomachs have been ruined eating these Army eggs!"

Katrina made a hasty sound of warning. "Be careful of your conversation in public places. Certain subjects are restricted to the briefing room."

Chaney said: "Quick! Switch to Aramaic. These peasants will never catch on."

Saltus began to laugh but just as suddenly shut it off. "I only know one word." He seemed embarrassed.

"Then don't repeat it," Chaney warned. "Katrina may have studied Aramaic—she reads everything."

"Hey—that's not fair."

"I do unfair things, I retaliate in kind, Commander. Last night, I sneaked into the briefing room while you were all asleep." He turned to the young woman. "I know your secret. I know one of the alternative targets."

"Do you, Mr. Chaney?"

"I do, Miss van Hise. I raided the briefing room and turned it inside out—a very thorough search, indeed. I found a secret map hidden under one of the telephones—the red phone. The alternative target is the Qumran monastery. We're going back to destroy the embarrassing scrolls—rip them from their jars and burn them. There." He sat back with barely concealed amusement.

The woman looked at him for a space, and Chaney had a sudden, intuitive torment. He felt uneasy.

When she broke her silence, her voice was so low it would not carry to the adjoining tables.

"You are almost right, Mr. Chaney. One of our alternatives *is* a probe into Palestine, and you were also selected for the team because of your knowledge of that general area."

Chaney was instantly wary. "I will have nothing to do with those scrolls. I'll not tamper with them."

"That will not be necessary. They are not an alternate target."

"What *is*?"

"I don't know the correct date, sir. Research has not been successful in determining the precise time and place, but Mr. Seabrooke believes it will be a profitable alternate. It is under active study." She hesitated and dropped her gaze to the table. "The general location in Palestine is or was a site known as the Hill of Skulls."

Chaney rocked in his chair.

In the long silence, Arthur Saltus groped for an understanding. "Chaney, what—?" He looked to the woman, then back to the man. "Hey—let *me* in on it!"

Chaney said quietly: "Seabrooke has picked a very hot alternative. If we can't go up *there* for the survey, our team is going *back* to film the Crucifixion."

Brian Chaney was the last of the four participants to return to the briefing room. He walked.

Kathryn van Hise had offered them a ride as they quit the mess hall and Arthur Saltus promptly accepted, scrambling into the front seat of the olive green sedan to sit close beside her. Chaney preferred the exercise. Katrina turned in the seat to look back at him as the car left the parking lot, but he was unable to read her expression: it may have been disappointment—and then again it may have been exasperation.

He suspected Katrina was losing her antipathy for him, and that was pleasing.

The sun was already hot in the hazy June sky and Chaney would have liked to go in search of the pool, but he decided against it only because he knew better than to be tardy a second time. As a satisfying substitute, he contented himself with watching the few women who happened to pass; he approved of the sharply abbreviated skirt that was the current style and, given another opportunity, would have included a forecast in his tables—but the stodgy old Bureau was likely to dismiss the subject matter as frivolous. Skirts had been climbing steadily for many years and now they were frequently one with the delta pants: a heady delight to the roving male eye. But with predictable military conservatism, the WAC skirts were not nearly as brief as those worn by civilians.

Happily, Katrina was a civilian.

The massive front door of the concrete building opened easily under his pull, moving on rolamite tracks. Chaney walked into the briefing room and stopped short at sight of the Major. A furtive signal from Saltus warned him to silence.

Major Moresby faced the wall, his back to the room and to Chaney. He stood at the far end of the long table, between the end of the table and the featureless wall with his fists knotted behind his back. The nape of his neck was flushed. Kathryn van Hise was busy picking up papers that had fallen—or been thrown—from the table.

Chaney closed the door softly behind him and advanced to the table, inspecting a stack of papers before his own chair. His reaction was one of sharp dismay. The papers were photocopies of his second scroll, the lesser of the two Qumran scrolls he had translated and published. There were nine sheets of paper faithfully reproducing the square Hebrew lettering of the *Eschatos* document from its opening line to its close. If he didn't know better, Chaney would have thought the Major was enraged at his temerity for tacking a descriptive Greek title on a Hebrew fantasy.

"Katrina! What are we doing with *this?*"

She finished the task of picking up the fallen pages and stacked them neatly on the table before the Major's chair.

"They are a part of today's study, sir."

"No!"

"Yes, sir." The woman slipped into her own chair and waited for Chaney and the Major to sit down.

The man did, after a moment. He glared at Chaney.

Chaney said: "Is this another of Seabrooke's idiotic ideas?"

"The matter is germane, Mr. Chaney."

"That matter is *not* germane, Miss van Hise. This has absolutely nothing to do with the Indic report, with the statistical tables, with the future surveys—nothing!"

"Mr. Seabrooke thinks otherwise."

Angrily: "Gilbert Seabrooke has holes in his head; his Bureau has holes in its measuring jars. Please tell him I said so. He should know better than to—" Chaney came to a full stop and glared at the young woman. "Is this *another* reason why I was chosen for the survey team?"

"Yes, sir. You are the only authority."

Chaney repeated the Aramaic word, and Saltus laughed despite himself.

She said: "Sir, Mr. Seabrooke believes it may have some slight bearing on the future survey, and we should be familiar with it. We should be familiar with every facet of the future that comes to our attention."

"But this has nothing to *do* with a future Chicago!"

"It may, sir."

"It may not! This is a fantasy, a fairy tale. It was written by a dreamer and told to his students—or to the peasants." Chaney sat down, containing his anger. "Katrina: this is a waste of time."

Saltus broke in. "More *midrash*, mister?"

"*Midrash*," Chaney agreed. He looked at the Major. "It has no biblical connection, Major. None whatever. This is a minor piece of prophecy fitted into a fantasy; it's the story of a man who lived twice—or of twins, the text isn't clear—who swept dragons from the sky. If the Brothers Grimm had discovered it first, they would have published it."

Katrina said stubbornly: "We are to study it."

Chaney was equally stubborn. "The turn of the century is only twenty-two years away but this document is addressed to the far future, to the end of the world. It depicts the end—the last days. I called it *Eschatos*, meaning 'The End of Things.' Does Seabrooke really think the end of the world is only twenty-two years away?"

"No, sir, I'm sure he doesn't believe that, but he has instructed us to study it thoroughly in preparation for the probe. There may be a tenuous connection."

"What tenuous connection? Where?"

"Those references to the blinding yellow light filling the sky, for one. That may be an allusion to the war in Southeast Asia. And there were other references to a cooling climate, and a series of plagues. The dragons may have a military connotation. Mr. Seabrooke mentioned specifically your point on Armageddon, in relation to the Arab-Israeli war. There are a number of incidents, sir."

Chaney permitted himself an audible groan.

Saltus said: "Hoist by your own petard, mister. I feel for you."

Chaney knew his meaning. The reviewers and the Moresbys of the world didn't *want* to believe his English translation of the Revelations scroll, but it appeared to be authentic. Now, Seabrooke was making noises like he wanted to believe *Eschatos*, or was willing to believe it.

Impatiently: "The blinding yellow light in the sky has *nothing* to do with the Asian war. In Hebrew fiction it was a romantic promise of health, wealth, of peace and prosperity for all. The yellow light is a benign sun, spilling contentment on the earth. The old prophet was saying simply that at last the earth belonged to men, to all men, and eternal peace was at hand. Utopia. No more than that.

"That utopia was to come *after* the end of things, after the last days, when a brand new world under a golden sun would be given to the peoples of Israel. It is a prophecy as old as time. It has nothing to do with our war in Asia, or the color of any soldier's skin." Chaney pointed to the door. "How cold is it out there now? *This* is swimming weather. And where are the plagues? Have you ever seen a dragon?"

Saltus: "And where is Armageddon?"

"The proper name is Har-Magedon. It's a mountain in Israel, Commander, the mountain of Megiddo rising above the Plain of Esdraelon. And the prophecies are a little too late—*all* the prophecies. Any number of decisive battles have already happened there and vanished into history. It was a favorite locale for the old fictioneers; it had such a bloody history it was firmly fixed in the native mind, it was a good site for still another story."

"Mister, you sure know how to throw cold water."

"Commander, I believe in being realistic; I believe in facts, not fantasy. I believe in statistics and firmly rooted continuities, not prophecies and dreams." Chaney stabbed the copied document with his finger. "The man who wrote this was a dreamer, and something of a plagiarist. Several passages were lifted from Daniel, and there is a hint of Micah."

"Do you think it's a fake?"

"No, definitely not. I had to make sure of that at the beginning. The scroll was found in the usual way: by university students searching old jars, in cave Q12. It was wrapped in the usual rotting linen of a type woven at Qumran, and that linen was submitted to the carbon-14 dating process—the tests were made at the Libby Institute in Chicago. Repeated tests established an age of nineteen hundred years, plus or minus seventy, for the linen.

"But we don't accept *that* as proof that the scroll inside the linen is of the same age. There are other methods of dating a manuscript." He bent over the copies and placed a finger on the opening line. "This text is written with square letters and contains no vowels—none at all. It reads from right to left down the page, right to left across the scroll. Square lettering came into use about the third century before Christ; before that a more flowing script was used but afterwards a square was common."

Chaney caught a movement from the corner of his eye. Major Moresby unbent, to peer closely at the copies.

"The Hebrew language used at that time had only twenty-two letters, and they were all consonants. Vowels hadn't been invented, and wouldn't be for another six or seven hundred years. This text contains the twenty-two standard consonants but nowhere on the scroll—above or below the lines, or within the words, or the margins—is there a sign to indicate where a consonant becomes a vowel. That was significant." He glanced at Moresby and discovered he had the man's close attention. "But there were other clues to work with. This scribe was familiar with the writings of Daniel, and of Micah. The text is not pure Hebrew; several Aramaic touches have slipped in—a word or a phrase having more impact than a Hebrew equivalent. The old Greek word *eschatos* doesn't appear, but it should have. I was surprised to find it missing, for the scribe had a knowledge of Greek drama, or melodrama." Chaney made a gesture. "The earliest date was about 100 B.C. It was not written before that.

"Setting a closing date isn't nearly as difficult, because the scribe betrays the limit of his knowledge. He was not alive and writing in 70 A.D. The text contains three direct references to a Temple, a great white Temple which appears to be the center of all important activity.

There were many temples in Palestine and in the surrounding lands, but only one *Temple*: the holiest of holy places, the Temple of Jerusalem. In this story the Temple is still standing, still in existence, and is the center of all activity. But in history *that* Temple stopped. The Roman armies invaded Judaea and destroyed it utterly in 70 A.D. In the course of putting down a Hebrew revolt they tore it apart to the last stone, and the Temple was no more."

Major Moresby said: "That was foretold."

Chaney ignored him. "So the date of composition was pinned down: not earlier than 100 B.C. and not later than 70 A.D. A satisfactory agreement with the radiocarbon tests. I'm satisfied the scroll is authentic, but the tale it tells is not—the story is pure fiction, built on symbols and myths known to the ancient Hebrews."

Arthur Saltus eyed the copies and then the woman. "Do we have to read all this, Katrina?"

"Yes, sir. Mr. Seabrooke has requested it."

Chaney said: "A waste of time, Commander."

Saltus grinned at him. "The Great White Chief has spoken, mister. I don't want to go back to that bucket in the South China Sea."

"Indic won't have me back—they sold me to the Great White Chief." Brian Chaney pushed the photocopied papers aside and reached for the hefty Indic report. He opened a page at random and found himself reading figures pertaining to a West German election three years earlier.

He remembered that election; people in his section had followed it with interest and had tried to place bets on it, without takers. Just before the report was closed and submitted to the Bureau, the National Democratic party had captured four point three percent of the popular vote—only seven-tenths of one percent short of the minimum needed to gain entrance to the Bundestag. The party had been accused of Neo-Nazism, and Chaney wondered if it had managed to overcome the Hitler image and win the necessary five percent in the last few years. In peacetime, Israeli papers would have carried the news; he would have noticed it. Perhaps they had published subsequent election news, despite their paper shortages and their domestic troubles—perhaps he had missed it. His nose had been buried in the translations for a long time. As the noses of Saltus and Moresby were buried in *Eschatos* now....

Chaney had often wondered about the anonymous scribe who had concocted that story. The long work on the scroll had imparted the feeling of almost knowing the man, of almost reading his mind. He sometimes thought the man had been a novice practicing his art—a probationer not yet tamped into the mold, or perhaps he was a defrocked priest who had lost his office because of his nonconformity. The man had never hesitated to employ Aramaic vernacular, where Aramaic was more colorful than his native Hebrew, and he told his story with zest, with poetic freedom.

*Eschatos:*

The sky was blue, new, and clear of dragons (winged serpents) when the man who was two men (twins?) lived on (under?) the earth. The man who was two men was at peace with the sun and his children multiplied (the tribes or families about him grew in size with the passage of time). He was known and welcomed in the white Temple, and may have dwelt there. His work took him frequently to distant Har-Magedon, where he was equally well known to those who lived on the mountain and those who tilled the plain below; he mingled with these peoples and instructed (counseled, guided) them in their daily lives; he was a wise man. He had a guest room (or house) with (alongside?) a mountain family and needed only to touch the tent rope (make sign) for food and water; it was supplied him without payment. (Form of repayment for his services?)

The man who was two men labored on the mountain.

His task (performed at unknown intervals) was an onerous one, and consisted of standing on the mountain top and sweeping the skies clean of muck (impurities, debris left over from the Creation) which tended to gather there. The mountain people were required to assist him in his work, in that they furnished him with ten *cor* of water (nine hundred gallons) drawn from an inexhaustible well (or cistern) near the base of the mountain; and each time the job was finished in the dark and light of a single day (from one sunset to the next). This task had been put to him by the nomadic Egyptian prophet (Moses?) by more than five times the Year of Jubilee (more than two hundred and fifty years earlier); and it was a sign and a promise the prophet gave to his children, the tribes: for so long as the skies were clean the sun would remain quiet, dragons would not hover, and the bitter cold that immobilized old men would be kept in its proper place at a distance.

The new prophet who came after the Egyptian (Aaron?) approved the pact, and it was continued; after him, Elijah approved the pact, and it was continued; and after him, Zephaniah approved the pact, and it was continued; after him, Micah approved the pact (chronological error) and it was continued. It is now. The skies were swept and the peoples prospered.

The man who was two men was a wondrous figure. He was a son (lineal descendant) of David.

His head was of the finest gold and his eyes were brilliant (word missing; probably gems), his breast and arms were of purest silver, his body was bronze, his legs were of iron, and his feet were of iron mixed with clay (entire description borrowed from Daniel). The man who was two men did not grow old, his age never changed, but on a day when he was working at his appointed task he was struck down by a sign. A stone was dislodged from the mountain and rolled down on him, crushing his feet and grinding the clay to dust, which blew away in the wind and he fell to earth grievously hurt. (Again, a whole incident borrowed from Daniel.) Work stopped. The mountain people carried him down to the plains people and the plains people carried him to the white Temple, where the priests and the physicians put him down in his injury (buried him?).

The first Year of Jubilee passed, and the second (a century), but he did not appear at his place on the mountain. His room (house) was not made ready for him, for the new children had forgotten; the people did not fetch water and the well (cistern) ran low; the skies were not cleansed. Debris gathered above Har-Magedon. The first dragon was seen there, and another, and they spawned in the muck until the skies were dark with their wings and loud with their thunder. A chilling cold crept over the land and there was ice on the streams. The tribes were thin (depopulated) and were hungry; they fought one another for food, and it came to pass that touching the tent rope was no more honored in the land, and kinsman and traveler alike were turned away or driven into the desert for the jackals. The messengers

(?) stopped and there was no more traffic between tribes and the towns of the tribes, and the roads were covered with weed and grass.

The elders lost the faith of their fathers and built a wall around the tribe, and then another and another, until the walls were a hundred and a hundred in number and every house was set apart from its neighbor, and families were set apart from one another. The elders caused great walls to be built and they did not traffic; the cities fell poor and made war on one another, and the sun was not quiet.

A plague came down from the muck above Har-Magedon, a dropping from the dragons to cover the land like a foul mist before dawn. The plague was a vile sickness of the eye, of the nose, of the throat, of the head, of the heart and the soul of a man, and his skin fell; the plague did make men over into a likeness of the four beasts, and they were loathsome in their misery and their brothers fled in terror before them.

And with this the voice of Micah cried out, saying, this was the end of the days; and the voice of Elisha cried out, saying, this was the end of the days; and the spirit and ghost of Ezekiel cried out, and was seen within the gates of the city, telling the lamentations and mourning, for this was the end of the days.

And it was so.

(The following line of text consisted of but a single word, an Aramaism indicating darkness, or time, or generation. It could be translated as Interregnum.)

The man who was two men rose up from his bed (tomb?) in the underworld, and was angry at what he found in the land. He broke the earth of the Temple (emerged from his tomb below? or within?) and came forth in fury to banish the dragons from the mountain. He raised up his rod and struck the walls, bidding the families to go free and live; he gave food and comfort to the traveler and counseled him, and guided his hand to the tent rope; he bade his kinsman enter his (room? house?) and take rest; he labored without stop to undo the sore misery on the land.

When the sun was quiet again, the man who was two men worked to refill the well (cistern) and he swept the skies clear of debris. The dragons fled from their foul nests, and the plague fled with them to another part of the world. The man turned his eye up to the Temple and there was a great, blinding yellow light filling the heavens from the rim of the world to the rim: and it was a sign and a promise from the holy prophets to the laborer that the world was made new again, and was at peace with itself. Flowers bloomed and there was fruit on the vine. The sun was quiet.

The man who was two men rested in his earth-place (tomb?) and was content.

Brian Chaney pulled himself from his reverie to look down the table at his companions.

Arthur Saltus was reading the photocopied pages in a desultory manner, his interest barely caught by the narrative. Major Moresby was scribbling in a notebook—his only support to a retentive memory—and had gone back to the beginning of the translation to read it a second time. Chaney suspected he was hooked. Kathryn van Hise was across the table from him, sitting motionless with her fingers interlaced on the tabletop. The young woman had been surreptitiously watching him while he day-dreamed, but turned her glance down when he looked directly at her.

Chaney wondered what she really thought of all this? Apart from her superior's opinions, apart from the stance officially adopted by the Bureau, what did *she* think? At breakfast she had exhibited some embarrassment—it may have been alarm—at the prospect of filming the alternate target, filming the Crucifixion, but other than that he'd found no sign of her personal beliefs or attitudes toward the future survey. She had revealed pride and triumph in the engineers' accomplishments and she was fanatically loyal to her employer—but what did *she* think? Did she have any mental reservations?

He failed utterly to understand Seabrooke's interest in the second scroll.

Every scholar recognized it as *midrash*; there had been no controversy over the second scroll and had it been published alone he would have escaped the notoriety. He thought Gilbert Seabrooke something of a lunatic to even introduce it into the briefing room. There was no meat here for the survey. There was nothing in the *Eschatos* relating to the coming probe of the turn of the century; the story was firmly rooted in the first century before Christ and did not look or hint beyond 70 A.D. Actually it didn't peer beyond its own century. It made no claim or pretense to genuine prophecy as did, say, the Book of Daniel—whose scribe pretended to be alive about five hundred years before he was born, only to betray himself by his faulty grasp of history. Gilbert Seabrooke was reading imaginary lines between the lines, grabbing at rays of yellow light and the droppings of dragons.

One of the three telephones rang.

Kathryn van Hise jumped from her chair to answer and the three men turned to watch her.

The conversation was short. She listened carefully, said *Yes, sir* three or four times, and assured the caller that the studies were proceeding at a satisfactory pace. She said *Yes, sir* a final time and hung up the instrument. Moresby was half out of his chair in anticipation.

Saltus said: "Well, come *on*, Katrina!"

"The engineers have concluded their testing and the vehicle is now on operational status. Field trials will begin very soon, gentlemen. Mr. Seabrooke suggested that we take the day off as a token of celebration. He will meet us at the pool this afternoon."

Arthur Saltus yelled, and was halfway to the door.

Brian Chaney dropped his copy of the *Eschatos* scroll into a wastebasket and prepared to follow him.

He looked to the woman and said: "Last one in is a wandering Egyptian."

Brian Chaney came up from a shallow dive and paddled to the edge of the pool; he clung to the tiled rim for a space and attempted to wipe the gentle sting of chlorine from his eyes. The sun was hot, and the air warmer than the water. Two of his companions played in the water behind him while a third—the Major—sat in the shade and stared solemnly at a chess board, waiting for anyone to come along and challenge him. The pieces were set out. The recreation area held a few others beside themselves but none seemed interested in chess.

Chaney glanced over his shoulder at the pair playing in the water, and felt the smallest pain of jealousy. He climbed from the pool and reached for a towel.

Gilbert Seabrooke said: "Afternoon, Chaney."

The Director of Operations sat nearby under a gaudy beach umbrella, sipping a drink and watching the bathers. It was his first appearance.

Chaney stretched the towel over his back and ran across the hot tiles. "Good afternoon. You're the red telephone." They shook hands.

Seabrooke smiled briefly. "No; that's our line to the White House. Please don't pick it up and call the President." A wave of the hand extended an invitation to the other chair beneath the umbrella. "Refreshments?"

"Not just yet, thanks." He studied the man with an open curiosity. "Has someone been carrying tales?" His glance went briefly to the woman in the water.

Seabrooke's smooth reply attempted to erase the sting. "I receive daily reports, of course; I try to keep on top of every activity on this station. And I'm quite used to people misunderstanding my motives and actions." Again the smallest of stingy smiles. "I make it a practice to explore every possible avenue to attain whatever goal is in view. Please don't be upset by my interest in your outside activities."

"They have no relation to *this* activity."

"Perhaps, and perhaps not. But I refuse to ignore them for I am a methodical man."

Chaney said: "And a persistent one."

Gilbert Seabrooke was tall, thin, taut, and looked like that well-known fellow in the State Department—or perhaps it was that other fellow who sat on the Supreme Court. He wore the carefully cultivated statesman image. His hair was silver gray and parted precisely in the middle, with the ends brushed backward at a conservative angle; his eyes appeared gray, although upon closer inspection they were an icy blue-green; the lips were firm, not used to laughter, while the chin was strong and clean with no hint of a double on the neckline. He carried his body as rigidly erect as a military man, and his pipe jutted out straight to challenge the world. He was Establishment.

Chaney had vague knowledge of his political history.

Seabrooke had been governor of one of the Dakotas—memory refused to reveal which one—and was only narrowly defeated in his bid for a third term. The man quickly turned up in Washington after the defeat and was appointed to a post in Agriculture: his party took care of its faithful. Some years later he moved to another post in Commerce, and after several years he dropped into a policy-making office in the Bureau of Standards. Today he sat beside the pool, directing everything on station.

Chaney asked: "How's the battle going?"

"Which battle?"

"The one with the Senate subcommittee. I suspect they're counting the dollars and the minutes."

The tight lips quavered, almost permitting a smile. "Eternal vigilance results in a healthy exchequer, Chaney. But I *am* having some little difficulty with those people. Science tends to frighten those who are infrequently exposed to it, while the practitioners of science are often the most misunderstood people in the world. The project could be different if more imagination were brought into play. If our researches were directly connected to the hostilities in Asia, if they would result in practical military hardware, we would be drowning in funds." A gesture of discontent. "But we must fight for every dollar. The military people and their war command priority."

Chaney said: "But there *is* a connection."

"I said this would be different if more imagination were brought into play," Seabrooke reminded him dryly. "At this point, imagination is sadly lacking; the military mind often does not recognize a practical use until that use is thrust under the nose. You may see an application and I believe I see one, but neither the Pentagon nor the Congress will recognize it for another dozen years. We must pinch pennies and depend upon the good will of the President for our continued existence."

"Ben Franklin's rocking chair didn't catch on for the longest time," Chaney said. But he saw a military application, and hoped the military never discovered it.

Seabrooke watched the woman in the water, following her lithe form as she raced away from Arthur Saltus.

"I understand that you experienced some difficulty in making up your mind."

Chaney knew his meaning. "I'm not an unduly brave man, Mr. Seabrooke. I have my share of brass and bravado when I'm standing on familiar ground, but I'm not a really brave man. I doubt that I could do what either of *those* men do every day, in their tours of duty." A tiny fear of the future turned like a worm in his mind. "I'm not the hero type—I believe discretion is the better part of valor, I want to run while I'm still able."

"But you stayed on in Israel under fire."

"I did, but I was scared witless all the while."

Seabrooke turned. "Do you believe Israel will be defeated? Do you believe this will end at Armageddon?"

Flatly: "No."

"You don't find it suggestive—?"

"No. That land has been a battleground for something like five thousand years—ever since the first Egyptian army marching north met the first Sumerian army marching south. Doom-criers marched with them, but don't fall into that trap."

"But those old biblical prophets are rather severe, rather disturbing."

"Those old prophets lived in a hard age and a hard land; they almost always lived under the boot of an invader. Those old prophets owed allegiance to a government and a religion which were at odds with every other nation within marching distance; they invited punishment by demanding independence." He repeated the warning. "Don't fall into that trap. Don't try to take those prophets out of their age and fit them into the twentieth century. They are obsolete."

Seabrooke said: "I suppose you're right."

"I can predict the downfall of the United States, of every government on the North American continent. Will you hang a medal on me for that?"

Seabrooke was startled. "What do you mean?"

"I mean that all this will be dust in ten thousand years. Name a single government, a single nation which has endured since the birth of civilization—say, five or six thousand years ago."

Slowly: "Yes. I see the point."

"Nothing endures. The United States will not. If we are fortunate we may endure at least as long as Jericho."

"I know the name, of course."

Chaney doubted it. "Jericho is the oldest town in the world, the city half as old as time. It was built in the Natufian period, but has been razed or burned and then rebuilt so many times that only an archeologist can tell the number. But the town is still there and has been continuously inhabited for at least six thousand years. The United States should be as lucky. We *may* endure."

"I fervently hope so!" Seabrooke declared.

Chaney braced him. "Then drop this *Eschatos* nonsense and worry about something worthwhile. Worry about our violent swing to the extreme right; worry about these hippy-hunts; worry about a President who can't control his own party, much less the country."

Seabrooke made no comment.

Brian Chaney had pivoted in his chair and was again watching Kathryn van Hise playing in the water. Her tanned flesh, only partially enclosed in a topless swim suit, was the target of many eyes. Those transparent plastic cups some women now wore in place of a bra or a halter was only one of the many little jolts he'd known on his return to the States. Israeli styles were much more conservative and he had half forgotten the American trend after three years' absence. Chaney looked at the woman's wet body and felt something more than a twinge of jealousy; he wasn't entirely sure the cups were decent. The swing to the ultra-conservative right was bound to catch up with feminine clothing sooner or later, and then he supposed legs would be covered to the ankle and the transparent cups and blouses would be museum pieces.

There would likely be other reactions in the coming years which would make some of *his* forecasts obsolete; the failure to anticipate a weak Administration was already throwing parts of the Indic report open to question. His recommendation for a renewable term trial marriage would probably be ignored—the program itself might be repealed before it got started if the howls frightened Congress. The vociferous minority might easily swell to a majority.

To move off an uncomfortable spot of dead silence, he asked casually: "The TDV is operational?"

"Oh, yes. It has been operational since an early hour this morning. The years of planning and building and testing are done. We are ready to forge ahead."

"What took you so long?"

Seabrooke turned heavily to look at him. Blue-green eyes were hard. "Chaney, nine men have already died by that vehicle. Would you have cared to be the tenth?"

Shock. "*No.*"

"No. Nor would anyone else. The engineers had to test again and again until every last doubt was erased. If any doubt *had* remained, the project would have been canceled and the vehicle dismantled. We would have burned the blueprints, the studies, the cuff-notes, everything. We would have wiped away every trace of the vehicle. You know the rule: two objects cannot occupy the same space at the same time."

"That's elementary."

A curt nod. "It is so elementary that our engineers overlooked it, and nine men died when the vehicle returned to its point of origin, its precise second of launch, and attempted to occupy the same space." His voice dropped. "Chaney, the most dreadful sight I have ever seen was the crash of an airliner on a Dakota hillside. I was with a hunting party less than a mile away and watched it fall. I was among the first to reach the wreckage. There was no possibility of anyone surviving— none." Hesitation. "The explosion in our laboratory was the second worst sight. I was not there—I was in another building—but when I reached the laboratory I found a terrible repetition of that hillside catastrophe. No man, no single piece of equipment was left intact. The room was shattered. We lost the engineer traveling with the vehicle and eight others on duty in the laboratory. The vehicle returned to the exact moment, the exact millisecond of its departure and destroyed itself. It was an incredible disaster, an incredible oversight—but it happened. Once."

After a space, Seabrooke picked up the thread of his recital. "We learned a bitter lesson. We rebuilt the laboratory with thicker, reinforced walls and we rebuilt the vehicle; we programmed a new line of research accenting the safety factor. That factor settled itself at just sixty-one seconds, and we were satisfied."

Chaney said: "They've been counted for me, again and again. I'll lose a minute on every trip."

"A passenger embarking for any distant point, *you*, will leave at twelve o'clock, let us say, and return not sooner than sixty-one seconds after twelve. The amount of elapsed time in the field will not affect the return; if you stayed there ten years you would return sixty-one seconds *after* you launched. If we could not be absolutely certain of that we would close shop and admit defeat."

"Thank you," Chaney said soberly. "I like my skin. How are you protecting those men now?"

"By reinforced walls and remote observation. The engineers work in an adjoining room but five feet of steel and concrete will separate you. They operate and observe the TDV by closed circuit television; indeed, they observe not only the operations room itself but the corridor to it and the storeroom and fallout shelter: everything on that level of basement."

Curiously: "How do you really *know* the vehicle is moving? Is it displacing anything?"

"It does not move, does not travel in the sense of passing through space. The vehicle will always remain in its original location, unless we choose to move it elsewhere. But it does operate, and in operation it displaces temporal strata just as surely as those people in the pool are displacing water by plunging into it."

"How did you prove that?"

"A camera was mounted in the fore of the vehicle, looking through a port into the operations room. A clock and a day-calendar hang on a wall in direct line of sight of that camera. The camera has not only photographed past hours and dates but has taken pictures of the wall *before* the clock was placed there. We know the TDV has probed at least twelve months into the past."

"Any effect on the monkeys?"

"None. They are quite healthy."

"What have you done to prevent another accident—a different kind of an accident?"

Sharply: "Explain that."

Chaney said carefully: "What will happen if that machine probes back into the past before the basement was dug? What will happen if it burrows into a bed of clay?"

"That simply will not be *allowed* to happen," was the quick reply. "The lower limit of displacement is December 30, 1941. A probe beyond that date is prohibited." The Director emptied his glass and put it aside. "Chaney, the site has been carefully researched to determine a lower limit; every phase of this operation has been researched so that nothing is left to chance. The first building on the site was a crude structure resembling a cabin. It burned to the ground in February, 1867."

"You went back that far?"

"We were prepared to go farther if necessary; we had access to records dating back to the Black Hawk war in 1831. A farmhouse *with* a basement was built on the site during the summer of 1901, and remained in place until demolition in 1941 when the government acquired this land for an ordnance depot. It has since been government owned and occupied, and the site remained vacant until the laboratory was built. The engineers were very careful to locate that basement. Today the TDV floats in a sealed tank of polywater three feet above the original basement floor, in a space that could have been occupied by nothing else. We even pinpointed the former location of the furnace and the coal room."

"And so the deadline is 1941? Why not 1901?"

"The lower limit is December 30, 1941, well after the date of demolition. The safety factor above all."

"I'd like to see that tank of polywater."

"You will. It is necessary that you become quite familiar with every aspect of the operation. Have you been visiting the doctor for your physicals?"

"Yes."

"Have you had weapons training?"

"No. Will *that* be necessary?"

Seabrooke said: "The safety factory, Chaney. It's wise to anticipate. The training may be wasted, but it's still wise to prepare yourself in every way."

"That sounds pessimistic. Wasted in what way?"

"Excuse me; you've been out of the country. All weapons for civilians will probably be prohibited in the near future. President Meeks favors that, you know."

Chaney said absently: "That will please the Major. He doesn't believe civilians have enough sense to point a gun in the right direction."

He was looking across the pool. Katrina had left the water and was now perched on the tiled rim of the opposite side, freeing her hair from the confines of a plastic cap. Arthur Saltus was as close as their two wet suits would permit, but none of the loungers about the pool were staring at him. Two other women in the water weren't drawing half the attention—but neither were they as exposed as Katrina. Military codes extended to the swimming pool whether WACS liked it or not.

Chaney continued to stare at the woman—and at Saltus hard by—but a part of his mind dwelt on Gilbert Seabrooke, on Seabrooke's matter-of-fact statements. He thought about the machine, the TDV. He *tried* to think about the TDV. Every effort to visualize it was a failure. Every attempt to understand its method of operation was a similar failure—he lacked the engineering background to comprehend it. It worked: he accepted that. His own ears told him that every time they rammed through a test.

Drawing an enormous amount of power and piloted by a remote guidance, the vehicle displaced—what? Temporal strata. Time layers. The machine didn't move through space, it didn't leave the basement tank, but it—or the camera mounted in the nose—peered and probed into time while photographing a clock and a calendar. Soon now, it would transmit humans into tomorrow and those humans were expected to do more than merely look through the nose at a clock. (But it had also killed nine men when it doubled back on itself.) Despite an effort to control it, his skin crawled. The cold shock would not leave him.

Chaney said shortly: "You picked a hell of a crew."

"Why do you think so?"

"Not an engineer in the lot—not a hard scientist in the lot. Moresby and I love each other like a cobra and a mongoose. I think I'm the mongoose. Want to try again?"

"I know what I'm doing, Chaney. The engineers and the physical scientists will come later, when the probes demand engineers and physical scientists. When did the first geologist reach the moon? The first selenographer? *This* survey demands your kind of man, and Moresby, and Saltus. You and Moresby were chosen because each of you is supreme in your field, and because you are natural opposites. I like to think the pair of you are delicate balances, with Saltus the neutral weight in center. And I say again, I know what I am doing."

"Moresby thinks I'm some kind of a nut."

"Yes. And what do you think of him?"

Sudden glee: "*He's* some kind of a nut."

Seabrooke permitted himself a wintry smile. "Forgive me, but there is a measure of truth to both suppositions. The Major *also* has a hobby which has embarrassed him."

Chaney groaned aloud. "Those damned prophets!" He looked around at the Major. "Why doesn't he collect toy soldiers, or be the best chess player in the world?"

"Why don't you write cookbooks?"

Chaney glanced down at his chest. "See how neatly the blade entered between the ribs? Notice that the haft stands out straight and true? A marksman's thrust."

Seabrooke said: "You like to read the past, while the Major prefers to read the future. I will admit yours is the more valuable vocation."

"Another futurist. You collect futurists."

"He places an inordinate faith in prognostication. He begins with so simple an act as reading his horoscope in the daily papers, and conducting himself accordingly. After his arrival here he admitted to Kathryn the mission was no surprise to him, because a certain horoscope had advised him to prepare himself for a momentous change in his daily affairs."

Chaney said: "*That* is as old as time; the earliest Egyptians, the Sumerians, the Akkadians, all were crazy about astrology. It's the most enduring religion."

"I suppose you are familiar with the small booklets known as farmer's almanacs?"

A nod. "I know of them."

"Moresby buys them regularly, not only to learn how their minute prophecies may affect him but to anticipate the weather a year in advance. I will admit I have looked into that last, and the Major has a remarkable record of correlating military operations with weather conditions—when he's stationed in the United States, you understand. One would suppose the weather works for him. And on some previous military posts, he has been known to plant a garden in strict accordance with the guidelines laid down in those almanacs—phases of the moon and so forth."

Skeptically: "Did the spinach come up?"

The firm lips twitched and toyed with a smile, then controlled themselves. "Finally, there is his library. Moresby owns a small collection of books, perhaps forty or fifty in all, which he moves with him from post to post. Books by such people as Nostradamus, Shipton, Blavatsky, Forman, and that Cromwell woman in Washington. He has an autographed copy by someone named Guinness; he met the author at some lecture or other. I inquired into that because of the security angle but Guinness proved harmless. Just recently he added your volume to the collection."

Chaney said: "He wasted his money."

"Do you also believe I've wasted mine?"

"If you were looking for prophetic visions, yes. If you were interested in a biblical curiosity, no. The future should bring some great debates on that Revelations scroll; a dozen or so applecarts have been upset."

Seabrooke peered at him. "But do you see how I'm using Moresby?"

"Yes. Just as you're using me."

"Quite so. I like to think I've assembled the best possible team for the most important undertaking of the twentieth century. There are no real and solid guidelines to the future, there are only speculative studies and pseudo-speculative literature. We're making use of both, and making use of trustworthy men who are actively involved in both. One or both of you will have a solid foot on the ground when you surface twenty-two years hence. What more can we do, Chaney?"

"You've taken hold of a wolf by the ears. You might look around for a way to let go—an escape route."

A moment of thoughtful silence. "A wolf by the ears. Yes, I have done that. But Chaney, I have no desire to let go; I am fascinated by this thing, I will *not* let go. This step is comparable to the very first rocket into space, the very first orbital flight, the very first man on the moon. I could not let go if I wanted to!"

Chaney was impressed by the vehemence, the passionate eagerness. "Why don't *you* go up to the future?"

Seabrooke said quietly: "I tried. I volunteered, but I was pushed aside." His voice betrayed the hurt. "I was washed out in the first physical examination by a heart murmur. Once again this is comparable to space flight, Chaney. Old men, disabled men, feeble men will never know the TDV. We have been shut out."

The man's gaze wandered back to Katrina, and Chaney joined him in the watchfulness. Her skimpy suit was beginning to dry under the June sun and some of the more interesting rubs and contours were smoothing out, losing the revealing contours beneath. Beside her, skin touching skin, Arthur Saltus monopolized her attention.

Chaney felt that he had been shut out.

After a while he asked a question that had been playing in the back of his mind.

"Katrina said you had a couple of alternatives in mind, if this future probe didn't work. What alternates?" And he waited to see if the woman had reported a breakfast table conversation to the Director.

"A confidence, Chaney?"

"Certainly."

"I know the President a bit better than you do."

"I'll grant you that."

"I know what he will not buy."

Chaney had a premonition. "He won't buy your alternatives? Either of them?"

"Buy them? He will be outraged by them. Shock waves will be felt all this distance from Washington." Seabrooke hit the table and his empty glass was upset. "I wanted to visit the future, see the future, *smell* the future, but I was rejected the first day by the medics; I was shipwrecked before I got aboard and that hurt me more than I can say. The only other way left to me, Chaney, was to see that future through your eyes—your camera, your tapes, your observations and reactions. I can live in it through you and Moresby and Saltus, and I am *determined* to do that! There is nothing else left to me.

"To that end, I prepared two alternatives to submit to the President. I made sure each of the alternate probes would be unacceptable to him, and he would direct me to proceed with the original plan. I want the future!"

Chaney asked: "Outrageous?"

A short nod. "The President is a religious man; he practices his faith. He will never permit a probe to the scene of the Crucifixion with film and tape."

"No—he won't do that." Chaney considered it. "But because of political consequences, not religious ones. He's afraid of the people and afraid of the politicians."

"If that be true, the second alternative would be more frightening."

Warily: "Where—or what?"

"The second alternative is Dallas in November, 1963. I propose to record the Kennedy assassination in a way not done before. I propose to station a cameraman on the sixth floor of that book depository, overlooking the route; I propose to station a second cameraman in that grove atop the knoll, to settle a controversy; I propose to station a third cameraman—*you*—on the curb alongside the Kennedy car, at the precise point necessary to record the shots from the window or the trees. We will have an accurate filmed record of the crime, Chaney."

The TDV was a keen disappointment.

Brian Chaney knew dismay, disillusionment. Perhaps he had expected too much, perhaps he had expected a sleek machine gleaming with chrome and enamel and glass, still new from an assembly line; or perhaps he had expected a mechanical movie monster, a bulging leviathan sprouting cables like writhing tentacles and threatening to sink through the floor of its own massive weight. Perhaps he had let his imagination run away with him.

The vehicle was none of those things. It was a squat, half-ugly can with the numeral 2 chalked on the side. It was unromantic. It was strictly functional.

The TDV resembled nothing more than an oversized oil drum hand-fashioned from scrap aluminum and pieces of old plastic—materials salvaged from a scrap pile for this one job. Chaney thought of a Model-T Ford he'd seen in a museum, and a rickety biplane seen in another; the two relics didn't seem capable of moving an inch. The TDV was a plastic and aluminum bucket resting in a concrete tank filled with polywater, the whole apparatus occupying a small space in a nearly bare basement room. The machine didn't seem capable of moving a minute.

The drum was about seven feet in length, and of a circumference barely large enough to accommodate a fat man lying down; the man inside would journey through time flat on his back; he would recline full-length on a wetwork sling while grasping two handrails near his shoulders, with his feet resting on a kickbar at the bottom of the drum. A small hatch topside permitted entry and egress. The upper end of the drum had been cut away—it appeared to be an afterthought—and the opening fitted with a transparent bubble for observing the clock and the calendar. A camera and a sealed metal cube rested in the bubble. Several electric cables, each larger than a swollen thumb, emerged from the bottom end of the vehicle and snaked across the basement floor to vanish into the wall separating the operations room from the laboratory. A stepstool rested beside the polywater tank.

The contrivance looked as if it had been pieced together in a one-man machine shop on the backlot.

Chaney asked: "*That* thing works?"

"Most assuredly," Seabrooke replied.

Chaney stepped over the cables and walked around the vehicle, following the invitation of an engineer. The clock and the calendar were securely fastened to a nearby wall, each protected by a clear plastic bubble. Above them—like perched and hovering vultures—were two small television cameras looking down on the basement room. A metal locker, placed near the door and securely fastened to the wall, was meant to contain their clothing. Light fixtures recessed in a high ceiling bathed the room in a cold, brilliant light. The room itself seemed chilly and strangely dry for a basement; it held a sharp smell that might be ozone, together with an unpleasant taste of disturbed dust.

Chaney put the flat of his hand against the aluminum hull and found it cold. There was a minute discharge of static electricity against his palm.

He asked: "How did the monkeys run it?"

"They didn't, of course," the engineer retorted with annoyance. (Perhaps he lacked a sense of humor.) "This vehicle is designed for dual operation, Mr. Chaney. All the tests were launched from the lab, as you will be on the out-stage of the journey. We will kick you forward."

Chaney searched that last for a double meaning.

The engineer said: "When the vehicle is programmed for remote, it can be literally kicked to or away from its target date by depressing the kickbar beneath your feet. We will launch you forward, but you will effect your own return when the mission is completed. We recall only in an emergency."

"I suppose it will wait up there for us?"

"It will wait there for you. After arrival on target the vehicle will lock on point and remain there until it is released, by you or by us. The vehicle cannot move until propelled by an electrical thrust and that thrust must be continuous. The tachyon generators provide the thrust against a deflecting screen which provides the momentum. The TDV operates in an artificially created vacuum which precedes the vehicle by one millisecond, in effect creating its own time path. Am I making myself clear?"

Chaney said: "No."

The engineer seemed pained. "Perhaps you should read a good book on tachyon deflector systems."

"Perhaps. Where will I find one?"

"You won't. They haven't been written."

"But it all sounds like perpetual motion."

"It isn't, believe me. This baby eats power."

"I suppose you *need* that nuclear reactor?"

"All of it—it serves this lab alone."

Chaney revealed his surprise. "It doesn't serve the station outside? How much does it take to kick this thing into the future?"

"The vehicle requires five hundred thousand kilos per launch."

Chaney and Arthur Saltus whistled in unison. Chaney said: "Is that power house protected? What about wiring? Transformers? Electrical systems are vulnerable to about everything: sleet storms, drunken drivers ramming poles, outages, one thing after another."

"Our reactor is set in concrete, Mr. Chaney. Our conduits are underground. Our equipment is rated for at least twenty years continuous service." A wave of the hand to indicate superior judgment, superior knowledge. "You needn't concern yourself; our future planning is complete. There will be power to spare for the next five hundred years, if need be. The power *will* be available for any launch and return."

Brian Chaney was skeptical. "Will cables and transformers last five hundred years?"

Again the quick annoyance. "We don't expect them to. All equipment will be replaced each twenty or twenty-five years according to a prearranged schedule. This is a completely planned operating system."

Chaney kicked at the concrete tank and hurt his toe. "Maybe the tank will leak."

"Polywater doesn't leak. It has the consistency of thin grease, and is suspended in capillary tubes. This is ninety-nine percent of the world's supply right here." He followed Chaney's lead and kicked the tank. "No leak."

"What does the TDV push against? That polywater?"

The engineer looked at him as if he were an idiot. "It *floats* on the polywater, Mr. Chaney. I *said* the thrust against a screen, a molybdenum screen provides the momentum to displace temporal strata."

Chaney said: "Ah! I see it now."

"I don't," Arthur Saltus said mournfully. He stood at the nose of the vehicle with his nose pressed against the transparent bubble. "What guides this thing? I don't see a tiller or a wheel."

The engineer gave the impression of wanting to leave the room, of wanting to hand over the instruction tour to some underling. "The vehicle is guided by a mercury proton gyroscope, Mr. Saltus." He pointed past the Commander's nose to a metal cube within the bubble, nestled alongside the camera. "That instrument. We borrowed the technique from the Navy, from their program to guide interplanetary ships in long-flight."

Arthur Saltus seemed impressed. "Good, eh?"

"Superior. Gyroscopes employing mercury protons are not affected by motion, shock, vibrations, or upset; they will operate through any violence short of destruction. *That* unit will take you there and bring you back to within sixty-one seconds of your launch. Rely on it."

Saltus said: "How?" and Major Moresby seconded him. "Explain it, please. I am interested."

The engineer looked on Moresby as the only partly intelligent nonengineer in the room. "Sensing cells in the unit will relay back to us a continuous signal indicating your time path, Mr. Moresby. It will signal any deviation from a true line; if the vehicle wavers we will know it immediately. Our computer will interpret and correct immediately. The computer will send forward the proper corrective signals to the tachyon deflector system and restore the vehicle to its right time path, all in less than a second. You will not be aware of the deviation or the correction, of course."

Saltus: "Do you guarantee we'll hit the target?"

"Within four minutes of the annual hour, Mr. Saltus. This system does not permit a tracking error greater than plus or minus four minutes per year. That is *on* target. The Soviet couldn't do any better."

Chaney was startled. "Do they have one?"

"No," Gilbert Seabrooke interposed. "That was a figure of speech. We all have pride in our work."

Seniority was all. Major Moresby made the first trial test, and then Commander Saltus.

When his turn came, Chaney undressed and stored his clothing in the locker. The hovering presence of the engineer didn't bother him but the prying eyes of the two television cameras did. He couldn't know who was on the other side of the wall, watching him. Wearing only his shorts—the one belated concession to modesty—and standing in his bare feet on the concrete floor, Chaney fought away the impulse to bolster his waning ego by thumbing his nose at the inquisitive cameras. Gilbert Seabrooke probably wouldn't approve.

Following instructions, he climbed into the TDV.

Chaney wriggled through the hatch, lowered himself onto the sling-like bed, and promptly banged his head against the camera mounted inside the bubble. It hurt.

"Damn it!"

The engineer said reprovingly: "Please be more careful of the camera, Mr. Chaney."

"You could hang that thing *outside* the bucket."

Inching lower onto the flimsy bed, he discovered that when his feet reached the kickbar there was insufficient room to turn his head without striking either the camera or the gyroscope, nor could he push out his elbows. He squinted up at the engineer in protest but the man's face disappeared from the opening as the hatch was slammed shut. Chaney had a moment of panic but fought it away; the drum was no worse than a cramped tomb—and better in one small respect: the transparent bubble admitted light from the ceiling fixtures. Still following the detailed instructions, he reached up to snug the hatch and was immediately rewarded by a blinking green bull's eye above his head. He thought that was nice.

Chaney watched the light for a space but nothing else happened.

Aloud: "All right, *move* it." The sound of his voice in the closed can startled him.

Twisting around at the expense of a strained neck muscle and another glancing blow off the camera, he peered through the bubble at the outside room but saw no one. It was supposed to be empty during a launch. He guessed that his companions were in the lab beyond the wall, watching him on the monitors as he had watched them. The sounds had been thunderously loud in there, causing acute pain to his eardrums.

Chaney's gaze came back to the green light against the hull above his head, and discovered that a red light beside it was now blazing, blinking in the same monotonous fashion as its brother. He stared at the two lights and wondered what he was supposed to do next. Instructions hadn't gone beyond that point.

He was aware that his knees were raised and that his legs ached; the interior of the bucket wasn't designed for a man who stood six feet four *and* had to share the space with a camera and gyroscope. Chaney lowered his knees and stretched out full length on the webbed sling, but he had forgotten the kickbar until his bare feet struck it. The red light winked out.

After a while someone rapped on the plastic bubble, and Chaney twisted around to see Arthur Saltus motioning for him to come out.

He opened the hatch and sat up. When he was in a comfortable position, he found that he could rest his chin on the rim of the hatch and look down into the room.

Saltus stood there grinning at him. "Well, mister, what did you think of *that?*"

"There's more room in a Syrian coffin," Chaney retorted. "I've got bruises."

"Sure, sure, civilian, tight quarters and everything, but what did you *think* of it?"

"Think of what?"

"Well, the—" Saltus stopped to gape in disbelief. "Civilian, do you mean to sit there like an idiot and tell me you weren't watching that clock?"

"I watched the lights; it was like Christmas time."

"Mister, they ran you through your test. You saw *ours*, didn't you? You checked the time?"

"Yes, I watched you."

"Well, you jumped into the future! One hour up!"

"The hell I did."

"The hell you didn't, civilian. What did you think you were doing in there—taking a nap? You were supposed to watch the clock. You went up an hour, and then you kicked yourself back. That stuffy old engineer was mad—you were supposed to wait for *him* to do it."

"But I didn't hear anything, feel anything."

"You *don't* hear anything in there; just out here, on the outside looking in. Man, we heard it! Pow, pow, the airhammer. And the guy was supposed to tell you there was no sense of motion: just climb in, and climb out. Shoot an hour." Saltus made a face. "Civilian, sometimes you disappoint me."

"Sometimes I disappoint myself," Chaney said. "I've missed the most exciting hour of my life. I guess it was exciting. I was looking at the lights and waiting for something to happen."

"It did happen." Saltus stepped down from the stool. "Come on out of there and get dressed. We have to listen to a lecture from old windbag in the lab—and after that we inspect the ship's stores. The fallout shelter, food and water and stuff; we might have to live off the stores when we get up there to the brink of 2000. What if everything is rationed, and we don't have ration cards?"

"We can always call Katrina and ask for some."

"Hey—Katrina will be an old woman, have you thought of that? She'll be forty-five or fifty, maybe—I don't know how old she is now. An *old* woman—damn!"

Chaney grinned at his concept of ancient age. "You won't have time for dating. We have to hunt Republicans."

"Guess not—nor the opportunity. We're not supposed to go looking for anybody when we get up there; we're not supposed to look for her or Seabrooke or even us. They're afraid we'll find *us*." He made a weary gesture. "Get your pants on. Damned lecture. I hate lectures— I always fall asleep."

A team of engineers lectured. Major Moresby listened attentively. Chaney listened with half an ear, attention wandering to Kathryn van Hise who was seated at one side of the room. Arthur Saltus slept.

Chaney wished the information given him had been printed on the usual mimeographed papers and passed around a table for study. That method of dissemination was the more effective for him; the information stayed with him when he could read it on a printed page and refer back to the sentence or the paragraph above to underscore a point. It was more difficult to call back a spoken reference without asking questions, which interrupted the speaker and the chain of thought and the drone which kept Saltus sleeping. The ideal way would be to set down the lecture in Aramaic or Hebrew and hand it to him to translate; *that* would insure his undivided attention to learn the message.

He gave one eye and one ear to the speaker.

Target dates. Once a target date was selected and the pertinent data was at hand, computers determined the exact amount of energy needed to achieve that date and then fed the amount into the tachyon generator in one immense surge. The resulting discharge against the deflector provided momentum by displacing temporal strata ahead of the vehicle along a designated time path; the displaced strata created a vacuum into which the vehicle moved toward the target date, always under the guidance of the mercury proton gyroscope. (Chaney thought: perpetual motion.)

The engineer said: "You can be no more than eighty-eight minutes off the designated hour of the target date, 2000. That is four minutes per year; that is to be anticipated. But there is another significant time element to be noted in the field, one that you must not forget. Fifty hours. You may spend up to fifty hours in the field on any date, but you may *not* exceed that amount. It is an arbitrary limit. To be sure, gentlemen, the safety of the displaced man is of first importance up to a point. Up to a point." He stared at the sleeping Saltus. "After that point the repossession of the vehicle will be of first importance."

"I read you," Chaney told him. "We're expendable; the bucket isn't."

"I cannot agree to that, Mr. Chaney. I prefer to say that at the expiration of fifty hours the vehicle will be recalled to enable a second man to go forward, if that is deemed advisable, to effect the recovery of the first."

"*If* he can be found," Chaney added.

Flatly: "You are not to remain on target beyond the arbitrary fifty-hour limit. We have only one vehicle; we don't wish to lose it."

"That is quite sufficient," Moresby assured him. "We can do the job in half that time, after all."

Upon completion of their assignment, each of them would return to the laboratory sixty-one seconds after the original launch, whether they remained on target one hour or fifty. The elapsed time in the field did not affect their return. They would be affected only by the elapsed time while *in* the field; those few hours of natural aging could not be recaptured or neutralized of course.

The necessities and some few of the luxuries of life were stored in the shelter: food, medicines, warm clothing, weapons, money, cameras and recorders, shortwave radios, tools. If storage batteries capable of giving service for ten or twenty years were developed in the near future, they would also be stocked for use. The radios were equipped to send and receive on both military and civilian channels; they could be powered by electricity available in the shelter or by batteries when used with a conversion unit. The shelter was fitted with lead-in wires, permitting the radios to be connected to an outside antenna, but once outside on the target minitennas built into the instruments would serve for a range of approximately fifty miles. The shelter was stocked with gasoline lanterns and stoves; a fuel tank was built into an outside wall.

After emerging from the vehicle, each man was to close the hatch and carefully note the time and date. He was to check his watch against the wall clock for accuracy and to determine the plus-or-minus variation. Before leaving the basement area to enter his target date he was to equip himself from the stores, and note any sign of recent use of the shelter. He was forbidden to open any other door or enter any other room of the building; in particular, he was forbidden to enter the laboratory where the engineers would be preparing his return passage, and forbidden to enter the briefing room where someone might be waiting out the arrival and departure.

He was to follow the basement corridor to the rear of the building, climb a flight of stairs and unlock the door for exit. He would be instructed where to locate the two keys necessary to turn the twin locks of the door. Only the three of them would ever use that door.

Chaney asked: "Why?"

"That has been designated the operations door. No other personnel are authorized to use it: field men only."

Beyond the door was a parking lot. Automobiles would be kept there continuously for their exclusive use; they would be fueled and ready on any target date. They were cautioned not to drive a new model car until they became thoroughly familiar with the controls and handling of it. Each man would be furnished the properly dated papers for gate passage, and was to carry a reasonable sum of money sufficient to meet anticipated expenses.

Saltus was awake. He poked at Chaney. "You can fly to Florida in fifty hours—have a swim and still get back in time. Here's your chance, civilian."

"I can walk to Chicago in fifty," Chaney retorted.

Their mission was to observe, film, record, verify; to gather as much data as possible on each selected date. Observations should also be made (and a permanent record left in the shelter) that would benefit the next man on his target. They were to bring in with them all exposed films and tapes but the instruments were to be stored in the shelter for the following man to use. A number of small metal discs each weighing an ounce would be placed in the vehicle before launch; the proper number of discs was to be thrown overboard before returning to compensate for the tapes and films being brought back.

Were there any questions?

Arthur Saltus stared at the engineer with sleepy eyes. Major Moresby said: "None at the moment, thank you." Chaney shook his head.

Kathryn van Hise claimed their attention. "Mr. Chaney, you have another appointment with the doctor in half an hour. When you are finished there, please come to the rifle range; you really should begin weapons training."

"I'm not going to run around Chicago shooting up the place—they have enough of that now."

"This will be for your own protection, sir."

Chaney opened his mouth to continue the protest, but was stopped. The sound was something like a massive rubber band snapped against his eardrums, something like a hammer or a mallet smashing into a block of compressed air. It made a noise of impact, followed by a reluctant sigh as if the hammer was rebounding in slow motion through an oily fluid. The sound hurt.

He looked around at the engineers with a question, and found the two men staring at each other with blank astonishment. With a single mind they deserted the room on the run.

Saltus said: "*Now* what the hell?"

"Somebody went joyriding," Chaney replied. "They'd better count the monkeys—one may be missing."

Katrina said: "There were no tests scheduled."

"Can that machine take off by itself?"

"No, sir. It must be activated by human control."

Chaney had a suspicion and glanced at his watch. The suspicion blossomed into conviction and despite himself he failed to suppress a giggle. "That was me, finishing my test. I hit that kickbar by accident just an hour ago."

Saltus objected. "My test didn't make a noise like that. William didn't."

Chaney showed him the watch. "You said I went up an hour. That's *now*. Did you kick yourself back?"

"No—we waited for the engineers to pull us back."

"But I kicked; I propelled myself from *here*, from a minute ago." He looked at the door through which the two men had run. "If that computer has registered a power loss, I did it. Do you suppose they'll take it out of my pay?"

They were outside in the warm sunshine of a summer afternoon. The Illinois sky was dark and clouded in the far west, promising a night storm.

Arthur Saltus looked at the storm clouds and asked: "I wonder if those engineers were sweeping bilge? Do you think they really know what they're talking about? Power surges and time paths and water that won't leak?"

Chaney shrugged. "A hair perhaps divides the false from the true. They have the advantage."

Saltus gave him a sharp glance. "You're borrowing again—and I think you've changed it to boot."

"A word or two," Chaney acknowledged. "Do you recall the rest of it? The remaining three lines of the verse?"

"No."

Chaney repeated the verse, and Saltus said: "Yes."

"All right, Commander. That machine down there is our Alif; the TDV is an Alif. With it, we can search for the treasure house."

"Maybe."

"No maybes: we *can*. We can search out *all* the treasure houses in history. The archeologists and the historians will go crazy with joy." He followed the man's gaze to the west, where he thought he heard low thunder. "If this wasn't a political project it wouldn't be wasted on Chicago. The Smithsonian would have a different use for the vehicle."

"Hah—I can read your mind, civilian! You wouldn't go up at all, you'd go back. You'd go scooting back to the year Zero, or some such, and watch those old scribes make scrolls. You've got a one-track mind."

"Not so," Chaney denied. "And there was no year Zero. But you're right about one thing: I wouldn't go up. Not with all the treasure houses of history waiting to be opened, explored, cataloged. I wouldn't go up."

"Where then, mister? Back where?"

Chaney said dreamily: "Eridu, Larsa, Nippur, Kish, Kufah, Nineveh, Uruk…"

"But those are just old—old cities, I guess."

"Old cities, old towns, long dead and gone—as Chicago will be when its turn comes. They are the treasure houses, Commander. I want to stand on the city wall at Ur and watch the Euphrates flood; I want to know how *that* story got into Genesis. I want to stand on the plains before Uruk and see Gilgamesh rebuild the city walls; I want to *see* that legendary fight with Enkidu.

"But more, I want to stand in the forests of Kadesh and see Muwatallis turn back the Egyptian tide. I think you'd both like to see that. Muwatallis was out-manned, out-wheeled, lacking everything but guts and intelligence; he caught Ramses' army separated into four divisions and what he did to them changed the course of Western history. It happened three thousand years ago but if the Hittites *had* lost—if Ramses had beaten Muwatallis—we'd likely be Egyptian subjects today."

Saltus: "I can't speak the language."

"You would be speaking it—or some local dialect—if Ramses had won." A gesture. "But that's what *I'd* do if I had the Alif and the freedom of choice."

Arthur Saltus stood lost in thought, looking at the western cloudbank. The thunder was clearly heard.

After a space he said: "I can't think of a blessed thing, mister. Not one thing I'd want to see. I may as well go up to Chicago."

"I stand in awe before a contented man," Chaney said. "The dust bin of history is no more than that."

**8**

Brian Chaney was splashing in the pool the next morning before most of the station personnel had finished their breakfasts. He swam alone, enjoying the luxury of solitude after his customary walk from the barracks. The early morning sun was blindingly bright on the water, a contrast from the night just past: the station had been raked by a severe thunderstorm during the night, and blown debris still littered the streets.

Chaney turned on his back and filled his lungs with air, to float lazily on the surface of the pool. He was contented. His eyes closed to shut out the brightness.

He could almost imagine himself back on the Florida beach—back to that day when he loafed at the water's edge, watching the gulls and the distant sail and doing nothing more strenuous than speculating on the inner fears of the critics and readers who had damned him and damned his translation of the Revelations scroll. Yes, and back to the day before he'd met Katrina. Chaney hadn't been aware of a personal vacuum then, but when they parted—when this mission was finished—he would be aware of one. He would miss the woman. Parting company with Katrina would hurt, and when he went back to the beach he'd be keenly aware of the new vacuum.

He had been unnecessarily rude to her when she first approached him, and he regretted that now; he had believed her to be only another newspaper woman there to badger him. He wasn't on civilized speaking terms with newspaper people. Nor did Chaney like to admit to jealousy—a childish emotion—but Arthur Saltus had aroused in him some response suspiciously close to jealousy. Saltus had moved in and boldly taken possession of the woman, another hurt.

But that wasn't the only hurt.

His trigger finger was sore, stiff, and his shoulder hurt like sin; they had assured him it was a light rifle but after an hour of firing it, Chaney wholly disbelieved them. Even in his sleep the bullying figure of the Major stood over him, needling him: "Squeeze it, squeeze it, don't yank—don't jerk—squeeze it!" Chaney squeezed it and four or five times out of ten managed to hit the target. He thought that remarkable, but his companions did not. Moresby was so disgusted he tore the rifle from Chaney's grasp and put five shots through the bull's eye in the space between one breath and the next.

The hand gun was worse. The Army model automatic seemed infinitely lighter when compared to the rifle, but because he could not use his left hand to lift and steady the barrel he missed the target eight times out of ten. The two good shots were only on the rim of the target.

Moresby muttered: "Give the civilian a shotgun!" and stalked away.

Arthur Saltus had taught him camera techniques.

Chaney was familiar with the common hand cameras and with the mounted rigs used in laboratories to copy documents, but Saltus introduced him to a new world. The holograph camera was new. Saltus said that film had been relegated to the cheap cameras; the holograph instruments used a thin ribbon of embossed nylon which would withstand almost any abuse and yet deliver a recognizable picture. He scoured a nylon negative with sandpaper, then made a good print. Adequate lighting was no longer a problem; the holograph would produce a satisfactory picture taken in the rain.

Chaney experimented with a camera strapped to his chest, with the lens peering through a buttonhole in his jacket where a button should be; there was another that fitted over his left shoulder, with the lens appearing to be a lodge emblem attached to his lapel—a remote cable ran down the inside of his coat sleeve and the plunger nestled in the palm of his hand. A fat belt buckle held a camera. A bowler hat concealed a camera. A folded newspaper was actually a motion picture camera in camouflage, and a smart looking attaché case was another. Microphones for the tape recorders—worn under the coat, or in the pocket—were buttons or emblems or tie clasps or stays tucked inside shirt collars.

He usually managed a decent picture—it was difficult to produce a poor one with the holograph instruments, but Saltus was often dissatisfied, pointing out this or that or the other thing which would have resulted in a sharper image or a more balanced composition. Katrina was photographed hundreds of times during the practice. She appeared to endure it with patience.

Chaney expelled a burst of air and started to sink. He flipped over on his stomach and swam under water to the edge of the pool. Grasping the tiled rim, he hauled himself out of the water and stared up in surprise at the grinning face of Arthur Saltus.

"Morning, civilian. What's new in ancient Egypt?"

Chaney peered past him. "Where is—?" He stopped.

"I haven't seen her," Saltus responded. "She wasn't in the mess hall—I thought she was here with *you*."

Chaney wiped his face with a towel. "Not here. I've had the pool to myself."

"Hah—maybe old William is beating our time; maybe he's playing chess with her in a dark corner somewhere." Saltus grinned at that thought. "Guess what, mister?"

"What now?"

"I read your book last night."

"Shall I run for cover, or stand up for a medal?"

"No, no, not *that* one. I'm not interested in those old scrolls. I mean the other book you gave me, the one about the desert tribes—old Abraham, and all. Damn but that man made some fine pictures!" He sat down beside Chaney. "Remember that one of the Nabataean well or cistern or whatever it was, down there at the foot of the fortress?"

"I remember it. Well built. It served the fortress through more than one siege."

"Sure. The guy made that one with natural lighting. No flash, no sun reflectors, nothing, just natural light; you can see the detail of the stonework and the water level. And it was on film, too—he wasn't using nylon."

"You can determine that by examination?"

"Well, of course! *I* can. Listen, mister, that's good photography. That man is good."

"Thank you. I'll tell him next time I see him."

Saltus said: "Maybe I'll read your book someday. Just to find out why they're shooting at you."

"It doesn't have pictures."

"Oh, I can read all the easy words." He stretched out his legs and stared up at the underside of the gaudy beach umbrella. A spider was beginning a web between the metal braces. "This place is dead this morning."

"What's to do? Other than a rousing game with the Major, or another session at the rifle range?"

Saltus laughed. "Shoulder hurt? That will wear away. Say, if I could find Katrina, I'd throw her into the pool and then jump in with her—that's where the action is!"

Chaney thought it wisest not to answer. His gaze went back to the sun-bright waters of the pool, now empty of swimmers and slowly regaining placidity. He remembered the manner in which Saltus had played there with Katrina, but the memory wasn't a pleasant one. He hadn't joined in the play because he felt self-conscious for the first time in his life, because his physique was a poor one compared to the muscular body of the Commander, because the woman seemed to prefer the younger man's company to his. That was hurtful to admit.

Chaney caught a quick movement at the gate.

"The Major has found us."

Major Moresby hustled into the recreation area and strode toward the pool, seeking them. Halfway across the patio he found them beneath the umbrella and turned hard. He was breathing heavily and his face flushed with excitement.

"Get up off your duff!" he barked at the Commander. And to

Chaney: "Get your clothes on. Urgent. They want us in the briefing room *now*. I have a car waiting."

"Hey—what goes?" Saltus was out of the chair.

"We do. Somebody has made the big decision. Damn it, Chaney, move!"

"The field trials?" Saltus demanded. "The field trials? This morning? Now?"

"This morning, now," Moresby acknowledged. "Gilbert Seabrooke brought the decision; they roused me out of bed. We're moving up, after all!" He turned on Chaney. "Will you haul your ass out of that chair, civilian? Move it! I'm waiting, everybody is waiting, the vehicle is cranked up and waiting."

Chaney jumped from the chair, heart pounding against his rib cage.

Moresby: "Katrina said to use the car. You are *not* to waste time walking, and that is an order."

Chaney's reflexes were slower, but he was already racing for the bath house to change. They ran with him. "I'm not walking."

"Where are we going?" Saltus demanded breathlessly. "I mean when? *When* in Joliet? Did you get the word?"

"Katrina gave the word. You won't like it, Art."

Arthur Saltus stopped abruptly in the doorway and Chaney collided with him.

"Why won't I like it?"

"Because it's a political thing, a damned political thing, after all! Katrina said the decision came down early this morning from the White House—from *him*. We should have expected something like that."

Slow repeat: "Why won't I like it?"

Moresby said with disdain: "We're going up two years to a date in November. November 6, 1980, a Thursday. The President wants to know if he'll be reelected." Arthur Saltus stared in open-mouthed astonishment. After a space of disbelief he turned to Chaney. "What was that word again, mister? In Aramaic?"

Brian Chaney told him.

**9**

BRIAN CHANEY
JOLIET, ILLINOIS
6 NOVEMBER 1980

IF WE OPEN A QUARREL BETWEEN THE PAST
AND THE PRESENT,
WE SHALL FIND THAT WE HAVE LOST THE FUTURE.
—WINSTON CHURCHILL

Chaney had no forewarning of something amiss.

The red light blinked out. He reached up to unlock the hatch and throw it open. The green light went dark. Chaney grasped the two handrails and pulled himself to a sitting position, with his head and shoulders protruding through the hatchway. He was alone in the room, as he expected to be. He struggled through the hatch and climbed over the side, easing himself down the hull until his feet touched the stool. The vehicle felt icy cold. Chaney reached up to slam shut the hatch, then cast a curious glance at the monitoring cameras. He hoped those future engineers approved his obedience to the ritual.

Chaney looked at his watch: 10:03. That was expected. He had kicked off less than a minute ago, the third and last to move up. He sought out the calendar and clock on the wall to verify the date and the time: 6 *Nov* 80. The clock read 7:55. A thermometer had been added to the instrument group to record outside temperature: 31 degrees F.

Chaney hesitated, unsure of his next move. The time was not right; it should have been ten o'clock, plus or minus eight minutes. He made a mental note to tell the engineers what he thought of their guidance system.

The first of the field trials had been launched at a few minutes past nine, with Major Moresby claiming his due. Thirty minutes later Arthur Saltus followed the Major into the future, and thirty minutes after him Chaney climbed into the bucket and was kicked off. All arrivals on target were supposed to be identical with departure times, plus or minus eight minutes. Chaney had expected to surface about ten and find the others waiting for him. They were scheduled to regroup in the fallout shelter, equip themselves, and travel to the target city in separate automobiles to effect a wider coverage of the area.

Katrina had given each of them explicit instructions and then wished them well.

Saltus had said: "Aren't you coming down to see us off?"

She'd replied: "I will wait in the briefing room, sir."

The wall clock moved to 7:56.

Chaney abandoned his irresolution. Rounding the hull of the vehicle, he opened the locker and reached for the suit hung there only minutes before. Small surprise. His suit had been cleaned and pressed and was now hanging in a paper sheath provided by the dry cleaner. Next to his were similar packages belonging to Moresby and Saltus. His name was written across the sheath and he recognized the woman's handwriting. *He* was first in: seniority.

Chaney ripped away the paper and dressed quickly, aware of the chill in the room. The white shirt he found in the locker was a new one and he looked with some interest at the wavy, patterned collar. Style, 1980. The sheath was jammed back into the locker as a mocking message.

Leaving the vehicle room, Chaney strode down the well-lighted corridor to the fallout shelter, conscious of the cameras watching his every step. The basement, the entire building, was cloaked in silence; the lab engineers would avoid contact with him as he must avoid them—but they had the advantage: they could examine a quaint specimen from two years in the past while he could only speculate on who was on the other side of the wall. Their door was shut. Chaney pushed the shelter door open and the overhead lights flashed on in automatic response. The room was empty of life.

Another clock above a workbench read 8:01.

Chaney strode into the shelter to stop, turn, stare, inspect everything open to his gaze. Except for a few new objects on the workbench the room was precisely the same as he'd last seen it, a day or two before. He was expected. Three tape recorders had been removed from the stores and set out on the bench, along with an unopened box of fresh tape; two still cameras designed to be worn over the shoulder were there, together with a motion picture camera for Arthur Saltus and new film for all three instruments. Three long envelopes rested atop the cameras, and again he recognized Katrina's handwriting.

Chaney tore his open, hoping to find a personal note, but it was curiously cool and impersonal. The envelope gave up a gate pass and identification papers bearing the date, 6 November 1980. A small photograph of his face was affixed to the identification. The brief note advised him not to carry arms off the station.

He said aloud: "Saltus, you've shut me out!" This evidence suggested the woman had made a choice in the intervening two years—unless he was imagining things.

Chaney prepared himself for the outside. He found a heavy coat and a rakish cap in the stores that were good fits, then armed himself with camera, recorder, nylon film and tape. He took from a money box what he thought would be an adequate supply of cash (there was a shiny new dime and several quarters bearing the date 1980; the portraits on the coins had not been changed), and a drawer yielded a pen and notebook, and a flashlight that worked. A last careful survey of the room suggested nothing else that would be useful to him, and he made ready to leave.

A clock told 8:14.

Chaney scrawled a quick note on the back of his torn envelope and propped it against the motion picture camera: *Arrived early for a swim. Will look for you laggards in town. Protons are perfidious.*

He stuffed the ID papers in his pocket and quit the shelter. The corridor was as silent and empty as before. Chaney climbed the stairway to the operations door and stopped with no surprise to read a painted sign.

DO NOT CARRY WEAPONS BEYOND THIS DOOR. FEDERAL LAW PROHIBITS THE POSSESSION OF FIREARMS BY ALL EXCEPT LAW ENFORCEMENT OFFICERS, AND MILITARY PERSONNEL ON ACTIVE DUTY. DISARM BEFORE EXITING.

Chaney fitted two keys into the twin locks and shoved. A bell rang somewhere behind him. The operations door rolled easily on rolamite tracks. He stepped outside into the chill of 1980. The time was 8:19 on a bleak November morning and there was a sharp promise of snow in the air.

He recognized one of the three automobiles parked in the lot beyond the door: it was the same car Major Moresby had driven a short while ago—or two years ago—when he hustled Chaney and Saltus from the pool to the lab. The keys were in the ignition lock. Walking to the rear of the vehicle, he stared for a moment at the red and white license plate to convince himself he *was* where he was supposed to be: Illinois 1980. Two other automobiles parked beyond the first one appeared to be newer, but the only visible change in their design appeared to be fancy grills and wheel caps. So much for public taste and Detroit pandering.

Chaney didn't enter the car immediately.

Moving warily, half fearful of an unexpected meeting, he circled the laboratory building to reconnoiter. Nothing seemed changed. The installation was just as he remembered it: the streets and sidewalks well repaired and clean—policed daily by the troops on station—the lawns carefully tended and prepared for the approach of winter, the trees now bare of foliage. The heavy front door was closed and the familiar black and yellow fallout shelter sign still hung above it. There was no guard on duty. On an impulse, Chaney tried the front door but found it locked—and that was a commentary of some kind on the usefulness of the fallout shelter below. He continued his inspection tour all the way around again to the parking lot.

Something *was* changed behind the lot.

Chaney eyed the space for a moment and then recognized the difference. What had been nothing more than a wide expanse of lawn two years ago was now a flower garden; the flowers were wilted with the nearness of winter and many of the dead blossoms and vines had been cleared away, but in the intervening two years someone—Katrina?—had caused a garden to be planted in an otherwise empty plot of grass.

Chaney left a sign for Major Moresby. He placed a shiny new quarter on the concrete sill of the locked door. A moment later he turned the key in the ignition and drove off toward the main gate.

The gatehouse was lighted on the inside and occupied by an officer and two enlisted men in the usual MP uniforms. The gate itself was shut but not locked. Beyond it, the black-topped road stretched away into the distance, aiming for the highway and the distant city. A white line had been newly painted—or repainted—down the center of the road.

"Are you going off station, sir?"

Chaney turned, startled by the sudden question. The officer had emerged from the gatehouse.

He said: "I'm going into town."

"Yes, sir. May I see your pass and identification?"

Chaney passed over his papers. The officer read them twice and studied the photograph affixed to the ID.

"Are you carrying weapons, sir? Are there any weapons in the car?"

"No, to both."

"Very good, sir. Remember that Joliet has a six o'clock curfew; you must be free of the city limits before that hour or make arrangements to stay overnight."

"Six o'clock," Chaney repeated. "I'll remember. Is it the same in Chicago?"

"Yes, sir." The officer stared at him. "But you can't enter Chicago from the south since the wall went up. Sir, are you going to Chicago? I will have to arrange for an armed guard."

"No—no, I'm not going there. I was curious."

"Very well, sir." He waved to a guard and the gate was opened. "Six o'clock, sir."

Chaney drove away. His mind was not on the road.

The warning indicated that a part of the Indic report had correctly called the turn: the larger cities had taken harsh steps to control the growing lawlessness, and it was likely that many of them had imposed strict dusk-to-dawn curfews. A traveler not out of town before dusk would need hotel accommodations to keep him off the streets. But the reference to the Chicago wall puzzled him. *That* wasn't foreseen, nor recommended. A wall to separate what from what? Chicago had been a problem since the migrations from the south in the 1950s— but a wall?

The winding private road led him to the highway. He pulled up to a stop sign and waited for a break in traffic on route 66. Across the highway, an officer in a parked state patrol car eyed his license plate and then glanced up to inspect his face. Chaney waved, and pulled into traffic. The state car did not leave its position to follow him.

A second patrol car was parked at the outskirts of town, and Chaney noted with surprise that two men in the back seat appeared to be uniformed national guardsmen. The bayonet-tipped rifles were visible. His face and his license were given the same scrutiny and their attention moved on to the car behind him.

He said aloud (but to himself): "Honest, fellas, *I'm* not going to start a revolution."

The city seemed almost normal.

Chaney found a municipal parking lot near the middle of town and had to search for the rare empty space. He was outraged to learn it cost twenty-five cents an hour to park, and grudgingly put two of Seabrooke's quarters into the meter. A clerk sweeping the sidewalk before a shuttered store front directed him to the public library.

He stood on the steps and waited until nine o'clock for the doors to open. Two city squad cars passed him while he waited and each of them carried a guardsman riding shotgun beside the driver. They stared at him and the clerk with the broom and every other pedestrian.

An attendant in the reading room said: "Good morning. The newspapers aren't ready."

She hadn't finished the chore of rubber-stamping the library name on each of the front pages, or of placing the steel rods through the newspaper centerfolds. A hanging rack stood empty, awaiting the dailies. An upside-down headline read: JCS DENIED BAIL.

Chaney said: "No hurry. I would like the Commerce and Agriculture yearbooks for the past two years, and the Congressional Record for six or eight weeks." He knew that Saltus and the Major would buy newspapers as soon as they reached town.

"All the governmental publications are in aisle two, on your left. Will you need assistance?"

"No, thanks. I know my way through them."

He found what he wanted and settled down to read.

The lower house of Congress was debating a tax reform bill. Chaney laughed to himself and noted the date of the Record was just three weeks before election. In some few respects the debate seemed a filibuster, with a handful of representatives from the oil and mineral states engaging in a running argument against certain of the proposals on the pious grounds that the so-called reforms would only penalize those pioneers who risk capital in the search for new resources. The gentleman from Texas reminded his colleagues that many of the southwestern fields had run dry—the oil reserves exhausted—and the Alaskan fields were yet ten years from anticipated capacity. He said the American consumer was facing a serious oil and gasoline shortage in the near future; and he got in a blow at the utility people by reminding that the hoped-for cheap power from nuclear reactors was never delivered.

The gentleman from Oregon once injected a plea to repeal the prohibition on cutting timber, claiming that not only were outlaw lumberjacks doing it, but that foreign opportunists were flooding the market with cheap wood. The presiding officer ruled that the gentleman's remarks were not germane to the discussion at hand.

The Senate appeared to be operating at the customary hectic pace.

The gentleman from Delaware was discussing the intent of a resolution to improve the lot of the American Indian, by explaining that his resolution would direct the Bureau of Indian Affairs to act on a previous resolution passed in 1954, directing them to terminate government control of the Indians and return their resources to them. The gentleman complained that no worthwhile action had been taken on the 1954 resolution and the plight of the Indian was as sorry as ever; he urged his fellows to give every consideration to the new resolution, and hoped for a speedy passage.

The sergeant-at-arms removed several people from the balcony who were disturbing the chamber.

The gentleman from South Carolina inveighed against a phenomenon he called "an alarming tide of ignorants" now flowing from the nation's colleges into government and industry. He blamed the shameful tide on "the radical-left revamping and reduction of standard English courses by misguided professors in our institutions of higher learning," and urged a return to the more rigorous disciplines of yesteryear when every student could "read, write, and talk good American English in the tradition of their fathers."

The gentleman from Oklahoma caused to be inserted in the Record a complete news item circulated by a press wire service, complaining that the nation's editors had either ignored it or relegated it to the back pages, which was a disservice to the war effort.

GRINNELL ASSESSES ARMS

Saigon (AP): General David W. Grinnell arrived in Saigon Saturday to assess what progress South Asian Special Forces have made in assuming a bigger share of the fighting chores.

Grinnell, making his third visit to the war zone in two years, said he was keenly interested in the course of the so-called Asian Citizen Program, and planned to talk to the fighting men in the countryside to find out first-hand how things were going.

With additional American troop commitments pegged in part on the effectiveness of South Asian Special Forces (SASF), Grinnell's visit sparked rumors of a fresh troop build-up in the hard hit northern sectors. Unofficial estimates set a figure of two million Americans now in combat in the Asian Theater, which the military command refuses to confirm or deny.

Asked about new arrivals, Grinnell said: "That is something the

President will have to decide at the proper time." General Grinnell will confer with American military and civilian officials on all fighting fronts before returning to Washington next week.

Chaney closed the record with a sense of despair and pushed the stack aside. Wanting to lose himself in less depressing but more familiar matters, he opened a copy of the current Commerce yearbook and sought out the statistical tables that were his stock in trade.

The human lemmings hadn't changed their habits. A bellwether indicating the migration patterns from one area to another was the annual ton-miles study of interstate shipments of household goods; the family that removed together grooved together. The flow continued into California and Florida, as he had forecast, and the adjoining tables revealed corresponding increases in tonnage for consumer durables and foodstuffs not indigenous to those states. The shipment of automobiles (assembled, new) into California had sharply decreased, and that surprised him. He had supposed that the proposal to ban automobiles in the state by 1985 would only result in an accelerated flow—a kind of hoarding—but the current figures suggested that state officials had found a way to discourage hoarding and depress the market at the same time. Prohibitive taxation, most likely. New York City should note the success of the program.

Chaney began filling his notebook.

The measured tolling of a bell somewhere outside the library brought him up from the book with surprise, and a flurry of aged men from the newspaper racks toward the door underscored the passage of time. It was the noon hour.

Chaney put away the government publications and cast a speculative eye on the attendant. A girl had replaced the older woman on duty earlier. He studied her for a space and decided on an approach least likely to arouse suspicion.

"Excuse me."

"Yes?" The girl looked up from a copy of *Teen Spin*.

Chaney consulted his notebook. "Do you remember the date of the Chicago wall? The *first* date—the earliest beginning? I can't pin it down."

The girl stared into the air above his head and said: "I think it was in August...no, no, it was the last week of July. I'm pretty sure it was the last of July." Her gaze came down to his. "We have the news magazines on file if you want me to get it for you."

Chaney caught the hint. "Don't bother; I'll look. Where are those files?"

She pointed behind him. "Fourth aisle, next to the windows. They may not be in chronological order."

"I'll find them. Thank you." Her head was already bending over the magazine as he turned away.

The Chicago wall ran down the middle of Cermak Road.

It stretched from Burnham Park on the lakefront (where it consisted only of barbed wire), westward to Austin Avenue in Cicero (where it finally ended in another loose skein of barbed wire in a white residential neighborhood). The wall was built of cement and cinder blocks; of wrecked or stolen automobiles, burned-out shells of city buses, sabotaged police cars, looted and stripped semi-trailer trucks; of upended furniture, broken concrete, bricks, debris, garbage, excretion. Two corpses were a part of it between Ashland and Paulina Street. The barrier began going up on the night of July twenty-ninth, the third night of widespread rioting along Cermak Road; it was lengthened and reinforced every night thereafter as the idea spread until it was a fifteen mile barricade cutting a city in two.

The black community south of Cermak Road had begun the wall at the height of the rioting, as a means of preventing the passage of police and fire vehicles. Both blacks and belligerent whites completed it. The corpses near Paulina Street had been foolish men who attempted to cross it.

There was no traffic over the wall, nor through it, nor along the north-south arteries intersecting Cermak Road. The Dan Ryan Expressway had been dynamited at 35th Street and again at 63rd Street; the Stevenson Expressway was breached at Pulaski Road. Aerial reconnaissance reported that nearly every major street in the sector was blocked or otherwise unfit for vehicular traffic; fires raged unchecked on South Halsted, and cattle had been loosed from their pens in the stockyards. Police and Army troops patrolled the city above the wall, while black militants patrolled below it. The government made no effort to penetrate the barrier, but instead appeared to be playing a waiting game. Rail and highway traffic from the east and south was routed in a wide swing around the zone, entering the city above the wall to the west; civilian air traffic was restricted to higher elevations. Road blocks were thrown up at the Indiana line, and along Interstate 80.

Chicago above the wall counted three hundred dead and two thousand-plus injured during the rioting and the building of the barricade. No one knew the count below the wall.

By the second week of August, troops had encircled the affected area and had dug in for a siege; none but authorized personnel were permitted to enter and none but white refugees were permitted to leave. Incomplete figures placed the number of emerging refugees at about six hundred thousand, although that figure was well below the known white population living in the rebellious zone. Attempts were being made daily—with small success—to rescue white families believed to be still alive in the area. Penetration was not possible from the north but search parties from the western and southern boundaries made several sallies into the area, sometimes working as far north as Midway Airport. Refugees were being relocated to downstate cities in Illinois and Indiana.

North Chicago was under martial law, with a strict dusk-to-dawn curfew. Violators moving on the streets at night were shot on sight and identified the following day, when the bodies could be removed. South Chicago had no curfew but shootings continued day and night.

At the end of October with the election only a week away, the northern half of the city was relatively quiet; firing across the wall under cover of darkness had fallen off to nuisance shooting, but the police and troops had been issued new orders not to fire unless fired upon. City water service into the zone continued but electricity was curtailed.

On the Sunday morning before election, a party of about two hundred unarmed blacks had approached Army lines at Cicero Avenue and asked for sanctuary. They were turned back. Washington announced the siege was effective and was already putting an end to the rebellion. Hunger and pestilence would destroy the wall.

Chaney strode across the room to the newspaper rack.

Thursday morning editions confirmed their projections published the day before: President Meeks had carried all but three states and won reelection by a landslide. A local editorial applauded the victory and claimed it was earned by "the President's masterful handling of the Chicago Confrontation."

Brian Chaney emerged from the library to stand on the steps under a cold November sun. He knew a sense of fear, of confusion—an uncertainty of where to turn. A city police cruiser passed the building, with an armed guardsman riding beside the driver.

Chaney knew why they both stared at him.

**10**

He wandered aimlessly along the street looking in store windows which were not boarded over, and at parked automobiles along the curb. None of the obviously newer cars were much changed from the older models parked ahead and behind; it was a personal satisfaction to see Detroit edging away from the annual model change and back to the more sensible balance of three decades ago.

Chaney stopped by the post office to mail a postcard to an old friend at the Indiana Corporation, and found the cost had climbed to ten cents. (He also made a mental note *not* to tell Katrina. She would probably claim he had fouled up the future.)

A grocery store window was entirely plastered over with enormous posters proclaiming deep price cuts on every item: ten thousand and one cut-rate bargains from wall to wall. Being a curious futurist, he walked in to inspect the bargains. Apples were selling at two for a quarter, bread at forty-five cents a pound loaf, milk at ninety-nine cents a half gallon, eggs at one dollar a dozen, ground beef at a dollar and twenty-nine cents a pound. The beef was well larded with fat. He bent over the meat counter to check the price of his favorite steak and discovered it was two dollars and forty-nine cents a pound. On an impulse, he paid ninety cents for an eight-ounce box of something called *Moon Capsules* and found them to be vitamin-enriched candies in three flavors. The advertising copy on the back panel claimed that NASA fed the capsules to the astronauts living on the moon, for extra jump-jump-jumping power.

The store boasted an innovation that was new to him.

A customers' lounge was fitted out with soft chairs and a large television, and Chaney dropped into a chair to look at the colored glass eye, curious about the programming. He was quickly disappointed. The television offered him nothing but an endless series of commercials featuring the products available in the store; there was no entertainment to break their monotony. He timed the series: twenty-two commercials in forty-four minutes, before an endless tape began repeating itself.

Only one made a lasting impression.

A splendidly beautiful girl with glowing golden skin was stretched out nude on a pink-white cloud; a sensuous cloud of smoke or wisp formed and changed and reformed itself to caress her saffron body with loving tongues of vapor. The girl was smoking a golden cigarette. She lay in dreamy indolence, eyes closed, her thighs sometimes moving with euphoric languor in response to a kiss of cloud. There was no spoken message. At spaced intervals during the two minutes, five words were flashed across the screen beneath the nude: *Go aloft with Golden Marijane.*

Chaney decided the girl's breasts were rather small and flat for his tastes.

He quit the store and returned to his car, finding an overtime parking ticket fastened to the windshield. The fine was two dollars, if paid that same day. Chaney scribbled a note on a page torn from his notebook and put it inside the envelope in lieu of two dollars; the ticket was then dropped into a receptacle fastened to a nearby meter post. He thought the local police would appreciate his thought.

That done, he wheeled out of the lot and retraced his route toward the distant station. The sunset curfew was yet some hours away but he was done with Joliet—nearly done with 1980. It seemed much colder and inhospitable than the temperature would suggest.

A state patrol car parked on the outskirts watched him out of town.

The gatehouse was lighted on the inside and occupied by an officer and two military policemen; they were not the same men who had checked him out earlier in the day but the routine was the same.

"Are you coming on station, sir?"

Chaney looked across the hood of his car at the gate just beyond the bumper. "Yes, I thought I would."

"May I see your pass and identification?"

Chaney gave up the necessary papers. The officer read them twice and studied the photograph affixed to one, then raised his eyes to compare the photograph to the face.

"You have been visiting in Joliet?"

"Yes.'"

"But not Chicago?"

"No."

"Did you acquire weapons while you were off-station?"

"No."

"Very well, sir." He waved to the guard and the gate was opened for him. "Please drive through."

Brian Chaney drove through and steered the car to the parking lot behind the laboratory building. The other two automobiles were absent, as was the shiny quarter marker.

He unloaded the paraphernalia from his pockets and from under his coat, only to realize with dismay that he hadn't taken a single photograph: not one fuzzy picture of a scowling policeman or an industrious sidewalk sweeper. That omission was apt to be received with something less than enthusiasm. Chaney fitted a tape cartridge into the recorder and flipped open his notebook; he thought he could easily fill two or three tapes with an oral report for Katrina and Gilbert Seabrooke. His personal shorthand was brief to the extreme—and unreadable by anyone else—but long experience in the tank enabled him to flesh out a report that was a reasonable summary of the Commerce and Agriculture yearbooks. Facts were freely interspersed with opinions, and figures with educated guesses, until the whole resembled a statistical and footnoted survey of that which Seabrooke wanted: a solid glimpse forward.

On the last tape he repeated all that he remembered from the pages of the Congressional Record, and after a pause asked Katrina if she knew what General Grinnell was doing now? The old boy got around a lot.

Chaney left the gear on the seat and got out of the car to stretch his legs. He looked at the western sky to measure the coming of darkness, and guessed that he had an hour or two before sunset. His watch read 6:38 but it was two hours faster than the clock in the basement; the engineering limit of fifty hours was far away.

The inquisitive futurist decided on a tour.

Walking with an easy stride he followed the familiar route to the barracks but was surprised to find it dark—padlocked. That gave him pause. The building deserted? Was he gone from this place? Moresby, Saltus, himself, gone from the station?

This day, this hour, this *now* was two years after the successful tests of the TDV, two years after the animals had stopped riding into time and men had taken their places; this was two years after the launching of the field trials and the scheduled launch of the Chicago survey. All that work was over and done—mission completed. Wasn't it then reasonable to assume the team was disbanded and returned to their own corners of the world? Moresby, Saltus, himself, now working elsewhere? (Perhaps he should have sent that postcard to himself at Indic.)

Neither Gilbert Seabrooke nor Katrina had ever dropped a hint of future plans for the team; he had assumed they would be disbanded when the Chicago probe was concluded and he hadn't considered staying on. He couldn't imagine himself wanting to stay on. Well— with *one* reservation, of course. He *would* entertain the idea of a probe into the opposite direction: it would be sheer delight to poke and peer and pry into old Palestine before the arrival of the Roman Tenth Legion—well before their arrival.

He found himself on E Street.

The recreation area appeared not to have changed at all. The post theater wasn't yet opened, its parking lot was empty. The officers' club was already brightly lit and filled with music, but the second club nearby for enlisted men was dark and silent. The pool area was closed for the winter and its gate secured by a lock. Chaney peered through the fencing but saw nothing more than a deserted patio and a canvas covering stretched over the pool. The chairs and benches together with the tables and umbrellas had been stored away, leaving nothing but memories clashing with a cold November evening.

He turned away from the fence to begin an aimless wandering about the station. It seemed normal in every respect. Automobiles passed him, most of them going to the commissary; he was the only man on foot. The sound of an aircraft brought his head up, his eyes searching the sky. The plane was not visible—he supposed it was above the thickening cloud cover—but he could follow its passage by the sound; the craft was flying an air corridor between Chicago and St. Louis, a corridor which paralleled the railroad tracks below. In a few minutes it was gone. A drop of moisture struck his upturned face, and then another, the first few flakes of promised snow. The smell of snow had been in the air since morning.

Chaney turned about to retrace his steps.

Three automobiles waited side by side in the parking lot behind the lab. His companions were back, neither of them languishing in a Joliet jail—but he suspected it would be terribly easy to get into jail. Chaney lifted the hood of the nearest car and laid his hand on the motor block. He almost burned the skin from his palm. The hood was snapped shut, and he gathered up the gear from the seat of his own car.

The twin keys were fitted into the locks of the operations door and turned. A bell rang somewhere below as the door eased open.

"Saltus! Hello, down there—Saltus!"

The hurtful sound hit him with near physical impact. The sound was something like a massive rubber band snapped against his eardrums, something like a hammer smashing into a block of compressed air. It struck and rebounded with a tremulous sigh. The vehicle kicked back following its time path to home base. The sound hurt.

Chaney jumped through the door and pulled it shut behind him.

"Saltus?"

A sandy-haired muscular figure stepped through the open doorway of the fallout shelter below.

"Where the hell have *you* been, civilian?"

Chaney went down the steps two or three at a time. Arthur Saltus waited at the bottom with a handful of film.

"Out there—out there," Chaney retorted. "Knocking around this forsaken place, staring through the fences, sniffing at the cracks and peeping in windows. I couldn't find a spoor. I think we're gone from here, Commander—dismissed and departed, the barracks padlocked. I hope we get a decent bonus."

"Civilian, have you been drinking?"

"No—but I could use one. What's in the stores?"

"You've been drinking," Saltus said flatly. "So what happened to you? We looked all over town."

"You didn't look in the library."

"Oh, hell! You would, and we didn't. Research stuff. What did you think of 1980, mister?"

"I don't like it, and I'll be liking it even less when I'm living in it. That milquetoast was reelected and the country is going to hell in a handbasket. A forty-eight state sweep! Did you see the election results?"

"I saw them, and by this time William has passed the news to Seabrooke and Seabrooke is calling the President. He'll celebrate tonight. But *I'm* not going to vote for him, mister—I *know* I didn't vote for him. And if I'm living Stateside then—now—I'm going to choose one of those three states that voted for the other fellow, old What's-his-name, the actor fellow."

"Alaska, Hawaii, and Utah."

"What's Utah like?"

"Dry, lonely, and glowing with radioactivity."

"Make it Hawaii. Will you go back to Florida?"

Chaney shook his head. "I'll feel safer in Alaska."

Quickly: "You didn't get into trouble?"

"No, not at all; I walked softly and carried a sweet smile on my face. I was polite to a mousy librarian. Didn't sass the cops or buy any pork in a grocery store." He laughed at a memory. "But someone will have to explain a parking ticket when they trace the license number back to this station."

Saltus looked his question.

Chaney said: "I got a ticket for overtime parking. It was an envelope affair; I was supposed to put two dollars in the envelope and drop it in a collection box. I didn't. Commander, I struck a blow for liberty. I wrote a note."

Saltus eyed him. "What was in the note?"

"We shall overcome."

Saltus tried to stifle startled laughter, but failed. After a space he said: "Seabrooke will fire you, mister!"

"He won't have the chance. I expect to be far away when 1980 comes. Did you read the papers?"

"Papers! We bought *all* the papers! William grabbed up every new one he could find—and then read his horoscope first. He was down in the mouth; he said the signs were bad—negative." Saltus turned and waved toward newspapers spread out on the workbench. "I was photographing those when you came in. I'd rather copy them than read them onto a tape; I can blow the negs up to life size when we get back—larger than life, if they want them that way."

Chaney crossed to the bench and bent over to scan a page under the camera lens. "I didn't read anything but the election results, and an editorial."

After a moment he said excitedly: "Did you read this? China invaded Formosa—captured it!"

"Get the rest, read the rest of it," Saltus urged him. "That happened weeks ago, and *now* there's hell to pay in Washington. Canada has formally recognized the take-over and is sponsoring a move to kick Formosa out of the United Nations—give the seat to China. There's talk of breaking off diplomatic relations and stationing troops along the Canadian border. Civilian, that will be a real mess! I don't give a damn for diplomats and diplomatic relations, but we need another hostile like we need an earthquake."

Chaney tried to read between the lines. "China *does* need Canadian wheat, and Ottawa *does* like Chinese gold. That's been a thorn in Washington's side for thirty years. Are you a stamp collector?"

"Me? No."

"Not too many years ago, American citizens were forbidden to buy Chinese stamps from Canadian dealers; it was a crime to purchase or possess. Washington was being silly." He fell silent and finished reading the news story. "If these facts are reliable, Ottawa has made a whopping deal; they will deliver enough wheat to feed two or three Chinese provinces. The cash price wasn't made public, and that's significant—China bought more than wheat. Diplomatic recognition and Canadian support for a seat in the United Nations were probably included in the sale contract. That's smart trading, Commander."

"They're damned good shots, too. I told you that. I hate their guts but I don't downgrade them." He flipped a newspaper page and repositioned his camera. "What time did you get in this morning? How come you were early?"

"Arrival was at 7:55. I don't know why."

"Old William was upset, mister. We were supposed to be first but you fouled up the line of seniority."

Chaney said impatiently: "I can't explain it; it just happened. That gyroscope isn't as good as the engineers claimed it to be. Maybe the mercury protons need fixing, recharging or something. Did you hit the target?"

"Dead on. William was three or four minutes off. Seabrooke won't like it, I'll bet."

"I wasn't jumping with joy; I expected to find you and the Major waiting for me. And I wonder now what will happen on a long launch? Can those protons even *find* 2000?

"If they can't, mister, you and me and old William will be wandering around in a fog without a compass; we'll just have to kick backwards and report a scrub."

The camera was moved again and another page copied.

"Hey—did you see the girls?"

"Two librarians. They were sitting down."

"Mister, you missed something good. They wear their hair in a funny way—I can't describe it—and their skirts aren't long enough to cover their sterns. Really, now, in November! Most of them wore long stockings to keep their legs warm while their sterns were freezing, and most of the time the stockings matched their lipstick: red and red, blue and blue, whatever. This year's fad, I guess. Ah, those girls!" He moved the camera and turned a page.

"I talked to them, I took pictures of them, I coaxed a phone number, I took a blond lovely to lunch—it only cost eight dollars for the two of us. That's not too much, everything considered. The people here are just like us, mister. They're friendly, and they speak English. That town was one sweet liberty port!"

"But they should be like us," Chaney protested. "They're only two years away."

"That was a joke, civilian."

"Excuse me."

"Didn't they have jokes in the tank?"

"Of course they did. One of the mathematicians came up with proof that the solar system didn't exist."

Saltus turned around to stare. "Paper proof?"

"Yes. It filled three pages, as I recall. He said that if he faced the east and recited it aloud, everything would go *poof*."

"Well, I hope he doesn't do that; I hope to hell he doesn't make a test run just to see if it works. I've got a special reason." Saltus studied the civilian for a long space. "Mister, do you know how to keep your mouth shut?"

Cautiously: "Yes. Is this a confidence?"

"You can't even tell William, or Katrina."

Chaney was uneasy. "Does it involve me? My work?"

"Nope—you have nothing to do with it, but I want a promise you'll keep quiet, no matter what. *I'm* not going to report it when I go back. It's something to keep."

"Very well. I'll keep it."

Saltus said: "I stopped in at the courthouse and had a look at the records—the vital statistics stuff—your kind of stuff. I found what I was looking for last March, eight months ago." He grinned. "My marriage license."

It was a kick in the stomach. "Katrina?"

"The one and only, the fair Katrina. Mister, I'm a married man! Me, a married man, chasing the girls and even taking one to lunch. Now, how will I explain that?"

Brian Chaney remembered the note found propped against his

camera: it *had* sounded cool, impersonal, even distant. He recalled the padlocked barracks, the emptiness, the air of desertion. He and Major Moresby were gone from this place.

He said: "Let us therefore brace ourselves to our duties, be they favorable or not. John Wesley, I think."

Chaney kept his face turned away to mask his emotions; he suspected the sharp sense of loss was reflected on his face and he didn't care to stumble through an explanation or an evasion. He put away the heavy clothing worn on the outside and then replaced the unused camera and the nylon films. The reels of tape were removed from the recorder, and the recorder put back in the stores. As an afterthought, he replaced the identification papers and the gate pass in the torn envelope—alongside Katrina's note—and propped the envelope on the bench where she would find it.

Saltus had finished his task and was removing film from the copying camera. He had left the newspapers flung over the bench in disarray.

Chaney gathered them up into an orderly pile. When he had finished the housekeeping chore, a right-side-up headline said: JCS DENIED BAIL.

"Who is JCS? What did he do?"

Saltus stared in disbelief. "Damn it, civilian, didn't you do *anything* out there?"

"I didn't bother with the papers."

Incredulously: "What the hell—are you blind? Why do you think the cops were patrolling the town? Why do you think the state guards were riding shotgun?"

"Well—because of that Chicago business. The wall."

"Bigod!" Arthur Saltus stalked across the room to face him, suddenly impatient with his naivete. "No offense, mister, but sometimes I think you never left that ivory tower, that cloud bank in Indiana. You don't seem to know what's going on in the world—you've got your nose buried too deep in those damned old tables. Shape up, Chaney! Shape up before you get washed out." He jabbed a long index finger at the newspapers stacked on the bench. "This country is under martial law. JCS is the Joint Chiefs of Staff. General

Grinnell, General Brandon, Admiral Elstar, the top dogs. They tried to pull a fast one but got caught, they—that French word."

"Which French word?"

"For take-over."

Chaney was stunned. "Coup."

"*That's* the word. Coup. They marched into the White House to arrest the President and the Vice President, they tried to take over the government at gun point. Our own government, mister! You hear about that sort of thing down in South America all the time, but now, right here in *our* country!" Saltus stopped talking and made a visible effort to control himself. After a moment he said again: "No offense, mister. I lost my temper."

Chaney wasn't listening. He was running across the basement room to the stacked newspapers.

It happened not at the White House, but at the Presidential retreat at Camp David.

A power failure blacked out the area shortly before midnight on Monday night, election eve. The President had closed his reelection campaign and flown to Camp David to rest. An emergency lighting system failed to operate and the Camp remained in darkness. Two hundred troops guarding the installation fell back upon the inner ring of defenses according to a prearranged emergency plan, and took up positions about the main buildings occupied by the President, the Vice President, and their aides. They elected not to go underground as there was no indication of enemy action. Admiral Elstar was with the Presidential party, discussing future operations in the South Asian seas.

Thirty minutes after the blackout, Generals Grinnell and Brandon arrived by car and were admitted through the lines. At General Grinnell's command, the troops about-faced and established a ring of quarantine about the buildings; they appeared to be expecting the order. The two generals then entered the main building—with drawn weapons—and informed the President and the Vice President they were under military arrest, together with all civilians in the area. Admiral Elstar joined them and announced that the JCS were taking control of the government for an indefinite period of time; he expressed dissatisfaction with civilian mismanagement of the country and the war effort, and said the abrupt action was forced upon the Joint Chiefs. The President appeared to take the news calmly and offered no resistance; he asked the members of his party to avoid violence and cooperate with the rebellious officers.

The civilians were herded into a large dining room and locked in. As soon as they were alone the aides brought out gas masks which had previously been concealed there; the party donned the masks and crawled under heavy dining tables to wait. Mortar fire was heard outside.

Electric power was restored at just one o'clock. The firing stopped.

FBI agents also wearing masks breached the door from the opposite side and informed the President the rebellion was ended. The Joint Chiefs of Staff and the disloyal troops had been taken under cover of a gas barrage, by an undisclosed number of agents backed by Federal marshals. Casualties among the troops were held to a minimum. The Joint Chiefs were unharmed.

Helicopters ferried the Presidential party back to Washington, where the President requested immediate reactivation of the TV networks to announce the news of the attempted coup and its subsequent failure. Congress was called into an emergency session, and at the request of the President declared the country under martial law. The affair was done.

A White House spokesman admitted that the plot was known well in advance, but refused to reveal the source of the tip. He said the action was allowed to go as far as it did only to ascertain the number and the identities of the troops who supported the Joint Chiefs. The spokesman denied rumors that those troops had been nerve-gassed. He said the plotters were being charged with treason and were being held in separate jails; he would not disclose the locations other than to say they were dispersed away from Washington. The spokesman declined to answer questions regarding the number of FBI agents and Federal marshals involved in the action; he shrugged off unofficial reports that thousands had been mustered.

The only reliable information known was that large numbers of them had lain in concealment about Camp David for several days prior to the action. The spokesman would say only the two groups had courageously rescued the President and his party.

Brian Chaney was unaware that the lights dimmed and the hurtful rubber band smashed against his eardrums; he didn't hear the massive mallet smash into the block of compressed air and then rebound with a soft, oily sigh. He didn't know that Arthur Saltus had left him until he turned around and found himself alone.

Chaney stared around the empty shelter and shouted aloud: "Saltus!"

There was no answer.

He strode to the door and shouted into the corridor. "Saltus!"

Booming echoes, and then silence. The Commander was emerging from the vehicle at home base.

"Listen to the word from the ivory tower, Saltus! Listen to me! What do you want to bet the President didn't risk *his* precious skin under a dining room table? What do you want to bet that he sent a double to Camp David? He's no Greatheart, no Bayard; he couldn't be certain of the outcome." Chaney stepped into the corridor.

"*We* tipped him off, you idiot—*we* passed the word. *We* told him of the plot and of his reelection. Do you really think he has the guts to expose himself? Knowing that he would be reelected the next day for another four-year ride? Do you think that, Saltus?"

Monitoring cameras looked at him under bright lights.

In the closed-off operations room, the TDV came back for him with an explosive burst of air.

Chaney turned on his heel and walked into the shelter. The newspapers were stacked, the gear was stored away, the clothing was neatly hung on racks. He had arrived and was preparing to leave with scarcely a trace of his passage.

The torn envelope caught his eye—the instructions from Katrina, and his identification papers, his gate pass. Cool, impersonal, distant—impassive, reserved. The wife of Arthur Saltus giving him last minute instructions for the field trial. She still lived on station; she still worked for the Bureau and the secret project—and unless the Commander had been reassigned to the war theater he was living with her.

But the barracks were dark, padlocked.

Brian Chaney knew the strong conviction that he was gone—that he and the Major had left the station. He didn't believe in crystal balls, in clairvoyance, hunches, precognition—Major Moresby could have all that claptrap to add to his library of phony prophets, but this one conviction was deeply fixed in his mind.

He was not *here* in November, 1980.

Chaney sensed a subtle change in relationships. It was nothing he could clearly identify, mark, pin down, but a shade of difference was there.

Gilbert Seabrooke had sponsored a victory party on the night of their return, and the President telephoned from the White House to offer his congratulations on a good job well done. He spoke of an award, a medal to convey the grateful appreciation of a nation—even though the nation could not be informed of the stunning breakthrough. Brian Chaney responded with a polite *thank you*, and held his tongue. Seabrooke hovered nearby, watchful and alert.

The party wasn't as successful as it might have been. Some indefinable element of spontaneity was missing, some elusive spark which, when struck, changes over an ordinary party into a memorable evening of pleasure. Chaney would remember the celebration, but not with heady delight. He passed over the champagne in favor of bourbon, but drank that sparingly. Major Moresby seemed withdrawn, troubled, brooding over some inner problem, and Chaney guessed he was already preoccupied with the startling power struggle which was yet two years away. Moresby had made a stiff, awkward little speech of thanks to the President, striving to assure him without words of his continued loyalty. Chaney was embarrassed for him.

Arthur Saltus danced. He monopolized Katrina, even to the point of ignoring her whispered suggestions that he give unequal time to Chaney and the Major. Chaney didn't want to cut in. On another evening, another party before the field trials, he could have cut in as often as he dared, but now he sensed the same subtle change in Kathryn van Hise which was sensed in the others. The mountain of information brought back from Joliet, November 1980, had altered many viewpoints and the glossy overlay of the party could not conceal that alteration.

There was a stranger at the party, the liaison agent dispatched by the Senate subcommittee. Chaney discovered the man surreptitiously watching him.

The briefing room offered the familiar tableau.

Major Moresby was again studying a map of the Chicago area. He used a finger to mark the several major routes and backroads between Joliet and the metropolis; the finger also traced the rail line through the Chicago suburbs to the Loop. Arthur Saltus was studying the photographs he'd brought back from Joliet. He seemed particularly pleased with a print of an attractive girl standing on a windy street corner, half watching the cameraman and half watching for a car or a bus coming along the street behind. The print revealed an expert's hand in composition and cropping, with the girl limned in sunny backlighting.

Kathryn van Hise said: "Mr. Chaney?"

He swung around to face her. "Yes, Miss van Hise?"

"The engineers have given me firm assurance *that* mistake will not happen again. They have used the time since your return to rebuild the gyroscope. The cause has been traced to a vacuum leakage but that has been repaired. The error is to be regretted, but it will not happen again."

"But I *like* getting there first," he protested. "That's the only way I can assert seniority."

"It will not happen again, sir."

"Maybe. How do they *know* it won't?"

Katrina studied him.

"The next targets will each be a year apart, sir, to obtain a wider coverage. Would you care to suggest a tentative date?"

He betrayed surprise. "We may choose?"

"Within reason, sir. Mr. Seabrooke has invited each of you to suggest an appropriate date. The original plan of the survey must be followed, of course, but he would welcome your ideas. If you would rather not suggest a date, Mr. Seabrooke and the engineers will select one."

Chaney looked down the table at Major Moresby.

"What did you take?"

Promptly: "The Fourth of July, 1999."

"Why that one?"

"It has significance, after all!"

"I suppose so." He turned to Saltus. "And you?"

"My birthday, civilian: November 23rd, 2000. A nice round number, don't you think? I thought so anyway. That will be my fiftieth birthday, and I can't think of a better way to celebrate." His voice dropped to a conspiratorial whisper. "I might take a jug with me. Live it up!"

Chaney considered the possibilities.

Saltus broke in. "Now, look here, mister—don't tell Seabrooke you want to visit Jericho on the longest day of summer, ten thousand years ago! *That* will get you the boot right through the front gate. Play by the rules. How would you like to spend Christmas in 2001? New Year's Eve?"

"No."

"Party-pooper. Wet blanket. What do you want?"

"I really don't care. Anything will do."

"Pick *something*," Saltus urged.

"Oh, just say 2000-plus. It doesn't much matter."

Katrina said anxiously: "Mr. Chaney, is something wrong?"

"Only that," he said, and indicated the photographs heaped on the table before Arthur Saltus, the new packets of mimeographed papers neatly stacked before each chair. "The future isn't very attractive right now."

"Do you wish to withdraw?"

"*No.* I'm not a quitter. When do we go up?"

"The launch is scheduled for the day after tomorrow. You will depart at one-hour intervals."

Chaney shuffled the papers on the table. "I suppose these will have to be studied now. We'll have to follow up."

"Yes, sir. The information you have developed on the trials has now become a part of the survey, and it is desirable that each segment be followed to its conclusion. We wish to know the final solutions, of course, and so you must trace these new developments." She hesitated. "*Your* role in the survey has been somewhat modified, sir."

He was instantly wary, suspicious. "In what way?"

"You will not go into Chicago."

"Not—But what the hell *am* I supposed to do?"

"You may visit any other city within range of your fifty-hour limit: Elgin, Aurora, Joliet, Bloomington, the city of your choice, but Chicago is now closed to you."

He stared at the woman, knowing humiliation. "But this is ridiculous! The problem may be cleared away, all but forgotten twenty-two years from now."

"It will not be forgotten so easily, sir. It *will* be wise to observe every precaution. Mr. Seabrooke has decided you may not enter Chicago."

"I'll resign—I'll quit!"

"Yes, sir, you may do that. The Indic contract will be returned to you."

"I *won't* quit!" he said angrily.

"As you wish."

Saltus broke in. "Civilian—sit down."

Chaney was surprised to discover himself standing. He sat down, knowing a mixture of frustration and humbled pride. He knotted his fingers together in his lap and pressed until they hurt.

After a space he said: "I'm sorry. I apologize."

"Apology accepted," Saltus agreed easily. "And don't let it trouble you. Seabrooke knows what he's doing—he doesn't want you naked and shivering in some Chicago jail, and he *doesn't* want some damned fool chasing you with a gun."

Major Moresby was eyeing him.

"I don't quite read you, Chaney. You've got more guts than I suspected, or you're a damned fool."

"When I lose my temper I'm a damned fool. I can't help myself." He felt Katrina watching him and turned back to her. "What am I supposed to do up there?"

"Mr. Seabrooke wishes you to spend the greater part of your time in a library copying pertinent information. You will be equipped with a camera having a copying lens when you emerge on target; your specific assignment is to photograph those books and periodicals which are germane to the information discovered in Joliet."

"You want me to follow the plots and the wars and the earthquakes through history. Make a copy of everything—steal a history book if I have to."

"You may purchase one, sir, and copy the pages in the room downstairs."

"That sounds exciting. A really wild visit to the future. Why not bring back the book with me?"

She hesitated. "I will have to ask Mr. Seabrooke. It seems reasonable, if you compensate for the weight."

"Katrina, I want to go outside and see *something*—I don't want to spend the time in a hole."

She said again: "You may visit any other city within range of your fifty-hour limit, sir. If it is safe."

Morosely: "I wonder what Bloomington is like."

"Girls!" Saltus answered. "One sweet liberty port!"

"Have you been there?"

"No."

"Then what are you talking about?"

"Just trying to cheer you up, civilian. I'm helpful that way." He picked up the photograph of the girl on the Joliet street corner and waggled it between thumb and forefinger. "Go up in the summertime. It's nicer then."

Chaney looked at him with a particular memory in the front of his mind. Saltus caught it and actually blushed. He dropped the photograph and betrayed his fleeting guilt by sneaking a sidelong glance at Katrina.

She said: "We hope for a thorough coverage, sir."

"I wish I had more than fifty hours in a library. A decent research job requires several weeks, even months."

"It may be possible to return again and again, at proper intervals of course. I will ask Mr. Seabrooke."

Saltus: "Hey—what about that, Katrina? So what happens *after* the survey? What do we do next?"

"I can't give you a meaningful answer, Commander. At this point in the operation nothing beyond the Chicago probe is programmed. Nothing more could be programmed until we knew the outcome of these first two steps. A final answer cannot be made until you return from Chicago."

"Do you *think* we'll do something else?"

"I would imagine that other probes will be prepared when this one is satisfactorily completed and the resultant data analyzed." But then she added a hasty postscript. "That is only my opinion, Commander. Mr. Seabrooke has said nothing of possible future operations."

"I like your opinion, Katrina. It's better than a bucket in the South China Sea."

Chaney asked: "What happened to the alternatives? To Jerusalem, and Dallas?"

Moresby broke in. "What's this?"

The young woman explained them to Moresby and Saltus. Chaney realized that only he had been told of both alternate programs, and he wondered now if he had let a cat out of the bag by mentioning them.

Katrina said: "The alternatives are being held in abeyance; they may never be implemented." She looked at Brian Chaney and paused. "The engineers are studying a new matter related to vehicle operations; there appears to be a question whether the vehicle may operate in reverse prior to the establishment of a power source."

"Hey—what's *that* in English?"

"It means I can't go back to old Jericho," Chaney told him. "No electricity back there. I *think* she said the TDV needs power all along the line to move anywhere."

Moresby: "But I understood you to say those test animals had been sent back a year or more?"

"Yes, sir, that is correct, but the nuclear reactor has been operating for more than two years. The previous lower limit of the TDV was December 30, 1941, but now that may have to be drastically revised. If it is found that the vehicle may not operate prior to the establishment of its power source, the lower limit will be brought forward to an arbitrary date of two years ago. We do not wish to lose the vehicle."

Chaney said: "One of those bright engineers should sit down to his homework—lay out a paradox graph, or map, or whatever. Katrina, if you keep this thing going, you're going to find yourself up against a wall sooner or later."

She colored and betrayed a minute hesitation before answering him. "The Indiana Corporation has been approached on the matter, sir. Mr. Seabrooke has proposed that all our data be turned over to them for a crash study. The engineers are becoming aware of the problems."

Saltus looked around at Chaney and said: "Sheeg!"

Chaney grinned and thought to offer an apology to Moresby and the woman. "That's an old Aramaic word. But it expresses my feelings quite adequately." He considered the matter. "I can't decide what I would rather do: stay here and make paradoxes, or go back there and solve them."

Saltus said: "Tough luck, civilian. I was almost ready to volunteer. *Almost*, I said. I *think* I'd like to stand on the city wall at Larsa with you and watch the Euphrates flood; I *think* I'd like—What?"

"The city wall at Ur, not Larsa."

"Well, wherever it was. A flood, anyway, and you said it got into the Bible. You have a smooth line, you *could* persuade me to go along." An empty gesture. "But I guess that's all washed out now—you'll never go back."

"I don't believe the White House would authorize a probe back that far," Chaney answered. "They would see no political advantage to it, no profit to themselves."

Major Moresby said sharply: "Chaney, you sound like a fool!"

"Perhaps. But if we *could* probe backward I'd be willing to lay you money on certain political targets, but nothing at all on others. What would the map of Europe be like if Attila had been strangled in his crib?"

"Chaney, after all!"

He persisted. "What would the map of Europe be like if Lenin had been executed for the anti-Czarist plot instead of his older brother? What would the map of the United States be like if George the Third had been cured of his dementia? If Robert E. Lee had died in infancy?"

"Civilian, they sure as hell won't let you go back *anywhere* with notions like that."

Dryly: "I wouldn't expect a bonus for them."

"Well, I guess not!"

Kathryn van Hise stepped into the breach.

"Please, gentlemen. Appointments have been made for your final physical examinations. I will call the doctor and inform him you are coming now."

Chaney grinned and snapped his fingers. "*Now.*"

She turned. "Mr. Chaney, if you will stay behind for a moment I would like more information on your field data."

Saltus was quickly curious. "Hey—what's this?"

She paged through the pile of mimeographed papers until she found the transcript of Chaney's tape recording. "Some parts of this report need further evaluation. If you care to dictate, Mr. Chaney, I will take it in shorthand."

He said: "Anything you need."

"Thank you." A half turn to the others at the table. "The doctor will be waiting, gentlemen."

Moresby and Saltus pushed back their chairs. Saltus shot Chaney a warning glance, reminding him of a promise. The reminder was answered with a confirming nod.

The men left the briefing room.

Brian Chaney looked across the table at Katrina in the silence they left behind. She waited quietly, her fingers laced together on the table top.

He remembered her bare feet in the sand, the snug delta pants, the see-through blouse, the book she carried in her hand and the disapproving expression she wore on her face. He remembered the startlingly brief swim suit worn in the pool, and the way Arthur Saltus had monopolized her.

"That was rather transparent, Katrina."

She studied him longer, not yet ready to speak. He waited for her to offer the next word, holding in his mind the image of that first glimpse of her on the beach.

At length: "What happened up there, Brian?"

He blinked at the use of his given name. It was the first time she had used it.

"Many, many things—I think we covered it all in our reports."

Again: "What happened up there, Brian?"

He shook his head. "Seabrooke will have to be satisfied with the reports."

"This is not Mr. Seabrooke's matter."

Warily: "I don't know what else I can tell you."

"Something happened up there. I am aware of a departure from the norm that prevailed before the trials, and I think you are too. Something has created a disparity, a subtle disharmony which is rather difficult to define."

"The Chicago wall, I suppose. And the JCS revolt."

"They were shocks to us all, but what else?"

Chaney gestured, searching for an escape route. "I found the barracks closed, locked. I think the Major and myself have left the station."

"But not Commander Saltus?"

"He may be gone—I don't know."

"You don't seem very sure of that."

"I'm not sure of anything. We were forbidden to open doors, look at people, ask questions. I didn't open doors. I know only that our barracks have been closed—and I don't think Seabrooke let us move in with him."

"What would you have done if it was permissible to open doors?"

Chaney grinned. "I'd go looking for you."

"You believe I was on the station?"

"Certainly! You wrote notes to each of us—you left final instructions for us in the room downstairs. I knew your handwriting."

Hesitation. "Did you find similar evidence of anyone else being on station?"

Carefully: "No. Your note was the only scrap."

"Why has the Commander's attitude changed?"

Chaney stared at her, almost trapped. "Has it?"

"I think you are aware of the difference."

"Maybe. Everybody looks at me in a new light. I'm feeling paranoiac these days."

"Why has your attitude changed?"

"Oh? Mine too?"

"You are fencing with me, Brian."

"I've told you everything I *can* tell you, Katrina."

Her laced fingers moved restlessly on the tabletop. "I sense certain mental reservations."

"Sharp girl."

"Was there some—some personal tragedy up there? Involving any one of you?"

Promptly: "No." He smiled at the woman across the table to rob his next words of any sting. "And, Katrina—if you are wise, if you are very wise, you won't ask any more questions. I hold certain mental reservations; I *will* evade certain questions. Why not stop now?"

She looked at him, frustrated and baffled.

He said: "When this survey is completed I want to leave. I'll do whatever is necessary to complete the work when we return from the probe, but then I'm finished. I'd like to go back to Indic, if that's possible; I'd like to work on the new paradox study, if that's permissible, but I don't want to stay here. I'm finished here, Katrina."

Quickly: "Is it because of something you found up there? Has something turned you away, Brian?"

"Ah— No more questions."

"But you leave me so unsatisfied!"

Chaney stood up and fitted the empty chair to the table. "Every thing comes to every man, if he but has the years. That sounds like Talleyrand, but I'm not sure. *You* have the years, Katrina. Live through just two more of them and you'll know the answers to all your questions. I wish you luck, and I'll think of you often in the tank—if they'll let me back in."

A moment of silence, and then: "Please don't forget your doctor's appointment, Mr. Chaney."

"I'm on my way."

"Ask the others to be here at ten o'clock in the morning for a final briefing. We must evaluate these reports. The probe is scheduled for the day after tomorrow."

"Are you coming downstairs to see us off?"

"No, sir. I will wait for you here."

## 12

DUMAH, BEWARE!
SOMEONE IS CRYING OUT TO ME FROM SEIR,
WATCHMAN, HOW MUCH OF THE NIGHT IS GONE?
WATCHMAN, HOW MUCH OF THE NIGHT IS GONE?
THE WATCHMAN SAID:
MORNING COMES, AND NIGHT AGAIN TOO.
IF YOU WOULD KNOW MORE
COME BACK, COME BACK, AND ASK ANEW.

—THE FIRST BOOK OF ISAIAH

Moresby was methodical.

The red light blinked out. He reached up to unlock the hatch and throw it open. The green light went dark. Moresby grasped the two handrails and pulled himself to a sitting position, with his head and shoulders protruding through the hatchway. He was alone in the lighted room, as he expected to be. The air was cool and smelled of ozone. Moresby struggled out of the hatch and climbed over the side; the stepstool was missing as he slid down the hull to the floor. He reached up to slam shut the hatch, then quickly turned to the locker for his clothing. Two other suits belonging to Saltus and Chaney also hung there in paper sheaths waiting to be claimed. He noted the locker had collected a fine coat of dust. When he was fully dressed, he smoothed out the imaginary wrinkles in the Air Force dress uniform he had elected to wear.

Moresby checked his watch: 10:05. He sought out the electric calendar and clock on the wall to verify the date and time: *4 July 99*.

The clock read 4:10, off six hours from his launching time. Temperature was an even 70 degrees.

Moresby decided the clock was in error, he would rely on his watch. His last act before leaving the room was to direct a smart salute toward the twin lenses of the monitoring cameras. He thought that would be appreciated by those on the other side of the wall.

Moresby strode down the corridor in eerie silence to the shelter; fine dust on the floor was kicked up by his feet. The shelter door was pushed open and the overhead lights went on in automatic response. He stared around, inspecting everything. There was no ready evidence that anyone had used the shelter in recent years; the stores were as neatly stacked as he had found them during his last inspection. Moresby lit a gasoline lantern to check its efficiency after so long a time; he watched its steady flame with satisfaction and then put it out. The supplies were dependable, after all. As an afterthought, he broke open a container of water to sample the quality: it tasted rather flat, insipid. But that was to be expected if the water had not been replaced this year. He considered that something of an oversight.

Three yellow cartons rested on the work bench—cartons which had not been there before.

He opened the first box and found a bullet-proof vest made from some unfamiliar nylon weave. The presence of the vests on the bench was significant. He slipped out of his military jacket only long enough to don the vest and then turned to work.

Moresby chose a tape recorder, inserted a cartridge, tested the machine, and crisply recorded those observations made thus far: the stepstool was missing, the basement had collected dust, the water had not been refreshed, the clock-time of his arrival was off six hours and five minutes. He did not offer personal opinions on any observation. The recorder was put aside on the bench. His next act was to select a radio, connect the leads of the exterior antenna to the terminal screws on the chassis, and plug it into a wall socket. The tape recorder was moved to within easy listening distance and turned on. Moresby snapped on the radio and tuned in a military channel.

Voice: "...moving around the northwest corner in a southerly direction—moving toward you. Estimated strength, twelve to fifteen men. Watch them, Corporal, they're packing mortars. Over." The sound of gunfire was loud behind the voice.

Voice: "Roger. We've got a hole in the fence at the northwest—some bastard tried to put a truck through. It's still burning, maybe that'll stop them. Over."

Voice: "You *must* hold them, Corporal. I can't send you any men—we have a double red here. Out."

The channel fell silent, closing off the firefight.

Moresby was not given to panic or reckless haste. Feeling little surprise, he began methodically to equip himself for the target. An Army-issue automatic, together with its belt and extra ammunition, was strapped around his waist; he selected a rapid-fire rifle after examining its make and balance, then emptied several boxes of cartridges in his jacket pockets. All insignia marking him an officer were removed from his uniform, but there was little he could do now about the uniform itself.

The stores offered him no battle helmets or liners. Moresby slung a canteen of the insipid water over his shoulder and a pack of rations across his back. He decided against the tape recorder because of its extra bulk, but reached for the radio as he studied a map of Illinois. A sudden hunch told him the skirmish would be somewhere near Chicago; the Air Force had long been worried about the defense of that city because it was the hub of railroad and highway traffic—and there was the always-threatening problem of foreign shipping traversing the Great Lakes to tie up at Chicago ports. Surveillance of that shipping had always been inadequate.

He was reaching out to disconnect the antenna when the channel came alive.

Voice: "Eagle One! The bandits have hit us—hit us at the northwest corner. I count twelve of them, spread out over the slope below the fence. They've got two—damn it!—two mortars and they're lobbing them in. Over." The harsh, half-shrieking voice was punctuated by the dull thump of mortar fire.

Voice: "Have they penetrated the fence? Over."

Voice: "Negative—negative. That burning truck is holding them. I think they'll try some other way—blow a hole in the fence if they can. Over."

Voice: "*Hold* them, Corporal. They are a diversion; we have the main attack here. Out."

Voice: "Damn it, Lieutenant—" Silence.

Moresby reached again for the leads to sever the radio from the topside antenna, but was stopped by an idea. He switched to an alternate military channel, one of six on the instrument, and punched the *send* button.

"Moresby, Air Force Intelligence, calling Chicago or the Chicago area. Come in, Chicago."

The channel remained silent. He repeated himself, waited impatiently for the sweep hand of his watch to make a full circle, and then made a third attempt. There was no response. Another military channel was selected.

"Moresby, Air Force Intelligence, calling Chicago or the Chicago area. Come in please."

The radio crackled with static or small arms fire. A weak voice, dimmed by distance or a faulty power supply: "Nash here. Nash here, west of Chicago. Use caution. Come in, Moresby. Over."

He stepped up the gain. "Major William Moresby, Air Force Intelligence on special duty. I am trying to reach Joliet or Chicago. Please advise the situation. Over."

Voice: "Sergeant Nash, sir, Fifth Army, HQ Company. Chicago negative, repeat negative. Avoid, avoid. You can't get in there, sir— the lake is hot. Over."

Moresby was startled. "*Hot?* Please advise. Over."

Voice: "Give me your serial number, sir."

Moresby rattled it off, and repeated his question.

Voice: "Yes, sir. The ramjets called in a Harry on the city. We're pretty certain they called it in, but the damned thing fell short and dropped into the lake off Glencoe. You can't go in anywhere there, sir. The city has been fired, and that lake water sprayed everything for miles up and down the shoreline. It's *hot*, sir. We're picking up civilian casualties coming out, but there isn't much we can do for them. Over."

Moresby: "Did you get your troops out? Over."

Voice: "Yes, sir. The troops have pulled back and established a new perimeter. I can't say where. Over."

A wash of static rattled the small speaker.

Moresby wished desperately for fuller information, but he knew better than to reveal his ignorance by asking direct questions. The request for his serial number had warned him the distant voice was suspicious, and had he stumbled over the number contact would have been lost. It suggested these radio channels were open to the enemy.

Moresby: "Are you certain those devils called in the Harry? Over."

Voice: "Yes, sir, reasonably certain. Border Patrol uncovered a relay station in Nuevo Leon, west of Laredo. They think they've found another one in Baja California, a big station capable of putting a signal overseas. Navy pinned down a launching complex at Tienpei. Over."

Moresby, fuming: "Damn them! We can expect more of the same if Navy doesn't take it out quickly. Do you know the situation at Joliet? Over."

Voice: "Negative, sir. We've had no recent reports from the south. What is your location? Be careful in your answer, sir. Over."

Moresby took the warning. "Approximately eight miles out of Joliet. I am well protected at the moment. I've heard mortar fire but haven't been able to locate it. I think I will try for the city, Sergeant. Over."

Voice: "Sir, we've taken a fix on you and believe we *know* your location. You are very well protected there. You have a strong signal. Over."

Moresby: "I have electricity here but I will be on battery when I leave cover. Over."

Voice: "Right, sir. If Joliet is closed to you, the O.D. suggests that you circle around to the northwest and come in here. Fifth Army HQ has been reestablished west of the Naval Training Station, but you'll pass through our lines long before that point. Look for the sentries. Use care, sir. Be alert for ramjets between your position and ours. They are heavily armed. Over."

Moresby: "Thank you, Sergeant. I'll go for the target of opportunity. Over and out."

Moresby snapped off the radio and disconnected the leads. That done, he turned off the tape recorder and left it on the bench for his return.

He studied the map once again, tracing the two roads which led to the highway and the alternate highway into Joliet. The enemy would be well aware of those roads, as well as the railroad, and if their action reached this far south they would have patrols out. It wouldn't be safe to use an automobile; large moving targets invited trouble.

A last searching examination of the room gave him no other article he thought he would need. Moresby took a long drink of water from the stores and quit the shelter. The corridor was dusty and silent, yet bright under lights and the monitoring cameras. He eyed the closed doors along the passageway, wondering who was behind them—watching. Obeying orders, he didn't so much as touch a knob to learn if they were locked. The corridor ended and a flight of stairs led upward to the operations exit. The painted sign prohibiting the carrying of arms beyond the door had been defaced: a large slash of black paint was smeared from the first sentence to the last, half obliterating the words and voiding the warning. He would have ignored it in any event.

Moresby again noted the time on his watch and fitted the keys into first one lock and then the other. A bell rang below him as he pushed out into the open air.

The northeast horizon was bright with the approaching dawn. It was ten minutes before five in the morning. The parking lot was empty.

He knew he had made a mistake.

The first and second sounds he heard were the booming thump of the mortar to the northwest, and a staccato tattoo of small arms fire near at hand—near the eastern gate. Moresby slammed shut the door behind him, made sure it had locked itself, and fell to the ground all in one blurring motion. The nearness of the battle was a shock. He pushed the rifle out in front of his face and crawled toward the corner of the building, searching for any moving object.

He saw no moving thing in the space between the lab building and the nearest structure across the way. Firing was louder as he reached the corner and rounded it.

A strong wind drove over the roof of the laboratory, blowing debris along the company street and bowing the tops of the trees planted along the thoroughfare. The wind seemed to be coming from everywhere, from every direction, moaning with a mounting intensity as it raced toward the northeast. Moresby stared that way with growing wonder and knew he'd made another mistake in guessing the coming dawn. That was not the sun. The red-orange brightness beyond the horizon was fire and the raging wind told him Chicago was being caught up in an enormous firestorm. When it grew worse, when steel melted and glass liquefied, a man would be unable to stand upright against the great inward rush of the feeding winds.

Moresby searched the street a second time, searched the parking lot, then jumped suddenly to his feet and ran across the street to the safety of the nearest building. No shot followed him. He hugged the foundation wall, turned briefly to scan his back trail, and darted around a corner. Shrubbery offered a partial concealment. When he stopped to catch his breath and reconnoiter the open yard ahead, he discovered he had lost the military radio.

The continued booming of the mortars worried him.

It was easy to guess the Corporal's guard holding the northwest corner was outnumbered, and probably pinned down. The first voice on the radio said *he* had a hell of a fight on his hands—"double red" was new terminology but quickly recognizable—down there near the gate or along the eastern perimeter, and men could not be spared for the defense of the northwestern corner. A wrong decision. Moresby thought that officer guilty of a serious error in judgment. He could hear light rifle fire at the gate—punctuated at intervals by a shotgun, suggesting civilians were involved in the skirmish—but those mortars were pounding the far corner of the station and they made a deadly difference.

Moresby left the concealing shrubbery on the run. There had been no other activity about the laboratory, no betraying movement of invader or defender.

He moved north and west, taking advantage of whatever cover offered itself, but occasionally sprinting along the open street to gain time—always watchfully alert for any other moving man. Moresby was painfully aware of the gap in intelligence: he didn't know the identity of the bandits, the ramjets, didn't know friend from foe save for the uniform he might be wearing. He knew better than to trust a man without uniform inside the fence: shotguns were civilian weapons. He supposed this damned thing was some civil uprising.

The mortar fired again, followed by a second shell. If that pattern repeated itself, they were side by side working in pairs. Moresby fell into a jogging trot to hold his wind. He worried about the Chinese thrust, about the Harry called in on Chicago. Who would bring *them* in on an American city? Who would ally himself with the Chinese?

In a surprisingly short time he passed a series of old barracks set back from the street, and recognized one of them as the building he had lived in for a few weeks—some twenty-odd years ago. It now appeared to be in a sorry state. He jogged on without pause, following the sidewalk he'd sometimes used when returning from the mess hall. The hot wind rushed with him, overtaking him and half propelling him along his way. That fire over the horizon was feeding on the wind, on the debris being sucked into it.

On a vagrant impulse—and because it lay in his direction—Moresby turned sharply to cut across a yard to E Street: the swimming pool was near at hand. He glanced at the sky and found it appreciably lighter: the real dawn was coming, bringing promise of a hot July day.

Moresby gained the fence surrounding the patio and the pool and stopped running, because his breath was spent. Cautiously, rifle ready, he moved through the entranceway to probe the interior. The recreation area was deserted. Moresby walked over to the tiled rim and looked down: the pool was drained, the bottom dry and littered with debris—it had not been used this summer. He expelled a breath of disappointment. The next to last time he'd seen the pool—only a few days ago, after all, despite those twenty years—Katrina had played in the blue-green water wearing that ridiculous little suit, while Art had chased her like a hungry rooster, wanting to keep his hands on her body. A nice body, that. Art knew what he was doing. And Chaney sat on the sun deck, mooning over the woman—the civilian lacked the proper initiative; wouldn't fight for what he wanted.

The mortars boomed again in the familiar one-two pattern. Moresby jumped, and spun around.

Outside the patio fence he saw the automobile parked at the curb a short distance up the street, and cursed his own myopic planning.

The northwest corner was a mile or more away, an agonizing distance when on foot.

Moresby stopped in dismay at sight of the dashboard.

The car was a small one—painted the familiar olive drab—more closely resembling the German beetle than a standard American compact, but its dash was nearly bare of ornament and instrument controls. There was no key, only a switch indicating the usual on-off positions; the vehicle had an automatic drive offering but three options: park, reverse, forward. A toggle switch for headlights, another for the windshield wipers completed the instrument cluster.

Moresby slid in under the wheel and turned the switch on. A single idiot light blinked at him briefly and stayed out. Nothing else happened. He pushed the selector lever deeper into park, flicked the switch off and on again, but without result other than a repetitious blinking of the idiot light. Cursing the balky car, he yanked at the lever—pulling it into forward—and the car quickly shot away from the curb. Moresby fought the wheel and kicked hard on the brake, but not before the vehicle had ricocheted off the opposite curb and dealt a punishing blow to his spine. It came to a skidding stop in the middle of the street, throwing his chest against the wheel. There had been no audible sound of motor or machinery in motion.

He stared down at the dashboard in growing wonder and realized he had an electric vehicle. Easing off on the brake, he allowed the car to gather forward momentum and seek its own speed. This time it did not appear to move as fast, and he went down gently on the accelerator. The car responded, silently and effortlessly.

Moresby gunned it, running for the northwest fence. Behind him, the rattle of gunfire around the gate seemed to have lessened.

The truck was still burning. A column of oily black smoke climbed into the early morning sky.

Major Moresby abandoned the car and leaped for the ground when he was within fifty yards of the perimeter. A second hole had been torn in the fence, blasted by short mortar fire, and in his first quick scan of the area he saw the bodies of two aggressors sprawled in the same opening. They wore civilian clothing—dirty shirts and levis— and the only mark of identification visible on either corpse was a ragged yellow armband. Moresby inched toward the fence, seeking better information.

The mortar was so near he heard the cough before the explosion. Moresby dug his face into the dirt and waited. The shell landed somewhere behind him, up slope, throwing rocks and dirt into the sky; debris pelted the back of his neck and fell on his unprotected head. He held his position, frozen to the ground and waiting stolidly for the second mortar to fire.

It never fired.

After a long moment he raised his head to stare down the slope beyond the ruptured fence. The slope offered poor shelter, and the enemy had paid a high price for that disadvantage: seven bodies were scattered over the terrain between the fence and a cluster of tree stumps two hundred yards below. Each of those bodies was dressed alike: street clothing, and a yellow band worn on the left arm.

Ramjets.

Moresby slid his gaze away to study the terrain.

The land sloped gently away from his own position and away from the protective fence, dropping down two hundred yards before leveling off into tillable area. Flat land at the bottom looked as though it had been plowed in the spring, but no crop grew there now. A billboard stood at the base of the slope looking toward the main line of the Chicago and Mobile Southern Railroad, another five hundred yards beyond the plowed area. Thirty yards north of the billboard and five yards higher up the slope was a cluster of seven or eight tree stumps that had been uprooted from the soil and dumped to one side out of the way; the farmer had cleared his tillable area but hadn't yet burned the unwanted stumps. The wheel marks of an invading truck showed clearly on the field.

Moresby studied the billboard and then the stumps. If he were directing the assault he would place a mortar behind each one; they were the only available cover.

Moving cautiously, he brought up the rifle and put two quick shots through the billboard near its bottom. Another two shots followed, biting into the tall grass and weeds immediately below the board. He heard a shout, a cry of sudden pain, and saw a man leap from the weeds to run for the stumps. The bandit staggered as he ran, holding pain in his thigh.

He was a soft target. Moresby waited, leading him.

When the running man was just halfway between the billboard and the nearest stump, he fired once—high, aiming for the chest. The falling body tumbled forward under its own headlong momentum and crashed to earth short of the stump.

The cough of the mortar was a grotesque echo.

Moresby delayed for a second—no more—and thrust his face into the dirt. There had been a furtive movement behind the stumps. The shell burst behind him, striking metal now instead of dirt, and he spun around on his belly to see the electric car disintegrate. Direct hit. Fragments rained down on him and he threw up his hands to protect his head and the back of his neck. His fingers stung.

The rain stopped. Moresby sat up and threw an angry brace of shots at the stumps, wanting to put the fear of God into the mortarman. He fell back quickly to await the cough of the second mortar. It did not come. A stillness; other than the headlong rush of the wind and the tiny sound of sporadic firing at the main gate. Moresby felt a sudden heady elation: that back-up mortar was out of action. *One down.* Deliberately sitting up, deliberately taking aim, he emptied the rifle at the offending tree stumps. There was no answering fire, despite the target he offered. He had nothing more than a mortar to contend with—a mortar manned by a civilian. A poor goddamned civilian.

Moresby discovered a trickle of blood on his fingers and knew the keen exuberance of battle. A shout declared his gleeful discovery. He rolled to the ground to reload his weapon and shouted again, hurling a taunt at the enemy.

He searched the area behind the fence for the defenders, the Corporal's guard he'd picked up on the radio. They should have joined him when he opened fire down slope. His searching glance picked out three men this side of the fence, near the burning truck, but *they* couldn't have joined in. The empty shoes and helmet liner of a fourth man lay on the scarred ground ten yards away. He caught a flicker of movement in a shell hole—it may have been no more than the bat of an eye, or the quiver of parched lips—and found the only survivor. A bloodless face stared over the rim of the hole at him.

Moresby scrabbled across the exposed slope and fell into the hole with the soldier.

The man wore Corporal's stripes on his only arm and clutched at a strap which had once been attached to a radio; the remainder of each had been blown away. He didn't move when Moresby landed hard beside him and burrowed into the bloodied pit. The Corporal stared helplessly at the place where Moresby had been, at the boiling column of oily smoke rising above the truck, at the coming sun, at the sky. His head would not turn. Moresby threw away his useless rations pack and tilted the canteen to the Corporal's mouth. A bit of water trickled between his lips but the greater part of it ran down his chin and would have been lost, had Moresby not caught it in his hand and rubbed it over the man's mouth. He attempted to force more between the lips.

The Corporal moved his head with a feeble negative gesture and Moresby stopped, knowing he was choking on the water; instead, he poured more into his open palm and bathed the Corporal's face, pulling down the wide eyelids with a wet caressing motion of his fingers. The bright and hurtful sky was shut out.

Wind roared across the face of the slope and over the plowed field below, sweeping toward the lakefront.

Moresby raised his eyes to study the slope and the field. A carelessly exposed foot and ankle were visible behind a tree stump. Calmly— without the haste that might impair his aim—he brought up his rifle and put a single slug into the ankle. He heard a bellowing cry of pain, and the curse directed at him. The target vanished from sight. Moresby's gaze came back to the empty shoes and helmet liner beyond the shell hole. He decided to move—knew he *had* to move now to prevent that mortar from coming in on him.

He fired again at the stumps to keep the mortarman down, then sprinted for the ruptured hole in the fence where the bodies of the two aggressors lay. He fell on his belly, fired another round and then jumped on all fours against the nearest body, burrowing down behind it as a shield against the mortarman. The raging wind blew over the hole.

Moresby plucked at the bandit's shirt, tearing away the armband and bringing it up to his eyes for a careful inspection.

It was no more than a strip of yellow cotton cloth cut from a bolt of goods, and bearing a crude black cross in India ink. There was no word, slogan, or other point of identification to establish a fealty. Black cross on yellow field. Moresby prodded his memory, wanting to fit that symbol into some known civilian niche. It *had* to fit into a neat little slot somewhere. His orderly mind picked and worried at the unfamiliar term: *ramjet*.

Nothing. Neither sign nor name were known prior to the launch, prior to 1978.

He rolled the stiffening body over on its back the better to see the face, and knew jarring shock. The black and bloodied face was still twisted in the agony of death. Two or more slugs had torn into the man's midsection, while another had ripped away his throat and showered his face with his own blood; it had not been instantaneous death. He had died in screaming misery alongside the man next to him, vainly attempting to break through the fence and take the defenders up the slope.

Major Moresby was long used to death in the field; the manner of this man's dying didn't upset him—but the close scrutiny of his enemy jolted him as he'd not been jolted before. He suddenly understood the crude black cross etched on the yellow field, even though he'd not seen it before today. This was a civilian rebellion—organized insurrection.

Ramjets were Negro guerrillas.

The mortar coughed down the slope and Major Moresby burrowed in behind the body. He waited impatiently for the round to drop somewhere behind him, above him, and then by God he'd *take* that mortar.

The time was twenty minutes after six in the morning, 4 July 1999. The rising sun burned the horizon.

A ramjet mortarman with a shattered ankle peered warily over a tree stump, and counted himself the victor.

## 13

YESTERDAY THIS DAY'S MADNESS DID PREPARE;
TOMORROW'S SILENCE, TRIUMPH, OR DESPAIR:
DRINK! FOR YOU KNOW NOT WHENCE YOU CAME, NOR WHY;
DRINK! FOR YOU KNOW NOT WHY YOU GO, NOR WHERE.

—OMAR KHAYYAM

Saltus was prepared to celebrate.

The red light blinked out. He reached up to unlock the hatch and throw it open. The green light went dark. Saltus grasped the two handrails and pulled himself to a sitting position with his head and shoulders protruding through the hatchway. He was alone in the room as he expected to be, but he noted, with mild surprise that some of the ceiling lights had burned out. Sloppy housekeeping. The air was chill and smelled of ozone. He struggled out of the hatch and climbed over the side; the stepstool was missing and he slid down the hull to the floor. Saltus reached up to slam shut the hatch, then turned to the locker for his clothing.

Another suit belonging to Chaney hung there in its paper sheath waiting to be claimed. He noted the locker had collected a heavy amount of dust and a fine film of it had even crept inside. Wretched housekeeping. When Saltus was dressed in the civvies he had elected to wear, he took out a pint of good bourbon from its place of concealment in the locker and surreptitiously slipped the bottle into a jacket pocket.

He thought he was adequately prepared for the future.

Arthur Saltus checked his watch: 11:02. He sought out the electric calendar and clock on the wall to verify the date and time: *23 Nov 00*. The clock read 10:55. Temperature was a cold 13 degrees. Saltus guessed his watch was wrong; it had been wrong before. He left the room without a glance at the cameras, secretively holding his hand against the bottle to mask the pocket bulge. He didn't think the engineers would approve of his intentions.

Saltus walked down the corridor in eerie silence to the shelter; dust on the floor muffled his footfalls and he wondered if William had found that same dust sixteen months earlier. The old boy would have been annoyed. The shelter door was pushed open and the overhead lights went on in automatic response—but again, some of them were burned out. Somebody rated a gig for poor maintenance. Saltus stopped just inside the door, pulled the bottle from his pocket and ripped away the seal from the cap.

A shout rattled the empty room.

"Happy birthday!"

For a little while, he was fifty years old.

Saltus swallowed the bourbon, liking its taste, and wiped his mouth with the back of his hand; he stared around the shelter with growing curiosity. Somebody had been at the ship's stores—somebody had helped himself to the provisions set by for *him* and then had carelessly left the debris behind for *him* to find. The place was overrun with privateers and sloppy housekeepers.

He discovered a gasoline lantern on the floor near his feet and reached down quickly to determine if it was warm. It was not, but a jostling shake told him there was fuel remaining in the tank. Many boxes of rations had been cut open—emptied of their contents—and the cartons stacked in a disorderly pile along the wall near the door. A few water containers rested beside the cartons and Saltus grabbed up the nearest to shake it, test it for use. The can was empty. He took another long pull from his birthday bottle and roamed around the room, making a more detailed inspection of the stores. They weren't in the ship-shape order he remembered from his last inspection.

A sealed bag of clothing had been torn open, a bag holding several heavy coats and parkas for winter wear. He could not guess how many had been taken from the container.

A pair of boots—no, two or three pair—were missing from a rack holding several similar pairs. Another bundle of warm lined mittens appeared to have been disturbed, but it was impossible to determine how many were gone. Somebody had visited the stores in winter. That somebody should not have been the Major—he was scheduled for the Fourth of July, unless that gyroscope went crazy and threw him off by half a year. Saltus turned again to count the used ration boxes and the water cans: not enough of them had been emptied to support a big man like William for the past sixteen months—not unless he was living outside most of the time and supporting himself from the land. The used-up stores *might* have carried him through a single winter, supplementing game from outside. It seemed an unlikely possibility.

Saltus worked his way around the room to the bench. It was littered with trash.

Three yellow cartons rested on the bench top, cartons he'd not seen there on previous visits. The first one was empty, but he tore away the lid flaps of the next to discover a bullet-proof vest made of an unfamiliar nylon weave. He did not hesitate. The garment looked flimsy and unreliable but because Katrina always knew what she was doing, he put on the protective vest beneath his civilian jacket. Saltus sipped at his bourbon and eyed the mess on the bench. It wasn't like William to leave things untidy—well, not *this* untidy. Some of it was his work.

A tape recorder and another gasoline lantern were on the bench. A moment later he discovered empty boxes which had contained rifle cartridges, another box for the tape now in the recorder, an opened map, and the insignia removed from the Major's dress uniform. Saltus thought he knew what that meant. He touched the lantern first but found it cold although the fuel tank was full, and then leaned over the bench to examine the recorder. Only a few minutes of tape had been spun off.

Saltus depressed the voice button, said: "Mark," and rewound the tape to its starting point.

Another push and the tape rolled forward.

Voice: "Moresby here. Four July 1999. Time of arrival 10:05 on my watch, 4:10 by the clock. Six hours and five minutes discrepancy. Dust everywhere, stool missing from operations room; shelter unoccupied and stores intact, but the water is stale. Am preparing for the target."

Brief period of miscellaneous sounds.

Arthur Saltus had another drink while he waited. He stared again at William's discarded military insignia.

Voice: "...moving around the northwest corner in a southerly direction—moving toward you. Estimated strength, twelve to fifteen men. Watch them, Corporal, they're packing mortars. Over." The sound of gunfire was loud behind the voice.

Voice: "Roger. We've got a hole in the fence at the northwest— some bastard tried to put a truck through. It's still burning; maybe that'll stop them. Over."

Voice: "You *must* hold them, Corporal. I can't send you any men— we have a double red here. Out."

The channel fell silent, closing off the firefight.

Arthur Saltus stared at the machine in consternation, knowing the first suspicions of what might have happened. He listened to the small sounds of Moresby working about the bench, guessing what he was doing; the sound of cartridges being emptied from boxes was quickly recognizable; a rattle of paper was the map being unfolded.

Voice: "Eagle one! The bandits have hit us—hit us at the northwest corner. I count twelve of them, spread out over the slope below the fence. They've got two—damn it!—two mortars and they're lobbing them in. Over." The harsh, half-shrieking voice was punctuated by the dull thump of mortar fire.

Voice: "Have they penetrated the fence? Over."

Voice: "Negative—negative. That burning truck is holding them. I think they'll try some other way—blow a hole in the fence if they can. Over."

Voice: "*Hold* them, Corporal. They are a diversion; we have the main attack here. Out."

Voice: "Damn it, Lieutenant—" Silence.

The pause was of short duration.

Voice: "Moresby, Air Force Intelligence, calling Chicago or the Chicago area. Come in, Chicago."

Arthur Saltus listened to Moresby's efforts to make radio contact with the world outside, and listened to the ensuing dialogue between Moresby and Sergeant Nash holding somewhere west of Chicago. He sucked breath in a great startled gasp when he heard the Chicago statement—it hit him hard in the belly—and listened in near-disbelief at the exchange which followed. Baja California clearly indicated the shortwave signals were being bounced to the Orient: *that* was where the Harrys were and *that* was where they had been called in from. The Chinese at last were retaliating for the loss of their two railroad towns. It was likely that now—sixteen months after the strike—Lake Michigan and the lands adjoining it were as radioactive as the farming area around Yungning. They had retaliated.

But who called it in? Who were the bandits? What in hell were ramjets? That was a kind of aircraft.

Voice: "...Fifth Army HQ has been reestablished west of the Naval Training Station, but you'll pass through our lines long before that point. Look for the sentries. Use care, sir. Be alert for ramjets between your position and ours. They are heavily armed. Over."

Moresby thanked the man and went out.

The tape repeated a snapping sound that was Moresby shutting off his radio, and a moment later the tape itself went silent as he stopped the recorder. Arthur Saltus waited—listening for a postscript of some kind when William returned from his target and checked in. The tape went on and on repeating nothing, until at last his own voice jumped out at him: "Mark."

He was dissatisfied. He let the machine run through the end of the reel but there was nothing more. Moresby had not returned to the shelter—but Saltus knew he would *not* attempt to reach Fifth Army headquarters near Chicago, not in the bare fifty hours permitted him on target with a firefight underway somewhere outside. He might try for Joliet if the route was secure but he certainly wouldn't penetrate far into hostile territory with a deadline over his head. He had gone out; he hadn't come back inside.

But yet Saltus was dissatisfied. Something nagged at his attention, something that wasn't quite right, and he stared at the tape recorder for a long time in an effort to place the wrongness. Some insignificant little thing didn't fit smoothly into place. Saltus rewound the tape to the beginning and played it forward a second time. He put down the birthday bottle to listen attentively.

When it was finished he was certain of a wrongness; *something* on the tape plucked at his worried attention.

And yet a third time. He hunched over the machine.

In order:

William making his preliminary report; two voices, worried over the bandits and the mortars at the northwest corner, plus the fighting at the main gate; William again, calling Chicago; Sergeant Nash responding, with a dialogue on the Chicago situation and an invitation to join them at the relocated headquarters. A farewell word of thanks from William, and a snap of the radio being shut off; a moment later the tape itself went silent when William turned off the recorder and left the shelter—

There—*that* was it.

The tape went dead when the recorder was turned off. There were no after-sounds of activity about the bench, no final message—there was nothing to indicate William had ever touched the recorder again. He had shut off the radio and the recorder in one-two order and quit the room. The tape should have ended there, stopped there. It did not. Saltus looked at his watch, squinting at the sweep hand. He ran the tape forward yet another time, from the point when William had shut it off to the point when *he* turned it on again and said: "Mark."

The elapsed time was one minute, forty-four seconds. Someone *after* William had done that. Someone else had opened the shelter, pilfered the stores, donned winter clothing, and listened to the taped report. Someone else had let the machine run on another minute and forty-four seconds before shutting it off and taking his leave. The visitor may have returned, but William never did.

Arthur Saltus felt that fair warning. He closed the corridor door and thumbed a manual switch to keep the shelter lights on. An Army-issue automatic was taken from the stores and strapped around his waist.

Another mouth-filling pull from the bottle, and he rolled the tape back to his "Mark."

"Saltus checking in. That was my mark and this is my birthday, 23 November, in the nice round number year of 2000. I am fifty years old but I don't look a day over twenty-five—chalk it up to clean living. Hello, Katrina. Hello, Chaney. And hello to you, Mr. Gilbert Seabrooke. Is that nosey little man from Washington still knocking around back there?

"I arrived at 10:55 or 11:02 something, depending on which timepiece you read. I say something because I don't yet know if it's ack-emma or the other—I haven't put my nose outside to test the wind. I have lost all faith in engineers and mercury protons, but they'd better not cheat *me* out of my full birthday. When I walk out that door I want to see bright sunshine on the greensward—morning sunshine. I want birds singing and rabbits rabbiting and all that jazz.

"Katrina, the housekeeping is awfully sloppy around here: it's poor ship. Dust on the furniture, the floors, lights burned out, empty boxes littering the place—it's a mess. Strangers have been wandering in and out, helping themselves to the drygoods and pinching the groceries. I guess somebody found a key to the place.

"Everything you heard before my mark was William's report. He didn't come back to finish it, and he *didn't* go up to Chicago or anywhere near there—you can rely on that." The bantering tone was dropped. "He's outside."

Arthur Saltus began a straightforward recital of all that he'd found. He ticked off the missing items from the stores, the number of empty boxes stacked haphazardly along the wall, the used water cans, the two lanterns which had seen but little service—William may have tested the one found on the bench—the debris on the floor, the insignia, and the peculiarity of the tape being rolled forward. He invited his listeners to make the same time-delay test he'd made and then offer a better explanation if they didn't care for his.

He said: "And when you come up here, civilian, just double-check the stores, count the empties again to see if our visitor has been back. And hey—arm yourself, mister. You'd damned well better shoot straight if you have to shoot at all. Remember *something* we taught you."

Saltus flicked off the machine to prevent the tape from listening to him take a drink—as difficult as that might be—and then flicked it on again.

"I'm going topside to search for William—I'm going to try tailing him. Lord only knows what I'll find after sixteen months but I'm going to try. It's likely he did one of two things: either he'd go for Joliet to find out what he could about that Chicago thing, or he'd jump into the squabble if it was alongside.

"If the squabble was here—on the station—I think he'd run for the northwest corner to help the Corporal; he'd *have* to get into the fight." Short pause. "I'm going up to take a look at that corner, but if I don't find anything I'll run into Joliet. I'm in the same boat now with old William—I've got to know what happened to Chicago." He stared solemnly at the empty space in his bottle and added: "Katrina, this sure knocks hell out of your survey. All that studying for nothing."

Saltus stopped talking but let the machine run on.

He plugged in a radio and connected the leads to the outside antenna. After a period of band searching, he reported back to the tape recorder.

"Radio negative. Nothing at all on the GI channels." Another slow sweep of the bands. "That's damned funny, isn't it? Nobody's playing the top ten platters."

Saltus switched over to the civilian wavelengths and monitored them carefully. "The forty- and eighty-meter bands are likewise negative. Everybody is keeping their mouths shut. What do you suppose they're scared of?" He went back to a military channel and turned up the gain to peak, hearing nothing but an airy whisper. The lack of communications nettled him.

The *send* button was depressed.

"Navy boot, come in. Come in, boot, you know me—I caddied for the Admiral at Shoreacres. Saltus calling Navy boot. Over."

He reported himself two or three times on several channels.

The radio crackled a sudden command. "Get off the air, you idiot! They'll get a fix on you!" It went silent.

Saltus was so startled he turned off the radio.

To the tape recorder: "Chaney, did you hear that? There *is* somebody out there! They don't have much going for them—the power was weak, or they were a long ways off—but there *is* somebody out there. Scared spitless, too. The ramjets must have them on the run." He stopped to consider that. "Katrina, try to find out what a ramjet is. Our Chinese friends *can't* be here; they don't have the transport, and they couldn't get through the Pacific minefields if they did. And keep *that* under your hat, civilian—it's top secret stuff."

Arthur Saltus equipped himself for the target, always remembering to keep an eye on the door.

He helped himself to a parka and pulled the hood over his head; he removed the light shoes he'd been wearing the summer he left and found a pair of hiking boots the proper size. Mittens were tucked into a pocket. Saltus slung a canteen of water over one shoulder and a pack of rations on his back. He picked out a rifle, loaded it, and emptied two boxes of cartridges into his pockets. The map was of little interest—he knew the road to Joliet, he'd been there only last Thursday to look into a little matter for the President. The President had thanked him. He loaded a camera and found room to pack away a fresh supply of nylon film.

Saltus decided against taking a radio or recorder, not wanting to be further encumbered; it would be awkward enough as it was and all signs clearly indicated the survey was sunk without a trace. Chicago was lost, forbidden, and Joliet might be a problem. But there was something he could do with the recorder and William's brief message—something to insure its return to home base. A last searching examination of the room gave him no other thing he thought he would need. The lights were turned off.

Saltus took a long pull on his dwindling supply of bourbon and quit the shelter. The corridor was dusty and vacant, and he fancied he could see his own footprints.

He carried the tape recorder with its dangling cord back to the operations room where the vehicle waited in its polywater tank. A thorough search of the room failed to reveal an electric outlet; even the service for the clock and the calendar came through the wall behind the encased instruments, wholly concealed.

"Damn it!" Saltus spun around to stare up at the two glass eyes. "Why can't you guys do something right? Even your lousy proton gyroscope is—is sheeg!"

He strode out of the room, marched along the dusty corridor to the adjoining laboratory door, and gave it a resounding kick to advertise his annoyance. *That* ought to shake up the engineers.

His jaw dropped when the door swung open under the blow.

Nobody slammed it shut again. Saltus edged closer and peered inside. Nobody shoved him back. The lab was empty. He walked in and stared around: it was his first sight of the working side of the project and the impression was a poor one.

Here too some of the ceiling lights had burned out, without being replaced. A bank of three monitoring sets occupied a wall bench at his left hand; one of them was blanked out but the remaining two gave him a blurred and unsatisfactory image of the room he had just quit. The vehicle was recognizable only because of its shape and its supporting tank. The two images lacked quality, as though the tubes were aged beyond caring. He turned slowly on the ball of his foot and scanned the room but found nothing to suggest recent occupancy. The tools and equipment were there—and still functioning—but the lab personnel had vanished, leaving nothing but dust and marks in the dust. A yellow bull's eye on a computer panel stared at him for an intruder.

Saltus put down the recorder and plugged it in.

He said without preamble: "Chaney, the treasure house is empty, deserted—the engineers are gone. Don't ask me why or where— there's no sign, no clue, and they didn't leave notes. I'm in the lab now but there's nobody here except the mice and me. The door was open, sort of, and I wandered in." He sipped whiskey, but this time didn't bother to conceal it from the tape.

"I'm going topside to look for William. Wait for me, Katrina, you lovely wench! Happy birthday, people."

Saltus pulled the plug from the receptacle, wrapped the cord around the recorder and walked back to the other room to drop the machine into the TDV. To compensate for the added weight, he pulled loose the heavy camera in the nose bubble and threw it overboard after first salvaging the film magazine. He hoped the liaison agent from Washington would cry over the loss. Saltus slammed shut the hatch and left the room.

The corridor ended and a flight of stairs led upward to the operations exit. The painted sign prohibiting the carrying of arms beyond the door had been defaced: a large slash of black paint was smeared from the first sentence to the last, half obliterating the words and voiding the warning.

Saltus noted the time on his watch and fitted the keys into the locks. A bell rang behind him as he pushed open the door. The day was bright with sunshine and snow.

It was five minutes before twelve in the morning. His birthday was only just begun.

An automobile waited for him in the parking lot.

**14**

Arthur Saltus stepped out warily into the snow. The station appeared to be deserted: nothing moved on any street as far as the eye could see.

His gaze came back to the parked automobile.

It was a small one resembling the German beetle and olive drab in color, but he tardily recognized it as an American make by the name stamped on each hubcap. The car had been there since before the snow: there were no tracks of movement, of betrayal. A thinner coating of snow lay over the hood and roof of the vehicle and one window was open a crack, allowing moisture to seep inside.

Saltus scanned the parking lot, the adjoining flower garden and the frigid empty spaces before him but discovered no moving thing. He held himself rigid, alert, intently watching, listening, and sniffing the wind for signs of life. No one and nothing had left tell-tale prints in the snow, nor sounds nor smells on the wind. When he was satisfied of that, he stepped away from the operations door and eased it shut behind him, making sure it was locked. Rifle up, he inched toward a corner of the lab building and peered around. The company street was trackless and deserted, as were the walks and lawns of the structures across the street. Shrubbery was bent under the weight of snow. His foot struck a covered object when he took a single step away from the protective corner.

He looked down, bent, and picked a radio out of the snow. It had been taken from the stores below.

Saltus turned it over looking for damage but saw none; the instrument bore no marks to suggest it had been struck by gunfire, and after a hesitation he concluded that Moresby had simply dropped it there to be rid of the extra weight. Saltus resumed his patrol, intent on circling the building to make certain he was alone. The sun-bright snow was unmarred all the way around. He was relieved, and paused again to sample the bourbon.

The automobile claimed his attention.

The dash puzzled him: it had an off-on switch instead of the usual key, and but one idiot light; there were no gauges to give useful information on fuel, oil, water temperature, or tire pressures, nor was there a speedometer. Propelled by a sudden exciting idea, Saltus climbed out of the little car and raised the hood. Three large silver-colored storage batteries were lined up against a motor so compact and simple it didn't appear capable of moving anything, much less an automobile. He dropped the hood and got back into the seat. The switch was flipped to the on position. There was no sound but the idiot light briefly winked at him. Saltus very gently pulled the selector lever to drive position and the car obediently crept forward through the snow toward the empty street. He pushed down on the accelerator with growing exhilaration and deliberately threw the car into a skid on the snow-packed street. It lurched and swung in a giddy manner, then came back under control when Saltus touched the steering wheel. The little automobile was fun.

He followed a familiar route to the barracks where he'd lived with William and the civilian, swinging and dancing from side to side on the slippery surface because the car seemed to obey his every whim. It would spin in a complete circle and come to rest with the nose pointing in the proper direction, it would slide sideways without threatening to topple, it would bite into the snow and leap forward with a minimum of slippage if just one wheel had a decent purchase. He thought that four-wheel-drive electric cars should have been invented a century ago.

Saltus stopped in dismay at the barracks—at the place where the barracks had been. He very nearly missed the site. All the antiquated buildings had burned to their concrete foundations, nearly hiding them from sight. He got out of the car to stare at the remains and at the lonely shadows cast by the winter sun.

Feeling depressed, Saltus drove over to E Street and turned north toward the recreation area.

He parked the car outside the fence surrounding the patio and prowled cautiously through the entranceway to scan the interior. The unmarked snow was reassuring but it did not lull him into a false sense of security. Rifle ready, pausing every few steps to look and listen and smell the wind, Saltus advanced to the tiled rim of the pool and looked down. It was nearly empty, drained of water, and the diving board taken away.

*Nearly* empty: a half dozen long lumps huddled under the blanket of snow at the bottom, lumps the shape of men. Two GI helmet liners lay nearby, recognizable by their shapes despite the covering snow. A naked, frozen foot protruded through the blanket into the cold sunshine.

Saltus turned away, expelling a breath of bitter disappointment; he wasn't sure what he had expected after so long a time, but certainly not that—not the bodies of station personnel dumped into an uncovered grave. The GI liners suggested their identities and suggested they had been dumped there by outsiders—by ramjets. Survivors on station would have buried the bodies.

He remembered the beautiful image of Katrina in that pool—Katrina, nearly naked, scantily clad in that lovely, sexy swim suit—and himself chasing after her, wanting the feel of that wet and splendid body under his hands again and again. She had teased him, run away from him, knowing what he was doing but pretending not to be aware: *that* added to the excitement. And Chaney! The poor out-gunned civilian sat up on the deck and burned with a green, sulphurous envy, wanting to but not daring to. Damn, but that was a day to be remembered!

Arthur Saltus scanned the street and then climbed back into the car.

There were two large holes in the fence surrounding the station at the northwest corner. Action from outside had caused both penetrations. The shell of a burned-out truck had caused one of them, and that rusted shell still occupied the hole. A mortar had torn through the other. There was a shallow cavity in the earth directly beneath the second hole, a cavity scooped out by another exploding mortar round. Snow-covered objects that might be the remains of men dotted the slope on both sides of the fence. There was the recognizable hulk of a thoroughly demolished automobile.

Saltus probed the wreckage of the car, turning over wheels with shredded tires, poking among the jumble of machined parts, picking up to examine with mild wonder a windshield fashioned of transparent plastic so sturdy it had popped out of place and fallen undamaged several feet away from the hulk. He compared it to the windshield of his own car, and found it to be identical. The batteries had been carried away—or were entirely demolished; the little motor was a mass of fused metal.

As best he could, Saltus scraped snow from the ground in search of something to indicate that William Moresby had died here. He thought it likely that William had found his car in the parking lot— a twin to his own vehicle—and drove it north to the scene of the skirmish. To *here*. It would be a hell of a note if the man had died before he got out of the car. Old William deserved a better break than that.

He found nothing—not even a scrap of uniform in the debris, and for the moment that was encouraging.

Down the slope a cluster of tree stumps and a sagging billboard were visible. Saltus went down to see them. A snow-blanketed body lay smashed against a stump but that was all; there was no weapon with it. The blown remains of one mortar lay around in front of the billboard and from the appearance of the piece, he would guess that a faulty shell had exploded within the tube, destroying the usefulness of the weapon and probably killing the operator. There was no corpse here to back up that guess, unless it was the one hurled against the tree stump. The second of the two mortars mentioned on the tape was missing—taken away. The winners of *this* skirmish had to be the ramjets; they had picked up their remaining mortar and retired—or had penetrated the hole to invade the station.

Saltus picked his way back up the slope and walked through the hole in the fence. The snow pattern dipped gracefully, following the rounded rough-bottomed contour of the cavity. His foot turned on something unseen at the bottom of the hole and he struggled to save his balance. A cold wind blew across the face of the slope, numbing his fingers and stinging his face.

He began the distasteful task of scraping snow off each of the fallen man-objects, brushing away just enough to catch a glimpse of the rotting cloth of the uniform. The defenders had worn Army tans, and one of them still carried a GI dogtag around his neck; in another place he turned up a Corporal's stripes attached to a bit of sleeve, and not far away was an empty pair of shoes. William Moresby's dress blues were not found.

An oversight nagged at him.

Saltus retraced his steps down the slope, annoyed at the oversight and annoyed again by the futility of it: he uncovered the remains of civilians wearing nondescript civilian clothing, and one yellow armband. A faded black cross on a rotting patch of yellow goods meant nothing to him but he folded it away for later examination. Katrina would want to see it. The ramjets themselves were beyond identification; sixteen months of exposure had made them as unrecognizable as those other bodies above the fence line. The only thing new he'd learned was that civilians were the bandits on the tape, civilians equipped with mortars and some kind of central organization—maybe the same group that had called in the Harry on Chicago. Ramjets allied with the Chinese—or at least inviting their cooperation.

To Saltus the scene read civil war.

He stopped at the next thought, staring with hard surprise at the covered bodies. Ramjets blowing Chicago—in retaliation? Ramjets losing in Chicago twenty years ago, trapped behind their own wall, but striking back in harsh retaliation *now*? Ramjets working with the

Chinese, welded together by a mutual hatred of the white establishment?

He picked again at the body against the stump, but the color of the man's skin was lost.

Arthur Saltus climbed the slope.

The world was strangely silent and empty—deserted. He'd seen no traffic on the distant highway nor on the nearer railroad; the sky was uncommonly bare of aircraft. He stayed continually on the alert for danger, but sighted no one, nothing—even animal tracks were missing from the snow. Deserted world—or more likely, a concealed world. That angry voice on the radio had ordered him to silence lest he betray his cover.

Saltus stayed only a few minutes longer on the cold upper slope, standing amid the debris of the smashed car. He hoped to God that William had jumped clear before the mortar smashed in. The old boy deserved at least a couple of whacks at the bandits before his doom prophets caught up to him.

He was finally convinced the Major had died there.

Saltus drove by the mess hall with little more than a passing glance. Like the barracks, the wooden parts of the structure were burned to the concrete block foundation. He thought it likely the ramjets had swept the station after the fence was breached, burning what was flammable and stealing or destroying the remainder. It was a blessing that the lab had been built to withstand war and earthquake, or he would have emerged into a room open to the sky and climbed down from the vehicle into snow. He hoped the bandits had long since starved to death—but at the same time remembered the pilfered stores in the shelter.

*That* bandit hadn't starved, but neither had he fed his fellows. How had he gotten through the locked door? He would need both keys and he would have to take them from William—but a direct hit on the car would have scattered the keys as thoroughly as the parts of the auto itself. Assuming possession of the keys, why hadn't the bandit thrown open the doors to his companions? Why hadn't the stores been looted, cleaned out, the lab ransacked? Was the man so selfish that he had fed only himself and let the rest go hang? Perhaps. But more than one pair of boots was missing.

Saltus turned a corner at a fast clip, skidding in the snow and then straightening his course toward the front gate. It was a small comfort to find the gatehouse still standing: concrete blocks were difficult to burn or destroy. The gate itself was torn open and twisted back out of the way. He drove through it and concentrated on the barely visible pattern of the road ahead; the smooth unbroken expanse of snow flanked by shallow ditches to either side guided him. Only last Thursday he and William had raced over the road hell-bent for a day in Joliet.

A bearded man leaped out of the gatehouse and put a shot through the rear window of the car.

Arthur Saltus didn't take the time to decide if he was astonished or outraged—the shot did frighten him, and he reacted automatically to danger. Slamming the accelerator to the floor, he spun hard on the wheel and threw the car into a sickening skid. It lurched and swung around in a dizzy arc, coming to rest with its blunt nose aimed at the gatehouse. Saltus floored the accelerator. The rear wheels spun uselessly on the slick snow, found a purchase only when they had burned down to the pavement, then thrust the car forward in a burst of speed that caught him unprepared. It careened wildly through the gate. He rammed the nose hard against the gatehouse door and leaped clear, hugging the side of the vehicle.

Saltus pumped two quick shots through the sagging door, and was answered by a scream of pain; he fired again and then scrambled over the hood to crouch in the doorway. The screaming man lay on the floor tearing at his bloodied chest. A tall, gaunt black man was backed against the far wall taking aim at him. Saltus fired without raising the rifle, and then deliberately turned and put a finishing shot through the head of the man writhing on the floor. The screaming stopped.

For a moment the world was wrapped in silence.

Saltus said: "Now, what the hell—"

An incredibly violent blow struck him in the small of his back, robbing him of breath and speech, and he heard the sound of a shot from an unimaginable distance away. He stumbled and went to his knees while a raging fire burned up his spine into his skull. Another distant shot shattered the peace of the world, but this once he felt nothing. Saltus turned on his knees to meet the threat.

The ramjet was climbing over the hood of the little fun car to get at him.

Caught up like a man swimming in mud, Saltus raised the rifle and tried to take aim. The weapon was almost too heavy to lift; he moved in a slow, agonizing motion. The ramjet slid down the hood and jumped through the doorway, reaching for him or his rifle. Saltus squinted at the face but it refused to come into clear focus. Somebody behind the face loomed over him as large as a mountain; somebody's hands grasped the barrel of the rifle and pulled it away. Saltus squeezed the trigger.

The looming face changed: it disintegrated in a confusing jumble of bone, blood, and tissue, coming apart like William's electric car under a mortar barrage. The face out of focus disappeared while a booming thunder filled the gatehouse and rattled the broken door. A large piece of the mountain teetered over him, threatening to bury him when it came down. Saltus tried to crawl away.

The toppling body knocked him off his knees and knocked away his weapon. He went down beneath it, still fighting for breath and praying not to be crushed.

Arthur Saltus opened his eyes to find the daylight gone. An intolerable burden pinned him to the gatehouse floor and an overpowering hurt wracked his body.

Moving painfully but gaining only an inch or two at a time, he crawled from under the burden and tried to roll it aside. After minutes or hours of strenuous effort he climbed as far as his knees and threw off the knapsack hammering at his back; he spilled as much water as he drank before the canteen followed. His rifle lay on the floor at his knee, but he was astonished to discover that his hand and arm lacked the strength to pick it up. It may have taken another hour to draw the service automatic from under his coat and place it on the hood of the car.

An unbelievable time was spent in crawling over the same hood to get outside. The gun was knocked to the ground. Saltus bent over, touched it, fingered it, grew dizzy and had to abandon the weapon to save himself. He grabbed at the door handle and hauled himself upright. After a while he tried it again, and only managed to seize the gun and stand upright before the recurring wave of nausea struck him. His stomach doubled up and ejected.

Saltus climbed into the car and backed it off from the gatehouse door. Opening the near window to get the cold bracing air, he tugged at the drive selector and steered a tortuous course from gate to parking lot. The car glanced off one curb and skidded across the snow to jump the other curb; it would have thrown its occupant if it had been traveling at greater speed. Saltus had lost the strength to push down on the brake, and the little car stopped only when it slammed into the concrete wall of the laboratory. He was thrown against the wheel and then out into the snow. A spotted trail of blood marked his erratic path from the car to the door with the twin locks.

The door opened easily—so easily that a dim corner of his fogged consciousness nagged at him: had he inserted *both* keys into the locks before the door swung? Had he inserted *any* key?

Arthur Saltus fell down the flight of stairs because he could not help himself.

The gun was gone from his hand but he couldn't remember losing it; his bottle of birthday bourbon was gone from his pocket but he couldn't remember emptying it or throwing away the bottle; the keys to the door were lost. Saltus lay on his back on the dusty concrete, looking at the bright lights and looking up the stairs at the closed door. He didn't remember closing that door.

A voice said: "Fifty hours."

He knew he was losing touch with reality, knew he was drifting back and forth between cold, painful awareness and dark periods of feverish fantasy. He wanted to sleep on the floor, wanted to stretch out with his face on the cold concrete and let the raging fire in his spine burn itself out. Katrina's vest had saved his life—barely. The slug—more than one?—was lodged in his back, but without the vest it would have torn all the way through his chest and blown away the rib cage. Thanks, Katrina.

A voice said: "Fifty hours."

He tried to stand up, but fell on his face. He tried to climb to his knees, but pitched forward on his face. There was not much strength left to him. In time with the measured passing of an eternity, he crawled to the TDV on his belly.

Arthur Saltus struggled for an hour to climb the side of the vehicle. His awareness was slipping away in a sea of nauseous fantasy: he had the hallucinatory notion that someone pulled off his heavy boots—that someone removed the heavy winter garments and tried to take off his clothing. When at last he fell head first through the vehicle's open hatch, he had the fever-fantasy that someone out there had helped him over the side.

A voice said: "Push the kickbar."

He lay on his stomach on the webbing facing in the wrong direction, and remembered that the engineers wouldn't recover the vehicle until the end of fifty hours. They had done that when William failed to return. Something was under him, hurting him, putting a hard new pressure on a rib cage already painfully sore. Saltus pulled the lump from beneath him and found a tape recorder. He pushed it toward the kickbar but it fell inches short of the goal. The hallucination slammed shut the hatch cover.

He said thickly: "Chaney...the bandits have burned the treasure house..."

The tape recorder was thrown at the kickbar.

The time was forty minutes after two in the morning, 24 November 2000. His fiftieth birthday was long past.

## 15

THE MEEK, THE TERRIBLE MEEK,
THE FIERCE AGONIZING MEEK,
ARE ABOUT TO ENTER INTO THEIR INHERITANCE.

—CHARLES RANN KENNEDY

Chaney was apprehensive.

The red light blinked out. He reached up to unlock the hatch and throw it open. The green light went dark. Chaney grasped the two handrails and pulled up to a sitting position, with his head and shoulders protruding through the hatchway. He hoped he was alone in the room—the vehicle was in darkness. The air was sharply cold and smelled of ozone. He struggled out of the hatch and climbed over the side. Saltus had warned him the stool was gone so he slid cautiously to the floor, and clung to the polywater tank for a moment of orientation. The blackness around him was complete: he saw nothing, heard nothing but the hoarse sound of his own breathing.

Brian Chaney reached up to slam shut the hatch but then stopped himself—the TDV was his only lifeline to home base and it was wiser to keep that hatch open and waiting. He stretched out his hand to grope for the locker; he remembered its approximate location, and took a few hesitant steps in the darkness until he bumped into it. His suit hung in a dusty paper sheath, prepared by a dry cleaner now many years behind him, and his shoes were on the bottom beneath the suit. An automatic pistol—put there at the insistence of Arthur Saltus—now was an ungainly lump in the pocket of his jacket.

The weapon underscored his apprehension.

Chaney didn't bother to check his watch: it lacked an illuminated dial and there was nothing to be seen on the wall. He quit the darkened room.

He moved slowly down the corridor in a black eerie silence to the shelter; dust stirred up by his feet made him want to sneeze. The shelter door was found by touch and pushed open but the overhead lights failed in their automatic response. Chaney felt for the manual switch beside the door, flicked it, but stayed in darkness: the electric power was out and the lecturing engineer was a liar. He listened intently to the unseen room. He had no matches or lighter—the penalty paid by a non-smoker when light or fire was needed—and stood there for a moment of indecision, trying to recall where the smaller items were stored. He thought they were in metal lockers along the far wall, near the racks of heavy clothing.

Chaney shuffled across the floor, wishing he had that cocksure engineer here with him.

His feet collided with an empty carton, startling him, and he kicked it out of the way. It struck another object before it came to rest: Saltus had complained of sloppy housekeeping, and Katrina had written a memo. After a period of cautious groping the ungainly bulge in his jacket pocket struck the leading edge of the bench, and he put forth both hands to explore the working surface. A radio—plugged in and wired to the antenna—a lantern, a few small empty boxes, a large one, a number of metal objects his fingers could not immediately identify, and a second lantern. Chaney barely hesitated over the objects and continued his probe. His roving fingers found a box of matches; the fuel tanks of both lanterns jostled with reassuring sounds. He lit the two lanterns and turned to look at the room. Chaney didn't like to think of himself as a coward but his hand rested in the gun pocket as he turned and peered into the gloom.

The raider had returned to pilfer the stores.

From the looks of the place the man must have spent the last few winters here, or had invited his friends in with him.

A third lantern rested on the floor near the door and he would have knocked that one over if he had stepped sideways in the darkness. A box of matches lay ready beside it. An incredible number of empty food cartons were stacked along a wall together with a collection of water cans, and he wondered why the man hadn't hauled the boxes outside and burned them to be rid of an untidy mess. Chaney counted the cans and boxes with growing wonder and tried to guess at the many years separating Arthur Saltus from his own recent arrival. *That* reminded him to look at his watch: five minutes before nine. He had the uneasy suspicion that the TDV had sent him askew once again. A plastic bag had been opened—as Saltus had reported—and a number of winter garments were missing from the racks. Several pairs of boots were gone from their shelves. The bundle of mittens was broken open and one had fallen to the floor, unnoticed in the darkness.

But there was no spilled food on the floor despite the litter of cartons and cans; every scrap had been taken up and used. Nor were there signs of mice or rats.

He whirled to the gun rack. Five rifles had been taken plus an undetermined number of the Army-issue automatics. He supposed—without count—that an appropriate amount of ammunition had gone with them. Major Moresby and Saltus would have accounted for two of the rifles.

The tiny metal objects on the workbench were the insignia Moresby had removed from his uniform, and Saltus had explained the reason for their removal in combat zones. The empty boxes had contained reels of tape, nylon film, and cartridges; the one remaining larger box was his bullet-proof vest. The map revealed the usual layer of dust. The radio was now useless—unless the supply of batteries had survived the intervening years.

Years: time.

Chaney picked up both lanterns and walked back to the room housing the TDV. He crossed to the far wall and bent down to read the calendar and clock. Each had stopped when the power line went out.

The clock read a few minutes of twelve noon, or twelve midnight. The calendar stopped measuring time on 4 Mar 09. Only the thermometer gave a meaningful reading: 52 degrees.

Eight and one half years after Arthur Saltus lived his disastrous fiftieth birthday, ten years after Major Moresby died in the skirmish at the fence, the nuclear power plant serving the laboratory failed or the lines were destroyed. They may have destroyed themselves for lack of replacement; the transformers may have blown out; the nuclear fuel may have been used up; any one or a hundred things could have happened to interrupt transmission. The power was gone.

Chaney had no idea how long ago it had failed: he knew only that he was somewhere beyond March 2009.

The outage may have happened last week, last month, last year, or at any time during the last hundred years. He hadn't asked the engineers the precise date of *his* target but had assumed they would fling him into the future one year following Saltus, to reconnoiter the station. The assumption was wrong—or the vehicle had strayed once more. Chaney ruefully concluded that it didn't matter, it really didn't matter at all. The ill-starred survey was nearly finished; it *would* be finished as soon as he made a final tour of the station and went back with his report.

He carried the lanterns back to the shelter.

The radio took his attention. Chaney dug out a sealed carton of batteries and fitted the required number into the conversion unit. The band selector was swept over the military channels and back again, without result. He turned up the gain to peak and held the instrument to his ear but it refused to give him even the airy whisper of dead air; the lack of hiss or static told him that the batteries had not survived the passage of time. Chaney dismissed the radio as of no further value and prepared himself for the target.

He was disappointed there was no note from Katrina, as he'd found on the field trial.

The bullet-proof vest went on first. Arthur Saltus had warned him of that, had shown him the valued protection of that: Saltus lived only because he'd worn one.

Because he didn't know the season of the year—only the temperature—Chaney donned a pair of boots and helped himself to a heavy coat and a pair of mittens. He picked out a rifle, loaded it as Moresby had taught him to do, and emptied a box of cartridges in his pocket. The map was of no interest: the probes into Joliet and Chicago had been hastily canceled and *now* he was restricted to the station itself. Check it out quickly and jump for home base. Katrina had said the President and his Cabinet were awaiting a final report before concluding a course of remedial action. They called it "formulating a policy of positive polarization," whatever that was.

A last tour of the station and the survey was ended; that much of the future would be known and mapped.

Chaney slung a canteen of water over his shoulder, then stuffed a knapsack with rations and matches and hung it from the other shoulder; he didn't expect to be outside long enough to use either one. He was pleased the aged batteries didn't work—that was excuse enough to leave radio and recorder behind—but he fitted film into the camera because Gilbert Seabrooke had asked for a record of the destruction of the station. The verbal description offered by Saltus had been a depressing one. One last searching examination of the room gave him no other article he thought he would need.

Chaney licked his lips, now dry with apprehension, and quit the shelter.

The corridor ended and a flight of stairs led up to the operations exit. The painted sign prohibiting the carrying of arms beyond the door had been defaced: a large slash of black paint was smeared from the first sentence to the last, half obliterating the words and voiding the warning. Chaney noted the time, and set the two lanterns down on the top step to await his return. He fitted the keys into the twin locks and stepped out hesitantly into the open air.

The day was bright with sunshine but sharply chill. The sky was new, blue, and clear of aircraft; it looked freshly scrubbed, a different sky than the hazy polluted one he had known almost all his life. Patches of light frost clung to the protected spots not yet touched by the sun.

His watch read 9:30, and he guessed the time was about right—the bright morning outside was still new.

A two-wheeled cart waited in the parking lot.

Chaney eyed the crude apparition, prepared for almost anything but that. The cart was not too skillfully made, having been put together with used lumber, an axle, and a pair of wheels taken from one of the small electric cars Saltus had described. Strands of machine wire had been employed to hold the four sides together where nails failed to do an adequate job, and to fasten the bed to the axle; the tires were long rotted away and the cart rode on metal rims. No skilled carpenter had fitted it together.

The second object to catch his eye was a heaped mound of clay in the adjoining area that had once been a flower garden. Unusually tall grass and weeds grew everywhere, partially obscuring a view of the station and almost blocking sight of the yellow mound; the grass grew high around the parking lot, and beyond it, and in the open spaces surrounding the buildings across the street. Weeds and grass filled the near distance as far as the eye could see, and he was reminded of the buffalo grass said to have grown here when Illinois was an Indian prairie. Time had done that—time and neglect. The station lawns had long gone unattended.

Moving warily, stopping often to scan the area around him, Chaney approached the mound.

When he was yet a distance away he discovered a faint trail running from the edge of the lot, through the garden and toward the mound itself. The next discovery was equally blunt. Alongside the path— almost invisible in the high grass—was a water channel, a crude aqueduct made from guttering ripped from some building and twisted into shape to serve this purpose. Chaney stopped short in surprise and stared at the guttering and the nearby mound, already guessing at what he would find. He continued the stealthy approach.

He came suddenly into a clearing in the rampant grass and found the artifact: a cistern with a crude wooden lid. A bucket and a length of rope rested beside it.

Chaney slowly circled the cistern and the clay that had come from the excavation, to stumble over yet another channel made of the same guttering; the second aqueduct ran through the weeds and grass toward the lab building—probably to catch the run-off from the roof. The clay mound was not fresh. Struck with an overwhelming curiosity, he knelt down and pried away the lid to find a cistern half filled with water. The walls of the pit were lined with old brick and rough stone slabs but the water was remarkably clean, and he looked to see why. Filters made of screenwire torn from a window were fitted over the ends of each gutter to protect the cistern from incoming debris and small animals. The gutters themselves were free of leaves and kash, and an effort had been made to seal the joints with a tarry substance.

Chaney put down the rifle and bent to study the cistern in wonder. It was already recognizable.

Like the cart, it had not been fashioned by skilled hands. The shape of the thing—the lines of it—were easily familiar: the sides not quite perpendicular, the mouth not evenly rounded, and the shaft appearing to be larger near the bottom than at the top. It was odd, amateurish, and sunk without a plumb line—but it was a reasonably faithful copy of a Nabataean cistern and it might be expected to hold water for a century or more. In this place it was startling. Chaney replaced the lid and climbed to his feet.

When he turned around he saw the grave.

It shocked him. The site had been concealed from him until now by the high growth of the garden, but again a faint path led to it from the clearing at the cistern. The mound above the grave was low, aged, and covered by a short weedy grass; the cross above it was nailed together and coated with fading white paint. Dim lettering was visible on the crossarm.

Chaney moved in and knelt again to read it.

*A ditat Deus K*

The gatehouse door had been loosed from its hinges and taken away—perhaps to build the cart.

Chaney peered warily through the opening, alert for danger but dreading the possibility of it, then stepped inside for a closer examination. The room was bare. No trace remained of the men who had died there: bone, weapon, scrap of cloth, nothing. Some of the window glass had been knocked out but other panes were intact; the screenwire had been taken from two of the windows. An empty place.

He backed out and turned to stare at the gate.

It was shut and padlocked, effectively blocking admittance to all but a determined climber, and an effort had been made to repair the damage done to it. Chaney noted all that in a single glance and went forward to study the additional stoppers—the added warnings. Three grisly talismans hung on the outside of the gate facing the road: three skulls, taken from the bodies of the men who'd died in the gatehouse so long ago. The warning to would-be trespassers was strikingly clear.

Chaney stared at the skulls, knowing the warnings to be as old as time; he knew of similar monitions which had guarded towns in Palestine before the Roman conquest, monitions which had been used as late as the eighteenth century in some of the more remote villages of the Negev.

He saw no one in the area: the entrance and its approaches were deserted, the warning well taken. Weeds and waist-high grass grew in the ditches and the fields on either side of the road leading to the distant highway but the grass had not been disturbed by the passage of men. The blacktopped road was empty, the white line down the center long since weathered away and the asphalt surface badly damaged by the years. An automobile using that road now would be forced to move at a snail's pace.

Chaney photographed the scene and quit the area.

Walking north with an easy stride, he followed the familiar route to the barracks where he'd lived that short while with Saltus and Moresby. The site was almost passed over because it was covered by a tangle of weeds and grass; no buildings rose above the jungle.

Forcing his way through the tangle—and flushing from its nesting place a quick, furry thing he tardily recognized as a rabbit—Chaney stumbled upon the burned-out base of a building nearly lost in the undergrowth. He couldn't recognize it as his own barracks, nor point to the location of his small room if it *had* been the barracks; only the long narrow rectangle of the foundation suggested the kind of dwelling it was. Chaney peered over the wall. A narrow band of frost lined the cement blocks at the groundline on the north side, pointing up the chill in the air. Patches of blue wildflowers grew in the sunlight and—much to his surprise—other patches of wild, red strawberries sprouted everywhere along the sunnier side of the foundation. He thought to glance at the sky, measuring the progress of the sun and the season, then stared again at the strawberries. It *should* be early summer.

Chaney photographed it and went back to the street. An abandoned place. He continued north.

E Street was easily identified without the need of the rusted sign standing on a pole at a corner. He stayed alert, walking cautiously and listening hard for any sound around him. The station was quiet under the sun.

The recreation area was harshly changed.

Chaney crept silently in the entrance and across the broken concrete patio to the rim of the swimming pool. He looked down. A few inches of dirty water covered the bottom—residue from the rains—together with a poor collection of rusted and broken weapons and an appreciable amount of debris blown in by the wind: the pool had become a dumping ground for trash and armament. The sodden corpse of some small animal floated in a corner. A lonely place. Chaney very carefully put away the memory of the pool as he'd known it and backed away from the edge. The area now seemed unkempt, ugly, and not a scene to be compared with more pleasant times.

He left quickly, bearing north and west. The far corner was a mile or more away as he remembered the map of the station, but he thought he could walk the distance in a reasonable time.

Chaney found the motor pool before he'd progressed a half dozen long blocks. Less than twenty cars littered the great blacktopped lot, but not one was operable: they had been wantonly stripped of parts and many of them were no more than burned-out shells. The hood of every vehicle was propped open, and the batteries taken; not one of the small motors was left intact to provide him with an idea of the plant. Chaney poked about the lot because he was curious, and because Arthur Saltus had told him about the little electric cars. He wished he could drive one. There were no trucks on the lot nor had he seen one anywhere on the station, although a number of them had been working the post during his training period. He supposed they had been transferred to Chicago to meet the emergency—or had been stolen when the ramjets overran the station.

Chaney emerged from the lot and stopped abruptly on the street. It may have been an illusion brought on by tension, but he thought he glimpsed movement in the high grass across the street. He slipped the safety on the rifle and walked to the curb. Nothing was visible in the heavy undergrowth.

There were no holes in the fence at the corner.

The burned and rusted shell of a truck occupied a place that had once been a hole, but now that truck was a part of the repaired fence. Barbed wire had been strung back and forth across the opening, pulled taut over, under, and through the wreck itself in such fashion that the truck became an integral part of the barrier; yet other strands of wire were laced vertically through the fencing, making it impossible for even a small boy to crawl through. He went along the fence to examine the second hole. It had been repaired and rebuilt in as thorough a manner as the first, and an old cavity in the ground had been filled in. The barricade was intact, impenetrable.

Everywhere the weeds and grass grew tall, actually concealing the lower third of the fence from a man standing only a few feet away. Chaney was not surprised to find the same gruesome talismans guarding the northwest corner; he had expected to find them. The skeletal owners of the skulls were missing, but nowhere on the station had he seen a human body—someone had buried them all, friend and foe alike. The three skulls hung at the top of the fencing, glaring down at the plain below and at the rusted railroad beyond.

Chaney turned away.

He prowled through the high grass, looking for anything. Arthur Saltus had found no trace of the Major but yet Chaney could not help himself; he searched for any trifle that would indicate the man's presence on the scene. It was impossible to give up Major Moresby without some effort, some attempt to place him there.

From somewhere in the distance the shrill, playful shout of a child pierced the morning.

Chaney jumped with astonishment and nearly lost his footing on a chunk of metal buried in the grass. He turned quickly to scan the corner of the station he thought empty, then searched backward over the route he'd traveled from the motor pool. The child was heard again—and then a woman's voice calling to it. Behind him. Down the slope. Chaney felt an eager, mounting excitement as he spun about and ran to the fence. They were out there beyond the fence.

He found them at once: a man, a woman, and a child of three or four years, trudging along the railway tracks in the middle distance. The man was carrying nothing but a stout stick or club, while the woman was toting a bag. The youngster ran along behind them, playing some game of his own devising.

Chaney was so glad to see them he forgot his own danger and yelled at the top of his voice. The rifle was a burden and he dropped it, to wave both hands.

Ignoring the barbed wire, he climbed part way up the fence to show himself and gain their attention. He shouted again, and beckoned them to come toward him.

The result left him utterly dumbfounded.

The adult members of the family looked around with some surprise, stared up and down the tracks, across fields, and discovered him at last clinging to the fence alongside the talismans. They stood motionless, frozen by fear, for only a tick in time. The woman cried out as though in pain and dropped the bag; she ran to protect the child. The man sprinted after her—passed her—and caught up the child in a quick scooping motion. The stick fell from his hands. He turned only once to stare at Chaney hanging on the fence and then raced away along the tracks. The woman stumbled—nearly fell—then ran desperately to keep pace with the man. The father shifted his small burden to one shoulder, then used his free hand to help the woman—urging her, hurrying her. They ran from him with all the speed and strength they possessed, the child now crying with consternation. Fear ran with them.

"Come back!"

He clung to the prickly fence and watched them out of sight. The billboard and high grasses hid them, shut them off, and the childish crying was hushed. Chaney hung there, his fingers curling through the holes of the fencing.

"Please come back!"

The northwest corner of the world stayed empty. He climbed down from the fence with bloodied hands.

Chaney picked up the rifle and turned away, plowing a path through the weeds and grass toward the distant road and the cluster of buildings at the heart of the station. He lacked the courage to look back. He had never known anyone to run from him—not even those beggar children who had squatted on the sands of the Negev and watched him pry into the sands of their forgotten history. They were timid and mistrustful, those Bedouin, but they hadn't run from him. He walked back without pause, refusing to look again at the stripped automobiles, the recreation area with its pool-sized midden, the burned out barracks and the attending wildflowers—refusing to look at any of it, not wanting to see anything more of the world that had been or the new one discovered today. He walked with the taste of wormwood in his mouth.

Elwood Station was an enclosed world, a fenced and fright-inducing world standing like an island of dogged isolation amid the survivors of that violent civil war. There *were* survivors. They were out there on the outside and they had fled from him—on the inside. Their fears centered on the station: *here* was the devil they knew. *He* was the devil they'd glimpsed.

But the station had a resident—not a visitor, not a raider from beyond the fence who plundered the stores in the wintertime, but a permanent resident. A resident devil who had repaired the fence and hung out the talisman to keep the survivors away, a resident christian who had dug a grave and erected a cross above it.

Chaney stood in the middle of the parking lot.

Before him: the impenetrable walls of the laboratory stood out like a great gray temple in a field of weeds. Before him: a mound of yellow clay heaped beside the Nabataean cistern stood out like an anachronistic thumb, with a single grave hard by. Before him: a two-wheeled cart made of reclaimed lumber and borrowed wheels.

Somewhere behind him: a pair of eyes watching.

# 16

Brian Chaney took the keys from his pocket and unlocked the operations door. Two lanterns rested on the top step, but no bells rang below as the door swung. A rush of clammy air fell through the doorway to be lost in the crisp, cleaner air outside. The sun rode high—near the zenith—but the day stayed chilly with little promise of becoming warmer. Chaney was thankful for the heavy coat he wore.

Quiet sun, clean sky, unseasonably cold weather: he could report that to Gilbert Seabrooke.

He propped the heavy door open by shoving the cart against it, and then went below for the first armload of rations. The rifle was left beside the cart, all but forgotten. Carton after carton of foodstuffs was hauled up the stairs and piled in the cart, until his arms were weary of carrying and his legs of climbing; but medicines and matches were forgotten and he made another trip. A few tools for himself were included as a tardy afterthought. Chaney very nearly overestimated himself: the cart was so heavily loaded after the last trip that he had difficulty moving it from the doorway, and so a few of the heavier boxes had to be left behind.

He left the parking lot, pushing the cart.

It cost him more than three hours and most of his determination to reach the northwest corner of the fence the second time that day. The load moved fairly well as long as paved streets served him but when he left the end of the street and struck off through the high grass on his own back trail, progress was miserable. The cart was only slightly easier to pull than push. Chaney didn't remember seeing a machete in the stores, but he wished for a dozen of them—and a dozen bearers to work in front of him hacking a trail through the weedy jungle. The load was back-breaking.

When at last he reached the fence he fell down and gasped for breath. The sun was long past noon.

The fence was assaulted with a crowbar. The task seemed easier where the fencing had been patched over the remains of the truck; it was not as stout there, not as resistant to the bar as the undamaged sections, and he concentrated on that place. He ripped away the barbed wire and pulled it free of the truck shell, then pried out the ends of the original fencing and rolled it back out of the way. When it was done his hands were bleeding again from many cuts and scratches, but he had forced an opening large enough to roll the cart through beside the truck. The wall was breached.

The heavy cart got away from him on the downward slope.

He ran with it, struggling to halt the plunge down the hillside and shouting at it with an exhausted temper but the cart ignored his imprecations and shot down through tall grass that was no barrier at all—now—until at last it reached the plain below and flipped end for end, spilling its load in the weeds. Chaney roared his anger: the Aramaic term so well liked by Arthur Saltus, and then another phrase reserved for asses and tax collectors. The cart—like the ass, but unlike the collector—did not respond.

Laboriously he righted the cart, gathered up the spill, and trudged across the field to the railroad.

The dropped walking stick was a marker.

His small treasure was left there for finding, laid out along the railroad right-of-way for the frightened family or any other traveler who might pass that way. He put the matches and the medicines atop the largest carton and then covered them with his overcoat to protect them from the weather. Chaney spent only a little while scanning the distances along the tracks for sight of a man—he was certain his shouting and his cursing would have frightened away anyone in the area. As before, he was alone in an empty world. From somewhere in the timber he heard a bird calling, and he would have to be content with that.

In the late afternoon hours when the thin heat of the sun was beginning to fade he pulled the empty cart up the hill and through the gaping hole in the fence for a last time, stopping only to retrieve the crowbar. Chaney didn't dare look back. He was afraid of what he might find—or not find. To suddenly turn and look, to discover someone already at the boxes would be his undoing—he knew he would behave as before and again frighten the man away. But to turn and see the same untenanted world again would only deepen his depression. He would not look back.

Chaney followed his own trail through the verdant grass, seeking the beginning of the paved road. Some small animal darted away at his approach.

He stood at the edge of the parking lot, looking at the abandoned garden and thinking of Kathryn van Hise. But for her, he would be loafing on the beach and thinking of going back to work in the tank— but only thinking of it; perhaps in another week or so he'd get up off his duff and look up train schedules and connections to Indianapolis, if they still existed in an age of dying rails. The only weight on his mind would be the reviewers who read books too hastily and leaped to fantastic conclusions. But for her, he would have never heard of Seabrooke, Moresby, Saltus—unless their names happened to be on a document coming into the tank. He wouldn't have jumped into Joliet two years ahead of his time and found a wall; he wouldn't have jumped into *this* dismal future, whatever year *this* might be, and found a catastrophe. He would have plodded along in his own slow, myopic way until the hard future slammed into him—or he into it.

He thought he was done here: done with the aborted survey and done with the very quiet and nearly deserted world of 2000-

something. He could do no more than tell Katrina, tell Seabrooke, and perhaps listen while they relayed the word to Washington. The next move would be up to the politicians and the bureaucrats—let them change the future if they could, if they possessed the power.

His role was completed. He could tape a report and label it *Eschatos*.

The mound of yellow clay claimed his attention and he followed the gutter through the grass to the cistern, wanting to photograph it. He still marveled at finding a Nabataean artifact thrust forward into the twenty-first century, and he suspected Arthur Saltus was responsible: it had been copied from the book he'd lent Saltus, from the pages of *Pax Abrahamitica*. With luck, it would trap and hold water for another century or so, and if he could measure the capacity he would probably find the volume to be near ten *cor*. Saltus had done well for an amateur.

Chaney turned to the grave.

He would not photograph that, for the picture would raise questions he didn't care to answer. Seabrooke would ask if there'd been an inscription on the crossarm, and why hadn't he photographed the inscription? Katrina would sit by with pencil poised to record his verbal reading.

## A *ditat Deus K*

Down there: Arthur or Katrina?

How could he tell Katrina that he'd found her grave? Or her husband's grave? Why couldn't *this* have been the final resting place of Major Moresby?

A bird cried again in some far off place, pulling his gaze up to the distant trees and the sky beyond.

The trees were in new leaf, telling the early summer; the grass was soft tender green, not yet wiry from the droughts of midsummer: a fresh world. Gauzy clouds were gathering about the descending sun, creating a mirage of reddish-gold fleece. Eastward, the sky was wondrously blue and clean—a newly scrubbed sky, disinfected and sterilized. At night the stars must appear as enormous polished diamonds.

Arthur or Katrina?

Brian Chaney knelt briefly to touch the sod above the grave, and mentally prepared himself to go home. His depression was deep.

A voice said: "Please...Mr. Chaney?"

The shock immobilized him. He was afraid that if he turned quickly or leaped to his feet, a nervous finger would jerk the trigger and he would join Moresby in the soil of the station. He held himself rigidly still, aware that his own rifle had been left in the cart. Oversight; carelessness; stupidity. One hand rested on the grave; his gaze remained on the small cross.

"Mr. Chaney?"

After the longest time—a disquieting eternity—he turned only his head to look back along the path.

Two strangers: two *almost* strangers, two people who mirrored his own uncertainty and apprehension.

The nearer of the two wore a heavy coat and a pair of boots taken from the stores; his head and hands were bare and the only weapon he carried was a pair of binoculars also borrowed from the stores. He was tall, thin, lanky—only a few inches less than Chaney's height, but he lacked the sandy hair and muscular body of his father; he lacked the bronzed skin and the silver filling in his teeth, he lacked the squint of eye that would suggest a seafarer peering into the sun. He lacked the buoyant youthfulness. If the man had possessed those characteristics instead of lacking them, Chaney would say he was looking at Arthur Saltus.

"How do you know my name?"

"You are the only one unaccounted for, sir."

"And you had my description?"

Softly: "Yes, sir."

Chaney turned on his knees to face the strangers. He realized they were as much afraid of him as he was of them. When had they last seen another man here?

"Your name is Saltus?"

A nod. "Arthur Saltus."

Chaney shifted his gaze to the woman who stood well behind the man. She stared at *him* with a curious mixture of fascination and fright, poised for instant flight. When had she last seen another man here?

Chaney asked: "Kathryn?"

She didn't respond, but the man said: "My sister."

The daughter was like the mother in nearly every respect, lacking only the summer tan and the delta pants. She was bundled in a great coat against the chill and wore the common boots that were much too large for her feet. A pair of binoculars hung around her neck: *he* felt closely observed. Her head was bare, revealing Katrina's great avalanche of fine brown hair; her eyes were the same soft—now frightened—delightful shade. She was a small woman, no more than a hundred pounds when free of the bulky boots and coat, and gave every appearance of being quick and alert. She also gave the appearance of being older than Katrina.

Chaney looked from one to the other: the two of them, brother and sister, were years beyond the people he had left in the past, years beyond their parents.

He said at last: "Do you know the date?"

"No, sir."

Hesitation, then: "I think you were waiting for me."

Arthur Saltus nodded, and there was the barest hint of affirmation from the woman.

"My father said you would be here—sometime. He was certain you would come; you were the last of the three."

Surprise: "No one else, after us?"

"No one."

Chaney touched the grave a last time, and their eyes followed his hand. He had one more question to ask before he would risk getting to his feet.

"Who lies here?"

Arthur Saltus said: "My father."

Chaney wanted to cry out: how? when? why? but embarrassment held his tongue, embarrassment and pain and depression; he bitterly regretted the day he'd accepted Katrina's offer and stepped into this unhappy position. He climbed to his feet, avoiding sudden moves that could be misinterpreted, and was thankful he hadn't taken a picture of the grave—thankful he wouldn't have to tell Katrina, or Saltus, or Seabrooke, what he'd found here. He would make no mention of the grave at all.

Standing, Chaney searched the area carefully, looking over their heads at the weedy garden, the parking lot, the company street beyond the lot and all of the station open to his eye. He saw no one else.

Sharp question: "Are you two alone here?"

The woman had jumped at his tone and seemed about to flee, but her brother held his ground.

"No, sir."

A pause, and then: "Where is Katrina?"

"She is waiting in the place, Mr. Chaney."

"Does she know I am here?"

"Yes, sir."

"She knew I would ask about her?"

"Yes, sir. She thought you would."

Chaney said: "I'm going to break a rule."

"She thought you would do that, too."

"But she didn't object?"

"She gave us instructions, sir. If you asked, we were to say that she *told* you where she would wait."

Chaney nodded his wonder. "Yes—she did that. She did that twice." He moved back along the path by way of the cistern and they carefully retreated before him, still uncertain of him. "Did you do this?"

"My father and I dug it, Mr. Chaney. We had your book. The descriptions were very clear."

"I'd tell Haakon, if I dared."

Arthur Saltus stepped aside when they reached the parking lot and allowed Chaney to go ahead of him. The woman had darted off to one side and now kept a prudent distance. She continued to stare at him, a stare that might have been rude under other circumstances, and Chaney was very sure she'd seen no other man for too many years. He was equally certain she'd never seen a man like him inside the protective fence: that was her apprehension.

He ignored the rifle resting in the cart.

Brian Chaney fitted the keys into the twin locks and swung the heavy door. His two lanterns rested on the top step, and as before a rush of musty air fell out into the waning afternoon sunlight. Chaney paused awkwardly on the doorsill wondering what to say—wondering *how* to say goodbye to these people. Only a damned fool would say something flippant or vacuous or inane; only a damned fool would utter one of the meaningless clichés of *his* age; but only a stupid fool would simply walk away from them without saying anything.

He glanced again at the sky and at the golden fleece about the sun, at the new grass and leaves and then at the aging mound of yellow clay. At length his gaze swung back to the man and woman who waited on him.

He said: "Thank you for trusting me."

Saltus nodded. "They said you could be trusted."

Chaney studied Arthur Saltus and almost saw again the unruly sandy hair and the peculiar set to his eyes—the eyes of a man long accustomed to peering against the sun-bright sea. He looked long at Kathryn Saltus but could *not* see the transparent blouse or the delta pants: on her those garments would be obscene. Those garments belonged to a world long gone. He searched her face for a moment too long, and was falling head over heels when reality brought him up short.

Harsh reality: she lived *here* but he belonged back there. It was folly to entertain even dreams about a woman living a hundred years ahead of him. Hurtful reality.

His conscience hurt when he closed the door because he had no more to say to them. Chaney turned away and went down the steps, putting behind him the quiet sun, the chill world of 2000-plus, the unknown survivors beyond the fence who had fled in terror at sight and sound of him, and the half-familiar survivors within the fence who were sharp reminders of his own loss. His conscience hurt, but he didn't turn back.

The time was near sunset on an unknown day.

It was the longest day of his life.

# 17

The briefing room was subtly different from that one he'd first entered weeks or years or centuries ago.

He remembered the military policeman who'd escorted him from the gate and then opened the door for him; he remembered his first glance into the room—his lukewarm reception, his tardy entrance. He'd found Kathryn van Hise critically eyeing him, assessing him, wondering if he would measure up to some task ahead; he'd found Major Moresby and Arthur Saltus playing cards, bored, impatiently awaiting his arrival; he'd found the long steel table positioned under lights in the center of the room—all waiting on him.

He had given his name and started an apology for his tardiness when the first hurtful sound stopped him, chopped him off in midsentence and hammered his ears. He had seen them turn together to watch the clock: sixty-one seconds. All that only a week or two ago—a century or two ago—before the bulky envelopes were opened and a hundred flights of fancy loosed. The long journey from the Florida beach had brought him twice to this room, but *this* time the lantern poorly illuminated the place.

Katrina was there.

The aged woman was sitting in her accustomed chair to one side of the oversized steel table—sitting quietly in the darkness beneath the extinct ceiling lights. As always, her clasped hands rested on the tabletop in repose. Chaney put the lantern on the table between them and the poor light fell on her face.

Katrina.

Her eyes were bright and alive, as sharply alert as he remembered them, but time had not been lenient with her. He read lines of pain, of unknown troubles and grief; the lines of a tenacious woman who had endured much, had suffered much, but had never surrendered her courage. The skin was drawn tight over her cheekbones, pulled tight around her mouth and chin and appeared sallow in lantern light. The lustrous, lovely hair was entirely gray. Hard years, unhappy years, lean years.

Despite all that he knew a familiar spark within him: she was as beautiful in age as in youth. He was pleased to find that loveliness so enduring.

Chaney pulled out his own chair and slid down, never taking his eye off her. The old woman sat without moving, without speaking, watching him intently and waiting for the first word.

He thought: she might have been sitting there for centuries while the dust and the darkness grew around her; waiting patiently for him to come forward to the target, waiting for him to explore the station, fulfill his last mission, end the survey, and *then* come opening doors to find the answers to questions raised above ground. Chaney would not have been too surprised to find her waiting in ancient Jericho if he'd gone back ten thousand years. She would have been there, placidly waiting in some temple or hovel, waiting in a place where he would find her when he began opening doors.

The dusty briefing room was as chill as the cellar had been, as chill as the air outside, and she was bundled in one of the heavy coats. Her hands were encased in a pair of large mittens intended for a man—and if he bent to look, he would find the oversize boots. She appeared bent over, small in the chair and terribly tired.

Katrina waited on him.

Chaney struggled for something to say, something that wouldn't sound foolish or melodramatic or carry a ring of false heartiness. She would despise him for that. Here again was the struggle of the outer door, and here again he was fearful of losing the struggle. He had left her here in this room only hours ago, left her with that sense of dry apprehension as he prepared himself for the third—now final—probe into the future. She had been sitting in the same chair in the same attitude of repose.

Chaney said: "I'm *still* in love with you, Katrina."

He watched her eyes, and thought they were quickly filled with humor and a pleasurable laughter.

"Thank you, Brian."

Her voice had aged as well: it sounded more husky than he remembered and it reflected her weariness.

"I found patches of wild strawberries at the old barracks, Katrina. When do strawberries ripen in Illinois?"

There *was* laughter in her eyes. "In May or June. The summers have been quite cold, but May or June."

"Do you know the year? The number?"

A minute movement of her head. "The power went out many years ago. I'm sorry, Brian, but I have lost the count."

"I don't suppose it really matters—not now, not with what we've already learned. I agree with Pindar."

She looked her question.

He said: "Pindar lived about twenty-five hundred years ago but he was wiser than a lot of men alive today. He warned man of peering too far into the future, he warned of not liking what would be found." An apologetic gesture; a grin. "Bartlett again: my vice. The Commander was always teasing me about my affair with Bartlett."

"Arthur waited long to see you. He hoped you would come early, that he might see you again."

"I would have liked—Didn't anyone *know?*"

"No."

"But why not? That gyroscope was tracking me."

"No one knew your arrival date; no one would guess. The gyroscope device could not measure your progress after the power failed *here*. We knew only the date of failure, when the TDV suddenly stopped transmitting signals to the computer *there*. You were wholly lost to us, Brian."

"Sheeg! Those goddam infallible engineers and their goddam infallible inventions!" He caught himself and was embarrassed at the outburst. "Excuse me, Katrina." Chaney reached across the table and closed his hands over hers. "I found the Commander's grave outside— I wish I *had* been on time. And I had already decided not to tell you about that grave when I went back, when I turned in my report." He peered at her. "I *didn't* tell anyone, did I?"

"No, you reported nothing."

A satisfied nod. "Good for me—I'm still keeping my mouth shut. The Commander made me promise not to tell you about your future marriage, a week or so ago when we returned from the Joliet trials. But you tried to pry the secret out of me, remember?"

She smiled at his words. "A week or so ago."

Chaney mentally kicked himself. "I have this bad habit of putting my foot in my mouth."

A little movement of her head to placate him. "But I guessed at your secret, Brian. Between your manner and Arthur's deportment, I guessed it. You put yourself away from me."

"I think you had already made up your mind. The little signs were beginning to show, Katrina." He had a vivid memory of the victory party the night of their return.

She said: "I had almost decided at that time, and I *did* decide a short while afterward; I *did* decide when he came back hurt from his survey. He was so helpless, so near death when you and the doctor took him from the vehicle I decided on the spot." She glanced at his enfolding hands and then raised her eyes. "But I was aware of your own intentions. I knew you would be hurt."

He squeezed her fingers with encouragement. "Long ago and far away, Katrina. I'm getting over it."

She made no reply, knowing it to be a half-truth.

"I met the children—" He stopped, aware of the awkwardness. "Children they are *not*—they're older than I am! I met Arthur and Kathryn out there but they were afraid of me."

Katrina nodded and again her gaze slid away from him to rest on his enveloping hands.

"Arthur is ten years older than you, I think, but Kathryn should be about the same age. I am sorry I can't be more precise than that; I am sorry I can't tell you how long my husband has been dead. We no longer know time here, Brian; we only live from one summer to the next. It is not the happiest existence." After a while her hands moved inside his, and she glanced up again. "They were afraid of you because they've known no other man since the station was overrun, since the military personnel left here and we stayed within the fence for safety. For a year or two we dared not even leave this building."

Bitterly: "The people out there were afraid of me, too. They ran away from me."

She was quickly astonished, and betrayed alarm.

"Which people? Where?"

"The family I found outside the fence—down there by the railroad tracks."

"There is no one alive out there."

"Katrina, there *is*—I saw them, called to them, begged them to come back, but they ran away in fear."

"How many? Were there many of them?"

"Three. A family of three: father, mother, and a little boy. I found them walking along the railroad track out there beyond the northwest corner. The little fellow was picking up something—pieces of coal, perhaps—and putting them in a bag his mother carried; they seemed to be making a game of it. They were walking in peace, in contentment until I called to them."

Tersely: "Why did you do that? Why did you call attention to yourself?"

"Because I was lonely! Because I was sick and hurt at sight of an empty world! I yelled out because those people were the only living things I'd found here, other than a frightened rabbit. I wanted their company, I wanted their news! I would have given them everything I owned for only an hour of their time. Katrina, I wanted to *know* if people were still living in this world." He stopped and took tighter rein on his emotions. More quietly: "I wanted to talk to them, to ask questions, but they were afraid of me—scared witless, shocked by sight of me. They ran like that frightened rabbit and I never saw them again. I can't tell you how much that hurt me."

She pulled her hands from his and dropped them into her lap. "Katrina—"

She wouldn't look up at once, but steadfastly kept her gaze on the tabletop. The movement of her hands had left small trails in the dust. He thought the tiny bundle of her seemed more wilted and withdrawn than before: the taut skin on her face appeared to have aged in the last few minutes—or perhaps that age had been claiming her all the while they talked.

"Katrina, please."

After a long while she said: "I am sorry, Brian. I will apologize for my children, and for that family. They dared not trust you, none of them, and the poor family felt they had good reason to fear you." Her head came up and he felt shock. "Everyone fears you; no one will trust you since the rebellion. I am the only one here who does not fear a black man."

He was hurt again, not by her words but because she was crying. It was painful to watch her cry.

Brian Chaney came into the briefing room a second time. He was carrying another lantern, two plastic cups, and a container of water from the stores. He would have brought along a bottle of whiskey if that had been available, but it was likely that the Commander had long ago consumed the whiskey on his successive birthdays.

The old woman had wiped her eyes dry.

Chaney filled both cups and set the first one on the table before her. "Drink up—we'll drink a toast."

"To what, Brian?"

"To what? Do we need an excuse?" He swung his arm in an expansive gesture which took in the room. "To that damned clock up there: knocking off sixty-one seconds while my ears suffered. To that red telephone: I never used it to call the President and tell him he was a dunce. To us: a demographer from the Indiana Corporation, and a research supervisor from the Bureau of Standards—the last two misfits sitting at the end of the world. We're out of place and out of time, Katrina: they don't need demographers and researchers here—they don't have corporations and bureaus here. Drink to us."

"Brian, you are a clown."

"Oh, yes." He sat down and looked at her closely in the lantern light. "Yes? I am that. And I think you are *almost* smiling again. Please smile for me."

Katrina smiled: pale shadow of an old smile.

Chaney said: "Now *that* is why I still love you!" He lifted his cup. "To the most beautiful researcher in the world—and you may drink to the most frustrated demographer in the world. Bottoms up!" Chaney emptied the cup, and thought the water tasted flat—stale.

She nodded over the rim of her cup and sipped.

Chaney stared at the long table, the darkened lights overhead, the stopped clock, the dead telephones. "I'm supposed to be working—making a survey."

"It doesn't matter."

"Have to keep Seabrooke happy. I can report a family out there: at least *one* family alive and living in peace. I suppose there are more—there has to be more. Do you know of anyone else? Anyone at all?"

Patiently: "There were a few at first, those many years ago; we managed to keep in touch with some survivors by radio before the power failure. Arthur located a small group in Virginia, a military group living underground in an Army command post; and later he contacted a family in Maine. Sometimes we would make brief contact with one or two individuals in the west, in the mountain states, but it was always poor news. Each of them survived for the same reasons: by a series of lucky circumstances, or by their skills and their wits, or because they were unusually well protected as we were. Their numbers were always small and it was always discouraging news."

"But *some* survived. That's important, Katrina. How long have you been alone on the station?"

"Since the rebellion, since the Major's year."

Chaney gestured. "That could be—" He peered at her, guessing at her age. "That could be thirty years ago."

"Perhaps."

"But what happened to the other people here?"

She said: "Almost all the military personnel were withdrawn at the beginning; they were posted to overseas duty. The few who remained did not survive the attack when the rebels overran the station. A very few civilian technicians stayed with us for a time, but then left to rejoin their families—or search for their families. The laboratory was already empty in Arthur's year. We had been ordered underground for the duration."

"The duration. How long was that?"

The sharp old eyes studied him. "I would think it is ending just now, Brian. Your description of the family outside the fence suggests it is ending now."

Bitterly: "And nobody around but you and me to sign the peace treaty and pose for the cameras. Seabrooke?"

"Mr. Seabrooke was relieved of his post, dismissed, shortly after the three launches. I believe he returned to the Dakotas. The President had blamed *him* for the failure of the survey, and he was made the scapegoat."

Chaney struck the table with a fist.

"I *said* that man was a dunce—just one more in a long line of idiots and dunces inhabiting the White House! Katrina, I don't understand how this country has managed to survive with so many incompetent fools at the top."

Softly-spoken reminder: "It hasn't, Brian."

He muttered under his breath and glared at the dust on the table. Aloud: "Excuse me."

She nodded easily but said nothing.

A memory prodded him. "What happened to the JCS, to those men who tried to take Camp David?"

She closed her eyes for a moment, as if to close off the past. Her expression was bitter. "The Joint Chiefs of Staff were executed before a firing squad, a public spectacle. The President had declared a business moratorium on the day of the execution; government offices closed and the children were let out of school, all to witness the spectacle on the networks. He was determined to give the country a warning. It was ghastly, depressing, and I hated him for it."

Chaney stared at her. "And I have to go back and tell him what he's going to do. What a hell of a chore *this* survey is!" He hurled the drinking cup across the room, unable to stifle the angry impulse. "Katrina, I wish you had never found me on the beach. I wish I had walked away from you, or thrown you into the sea, or kidnapped you and ran away to Israel—anything."

She smiled again, perhaps at the memory of the beach. "But that would have accomplished nothing, Brian. The Arab Federation overran Israel and drove the people into the sea. We wouldn't have escaped anything."

He uttered a single word and then had to apologize again, although the woman didn't understand the epithet. "The Major certainly jumped into the beginning of hell."

She corrected him. "The Major jumped into the end of it; the wars had been underway for nearly twenty years and the nation was on the brink of disaster. Major Moresby came forward only in time to witness the end for us, for the United States. After him, the government ceased to be. After twenty years we were wholly exhausted, used up, and could not defend ourselves against anyone."

The old woman spoke with a dry weariness, a long fatigue, and he could listen to her voice and her spirit running down as she talked.

The wars began just after the Presidential election of 1980, just after the field trials into Joliet. Arthur Saltus had told her of the two Chinese railroad towns blown off the map, and suddenly one day in December the Chinese bombed Darwin, Australia, in long-delayed retaliation. The whole of northern Australia was made uninhabitable by radiation. The public was never told of the first strike against the railroad towns but only of the second: it was painted an act of brutal savagery against an innocent populace. Radioactivity spread across the Arafura Sea to the islands to the north, and drifted toward the Philippines. Great Britain appealed to the United States for aid.

The reelected President and his Congress declared war on the Chinese Peoples' Republic in the week following his inauguration, after having waged an undeclared war since 1954. The Pentagon had privately assured him the matter could be terminated and the enemy subdued in three weeks. Some months later the President committed massive numbers of troops to the Asian Theater: now involving eleven nations from the Philippine Republic westward to Pakistan, and to the defense of Australia. He was then compelled to send troops to Korea, to counteract renewed hostilities there, but lost them all when the Chinese and the Mongolians overran the peninsula and ended foreign occupation.

She said tiredly: "The President was reelected in 1980, and again for a third term in 1984. After Arthur brought back the terrible news from Joliet, the man seemed unable to control himself and unable to do anything right. The third-term prohibition was repealed at his urging, and some time during that third term the Constitution was suspended altogether 'for the duration of the emergency.' The emergency never ended. Brian, that man was the last elected President the country ever had. After him there was nothing."

Chaney said bitterly: "The meek, the terrible meek. I hope he is still alive to see this!"

"He isn't, he wasn't. He was assassinated and his body thrown into the burning White House. They burned Washington to destroy a symbol of oppression."

"Burned it! Wait until I tell him *that*."

She made a little gesture to hush him or contradict him. "All that and more, much more. Those twenty years were a frightful ordeal; the last few years were numbing. Life appeared to stop, to give way to savagery. We missed the little things at first: passenger trains and airliners were forbidden to civilian traffic, mail deliveries were cut back to twice a week and then halted altogether, the news telecasts were restricted to only one a day and then as the war worsened, further restricted to only local news not of a military nature. We were isolated from the world and nearly isolated from Washington.

"Our trucks were taken away for use elsewhere; food was not brought in, nor medicines, nor clothing, nor fuel, and we fell back on the supplies stored on station. The military personnel were transferred to other posts or to points overseas, leaving only a token crew to guard this installation.

"Brian, that guard was compelled to fire on nearby townspeople attempting to raid our stores: the rumor had been spread that enormous stockpiles of food were here, and they were desperately hungry."

Katrina looked down at her hands and swallowed painfully. "The twenty years finally ended for *us* in a shocking civil war."

Chaney said: "Ramjets."

"They were called that, once they came into the open, once their statement of intent was publicized: Revolution And Morality. Sometimes we would see banners bearing the word RAM, but the name soon became something dirty—something akin to that other name they were called for centuries: it was a very bitter time and you would have suffered if you had remained on station.

"Brian, people everywhere were starving, dying of disease, rotting in neglect and misery, but those people possessed a leadership we now lacked. Ramjets had efficient leadership. Their leaders used them against us and it was our turn to suffer. There *was* revolution but little or no morality; whatever morality they may have possessed was quickly lost in the rebellion and we all suffered. The country was caught up in a senseless savagery."

"That's when Moresby came up?"

A weary nod.

Major Moresby witnessed the beginning of the civil war when he emerged on his target date. *They* had chosen the same date for the outbreak of the rebellion—they had selected the Fourth of July as *their* target in a bid for independence from white America and the bombing of Chicago was intended to be the signal. Ramjet liaison agents in Peiping had arranged that: Chicago—not Atlanta or Memphis or Birmingham—was the object of their greatest hatred after the wall. But the plan went awry.

The rebellion broke out almost a week earlier—quite by accident—when triggered by a riot in the little river town of Cairo, Illinois. A traffic arrest there, followed by a street shooting and then a wholesale jail delivery of black prisoners, upset the schedule: the revolt was quickly out of control. The state militia and the police were helpless, depleted in number, their reserve manpower long since spent overseas; there was no regular army left standing in the United States except for token troops at various posts and stations, and even the ceremonial guards at national monuments had been removed and assigned to foreign duty. There was no remaining force to prevent the rebellion. Major Moresby climbed out of the vehicle and into the middle of the holocaust.

The agony went on for almost seventeen months.

The President was assassinated, Congress fled—or died while trying to flee—and Washington burned. They burned many of the cities where they were numerically strong. In their passion they burned themselves out of their homes and destroyed the fields and crops which had fed them.

The few remaining lines of transportation which were open up to that moment ceased entirely. Trucks were intercepted, looted and burned, their drivers shot. Buses were stopped on interstate highways and white passengers killed. Railroad trains were abandoned wherever they stopped, or wherever the tracks were torn up, engineers and crews were murdered wherever they were caught. Desperate hunger soon followed the stoppage of traffic.

Katrina said: "Everyone here expected the Chinese to intervene, to invade, and we knew we could not stop them. Brian, our country had lost or abandoned twenty million men overseas; we were helpless before any invader. But they did not come. I thank God they did not come. They were prevented from coming when the Soviet turned on them in a holy war in the name of Communism: that long, long border dispute burst into open warfare and the Russians drove on Lop Nor." She made a little gesture of futility. "We never learned what happened; we never learned the outcome of anything in Europe. Perhaps they are still fighting, if anyone is left alive to fight. Our contact with the Continent was lost, and has never been restored to our knowledge. We lost contact with that military group in Virginia when the electricity failed. We were alone."

He said in wonder: "Israel, Egypt, Australia, Britain, Russia, China—all of them: the world."

"All of them," she repeated with a dull fatigue. "And our troops were wasted in nearly every one of them, thrown away by a man with a monumental ego. Not more than a handful of those troops ever returned. We were done."

Chaney said: "I guess the Commander came up at the end—seventeen months later."

"Arthur emerged from the TDV on his target date, just past the end of it: the beginning of the second winter after the rebellion. We think the rebellion *had* ended, spent and exhausted on its own fury. We think the men who assaulted him at the gatehouse were stragglers, survivors who had managed through the first winter. He said those men were as surprised by his appearance, as he was by theirs; they might have fled if he had not cornered them." Katrina laced her fingers on the tabletop in familiar gesture and looked at him. "We saw a few armed bands roaming the countryside that second winter. We repaired the fence, stood guard, but were not again molested: Arthur put out warnings he had found in the book you gave him. By the following spring, the bands of men had dwindled to a few scavengers prowling the fields for game—but after that we saw no one. Until you came, we saw no one."

He said: "So ends the bloody business of the day."

# 18

Katrina peered across the table and sought to break the unhappy silence between them.

"A family, you said? Father, mother, and child? A healthy child? How old was he?"

"I don't know: three, maybe four. The kid was having himself a fine time—playing, hollering, picking up things—until I scared off his parents." Chaney still felt bitter about that encounter. "They all looked healthy enough. They *ran* healthy."

Katrina nodded her satisfaction. "It gives one hope for the future, doesn't it?"

"I suppose so."

She reprimanded him: "You *know* so. If those people were healthy, they were eating well and living in some degree of safety. If the man carried no weapon, he thought none was needed. If they had a child and were together, family life has been reestablished. And if that child survived his birth and was thriving, it suggests a quiet normalcy has returned to the world, a measure of sanity. All that gives me hope for the future."

"A quiet normalcy," he repeated. "The sun in that sky was quiet. It was cold out there."

The dark eyes peered at him. "Have you ever admitted to yourself that you could be wrong, Brian? Have you even thought of your translations today? You were a stubborn man; you came close to mocking Major Moresby."

Chaney failed to answer: it was not easy to reassess the *Eschatos* scroll in a day. A piece of his mind insisted that ancient Hebrew fiction was only fiction.

They sat in the heavy silence of the briefing room, looking at each other in the lantern light and knowing this was coming to an end. Chaney was uneasy. There had been a hundred—a thousand—questions he'd wanted to ask when he first walked into the room, when he first discovered her, but now he could think of little to say. Here was Katrina, the once youthful, radiant Katrina of the swimming pool—and outside was Katrina's family waiting for him to leave.

He wanted desperately to ask one more question but at the same time he was afraid to ask: what happened to *him* after his return, after the completion of the probe? What had happened to *him*? He wanted to know where he had gone, what he had done, how he had survived the perilous years—he wanted to know *if* he had survived those years. Chaney was long convinced that he was not on station in 1980, not there at the time of the field trials, but where was he then? She might have some knowledge of him after he'd finished the mission and left; she might have kept in touch. He was afraid to ask. Pindar's advice stopped his tongue.

He got up suddenly from his chair. "Katrina, will you walk downstairs with me?"

She gave him a strange look, an almost frightened look, but said: "Yes, sir."

Katrina left her chair and came around the table to him. Age had slowed her graceful walk and he was acutely distressed to see her move with difficulty. Chaney picked up a lantern, and offered her his free arm. He felt a flush of excitement as she neared him, touched him.

They descended the stairs without speaking. Chaney slowed his pace to accommodate her and they went down slowly, one cautious step at a time. Kathryn van Hise held on to the rail and moved with the hesitant pace of the aged.

They stopped at the opened door to the operations room. Chaney held the lantern high to inspect the vehicle: the hatch was open and the hull of the craft covered by dust; the concrete cradle seemed dirty with age.

He asked suddenly: "How much did I report, Katrina? Did I tell them about you? Your family? Did I tell them about that family on the railroad tracks? What did I say?"

"Nothing." She wouldn't look up at him.

"What?"

"You reported nothing."

He thought her voice was strained. "I had to say something. Gilbert Seabrooke will demand *something*."

"Brian—" She stopped, swallowed hard, and then began again. "You reported nothing, Mr. Chaney. You did not return from your probe. We knew you were lost to us when the vehicle failed to return at sixty-one seconds: you were wholly lost to us."

Brian Chaney very carefully put the lantern down and then turned her around and pulled her head up. He wanted to see her face, wanted to see why she was lying. Her eyes were wet with threatened tears but there was no lie there.

Stiffly: "Why not, Katrina?"

"We have no power, Mr. Chaney. The vehicle is helpless, immobile."

Chaney swung his head to stare at the TDV and as quickly swung back to the woman. He wasn't aware that he was holding her in a painful grip.

"The engineers can pull me back."

"No. They can do nothing for you: they lost you when that device stopped tracking, when the computer went silent, when the power failed here and you overshot the failure date. They *lost* you; they lost the vehicle." She pulled away from his hard grasp, and her wavering gaze fell. "You didn't come back to the laboratory, Mr. Chaney. No one saw you again after the launch; no one saw you again until you appeared here, today."

Almost shouting: "Stop calling me Mr. Chaney!"

"I am...I am terribly sorry. You were as lost to us as Major Moresby. We thought..."

He turned his back on the woman and deliberately walked into the operations room. Brian Chaney climbed up on the polywater tank and thrust a leg through the open hatch of the TDV. He didn't bother to undress or remove the heavy boots. Wriggling downward through the hatch, he slammed it shut over his head and looked for the blinking green light. There was none. Chaney stretched out full length on the web sling and thrust his heels against the kickbar at the bottom. No red light answered him.

He knew panic.

He fought against that and waited for his nerves to rest, waited for a stolid placidity to return. The memory of his first test came back: he'd thought then the vehicle was like a cramped tomb, and he thought so now. Lying on the webbed sling for the first time—and waiting for something spectacular to happen—he had felt an ache in his legs and had stretched them out to relieve the ache. His feet had struck the kickbar, sending him back to the beginning before the engineers were ready; they had been angry with him. And an hour later, in the lecture room, everyone heard and saw the results of his act: the vehicle kicked backward as he thrust out his feet, the sound struck his eardrums and the lights dimmed. The astonished engineers left the room on the run, and Gilbert Seabrooke proposed a new study program to be submitted to Indic. The TDV sucked power from its present, not its past.

Chaney reached up to snug the hatch. It was snug. The light that should have been blinking green stayed dark. Chaney put the heavy boots against the bar and pushed. The red light stayed dark. He pushed again, then kicked at the bar. After a moment he twisted around to peer through the plastic bubble into the room. It was dimly lit by the lantern resting on the floor.

He shouted: "Goddammit, go!" And kicked again.

The room was dimly lit by lantern light.

He walked slowly along the corridor in the feeble light of the lantern, walked woodenly in shock tinged with fear. The failure of the vehicle to move under his prodding had stunned him. He wished desperately for Katrina, wished she was standing by with a word or a gesture he might seize for a crutch, but she wasn't visible in the corridor. She had left him while he struggled with the vehicle, perhaps to return to the briefing room, perhaps to go outside, perhaps to retire to whatever sort of shelter she shared with her son and daughter. He was alone, fighting panic. The door to the engineering laboratory was standing open, as was the door to the storeroom, but she wasn't waiting for him in either place. Chaney listened for her but heard nothing, and went on after the smallest pause. The dusty corridor ended and a flight of stairs led upward to the operations exit.

He thought the sign on the door was a bitter mockery—one of the many visited on him since he'd sailed for Israel a century or two ago. He regretted the day he had read and translated those scrolls—but at the same time he wished desperately he knew the identity of that scribe who had amused himself and his fellows by creating the *Eschatos* document. A single name would be enough: an Amos or a Malachi or an Ibycus.

He would hoist a glass of water from the Nabataean cistern and salute the unknown genius for his wit and wisdom, for his mockery. He would shout to the freshly scrubbed sky: "Here, damn your eyes, Ibycus! Here, for the long-dead dragons and the ruptured fence and the ice on the rivers. Here, for my head of gold, my breast of silver, my legs of iron and my feet of clay. My feet of clay, Ibycus!" And he would hurl the glass at the lifeless TDV.

Chaney turned the keys in the locks and pushed out into the chill night air. The darkness surprised him; he hadn't realized he'd spent so many bittersweet hours inside with Katrina. The parking lot was empty but for the cart and his discarded rifle. Katrina's children hadn't waited for him, and he was aware of a small hurt.

He stepped away from the building and then turned back to look at it: a massive white concrete temple in the moonlight. The barbaric legions had failed to bring it down, despite the damage caused elsewhere on the station.

The sky was the second surprise: he had seen it by day and marveled, but at night it was shockingly beautiful. The stars *were* bright and hard as carefully polished gems, and there were a hundred or a thousand more than he'd ever seen before, he had never known a sky like that in his lifetime. The entire eastern rim of the heavens was lighted by a rising moon of remarkable brilliance.

Chaney stood alone in the center of the parking lot searching the face of the moon, searching out the Sea of Vapors and the pit known as Bode's Crater. The pulsating laser there caught his eye and held it. That one thing had not changed—that one monument not destroyed. The brilliant mote still flashed on the rim of Bode's Crater, marking the place where two astronauts had fallen in the Seventies, marking their grave and their memorial. One of them had been black. Brian Chaney thought himself lucky: he had air to breathe but those men had none.

He said aloud: "You weren't so damned clever Ibycus! You missed *that* one—your prophets didn't show you the *new* sign in the sky."

Chaney sat down in the tilted cart and stretched out his legs for balance. The rifle was an unpleasant lump under his spine and he threw it aside to be rid of it. In a little while he leaned backward and rested against the bed of the cart. The whole of the southeast sky was before him. Chaney thought he should go looking for Katrina, for Arthur and Kathryn, and a place to sleep. Perhaps he would do that after a while, but not now, not now.

The stray thought came that the engineers had been right about one thing: the polywater tank hadn't leaked.

Elwood Station was at peace.

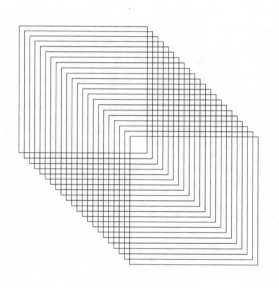

INTRODUCED
BY JACK DANN

# THERE WILL BE TIME

BY POUL ANDERSON

# INTRODUCTION

The year was 1976. George Zebrowski and I were asked to write "chapters" for one of the earliest shared world anthology novels. It was called *A World Named Cleopatra* and was created by Poul Anderson. Poul had already written the first story set on the planet Cleopatra and provided us with a "bible" that described everything we needed to know about the world: its size, solar system, surface gravity, atmosphere, weather patterns, geography, geology, flora and fauna, history, and some of the names of the wondrous things he had discovered there. Poul had done the hard work; all that was left for this sorcerer's apprentice was to create a story that might live and breathe and become part of an imaginary place that Poul had made...real.

But reading Poul's bible and lovingly wrought novella was a revelation to this (then) young writer, for *A World Named Cleopatra* was more than a rigorous short course by a master in planet building and science fictional extrapolation. It was a way of thinking about the process of writing, which itself is the rigorous creation and construction of science fictional, historical or contemporary worlds.

Poul Anderson has referred to planet-building as one of the "joyous arts."

Perhaps the same could be said of the act of writing.

Indeed, there is joy in all of Anderson's work, joy and a certain nostalgic poignancy, a gentle evocation of the profound sadness and loss that life brings to all of us. If I were to compare Poul Anderson with another writer, it would be Loren Eiseley, the great naturalist who examined the world with the mind of a scientist and the heart of a poet reveling in wonder. And Poul Anderson, fictional world builder, is also a poet. His bardic roots reach back to the great epics such as *Gilgamesh, Beowulf, The Volsunga Saga, Hrolf's Saga Krakam, The Elder Edda*, and, of course, the *Iliad* and the *Odyssey*.

In an essay called "Star-flights and Fantasies," written for *The Craft of Science Fiction*, a fine (and now all but unknown) anthology edited by Reginald Bretnor, Anderson described the hallmarks of the epic form.

I think they provide a pretty fair description of his own work:

"Largeness—diversity—marvels—seriousness, possibly leavened by humor, a conviction that life is worth living—attention turned outward to the surrounding world—the supposition that man can either bend fate, or can in his heart resist being bent by it—endurance—achievement—a narrative that keeps moving—bold use of language...."

Sandra Meisel, the foremost Anderson critic, called him "a literalist of the imagination" and went on to say: "He makes what is magical real and what is real magical. Of such power is poetry born."

And the late author and critic James Blish said, "To be a bard is not necessarily the same thing as being a poet. But Anderson is both."

✳

Blish also called Poul Anderson "the enduring explosion." He said that in 1971, but it is as true today as it was then. Anderson is the author of some fifty novels and over two hundred stories—all of consistently high quality. He has written groundbreaking classic science fiction and fantasy, as well as historical fiction, contemporary novels, young adult fiction, criticism, nonfiction (including books on the possibilities of life on other worlds, thermonuclear war, and space exploration), poetry, and award- winning mysteries. He is also an anthologist and a translator who speaks several Scandinavian languages. He has been honored with seven Hugo awards, three Nebula awards, the Tolkein Memorial Award, the Cock Robin Award, two Morley-Montgomery Prizes for scholarship in Sherlock Holmes; and he is a knight of Mark Twain.

Poul Anderson was born in Bristol, Pennsylvania in 1926. His parents were Danish, hence his unusual first name. The late fantasy editor and author Lin Carter said that "Poul himself pronounces it to sound about halfway between 'pole' and 'powl'—but I have never met anyone except Poul himself who can quite pronounce it." Anderson grew up in Texas and Minnesota and spent some time in Denmark. Throughout his career, he has integrated an interest in Scandinavian literature and culture into his fiction, which is all the richer for it.

He began his science fiction career as an undergraduate. As he tells it: "At the University of Minnesota, I majored in physics, graduating with honors in 1948. But apart from a little assisting here and there, I have not worked in the field. What happened was that writing, which had been a hobby for a long time, began to pay off while I was in college with some sales to *Astounding Science Fiction*. I decided to take a year off, living by the typewriter...."

Anderson is still living by the typewriter...or perhaps it's a computer now.

He published a novel for younger readers in 1952, then followed this first novel with two more books, *Brain Wave* and *The Broken Sword*, in 1954. They were both major books, which established him as an important new name in science fiction and fantasy. *Brain Wave* is Wellsian in technique: Anderson asks the reader to accept one fantastic premise—that for millions of years Earth has been passing through a field that inhibits intelligence—and then extrapolates the consequences of what might happen when we finally pass out of that field. *The Broken Sword* is a dark and savage portrayal of the interaction of men with the world of Faerie, which is consistent with Edda and Norse saga. Michael Moorcock considers it to be Anderson's finest fantasy.

Anderson's enduring explosion expanded into a virtual universe of stories and novels, many of which will certainly last well beyond the author's times. His fascination with myth, history, and science can be seen in the enormous variety of books he produced...and continues to produce. Many of his stories and novels are linked into galaxy-spanning future histories, such as the *Technic History* series that begins with *War of the Wing-Men* (later retitled *The Man Who Counts*) in 1958 and includes story collections such as *Trader to the Stars* (1964) and *The Earth Book of Stormgate* (1978) and novels such as *Satan's World* (1969) and *The Day of Their Return* (1973); and the Psychotechnic League series, which can be found in collections such as *The Psychotechnic League* (1981) and *Starship* (1982) and novels such as *Star Ways*, which was later published under the title *The Peregrine* in 1978, and *Virgin Planet* (1959). There is also the Time Patrol series of stories, which have been collected in the omnibus *The Time Patrol* (1991), and there are other linked sequences of stories and novels; but with a writer so prolific and consistently good as Anderson, I leave it to the reader to discover—or rediscover—these books and stories. I can but point out some of his classic work such as *The Enemy Stars* (1959); the brilliant *The High Crusade* (1960), a lovely conceit about medieval knights who conquer the universe with battle-axes and broadswords; the much loved heroic fantasy *Three Hearts and Three Lions* (1961); *Twilight World* (1961); *After Doomsday* (1962); *The Byworlder* (1971); *The People of the Wind* (1973); *The Avatar* (1978); *Orion Shall Rise* (1983); *The Boat of a Million Years* (1989); *Harvest of Stars* (1993); *The Stars Are Also Fire* (1994); and his short story collections such as *Seven Conquests* (1969), *The Queen of Air and Darkness and Other Stories* (1973), and *The Best of Poul Anderson* (1976). There are over forty-five collections to choose from!

I would especially recommend his awesome cosmological journey, *Tau Zero* (1970), which James Blish called "the ultimate hard science fiction novel." It is the ultimate "trip" through time and space on a starship that cannot decelerate. Traveling at near-light speed, the characters witness the end of the universe...and what's beyond. Anderson's conception in *Tau Zero* is larger than life. But once the reader becomes used to the ideas, the characters, with all their faults and virtues, come forward as large as life. As Sandra Miesel suggests, "In Anderson's hands, the laws of nature assume poetic, symbolic, even metaphysical significance."

But for all of Anderson's critical and commercial success, he has still not received the attention he deserves. Critic and encyclopedist John Clute noted that "Poul Anderson is still not as well defined a figure in the pantheon of US sf as writers (like Isaac Asimov from the Golden Age of sf and Frank Herbert from a decade later) of about the same age and certainly no greater skill." I think a comparison can be made between Anderson and the late Fritz Leiber, both bardic storytellers. Leiber was a great science fiction and fantasy writer who did trail blazing and influential work such as the sword and sorcery series *Fafhrd and Gray Mouser*, the urban fantasy *Conjure Wife*, and the time travel novel *The Big Time*. But because Leiber was so versatile and wrote across so many genres, it was difficult to create a single commercial marketing focus. As a result, his work is not as well known as it should be. The same is true of Poul Anderson. But Anderson is more prolific than Leiber was, and there is the added complication that his future histories and fantasy world creations are woven through many novels and stories which were brought into print by many magazines and publishers. This has, unfortunately, muffled his impact on the market.

Poul Anderson's importance in the development of the fantasy and science fiction genres is reflected in his influence on other writers in the field. It is only a matter of time before his work is more widely recognized as part of the canon of science fiction.

❋

High level science fiction needs the perspective and insight of a historian and philosopher. What is required is a Stapeldonian sense of the cycles and permutations and rich variety of history combined with rigorous extrapolation and an ability to create characters we care for.

You'll find all of this in Poul Anderson's *There Will Be Time* (1972), a mature work from the same period as *Tau Zero*. It is one of the few science fiction novels that has not become an "antique future" over time. It doesn't matter that a few of the details of our "present" that Anderson extrapolated back in the revolutionary '60s are not spot-on; they are certainly close enough. The time in which this novel is set becomes just another interesting historical period to the reader in 1997.

Anderson writes: "*Certainly There Will Be Time* is very much a book of the so-called sixties, that `low dishonest decade,' to borrow W. H. Auden's phrase for the thirties. True, it begins earlier, but there draws on my years in the Midwest. It goes on to such issues as ecology, campus radicalism, and the threat of nuclear war. (They are with us yet, of course, but emphases have shifted and other things are now crowding in on our attention.) However, I tried to show that contemporary scene in a larger context, to bring bits of the past and future alive, and to convey some sense of the vastness of history."

As you begin this novel, note the loving attention the author gives to his characters; the narrator Robert Anderson comes alive immediately and will live in your mind long after you've finished this book. Anderson's fictional portraits bring to mind the best work of Clifford Simak and Edgar Pangborn.

*There Will Be Time* is Wellsian in form, for, as in *The Time Machine*, you are only asked to accept one fantastical premise: the possibility of the time traveler. Although this novel reads more like an adventure novel than a philosophical novel, it is an inquiry into the questions of progress, the good society, free will and determinism, human nature, and human history. Anderson is not afraid to be didactic, to invite the reader into a fictional dialogue; he not only ponders and extrapolates present history, but he questions our ideas about the nature of time travel itself and the difficulties of studying the past...and the future.

In a sense, this novel is a primer for future time travelers!

*There Will Be Time* is a novel of grand vistas and human character. Perhaps you'll feel a certain sadness when you've finished this book, as I did...a nostalgia for something lost, for the sensation of being in the middle of life, of seeing into it fully and experiencing its breadth and wonder.

A good story is like memory, like experience itself.

I commend this one to you....

Jack Dann
Melbourne, Australia
July 1, 1996

# THERE WILL BE TIME

BY POUL ANDERSON

# FOREWORD

BE AT EASE. I'm not about to pretend this story is true. First, that claim is a literary convention which went out with Theodore Roosevelt of happy memory. Second, you wouldn't believe it. Third, any tale signed with my name must stand or fall as entertainment; I am a writer, not a cultist. Fourth, it *is* my own composition. Where doubts or gaps occur in that mass of notes, clippings, photographs, and recollections of words spoken which was bequeathed me, I have supplied conjectures. Names, places, and incidents have been changed as seemed needful. Throughout, my narrative uses the techniques of fiction.

Finally, I don't believe a line of it myself. Oh, we could get together, you and I, and ransack official files, old newspapers, yearbooks, journals, and so on forever. But the effort and expense would be large; the results, even if positive, would prove little; we have more urgent jobs at hand; our discoveries could conceivably endanger us.

These pages are merely for the purpose of saying a little about Dr. Robert Anderson. I do owe the book to him. Many of the sentences are his, and my aim throughout has been to capture something of his style and spirit, in memoriam.

You see, I already owed him much more. In what follows, you may recognize certain things from earlier stories of mine. He gave me those ideas, those backgrounds and people, in hour after hour while we sat with sherry and Mozart before a driftwood fire, which is the best kind. I greatly modified them, in part for literary purposes, in part to make the tales my own work. But the core remained his. He would accept no share of payment. "If you sell it," he laughed, "take Karen out to an extravagant dinner in San Francisco, and empty a pony of akvavit for me."

Of course, we talked about everything else too. My memories are rich with our conversations. He had a pawky sense of humor. The chances are overwhelming that, in leaving me a boxful of material in the form he did, he was turning his private fantasies into a final, gentle joke.

On the other hand, parts of it are uncharacteristically bleak.

Or are they? A few times, when I chanced to be present with one or two of his smaller grandchildren, I'd notice his pleasure in their company interrupted by moments of what looked like pain. And when last I saw him, our talk turned on the probable shape of the future, and suddenly he exclaimed, "Oh, God, the young, the poor young! Poul, my generation and yours have had it outrageously easy. All we ever had to do was be white Americans in reasonable health, and we got our place in the sun. But now history's returning to its normal climate here also, and the norm is an ice age." He tossed off his glass and poured a refill more quickly than was his wont. "The tough and lucky will survive," he said. "The rest…will have had what happiness was granted them. A medical man ought to be used to that kind of truth, right?" And he changed the subject.

In his latter years Robert Anderson was tall and spare, a bit stoop-shouldered but in excellent shape, which he attributed to hiking and bicycling. His face was likewise lean, eyes blue behind heavy glasses, clothes and white hair equally rumpled. His speech was slow, punctuated by gestures of a pipe if he was enjoying his twice-a-day smoke. His manner was relaxed and amiable. Nevertheless, he was as independent as his cat. "At my stage of life," he observed, "what was earlier called oddness or orneriness counts as lovable eccentricity. I take full advantage of the fact." He grinned. "Come your turn, remember what I've said."

On the surface, his life had been calm. He was born in Philadelphia in 1895, a distant relative of my father. Though our family is of Scandinavian origin, a branch has been in the States since the Civil War. But he and I never heard of each other till one of his sons, who happened to be interested in genealogy, happened to settle down near me and got in touch. When the old man came visiting, my wife and I were invited over and at once hit it off with him.

His own father was a journalist, who in 1910 got the editorship of the newspaper in a small upper-Midwestern town (current population 10,000; less then) which I choose to call Senlac. He later described the household as nominally Episcopalian and principally Democratic. He had just finished his premedical studies when America entered the First World War and he found himself in the Army; but he never got overseas. Discharged, he went on to his doctorate and internship. My impression is that meanwhile he exploded a bit, in those hipflask days. It cannot have been too violent. Eventually he returned to Senlac, hung out his shingle, and married his longtime fiancée.

I think he was always restless. However, the work of general practitioners was far from dull—before progress condemned them to do little more than man referral desks—and his marriage was happy. Of four children, three boys lived to adulthood and are still flourishing.

In 1955 he retired to travel with his wife. I met him soon afterward. She died in 1958 and he sold their house but bought a cottage nearby. Now his journeys were less extensive; he remarked quietly that without Kate they were less fun. Yet he kept a lively interest in life.

He told me of those folk whom I, not he, have called the Maurai, as if it were a fable which he had invented but lacked the skill to make into a story. Some ten years later he seemed worried about me, for no reason I could see, and I in my turn worried about what time might be doing to him. But presently he came out of this. Though now and then an underlying grimness showed through, he was mostly himself again. There is no doubt that he knew what he was doing, for good or ill, when he wrote the clause into his will concerning me.

I was to use what he left me as I saw fit.

Late last year, unexpectedly and asleep, Robert Anderson took his death. We miss him.

—P. A.

The beginning shapes the end, but I can say almost nothing of Jack Havig's origins, despite the fact that I brought him into the world. On a cold February morning, 1933, who thought of genetic codes, or of Einstein's work as anything that could ever descend from its mathematical Olympus to dwell among men, or of the strength in lands we supposed were safely conquered? I do remember what a slow and difficult birth he had. It was Eleanor Havig's first, and she quite young and small. I felt reluctant to do a Caesarian; maybe it's my fault that she never conceived again by the same husband. Finally the red wrinkled animal dangled safe in my grasp. I slapped his bottom to make him draw his indignant breath, he let the air back out in a wail, and everything proceeded as usual.

Delivery was on the top floor, the third, of our county hospital, which stood at what was then the edge of town. Removing my surgical garb, I had a broad view out a window. To my right, Senlac clustered along a frozen river, red brick at the middle, frame homes on tree-lined streets, grain elevator and water tank rearing ghostly in

THERE WILL BE TIME

dawnlight near the railway station. Ahead and to my left, hills rolled wide and white under a low gray sky, here and there roughened by leafless woodlots, fence lines, and a couple of farmsteads. On the edge of sight loomed a darkness which was Morgan Woods. My breath misted the pane, whose chill made my sweaty body shiver a bit.

"Well," I said half aloud, "welcome to Earth, John Franklin Havig." His father had insisted on having names ready for either sex. "Hope you enjoy yourself."

Hell of a time to arrive, I thought. A worldwide depression hanging heavy as winter heaven. Last year noteworthy for the Japanese conquest of Manchuria, bonus march on Washington, Lindbergh kidnapping. This year begun in the same style: Adolf Hitler had become Chancellor of Germany.... Well, a new President was due to enter the White House, the end of Prohibition looked certain, and springtime in these parts is as lovely as our autumn.

I sought the waiting room. Thomas Havig climbed to his feet. He was not a demonstrative man, but the question trembled on his lips. I took his hand and beamed. "Congratulations, Tom," I said. "You're the father of a bouncing baby boy. I know—I just dribbled him all the way down the hall to the nursery."

My attempt at a joke came back to me several months afterward.

Senlac is a commercial center for an agricultural area; it maintains some light industry, and that's about the list. Having no real choice in the matter, I was a Rotarian, but found excuses to minimize my activity and stay out of the lodges. Don't get me wrong. These people are mine. I like and in many ways admire them. They're the salt of the earth. It's simply that I want other condiments too.

Under such circumstances, Kate's and my friends tended to be few but close. There was her banker father, who'd staked me; I used to kid him that he'd done so because he wanted a Democrat to argue with. There was the lady who ran our public library. There were three or four professors and their wives at Holberg College, though the forty miles between us and them was considered rather an obstacle in those days. And there were the Havigs.

These were transplanted New Englanders, always a bit homesick; but in the '30's you took what jobs were to be had. He taught physics and chemistry at our high school. In addition, he must coach for track. Slim, sharp-featured, the shyness of youth upon him as well as an inborn reserve, Tom got through his secondary chore mainly on student tolerance. They were fond of him; besides, we had a good football team. Eleanor was darker, vivacious, an avid tennis player and active in her church's poor-relief work. "It's fascinating, and I think it's useful," she told me early in our acquaintance. With a shrug: "At least it lets Tom and me feel we aren't altogether hypocrites. You may've guessed we only belong because the school board would never keep on a teacher who didn't."

I was surprised at the near hysteria in her voice when she phoned my office and begged me to come.

A doctor's headquarters were different then from today, especially in a provincial town. I'd converted two front rooms of the big old house where we lived, one for interviews, one for examination and treatments, including minor surgery. I was my own receptionist and secretary. Kate helped with paperwork—looking back from now, it seems impossibly little, but perhaps she never let on—and, what few times patients must wait their turns, she entertained them in the parlor. I'd made my morning rounds, and nobody was due for a while; I could jump straight into the Marmon and drive down Union Street to Elm.

I remember the day was furnace hot, never a cloud above or a breath below, the trees along my way standing like cast green iron. Dogs and children panted in their shade. No birdsong broke the growl of my car engine. Dread closed on me. Eleanor had cried her Johnny's name, and this was polio weather.

But when I entered the fan-whirring venetian-blinded dimness of her home, she embraced me and shivered. "Am I going crazy, Bob?" she gasped, over and over. "Tell me I'm not going crazy!"

"Whoa, whoa, whoa," I murmured. "Have you called Tom?" He eked out his meager pay with a summer job, quality control at the creamery.

"No, I...I thought—"

"Sit down, Ellie." I disengaged us. "You look sane enough to me. Maybe you've let the heat get you. Relax—flop loose—unclench your teeth, roll your head around. Feel better? Okay, now tell me what you think happened."

"Johnny. Two of him. Then one again." She choked. "The *other* one!"

"Huh? Whoa, I said, Ellie. Let's take this a piece at a time."

Her eyes pleaded while she stumbled through the story. "I, I, I was bathing him when I heard a baby scream. I thought that must be from a buggy or something, outside. But it sounded as if it came from the...the bedroom. At last I wrapped Johnny in a towel—couldn't leave him in the water—and carried him along for a, a look. And there was another tiny boy, there in his crib, naked and wet, kicking and yelling. I was so astonished I...dropped mine. I was bent over the crib, he should've landed on the mattress, but, oh, Bob, he didn't. He vanished. In midair. I'd made a, an instinctive grab for him. All I caught was the towel. Johnny was gone! I think I must've passed out for a few seconds. And when I hunted I—found— nothing—"

"What about the strange baby?" I demanded.

"He's...not gone...I think."

"Come on," I said. "Let's go see."

And in the room, immensely relieved, I crowed: "Why, nobody here but good ol' John."

She clutched my arm. "He looks the same." The infant had calmed and was gurgling. "He sounds the same. Except he can't be!"

"The dickens he can't. Ellie, you had a hallucination. No great surprise in this weather, when you're still weak." Actually, I'd never encountered such a case before, certainly not in a woman as levelheaded as she. But my words were not too implausible. Besides, half a GP's medical kit is his confident tone of voice.

She wasn't fully reassured till we got the birth certificate and compared the prints of fingers and feet thereon with the child's. I prescribed a tonic, jollied her over a cup of coffee, and returned to work.

When nothing similar happened for a while, I pretty well forgot the incident. That was the year when the only daughter Kate and I would ever have caught pneumonia and died, soon after her second birthday.

Johnny Havig was bright, imaginative, and a loner. The more he came into command of limbs and language, the less he was inclined to join his peers. He seemed happiest at his miniature desk drawing pictures, or in the yard modeling clay animals, or sailing a toy boat along the riverbank when an adult took him there. Eleanor worried about him. Tom didn't. "I was the same," he would say. "It makes for an odd childhood and a terrible adolescence, but I wonder if it doesn't pay off when you're grown."

"We've got to keep a closer eye on him," she declared. "You don't realize how often he disappears. Oh, sure, a game for him, hide-and-seek in the shrubbery or the basement or wherever. Grand sport, listening to Mommy hunt up the close and down the stair, hollering. Someday, though, he'll find his way past the picket fence and—" Her fingers drew into fists. "He could get run over."

The crisis came when he was four. By then he understood that vanishings meant spankings, and had stopped (as far as his parents knew. They didn't see what went on in his room). But one summer morning he was not in his bed, and he was not to be found, and every policeman and most of the neighborhood were out in search.

At midnight the doorbell rang. Eleanor was asleep, after I had commanded her to take a pill. Tom sat awake, alone. He dropped his cigarette—the scorch mark in the rug would long remind him of his agony—and knocked over a chair on his way to the front entrance.

A man stood on the porch. He wore a topcoat and shadowing hat which turned him featureless. Not that that made any difference. Tom's whole being torrented over the boy who held the man by the hand.

"Good evening, sir," said a pleasant voice. "I believe you're looking for this young gentleman?"

And, when Tom knelt to seize his son, hold him, weep and try to babble thanks, the man departed.

"Funny," Tom said to me afterward. "I couldn't have been focusing entirely on Johnny for more than a minute. You know Elm Street has good lamps and no cover. Even in a sprint, nobody could get out of sight fast. Besides, running feet would've set a dozen dogs barking. But the pavement was empty."

The child would say nothing except that he had been "around," and was sorry, and wouldn't wander again.

❅

Nor did he. In fact, he emerged from his solitariness to the extent of acquiring one inseparable friend, the Dunbar boy. Pete fairly hulked over his slight, quiet companion. He was no fool; today he manages the local A & P. But John, as he now wanted to be called, altogether dominated the relationship. They played his games, went to his favorite vacant lots and, later, his chosen parts of Morgan Woods, enacted the histories of his visionary worlds.

His mother sighed, in my cluttered carbolic-and-leather-smelling office: "I suppose John's so good at daydreaming that even for Pete, the real world seems pale by contrast. That's the trouble. He's too good at it."

This was in the second year following. I'd seen him through a couple of the usual ailments, but otherwise had no cause to suspect problems and was startled when Eleanor requested an appointment to discuss him. She'd laughed over the phone: "Well, you know Tom's Yankee conscience. He'd never let me ask you professional questions on a social occasion." The sound had been forlorn.

I settled back in my creaky swivel chair, bridged my fingers, and said, "Do you mean he tells you things that can't be true, but which he seems to believe are? Quite common. Always outgrown."

"I wonder, Bob." She frowned at her lap. "Isn't he kind of old for that?"

"Perhaps. Especially in view of his remarkably fast physical and mental development, these past months. However, practicing medicine has driven into my bones the fact that 'average' and 'normal' do not mean the same.... Okay. John has imaginary playmates?"

She tried to smile. "Well, an imaginary uncle."

I lifted my brows. "Indeed? Just what has he said to you?"

"Hardly anything. What do children ever tell their parents? But I've overheard him talking to Pete, often, about his Uncle Jack who comes and takes him on all sorts of marvelous trips."

"Uncle Jack, eh? What kind of trips? To this kingdom you once mentioned he's invented, which Leo the Lion rules over?"

"N-no. That's another weird part. He'll describe Animal Land to Tom and me; he knows perfectly well it's pure fantasy. But these journeys with his 'uncle'...they're different. What snatches I've caught are, well, realistic. A visit to an Indian camp, for instance.

They weren't storybook or movie Indians. He described work they had to do, and the smell of drying hides and dung fires. Or, another time, he claimed he'd been taken on an airplane ride. I can see how he might dream up an airplane bigger than a house. But why did he dwell on its having no propellers? I thought boys loved to go *eee-yowww* like a diving plane. No, his flew smooth and nearly noiseless. A movie was shown aboard. In Technicolor. He actually had a name for the machine. Jet? Yes, I think he said 'jet.'"

"You're afraid his imagination may overcome him?" I asked needlessly. When she nodded, swallowing, I leaned forward, patted her hand, and told her:

"Ellie, imagination is the most precious thing childhood has got. The ability to imagine in detail, like those Indians, is beyond valuation. Your boy is more than sane; he may be a genius. Whatever you do, never try to kill that in him."

I still believe I was right—totally mistaken, but right.

On this warm day, I chuckled and finished, "As for his, uh, jet airplane, I'll bet you a dozen doughnut holes Pete Dunbar has a few Buck Rogers Big Little Books."

All small boys were required to loathe school, and John went through the motions. No doubt much of it did bore him, as must be true of any kid who can think and is forced into lockstep. However, his grades were excellent, and he was genuinely gripped by what science and history were offered. ("A star passed near our sun and pulled out a ribbon of flaming gas that became the planets....The periods of world civilization are Egypt, Greece, Rome, the Middle Ages, and modern time, which began in 1492.")

His circle of friends, if not intimates, widened. Both sets of parents regretted that my Billy was four years older, Jimmy two and Stuart three years younger, than Johnny. At their stage of life, those gaps dwarfed the Grand Canyon. John shunned organized games, and by and large existed on the fringes of the tribe. For instance, Eleanor had to do the entire organizing of his birthday parties. Nevertheless, between his gentle manner and his remarkable fund of conversation— when someone else took the initiative and stimulated him—he was fairly well liked.

In his eighth year he caused a new sensation. A couple of older boys from the tough side of the tracks decided it would be fun to lie in wait for individuals on their way back from school and pummel them. Buses only carried farm children, and Senlac wasn't yet built solid; most walking routes had lonely spots. Naturally, the victims could never bring themselves to complain.

The sportsmen did, after they jumped John Havig. They blubbered that he'd called an army to his aid. And beyond doubt, they had taken a systematic drubbing.

The tale earned them an extra punishment. "Bullies are always cowards," said fathers to their sons. "Look what happened when that nice Havig boy stood up and fought." For a while he was regarded with awe, though he blushed and stammered and refused to give details; and thereafter we called him Jack.

Otherwise the incident soon dropped into obscurity. That was the year when France fell.

"Any news of the phantom uncle?" I asked Eleanor. Some families had gotten together for a party, but I wanted a respite from political talk.

"What?" She blinked, there where we stood on the Stocktons' screened porch. Lighted windows and buzzing conversation at our backs didn't blot out a full moon above the chapel of Holberg College, or the sound of crickets through a warm and green-odorous dark. "Oh." She dimpled. "You mean my son's. No, not for quite a while. You were right, that was only a phase."

"Or else he's learned discretion." I wouldn't have uttered my thought aloud if I'd been thinking.

Stricken, she said, "You mean he may have clammed up completely? He is reserved, he does tell us nothing important, or anybody else as far as I can learn—"

"I.e.," I said in haste, "he takes after his dad. Well, Ellie, you got yourself a good man, and your daughter-in-law will too. Come on, let's go in and refresh our drinks."

My records tell me the exact day when, for a while, Jack Havig's control broke apart.

Tuesday, April 14, 1942. The day before, Tom had made the proud announcement to his son. He had not mentioned his hope earlier, save to his wife, because he wasn't sure what would happen. But now he had the notice. The school had accepted his resignation, and the Army his enlistment, as of term's end.

Doubtless he could have gotten a deferment. He was over thirty, and a teacher, of science at that. In truth, he would have served his country better by staying. But the crusade had been preached, the wild geese were flying, the widowmaker whistled beyond the safe dull thresholds of Senlac. I also, middle-aged, looked into the possibility of uniform, but they talked me out of trying.

Eleanor's call drew me from bed before sunrise. "Bob, you've got to come, right away, please, please. Johnny. He's hysterical. Worse than hysterical. I'm afraid...brain fever or—Bob, come!"

I hurried to hold the thin body in my arms, try to make sense of his ravings, eventually give him an injection. Before then Jack had shrieked, vomited, clung to his father like a second skin, clawed himself till blood ran and beaten his head against the wall. "Daddy, Daddy, don't go, they'll kill you, I know, I know, I saw, I was there an' I saw, I looked in that window right there an' Mother was crying, Daddy, Daddy, Daddy!"

I kept him under graduated sedation for the better part of a week. That long was needed to quiet him down. He was a listless invalid until well into May.

This was absolutely no normal reaction. Other boys whose fathers were off to war gloried, or claimed they did. Well, I thought, Jack wasn't any of them.

He recovered and buckled down to his schoolwork. He was in Tom's company at every imaginable opportunity, and some that nobody would have imagined beforehand. This included furloughs, spent at home. Between times, he wrote almost daily letters to his father—

—who was killed in Italy, August 6, 1943.

A doctor cannot endure having made his inevitable grisly blunders unless he recalls enough rescues to offset them. I count Jack Havig among those who redeemed me. Yet I helped less as a physician than as a man.

My special knowledge did let me see that, beneath a tightheld face, the boy was seriously disturbed. Outside the eastern states, gasoline was not rationed in 1942. I arranged for a colleague to take over my practice, and when school closed, Bill and I went on a trip...and we took Jack along.

In Minnesota's Arrowhead we rented a canoe and entered that wilderness of lakes, bogs, and splendid timber which reaches on into Canada. For an entire month we were myself, my thirteen-year-old son, and my all but adopted son whom I believed to be nine years of age.

It's rain and mosquito country; paddling against a headwind is stiff work; so is portaging; to make camp required more effort than if we'd had today's ingenious gear and freeze-dried rations. Jack needed those obstacles, that nightly exhaustion. After fewer days than might have been awaited, the land could begin to heal him.

Hushed sunrises, light gold in the uppermost leaves and ashiver across broad waters; birdsong, rustle of wind, scent of evergreen; a squirrel coaxed to take food from a hand; the soaring departure of deer; blueberries in a bright warm opening of forest, till a bear arrived and we most respectfully turned the place over to him; moose, gigantic and unafraid, watching us glide by; sunsets which shone through the translucent wings of bats; dusk, fire and stories and Bill's young wonderings about things, which showed Jack better than I could have told him how big a world lies beyond our sorrows; a sleeping bag, and stars uncountable.

It was the foundation of a cure.

Back home again, I made a mistake. "I hope you're over this notion about your father, Jack. There's no such thing as foreknowing the future." He whitened, whirled, and ran from me. I needed weeks to regain his confidence.

His trust, at any rate. He confided nothing to me except the thoughts, hopes, problems of an ordinary boy. I spoke no further of his obsession, nor did he. But as much as time and circumstance allowed, I tried to be a little of what he so desperately lacked, his father.

We could take no more long excursions while the war lasted. However, we had country roads to tramp, Morgan Woods to roam and picnic in, the river for fishing and swimming, Lake Winnego and my small sailboat not far off. He could come around to my garage workshop and make a bird feeder for himself or a broom rack for his mother. We could talk.

I do believe he won to a measure of calm about Tom's death by the time it happened. Everybody assumed his premonition was coincidental.

Eleanor had already taken a job in the library, plus giving quite a few hours per week to the hospital. Widowhood struck her hard. She rallied gamely, but for a long while was subdued and unsocial. Kate and I tried to get her out, but she declined invitations more often than not.

When at last she began to leave her shell, it was mostly in the company of others than her old circle. I couldn't keep from remarking: "You know, Ellie, I'm damn glad to see you back in circulation. Still—forgive me—your new friends are kind of a surprise."

She reddened and looked away. "True," she said low.

"Perfectly good people, of course. But, uh, not what you'd call intellectual types, are they?"

"N-no....All right." She straightened in her chair. "Bob, let's be frank. I don't want to leave here, if only because of what you are to Jack. Nor do I want to be buried alive, the way I was that first couple of years. Tom influenced me; I don't really have an academic turn of mind like his. And...you who we went with...you're all married."

I abandoned as useless my intention in raising the matter—to tell her how alien her son was to those practical-minded, loud-laughing men who squired her around, how deeply he was coming to detest them.

He was twelve when the nuclear thunderbolts slew two cities and man's last innocence. Though the astonishing growth rate I had noted in him earlier had slowed down to average since 1942, its effects remained to make him precocious. That reinforced the extreme solitariness which had set in. No longer was Pete Dunbar, or any schoolmate, more than a casual associate. Politely but unshakably, Jack refused everything extracurricular. He did his lessons, and did them well, but his free time was his and nobody else's: his to read enormously, with emphasis on history books; to take miles-long hikes by himself; to draw pictures or to shape things with the tools I'd helped him collect.

I don't mean he was morbid. Lonely boys are not uncommon, and generally become reasonably sociable adults. Jack was fond of the Amos 'n' Andy program, for instance, though he preferred Fred Allen; and he had a dry wit of his own. I remember various of his cartoons he showed me, one in particular suggested by a copy of *The Outsider and Others* which I lent him. In a dark, dank forest were two human figures. The first, cowering and pointing, was unmistakably H. P. Lovecraft. His companion was a tweedy woman who snapped: "Of course they're pallid and mushroom-like, Howard. They *are* mushrooms."

While he no longer depended on me, we saw a good bit of each other; and the age difference between him and Bill was less important now, so that they two sometimes went together for a walk or a swim or a boat ride—even, in 1948, a return to northern Minnesota with Jim and Stuart.

Soon after he came back from this, my second son asked me: "Dad, what's a good book on, uh, philosophy?"

"Eh?" I laid down my newspaper. "Philosophy, at thirteen?"

"Why not?" Kate said across her embroidery. "In Athens he'd have started younger."

"Well, m-m, philosophy's a mighty wide field, Jim," I stalled. "What's your immediate question?"

"Oh," he mumbled, "free will and time and all that jazz. Jack Havig and Bill talked a lot about it on our trip."

I learned that Bill, being in college, had begun by posing as an authority, but soon found himself entangled in problems—was the history of the universe written before its beginning? if so, why do we know we make free choices? if not, how can we affect the course of the future...or the past?—which it didn't seem a high school kid could have pondered as thoroughly as Jack had done.

When I asked my protégé what he wanted for Christmas, he answered: "Something I can understand that explains relativity."

In 1949, Eleanor remarried. Her choice was catastrophic.

Sven Birkelund meant well. His parents had brought him from Norway when he was three; he was now forty, a successful farmer in possession of a large estate and fine house ten miles outside town, a combat veteran, and a recent widower who had two boys to raise: Sven, Jr., sixteen, and Harold, nine. Huge, red-haired, gusty, he blazed forth maleness—admitted Kate to me, though she couldn't stand him—and he was not unlettered either; he subscribed to magazines (*Reader's Digest*, *National Geographic*, *Country Gentleman*), read an occasional book, liked travel, and was a shrewd businessman.

And... Eleanor, always full of life, had been celibate for six years. You can't warn someone who's tumbled into love. Neither Kate nor

I tried. We attended the wedding and reception and offered our best wishes. Mostly I was conscious of Jack. The boy had grown haggard; he moved and talked like a robot.

In his new home, he rarely got a chance to see us. Afterward he would not go into detail about the months which followed. Nor shall I. But consider: Where Eleanor was a dropout from the Episcopal Church, and Jack a born agnostic, Birkelund was a Bible-believing Lutheran. Where Eleanor enjoyed gourmet cooking and Jack the eating, Birkelund and his sons wanted meat and potatoes. Tom spent his typical evening first with a book, later talking with her. If Birkelund wasn't doing the accounts, he was glued to the radio or, presently, the television screen. Tom had made a political liberal of her. Birkelund was an ardent and active American Legionnaire—he never missed a convention, and if you draw the obvious inference, you're right—who became an outspoken supporter of Senator Joseph McCarthy.

And on and on. I don't mean that she was disillusioned overnight. I'm sure Birkelund tried to please her, and gradually dropped the effort only because it was failing. The fact that she was soon pregnant must have forged a bond between them which lasted a while. (She told me, however, I being the family doctor, that in the later stages his nightly attentions became distasteful but he wouldn't stop. I called him in for a Dutch uncle lecture and he made a sulky compromise.)

For Jack the situation was hell from the word go. His stepbrothers, duplicates of their father, resented his invasion. Junior, whose current interests were hunting and girls, called him a sissy because he didn't like to kill and a queer because he never dated. Harold found the numberless ways to torment him which a small boy can use on a bigger one whose fists may not defend.

More withdrawn than ever, he endured. I wondered how.

In the fall of 1950, Ingeborg was born. Birkelund named her after an aunt because his mother happened to be called Olga. He expressed disappointment that she was a girl, but threw a large and drunken party anyway, at which he repeatedly declared, amidst general laughter, his intention of trying for a son the minute the doctor allowed.

The doctor and his wife had been invited, but discovered a prior commitment. Thus I didn't see, I heard how Jack walked out on the celebration and how indignant Birkelund was. Long afterward, Jack told: "He cornered me in the barn when the last guest had left who wasn't asleep on the floor, and said he was going to beat the shit out of me. I told him if he tried, I'd kill him. I meant that. He saw it, and went off growling. From then on, we spoke no more than we couldn't avoid. I did my chores, my share of work come harvest or whatever, and when I'd eaten dinner I went to my room."

And elsewhere.

The balance held till early December. What tipped it doesn't matter—something was bound to—but was, in fact, Eleanor's asking Jack if he'd given thought to the college he would like to attend, and Birkelund shouting, "He can damn well get the lead out and go serve his country like I did and take his GI if they haven't cashiered him," and a quarrel which sent her upstairs fleeing and in tears.

Next day Jack was not there.

He returned at the end of January, would say no word about where he had been or what he had done, and stated that he would leave for good if his stepfather took the affair to the juvenile authorities as threatened. I'm certain he dominated that scene, and won himself the right to be left in peace. Both his appearance and his demeanor were shockingly changed.

Again the household knew a shaky equilibrium. But six weeks later, upon a Sunday when Jack had gone for his usual long walk after returning from church, he forgot to lock the door to his room. Little Harold noticed, entered, and rummaged through the desk. His find, which he promptly brought to his father, blew apart the whole miserable works.

Snow fell, a slow thick whiteness filling the windows. What daylight seeped through was silver-gray. Outdoors the air felt almost warm—and how utterly silent.

Eleanor sat on our living-room couch and wept. "Bob, you've got to talk to him, you, you, you've got to help him…again….What happened when he ran away? What did he *do*?"

Kate laid arms around her and drew the weary head down to her own shoulder. "Nothing wrong, my dear," she murmured. "Oh, be very sure. Always remember, Jack is Tom's son."

I paced the rug, in the dull twilight against which we had turned on no lights. "Let's spell out the facts," I said, speaking bolder than I felt. "Jack had this mimeographed pamphlet that Sven describes as Communist propaganda. Sven wants to call the sheriff, the district attorney, anybody who can force Jack to tell who he fell in with while he was gone. You slipped out to the shed, drove off in the pickup, met the boy on the road, and brought him here."

"Y-y-yes. Bob, I can't stay. Ingeborg's at home.... Sven will call me an, an unnatural mother—"

"I might have a few words to say about privacy," I answered, "not to mention freedom of speech, press, and opinion." After a pause: "Uh, you told me you snaffled the pamphlet?"

"I—" Eleanor drew back from Kate's embrace. Through tears and hiccoughs, a strength spoke that I remembered: "No use for him to call copper if the evidence is gone."

"May I see it?" I asked.

She hesitated. "It's...a prank, Bob. Nothing s-s-significant. Jack's waiting—"

—in my office, by request, while we conferred. He had shown me a self-possession which chilled this winter day.

"He and I will have a talk," I said, "while Kate gets some coffee, and I expect some food, into you. But I've got to have something to talk about."

She gulped, nodded, fumbled in her purse, and handed me several sheets stapled together. I settled into my favorite armchair, left shank on right knee, a good head of steam in my pipe, and read the document.

I read it twice. And thrice. I quite forgot the women.

Here it is. You won't find any riddles.

But hark back. The date was the eleventh of March, in the year of Our Lord nineteen hundred and fifty-one.

Harry S Truman was President of the United States, having defeated Thomas E. Dewey for election, plus a former Vice President who would later have the manhood to admit that his party had been a glove on the hand of Moscow. This was the capital of a Soviet Union which my adored FDR had assured me was a town-meeting democracy, our gallant ally in a holy war to bring perpetual peace. Eastern Europe and China were down the gullet. Citizens in the news included Alger Hiss, Owen Lattimore, Judith Coplon, Morton Sobell, Julius and Ethel Rosenberg. Somehow, to my friends and myself, they did not make Joseph McCarthy less of an abomination. But under the UN flag, American young men were dying in battle—five and a half years after our V-days!—and their killers were North Korean and Chinese. Less than two years ago, the first Russian atomic bombs had roared. NATO, hardly older, was a piece of string in the path of hundreds of divisions. Most of us, in an emotional paralysis which let us continue our daily lives, expected World War III to break out at any instant.

I could not altogether blame Sven Birkelund for jumping to conclusions.

But as I read, and read, my puzzlement deepened.

Whoever wrote this thing knew Communist language—I'd been through some books on that subject—but was emphatically not a Communist himself. What, then, was he?

Hark back, I say. Try to understand your world of 1951.

Apart from a few extremists, America had never thought to question her own rightness, let alone her right to exist. We knew we had problems, but assumed we could solve them, given time and good will, and eventually everybody of every race, color, and creed would live side by side in the suburbs and sing folk songs together. *Brown vs. Board of Education* was years in the future; student riots happened in foreign countries, while ours worried about student apathy; Indochina was a place where the French were experiencing vaguely noticed difficulties.

Television was hustling in, and we discussed its possible effects. Nuclear-armed intercontinental missiles were on their way, but nobody imagined they could be used for anything except the crudest exchange of destructions. Overpopulation was in the news but would soon be forgotten. Penicillin and DDT were unqualified friends to man. Conservation meant preserving certain areas in their natural states and, if you were sophisticated about such matters, contour plowing on hillsides. Smog was in Los Angeles and occasionally London. The ocean, immortal mother of all, would forever receive and cleanse our wastes. Space flight was for the next century, when an eccentric millionaire might finance a project. Computers were few, large, expensive, and covered with blinking lights. If you followed the science news, you knew a little about transistors, and perhaps looked forward to seeing cheap, pocket-sized radios in the hands of Americans; they could make no difference to a peasant in India or Africa. All contraceptives were essentially mechanical. The gene was a locus on the chromosome. Unless he blasted himself back to the Stone Age, man was committed to the machine.

Put yourself in 1951, if you can, if you dare, and read as I did that jape on the first page of which appeared the notice "Copyright © 1970 by John F. Havig."

## WITHIT'S COLLEGIATE DICTIONARY

*Activist:* A person employing tactics in the cause of *liberation* which, when used by a *fascist*, are known as *McCarthyism* and *repression*.

*Aggression:* Any foreign policy advocated by a *fascist*.

*Black:* Of whole or partial sub-Saharan African descent; from the skin color, which ranges from brown to ivory. Not to be confused with *Brown, Red, White,* or *Yellow.* This word replaces the former "Negro," which today is considered insulting since it means "Black."

*Bombing:* A method of warfare which delivers high explosives from the air, condemned because of its effects upon women, children, the aged, the sick, and other noncombatants, unless these happen to have resided in Berlin, Hamburg, Dresden, Tokyo, Osaka, etc., though not Hiroshima or Nagasaki. Cf. *missile.*

*Brown:* Of Mexican descent; from the skin color, which ranges from brown to ivory. Not to be confused with *Black, Red, White,* or *Yellow.*

*Brutality:* Any action taken by a policeman. Cf. *Pig.*

*Chauvinism*: Belief of any Western *White* man that there is anything to be said for his country, civilization, race, sex, or self. *Chauvinist*: Any such man; hence, by extension, a fascist of any nationality, race, or sex.

*Colonialist*: Anyone who believes that any European- or North American-descended person has any right to remain in any territory outside Europe or North America where his ancestors happened to settle, unless these were Russian. Cf. *native*.

*Concentration camp*: An enclosed area into which *people* suspect to their government or to an occupying power are herded. No *progressive* country or *liberation* movement can operate a concentration camp, since by definition these have full support of the *people*. NB: Liberals consider it impolite to mention Nisei in this connection.

*Conformist*: One who accepts *establishment* values without asking troublesome questions. Cf. *nonconformist*.

*Conservative*: See *aggression, bombing, brutality, chauvinism, colonialist, concentration camp, conformist, establishment, fascist, imperialist, McCarthyism, mercenary, military-industrial complex, missile, napalm, pig, plutocrat, prejudice, property rights, racist, reactionary, repression, storm trooper, xenophobia.*

*Criminal*: A *fascist*, especially when apprehended and punished. Cf. *martyr.*

*Democracy*: A nation in which the government, freely elected, remains responsive to the popular will, e.g., Czechoslovakia.

*Development*: (1) In *fascist* countries, the bulldozing of trees and hillsides, erection of sleazy row houses, etc., or in general, the exploitation of the environment. (2) In *progressive* countries, the provision of housing for the masses, or in general, the utilization of natural resources to satisfy human needs.

*Ecology*: (1) Obsolete: The study of the interrelationships of living things with each other and with the general environment. (2) Everything non-human which is being harmed by the *establishment*, such as trees and falcons but not including rats, sparrows, algae, etc. Thus *progressive* countries have no ecology.

*Establishment*: The powers that be, when these are *conservative.*

*Fallout*: Radioactive material from a *nuclear weapon*, widely distributed if this is tested in the atmosphere, universally condemned for its deleterious effect upon public health and heredity, unless the test is conducted by a *progressive* country.

*Fascist*: A person who favors measures possibly conducive to the survival of the West.

*Freedom*: Instant gratification.

*Glory*: An outworn shibboleth, except when applied to a *hero* or *martyr*.

*Hero*: A person who sacrifices and takes risks in a *progressive* cause. Cf. *pig* and *storm trooper*.

*Honor*: See *glory*.

*Human rights*: All rights of the people to *freedom*, when held to take infinite precedence over *property rights*, since the latter are not human rights.

*Imperialist*: A person who advocates that any Western country retain any of its overseas territory.

*Liberation*: Foreign expulsion and domestic overthrow of Western governments, influences, and institutions. *Sacred liberation*: Liberation intended to result in a (*People's*) *Republic*.

*Love*: An emotion which, if universally felt, would automatically solve all human problems, but which some (see *conservative*) are by definition incapable of feeling.

*Martyr*: A person who suffers or dies in the cause of *liberation*. Not to be confused with a criminal or, collectively, with enemy personnel.

*McCarthyism*: Character assassination for political purposes, by asserting that some person is a member of the Communist conspiracy, especially when this is done by an admirer of Sen. Joseph McCarthy. Not to be confused with asserting that some person is a member of the *fascist* conspiracy, especially when this is done by an admirer of Sen. Eugene McCarthy.

*Mercenary:* A soldier who, for pay, serves a government not his own. Cf. *United Nations.*

*Military-industrial complex:* An interlocking directorate of military and industrial leaders, held to be in effective control of the USA. Not to be confused with military and industrial leaders of the USSR or the various (*People's*) *Republics.*

*Missile:* A self-contained device which delivers high explosives from the air, condemned for its effects upon women, children, the aged, the sick, and other noncombatants, unless these happen to have resided in Saigon, Da Nang, Hué, etc. Cf. *bombing.*

*Napalm:* Jellied gasoline, ignited and propelled against enemy *personnel,* condemned by all true liberals except when used by Israelis upon Arabs.

*Native:* A non-*White* inhabitant of a region whose ancestors dispossessed the previous lot.

*Nonconformist:* One who accepts *progressive* values without asking troublesome questions. Cf. *conformist.*

*Nuclear weapon:* A weapon employing some form of atomic energy, used by *fascist* governments for purposes of *aggression* and by *progressive* governments to further the cause of *peace.*

*One man, one vote:* A legal doctrine requiring that, from time to time, old gerrymanders be replaced with new ones. The object of this is the achievement of genuine *democracy.*

*Organic:* Of foods, grown only with natural manures, etc., and with no chemical sprays, etc., hence free of harmful residues and of earthborne diseases or serious insect infestation, since surrounding lands have been artificially fertilized and chemically sprayed.

*Peace:* The final solution of the *fascist* problem. *Peaceful coexistence:* A stage preliminary to *peace,* in which *aggression* is phased out and *sacred liberation* proceeds.

*People:* (Always used with the definite article and often capitalized.) Those who support *liberation.* Hence everyone not a *fascist* is counted among them, whether he wants to be or not.

*Personnel:* Members of a military or police organization, whether hostile or useful. Not to be confused with human beings.

*Pig*: (1) An animal known for its value, intelligence, courage, self-reliance, kindly disposition, loyalty, and (if allowed to follow its natural bent) cleanliness. (2) A policeman. Cf. *activist*.

*Plutocrat*: A citizen of a *republic* who, because of enormous wealth which he refuses to share with the *poor*, wields undue political power. Not to be confused with a Kennedy.

*Poor*: (Always used with the definite article and often capitalized.) That class of persons who are defined by someone as possessing less than their rightful wealth and privilege. The *progressive* definition includes all non-*fascist* Black, Brown, Red, and Yellow persons, regardless of income.

*Pot*: Marijuana. Must we go through that alcohol-tobacco tranquilizers-are-legal routine again?

*Prejudice*: Hostility or contempt for a person or group, on a purely class basis and regardless of facts. Not to be confused with judgment passed on enemies of the *people* (see *conservative*).

*Progressive*: Conducive to *liberation*.

*Property rights*: The alleged rights of persons who have earned or otherwise lawfully obtained property, or of taxpayers who have similarly acquired property which is then designated public, to be secure in the enjoyment thereof, irrespective of *human rights*.


*Racist*: A White person who, when any Black person rings a bell, fails to salivate.

*Reactionary*: Not *progressive*.

*Red*: ( 1 ) Of American Indian descent; from the skin color, which ranges from brown to ivory. Not to be confused with *Black*, *Brown*, *White*, or *Yellow*, nor with "Mexican," even though most Mexicans are of American Indian stock. (2) Struggling for *liberation* or struggling in its aftermath.

*Repression*: Denial of the right of free speech, e.g., by refusal to provide a free rostrum for an *activist*, or the right of a free press, e.g., by refusing to print, televise, or stock in libraries every word of an *activist*, or the right to be heard, e.g., by mob action against an *activist*. Not to be confused with protection of the *people* from *reactionary* infection.

*Republic*: A country whose government is chosen not on a basis of heredity or riches but by the electorate, from whom political power grows. *People's Republic*: One in which the electorate consists of a gun barrel.

*Self-determination*: The right of a culturally or ethnically distinct group to govern themselves, as in Biafra, East Pakistan, Goa, Katanga, the Sinai, Tibet, the Ukraine, etc.

*Storm trooper*: A person who sacrifices and takes risks in a *fascist* cause. Cf. *hero*.

*United Nations*: An international organization which employs Swedish, Indian, Irish, Canadian, etc. troops in other parts of the world than these so as to further *self-determination*.

*White*: Of Caucasoid descent; from the skin color, which ranges from brown to ivory. Not to be confused with *Black*, *Brown*, *Red*, or *Yellow*.

*Winds of change*: Poetic metaphor for the defeat of *reactionary* forces. Not applicable to any advance or restoration of these.

*Women's liberation*: A movement which opposes male *chauvinism*.

*Xenophobia*: Distrust of the ability of strangers to run your life for you.

*Yellow*: Of Mongoloid descent; from the skin color, which ranges from brown to ivory. Not to be confused with *Black*, *Brown*, *Red*, or *White*.

For a moment, as I entered, my office was foreign to me. That rolltop desk, gooseneck reading lamp, worn leather-upholstered swivel chair and horsehair-stuffed seat for visitors, shelf of reference books, framed diploma, door ajar on the surgery to give a glimpse of cabinets wherein lay instruments and drugs that Koch would mostly have recognized—all was out of place, a tiny island in time which the ocean was swiftly eroding away; and I knew that inside of ten years I'd do best to retire.

The snowfall had thickened, making the windows a pale dusk. Jack had turned the lamp on so he could read a magazine. Beyond its puddle of light, shadows lay enormous. The steam radiator grumbled. It turned the air dry as well as warm.

He rose. "Sorry to give you this bother, Dr. Anderson," he said.

I waved him back into the armchair, settled myself down, reached for a fresh pipe off the rack. That much smoking was hard on the mouth, but my fingers needed something to do.

Jack nodded at the pamphlet I'd tossed on the desk. "How do you like it?" he asked tonelessly.

I peered through the upper half of my bifocals. This was not the boy who knew he would lose his father, nor the youth who tried and failed to hide his wretchedness when his mother took unto him a stepfather—only last year. A young man confronted me, whose eyes were old.

They were gray, those eyes, in a narrow straight-nosed face upon a long head. The dark-blond hair, the slim, middle-sized, slightly awkward body were Tom's; the mouth, its fullness and mobility out of place in that ascetic countenance, was Eleanor's; the whole was entirely Jack Havig, whom I had never fathomed.

Always a careless dresser, he wore the plaid wool shirt and blue denims in which he had gone for that tramp across the hills. His attitude seemed alert rather than uneasy, and his gaze did not waver from mine.

"Well," I said, "it's original. But you must admit it's sort of confusing." I loaded the pipe.

"Yeah, I suppose. A souvenir. I probably shouldn't have brought anything back."

"From your, uh, trip away from home? Where were you, Jack?"

"Around."

I remembered a small stubborn person who gave the same reply, after an unknown had returned him to his father. It led me to recall much else.

My wooden match made a *scrit* and flare which seemed unnaturally strong. I got the tobacco burning, took a good taste and smell of it, before I had my speech put together.

"Listen, Jack. You're in trouble. Worse, your mother is." That jarred him. "I'm the friend of you both, I want to help, but damnation, you'll have to cooperate."

"Doc, I wish I could," he whispered.

I tapped the pamphlet. "Okay," I said, "tell me you're working on a science-fiction story or something, laid in 1970, and this is background material. Fine. I'd think you're needlessly obscure, but never mind; your business." Gesturing with the pipestem: "What is not your business is the fact it's mimeographed. Nobody mimeographs anything for strictly personal use. Organizations do. What organization is this?"

"None. A few friends." His neck stiffened. "Mighty few, among all those Gadarene swine happily squealing their slogans."

I stood. "How about a drink?"

Now he smiled. "Thanks. The exact prescription I want."

Pouring from a brandy bottle—sometimes it was needful for both a patient and myself, when I must pronounce sentence —I wondered what had triggered my impulse. Kids don't booze, except a little beer on the sly. Do they? It came to me afresh, here was no longer a kid.

He drank in the way of an experienced if not heavy drinker. How had he learned? He'd been gone barely a month.

I sat again and said: "I don't ask for secrets, Jack, though you know I hear a lot in my line of work, and keep them. I *demand* your help in constructing a story, and laying out a program of future behavior, which will get your mother off the hook."

He frowned. "You're right. The trouble is, I can't think what to tell you."

"The truth, maybe?"

"Doc, you don't want that. Believe me, you don't."

"'Beauty is truth, truth beauty—' Why did Keats hand the world that particular piece of BS? He'd studied medicine; he knew better. Jack, I'll bet you ten dollars I can relate a dozen true stories which'll shock you worse than you could ever shock me."

"I won't bet," he said harshly. "It wouldn't be fair to you."

I waited.

He tossed off his drink and held out the glass. In the yellow lamplight, gaunt against the winter window, his face congealed with resolution. "Give me a refill, please," he said, "and I will tell you."

"Great." The bottle shook a bit in my grasp as the liquor clucked forth. "I swear to respect any confidentiality."

He laughed, a rattling noise. "No need for oaths, Doc. You'll keep quiet."

I waited.

He sipped, stared past me, and murmured: "I'm glad. It's been such a burden, through my whole life, never to share the…the fact of what I am."

I streamed smoke from my lips and waited.

He said in a rush, "For the most part I was in the San Francisco area, especially Berkeley. For more than a year."

My fingers clenched on the pipe bowl.

"Uh-huh." He nodded. "I came home after a month's absence. But I'd spent about eighteen months away. From the fall of 1969 to the end of 1970."

After a moment, he added: "That's not a whole year and a half. But you've got to count my visits to the further future."

Steam hissed in the radiator. I saw a sheen of sweat on the forehead of my all but adopted son. He gripped his tumbler as tightly as I my pipe. Yet in spite of the tension in him, his voice remained level.

"You have a time machine?" I breathed.

He shook his head. "No. I move around in time by myself. Don't ask me how. I don't know."

His smile jerked forth. "Sure, Doc," he said. "Paranoia. The delusion that I'm something special in the cosmos. Okay, I'll give you a demonstration." He waved about. "Come here, please. Check. Make certain I've put no mirrors, trapdoors, gimmickry in your own familiar office."

Numbly, I felt around him, though it was obvious he'd had no chance to bring along, or rig, any apparatus.

"Satisfied?" he asked. "Well, I'll project myself into the future. How far? Half an hour? No, too long for you to sit here gnawing your pipe. Fifteen minutes, then." He checked his watch against my wall clock. "It's 4:17, agreed? I'll reappear at 4:30, plus or minus a few seconds." Word by word: "Just make sure nobody or nothing occupies this chair at that period. I can't emerge in the same space as another solid body."

I stood back and trembled. "Go ahead, Jack," I said through the thuttering in my veins.

Tenderness touched him. He reached to squeeze my hand. "Good old Doc. So long."

And he was gone. I heard a muted *whoosh* of air rushing in where he had sat, and nothing else. The chair stood empty. I felt, and no form occupied it.

I sat down once more at my desk, and stared for a quarter of an hour which I don't quite remember.

Abruptly, there he was, seated as he had been.

I struggled not to faint. He hurried to me. "Doc, here, take it easy, everything's okay, here, have a drink—"

Later he gave me a one-minute show, stepping back from that near a future to stand beside himself, until the first body vanished.

Night gathered.

"No, I don't know how it works," he said. "But then, I don't know how my muscles work, not in the way you know—and you'll agree your scientific information is only a glimmer on the surface of a mystery."

"How does it feel?" I asked, and noticed in surprise the calm which had come upon me. I'd been stunned longer on Hiroshima Day. Well, maybe the bottom of my mind had already guessed what Jack Havig was.

"Hard to describe." He frowned into darkness. "I...will myself backward or forward in time...the way I will to, oh, pick my glass off your desk. In other words, I order whatever-it-is to move me, the same as we order our fingers to do something, and it happens."

He searched for words before he went on: "I'm in a shadow world while I time-travel. Lighting varies from zero to gray. If I'm crossing more than one day-and-night period, it flickers. Objects look dim, foggy, flat. Then I decide to stop, and I stop, and I'm back in normal time and solidness....No air reaches me on my way. I have to hold my breath, and emerge occasionally for a lungful if the trip takes that long in my personal time."

"Wait," I said. "If you can't breathe en route, can't touch anything or be touched, can't be seen—how come you have the feeble vision you do? How can light affect you?"

"I don't know either, Doc. I've read physics texts, however, trying to get a notion about that as well as everything else. And, oh, it must be some kind of force which moves me. A force operating in at least four dimensions, nevertheless a force. If it has an electromagnetic component, I can imagine how a few photons might get caught in the field of it and carried along. Matter, even ionized matter, has rest mass and therefore can't be affected in this fashion....That's a layman's guess. I wish I dared bring a real scientist in on this."

"Your guess is too deep for me already, friend. Uh, you said a crossing isn't instantaneous, as far as you yourself are concerned. How long does it take? How many minutes per year, or whatever?"

"No particular relationship. Depends on me. I feel the effort I'm exerting, and can gauge it roughly. By, well, straining, I can move...faster...than otherwise. That leaves me exhausted, which seems to me to prove that time traveling uses body energy to generate and apply the thrusting force....It's never taken more than a few minutes, according to my watch; and that was a trip through several centuries."

"When you were a baby—" My voice halted.

He nodded anew. "Yeah, I've heard about the incident. Fear of falling's an instinct, isn't it? I suppose when my mother dropped me, I threw myself into the past by sheer reflex . . .and thereby caused her to drop me."

He took a swallow of brandy. "My ability grew as I grew. I probably have no limit now, if I can stop at need, along the way, to rest. But I am limited in the mass I can carry along. That's only a few pounds, including clothes. More, and I can't move; it's like being weighted down. If you grabbed me, for instance, I'd be stuck in normal time till you let go, because you're too much for me to haul. I couldn't just leave you behind; the force acts, or tries to act, on everything in direct contact with me." A faint smile. "Except Earth itself, if I happen to be barefoot. I suppose that much mass, bound together not only by gravitation but by other, even stronger forces, has a—what?—a cohesion?—of its own."

"You warned me against putting a solid object where you planned to, uh, materialize," I said.

"Right," he answered. "I can't, in that case. I've experimented. Traveling through time, I can move around meanwhile in space if I want. That's how I managed to appear next to myself. By the way, the surface I'm on may rise or sink, but I rise or sink likewise, same as when a person stands somewhere in normal time. And, aside from whatever walking I do, I stay on the same geographical spot. Never mind that this planet is spinning on its axis, and whirling around a sun which is rushing through a galaxy...I stay *here*. Gravitation again, I suppose....Yes, about solid matter. I tried entering a hill, when I was a child and thoughtless. I could go inside, all right, easy as stepping into a bank of fog. But then I was cut off from light, and I couldn't emerge into normal time, it was like being in concrete, and my breath ran out—" He shivered. "I barely made it back to the open air."

"I guess matter resists displacement by you," I ventured. "Fluids aren't too hard to shove aside when you emerge, but solids are."

"Uh-huh, that's what I figured. If I'd passed out and died inside that rock and dirt, I guess my body would've—well, been carried along into the future at the ordinary rate, and fallen back into normal existence when at last the hill eroded away from around it."

"Amazing how you, a mere tad, kept the secret."

"Well, I gather I gave my mother a lot of worries. I don't actually remember. Who does recall his first few years? Probably I needed a while to realize I was unique, and the realization scared me—maybe time traveling was a Bad Thing to do. Or perhaps I gloated. Anyway, Uncle Jack straightened me out."

"Was he the unknown who brought you back when you'd been lost?"

"Yes. I do remember that. I'd embarked on a long expedition into the past, looking for Indians. But I only found a forest. He showed up—having searched the area through a number of years—and we had it nice together. Finally he took my hand and showed me how to come home with him. He could've delivered me within a few minutes of my departure and spared my parents those dreadful hours. But I believe he wanted me to see how I'd hurt them, so the need for discretion would really get driven into me. It was."

His tone grew reminiscent: "We had some fine excursions later. Uncle Jack was the ideal guide and mentor. I'd no reason to disobey his commands about secrecy, aside from some disguised bragging to my friend Pete. Uncle Jack led me to better things than I'd ever have discovered for myself."

"You did hop around on your own," I reminded him.

"Occasionally. Like when a couple of bullies attacked me. I doubled back several times and outnumbered them."

"No wonder you showed such a growth rate....When you learned your father was going into the service, you hoped to assure yourself he'd return safe, right?"

Jack Havig winced. "Yes. I headed futureward and took quick peeks at intervals. Until I looked in the window and saw Mother crying.

Then I went pastward till I found a chance to read that telegram—oh, God. I didn't travel in time again for years. I didn't think I'd ever want to."

The silence of the snow lapped about us.

At length I asked: "When did you most recently meet this mentor?"

"In 1969. But the previous time had been . . . shortly before I took off and learned about my father. Uncle Jack was particularly good to me, then. We went to the old and truly kind of circus, sometime in the late nineteenth century. I wondered why he seemed so sad, and why he reexplained in such detail the necessity of keeping our secret. Now I know."

"Do you know who he is?"

His mouth lifted on the left side only. "Who do you suppose?"

"I resumed time traveling last year," he said after a while. "I had to have a refuge from that, that situation on the farm. They were jaunts into the past, at first. You've no idea how beautiful this country was before the settlers arrived. And the Indians—well, I have friends among them. I haven't acquired more than a few words of their language, but they welcome me and, uh, the girls are always ready, able, and eager."

I could not but laugh. "Sven the Younger makes a lot of your having no dates!"

He grinned back. "You can guess how those trips relieved me." Serious again: "But you can guess, too, how more and more the whole thing at home—what Birkelund is pleased to call my home—got to feel silly, futile, and stifling. Even the outside world. Like, what the devil was I doing in high school? There I was, full-grown, full of these marvels I'd seen, hearing teen-agers giggle and teachers drone!"

"I imagine the family flareup was what sent you into the future?"

"Right. I was half out of my mind with rage. Mainly I hoped to see Sven Birkelund's tombstone. Twenty years forward seemed like a good round number. But knowing I'd have a lot to catch up on, I made for late 1969, so as to be prepared to get the most out of 1970...The house was still in existence. Is. Will be."

"Sven?" I asked softly.

"I suppose he'll have survived." His tone was savage. "I don't care enough to check on that. In two more years, my mother will divorce him."

"And—?"

"She'll take the babies, both of them, back to Massachusetts. Her third marriage will be good. I mustn't add to her worries in this time, though. That's why I returned. I made my absence a month long to show Birkelund I mean business; but I couldn't make it longer than that, I couldn't do it to her."

I saw in him what I have seen in others, when those they care about are sick or dying. So I was hasty to say: "You told me you met your Uncle Jack, your other self."

"Yeah." He was glad to continue with practicalities. "He was waiting when I appeared in 1969. That was out in the woodlot, at night—I didn't want to risk a stray spectator—but the lot had been logged off and planted in corn. He'd taken a double room in the hotel—that is, the one they'll build after the Senlac Arms is razed—and put me up for a few days. He told me about my mother, and encouraged me to verify it by newspaper files in the library, plus showing me a couple of letters she'd recently written to him...to me. Afterward he gave me a thousand dollars—Doc, the prices in twenty years!—and he suggested I look around the country.

"News magazines indicated Berkeley was where it was at— uh, a future idiom. Anyway, San Francisco's right across the Bay and I'd always wanted to see it."

"How was Berkeley?" I asked, remembering visits to a staid university town.

He told me, as well as he was able. But no words, in 1951, could have conveyed what I have since experienced, that wild, eerie, hilarious, terrifying, grotesque, mind-bending assault upon every sense and common sense which is Telegraph Avenue at the close of the seventh decade of the twentieth century.

"Didn't you risk trouble with the police?" I inquired.

"No. I stopped off in 1966 and registered under a fake name for the draft, which gave me a card saying I was twenty-one in 1969.... The Street People hooked me. I came to them, an old-fashioned bumpkin, heard their version of what'd been going on, and nobody else's. For months I was among the radicals. Hand-to-mouth odd-job existence, demonstrations, pot, dirty pad, unbathed girls, the works."

"Your writing here doesn't seem favorable to that," I observed.

"No. I'm sure Uncle Jack wanted me to have an inside knowledge, how it feels to be somebody who's foresworn the civilization that bred him. But I changed."

"M-m-m, I'd say you rebounded. Way out into right field. But go on. What happened?"

"I took a trip to the further future."

"And?"

"Doc," he said most quietly, "consider yourself fortunate. You're already getting old."

"I'll be dead, then?" My heart stumbled.

"By the time of the blowup and breakdown, no doubt. I haven't checked, except I did establish you're alive and healthy in 1970." I wondered why he did not smile, as he should have done when giving me good news. Today I know; he said nothing about Kate.

"The war—*the* war—and its consequences come later," he went on in the same iron voice. "But everything follows straight from that witches' sabbath I saw part of in Berkeley."

He sighed and rubbed his tired eyes. "I returned to 1970 with some notion of stemming the tide. There were a few people around, even young people, who could see a little reality. This broadside...they helped me publish and distribute it, thinking me a stray Republican."

"Were you?"

"Lord, no. You don't imagine any political party has been any use whatsoever for the past three or four generations, do you? They'll get worse."

He had emptied his glass anew, but declined my offer of more. "I'd better keep a clear head, Doc. We do have to work out a cover yarn. I know we will, because my not-so-much-older self gave me to understand I'd handle my present troubles all right. However, it doesn't let us off going through the motions."

"Time is unchangeable?" I wondered. "We—our lives—are caught and held in the continuum—like flies in amber?"

"I don't know, I don't know," he groaned. "I do know that my efforts were wasted. My former associates called me a fink, my new friends were an insignificant minority, and, hell, we could hardly give away our literature."

"You mustn't expect miracles in politics," I said. "Beware of the man who promises them."

"True. I realized as much, after the shock of what I'd seen uptime had faded a bit. In fact, I decided my duty was to come back and stand by my mother. At least this way I can make the world a tiny bit less horrible."

His tone softened: "No doubt I was foolish to keep a copy of my flyer. But the dearest girl helped me put it together....Well. In a way, I've lucked out. Now one other human being shares my life. I've barely started to feel how lonely I was."

"You are absolutely unique?" I whispered.

"I don't know. I'd guess not. They're doubtless very rare, but surely more time travelers than me exist. How can I find them?" he cried. "And if we should join together, what can we do?"

**5**

Birkelund proved less of a problem than expected. I saw him in private, told him the writing was a leftover script from an amateur show, and pointed out that it was actually sarcastic—after which I gave him holy hell about his treatment of his stepson and his wife. He took it with ill grace, but he took it. As remarked earlier, he was by no means an evil man.

Still, the situation remained explosive. Jack contributed, being daily more short-tempered and self-willed. "He's changed so much," Eleanor told me in grief. "His very appearance. And I can't blame all the friction on Sven and his boys. Jack's often downright arrogant."

Of course he was, in his resentment of home, his boredom in school, his burden of foreknowledge. But I couldn't tell his mother that. Nor, for her sake, could he make more than overnight escapes for the next two or three years.

"I think," I said, "it'd be best if he took off on his own."

"Bob, he's barely eighteen," she protested.

He was at least twenty-one, probably more, I knew. "Old enough to join the service." He'd registered in the lawful manner on his birthday. "That'll give him a chance to find himself. It's possible to be drafted by request, so as to be in for the minimum period. The board will oblige if I speak to 'em."

"Not before he's graduated!"

I understood her dismay and disappointment. "He can take correspondence courses, Ellie. Or the services offer classes, which a bright lad like Jack can surely get into. I'm afraid this is our best bet."

He had already agreed to the idea. A quick uptime hop showed him he would be posted to Europe. "I can explore a lot of history," he said; then, chill: "Besides, I'd better learn about weapons and combat techniques. I damn near got killed in the twenty-first century. Couple members of a cannibal band took me by surprise, and if I hadn't managed to wrench free for an instant—"

The Army was ill-suited to his temperament, but he stuck out basic training, proceeded into electronics, and on the whole gained by the occasion. To be sure, much of that was due to his excursions downtime. They totaled a pair of extra years.

His letters to me could only hint at this, since Kate would read them too. It was a hard thing for me, not to open for her the tremendous fact, not to have her beside me when at last he came home and through hour upon hour showed me his notes, photographs, memories.

(Details were apt to be unglamorous—problems of vaccination, language, transportation, money, law, custom—filth, vermin, disease, cruelty, tyranny, violence— "Doc, I'd never dreamed how different medieval man was. Huge variations from place to place and era to era, yeah, but always the...Orientalness?...no, probably it's just that the Orient has changed less." However, he had watched Caesar's legions in triumph through Rome, and the greyhound shapes of Viking craft dancing over Oslo Fjord, and Leonardo da Vinci at work....He'd not been able to observe in depth. In fact, he was maddened by the superficial quality of almost all his experiences. How much can you learn in a totally strange environment, when you can barely speak a word and are liable to be arrested on suspicion before you can swap for a suit of contemporary clothes? Yet what would I not have given to be there too?)

How it felt like a betrayal of Kate, not telling her! But if Jack could keep silence toward his mother, I must toward my wife. His older *persona* had been, was, would be right in stamping upon the child a reflex of secrecy.

Consider the consequences, had it become known that one man— or one little boy—can swim through time. To be the sensation of the age is no fit fate for any human. In this case, imagine as well the demands, appeals, frantic attempts by the greedy, the power-hungry, the ideology-besotted, the bereaved, the frightened to use him, the race between governments to sequester or destroy him who could be the ultimate spy or unstoppable assassin. If he survived, and his sanity did, he would soon have no choice but to flee into another era and there keep his talent hidden.

No, best wear a mask from the beginning.

But then what use was the fantastic gift?

"Toward the end of my hitch, I spent more time thinking than roving," he said.

We'd taken my boat out on Lake Winnego. He'd come home, discharged, a few weeks earlier, but much remained to tell me. This was the more true because his mother needed his moral support in her divorce from Birkelund, her move away from scenes which were now painful. He'd matured further, not only in the flesh. Two of my years ago, a man had confronted me: but a very young man, still groping his way out of hurt and bewilderment. The Jack Havig who sat in the cockpit today was in full command of himself.

I shifted my pipe and put down the helm. We came about in a heel and *swoosh* and rattle of boom. Springtime glittered on blue water; sweetness breathed from the green across fields and trees, from apple blossoms and fresh-turned earth. The wind whooped. It was cool and a hawk rode upon it.

"Well, you had plenty to think about," I answered.

"For openers," he said, "how does time travel work?"

"Tell me, Mr. Bones, how *does* time travel work?"

He did not chuckle. "I learned a fair amount of basic physics in the course of becoming an electronics technician. And I read a lot on my own, including stuff I went uptime to consult—books, future issues of *Scientific American* and *Nature*, et cetera. All theory says that what I do is totally impossible. It starts by violating the conservation of energy and goes on from there."

"*E pur si muove.*"

"Huh?...Oh. Yeah. Doc, I studied the Italian Renaissance prior to visiting it, and discovered Galileo never did say that. Nor did he ever actually drop weights off the Leaning Tower of Pisa. Well." He sprawled back on the bench and opened another bottle of beer for each of us. "Okay. So there are hookers in the conservation of energy that official science doesn't suspect. Mathematically speaking, world lines are allowed to have finite, if not infinite discontinuities, and to be multi-valued functions. In many ways, time travel is equivalent to faster-than-light travel, which the physicists also declare is impossible."

I watched my tobacco smoke stream off on the breeze. Wavelets smacked. "You've left me a few light-years behind," I said. "I get nothing out of your lecture except an impression that you don't believe anything, uh, supernatural is involved."

He nodded. "Right. Whatever the process may be, it operates within natural law. It's essentially physical. Matter-energy relationships are involved. Well, then, why can I do it, and nobody else? I've been forced to conclude it's a peculiarity in my genes."

"Oh?"

"They'll find the molecular basis of heredity, approximately ten years from now."

"What?" I sat bolt upright. "This you've got to tell me more about!"

"Later, later. I'll give you as much information on DNA and the rest as I can, though that isn't a whale of a lot. The point is, our genes are not simply a blueprint for building a fetus. They operate throughout life, by controlling enzyme production. You might well call them the very stuff of life....What besides enzymes can be involved? This civilization is going to destroy itself before they've answered that question. But I suspect there's some kind of resonance—or something—in those enormous molecules; and if your gene structure chances to resonate precisely right, you're a time traveler."

"Well, an interesting hypothesis." I had fallen into a habit of understatement in his presence.

"I've empirical evidence," he replied. With an effort: "Doc, I've had quite a few women. Not in this decade; I'm too stiff and gauche. But uptime and downtime, periods when it's fairly easy and I can use a certain glamour of mysteriousness."

"Congratulations," I said for lack of anything better.

He squinted across the lake. "I'm not callous about them," he said. "I mean, well, if a romp is all she wants, like those Dakotan girls two-three centuries ago, okay, fine. But if the affair is anything more, I feel responsible. I may not plan to live out my life in her company— I wonder if I'll ever marry— but I check on her future for the next several years, and try to make sure she does well." His countenance twisted a bit. "Or as well as a mortal can. I've not got the moral courage to search out their deaths."

After a pause: "I'm digressing, but it's an important digression to me. Take Meg, for instance. I was in Elizabethan London. The problems caused by my ignorance were less than in most milieus, though I did need a while to learn the ropes and even the pronunciation of their English. A silver ingot I'd brought along converted more easily than usual to coin—people today don't realize how much suspicion and regulation there was in the oh-so-swashbuckling past—even if I do think the dealer cheated me. Well, anyhow, I could lodge in a lovely half-timbered inn, and go to the Globe Theatre, and generally have a ball.

"One day I happened to be in a slum district. A woman plucked my sleeve and offered me her daughter's maidenhead cheap. I was appalled, but thought I should at least meet the poor girl, maybe give her money, maybe try to get my landlord to take her on as a respectable servant....No way." (Another of his anachronistic turns of speech.) "She was nervous but determined. And after she'd explained, I had to agree that an alley lass of independent spirit probably was better off as a whore than a servant, considering what servants had to put up with. Not that anyone was likely to take her in such a capacity, class distinctions and antagonisms being what they were.

"She was cocky, she was good-looking, she said she'd rather it was me than some nasty and probably poxy dotard. What could I do? Disinterested benevolence just plain was not in her mental universe. If she couldn't see my selfish motive, she'd've decided it must be too deep and horrible for her, and fled."

He glugged his beer. "All right," he told me defiantly. "I moved into larger quarters and took her along. The idea of an age of consent didn't exist either. Forget about our high school kids; I'd certainly never touch one of them. Meg was a woman, young but a woman. We lived together for four years of her life.

"Of course, for me that was a matter of paying the rent in advance, and now and then coming back from the twentieth century. Not very often, I being stationed in France. Sure, I could leave whenever I wanted, and return with no AWOL time passed, but the trip to England cost, and besides, there were all those other centuries....Nevertheless, I do believe Meg was faithful. You should've seen how she fended off her relatives who thought they could batten on me! I told her I was in the Dutch diplomatic service....

"Oh, skip the details. I'm talking all around my subject. In the end, a decent young journeyman fell in love with her. I gave them a wedding present and my blessings. And I checked ahead, dropping in occasionally through the next decade, to make sure everything was all right. It was, as close as could be expected."

He sighed. "To get to the point, Doc, she bore him half a dozen children, starting inside a year of their marriage. She had never conceived by me. As far as I've determined, no woman ever has."

He had gotten a fertility test, according to which he was normal.

Neither of us wanted to dwell on his personal confession. It suggested too strongly how shaped our psyches are by whatever happens to be around us. "You mean," I said slowly, "you're a mutant? So much a mutant that you count as, as a different species?"

"Yeah. I think my genes are that strange."

"But a fellow time traveler—a female—"

"Right on, Doc." Another futurism.

He was still for a while, in the blowing sunlit day, before he said: "Not that that's important in itself. What is important—maybe the most important thing in Earth's whole existence—is to find those other travelers, if there are any, and see what we can do about the horrors uptime. I can't believe I'm a meaningless accident!"

"How do you propose to go about it?"

His gaze was cat-cool. "I start by becoming rich."

For years which followed, I am barely on the edge of his story.

He'd see me at intervals, I think more to keep our friendship alive than to bring me up to date—since he obviously wanted Kate's company as much as mine. But I have only indirect news of his career. Often, in absence, he would become a dream in my mind, so foreign was he to our day-by-day faster-and-faster-aging small-town life, the growing up of our sons, the adventure of daughters-in-law and grandchildren. But then he would return, as if out of night, and for hours I would again be dominated by that lonely, driven man.

I don't mean he was fanatical. In fact, he continued to gain in perspective and in the skill of savoring this world. His intellect ranged widely, though it's clear that history and anthropology must be his chief concerns. As a drop of fortune, he had a talent for learning languages. (He and I wondered how many time travelers were wing-clipped by the mere lack of that. ) Sardonic humor and traditional Midwestern courtesy combined to make his presence pleasant. He became quite a gourmet, while staying able to live on stockfish and hardtack without complaint. He kept a schooner in Boston, whereon he took Kate and me to the West Indies in celebration of our retirement. While the usages of his boyhood made him reticent about it, I learned he was deeply sensitive to beauty both natural and manmade; of the latter, he had special fondness for Baroque, Classical, and Chinese music, for fine ships and weapons, and for Hellenic architecture. (God, if You exist, I do thank You from my inmost heart that I have seen Jack Havig's photographs of the unruined Acropolis.)

I was the single sharer of his secret, but not his single friend. Theoretically he could have been intimate with everyone great, Moses, Pericles, Shakespeare, Lincoln, Einstein. But in practice the obstacles were too much. Besides language, custom, and law, the famous were hedged off by being busy, conspicuous, sought-after. No, Havig—I called him "Jack" to his face, but now it seems more natural to write his surname—Havig told me about people like his lively little

Meg (three hundred years dust), or a mountain man who accompanied Lewis and Clark, or a profane old *moustache* who had marched with Napoleon.

("History does not tend to the better, Doc, it does not, it does not. We imagine so because events have produced our glorious selves. Think, however. Put aside the romantic legends and look at the facts. The average Frenchman in 1800 was no more unfree than the average Englishman. The French Empire could have brought Europe together, and could have been liberalized from within, and there might have been no World War I in which Western civilization cut its own throat. Because that's what happened, you know. We're still busy bleeding to death, but we haven't far to go now.")

Mainly his time excursions were for fun, in that period between his acquiring the techniques and resources to make them effective, and his development of a search plan for fellow mutants. "To be honest," he grinned, "I find myself more and more fond of low-down life."

"Toulouse-Lautrec's Paris?" I asked at random. He had already told me that earlier decadences were overrated, or at least consisted of tight-knit upper classes which didn't welcome strangers.

"Well, I haven't tried there," he admitted. "An idea, maybe. On the other hand, Storyville in its flowering—" He wasn't interested in the prostitutes; if nothing else, he had by now seen enough of the human condition to know how gruesome theirs usually was. He went for the jazz, and for the company of people whom he said were more real than most of his own generation, not to speak of 1970.

Meanwhile he made his fortune.

You suppose that was easy. Let him look up the stock market quotations—1929 is an obvious year—and go surf on the tides of Wall Street.

The fact was different. For instance, what might he use for money?

While in Europe, he bought gold or silver out of his pay, which he exchanged for cash in various parts of the nineteenth and later eighteenth centuries. With that small stake, he could begin trading. He would take certain stamps and coins uptime and sell them to dealers; he would go downtime with a few aluminum vessels, which were worth more than gold before the Hall process was invented. But these and similar dealings were necessarily on a minute scale, both because the mass he could carry was limited and because he dared not draw overmuch attention to himself.

He considered investing and growing wealthy in that period, but rejected the idea. The rules and mores were too peculiar, too intricate for him to master in as much of his lifespan as he cared to spend. Besides, he wanted to be based in his own original era; if nothing else, he would need swift spatial transportation when he began his search. Thus he couldn't simply leave money in the semi-distant past at compound interest. The intervening years gave too many chances for something to go wrong.

As for a more manageable point like 1929, what gold he brought would represent a comparatively trifling sum. Shuttling back and forth across those frantic days, he could parlay it—but within strict limits, if he wasn't to be unduly noticed. Also, he must take assorted federal agencies into account, which in the years ahead would become ever better equipped to be nosy.

He never gave me the details of his operations. "Frankly," he said, "finance bores me like an auger. I found me a couple of sharp partners who'd front, and an ultra-solid bank for a trustee, and let both make more off my 'economic analyses' than was strictly necessary."

In effect, John Franklin Havig established a fund, including an arrangement for taxes and the like, which was to be paid over to "any collateral male descendant" who met certain unambiguous standards, upon the twenty-first birthday of this person. As related, the bank was one of those Eastern ones, with Roman pillars and cathedral dimness and, I suspect, a piece of Plymouth Rock in a reliquary. Thus when John Franklin Havig, collateral descendant, was contacted in 1954, everything was so discreet that he entered his millionaire condition with scarcely a ripple. The Senlac *Trumpet* did announce that he had received a substantial inheritance from a distant relative.

"I let the bank keep on managing the bucks," he told me. "What I do is write checks."

After all, riches were merely his means to an end.

No, several ends. I've mentioned his pleasures. I should add the help he gave his mother and, quietly, others. On the whole, he disdained recognized charities. "They're big businesses," he said. "Their executives draw down more money than you do, Doc. Besides, to be swinishly blunt, we have too many people. When you've seen the Black Death, you can't get excited about Mississippi sharecroppers." I scolded him amicably for being such a right-winger when he had witnessed *laissez-faire* in action, and he retorted amicably that in this day and age liberals like me were the ones who had learned nothing and forgotten nothing, and we had us a drink....But I believe that, without fuss, he rescued quite a few individuals; and it is a fact that he was a substantial contributor to the better conservationist organizations.

"We need a reserve of life, every kind of life," he explained. "Today for the spirit—a glimpse of space and green. Tomorrow for survival, flat-out survival."

The War of Judgment, he said, would by no means be the simple capitalist-versus-Communist slugfest which most of us imagined in the 1950's.

"I've only the vaguest idea yet of what actually will go on. Not surprising. I've had to make fugitive appearances—watching out for radioactivity and a lot else—and who in the immediate sequel is in any condition to give me a reasoned analysis? Hell, Doc, scholars argue today about what went wrong in 1914 to '18, and they aren't scrambling for a leftover can of dog food, or arming against the Mong who'll pour across a Bering Straits that all the dust kicked into the atmosphere will cause to be frozen."

His impression was that, like World War I, it was a conflict which everybody anticipated, nobody wanted, and men would have recoiled from had they foreseen the consequences. He thought it was less ideological than ecological.

"I have this nightmare notion that it came not just as a result of huge areas turning into deserts, but came barely in time. Do you know the oceans supply half our oxygen? By 1970, insecticide was in the plankton. By 1990, every ocean was scummy, and stank, and you didn't dare swim in it."

"But this must have been predicted," I said.

He leered. "Yeah. 'Environment' was very big for a while. Ecology Now stickers on the windshields of cars belonging to hairy young men—cars which dripped oil wherever they parked and took off in clouds of smoke thicker than your pipe can produce....Before long, the fashionable cause was something else, I forget what. Anyhow, that whole phase—the wave after wave of causes—passed away. People completely stopped caring.

"You see, that was the logical conclusion of the whole trend. I know it's stupid to assign a single blame for something as vast as the War of Judgment, its forerunners and aftermaths. Especially when I'm still in dark about what the events *were*. But Doc, I feel a moral certainty that a large part of the disaster grew from this particular country, the world's most powerful, the vanguard country for things both good and ill...never really trying to meet the responsibilities of power.

"We'll make halfhearted attempts to stop some enemies in Asia, and because the attempts are halfhearted we'll piss away human lives— on both sides—and treasure—to no purpose. Hoping to placate the implacable, we'll estrange our last few friends. Men elected to national office will solemnly identify inflation with rising prices, which is like identifying red spots with the measles virus, and slap on wage and price controls, which is like papering the cracks in a house whose foundations are sliding away. So economic collapse brings international impotence. The well-off whites will grow enough aware that we have distressed minorities, and give them enough, to bring on revolt without really helping them; and the revolt will bring on reaction, which will stamp on every remnant of progress. As for our foolish little attempts to balance what we drain from the environment against what we put back—well, I mentioned that car carrying the ecology sticker.

"At first Americans will go on an orgy of guilt. Later they'll feel inadequate. Finally they'll turn apathetic. After all, they'll be able to buy any anodyne, any pseudo-existence they want.

"I wonder if at the end, down underneath, they don't welcome their own multimillion-fold deaths."

Thus in February of 1964, Havig came into the inheritance he had made for himself. Shortly thereafter he set about shoring up his private past, and spent months of his lifespan being "Uncle Jack." I asked him what the hurry was, and he said, "Among other things, I want to get as much foreknowledge as possible behind me." I considered that for a while, and choked off my last impulse to ask him about the tomorrows of me and mine. I did not understand how rich a harvest this would bear until the day when they buried Kate.

I never asked Havig if he had seen her gravestone earlier. He may have, and kept silent. As a physician, I think I know how it is possible to possess such information and yet smile.

He didn't go straight from one episode with his childhood self to the next. That would have been monotonous. Instead, he made his pastward visits vacations from his studies at our state university. He didn't intend to be frustrated when again he sought a non-English-speaking milieu. Furthermore, he needed a baseline from which to extrapolate changes of language in the future; there/then he was also often a virtual deaf-mute.

His concentration was on Latin and Greek—the latter that *koine* which in its various forms had wider currency through both space and time than Classical Attic—plus French, German, Italian, Spanish, Portuguese (and English), with emphasis on their evolution—plus some Hebrew, Aramaic, Arabic—plus quite a bit of the numerous Polynesian tongues.

"They do have a civilization on the other side of the dark centuries," he told me. "I've barely glimpsed that, and can't make head or tail of what's going on. But it does look as if Pacific Ocean peoples dominate the world, speaking the damnedest *lingua franca* you can imagine."

"So there is hope!" gusted from me.

"I still have to find out for sure." His glance speared mine. "Look, suppose you were a time traveler from, well, Egypt of the Pharaohs. Suppose you came to today's world and touristed around, trying to stay anonymous. How much sense would anything make? Would the question 'Is this development good or bad?' even be meaningful to you? I haven't tried to explore beyond the early stages of the Maurai Federation. It'll be the work of years to understand that much."

He was actually more interested in bygone eras, which to him were every bit as alive as today or tomorrow. Those he could study beforehand—in more detail than you might think, unless you're a professional historiographer—and thus prepare himself to move around with considerable freedom. Besides, while the past had ghastlinesses enough, nothing, not the Black Death or the burning of heretics or the Middle Passage or the Albigensian Crusade, nothing in his mind matched the Judgment. "That's when the whole planet almost goes under," he said. "I imagine my fellow time travelers generally avoid it. I'm likeliest to find them in happier, or less unhappy, eras."

Given these activities, he was biologically about thirty when at last he succeeded. This was in Jerusalem, on the day of the Crucifixion.

**6**

He told me of his plan in 1964. As far as practicable, his policy was to skip intervals of the twentieth century equal to those he spent elsewhen, so that his real and calendar ages wouldn't get too much out of step. I hadn't seen him for a while. He no longer dwelt in Senlac, but made his headquarters in New York—a post office box in the present, a sumptuous apartment in the 1890's, financed by the sale of gold he bought after this was again made legal and carried downtime. He did come back for visits, though. Kate found that touching. I did too, but I knew besides what need he had of me, his only confidant.

"Why...you're right!" I exclaimed. "The moment you'd expect every traveler, at least in Christendom, to head for. Why haven't you done it before?"

"Less simple than you suppose, Doc," he replied. "That's a long haul, to a most thoroughly alien territory. And how certain is the date, anyway? Or even the fact?"

I blinked. "You mean you've never considered seeking the historical

Christ? I know you're not religious, but surely the mystery around him—"

"Doc, what he was, or if he was, makes only an academic difference. What counts is what people through the ages have believed. My life expectancy isn't enough for me to do the pure research I'd like. In fact, I'm overdue to put fun and games aside. I've seen too much human misery. Time travel has got to have some real value; it's got to be made to help." He barely smiled. "You know I'm no saint. But I do have to live in my own head."

He flew from New York to Israel in 1969, while the Jews were in firm control of Jerusalem and a visitor could move around freely. From his hotel he walked out Jericho Road, carrying a handbag, till he found an orange grove which offered concealment. There he sprang back to the previous midnight and made his preparations.

The Arab costume he had bought at a tourist shop would pass in Biblical times. A knife, more eating tool than weapon, was sheathed at his hip; being able to blink out of bad situations, he seldom took a firearm. A leather purse held phrase book (specially compiled, for pay, by an American graduate student), food, drinking cup, Halazone tablets, soap, flea repellent, antibiotic, and money. That last was several coins of the Roman period, plus a small ingot he could exchange if need be.

Having stowed his modern clothes in the bag, he drew forth his last item of equipment. He called it a chronolog. It was designed and built to his specifications in 1980, to take advantage of the superb solid-state electronics then available. The engineers who made it had perhaps required less ingenuity than Havig had put into his cover story.

I have seen the apparatus. It's contained in a green cracklefinish box with a carrying handle, about 24 by 12 by 6 inches. When the lid is opened, you can fold out an optical instrument vaguely suggestive of a sextant, and you can set the controls and read the meters. Beneath these lies a miniature but most sophisticated computer, running off a nickel-cadmium battery. The weight is about five pounds, which edges near half the limit of what a traveler can pack through time and helps explain Havig's reluctance to carry a gun.

Other items are generally more useful. But none approaches in value the chronolog.

Imagine. He projects himself backward or forward to a chosen moment. How does he know "when" he has arrived? On a short hop, he can count days, estimate the hour by sun or stars if a clock isn't on the spot. But a thousand years hold a third of a million dawns; and the chances are that many of them won't be identifiable, because of stormy weather or the temporary existence of a building or some similar accident.

Havig took his readings. The night was clear, sufficiently cold for his breath to smoke; Jerusalem's lights hazed the sky northward, but elsewhere the country lay still and dark save for outlying houses and passing cars; constellations wheeled brilliant overhead. He placed the moon and two planets in relation to them, set the precise Greenwich time and geographical locations on appropriate dim-glowing dials, and worked a pair of verniers till he had numbers corresponding to that Passover week of Anno Domini 33.

("The date does seem well established," he'd remarked. "At least, it's the one everybody would aim at." He laughed. "Beats the Nativity. The only thing certain about *that* is it wasn't at midwinter—not if shepherds were away from home watching their flocks!")

He had been breathing in and out, deep slow breaths which oxygenated his blood to the fullest. Now he took a lungful—not straining, which would have spent energy, just storing a fair amount— and launched himself down the world lines.

There was the sensation, indescribable, but which he had told me was not quite unlike swimming against a high tide. The sun rose in the west and skidded eastward; then, as he "accelerated," light became a vague pulsation of grayness, and everywhere around him reached shadow. It was altogether silent.

He glimpsed a shellburst—soundless, misty—but was at once past the Six Day War, or had that been the War of Independence or the First World War? Wan unshapes drifted past. On a cloudy night in the late nineteenth century he must reenter normal time for air. The chronolog could have given him the exact date, had he wanted to shoot the stars again; its detectors included sensitivities to those radiations which pierce an overcast. But no point in that. A couple of mounted men, probably Turkish soldiers, happened to be near. Their presence had been too brief for him to detect while traveling, even were it daylight. They didn't notice him in the dark. Horseshoes thumped by and away.

He continued.

Dim though it was, the landscape began noticeably changing. Contours remained about the same, but now there were many trees, now few, now there was desert, now planted fields. Fleetingly, he glimpsed what he guessed was a great wooden stadium wherein the Crusaders held tourneys before Saladin threw them out of their blood-smeared kingdom, and he was tempted to pause but held to his purpose. Stops for breath grew more frequent as he neared his goal. The journey drained strength; and, too, the idea that he might within hours achieve his dream made the heart hammer in his breast.

A warning light blinked upon the chronolog.

It could follow sun, moon, planets, and stars with a speed and precision denied to flesh. It could allow for precession, perturbation, proper motion, even continental drift; and when it identified an aspect of heaven corresponding to the destination, that could be nothing except the hour which was sought.

A light flashed red, and Havig stopped.

Thursday night was ending. If the Bible spoke truly, the Last Supper had been held, the agony in the garden was past, and Jesus lay in bonds, soon to be brought before Pilate, condemned, scourged, lashed to the cross, pierced, pronounced dead, and laid in the tomb.

("They tie them in place," Havig told me. "Nails wouldn't support the weight; the hands would tear apart. Sometimes nails are driven in for special revenge, so the tradition could be right as far as it goes." He covered his face. "Doc, I've seen them hanging, tongues black from thirst, bellies bloated—after a while they don't cry out any longer, they croak, and no mind is left behind their eyes. The stink, the stink! They often take days to die. I wonder if Jesus wasn't physically frail, he won to his death so soon....A few friends and kinfolk, maybe, hover on the fringes of the crowd, hardly ever daring to speak or even weep. The rest crack jokes, gamble, drink, eat picnic lunches, hold the kiddies up for a better view. What kind of a thing is man, anyway?"

(Put down your pride. Ours is the century of Buchenwald and Vorkuta—and Havig reminded me of what had gone on in the nostalgically remembered Edwardian part of it, in places like the Belgian Congo and the southern United States—and he told me of what has yet to happen. Maybe I don't envy him his time travel after all.)

Morning made an eastward whiteness. Now he had an olive orchard at his back, beyond which he glimpsed a huddle of adobe buildings. The road was a rutted dirt track. Afar, half hidden in lingering twilight, Jerusalem of the Herodian kings and the Roman proconsulate crouched on its hills. It was smaller and more compact than the city he remembered two millennia hence, mainly within walls though homesteads did spread beyond. Booths and felt tents crowded near the gates, erected by provincials come to the holy place for the holy days. The air was cold and smelled of earth. Birds twittered. "Beyond one or two hundred years back," Havig once said to me, "the daytime sky is always full of wings."

He sat panting while light quickened and vigor returned. Hungry, he broke off chunks of goat cheese and tortilla-like bread, and was surprised to realize that he was taking a perfectly ordinary meal on the first Good Friday in the world.

If it was. The scholars might have gotten the date wrong, or Jesus might be nothing more than an Osirian-Essene-Mithraic myth. Suppose he wasn't, though? Suppose he was, well, maybe not the literal incarnation of the Creator of these acres, those wildfowl, yonder universe…but at least the prophet from whose vision stemmed most of what was decent in all time to come. Could a life be better spent than following him on his ministry?

Well, Havig would have to become fluent in Aramaic, plus a million details of living, and he would have to forget his quest….He sighed and rose. The sun broke over the land.

He soon had company. Nevertheless he walked as an outsider.

("If anything does change man," he said, "it's science and technology. Just think about the fact—while it lasts—that parents need not take for granted some of their babies will die. You get a completely different concept of what a child is." He must have seen the memory of Nora flit across my face, for he laid a hand on my shoulder and said: "I'm sorry, Doc. Shouldn't have mentioned that. And never ask me to take a camera back to her, or a shot of penicillin, because I've tried altering the known past and something always happens to stop me.... Think of electric bulbs, or even candles. When the best you've got is a flickering wick in a bowl of oil, you're pretty well tied to daylight. The simple freedom to stay awake late isn't really that simple. It has all sorts of subtle but far-reaching effects on the psyche.")

Folk were up at dawn, tending livestock, hoeing weeds, stoking fires, cooking and cleaning, against the Sabbath tomorrow. Bearded men in ragged gowns whipped starveling donkeys, overloaded with merchandise, toward the city. Children, hardly begun to walk, scattered grain for poultry; a little older, they shooed gaunt stray dogs from the lambs. When he reached pavement, Havig was jostled: by caravaneers from afar, sheikhs, priests, hideous beggars, farmers, artisans, a belated and very drunken harlot, a couple of Anatolian traders, or whatever they were, in cylindrical hats, accompanying a man in a Grecian tunic, and then the harsh cry to make way and tramp-tramp-tramp, quickstep and metal, a Roman squad returning from night patrol.

I've seen photographs which he took on different occasions, and can well imagine this scene. It was less gaudy than you may suppose, who live in an age of aniline dyes and fluorescents. Fabrics were subdued brown, gray, blue, cinnabar, and dusty. But the sound was enormous—shrill voices, laughter, oaths, extravagant lies and boasts, plang of a harp, fragments of a song; shuffling feet, cropping unshod hoofs, creaking wooden wheels, yelping dogs, bleating sheep, grunting camels, always and always the birds of springtime. These people were not stiff Englishmen or Americans; no, they windmilled their arms, they shaped the air with their palms, backslapped, jigged, clapped hand to dagger in affront and almost instantly were good-humored again. And the smells! The sweet sweat of horses, the sour sweat of men; smoke, fragrant from cedar or pungent from dried dung; new-baked bread; leeks and garlic and rancid grease; everywhere the droppings and passings of animals, often the ammonia of a compost heap; a breath of musk and attar of roses, as a veiled woman went by borne in a litter; a wagonload of fresh lumber; saddle leather warming beneath the sun—Havig never praised this day when nails were beaten through living bodies; but nothing of what he inhaled made him choke, or hurt his eyes, or gave him emphysema or cancer.

The gates of Jerusalem stood open. His pulse beat high.

And then he was found.

It happened all at once. Fingers touched his back. He turned and saw a stocky, wide-faced person, not tall, clad similarly to him but also beardless, short-haired, and fair-skinned.

Perspiration sheened upon the stranger's countenance. He braced himself against the streaming and shoving of the crowd and said through its racket: "*Es tu peregrinator temporis?*"

The accent was thick—eighteenth-century Polish, it would turn out—but Havig had a considerable mastery of classical as well as later Latin, and understood.

"*Are you a time traveler?*"

For a moment he could not reply. Reality whirled about him. Here was the end of his search.

Or theirs.

His height was unusual in this place, and he had left his head bare to show the barbering and the Nordic features. Unlike the majority of communities in history, Herodian Jerusalem was sufficiently cosmopolitan to let foreigners in; but his hope had been that others like him would guess he was a stranger in time as well as in space, or he might spy one of them. And now his hope was fulfilled.

His first thought, before the joy began, was an uneasy idea that this man looked far too tough.

They sat in the tavern which was their rendezvous and talked: Waclaw Krasicki who left Warsaw in 1738, Juan Mendoza who left Tijuana in 1924, and the pilgrims they had found.

These were Jack Havig. And Coenraad van Leuven, a man-at-arms from thirteenth-century Brabant, who had drawn his sword and tried to rescue the Savior as the cross was being carried toward Golgotha, and was urged back by Krasicki one second before a Roman blade would have spilled his guts, and now sat stunned by the question: "How do you know that person really was your Lord?" And a gray-bearded Orthodox monk who spoke only Croatian (?) but seemed to be named Boris and from the seventeenth century. And a thin, stringy-haired, pockmarked woman who hunched glaze-eyed in her robe and cowl and muttered in a language that nobody could identify.

"This is *all*?" Havig asked unbelieving.

"Well, we have several more agents in town," Krasicki answered. Their conversation was in English, when the American's origin was known. "We're to meet Monday evening, and then again right after, hm, Pentecost. I suppose they'll turn up a few more travelers. But on the whole, yes, it seems like we'll make less of a haul than we expected."

Havig looked around. The shop was open-fronted. Customers sat cross-legged on shabby rugs, the street and its traffic before them, while they drank out of clay cups which a boy filled from a wineskin. Jerusalem clamored past. On Good Friday!

Krasicki wasn't bothered. He had mentioned leaving his backward city, country, and time for the French Enlightenment; in a whisper, he had labeled his partner Mendoza as a gangster. ("Mercenary" was what he said, but the connotation was plain.) "It's nothing to me if a Jewish carpenter who suffers from delirium is executed," he told Havig. With a nudge: "Nor to you, eh? We seem to have gotten one reasonable recruit, at any rate."

In fact, that was not the American's attitude. He avoided argument by asking: "Are time travelers really so few?"

Krasicki shrugged. "Who knows? At least they can't easily come here. It makes sense. You boarded a flying machine and arrived in hours. But think of the difficulties, the downright impossibility of the trip, in most eras. We read about medieval pilgrims. But how many were they, really, in proportion to population? How many died on the way? Also, I suppose, we'll fail to find some time travelers because they don't want to be found—or, maybe, it's never occurred to them that others of their kind are in search—and their disguises will be too good for us."

Havig stared at him, and at imperturbable Juan Mendoza, three-quarters-drunk Coenraad, filthy rosary-clicking Boris, unknown crazy woman, and thought: *Sure. Why should the gift fall exclusively on my type? Why didn't I expect it's given at random, to a complete cross-section of humanity? And I've seen what most humanity is like. And what makes me imagine I'm anything special?*

"We can't spend too many man-hours hunting, either," Krasicki said. "We are so few in the Eyrie." He patted Havig's knee. "Mother of God, how glad the Sachem will be that at least we found you!"

A third-century Syrian hermit and a second-century B.C. Ionian adventurer were gathered by two more teams. Report was given of another woman—she seemed to be a Coptic Christian—who vanished when approached.

"A rotten harvest," Krasicki grumbled. "However—" And he led the way, first to the stop after Pentecost, which yielded naught, then to the twenty-first century.

Dust drifted across desert. In Jerusalem nothing human remained except bones and shaped stones. But an aircraft waited, needle-nosed, stubby-winged, nuclear-powered, taken by Eyrie men from a hangar whose guardians had had no chance to throw this war vessel into action before the death was upon them.

"We flew across the Atlantic," Havig would tell me. "Headquarters was in...what had been...Wisconsin. Yes, they let me fetch my chronolog from where I'd hidden it, though I pleaded language difficulties to avoid telling them what it was. They themselves had had to cast about to zero in on the target date. That's a clumsy, lifespan-consuming process, which probably helps account for the dearth of travelers they found, and certainly explains their own organization's reluctance to make long temporal journeys. Return was easier, because they'd erected a kind of big billboard in the ruins, on which an indicator was set daily to the correct date.

"In late twenty-first-century America, things were barely getting started. The camp and sheds were inside a stockade and had been attacked more than once by, uh, natives or marauders. From then we moved on uptime to when the Sachem had sent his expedition out to that Easter."

I do not know if my friend ever looked upon Jesus.

**7**

After a hundred-odd years, the establishment was considerable. Fertility was increasing in formerly tainted soil, thus letting population build up. Grain-fields ripened across low hills, beneath a mild sky where summer clouds walked. Cultivation of timber had produced stands which made cupolas of darker green where birds nested and wind murmured. Roads were dirt, but laid out in a grid. Folk were about, busy. They had nothing except hand tools and animal-drawn machines; however, these were well-made. They looked much alike in their mostly homespun blue trousers and jackets—both sexes—and their floppy straw hats and clumsy shoes: weather-beaten and work-gnarled like any pre-industrial peasants, hair hacked off below the ears, men bearded; they were small by the standards of our time, and many had poor teeth or none. Yet they were infinitely better off than their ancestors of the Judgment.

They paused to salute the travelers, who rode on horseback from the airfield site, then immediately resumed their toil. An occasional pair of mounted soldiers, going by, drew sabers in a deferential but less servile gesture. They were uniformed in blue, wore steel helmets and breastplates, bore dagger at belt, bow and quiver and ax at croup, lance in rest with red pennon aflutter from the shaft, besides those swords.

"You seem to keep tight control," Havig said uneasily.

"What else?" Krasicki snapped. "Most of the world, including most of this continent, is still in a state of barbarism or savagery, where man survives at all. We can't manufacture what we can't get the materials and machinery for. The Mong are on the plains west and south of us. They would come in like a tornado, did we let down our defenses. Our troopers aren't overseeing the workers, they're guarding them against bandits. No, those people can thank the Eyrie for everything they do have."

The medieval-like pattern was repeated in town. Families did not occupy separate homes, they lived together near the stronghold and worked the land collectively. But while it looked reasonably clean, which was a welcome difference from the Middle Ages, the place had none of the medieval charm. Brick rows flanking asphalted streets were as monotonous as anything in the Victorian Midlands. Havig supposed that was because the need for quick though stout construction had taken priority over individual choice, and the economic surplus remained too small to allow replacing these barracks with real houses. If not—But he ought to give the Sachem the benefit of the doubt, till he knew more.... He saw one picturesque feature, a wooden building in a style which seemed half Asian, gaudily painted. Krasicki told him it was a temple, where prayers were said to Yasu and sacrifices made to that Oktai whom the Mong had brought.

"Give them their religion, make the priests cooperate, and you have them," he added.

Havig grimaced. "Where's the gallows?"

Krasicki gave him a startled glance. "We don't hold public hangings. What do you think we are?" After a moment: "What milksop measures do you imagine can pull anybody through years like these?"

The fortress loomed ahead. High, turreted brick walls enclosed several acres; a moat surrounded them in turn, fed by the river which watered this area. The architecture had the same stern functionality as that of the town. Flanking the gates, and up among the battlements, were heavy machine guns, doubtless salvaged from wreckage or brought piece by piece out of the past. Stuttering noises told Havig that a number of motor-driven generators were busy inside.

Sentries presented arms. A trumpet blew. Drawbridge planks clattered, courtyard flagstones resounded beneath horsehoofs.

Krasicki's group reined in. A medley of people hastened from every direction, babbling their excitement. Most, liveried, must be castle servants. Havig scarcely noticed. His attention was on one who thrust her way past them until she stood before him.

Enthusiasm blazed from her. He could barely follow the husky, accented voice: "Oktai's tail! You did find 'm!"

She was nearly as tall as him, sturdily built, with broad shoulders and hips, comparatively small bust, long smooth limbs. Her face bore high cheekbones, blunt nose, large mouth, good teeth save that two were missing. (He would learn they had been knocked out in a fight.) Her hair, thick and mahogany, was not worn in today's style, but waist-length, though now coiled in braids above barbarically large brass earrings. Her eyes were brown and slightly almond—some Indian or Asian blood—under the heavy brows; her skin, sun-tanned, was in a few places crossed by old scars. She wore a loose red tunic and kilt, laced boots, a Bowie knife, a revolver, a loaded cartridge belt, and, on a chain around her neck, the articulated skull of a weasel.

"Where 'ey from? You, yon!" Her forefinger stabbed at Havig. " 'E High Years, no?" A whoop of laughter. "You got aplen'y for tell me, trailmate!"

"The Sachem is waiting," Krasicki reminded her.

" 'Kay, I'll wait alike, but not 'e whole jokin' day, you hear?" And when Havig had dismounted, she flung arms around him and kissed him full on the lips. She smelled of sunshine, leather, sweat, smoke, and woman. Thus did he meet Leonce of the Glacier Folk, the Skula of Wahorn.

The office was the antechamber of a suite whose size and luxury it reflected. Oak paneling rose above a deep-gray, thick-piled carpet. Drapes by the windows were likewise furry and feelable: mink. Because of their massiveness, desk, chairs, and couch had been fashioned in this section of time; but the care lavished on them was in contrast to the austerity Havig had observed in other rooms opening on the hallways which took him here. Silver frames held some photographs. One was a period piece, a daguerreotype of a faded-looking woman in the dress of the middle nineteenth century. The rest were candid shots taken with an advanced camera, doubtless a miniature using a telescopic lens like his own. He recognized Cecil Rhodes, Bismarck, and a youthful Napoleon; he could not place the yellow-bearded man in a robe.

From this fifth floor of the main keep, the view showed wide across that complex of lesser buildings, that bustle of activity, which was the Eyrie, and across the land it ruled. Afternoon light slanted in long hot bars. The generator noise was a muted pecking.

"Let's have music, eh?" Caleb Wallis flipped the switches of a molecular recorder from shortly before the Judgment. Notes boomed forth. He lowered the volume but said: "That's right, a triumphal piece. Lord, I'm glad to have you, Havig!" The newcomer recognized the Entry of the Gods from *Das Rheingold.*

The rest of his group, including their guides, had been dismissed, not altogether untactfully, after a short interview had demonstrated what they were. "You're different," the Sachem said. "You're the one in a hundred we need worst. Here, want a cigar?"

"No, thanks, I don't smoke."

Wallis stood for a moment before he said, emphatically rather than loudly, "I am the founder and master of this nation. We must have discipline, forms of respect. I'm called 'sir.'"

Havig regarded him. Wallis was of medium height, blocky and powerful despite the paunch of middle life. His face was ruddy, somewhat flat-nosed, tufty-browed; gingery-gray muttonchop whiskers crossed upper lip and cheeks to join the hair which fringed his baldness. He wore a black uniform, silver buttons and insignia, goldwork on the collar, epaulets, ornate dagger, automatic pistol. But there was nothing ridiculous about him. He radiated assurance. His voice rolled deep and compelling, well-nigh hypnotic when he chose. His small pale eyes never wavered.

"You realize," Havig said at last, "this is all new and bewildering to me...sir."

"Sure! Sure!" Wallis beamed and slapped him on the back. "You'll catch on fast. You'll go far, my boy. No limit here, for a man who knows what he wants and has the backbone to go after it. And you're an American, too. An honest-to-God American, from when our country was herself. Mighty few like that among us."

He lowered himself behind the desk. "Sit down. No, wait a minute, see my liquor cabinet? I'll take two fingers of the bourbon. You help yourself to what you like."

Havig wondered why no provision for ice and soda and the rest had been made. It should have been possible. He decided Wallis didn't use such additions and didn't care that others might.

Seated in an armchair, a shot of rum between his fingers, he gazed at the Sachem and ventured: "I can go into detail about my biography, sir, but I think that could more usefully wait till I know what the Eyrie…is."

"Right, right." Wallis nodded his big head and puffed on the stogie. Its smoke was acrid. "However, let's just get a few facts straight about you. Born in—1933, did you say? Ever let on to anybody what you are?" Havig checked the impulse to mention me. The knowledgeable questions snapped: "Went back as a young man to guide your childhood? Went on to improve your station in life, and then to search for other travelers?"

"Yes, sir."

"What do you think of your era?"

"Huh? Why, uh, well…we're in trouble. I've gone ahead and glimpsed what's in store. Sir."

"Because of decay, Havig. You understand that, don't you?" Intensity gathered like a thunderhead. "Civilized man turning against himself, first in war, later in moral sickness. The white man's empires crumbling faster than Rome's; the work of Clive, Bismarck, Rhodes, McKinley, Lyautey, all Indian fighters and Boers, everything that'd been won, cast out in a single generation; pride of race and heritage gone; traitors—Bolsheviks and international Jews—in the seats of power, preaching to the ordinary white man that the wave of the future was black. I've seen that, studying your century. You, living in it, have you seen?"

Havig bristled. "I've seen what prejudice, callousness, and stupidity bring about. The sins of the fathers are very truly visited on the sons."

Wallis chose to ignore the absence of an honorific. Indeed, he smiled and grew soothing: "I know. I know. Don't get me wrong. Plenty of colored men are fine, brave fellows—Zulus, for instance, or Apache Indians to take a different race, or Japs to take still another. Any travelers we may find among them will get their chance to occupy the same honored position as all our proven time agents do, as you will yourself, I'm sure. Shucks, I admire your Israelis, what I've heard about them. A mongrel people, racially no relation to the Hebrews of the Bible, but tough fighters and clever. No, I'm just talking about the need for everybody to keep his own identity and pride. And I'm only mad at those classes it's fair to call niggers, redskins, Chinks, kikes, wops, you know what I mean. Plenty of pure-blooded whites among them, I'm sorry to say, who've either lost heart or have outright sold themselves to the enemy."

Havig forced himself to remember that that basic attitude was common, even respectable in the Sachem's birth-century. Why, Abraham Lincoln had spoken of the inborn inferiority of the Negro....He didn't suppose Wallis ordered crucifixions.

"Sir," he said with much care, "I suggest we avoid argument till we've made the terms of our thinking clear to each other. That may take a lot of effort. Meanwhile we can better discuss practical matters."

"Right, right," Wallis rumbled. "You're a brain, Havig. A man of action, too, though maybe within limits. But I'll be frank, brains are what we need most at this stage, especially if they have scientific training, realistic philosophies." He waved the cigar. "Take that haul today from Jerusalem. Typical! The Brabanter and the Greek we can probably train up to be useful fighting men, scouts, auxiliaries on time expeditions, that sort of thing. But the rest—" He clicked his tongue. "I don't know. Maybe, at most, ferrymen, fetching stuff from the past. And I can only hope the woman'll be a breeder."

"What?" Havig started half out of his chair. It leaped inside him. "We can have children?"

"With each other, yes. In the course of a hundred years we've proved that." Wallis guffawed. "Not with nontravelers, no, not ever. We've proved that even oftener. How'd you like a nice little servant girl to warm your bed tonight, hm? Or we have slaves, taken on raids—and don't go moralistic on me. Their gangs would've done the same to us, and if we didn't bring prisoners back here and tame them, rather than cut their throats, they and their brats would go on making trouble along our borders." His mood had reverted to serious. "Quite a shortage of traveler women here, as you'd expect, and not all of them willing or able to become mothers. But those who do—The kids are ordinary, Havig. The gift is not inherited."

Considering the hypothesis he had made (how far ago on his multiply twisted world line?), the younger man was unsurprised. If two such sets of chromosomes could interact to make a life, it must be because the resonances (?) which otherwise barred fertility were canceled out.

"Well, then, no use trying to breed a race from ourselves," Wallis continued wistfully. "Oh, we do give our kids educations, preference, leadership jobs when they're grown. I have to allow that, it being one thing which helps keep my agents loyal to me. But frankly, confidentially, I'm often hard put to find handsome-looking posts where somebody's get can do no harm. Because the parents are time travelers, it doesn't follow they're not chuckleheads fit only to bring forth more chuckleheads. No, we're a kind of aristocracy in these parts, I won't deny, but we can't keep it hereditary for very long. I wouldn't want that anyway."

Havig asked softly: "What do you want, sir?"

Wallis put aside his cigar and drink, as if his next words required the piety of folded hands on the desk before him. "To restore civilization. Why else did God make our kind?"

"But—in the future—I've glimpsed—"

"The Maurai Federation?" Fury flushed the wide countenance. A fist thudded down. "How much of it have you seen? Damn little, right? I've explored that epoch, Havig. You'll be taken to learn for yourself. I tell you, they're a bunch of Kanaka-white-nigger-Chink-Jap mongrels who'll come to power—are starting to come to power while we sit here—for no other reason than that they were less hard-hit. They'll work, and fight, and bribe, and connive to dominate the world, only so they can put bridle and saddle on the human race in general, the white race in particular, and stop progress forever. You'll see! You'll see!"

He leaned back, breathed hard, swallowed his whiskey, and stated: "Well, they won't succeed. For three-four centuries, yes, I'm afraid men will have to bear their yoke. But afterward—That's what the Eyrie is for, Havig. To prepare an afterward."

"I was born in 1853, upstate New York," the Sachem related. "My father was a poor storekeeper and a strict Baptist. My mother—that's her picture." He indicated the gentle, ineffectual face upon the wall, and for an instant a tenderness broke through. "I was the last of seven children who lived. So Father hadn't a lot of time or energy to spare for me, especially since the oldest boy was his favorite. Well, that taught me at an early age how to look out for myself and keep my mouth shut. Industry and thrift, too. I went to Pittsburgh when I was officially 17, knowing by then how much of the future was there. My older self had worked closer with me than I gather yours did. But then, I always knew I had a destiny."

"How did you make your fortune, sir?" Havig inquired. He was interested as well as diplomatic.

"Well, my older self joined the Forty-niners in California. He didn't try for more than a good stake, just enough to invest for a proper profit in sutlering when he skipped on to the War Between the States. Next he had me run over his time track, and when I came back to Pittsburgh the rest was easy. You can't call 'em land speculations when you know what's due to happen, right? I sold short at the proper point in '73, and after the panic was in a position to buy up distressed property that would become valuable for coal and oil. Bought into railroads and steel mills, too, in spite of trouble from strikers and anarchists and suchlike trash. By 1880, my real age about thirty-five, I figured I'd made my pile and could go on to the work for which God had created me."

Solemnly: "I've left my father's faith. I guess most time travelers do. But I still believe in a God who every now and then calls a particular man to a destiny."

And then Wallis laughed till his belly jiggled and exclaimed: "But my, oh, my, ain't them highfalutin words for a plain old American!

It's not glamour and glory, Havig, except in the history books. It's hard, grubby detail work, it's patience and self-denial and being willing to learn from the mistakes more than the successes. You see how I'm not young any more, and my plans barely started to blossom, let alone bear fruit. The doing, though, the doing, that's the thing, that's to be alive!"

He held out his empty glass. "Refill this," he said. "I don't ordinarily drink much, but Lord, how I've wanted to talk to somebody both new and bright! We have several shrewd boys, like Krasicki, but they're foreigners, except a couple of Americans who I've gotten so used to I can tell you beforehand what they'll say to any remark of mine. Go on, pour for me, and yourself, and let's chat awhile."

Presently Havig could ask: "How did you make your first contacts, sir?"

"Why, I hired me a lot of agents, throughout most of the nineteenth century, and had them go around placing advertisements in papers and magazines and almanacs, or spreading a word of mouth. They didn't say 'time traveler,' of course, nor know what I really wanted. That wording was very careful. Not that I made it myself. I'm no writer. Brains are what a man of action hires. I hunted around and found me a young Englishman in the '90's, starting out as an author, a gifted fellow even if he was kind of a socialist. I wanted somebody late in the period, to avoid, um-m, anticipations, you see? He got interested in my, ha, 'hypothetical proposition,' and for a few guineas wrote me some clever things. I offered him more money but he said he'd rather have the free use of that time travel idea instead."

Havig nodded; a tingle went along his nerves. "Some such thought occurred to me, sir. But, well, I hadn't your single-mindedness. I definitely don't seem to have accumulated anything like your fortune. And besides, in my period, time travel was so common a fictional theme, I was afraid of publicity. At best, it seemed I'd merely attract cranks."

"I got those!" Wallis admitted. "A few genuine, even: I mean travelers whose gift had made them a little tetched, or more than a little. Remember, a dimwit or a yokel, if he isn't scared green of what's happened to him and never does it again—or doesn't want to travel outside the horizon he knows—or doesn't get taken by surprise and murdered for a witch—he'll hide what he is, and that'll turn him strange. Or say he's a street urchin, why shouldn't he make himself rich as a burglar or a bookmaker, something like that, then retire to the life of Riley? Or say he's an Injun on the reservation, he can impress the devil out of his tribe and make them support him, but they aren't about to tell the palefaces, are they? And so on and so on. Hopeless cases. As for one like me, who is smart and ambitious, why, he'll lay low same as you and I did, won't he? Often, I'm afraid, too low for any of us to find."

"How...how many did you gather?"

"Sir."

"I'm sorry. Sir."

Wallis gusted a breath. "Eleven. Out of a whole blooming century, eleven in that original effort." He ticked them off. "Austin Caldwell the best of the lot. A fuzzy-checked frontier scout when he came to my office; but he's turned into quite a man, quite a man. He it was who nicknamed me the Sachem. I kind of liked that, and let it stick.

"Then a magician and fortuneteller in a carnival; a professional gambler; a poor white Southern girl. That was the Americans. Abroad, we found a Bavarian soldier; an investigator for the Inquisition, which was still going in Spain, you may know; a female Jew cultist in Hungary; a student in Edinburgh, working his heart out trying to learn from books what he might be; a lady milliner in Paris, who went off into time for her designs; a young peasant couple in Austria. We were lucky with those last, by the way. They'd found each other—maybe the only pair of travelers who were ever born neighbors—and had their first child, and wouldn't have left if the baby weren't small enough to carry.

"What a crew! You can imagine the problems of language and transportation and persuading and everything."

"No more than those?" Havig felt appalled.

"Yes, about as many, but unusable. Cracked, like I told you, or too dull, or crippled, or scared to join us, or whatever. One strapping housewife who refused to leave her husband. I thought of abducting her—the cause is bigger than her damn comfort—but what's the good of an unwilling traveler? A man, maybe you could threaten his kin and get service out of him. Women are too cowardly."

Havig remembered a flamboyant greeting in the courtyard, but held his peace.

"Once I had my first disciples, I could expand," Wallis told him. "We could explore wider and in more detail, learning better what needed to be done and how. We could establish funds and bases at key points of...m-m...yes, space-time. We could begin to recruit more, mainly from different centuries but a few additional from our own. Finally we could pick our spot for the Eyrie, and take command of the local people for a labor supply. Poor starved harried wretches, they welcomed warlords who brought proper guns and seed corn!"

Havig tugged his chin. "May I ask why you chose that particular place and year to start your nation, sir?"

"Sure, ask what you want," Wallis said genially. "Chances are I'll answer....I thought of the past. You can see from yonder picture I've been clear back to Charlemagne, testing my destiny. It's too long a haul, though. And even in an unexplored section like pre-Columbian America, we'd risk leaving traces for archeologists to discover. Remember, there could be Maurai time travelers, and what we've got to have is surprise. Right now, these centuries, feudalisms like ours are springing up everywhere, recovery is being made, and we take care not to look unique. Our subjects know we have powers, of course, but they call us magicians and children of the Those—gods and spirits. By the time that story's filtered past the wild people, it's only a vague rumor of still another superstitious cult."

Havig appreciated the strategy. "As far as I've been able to find out, sir, which isn't much," he said, "the, uh, the Maurai culture is right now forming in the Pacific basin. Anybody from its later stages, coming downtime, would doubtless be more interested in that genesis than in the politics of obscure, impoverished barbarians."

"You do your Americans an injustice," Wallis reproved him. "You're right, of course, from the Maurai standpoint. But actually, our people have had a run of bad luck."

There was some truth in that, Havig must agree. Parts of Oceania had been too unimportant for overdevelopment or for strikes by the superweapons; and those enormous waters were less corrupted than seas elsewhere, more quickly self-cleansed after man became again a rare species. Yet the inhabitants were no simple and simpering dwellers in Eden. Books had been printed in quantities too huge, distributed over regions too wide, for utter loss of any significant information. To a lesser degree, the same was true of much technological apparatus.

North America, Europe, parts of Asia and South America, fewer parts of Africa, hit bottom because they were overextended. Let the industrial-agricultural-medical complexes they had built be paralyzed for the shortest of whiles, and people would begin dying by millions. The scramble of survivors for survival would bring everything else down in wreck.

Now even in such territories, knowledge was preserved: by an oasis of order here, a half-religiously venerated community there. At last, theoretically, it could diffuse to the new barbarians, who would pass it on to the new savages... theoretically. Practice said otherwise. The old civilization had stripped the world too bare.

You could, for example, log a virgin forest, mine a virgin Mesabi, pump a virgin oil field, by primitive methods. Using your gains from this, you could go on to build a larger and more sophisticated plant capable of more intricate operations. As resources dwindled, it could replace lumber with plastics, squeeze iron out of taconite, scour the entire planet for petroleum.

But by the time of the Judgment, this had *been* done. That combination of machines, trained personnel, well-heeled consumers and taxpayers, went under and was not to be reconstructed.

The data needed for an industrial restoration could be found. The natural materials could not.

"Don't you think, sir," Havig dared say, "by their development of technological alternatives, the Maurai and their allies will do a service?"

"Up to a point, yes. I have to give the bastards that," Wallis growled. His cigar jabbed the air. "But that's as far as it goes. Far enough to put them hard in the saddle, and not an inch more. We're learning about their actual suppression of new developments. You will likewise."

He seemed to want to change the subject, for he continued: "Anyhow, as to our organization here. My key men haven't stuck around in uninterrupted normal time, and I less. We skip ahead—

overlapping—to keep leadership continuous. And we're doing well. Things snowball for us, in past, present, and future alike.

"By now we've hundreds of agents, plus thousands of devoted commoners. We ruled over what used to be a couple of whole states, though of course our traffic is more in time than space. Mainly we govern through common-born deputies. When you can travel along the lifespan of a promising boy, you can make a fine and trusty man out of him—especially when he knows he'll never have any secrets from you, nor any safety.

"But don't get me wrong. I repeat, we aren't monsters or parasites. Sometimes we do have to get rough. But our aim is always to put the world back on the path God laid out for it."

He leaned forward. "And we will," he almost whispered. "I've traveled beyond. A thousand years hence, I've seen—

"Are you with us?"

**8**

"By and large, the next several months were good," Havig would relate (would have related) to me. "However, I stayed cautious. For instance, I hedged on giving out exact biographical data. And I passed the chronolog off as a radionic detector and transmitter, built in case visitors to the past had such gear in use. Wallis said he doubted they did and lost interest. I found a hiding place for it. If they were the kind of people in the Eyrie I hoped they were, they'd understand when I finally confessed my hesitation about giving them something this helpful."

"What made you wary?" I asked.

His thin features drew into a scowl. "Oh…minor details at first. Like Wallis's whole style. Though, true, I didn't have a proper chance to get acquainted, because he soon hopped forward to the following year. Think how that lengthens and strengthens power!"

"Unless his subordinates conspire against him meanwhile," I suggested.

He shook his head. "Not in this case. He knows who's certainly loyal, among both his agents and his hand-reared commoners. A hard core of travelers shuttles in and out through time with him, on a complicated pattern which always has one of them clearly in charge.

"Besides, how'd you brew a conspiracy among meek commoner farmers and laborers, arrogant commoner soldiers and officials, or the travelers themselves? They're a wildly diverse and polyglot band, those I met in the castle and those stationed in outlying areas. Nearly all from post-medieval Western civilization—"

"Why?" I wondered. "Surely the rest of history has possibilities in proportion."

"Yeah, and Wallis said he did mean to extend the range of his recruiters. But the difficulties of long temporal trips, language and culture barriers, training whomever you brought back, seemed too great thus far. His Jerusalem search was an experiment, and aside from me had a disappointing result."

Havig shrugged. "To return to the main question," he said, "American English is the Eyrie's official language, which everybody's required to learn. But even so, with most I could never communicate freely. Besides accents, our minds were too different. From my angle, the majority of them were ruffians. From theirs, I was a sissy, or else too sly-acting for comfort. And they had, they have their mutual jealousies and suspicions. Simply being together doesn't stop them regarding each other as Limeys, Frogs, Boches, Guineas, the hereditary enemy. How would you give them a common cause?

"And, finally, why on Earth should they mutiny? Only a few are idealists of any kind; that's a rare quality, remember. But we lived— they live—like fighting cocks. The best of food, drink, time-imported luxuries, servants, bed partners, sports, liberal furloughs to the past, if reasonable precautions are observed, and ample pocket money provided. The work isn't hard. Those who need it get training in what history and technology are appropriate to their talents. The able-bodied learn commando skills. The rest become clerks, temporal porters, administrators, or researchers if they have the brains for it. That was our routine, by no means a dull one. The work itself was fascinating—or would be, I knew, as soon as my superiors decided I was properly trained. Think: a scout in time!

"No, on the whole I had no serious complaints. At first."

"You don't seem to have found your associates really congenial, however," I said.

"A few I did," he replied. "Wallis himself could charm as well as domineer: in his fashion, a spellbinding conversationalist, what with everything he'd experienced. His top lieutenant, Austin Caldwell, gray now but whipcord-tough still, crack shot and horseman, epic whiskey drinker, he had the same size fund of stories to draw on, plus more humor; in addition, he was a friendly soul who went out of his way to make my beginnings easier. Reuel Orrick, that former carnival magician, a delightful old rogue. Jerry Jennings, hardly more than an English schoolboy, desperately trying to find a new dream after his old ones broke apart in the trenches, 1918. A few more. And then Leonce." He smiled, though it was a haunted smile. "Especially Leonce."

They rode forth upon a holiday, soon after his arrival. He had barely gotten moved into his two-room castle apartment, and as yet had few possessions. She presented him with a bearskin rug and a bottle of Glenlivet from downtime. He wasn't sure if it was mere cordiality, like that which some others showed, or what. Her manner baffled him more than her dialect. A lusty kiss, within five minutes of first sight— then casual cheerfulness, and she sat by a different man practically every mess—But Havig found too much else to occupy his mind, those early days.

The proffered concubine was not among them. He didn't like the idea of a woman being ordered to his couch. This was an extra reason to welcome Leonce's invitation to a picnic, when they got their regular day off.

Bandits had been thoroughly suppressed in the vicinity, and mounted patrols assured they would not slip back. It was safe to go out unescorted. The pair carried pistols only as a badge which none but their kind were allowed.

Leonce chose the route, several miles through fields dreamy beneath the morning sun, until a trail left the road for a timberlot big enough to gladden Havig with memories of Morgan Woods. A scent of new-cut hay yielded to odors of leaf and humus. It was warm, but a breeze ruffled foliage, stroked the skin, made sunflecks dance in shadow. Squirrels streaked and chattered over branches. Hoofs beat slowly, muscles moved at leisure between human thighs.

On the way she had eagerly questioned him. He was glad to oblige, within the broad circle drawn by discretion. What normal man does not like to tell an attractive woman about himself? Especially when to her his background is fabulous! The language fence toppled. She had not been here long either, less than a year even if temporal trips were reckoned in. But she could speak his English fairly well by now when she wasn't excited; and his talented ear began to pick up hers.

"From the High Years!" she breathed, leaned in her stirrups and squeezed his arm. Her hands bore calluses.

"Uh, what do you mean by that?" he asked. "Shortly before the Judgment?"

"Ay-yeh, when men reached for moon an' stars an'—an' ever'thing." He realized that, despite her size and brashness, she was quite young. The tilted eyes shone upon him from beneath the ruddy hair, which today hung in pigtails tied with ribbons.

*When we doomed ourselves to become our own executioners*, he thought. But he didn't want to croak about that. "You look as if you come from a hopeful period," he said.

She made a *moue*, but at once grew pensive, cradled chin in fist and frowned at her horse's ears, until: "Well, yes an' no. Same's for you, I reckon."

"Won't you explain? I've heard you're from uptime of here, but I don't know more."

When she nodded, red waves of light ran over her mane. " 'Bout 'nother hun'erd 'n' fifty year. Glacier Folk."

After they entered the woods they could not ride abreast. Guiding, she led the way. He admired her shape from behind, and her grace in the saddle; and often she turned her head to flash him a grin while she talked.

Her homeland he identified as that high and beautiful country which he had known as Glacier and Waterton Parks and on across the Bitterroot Range. Today her ancestors were in its eastern part, having fled from Mong who conquered the plains for their own herds and ranches. Already they were hunters and trappers more than smallhold farmers, raiders of the lowland enemy, elsewhere traders who brought furs, hides, ores, slaves in exchange for foodstuffs and finished products. Not that they were united; feuds among families, clans, tribes would rage for generations.

But as their numbers and territory expanded, a measure of organization would evolve. Leonce tried to describe: "Look, you, I'm o' the Ranyan kin, who belong in the Wahorn troop. A kin's a...a gang o' families who share the same blood. A troop meets four times a year, under its Sherf, who leads 'em in killin' cattle for Gawd an' Oktai an' the rest o' what folk here-aroun' call the Those. Then they talk about things, an' judge quarrels, an' maybe vote on laws—the grownups who could come, men an' women both." Merriment pealed. "Ha! So we per-ten'. Mainly it's to meet, gossip, dicker, swap, gorge, booze, joke, show off...you know?"

"I think I do," Havig answered. Some such institution was common in primitive societies.

"In later time," she continued, "Sherfs, an' whatever troop people can go 'long, been meetin' likewise once a year, in the Congers. The Jinral runs that show: first-born to the line o' Injun Samal, in the Rover kin who belong to no troop. It'd be a blood-flood, that many diff'rent kin together, or would've been at the start, 'cep' it's at Lake Pendoray, which is peacoholy."

Havig nodded. The wild men became less wild as the advantages of law and order grew in their minds—no doubt after Injun Samal had knocked the heads of their chieftains together.

"When I left, things were perty quiet," Leonce said. "The Mong were gone, an' we traded of'ner'n we fought with the new lowlanders, who're strong an' rich. More 'n' more we were copyin' 'em." She sighed. "A hun'erd years after me, I've learned, the Glacier Folk are in the Nor'wes' Union. I don't want to go back."

"You seem to have had a rough life just the same."

"Ay-yeh. Could'a been worse. An' what the jabber, I got plen'y life to go....Here we are."

They tied their horses in a small meadow which fronted on a brook. Trees behind it and across the swirling, bubbling brown water stood fair against heaven; grass grew thick and soft, starred with late wildflowers. Leonce unpacked the lunch she had commanded to be prepared, a hearty enough collection of sandwiches and fruit that

Havig doubted he could get around his whole share. Well, they wanted a rest and a drink first anyway. He joined her, shoulder to shoulder; they leaned back against a bole and poured wine into silver cups.

"Go on," he reminded. "I want to hear about you."

Her lashes fluttered. He observed the tiny freckles across cheekbones and nose. "Aw, nothin' nex' to you, Jack."

"Please. I'm interested."

She laughed for delight. Yet the tale she gave him, in matter-of-fact phrases that begged no sympathy, had its grimness.

In most respects a Glacier family, which turned such fangs to the outer world, was affectionate and close-knit. An earlier tradition of equality between the sexes had never died there, or else had revived in an age when any woman might at any moment have to hunt or do battle. Of course, some specialization existed. Thus men took the heaviest manual labor, women the work demanding most patience. Men always offered the sacrifices; but what Leonce called skuling was a prerogative of the female only, if she showed a bent for it. "Foreknowin'," she explained. "Unravelin' dreams. Readin' an' writin'. Healin' some kinds o' sickness. Drivin' black fogs out o' heads. Sendin' ghosts back where they belong. That kind o' job. An'...m-m-m...ways to trick the eye, fool the mind—you know?"

But hers was no sleight-of-hand or ritual performance. No older self came to warn that child about keeping secrecy.

Her father was (would be) Wolfskin-Jem, a warrior of note. He died fighting off an attack whipped up by the Dafy kin, ostensibly to kill the "thing" which had been born to him, actually to end a long-smoldering feud. But his wife Onda escaped with their children, to find refuge among the Donnal troop. There followed years of guerrilla war and intrigue, before the Ranyans got allies and made their crushing comeback. Leonce, as a spy through time, played a key role. Inevitably, she became the new Skula.

Among friends she was regarded initially with respect, not dread. She learned and practiced the normal skills, the normal sports. But her gift marked her out, and awe grew around her as her ability did. From Onda she learned to be sparing of it. (Also, despite stoic fatalism, it hurt to foreknow the misfortunes of those she cared about.) Nevertheless, having such a Skula, Wahorn waxed mighty.

And Leonce, ever more, became lonely. Her siblings married and moved away, leaving her and Onda by themselves in Jem's old lodge. Both took lovers, as was the custom of unwedded women, but none of Leonce's sought marriage, if only because she seemed to be barren, and gradually they stopped seeking her at all. Former playmates sought her for help and advice, never pleasure. Reaching after comradeship, she insisted on accompanying and fighting in raids on the lowlands. The kindred of those who fell shunned her and mumbled questions about why the Skula had allowed deaths that surely one of her powers could have forbidden—or did she *want* them—? Then Onda died.

Not much later, Eyrie scouts tracked down a far-flung rumor to the source, herself. She welcomed them with tears and jubilation. Wahorn would never see her again.

"My God." Havig laid an arm around her. "You have had it cruel."

"Aw, was plen'y good huntin', skiin', feastin', singin', lots o' jokin' once I'd gotten here." She had downed a quantity of wine. It made her breath fragrant as she nuzzled him. "I don't sing bad. Wanna hear?"

"Sure."

She bounded to fetch an instrument like a dwarf guitar from a saddlebag, and was back in a second. "I play a bone flute too, but can't sing 'long o' that, hm? Here's a song I made myself. I used to pass a lot o' lone-time makin' songs."

A little to his astonishment, she was excellent. "—*Ride w'ere strides a rattle o' rocks, / Thunder 'e sun down t' dance on your lance*—" What he could follow raised gooseflesh on him.

"Wow," he said low when she had finished. "What else do you do?"

"Well, I can read an' write, sort o'. Play chess. Rules changed some from home to here, but I take mos' games anyhow. An' Austin taught me poker; I win a lot. An' I joke."

"Hm?"

She grinned and leaned into his embrace. "Figgered we'd joke after lunch, Jack, honeybee," she murmured. "But w'y not 'fore *an*' after? Hm-m-m-m?"

He discovered, with glee which turned to glory, that one more word would in the course of generations change its meaning.

"Yeah," he told me. "We moved in together. It lasted till…I left. Several months. Mostly they were fine. I really liked that girl."

"Not loved, evidently," I observed.

"N-n-no. I suppose not. Though what is love, anyway? Doesn't it have so infinitely many kinds and degrees and mutations and quantum jumps that—Never mind." He stared into the night which filled the windows of the room where we sat. "We had our fights, roof-shattering quarrels she'd end by striking me and taunting me because I wouldn't strike back, till she rushed out. Touchy as a fulminate cap, my Leonce. The reconciliations were every bit as wild." He rubbed weary eyes. "Not suitable to my temperament, eh, Doc? And I'll admit I was jealous, my jealousy brought on a lot of the trouble. She'd slept with many agents, and commoners for that matter, before I arrived, not to mention her highland lads earlier. She went on doing it too, not often, but if she particularly liked a man, this was her way to be kind and get closer to him. I had the same freedom, naturally, with other women, but…I…didn't…want it."

"Why didn't she get pregnant by an, uh, agent?"

His mouth twitched upward. "When she heard in the Eyrie what the situation was, she insisted on being taken to the last High Years, partly for a look around, like me going to Pericles' Greece or Michelangelo's Italy, but also to get a reversible sterilization shot. She wanted children in due course, when she felt ready to settle down— Glacier wives are chaste, it seems— but that wasn't yet and meanwhile she enjoyed sex, same as she enjoyed everything else in life. Judas priest, what a lay she was!"

"If she mainly stayed with you, however, there must have been a strong attraction on both sides," I said.

"There was. I've tried, as near as my privacy fetish will let me, to tell you what held me to her. From Leonce's side…hard to be sure. How well did we actually know each other? How well have any man and woman ever?—My learning and, yes, intelligence excited her. She had a fine mind, hit-or-miss educated but fine. And, I'll be frank, I doubtless had the top IQ in the Eyrie. Then, too, I suppose we felt the attraction of opposites. She called me sweet and gentle—not patronizingly, because I did do pretty well in games and exercises, being from a better-nourished era than average—but I was no stark mountaineer or roughneck Renaissance mercenary."

Again ghosts dwelt in his smile. "On the whole," he said, "she gave me the second best part of my life, so far and I think probably forever. I'll always be grateful to her, for that and for what followed."

Havig's suspicions developed slowly. He fought them. But piece by piece, the evidence accumulated that something was being withheld from him. It lay in the evasion of certain topics, the brushoff of certain questions, whether with Austin Caldwell's embarrassment, or Coenraad van Heuvel's brusque "I may not say what I have been told," or Reuel Orrick's changing the subject and proceeding to get weeping drunk, or the mild "In God's good time all shall be revealed to you, my son" of Padre Diego the Inquisitor, or an obscene command to shut up from various warrior types.

He was not alone in this isolation. Of those others whom he approached about it, most were complaisant, whether from prudence or indifference. But young Jerry Jennings exclaimed, "By Jove, you're right!"

So did Leonce, in more pungent words. Then after a moment she said: "Well, they can't give us new 'uns ever'thing in a single chew, can they?"

"Coenraad's as new as I am," he protested. "Newer than you."

Her curiosity piqued, she found her own methods of investigation. They were not what you'd think. She could match a tough, woman-despising man-at-arms goblet for goblet till he was sodden and pliable, while her head remained ice-clear. She could trap a sober person by an adroit question; it helped having been a shaman. And she appalled Havig by whispering to him at night, amidst schoolgirl giggles, how she had done what was strictly forbidden without permission, slipped into different periods of the Eyrie's existence to snoop, pry, and eavesdrop.

She concluded: "Near's I can learn, ol' Wallis's jus' feared you an' 'em like you might get mad at what some o' the agents do in some times an' places. Anyhow, till you're more used to the i-dear."

"I was arriving at the same notion myself," Havig said bleakly. "I've seen what earlier ages are like, what personalities they breed. The travelers who respond to his come-ons, or make themselves conspicuous enough for his searchers to hear about, are apt to be the bold—which in most cases means the ruthless. Coming here doesn't change them."

"Seems like orders is, you got to be led slow to the truth. I s'pose I'm only kep' from it 'cause of bein' by you." She kissed him. " 'S 'kay, darlya."

"You mean you'd condone robbery and—"

"Hush. We got to use who we can get. Maybe they do be rough. Your folk, they never were?"

Sickly, he remembered how...from Wounded Knee to My Lai, and before and after...he never disowned his nation. For where and when—if it had not abdicated all responsibility for the future—existed a better society?

(Denmark, maybe? Well, the Danes boasted about Viking ancestors, who were comfortably distant in time, but stayed notably silent about what happened during the slave uprising in the Virgin Islands, 1848, or less directly in Greenland. By 1950 or so, of course, they were free to relax into a smugness shared by the Swedes, who had not only traded with Hitler but let his troop trains roll through their land. And yet these were countries which did much good in the world.)

"'Sides," Leonce said candidly, "the weak go down, 'less they're lucky an' got somebody strong to guard 'em. An' in the end, come the Ol' Man, we're all weak." She thought for a minute. "Could be," she mused, "was I undyin', I'd never kill more'n a spud, an' it only for food. But I will die. I'm in the game too. So're you, darlya. Let's play for the best score we can make, hm?"

He pondered long upon that.

"But if nothing else," he told me, and I heard his anguish, "I had to try and make certain the gold was worth more than the tailings."

"Or the end could justify the means?" I responded. "Sure, I follow. To say it never does is a counsel of perfection. In the real world, you usually must choose the lesser evil. Speaking as an old doctor—no— well, yes, I'll admit I've given my share of those shots which end the incurable pain; and sometimes the choice has been harder. Go on, please do."

"I'd been promised a survey of the Maurai epoch," he said, "so I could satisfy myself it was, at best, a transition period, whose leaders became tyrants and tried to freeze the world. So I could agree that, when the Maurai hegemony began to crumble—perhaps hastened by our subversion—we ought to intervene, seize power, help turn men back toward achievement and advancement."

"Not openly, surely," I objected. "That, the sudden mass appearance of time travelers, would produce headlines nobody could mistake."

"True, true. We were to spend centuries building our strength in secret, till we were ready to act in disguise. It wasn't made clear exactly what disguise; but it was admitted that information was still sparse, because of the usual difficulties. Besides, I heard long philosophical arguments from guys like Padre Diego, about free will and the rest. I thought the logic stank, but said nothing."

"Had, um, Leonce already been taken uptime?"

"Yes. That's why she basically favored Wallis, in spite of her occasional naughtinesses. She told me about a world where progress had been made, more and more peaceful-looking for a long span of history. Except she could not agree this was necessarily progress. Granted, that world did have fleets of efficient sailing ships and electric-powered dirigibles, ocean ranches, solar energy screens charging accumulators, widescale use of bacterial fuel cells which ran off the wastes of living organisms, new developments in both theoretical and applied science, especially biology—"

He stopped for breath and I tried to inject a light note: "Don't tell me your pet Valkyrie used such terms!"

"No, no." He continued earnest. "I'm anticipating what I saw or had explained to me. Her impressions were more general. But she had that huntress and sorceress knack of close observation. She was quite able to trace the basic course of events."

"Which was?"

"Men did not go on to any fresh peak. Instead, what they reached was a plateau, where they stayed. The big-technological culture didn't improve further, it merely spread further.

"That was scarcely her ideal of the High Years restored, or Wallis's of unlimited growth and accomplishment.

"The tour skimmed fast through a later phase of what appeared to be retrogression and general violence. Eyrie agents don't dare explore it in detail till they have a larger and stronger organization. Nor can they understand what lies beyond. It seems peaceful once more, but it's not comprehensible. From the glimpse I had, I'm prepared to believe that."

"What was it like?" I asked. "Can you tell me?"

"Very little." His tone fell rough. "I haven't time. Sound strange, coming from me? Well, it's true. I'm a fugitive, remember."

"I gather your trip uptime did not remove your skepticism about Wallis's intentions," I said, more calmly than I felt. "Why?"

He ran fingers through his blond, sweat-darkened hair. "I'm a child of this century," he replied. "Think, Doc. Recall how intelligent men like, well, Bertrand Russell or Henry Wallace took extensive tours of Stalin's Russia, and came home to report that it did have its problems but those had been exaggerated and were entirely due to extraneous factors and a benevolent government was coping with everything. Don't forget, either, the chances are that most of their guides *did* think this, and were in full sincerity obeying instructions to shield a foreign visitor from what he might misinterpret." His grin was unpleasant. "Maybe the curse of my life is that I've lost the will to believe."

"You mean," I said, "you wondered if the world really would benefit from the rule of the Eyrie? And if maybe the Maurai were being slandered, you being shown nothing except untypical badness?"

"No, not exactly that, either. Depends on interpretation and—oh, here's a prime example."

Not every recruit was given as thorough a tour as Havig. Plainly Wallis deemed him to be both of particular potential value and in particular need of convincing.

By doubling back and forth through chronology, he got a look at documents in ultra-secret files. (He could puzzle them out, since Ingliss was an official second language of the Federation and spelling had changed less than pronunciation.) One told how scientists in Hinduraj had clandestinely developed a hydrogen-fusion generator which would end Earth's fuel shortage, and the Maurai had as clandestinely learned of it, sabotaged it, and applied such politico-economic pressures that the truth never became public.

The motive given was that this revolutionary innovation would have upset the Pax. Worse, it would have made possible a rebirth of the ancient rapacious machine culture, which the planet could not endure.

And yet...uptime of the Maurai dominion, Havig saw huge silent devices and energies...and men, beasts, grass, trees, stars bright through crystalline air...

"Were the Pacific sociologists and admirals sincere in their belief?" he said in a harsh whisper. "Or were they only preserving their top-dog status? Or both, or neither, or what?

"And is that farther future good? It could be a smooth running monstrosity, you know, or it could be undermining the basis of all life's existence, or—How could I tell?"

"What did you ask your guides?" I responded.

"Those same questions. The leader was Austin Caldwell, by the way, an honest man, hard as the Indians who once hunted his scalp but nevertheless honest."

"What did he tell you?"

"To stop my goddam quibbling and trust the Sachem. The Sachem had done grand thus far, hadn't he? The Sachem had studied and thought about these matters; he didn't pretend to know everything himself, but we'd share the wisdom he was gathering as it became ready, and he would lead us onto the right paths.

"As for me, Austin said, I'd better remember how slow and awkward it was, getting around like this, having to return across centuries whenever we needed transportation to a new area. I'd already had as much lifespan and trouble spent on me as I was worth, anyhow at my present stage of development. If I couldn't accept the discipline that an outfit must have which is embarked on dangerous endeavors— well, I was free to resign, but I'd better never show my hide near the Eyrie again.

"What could I do? I apologized and came back with them."

He was given a couple of days off, which he spent regaining his spirits in Leonce's company. The period of his training and indoctrination had brought winter's chances for old-fashioned sports outdoors and indoors. Thereafter he was assigned to reread Wallis's history of the future, ponder it in the light of what he had witnessed, and discuss any questions with Waclaw Krasicki, who was the most scholarly of the garrison's current directorate.

The Sachem admitted he was far from omniscient. But he had seen more than anyone else, on repeated expeditions with differing escorts. He had ranged more widely across Earth's surface as well as through Earth's duration than was feasible for subordinates, transport being as limited as it was. He had conducted interviews and interrogations, which others must not lest too many events of that sort arouse somebody's suspicions.

He knew the Eyrie would be here, under his control, for the next two centuries. He had met himself then, who told him how satisfactorily Phase One of the plan had been carried out. At that date, the vastly augmented force he was shown must evacuate this stronghold. Nuclei of renascent civilization were spreading across all America, the Maurai were everywhere, a realm like his could no longer stay isolated nor maintain the pretense its leaders were nothing extraordinary.

A new base had been (would be) constructed uptime. He visited it, and found it totally unlike the old. Here were modern materials, sleek construction—mostly underground—housing advanced machinery, automation, a thermonuclear powerplant.

This was in the era of revolt against the Maurai. They had in the end failed to convert to their philosophy the gigantically various whole of mankind. Doubts, discontents, rebelliousness among their own people led to vacillation in foreign policy. One defiant nation redeveloped the fusion energy generator; and it made no attempt at secrecy. Old countries and alliances were disintegrating, new being born in turmoil.

"Always we need patience as well as boldness and briskness," Wallis wrote. "We will have far more resources than we do in Phase One, and far more skill in employing them. That includes the use of time travel to multiply the size of a military force, each man doubling back again and again till the opposition is overwhelmed. But I am well aware this sort of thing has its limits and hazards. In no case can we hope to take over the whole world quickly. An empire which is to last thousands of years is bound to be slow in the building."

*Was* that how Phase Two would end: with a planet once more pastoralized, in order that the overlordship of the Eyrie men, in the fabulous engines they would have developed, be unchallengeable? Wallis believed it. He believed Phase Three would consist of the benign remolding of that society by its new masters, the creation of a wholly new kind of man. Ranging very far uptime, he had glimpsed marvels he could not begin to describe.

But he seemed vague in this part of his book. Exact information was maddeningly hard to gather. He meant to continue doing so, though more and more by proxy. In general, he recognized, his lifespan would be spent on Phase One. The self he met at its end was an aged man.

"Let us be satisfied to be God's agents of redemption," he wrote. "However, those who wish may cherish a private hope. Is it not possible that at last science will find a way to make the old young again, to make the body immortal? And by then, I have no doubt, time travel will be understood, may even be commonplace. Will not that wonderful future return and seek us out, who brought it into being, and give us our reward?"

Havig's mouth tightened. He thought: *I've seen what happens when you try to straitjacket man into an ideology.*

But later he thought: *There is a lot of flexibility here. We could conceivably end more as teachers than masters.*

And finally: *I'll stick around awhile, at least. The alternative to serving him seems to be to let my gift go for nothing, my life go down in futility.*

Krasicki summoned him. It was a steely-cold day. Sunlight shattered into brilliance on icicles hanging from turrets. Havig shivered as he crossed the courtyard to the office.

Uniformed, Krasicki sat in a room as neat and functional as a cell. "Be seated," he ordered. The chair was hard, and squeaked.

"Do you judge yourself ready for your work?" he asked.

A thrill went through Havig. His pulses hammered. "Y-yes. Anxious to start. I—" He straightened. "Yes."

Krasicki shuffled some papers on his desk. "I have been watching your progress," he said, "and considering how we might best employ you. That includes minimum risk to yourself. You have had a good deal of extratemporal experience on your own, I know, which makes you already valuable. But you've not hitherto been on a mission for us." He offered a stiff little smile. "The idea which came to me springs from your special background."

Havig somehow maintained a cool exterior.

"We must expand our capabilities, particularly recruiting," Krasicki said. "Well, you've declared yourself reasonably fluent in the Greek *koine*. You've described a visit you made to Byzantine Constantinople. That seems like a strategic place from which to begin a systematic search through the medieval period."

"Brilliant!" Havig cried, suddenly happy and excited. It rushed from him: "Center of civilization, everything flowed through the Golden Horn, and, and what we could do as traders—"

Krasicki lifted a palm. "Hold. Perhaps later, when we have more manpower, a wider network, perhaps then that will be worthwhile. But at present we're too sharply limited in the man-years available to us. We cannot squander them. Never forget, we must complete Phase One by a definite date. No, Havig, what is necessary is a quicker and more direct approach."

"What—?"

"Given a large hoard of coin and treasure, we can finance ourselves in an era when this is currency. But you know yourself how cumbersome is the transportation of goods through time. Therefore we must acquire our capital on the…on the spot?…yes, on the spot. And, as I said, quickly."

Havig's suspicions exploded in dismay. "You can't mean by robbery!"

"No, no, no." Krasicki shook his head. "Think. Listen. A raid on a peaceful city, massive enough to reap a useful harvest, that would be dangerously conspicuous. Could get into the history books, and that could wreck our cover. Besides, it would be dangerous in itself, too. Our men would have small numbers, not overly well supplied with firearms. They would not have powered vehicles. The Byzantine army and police were usually large and well-disciplined. No, I don't propose madness."

"What, then?"

"Taking advantage of chaos, in order to remove what would otherwise be stolen by merciless invaders for no good purpose."

Havig stared.

"In 1204," his superior went on, "Constantinople was captured by the armies of the Fourth Crusade. They plundered it from end to end; what remained was a broken shell." He waved an arm. "Why should we not take a share? It's lost to the owners anyway." He peered at the other's face before adding: "And, to be sure, we arrange compensation, give them protection from slaughter and rapine, help them rebuild their lives."

"Judas priest!" Havig choked. "A hijacking!"

Having briefed himself in the Eyrie's large microtape library, having had a costume made and similar details taken care of, he embarked.

An aircraft deposited him near the twenty-first-century ruins of

Istanbul and took off again into the air as quickly as he into the past. A lot of radioactivity lingered in these ashes. He hadn't yet revealed the fact of his chronolog and must find his target by the tedious process of counting sun-traverses, adding an estimate of days missed, making an initial emergence, and zeroing in by trial and error.

Leonce had been furious at being left behind. But she lacked the knowledge to be useful here, except as companion and consoler. Indeed, she would have been a liability, her extreme foreignness drawing stares. Havig meant to pass for a Scandinavian on pilgrimage—Catholic, true, but less to be detested than a Frenchman, Venetian, Aragonese, anyone from those western Mediterranean nations which pressed wolfishly in on the dying Empire. As a Russian he would have been more welcome. But Russians were common thereabouts, and their Orthodox faith made them well understood. He dared not risk a slip.

He didn't start in the year of the conquest. That would be too turbulent, and every outsider too suspect, for the detailed study he must make. The Crusaders actually entered Constantinople in 1203, after a naval siege, to install a puppet on its throne. They hung around to collect their pay before proceeding to the Holy Land. The puppet found his coffers empty, and temporized. Friction between East Romans and "Franks" swelled to terrifying proportions. In January 1204, Alexius, son-in-law of the deposed Emperor, got together sufficient force to seize palace and crown. For three months he and his people strove to drive the Crusaders off. Their hope that God would somehow come to their aid collapsed when Alexius, less gallant than they, despaired and fled. The Crusaders marched back through opened portals. They had worked themselves into homicidal self-righteousness about "Greek perfidy," and the horror began almost at once.

Havig chose spring, because it was a beautiful season, in 1195, because that was amply far downtime, for his basic job of survey. He carried well-forged documents which got him past the city guards, and gold pieces to exchange for *nomismae*. After finding a room in a good inn—nothing like the pigsty he'd have had to endure in the West—he started exploring.

His prior visit had been to halcyon 1050. The magnificence he now encountered, the liveliness and cosmopolitan colorfulness, were no less. However raddled her dominion, New Rome remained the queen of Europe.

Havig saw her under the shadow.

The house and shop of Doukas Manasses, goldsmith, stood on a hill near the middle of the city. Square-built neighbors elbowed it, all turning blind faces onto the steep, wide, well-paved and well-swept street. But from its flat roof you had a superb view, from end to end of the vast, towered walls which enclosed the city, and further: across a maze of thoroughfares, a countlessness of dwellings and soaring church domes; along the grand avenue called the Mesê to flowering countryside past the Gate of Charisius, on inward by columns which upbore statuary from the noblest days of Hellas, monasteries and museums and libraries which preserved works by men like Aeschylus and women like Sappho that later centuries would never read, through broad forums pulsing with life, to the Hippodrome and that sprawling splendid complex which was the Imperial Palace. On a transverse axis, vision reached from glittering blue across the Sea of Marmora to a mast-crowded Golden Horn and the rich suburbs and smaragdine heights beyond.

Traffic rivered. The noise of wheels, hoofs, feet, talk, song, laughter, sobbing, cursing, praying blended together into one ceaseless heartbeat. A breeze carried a richness of odors, sea, woodsmoke, food, animals, humanity. Havig breathed deep.

"Thank you, Kyrios Hauk," Doukas Manasses said. "You are most courteous to praise this sight." His manner implied mild surprise that a Frank would not sneer at everything Greek. To be sure, Hauk Thomasson was not really a Frank or one of the allied English, he was from a boreal kingdom.

"Less courteous than you, Kyrios Manasses, to show me it," Havig replied.

They exchanged bows. The Byzantines were not basically a strict folk—besides their passionate religion and passionate sense for beauty, they had as much bustling get-up-and-go, as much inborn gusto, as Levantines in any era—but their upper classes set store by ceremonious politeness.

"You expressed interest," Doukas said. He was a gray-bearded man with handsome features and nearsighted eyes. His slight frame seemed lost in the usual dalmatic robe.

"I merely remarked, Kyrios, that a shop which produced such elegance as does yours must be surrounded by inspiration." You could case public buildings easily enough, but your way to learn what private hands held what wealth was to go in, say you were looking for a gift to take home, and inspect a variety of samples.

Well, dammit, Doukas and his apprentices did do exquisite work.

"You are too kind," the goldsmith murmured. "Although I do feel— since all good stems from God—that we Romans should look more to His creation, less to conventionality, than we have done."

"Like this?" Havig pointed at a blossoming crabapple tree in a large planter.

Doukas smiled. "That's for my daughter. She loves flowers, and we cannot take her daily on an outing in the country."

Women enjoyed an honorable status, with many legal rights and protections. But perhaps Doukas felt his visitor needed further explanation: "We may indulge her too much, my Anna and I. However, she's our only. That is, I was wedded before, but the sons of sainted Eudoxia are grown. Xenia is Anna's first, and my first daughter."

On impulse he added: "Kyrios Hauk, think me not overbold. But I'm fascinated to meet a...friendly...foreigner, from so remote a country at that. It is long since there were many from your lands in the Varangian Guard. I would enjoy conversing at leisure. Would you honor our home at the evening meal?"

"Why—why, thank you." Havig thought what a rare chance this was to find things out. Byzantine trades and crafts were organized in tight guilds under the direction of the prefect. This man, being distinguished in his profession, probably knew all about his colleagues, and a lot about other businesses. "I should be delighted."

"Would you mind, my guest, if wife and child share our board?" Doukas asked shyly. "They will not interrupt. Yet they'd be glad to hear you. Xenia is, well, forgive my pride, she's only five and already learning to read."

She was a singularly beautiful child.

Hauk Thomasson returned next year and described the position he had accepted with a firm in Athens. Greece belonged to the Empire, and would till the catastrophe; but so much trade was now under foreign control that the story passed. His work would often bring him to Constantinople. He was happy to have this opportunity of renewing acquaintanceship, and hoped the daughter of Kyrios Manasses would accept a small present—

"Athens!" the goldsmith whispered. "You dwell in the soul of Hellas?" He reached up to lay both hands on his visitor's shoulders. Tears stood in his eyes. "Oh, wonderful for you, wonderful! To see those temples is the dream of my life….God better me, more than to see the Holy Land."

Xenia accepted the toy gratefully. At dinner and afterward she listened, rapt, till her nanny shooed her to bed. She was a sweet youngster, Havig thought, undeniably bright, and not spoiled even though it seemed Anna would bear no more children.

He enjoyed himself, too. A cultured, sensitive, observant man is a pleasure to be with in any age. This assignment was, for a while, losing its nightmare quality.

In truth, he simply skipped ahead through time. He must check up periodically, to be sure events didn't make his original data obsolete. Simultaneously he could develop more leads, ask more questions, than would have been practical in a single session.

But—he wondered a few calendar years later—wasn't he being more thorough than needful? Did he really have to make this many visits to the Manasses family, become an intimate, join them on holidays and picnics, invite them out to dinner or for a day on a rented pleasure barge? Certainly he was exceeding his expense estimate…. To hell with that. He could finance himself by placing foreknowledgeable bets on events in the Hippodrome. An agent working alone had broad discretion.

He felt guilty about lying to his friends. But it had to be. After all, his objective was to save them.

Xenia's voice was somewhat high and thin, but whenever he heard or remembered it, Havig would think of songbirds. Thus had it been since first she overcame her timidity and laughed in his presence. From then on, she chattered with him to the limit her parents allowed, or more when they weren't looking.

She was reed-slender. He had never seen any human who moved with more gracefulness; and when decorum was not required, her feet danced. Her hair was a midnight mass which, piled on her head, seemed as if it ought to bend the delicate neck. Her skin was pale and clear; her face was oval, tilt-nosed, its lips always a little parted. The eyes dominated that countenance, enormous, heavy-lashed, luminous black. Those eyes may be seen elsewhere, in a Ravenna mosaic, upon Empress Theodora the Great; they may never be forgotten.

It was a strange thing to meet her at intervals of months which for Havig were hours or days. Each time, she was so dizzyingly grown. In awe he felt a sense of that measureless river which he could swim but on which she could only be carried from darkness to darkness.

The house was built around a courtyard where flowers and oranges grew and a fountain played. Doukas proudly showed Havig his latest acquisition: on a pedestal in one corner, a bust of Constantine who made Rome Christian and for whom New Rome was named. "From the life, I feel sure," he said. "By then the art of portrayal was losing its former mastery. Nevertheless, observe his imperiously tight-held mouth—"

Nine-year-old Xenia giggled. "What is it, dear?" her father asked.

"Nothing, really," she said, but couldn't stop giggling.

"No, do tell us. I shan't be angry."

"He...he...he wants to make a very important speech, and he has gas!"

"By Bacchus," Havig exclaimed, "she's right!"

Doukas struggled a moment before he gave up and joined the fun.

"Oh, please, will you not come to church with us, Hauk?" she begged. "You don't know how lovely it is, when the song and incense and candleflames rise up to Christ Pantocrator." She was eleven and overflowing with God.

"I'm sorry," Havig said. "You know I am, am Catholic."

"The saints won't mind. I asked Father and Mother, and they won't mind either. We can say you're a Russian, if we need to. I'll show you how to act." She tugged his hand. "Do come!"

He yielded, not sure whether she hoped to convert him or merely wanted to share something glorious with her honorary uncle.

"But it's too wonderful!" She burst into tears and hugged her thirteenth birthday present to her before holding it out. "Father, Mother, see what Hauk gave me! This book, the p-p-plays of Euripides—all of them—for *me*!"

When she was gone to change clothes for a modest festival dinner, Doukas said: "That was a royal gift. Not only the cost of having the copy made and binding it as a codex. The thought."

"I knew she loves the ancients as much as you do," the traveler answered.

"Forgive me," Anna the mother said. "But at her age...may Euripides not be, well, stern reading?"

"These are stern times," Havig replied, and could no longer feign joy. "A tragic line may hearten her to meet fate." He turned to the goldsmith. "Doukas, I tell you again, I swear to you, I know through my connections that the Venetians at this very moment are negotiating with other Frankish lords—"

"You have said that." The goldsmith nodded. His hair and beard were nearly white.

"It's not too late to move you and your family to safety. I'll help."

"Where is safety better than these walls, which no invader has ever breached? Or where, if I break up my shop, where is safety from pauperdom and hunger? What would my apprentices and servants do? They can't move. No, my good old friend, prudence and duty alike tells us we must remain here and trust in God." Doukas uttered a small sad chuckle. " 'Old,' did I say? You never seem to change. Well, you're in your prime, of course."

Havig swallowed. "I don't think I'll be back in Constantinople for some while. My employers, under present circumstances—Be careful. Keep unnoticeable, hide your wealth, stay off the streets whenever you can and always at night. I know the Franks."

"Well, I, I'll bear your advice in mind, Hauk, if—But you go too far. This is New Rome."

Anna touched the arms of both. Her smile was uncertain. "Now that's enough politics, you men," she said. "Take off those long faces. We're making merry on Xenia's day. Have you forgotten?"

Time-skipping in an alley across the street, Havig checked the period of the first Latin occupation. Nothing terrible seemed to happen. The house drew back into itself and waited.

He went pastward to a happier year, took a night's lodging, forced himself to eat a hearty supper and get a lot of sleep. Next morning he omitted breakfast: a good idea when you may soon be in combat.

He jumped ahead, to the twelfth of April, 1204.

He could be no more than an observer through the days and nights of the sack. His orders were explicit and made sense: "If you can possibly avoid it, stay out of danger. Under no conditions mingle, or try to influence events. Absolutely never, and this is under penalties, never enter a building which is a scene of action. We want your report, and for that we need you alive."

Fire leaped and roared. Smoke drifted bitter. People huddled like rats indoors, or fled like rats outside, and some escaped but thousands were ridden down, shot down, chopped down, beaten, stomped, tortured, robbed, raped, by yelling sooty sweaty blood-spattered men whose fleas hopped about on silks and altar cloths they had flung across their shoulders. Corpses gaped in the gutters, which ran red till they clotted. Many of the bodies were very small. Mothers crept about shrieking for children, children for mothers; most fathers lay dead. Orthodox priests in their churches were kept in pain until they revealed where the treasury was hidden; usually there was none, in which case it was great sport to soak their beards in oil and set these alight. Women, girls, nuns of any age lay mumbling or whimpering after a row of men had violated them. Humiliations more ingenious might be contrived.

A drunken harlot sat on the patriarch's throne in Hagia Sophia, while dice games for plunder were played on the altars. The bronze horses of the Hippodrome were carted off to Venice's Cathedral of St. Mark; artwork, jewelry, sacred objects would be scattered across a continent; but at least these things were preserved. More was melted down or torn apart for the precious metals and stones, or smashed or burned for amusement. So perished much classical art, and nearly all classical writing, which Constantinople had kept safe until these days. It is not true that the Turks of 1453 were responsible. The Crusaders were there before them.

Afterward came the great silence, broken by furtive crying, and the stench, and the sickness, and the hunger.

In this wise, at the beginning of that thirteenth century which Catholic apologists call the apogee of civilization, did Western Christendom destroy its Eastern flank. A century and a half later, having devoured Asia Minor, the Turks entered Europe.

Havig time-skipped.

He would return to a safe date, seek out one of his chosen sites, and advance through the whole period of the sack, flickering in and out of normal time, until he knew what was to happen there. When he saw a Frankish band enter a place, he focused more sharply. In most cases they staggered out after a while, sated with death and torment, kicking prisoners who carried away their spoils. Those buildings he wrote off. You couldn't change the past or future, you could merely discover what parts were your own.

But in certain instances—and only a comparative few would be accessible to the Eyrie commandos; they hadn't many man-months to spend on this job—

Havig saw marauders frightened off, or cut down if need be, by submachine gun fire. The spectacle did not make him gloat. However, he knew a chilly satisfaction while he recorded the spot.

From it, the Eyrie men would cart their loot. They were dressed in conqueror style. Amidst this confusion, it was unlikely they would attract notice. A ship was arranged for, to bear the gains to a safe depot.

They would take care of the dwellers, Krasicki had promised. What to do would depend on circumstances. Some families need simply be left unharmed, with enough money to carry on. Others must be guided elsewhere and staked to a fresh beginning.

Paradoxes need not be feared. The tale of how veritable saints— or demons, if one was a Frank—had rescued so-and-so might live a while in folklore but would not get into any chronicle. Writers in Constantinople must be cautious for the next fifty-seven years, until Michael Paleologus ended the Latin kingdom and raised a ghost of Empire. By then, anecdotes would have been lost.

Havig didn't look into the immediate sequels of these agent actions. Besides the prohibition laid on him, he already was overburdened. Many sights he witnessed sent him fleeing downtime, weeping and vomiting, to sleep till he had the strength to continue.

The Manasses home was among the earliest he investigated. It wasn't quite the first; he wanted to gain experience elsewhere; but he knew he was going to be dulled later on.

He had cherished a hope it might be entirely overlooked. Some of his points were. It being unfeasible to check the Crusaders in the famous places, he had investigated lesser ones, whose aggregate wealth was what counted. And Constantinople was too big, too labyrinthine, too rich and strange for the pillagers to break down every door.

He felt no extreme fears. In this particular case, *something* would be done if need be, by himself if nobody else, and Caleb Wallis could take his destiny and stuff it. Nevertheless, when Havig from his alley saw a dozen filthy men lope toward that open entrance, the heart stumbled within him. When lead sleeted from it, and three Franks fell and were quiet, two lay sprattling and shrieking, and the rest howled and fled, Havig cheered.


His return was a sizable operation in itself.

Between the radioactivity and the time uncertainty, he couldn't proceed up to dead Istanbul and hunt around for an agreed-on hour at which the aircraft would meet him. Nor could he appear in an earlier epoch—the Eyrie's planes were not available then—or at a later one—the site would be reoccupied. He'd look too peculiar, and would still have the problem of reaching a geographical point where contact could be made.

"Now you tell me!" he muttered to himself. For a while he marveled that the obvious answer hadn't occurred when this whole project was being discussed. Use his twentieth-century *persona*. Cache some funds and clothes in a contemporary Istanbul hotel; feed the management a line about being involved in production of a movie; and there he was, set.

Well, he'd been overwhelmed by things to think about. And the idea hadn't come to anyone else. While Wallis employed some gadgets developed in the High Years, he and his lieutenants were nineteenth-century men who had organized an essentially nineteenth-century operation.

The plan called for Havig to double back downtime, make more money if he had to, engage passage on a ship to Crete, there find a specific isolated spot, and project himself uptime.

Actually, effort, cramped quarters, dirt, noise, smells, moldy hardtack, scummy water, weird fellow passengers, and all, he didn't care. He needed something to take his mind off what he had seen.

"Splendidly done," Krasicki said across the written report. "Splendidly. I'm sure the Sachem will give you public praise and reward, when next your two time-lines intersect."

"Hm? Oh. Oh, yeah. Thanks." Havig blinked.

Krasicki studied him. "You are exhausted, are you not?"

"Call me Rip van Winkle," Havig muttered.

Krasicki understood his gauntness, sunken eyes, slumped body, tic in cheek, if not the reference. "Yes. It is common. We allow for it. You have earned a furlough. In your home milieu, I suggest. Never mind about the rest of the Constantinople business. If we need more from you, we can always ask when you return here." His smile approached warmth. "Go, now. We'll talk later. I think we can arrange for your girl friend to accompany—Havig? Havig?"

Havig was asleep.

His trouble was that later, instead of enjoying his leave, he started thinking.

He woke with his resolve crystallized. It was early. Light over the high rooftops of the Rive Gauche, Paris, 1965, reached gray and as cool as the air, which traffic had not yet begun to trouble. The hotel room was shadowy. Leonce breathed warm and tousle-haired beside him. They had been night-clubbing late—among the *chansonniers*, which he preferred, now that her wish for the big glittery shows was slaked—and come back to make leisured and tender love. She'd hardly stir before a knock, some hours hence, announced coffee and croissants.

Havig was surprised at his own rousing. Well, more and more in the past couple of weeks, he'd felt he was only postponing the inevitable. His conscience must have gotten tired of nagging him and delivered an ultimatum.

Regardless of danger, he felt at peace, for the first time in that whole while.

He rose, washed and dressed, assembled his gear. It lay ready, two modules within his baggage. There was the basic agent's kit, an elaborated version of what he had taken to Jerusalem plus a gun. (The Eyrie's documents section furnished papers to get that past customs.) He had omitted items Leonce had in hers, such as most of the silver, in order to save the mass of the chronolog. (He had unobtrusively taken it back with him on this trip. She asked him why he lugged it around. When he said, "Special electronic gear," the incantation satisfied her.) Passport, vaccination certificate, and thick wallet of traveler's checks completed the list.

For a minute he stood above the girl. She was a dear, he thought. Her joy throughout their tour had been a joy to him. Dirty trick, sneaking out on her. Should he leave a note?...No, no reason for it. He could return to this hour. If he didn't, well, she knew enough contemporary English and procedure, and had enough funds, to handle the rest. (Her own American passport was genuine; the Eyrie had made her a birth certificate.) She might perhaps feel hurt if she knew what had gotten him killed.

Chances were he was simply courting a reprimand. In that case, she'd hear the full story; but he'd be there to explain, in terms of loyalty which she could understand.

Or would it much matter? That she called him "darlya" and spoke of love when he embraced her was probably just her way. Lately, though, she'd been holding his hand a lot when they were out together, and he'd caught her smiling at him when she thought he wasn't noticing.... He was a bit in love with her too. It could never last, but while it did—

He stooped. "So long, Big Red," he whispered. His lips brushed hers. Straightening, he picked up his two carrying cases and stole from the room. By evening he was in Istanbul.

The trip took this many hours out of his lifespan, mostly spent on the plane and airport buses. Time-hopping around among ticket agencies and the like made the calendrical interval a couple of days. He had told me through a wry grin: "Know where the best place usually is for unnoticed chronokinesis in a modern city? Not Superman's telephone booth. A public lavatory stall. Real romantic, huh?"

He ate a good though lonely dinner, and in his luxurious though lonely chamber took a sleeping pill. He needed to be rested before he embarked.

Constantinople, late afternoon on the thirteenth of April, 1204. Havig emerged in an alley downhill from his destination. Silence pressed upon him—no slap of buskins, clop of hoofs, rumble and squeal of cartwheels, no song of bells, no voices talking, chaffering, laughing, dreaming aloud, no children at their immemorial small games. But the stillness had background, a distant jagged roar which was fire and human shrieking, the nearer desperate bark of a dog.

He made ready. The gun, a 9-mm. Smith & Wesson mulekiller, he holstered at his waist. Extra ammunition he put in the deep pockets of his jacket. Kit and chronolog he strapped together in an aluminum packframe which went on his back.

Entering the street, he saw closed doors, shuttered windows. Most dwellers were huddled inside, hungry, thirsty, endlessly at prayer. The average place wasn't worth breaking into, except for the pleasures of rape, murder, torture, and arson. True, this was the district of the goldsmiths. But not every building, or even a majority, belonged to one. Residential sections were not based on economic status; the poor could be anywhere. With booths and other displays removed, you couldn't tell if a particular facade concealed wealth or a tenement house—

—until, of course, you clapped hands on a local person and wrenched the information out of him.

Evidently those who rushed the Manasses home were in advance of the mobs which would surely boil hither as soon as palace and church buildings were stripped. Were they here yet? Havig hadn't been sure of the exact time when he saw them.

He trotted around a corner. A man lay dead of a stab wound. His right arm reached across his back, pulled from its socket. A shabby-clad woman crouched above him. As Havig passed, she screamed: "Wasn't it enough that you made him betray our neighbor? In Christ's name, wasn't that enough?"

No, he thought. There was also the peculiar thrill in extinguishing a life.

He went on by. The agony he had seen earlier returned to him in so monstrous a flood that the tears of this widow were lost. He could do nothing for her; trousers, short hair, shaven chin marked him a Frank in her eyes. When he was born, she and her grief were seven hundred years forgotten.

At least, he thought, he knew how the Crusaders had located Doukas's shop. One among them must understand some Greek, and their band had decided to seek out this part of town ahead of the rush. He knew also that his scheduling was approximately right.

Yells, clangor, and a terrible stammer reverberated wall to wall, off the cobbles, up to soot-befouled heaven. He stretched lips over teeth. "Yeah," he muttered, "I got it *exactly* right."

He quickened his pace. His younger self would be gone by the time he arrived. Obvious: he had not seen his later self. He didn't want that house unwatched for many minutes.

Not after considering what sort of man the average Eyrie warrior was.

The street of his goal was steep. Gravity dragged at him. He threw his muscles against it. His bootsoles thudded like his heart. His mouth was dry. Smoke stung his nostrils.

There!

One of the wounded Crusaders saw him, struggled to his knees, raised arms. Blood shone its wild red, hiding the cross on the surcoat, dripping in thick gouts to the stones. "*Ami,*" croaked from a face contorted out of shape, on whose waxenness the beard stubble stood blue. "*Frère par Iesu*—" The other survivor could merely groan, over and over.

Havig felt an impulse to kick their teeth in, and immediate shame. Mortal combat corrupts, and war corrupts absolutely. He ignored the kneeling man, who slumped behind him; he lifted both hands and shouted in English:

"Hold your fire! I am from the Eyrie! Inspection! Hold your fire and let me in!" Not without a tightness in his own unriddled guts, he approached the doorway.

An oxcart stood by, the animal tethered to a bracket which had formerly upheld Doukas's sign, twitching its ears against flies and with mild interest watching the Crusaders die. It would have been arranged for beforehand, to bring gold and silver and precious stones, ikons and ornaments and bridal chaplets, down to the ship which waited. Havig wasn't the only traveler who had been busy in the years before today. An operation like this took a great deal of work.

Nobody guarded the entrance. Armed as they were, the agents could deal with interference, not that any such attempt would be made. Havig stopped. Scowling, he examined the door. It was massive, and had surely been barred. The Franks had doubtless meant to chop their way in. But at the point when Havig glimpsed them and halted for a clear look, it had stood open. That was one fact which had never stopped plaguing him.

From the way it sagged on its hinges, scorched and half splintered, Wallis's boys must have used a dynamite charge. That had been done so quickly that, in Havig's dim chronokinetic sight, their arrival had blurred together with that of the Franks a few minutes afterward.

Why had they forced an entrance? Such impatience would panic the household, complicate the task of assisting it to safety.

A scream fled down the rooms inside: "*No, oh, no, please!*" in Greek and Xenia's voice, followed by an oath and a guffaw. Havig crouched back as if stabbed.

In spite of everything, he had come late. At the moment of his arrival, the agents had already blown down the door and entered. They'd posted a man here to await the plunderers whom Havig had reported. Now he'd gone back within to join the fun.

For an instant which had no end, Havig cursed his own stupidity. Or naïveté—he was new to this kind of thing, bound to overlook essentials. To hell with that. Here he was and now he was, and his duty was to save whatever might be left.

His call must not have been noticed. He repeated it while he went through the remembered house. That sobbed-out cry for mercy had come from the largest chamber, which was the main workshop and storeroom.

Family, apprentices, and servants had been brought together there. It was more light and airy than usual in Byzantium, for a door and broad windows opened on the patio. Yonder the fountain still tinkled and twinkled, oranges glowed amid dark green leaves, Eastertide flowerbeds were budding, the bust of Constantine stood in eternal embarrassment. Here, on shelves and tables, everywhere crowded that beauty which Doukas Manasses had seen to the making of.

He sprawled near the entrance. His skull was split open. The blood had spread far, making the floor slippery, staining footwear which then left crimson tracks. But much had soaked into his robe and white beard. One hand still held a tiny anvil, with which he must have tried to defend his women.

Four agents were present, dressed as Crusaders. In a flash, Havig knew them. Mendoza, of the Tijuana underworld in his own century, who had been among those who went to Jerusalem, was in charge. He was ordering the natives to start collecting loot. Moriarty, nineteenth-century Brooklyn gangster, kept guard, submachine gun at the ready. Hans, sixteenth-century *Landsknecht*, watched Coenraad of Brabant, who had wanted to draw sword and save the Savior, struggle with Xenia.

The girl screamed and screamed. She was only fourteen. Her hair had fallen loose. Sweat and tears plastered locks to her face. Coenraad grasped her around the waist. His free hand ripped at her gown. A war hammer, stuck in his belt, dripped blood and brains.

"Me next," Hans grinned. "Me next."

Coenraad bore Xenia down to the wet floor and fumbled with his trousers. Anna, who had stood as if blind and deaf near the body of her husband, wailed. She scuttled toward her daughter. Hans decked her with a single blow. "Maybe you later," he said.

"Hard men, you two," Moriarty laughed. "Real hard, hey?"

The sequence had taken seconds. Havig's call had again failed to pierce their excitement. Mendoza was first to see him, and exclaim. The rest froze, until Coenraad let Xenia go and climbed to his feet.

She stared up. Never had he thought to see such a light as was born in her eyes. "Hauk!" She cried. "Oh, Hauk!"

Mendoza swung his gun around. "What is this?" he demanded.

Havig realized how far his own hand was from his own weapon. But he felt no fear—hardly any emotion, in fact, on the surface, beyond a cougar alertness. Down underneath roiled the fury, sorrow, horror, disgust he could not now afford.

"I might ask you the same," he replied slowly.

"Have you forgotten your orders? I know them. Your job is to gather intelligence. You are not to risk yourself at a scene of operations like this."

"I finished my job, Mendoza. I came back for a personal look."

"Forbidden! Get out, and we'll talk later about whether or not I report you."

"Suppose I don't?" Despite control, Havig heard his voice rise, high and saw-edged: "I've seen what I wasn't supposed to see in one lump, only piece by piece, gradually, so I'd make the dirty little compromises till it no longer mattered, I'd be in so deep that I'd either have to kill myself or become like you. Yes, I understand."

Mendoza's shrug did not move the tommygun barrel aimed at Havig's stomach. "Well? What do you expect? We use what human material we can find. These boys are no worse than the Crusaders— than man in most of history. Are they, Jack? Be honest."

"They are. Because they have the power to come into any time, any place, do anything, and never fear revenge. How do they spend their holidays, I wonder? I imagine the taste for giving pain and death must grow with practice."

"Listen—"

"And Wallis, his whole damned outfit, doesn't even try to control them!"

"Havig, you talk too much. Get out before I arrest you."

"They keep the few like me from knowing, till we've accepted that crock—about how the mission of the Eyrie is too important for us to waste lifespan on enforcing common humanity. Right?"

Mendoza spat. "Hokay, boy, you said plenty and then some. You're under arrest. You'll be escorted uptime and the Sachem will judge your case. Be good and maybe you'll get off easy."

For a moment it was tableau, very quiet save for Xenia's sobs where she cradled the head of her half-conscious mother. Her eyes never left Havig. Nor did those of the household he had known—hopeful young Bardas, gifted Ioannes, old Maria who had been Xenia's nurse, all and all of the dozen—nor those of Mendoza and Moriarty. Hans's kept flickering in animal wariness, Coenraad's in thwarted lechery.

Havig reached his decision, made his plan, noted the position of each man and weapon, in that single hard-held breath.

Himself appeared, sixfold throughout the room. The firefight exploded.

He cast himself back in time a few minutes while sidestepping, sped uptime while he drew his pistol, emerged by Hans. The gun cracked and kicked. The *Landsknecht's* head geysered into pieces. Havig went back again, and across the chamber.

Afterward he scarcely remembered what happened. The battle was too short, too ferocious. Others could do what he did, against him. Coenraad wasn't quick-witted enough, and died. Moriarty vanished from Havig's sight as the latter arrived. Mendoza's gun blasted, and Havig sprang futureward barely in time. Traveling, he saw Moriarty's shadow form appear. He backtracked, was there at the instant, shot the man and twisted off into time, away from Mendoza.

Then the Mexican wasn't present. Havig slipped pastward—a night when the family slept at peace under God—to gasp air and let the sweat stop spurting, the limbs stop shaking. At last he felt able to return and scan the period of combat in detail. Beyond a certain point, not long after the beginning, he found no Mendoza.

The fellow must have gone way uptime, maybe to the far side of the Judgment, for help.

This meant fast action was vital. Havig's friends could not time-hop. The enemy would be, no, were handicapped by the difficulty of reaching a precise goal without a chronolog. But they could cast around, and wouldn't miss by much.

Havig rejoined Earth at the earliest possible second. Moriarty threshed about, yammering anguish, like those men outside whom he, perhaps, had been the one to shoot. Never mind him. The Byzantines huddled together. Bardas lay dead, two others wounded in crossfire.

"I come to save you," Havig said into the reek of powder and fear, into their uncomprehending glazed-eye shock. He drew the sign of the cross, right to left in Orthodox style. "In the name of the Father, and of the Son, and of the Holy Ghost. In the name of the Virgin Mary and every saint. Come with me, at once, or you die."

He helped Xenia rise. She clung to him, face buried against his breast, fingers clutching. He rumpled the long black hair and remembered how he a child would grasp at a father bound for death. Across her shoulder he snapped: "Ioannes, Nicephorus, you look in the best shape. Carry your lady Anna. The rest of you who're hale, give aid to the hurt." English broke from him: "Goddammit, we've got to get out of here!"

Numbly, they obeyed. In the street he stopped to don the surcoat off a dead Crusader. His pack he gave a man to carry. From another corpse he took a sword. He didn't waste time unbuckling the scabbard belt. That weapon indicated a high enough rank that his party wasn't likely to meet interference.

Several streets down, dizziness overwhelmed him. He must sit, head between knees, till strength returned. Xenia knelt before him, hands anxiously trying to help. "Hauk," went her raw whisper. "Wh-wh-what's wrong, dearest Hauk?"

"We're safe," he finally said.

From the immediate threat, at least. He didn't suppose the Eyrie would spend man-years scouring Constantinople for him and these, once they had vanished into the multitudes. But he had still to safeguard their tomorrows, and his own. The knowledge gave him a glacial kind of resolution. He rose and led them further on their stumbling way.

"I left them at a certain monastery," he told me (long afterward on his own world line). "The place was jammed with refugees, but I foreknew it'd escape attention. In the course of the next several days, local time, I made better arrangements. A simple task—" he grimaced—"distasteful but simple, to hijack unidentifiable loot from ordinary Franks. I made presents to that monastery, and to the nunnery where I later took the women. This won favor for the people I'd brought, special favor out of the hordes, because with my donations the monks and nuns could buy bread to feed their poor."

"What about the hordes?" I asked softly.

He covered his face. "What could I do? They were too many."

I gripped his shoulder. "They are always too many, Jack."

He sighed and smiled a little. "Thanks, Doc."

I had exceeded my day's tobacco ration, but the hour was far into night and my nerves required some help. Drawing out my pipe, I made an evil-smelling ceremony of cleaning it. "What'd you do next?"

"Went back to the twentieth century—a different hotel—and slept a lot," he said. "Afterward…well, as for my Byzantines, I could do nothing in their immediate futures. I'd cautioned them against talking, told them to say they'd just fled from a raid. After a 'saint' had rescued them from 'demons,' it was a safe bet they'd obey. But as fail-safe, I did not tell the men where I led the women.

"Further than that, no transportation being available, and me not wanting to do anything which might make them noticeable, my best tactic was to leave them alone. The organized institutions where they were could care for them better than I'd know how.

"Besides, I had to provide for my own survival."

I reamed the pipe with needless force. "Yes, indeed," I said. "What did you do?"

He sipped his drink. While he dared not blur mind or senses, the occasional taste of Scotch was soothing. "I knew the last date on which I had publicly been J. F. Havig," he told me. "At the start of my furlough, in 1965, in conference with a broker of mine. True, there had been later appearances in normal time, like my 1969 trip to Israel, but those were brief. Nineteen sixty-five marked the end of what real continuity there was in my official persona.—Everything was in order, the broker told me. I didn't see how so complicated a financial and identity setup could be faked. Thus my existence was safe up to that point."

"The Eyrie couldn't strike at you earlier? Why not?"

"Oh, they could appear at a previous moment and lay a trap of some kind, no doubt. But it couldn't be sprung till later. On the whole, I doubted they'd even try that. None of them really know their way around the twentieth century, its upper echelons in particular, as I do."

"You mean, an event once recorded is unalterable?"

Now his smile chilled me. "I suspect all events are," he said. "I do know a traveler cannot generate contradictions. I've tried. So have others, including Wallis himself. Let me give you a single, personal example. Once in young manhood I thought I'd go back downtime, break my 'uncle's' prohibition, reveal to my father what I was and warn him against enlisting."

"And?" I breathed.

"Doc, remember that broken leg of mine you treated?"

"Yes. Wait! That was—"

"Uh-huh. I tripped on an electric cord somebody had carelessly left at the top of some stairs, the personal-time day before I planned to set out.... When I was well and ready to start afresh, I got an urgent call from my trust company and had to argue over assorted tedious details. Returning to Senlac, I found my mother had made her final break with Birkelund and needed my presence. I looked at those two innocent babies he and she had brought into this world, and got the message."

"Does God intervene, do you think?"

"No, no, no. I suppose it's simply a logical impossibility to change the past, same as it's logically impossible for a uniformly colored spot to be both red and green. And every instant in time is the past of infinitely many other instants. That figures.

"The pattern *is*. Our occasional attempts to break it, and our failures, are part of *it*."

"Then we're nothing except puppets?"

"I didn't say that, Doc. In fact, I can't believe we are. Seems to me, our free wills must be a part of the grand design too. But we'd better take care to stay within the area of unknownness, which is where our freedom lies."

"Could this be analogous to, well, drugs?" I wondered. "A man might deliberately, freely take a chemical which grabbed hold of his mind. But then, while its effects lasted, he would not be free."

"Maybe, maybe." Havig stirred in his chair, peered out into night, took another small swallow of whiskey. "Look, we may not have time for these philosophical musings. Wallis's hounds are after me. If not in full cry, surely at any rate alert for any spoor of me. They know something of my biography. They can find out more, and make spot checks if nothing else."

"Is that why you avoided me, these past years of my life?" I asked.

"Yes." Now he laid a comforting hand on me. "While Kate lived— You understand?"

I nodded dumbly.

"What I did," he said, hastening on to dry detail, "was return to that selfsame date of 1965, in New York, the last one I could be reasonably sure of. From there I backtracked, laying a groundwork. It took a while. I had to make sure that what I did would be so hard to trace that Wallis wouldn't assign the necessary man-years to the task. I worked through Swiss banks, several series of dummies, et cetera. The upshot was that John Havig's fortune got widely distributed, in the names of a number of people and corporations who in effect are me. John Havig himself, publicity-shy playboy, explained to his hired financiers that this was because—never mind. A song and dance which sounded enough like a tax-fraud scheme, though actually it wasn't, that they were glad to wash their hands of me and to know nothing important.

"John Havig, you recall, thereupon quietly dropped out of circulation. Since he had no intimates in the twentieth century, apart from his mother and his old hometown doctor, only these would ever miss him or wonder much; and it was easy to drop them an occasional reassuring letter."

"Postcards to me, mainly," I said. "You had me wondering, all right." After a pause: "Where were you?"

"Having covered my tracks as well as might be," he answered, "I went back to Constantinople."

In the burnt-out husk of New Rome, order was presently restored. At first, if nothing else, troops needed water and food, for which labor and some kind of civil government were needed, which meant that the dwellers could no longer be haried like vermin. Later, Baldwin of Flanders, lord over that fragment of the Empire which became his portion and included the city, desired to get more use than that out of his subjects. He was soon captured in war against the Bulgarians and died a prisoner, but the attitude of his brother and successor Henry I was the same. A Latin king could oppress the Greeks, squeeze them, humiliate them, tax them to poverty, dragoon them into his corvées or his armies. But for this he must allow them a measure of security in their work and their lives.

Though Xenia was a guest, the nunnery was strict. She met Havig in a chilly brick-walled gloom, under the disapproving gaze of a sister. Robed in rough brown wool, coifed, veiled, she was forbidden to touch her male visitor, let alone seek his arms, no matter how generous a benefaction he had brought along. But he saw her Ravenna eyes; and the garments could not hide how she had begun to grow and fill out; nor could every tone in her voice be flattened, which brought back to him the birds on countryside days with her and her father—

"Oh, Hauk, darling Hauk!" Shrinking back, drawing the cross, starting to genuflect and hesitating a-tremble: "I...I beg your pardon, your forgiveness, B-b-blessed One."

The old nun frowned and took a step toward them. Havig waved wildly. "No, no, Xenia!" he exclaimed. "I'm as mortal as you are. I swear it. Strange things did happen, that day last year. Maybe I can explain them to you later. Believe me, though, my dear, I've never been anything more than a man."

She wept awhile at that, not in disappointment. "I, I, I'm so g-glad. I mean, you...you'll go to Heaven when you die, but—" But today he was not among her stiff stern Byzantine saints.

"How is your mother?" Havig asked.

He could barely hear: "She...has taken the veil. She begs me to do l-l-likewise." The thin fingers twisted together till nails stood white; the look raised to him was terrified. "Should I? I waited for you—to tell me—"

"Don't get me wrong, Doc," Havig said. "The sisters meant well. Their rule was severe, however, especially considering the unsureness when overlords both temporal and spiritual were Catholic. You can imagine, can't you? She loved her God, and books had always been a main part of her life. But hers was the spirit of classical antiquity, as she dreamed that age had been—I never found the heart to disillusion her. And her upbringing— my influence too, no doubt—had turned her early toward the living world. Even lacking that background, a round of prayer and obedience inside the same cloisters, nothing else till death opened the door—was never for her. The ghastly thing which had struck her did not take away her birthright, which was to be a sun-child."

"What'd you do?" I asked.

"I found an elderly couple who'd take her in. They were poor, but I could help them financially; they were childless, which made them extra glad, extra kind to her; and he, a scribe, was a scholar of sorts. It worked out well."

"You made periodic checkups, of course."

Havig nodded. Gentleness touched his mouth. "I had my own projects going," he said. "Still, during the next year or so of my lifespan, the next three of Xenia's, I went back from time to time to visit her. The times got to be oftener and oftener."

The ship was a trimaran, and huge. From the flying bridge, Havig looked across a sweep of deck, beautifully grained hardwood whereon hatches, cargo booms, donkey engines, sunpower screens, and superstructure made a harmonious whole. There was no brightwork; Maurai civilization, poor in metals, must reserve them for the most basic uses. The cabins were shingled. Bougainvillea and trumpet flower vines rioted over them. At each forepeak stood a carven figure representing one of the Trinity—Tanaroa Creator in the middle, a column of abstract symbols; Lesu Haristi holding his cross to starboard; to port, shark-toothed Nan, for death and the dark side of life.

But they were no barbarians who built and crewed this merchantman. The triple hull was designed for ultimate hydrodynamic efficiency. The three great A-frame masts bore sails, true, but these were of esoteric cut and accompanied by vanes which got their own uses out of the wind; the entire rig was continuously readjusted by small motors, which biological fuel cells powered and a computer directed. The personnel were four kanakas and two wahines, who were not overworked.

Captain Rewi Lohannaso held an engineering degree from the University of Wellantoa in N'Zealann. He spoke several languages, and his Ingliss was not the debased dialect of some Merican tribe, but as rich and precise as Havig's native tongue.

A stocky brown man in sarong and bare feet, he said, slowly for the benefit of his passenger who was trying to master the modern speech: "We kept science after technology's world-machine broke down. Our problem was to find new ways to apply that science, on a planet gutted and poisoned. We've not wholly solved it. But we have come far, and I do believe we will go further."

The ocean rolled indigo, turquoise, aquamarine, and aglitter. Waves rushed, wavelets chuckled. Sunlight fell dazzling on sails and on the wings of an albatross. A pod of whales passed majestically across vision. The wind did not pipe in the ears, at the speed of the ship before it, but lulled, brought salty odors, stroked coolness across bare sun-warmed skins. Down on deck, a young man, off duty, drew icy-sweet notes from a bamboo flute, and a girl danced. Their nude bodies were as goodly to see as a cat or a blooded horse.

"That's why you've done a grand thing, Brother Thomas," Lohannaso said. "They'll jubilate when you arrive." He hesitated. "I did not radio for an aircraft to bring you and your goods to the Federation because the Admiralty might have obliged. And…frankly, dirigibles are faster, but less reliable than ships. Their engines are feeble; the fireproofing anticatalyst for the hydrogen is experimental."

("I think that brought home to me as much as anything did, the truth about Maurai society in its best days," Havig said to me. "They were—will not be back-to-nature cranks. On the contrary, beneath the easygoing affability, they may well be more development-minded than the U.S.A. today. But they won't have the fuel for heavier-than-air craft, anyhow not in their earlier stages; and they won't have the helium for blimps like ours. We squandered so much of everything.")

"Your discovery waited quite a few centuries," Lohannaso went on. "Won't hurt if it waits some extra weeks to get to Wellantoa."

("If I wanted to study the Maurai in depth, to learn what percentage of what Wallis said about them was true and what was lies or blind prejudice, I needed an entrée. Beginning when they first started becoming an important factor in the world, I could follow their history onward. But I had to make that beginning, from scratch. I could pose as a Merican easily enough —among the countless dialects English had split into, mine would pass—but why should they be interested in one more barbarian? And I'd no hope of pretending to be from a semi-civilized community which they had trade relations with.... Well, I hit on an answer." Havig grinned. "Can you guess, Doc? No? Okay. Through a twentieth-century dummy I acquired a mess of radioisotopes, like Carbon 14. I left them where they'd be safe—their decay must be real—and moved uptime. There I became Brother Thomas, from an inland stronghold which had preserved a modicum of learning. I'd discovered this trove and decided the Maurai should have it, so carted it myself to the coast....You see? The main thrust of their research was biological. It must be, both because Earth's ecology was in bad need of help, and because life is *the* sunpower converter. But they had no nuclear reactors to manufacture tracer isotopes wholesale. To them, my 'find' was a godsend.")

"Do you think I'll be accepted as a student?" Havig asked anxiously. "It would mean a lot to my people as well as me. But I'm such an outsider—"

Lohannaso laid an arm around his shoulder in the Maurai manner. "Never you sweat, friend. First, we're a trader folk. We pay for value received, and this value is beyond my guessing. Second, we want to spread knowledge, civilization, as wide as we can. We want allies ourselves, trained hands and brains."

"Do you actually hope to convert the whole of mankind?"

"Belay that! Anyhow, if you mean, Do we hope to make everybody into copies of us? The answer is, No. Mind, I'm not in Parliament or Admiralty, but I follow debates and I read the philosophers. One trouble with the old machine culture was that, by its nature, it did force people to become more and more alike. Not only did this fail in the end—disastrously—but to the extent it succeeded, it was a worse disaster." Lohannaso smote the rail with a mighty fist. "Damnation, Thomas! We *need* all the diversity, all the assorted ways of living and looking and thinking, we can get!"

He laughed and finished: "Inside of limits, true. The pirates have to be cleaned up, that sort of job. But otherwise—Well, this's getting too bloody solemn. Almost noon now. Let me shoot the sun and do my arithmetic, then Terai comes on duty and you and I'll go have lunch. You haven't lived till you've sampled my beer."

("I spent more than a year among the early Maurai," Havig told me. "Being eager to spread the gospel, they gave me exactly the sort of education I needed for my purposes. They were dear, merry people— oh, yes, they had their share of bad guys, and human failings and miseries, but on the whole, the Federation in that century was a happy place to be.

("That wasn't true of the rest of the world, of course. Nor of the past. I'd keep time-skipping to twentieth-century Wellington or Honolulu, and catching planes to Istanbul, and going back to see how Xenia was getting on.

("When at last I felt I'd reached the point of diminishing returns, as far as that particular future milieu was concerned, I came once more to Latin Constantinople. Xenia was eighteen. Shortly afterward, we married.")

Of their life together, in the five years of hers which were granted them, he told me little. Well, I haven't much I care to tell either, of what really mattered between Kate and me.

He did mention some practical problems. They were tripartite: supporting her decently, getting along in the environment to which she was confined, and staying hidden from the Eyrie.

As for the first, his undertaking wasn't quite simple. He couldn't start a business, in a world of guilds, monopolies, complicated regulations, and folk who even in a metropolis—before the printing press, regular mail service, electronic communications—were as gossipy as villagers. It took him considerable research and effort to establish the persona of an agent for a newly formed association of Danish merchant adventurers, more observer and contact man than factor and thus not in competition with the Franks. Finance was the least of his worries; a little gold, carried downtime, went a long way. But he must have a plausible explanation for his money.

As for the second, he thought about moving a good, safe distance off, perhaps to Russia or Western Europe, perhaps to Nicaea where a

Byzantine monarchy held out and would, at last, regain Constantinople. But no, there was little good and no safety. The Tartars were coming, and the Holy Inquisition. Sacked and conquered, this great city nevertheless offered as much as any place outside a hopelessly alien Orient; and here Xenia was among familiar scenes, in touch with friends and her mother. Besides, wherever they might go, they would be marked, she a Levantine who called herself a Roman, he something else. Because of his masquerade, they more or less had to buy a house in Pera, where foreigners customarily lived. But that town lay directly across the Golden Horn, with frequent ferries.

As for the third, he kept a low profile, neither conspicuously active nor conspicuously reclusive. He found a new pseudonym, Jon Andersen, and trained Xenia to use it and to be vague about her own origin. Helpfully, his Catholic acquaintances had no interest in her, beyond wondering why Ser Jon had handicapped himself by marrying a heretical Greek. If he must have her, why not as a concubine?

"How much of the truth did you tell Xenia?" I inquired.

"None." His brows bent. "That hurt, not keeping secrets but lying to her. It wouldn't have been safe for her to know, however, supposing she could've grasped the idea...would it? She was always so open-hearted. Hard enough for her to maintain the deceptions I insisted on, like the new identity I claimed I needed if I was to work for a new outfit. No, she accepted me for what I said I was, and didn't ask about my affairs once she realized that when I was with her I didn't want to think about them. *That* was true."

"But how did you explain her rescue?"

"I said I'd prayed to my patron saint, who'd evidently responded in striking fashion. Her memory of the episode was blurred by horror and bewilderment; she had no trouble believing." He winced. "It hurt me also, to see her light candles and plead like a well-behaved child for the baby of her own that I knew we could never have."

"Hm, apropos religion, did she turn Catholic, or you go through the motions of conversion to Orthodoxy?"

"No. I'd not ask her to change. There has not been a soul less hypocritical than Xenia. To me, it'd have been a minor fib, but I had to stay halfway respectable in the eyes of the Italians, Normans, and French; otherwise we could never have maintained ourselves at a reasonable standard. No, we found us an Eastern priest who'd perform the rite, and a Western bishop who'd grant me dispensation, for, hm, an honorarium. Xenia didn't care. She had principles, but she was tolerant and didn't expect I'd burn in hell, especially if a saint had once aided me. Besides, she was deliriously happy." He smiled. "I was the same, at first and most of the time afterward."

Their house was modest, but piece by piece she furnished and ornamented it with the taste which had been her father's. From its roof you looked across crowded Pera and ships upon the Golden Horn, till Constantinople rose in walls and towers and domes, seeming at this distance nearly untouched. Inland reached countryside where she loved being taken on excursions.

They kept three servants, not many in an age when labor to do was abundant and labor to hire came cheap. Havig got along well with his groom, a raffish Cappadocian married to the cook, and Xenia spoiled their children. Housemaids came and went, themselves taking considerable of the young wife's attention; our machinery today spares us more than physical toil. Xenia did her own gardening, till the patio and a small yard behind the house became a fairyland. Otherwise she occupied herself with needlework, for which she had unusual talent, and the books he kept bringing her, and her devotions, and her superstitions.

"From my viewpoint, the Byzantines were as superstitious as a horse," Havig said. "Magic, divining, guardianship against everything from the Evil Eye to the plague, omens, quack medicines, love philters, you name it, somebody swore by it. Xenia's shibboleth is astrology. Well, what the deuce, that's done no harm—she has the basic common sense to interpret her horoscopes in a reasonable fashion—and we'd go out at night and observe the stars together. You could do that in a city as well as anywhere else, before street lamps and everlasting smog. She is more beautiful by starlight even than daylight. O God, how I must fight myself not to bring her a telescope, just a small one! But it would have been too risky, of course."

"You did a remarkable job of, well, bridging the intellectual gap," I said.

"Nothing remarkable, Doc." His voice, muted, caressed a memory. "She was—is—younger than me, I'd guess by a decade and a half. She's ignorant of a lot that I know. But this works vice versa, remember. She's familiar with the ins and outs of one of the most glorious cosmopolises history will ever see. The people, the folkways, the lore, the buildings, the art, the songs, the books—why, she'd read Greek classics my age never did, that perished in the sack. She'd tell me about them, she'd sit chanting those tremendous lines from Aeschylus or Sophocles, till lightnings ran up and down my backbone; she'd get us both drunk on Sappho, or howling with laughter out of Aristophanes. Knowing what to look for, I often 'happened' to find books in a bazaar...downtime."

He stopped for breath. I waited. "The everyday, too," he concluded. "When you finished up in the office, weren't you interested in what Kate had been doing? And then—" he looked away—"there was us. We were always in love."

She used to sing while she went about her household tasks. Riding past the walls to the stable, he would hear those little minor-key melodies, floating out of a window, suddenly sound very happy.

On the whole, he and she were comparatively asocial. Now and then, to keep up his facade, it was necessary to entertain a Western merchant, or for Havig alone to attend a party given by one. He didn't mind. Most of them weren't bad men for their era, and what they told was interesting. But Xenia had all she could do to conceal her terrified loathing. Fortunately, no one expected her to be a twentieth century-style gracious hostess.

When she stepped from the background and welled and sparkled with life was when Eastern friends came to dinner. Havig got away with that because Jon Andersen, advance man for an extremely distant company, must gather information where he could, hunting crumbs from the tables of Venice and Genoa. He liked those persons himself: scholars, tradesmen, artists, artisans, Xenia's priest, a retired sea captain, and more exotic types, come on diplomacy or business, whom he sought out—Russians, Jews of several origins, an occasional Arab or Turk.

When he must go away, he both welcomed the change and hated the loss of lifespan which might have been shared with Xenia. Fairly frequent absences were needed for him to stay in character. To be sure, a man's office was normally in his house, but Jon Andersen's business would require him not only to go see other men in town, but irregularly to make short journeys by land or sea to various areas.

"Some of that was unavoidable, like accepting an invitation," he told me. "And once in a while, like every man regardless of how thoroughly married, I wanted to drift around on my own for part of a day. But mainly, you realize, I'd go uptime. I didn't —I don't know what good it might do, but I've got this feeling of obligation to uncover the truth. So first I'd project myself to Istanbul, where I kept a false identity with a fat bank account. There/then I'd fly to whatever part of the world was indicated, and head futureward, and continue my study of the Maurai Federation and civilization, its rise, glory, decline, fall, and aftermath."

Twilight stole slow across the island. Beneath its highest hill, land lay darkling save where firefly lanterns glowed among the homes of sea ranchers; but the waters still glimmered. White against a royal blue which arched westward toward Asia, seen through the boughs of a pine which a hundred years of weather had made into a bonsai, Venus gleamed. On the verandah of Carelo Keajimu's house, smoke drifted fragrant from a censer. A bird sat its perch and sang that intricate, haunting repertoire of melodies for which men had created it; yet this bird was no cageling, it had a place in the woods.

The old man murmured: "Aye, we draw to an end. Dying hurts. Nonetheless the forefathers were wise who in their myths made Nan coequal with Lesu. A thing which endured forever would become unendurable. Death opens a way, for peoples as well as for people."

He fell silent where he knelt beside his friend, until at last he said: "What you relate makes me wonder if we did not stamp our sigil too deeply."

("I'd followed his life," Havig told me. "He began as a brilliant young philosopher who went into statecraft. He finished as an elder statesman who withdrew to become a philosopher. Then I decided he could join you, as one of the two normaltime human beings I dared trust with my secret.

("You see, I'm not wise. I can skim the surface of destiny for information; but can I interpret, can I understand? How am I to know what should be done, or what can be done? I've scuttled around through a lot of years; but Carelo Keajimu lived, worked, thought to the depths of ninety unbroken ones. I needed his help.")

"That is," Havig said, "you feel that, well, one element of your culture is too strong, at the expense of too much else, in the next society?"

"From what you have told me, yes." His host spent some minutes in rumination. They did not seem overly long. "Or, rather, do you not have the feeling of a strange dichotomy...uptime, as you say...between two concepts which our Maurai ideal was to keep in balance?"

Science, rationality, planning, control. Myth, the liberated psyche, man an organic part of a nature whose rightness transcends knowledge and wisdom.

"It seems to me, from what you tell, that the present overvaluation of machine technology is a passing rage," Keajimu said. "A reaction, not unjustified. We Maurai grew overbearing. Worse, we grew self-righteous. We made that which had once been good into an idol, and thereby allowed what good was left to rot out of it. In the name of preserving cultural diversity, we tried to freeze whole races into shapes which were at best merely quaint, at worst grotesque and dangerous anachronisms. In the name of preserving ecology, we tried to ban work which could lay a course for the stars. No wonder the Ruwenzorya openly order research on a thermonuclear powerplant! No wonder disaffection at home makes us impotent to stop that!"

Again a quietness, until he continued: "But according to your report, Jack my friend, this is a spasm. Afterward the bulk of mankind will reject scientism, will reject science itself and only keep what ossified technology is needful to maintain the world. They will become ever more inward-turning, contemplative, mystical; the common man will look to the sage for enlightenment, who himself will look into himself. Am I right?"

"I don't know," Havig said. "I have that impression, but nothing more than the impression. Mostly, you realize, I don't understand so much as the languages. One or two I can barely puzzle out, but I've never had the time to spare for gaining anything like fluency. It's taken me years of lifespan to learn what little I have learned about you Maurai. Uptime, they're further removed from me."

"And the paradox is deepened," Keajimu said, "by the contrasting sights you have seen. In the middle of a pastoral landscape, spires which hum and shimmer with enigmatic energies. Noiseless through otherwise empty skies glide enormous ships which seem to be made less of metal than of force. And…the symbols on a statue, in a book, chiseled across a lintel, revealed by the motion of a hand…they are nothing you can comprehend. You cannot imagine where they came from. Am I right?"

"Yes," Havig said miserably. "Carelo, what should I do?"

"I think you are at a stage where the question is, What should I learn?"

"Carelo, I, I'm a single man trying to see a thousand years. I can't! I just, well, feel this increasing doubt…that the Eyrie could possibly bring forth those machine aspects….Then what will?"

Keajimu touched him, a moth-wing gesture. "Be calm. A man can do but little. Enough if that little be right."

"What's right? *Is* the future a tyranny of a few technic masters over a humankind that's turned lofty-minded and passive because this world holds nothing except wretchedness? If that's true, what can be done?"

"As a practical politician, albeit retired," Keajimu said with that sudden dryness which could always startle Havig out of a mood, "I suspect you are overlooking the more grisly possibilities. Plain despotism can be outlived. But we Maurai, in our concentration on biology, may have left a heritage worse than the pain it forestalls."

"What?" Havig tensed on his straw mat.

"Edged metal may chop firewood or living flesh," Keajimu declared. "Explosives may clear away rubble or inconvenient human beings. Drugs—well, I will tell you this is a problem that currently troubles our government in its most secret councils. We have chemicals which do more than soothe or stimulate. Under their influence, the subject comes to believe whatever he is told. In detail. As you do in a dream, supplying every necessary bit of color or sound, happiness or fear, past or future....To what extent dare we administer these potions to our key troublemakers?

"I am almost glad to learn that the hegemony of the Federation will go under before this issue becomes critical. The guilt cannot, therefore, be ours." Keajimu bowed toward Havig. "But you, poor time wanderer, you must think beyond the next century. Come, this evening know peace. Observe the stars tread forth, inhale the incense, hear the songbird, feel the breeze, be one with Earth."

I sat alone over a book in my cottage in Senlac, November 1969. The night outside was brilliantly clear and ringingly cold. Frostflowers grew on my windowpanes.

A Mozart symphony lilted from a record player, and the words of Yeats were on my lap, and a finger or two of Scotch stood on the table by my easy chair, and sometimes a memory crossed my mind and smiled at me. It was a good hour for an old man.

Knuckles thumped the door. I said an uncharitable word, hauled my body up, constructed excuses while I crossed the rug. My temper didn't improve when Fiddlesticks slipped between my ankles and nearly tripped me. I only kept the damn cat because he had been Kate's. A kitten when she died, he was now near his ending—

As I opened the door, winter flowed in around me. The ground beyond was not snow-covered, but it was frozen. Upon it stood a man who shivered in his inadequate topcoat. He was of medium height, slim, blond, sharp-featured. His age was hard to guess, though furrows were deep in his face.

Half a decade without sight of him had not dimmed my memories. "Jack!" I cried. A wave of faintness passed through me.

He entered, shut the door, said in a low and uneven voice, "Doc, you've got to help me. My wife is dying."

# 12

"Chills and fever, chest pain, cough, sticky reddish sputum...yes, sounds like lobar pneumonia," I nodded. "What's scarier is that development of headache, backache, and stiff neck. Could be meningitis setting in."

Seated on the edge of a chair, mouth writhing, Havig implored, "What to do? An antibiotic—"

"Yes, yes. I'm not enthusiastic about prescribing for a patient I'll never see, and letting a layman give the treatment. I would definitely prefer to have her in an oxygen tent."

"I could ferry—" he began, and slumped. "No. A big enough gas container weighs too much."

"Well, she's young," I consoled him. "Probably streptomycin will do the trick." I was on my feet, and patted his stooped back. "Relax, son. You've got time, seeing as how you can return to the instant you left her."

"I'm not sure if I do," he whispered; and this was when he told me everything that had happened.

In the course of it, fear struck me and I blurted my confession. More than a decade back, in conversation with a writer out California way, I had not been able to resist passing on those hints Havig had gotten about the Maurai epoch on his own early trips thence. The culture intrigued me, what tiny bit I knew; I thought this fellow, trained in speculation, might interpret some of the puzzles and paradoxes. Needless to say, the information was presented as sheer playing with ideas. But presented it was, and when he asked my permission to use it in some stories, I'd seen no reason not to agree.

"They were published," I said miserably. "In fact, in one of them he even predicted what you'd discover later, that the Maurai would mount an undercover operation against an underground attempt to build a fusion generator. What if an Eyrie agent gets put on the track?"

"Do you have copies?" Havig demanded.

I did. He skimmed them. A measure of relief eased the lines in his countenance. "I don't think we need worry," he said. "He's changed names and other items; as for the gaps in what you fed him, he's guessed wrong more often than right. If anybody who knows the future should chance to read this, it'll look at most like one of science fiction's occasional close-to-target hits." His laugh rattled. "Which are made on the shotgun principle, remember!…But I doubt anybody will. These stories never had wide circulation. They soon dropped into complete obscurity. Time agents wouldn't try to scan the whole mass of what gets printed. Assuredly, Wallis's kind of agents never would."

After a moment: "In a way, this reassures me. I begin to think I've been over-anxious tonight. Since nothing untoward has happened thus far to you or your relative, it scarcely will. You've doubtless been checked up on, and dismissed as of no particular importance to my adult self. That's a major reason I've let a long time pass since our last meeting, Doc—your safety. This other Anderson—why, I've never met him at all. He's a connection of a connection."

Again a silence until, grimly: "They haven't even tried to strike at me through my mother, or bait a trap with her. I suppose they figure that's too obvious, or too risky in this era they aren't familiar with— or too something-or-other—to be worthwhile. Stay discreet, and you should be okay. But you've got to help me!"

—Night was grizzled with dawn when at last I asked: "Why come to me? Surely your Maurai have more advanced medicine."

"Yeah. Too advanced. Nearly all of it preventive. They consider drugs as first aid. So, to the best of my knowledge, theirs are no better than yours for something like Xenia's case."

I rubbed my chin. The bristles were stiff and made a scratchy noise. "Always did suspect there's a natural limit to chemotherapy," I remarked. "Damn, I'd like to know what they do about virus diseases!"

Havig stirred stiffly. "Well, give me the ampoules and hypodermic and I'll be on my way," he said.

"Easy, easy," I ordered. "Remember, I'm no longer in practice. I don't keep high-powered materials around. We've got to wait till the pharmacy opens—no, you will not hop ahead to that minute! I want to do a bit of thinking and studying. A different antibiotic might be indicated; streptomycin can have side effects which you'd be unable to cope with. Then you need a little teaching. I'll bet you've never made an injection, let alone nursed a convalescent. And first off, we both require a final dose of Scotch and a long snooze."

"The Eyrie—"

"Relax," I said again to the haggard man in whom I could see the despair-shattered boy. "You just got through deciding those bandits have lost interest in me. If they were onto your arrival at this point in time, they'd've been here to collar you already. Correct?"

His head moved heavily up and down. "Yeah. I s'pose."

"I sympathize with your caution, but I do wish you'd consulted me at an earlier stage of your wife's illness."

"Don't I?…At first, seemed like she'd only gotten a bad cold. They're tougher then than we are today. Infants die like flies. Parents don't invest our kind of love in a baby, not till it's past the first year or two. By the same token, though, if you survive babyhood the chances are you'll throw off later sicknesses. Xenia didn't go to bed, in spite of feeling poorly, till overnight—" He could not finish.

"Have you checked her personal future?" I asked.

The sunken eyes sought me while they fought off sleep. The exhausted voice said: "No. I've never dared."

Nor will I ever know how well-founded was his fear of foreseeing when Xenia would die. Did ignorance save his freedom, or merely his illusion of freedom? I know nothing except that he stayed with me for a pair of days, dutifully resting his body and training his hands, until he could minister to his wife. In the end he said good-by, neither of us sure we would come together again; and he drove his rented car to the city airport, and caught his flight to Istanbul, and went pastward with what I had given him, and was captured by the Eyrie men.

It was likewise November in 1213. Havig had chosen that month out of 1969 because he knew it would be inclement, his enemies not likely to keep a stakeout around my cottage. Along the Golden Horn, the weather was less extreme. However, a chill had blown down from Russia, gathering rain as it crossed the Black Sea. For defense, houses had nothing better than charcoal braziers; hypocausts were too expensive for this climate and these straitened times. Xenia's slight body shivered, day after day, until the germs awoke in her lungs.

Havig frequently moved his Istanbul lair across both miles and years. As an extra safety factor, he always kept it on the far side of the strait from his home. Thus he must take a creaky-oared ferry, and walk from the dock up streets nearly deserted. In his left hand hung the chronolog, in his right was clutched a flat case containing the life of his girl. Raindrops spattered out of a lowering grayness, but the mists were what drenched his Frankish cloak, tunic, and trousers, until they clung to his skin and the cold gnawed inward. His footfalls resounded hollow on slickened cobblestones. Gutters gurgled. Dim amidst swirling vapors, he glimpsed himself hurrying down to the waterfront, hooded against the damp, too frantic to notice himself. He would have been absent a quarter hour when he returned to Xenia. Though the time was about three o'clock in the afternoon, already darkness seeped from below.

His door was closed, the shutters were bolted, wan lamplight shone through cracks.

He knocked, expecting the current maid—Eulalia, was that her name?—to lift the latch and grumble him in. She'd be surprised to see him back this soon, but the hell with her.

Hinges creaked. Gloom gaped beyond. A man in Byzantine robe and beard occupied the doorway. The shotgun in his grasp bulked monstrous. '"Do not move, Havig," he said in English. "Do not try to escape. Remember, we hold the woman."

Save for an ikon of the Virgin, their bedroom was decorated in gaiety. Seen by what light trickled in a glazed window, the painted flowers and beasts jeered. It was wrong that a lamb should gambol above Xenia where she lay. She was so small and thin in her nightgown. Skin, drawn tight across the frail bones, was like new-fallen snow dappled with blood. Her mouth was dry, cracked, and gummed. Only the hair, tumbling loose over her bosom, and the huge frightened eyes had luster.

The man in East Roman guise, whom Havig did not know, held his left arm in a practiced grip. Juan Mendoza had the right, and smirked each time he put backward pressure on the elbow joint. He was dressed in Western style, as was Waclaw Krasicki, who stood at the bedside.

"Where are the servants?" Havig asked mechanically.

"We shot them," Mendoza said.

"What—"

"They didn't recognize a gun, so that wouldn't scare them. We couldn't let a squawk warn you. Shut up."

The shock of knowing they were dead, the hope that the children had been spared and that an orphanage might take them in, struck Havig dully, like a blow on flesh injected with painkiller. Xenia's coughing tore him too much.

"Hauk," she croaked, "no, Jon, Jon—" Her hands lifted toward him, strengthless, and his were caught immobile.

Krasicki's broad visage had noticeably aged. Years of his lifespan must have passed, uptime, downtime, everywhen an outrage was to be engineered. He said in frigid satisfaction: "You may be interested to know what a lot of work went on for how long, tracking you down. You've cost us, Havig."

"Why…did…you bother?" the prisoner got out.

"You did not imagine we could leave you alone, did you? Not just that you killed men of ours. You're not an ignorant lout, you're smart and therefore dangerous. I've been giving this job my personal attention."

Havig thought drearily: *What an overestimate of me.*

"We must know what you've been doing," Krasicki continued. "Take my advice and cooperate."

"How did you—?"

"Plenty of detective work. We reasoned, if a Greek family was worth to you what you did, you'd keep in touch with them. You covered your trail well, I admit. But given our limited personnel, and the problems in working here, and everything else we had to do throughout history—you needn't feel too smug about your five-year run. Naturally, when we did close in, we chose this moment for catching you. The whole neighborhood knows your wife is seriously ill. We waited till you went out, expecting you'd soon be back." Krasicki glanced at Xenia. "And cooperative, no?"

She shuddered and barked, as an abandoned dog had barked while her father was slain. Blood colored the mucus she cast up.

"Christ!" Havig screamed. "Let me go! Let me treat her!"

"Who are they, Jon?" she pleaded. "What do they want? Where is your saint?"

"Besides," Mendoza said, "Pat Moriarty was a friend of mine." He applied renewed pressure, barely short of fracturing.

Through the ragged darknesses which pain rolled across him, Havig heard Krasicki: "If you behave, if you come along with us, not making trouble, okay, we'll leave her in peace. I'll even give her a shot from that kit I guess you went to fetch."

"That...isn't...enough....Please, please—"

"It's as much as she'll get. I tell you, we've already wasted whole man-years on your account. Don't make us waste more, and take added risks. Look, would you rather we broke her arms?"

Havig sagged and wept.

Krasicki kept his promise, but his insertion of the needle was clumsy and Xenia shrieked. "It's well, it's well, my darling, everything's well, the saints watch over you," Havig cried from the far side of a chasm which roared. To Krasicki: "Listen, let me say good-by to her, you've got to, I'll do anything you ask if you let me say good-by."

Krasicki shrugged. "Okay, if you're quick."

Mendoza and the other man kept their hold on Havig while he stooped above his girl. "I love you," he told her, not knowing if she really heard him through the fever and terror. The mummy lips that his touched were not those he remembered.

"All right," Krasicki said, "let's go."

Uptime bound, Havig lost awareness of the men on either side of him. They had substance to his senses, like his own body, but only the shadow-flickers in the room were real. He saw her abandoned, reaching and crying; he saw her become still; he saw someone who must have grown worried and broken down the door step in, days later; he saw confusion, and then the chamber empty, and then strangers in it.

So he might have resisted, willed himself to stay in normal time at their first stop for air, an inertness which his captors could not move. But there are ways to erode any will. Better not arrive at the Eyrie crippled alike in body and spirit, ready for whatever might occur to Caleb Wallis. Better keep the capability of revenge.

That thought was vague. The whole of him was drowned in her death. He scarcely noticed how the shadows shifted—the house which had been hers and his torn down for a larger, which caught fire when the Turks took Pera, and was succeeded by building after building filled with faces and faces and faces, until the final incandescence and the drifting radioactive ash—nor their halt among ruins, their flight across the ocean, their further journey to that future where the Sachem waited. In him was nothing except Xenia, who saw him vanish and lay back to die alone, unshriven.

While summer blanketed the Eyrie in heat and brazen light, the tower room where Havig was confined stored cool dimness in its bricks. It was bare save for a washstand, a toilet, a mattress, and two straight chairs. A single window gave upon the castle, the countryside, the peasants at labor for their masters. When you had looked out into yonder sunshine, you were blind for a while.

A wire rope, welded at the ends, stretched five feet from a ring locked around his ankle to a staple in the wall. That sufficed. A time traveler bore along whatever was in direct contact with him, such as clothing. In effect, Havig would have had to carry away the entire keep. He did not try.

"Sit down, do sit down," Caleb Wallis urged.

He had planted his broad bottom in one of the chairs, beyond reach of his prisoner. Black, epauletted uniform, neatly combed gingery whiskers, bare pate were an assertion of lordship over Havig's grimed archaic clothes, stubbly jaws, bloodshot and murk-encircled eyes.

Wallis waved his cigar. "I'm not necessarily mad at you," he said. "In fact, I kind of admire your energy, your cleverness. I'd like to recall them to my side. That's how come I ordered the boys to let you rest before this interview. I hope the chow was good? Do sit down."

Havig obeyed. He had not ceased to feel numb. During the night he had dreamed about Xenia. They were bound somewhere on a great trimaran whose sails turned into wings and lifted them up among stars.

"We're private here," Wallis said. An escort waited beyond the door, which stood thick and shut. "You can talk free."

"Supposing I don't?" Havig replied.

The eyes which confronted him were like bullets. "You will. I'm a patient man, but I don't aim to let you monkey any further with my destiny. You're alive because I think maybe you can give us some compensation for the harm you've done, the trouble you've caused. For instance, you know your way around in the later twentieth century. And you have money there. That could be mighty helpful. It better be."

Havig reached inside his tunic. He thought dully: *How undramatic that a new-made widower, captive and threatened with torture, should be unbathed, and on that account should stink and itch.* He'd remarked once to Xenia that her beloved classical poets left out those touches of animal reality; and she'd shown him passages in Homer, the playwrights, the hymners, oh, any number of them to prove him wrong, her forefinger danced across the lines, and bees hummed among her roses....

"I gather you were keeping a wench in Constantinople, and she fell sick and had to be let go," Wallis said. "Too bad. I sympathize, kind of. Still, you know, lad, in a way you brought it on yourself. And on her." The big bald head swayed. "Yes, you did. I'm not telling you God has punished you. That could be, but nature does give people what they deserve, and it is not fitting for a proper white man to bind himself to a female like that. She was Levantine, you know. Which means mongrel—Armenian, Asiatic, hunky, spig, Jew, probably a touch of nigger—" Again Wallis's cigar moved expansively. "Mind, I've nothing against you boys having your fun," he said with a jovial wink. "No, no. Part of your pay, I guess, sampling damn near anyone you want, when you want her, and no nonsense afterward out of her or anybody else." He scowled. "But you, Jack, you *married* this'n."

Havig tried not to listen. He failed. The voice boomed in on him:

"There's more wrongness in that than meets the eye. It's what I call a symbolic thing to do. You bring yourself down, because a mixed-breed can't possibly be raised to your level. And so you bring down your whole race." The tone harshened. "Don't you understand? It's always been the curse of the white man. Because he is more intelligent and sensitive, he opens himself to those who hate him. They divide him against himself, they feed him lies, they slide their slimy way into control of his own homelands, till he finds he's gotten allied with his natural enemy against his brother. Oh, yes, yes, I've studied your century, Jack. That's when the conspiracy flowered into action, wrecked the world, unlocked the gates for Mong and Maurai....You know what I think is one of the most awful tragedies of all time? When two of the greatest geniuses the white race ever produced, its two possible saviors from the Slav and the Chinaman, were lured into war on different sides. Douglas MacArthur and Adolf Hitler."

Havig knew—an instant later, first with slight surprise, next with a hot satisfaction—that he had spat on the floor and snapped: "If the General ever heard you say that, I wouldn't give this for your life, Wallis! Not that it's worth it anyway."

Surprisingly, or maybe not, he provoked no anger. "You prove exactly what I was talking about." The Sachem's manner verged on sorrow. "Jack, I've got to make you see the plain truth. I know you have sound instincts. They've only been buried under a stack of cunning lies. You've *seen* that nigger empire in the future, and yet you can't see what ought to be done, what must be done, to put mankind back on the right evolutionary road."

Wallis drew upon his cigar till its end glowed beacon-red, exhaled pungent smoke, and added benign-voiced: "Of course, you're not yourself today. You've lost this girl you cared about, and like I told you, I do sympathize." Pause. "However, she'd be long dead by now regardless, wouldn't she?"

He grew utterly intense. "Everybody dies," he said. "Except us. I don't believe we travelers need to. You can be among us. You can live forever."

Havig resisted the wish to reply, "I don't want to, if you're included in the deal." He waited.

"They're bound to find immortality, far off in the world we're building," Wallis said. "I'm convinced. I'll tell you something. This is confidential, but either I can trust you eventually or you die. I've been back to the close of Phase One, more thoroughly than I'd been when I wrote the manual. You remember I'll be old then. Sagging cheeks, rheumy eyes, shaky liver-spotted hands…not pleasant to see yourself old, no, not pleasant." He stiffened. "This trip I learned something new. At the end, I am going to disappear. I will never be seen any more, aside from my one short visit I've already paid to Phase Two. Never. And likewise a number of my chief lieutenants. I didn't get every name of theirs—no use spending lifespan on that—but I wouldn't be bowled over if you turned out to be among them."

Faintly, the words pricked Havig's returning apathy. "What do you suppose will have happened?" he asked.

"Why, the thing I wrote about," Wallis exulted. "The reward. Our work done, we were called to the far future and made young forever. Like unto gods."

In the sky outside, a crow cawed.

The trumpet note died from Wallis's words. "I hope you'll be included, Jack," he said. "I do. You're a go-getter. I don't mind admitting your talk about your experiences on your own hook in Constantinople was what gave Krasicki the idea of our raid. And you did valuable work there, too, before you went crazy. That was our best haul to date. It's given us what we need to expand into the period. Believe me, Caleb Wallis is not ungrateful.

"Sure," he purred, "you were shocked. You came new to the hard necessities of our mission. But what about Hiroshima, hey? What about some poor homesick Hessian lad, sold into service, dying of lead in his belly for the sake of American independence? Come to that, Jack, what about the men, your comrades in arms, who you killed?

"Let's set them against this girl you happened to get infatuated with. Let's chalk off your services to us against the harm you've done. Even-

Steven, right? Okay. You must've been busy in the years that followed. You must've collected a lot of information. How about sharing it? And leading us to your money, signing it over? Earning your way back into our brotherhood?"

Sternness: "Or do you want the hot irons, the pincers, the dental drills, the skilled attentions of professionals you know we got—till what's left of you obliges me in the hope I'll let it die?"

Night entered first the room, then the window. Havig gazed stupidly at the recorder and the supper which had been brought him, until he could no longer see them.

He ought to yield, he thought. Wallis could scarcely be lying about the future of the Eyrie. If you can't lick 'em, join 'em, and hope to be an influence for mercy, in the name of Xenia's timid ghost.

Yet if—for example—Wallis learned about the Maurai psychodrugs, which the Maurai themselves dreaded, and sent men uptime—

Well, Julius Caesar butchered and subjugated to further his political career. In the process he laid the keel of Western civilization, which in its turn gave the world Chartres Cathedral, St. Francis of Assisi, penicillin, Bach, the Bill of Rights, Rembrandt, astronomy, Shakespeare, an end to chattel slavery, Goethe, genetics, Einstein, woman suffrage, Jane Addams, man's footprints on the moon and man's vision turned to the stars…yes, also the nuclear warhead and totalitarianism, the automobile and the Fourth Crusade, but on the whole, on balance, in an aspect of eternity—

Dared he, mere Jack Havig, stand against an entire tomorrow for the sake of a little beloved dust?

Could he? An executioner would be coming to see if he had put something on tape.

He had better keep in mind that Jack Havig counted for no more in eternity than Doukas Manasses, or Xenia, or anybody.

Except: he did not have to give the enemy a free ride. He could make them burn more of their lifespans. For whatever that might be worth.

A hand shook him. He groped his way out of uneasy sleep. The palm clapped onto his mouth. In blackness: "Be quiet, you fool," whispered Leonce.

## 13

A pencil flashlight came to life. Its beam probed until the iron sheered on Havig's ankle. "Ah," she breathed. "That's how they bottle you? Like I reckoned. Hold this." She thrust the tube at him. Dizzy, rocked by his heartbeat, scarcely believing, he could not keep it steady. She said a bad word, snatched it back, took it between her teeth, and crouched over him. A hacksaw began to grate.

"Leonce—my dear, you shouldn't—" he stammered.

She uttered an angry grunt. He swallowed and went silent. Stars glistened in the window.

When the cable parted, leaving him with only the circlet, he tottered erect. She snapped off the light, stuck the tube in her shirt pocket—otherwise, he had glimpsed, she wore jeans and hiking shoes, gun and knife—and grasped him by the upper arms. "Listen," she hissed. "You skip ahead to sunrise. Let 'em bring you breakfast before you return to now. Got me? We want 'em to think you escaped at a later hour. Can you carry it off? If not, you're dead."

"I'll try," he said faintly.

"Good." Her kiss was brief and hard. "Be gone."

Havig moved uptime at a cautious pace. When the window turned gray he emerged, arranged his tether to look uncut to a casual glance, and waited. He had never spent a longer hour.

A commoner guard brought in a tray of food and coffee. "Hello," Havig said inanely.

He got a surly look and a warning: "Eat fast. They want to talk to you soon."

For a sick instant, Havig thought the man would stay and watch. But he retired. After the door had slammed, Havig must sit down for a minute; his knees would not upbear him.

Leonce—He gulped the coffee. Will and strength resurged. He rose to travel back nightward.

The light-gleam alerted him to his moment. As he entered normal time, he heard a hoarse murmur across the room: "— Can you carry it off? If not, you're dead."

"I'll try."

"Good." Pause. "Be gone."

He heard the little rush of air filling a vacuum where his body had been, and knew he had departed. "Here I am," he called low.

"Huh? Ah!" She must see better in the dark than he, because she came directly to him. "All 'kay?"

"Yes. Maybe."

"No chatter," she commanded. "They may decide to check these hours, 'spite of our stunt. Here, hold my hand an' slip downtime. Don't hurry yourself. I know we'll make it. I just don't want 'em to find out how."

Part of the Eyrie's training was in such simultaneous travel. Each felt a resistance if starting to move "faster" or "slower" than the partner, and adjusted the chronokinetic rate accordingly.

A few nights earlier, the chamber was unoccupied, the door unlocked. They walked down shadow stairs, across shadow courtyard, through gates which, in this period of unchallenged reign, were usually left open. At intervals they must emerge for breath, but that could be in the dark. Beyond the lowered drawbridge, Leonce lengthened her stride. Havig wondered why she didn't simply go to a day before the castle existed, until he realized the risk was too great of encountering others in the vicinity. A lot of men went hunting in the primeval forest which once grew here.

Dazed with fatigue and grief, he would do best to follow her lead. She'd gotten him free, hadn't she?

She really had. He needed a while to conceive of that.

They sat in the woods, one summer before Columbus was born. The trees, oak and elm and birch mingled together, were gigantic; their fragrance filled the air, their leaves cast green shadows upon the nearly solid underbrush around them. Somewhere a woodpecker drummed and a bluejay scolded. The fire glowed low which Leonce had built. On an improvised spit roasted a grouse she had brought down out of a thousandfold flock which they startled when they arrived.

"I can never get over it," she said, "what a wonderful world this is before machine man screws things up. I don't think a lot o' the High Years any more. I've been then too often."

Havig, leaned against a bole, had a brief eerie sense of *déjà vu*. The cause came to him: this setting was not unlike that almost a millennium hence, when he and she—He regarded her more closely than hitherto. Mahogany hair in a kind of Dutch bob, suntan faded, the Skula's weasel skull left behind and the big body in boyish garb, she might have come straight from his home era. Her English had lost most of the Glacier accent, too. Of course, she still went armed, and her feline gait and haughty bearing hadn't changed.

"How long for you?" he inquired.

"Since you left me in Paris? 'Bout three years." She frowned at the bird, reached and turned it above the coals.

"I'm sorry. That was a shabby way to treat you. Why did you want to spring me?"

Her scowl deepened. "S'pose you tell me what happened."

"You don't know?" he exclaimed in amazement. "For heaven's sake, if you weren't sure why I was under arrest, how could you be sure I didn't deserve—"

"Talk, will you?"

The story stumbled forth, in bare outline. Now and then, during it, the tilted eyes sought him, but her countenance remained expressionless. At the end she said: "Well, seems my hunch was right. I haven't thrown away much. Was gettin' more an' more puked at that outfit, as I saw how it works."

She might have offered a word for Xenia, he thought, and therefore he matched her brusqueness: "I didn't believe you'd object to a spot of fighting and robbery."

"Not if they're honest, strength 'gainst strength, wits 'gainst wits. But those…jackals…they pick on the helpless. An' for sport more'n for gain." In a kind of leashed savagery, she probed the fowl with her knife point. A drop of fat hit the coals; yellow flame sputtered and flared. " 'Sides, what's the sense o' the whole business? Why *should* we try to fasten machines back on the world? So Cal Wallis can be promoted to God j.g.?"

"When you learned I'd been located and was being held, that touched off the rebellion which had been gathering in you?" Havig asked.

She didn't reply directly. "I went downtime, like you'd guess, found when the room was empty, went uptime to you. First, though, I'd spent some days future o' that, not to seem involved in your escape. Ha, ever'body was runnin' 'round like guillotined chickens! I planted the notion you must've co-opted a traveler while you were in the past." The broad shoulders lifted and dropped. "Well, the hooraw blew over. Evidently it didn't seem worth mentionin' to the earlier Wallis, on his inspection tour. Why admit a failure? His next appearance beyond your vanishment was years ahead, an' nothin' awful had happened meanwhile. You didn't matter. Nor will I, when I never return from my furlough. I s'pose they'll reckon I died in an accident." She chuckled. "I do like sports cars, an' drive like a bat out o' Chicago."

"In spite of, uh, opposing a restoration of machine society?" Havig wondered.

"Well, we can enjoy it while we got it, can't we, whether or not it'll last or ought to?" She observed him steadily, and her tone bleakened. "That's 'bout all we can do, you an' me. Find ourselves some nice hidey-holes, here an' there in space-time. Because we're sure not goin' to upset the Eyrie."

"I'm not certain its victory is predestined," Havig said. "Maybe wishful thinking on my part. After what I've seen, however—" His earnestness helped cover the emptiness in him where Xenia had been. "Leonce, you do wrong to put down science and technology. They can be misused, but so can everything. Nature never has been in perfect balance—there are many more extinct species than live—and primitive man was quite as destructive as modern. He simply took longer to use up his environment. Probably Stone Age hunters exterminated the giant mammals of the Pleistocene. Certainly farmers with sickles and digging sticks wore out what started as the Fertile Crescent. And nearly all mankind died young, from causes that are preventable when you know how.... The Maurai will do more than rebuild the foundation of Earth's life. They'll make the first attempt ever to *create* a balanced environment. And that'll only be possible because they do have the scientific knowledge and means."

"Don't seem like they'll succeed."

"I can't tell. That mysterious farther future…it's got to be studied." Havig rubbed his eyes. "Later, later. Right now I'm too tired. Let me borrow your Bowie after lunch and cut some boughs to sleep on for a week or three."

She moved, then, to come kneel before him and lay one hand on his neck, run fingers of the other through his hair. "Poor Jack," she murmured. "I been kind o' short with you, haven't I? Forgive. Was a strain on me also, this gettin' away an'—Sure, sleep. We have peace. Today we have peace."

"I haven't thanked you for what you did," he said awkwardly. "I'll never be able to thank you."

"You bugbrain!" She cast arms around him. "Why do you think I hauled you out o' there?"

"But—but—Leonce, I've seen my wife die—"

"Sure," she sobbed. "How I…I'd like to go back…an' meet that girl. If she made you happy—Can't be, I know. Well, I'll wait, Jack. As long as needful, I'll wait."

They weren't equipped to stay more than a short while in ancient America. They could have gone uptime, bought gear, ferried it back. But after what they had suffered, no idle idyll was possible for them.

More important was the state of Havig's being. The wound in him healed slowly, but it healed, and left a hard scar: the resolve to make war upon the Eyrie.

He didn't think it was merely a desire for vengeance upon Xenia's murderers. Leonce assumed this, and leagued herself with him because a Glacier woman stood by her man. He admitted that to a degree she was correct. (Is the impulse always evil? It can take the form of exacting justice.) Mainly, he believed that he believed, a brigand gang must be done away with. The ghastlinesses it had already made, and would make, were unchangeable; but could not the sum of that hurt be stopped from mounting, could not the remoter future be spared?

"A thing to puzzle over," he told Leonce, "is that no time travelers seem to be born in the Maurai era or afterward. They might stay incognito, sure, same as the majority of them probably do in earlier history—too frightened or too crafty to reveal their uniqueness. Nevertheless...every single one? Hardly sounds plausible, does it?"

"Did you investigate?" she asked.

They were in a mid-twentieth-century hotel. Kansas City banged and winked around them, early at night. He was avoiding his former resorts until he could be sure that Wallis's men would not discover these. The lamplight glowed soft over Leonce where she sat, knees drawn close to chin, in bed. She wore a translucent peignoir. Otherwise she gave him no sign that she was anything more in her heart than his sisterlike companion. A huntress learns patience, a Skula learns to read souls.

"Yes," he said. "I've told you about Carelo Keajimu. He has connections across the globe. If he can't turn up a traveler, nobody can. And he drew blank."

"What does this mean?"

"I don't know, except—Leonce, we've got to take the risk. We've got to make an expedition uptime of the Maurai."

Again practical problems consumed lifespan.

Think. One epoch does not suddenly and entirely replace another. Every trend is blurred by numberless counter-currents. Thus, Martin Luther was not the first Protestant in the true sense—doctrinal as well as political—of that word. He was simply the first who made it stick. And his success was built on the failures of centuries, Hussites,

Lollards, Albigensians, on and on to the heresies of Christendom's dawn; and those had origins more ancient yet. Likewise, the thermonuclear reactor and associated machines were introduced, and spread widely, while mysticism out of Asia was denying, in millions of minds, that science could answer the questions that mattered.

If you want to study an epoch, in what year do you begin?

You can move through time, but once at your goal, what have you besides your feet for crossing space? Where do you shelter? How do you eat?

It took a number of quick trips futureward to find the start of a plan.

Details are unimportant. On the west coast of thirty-first century North America, a hybrid Ingliss-Maurai-Spanyol had not evolved too far for Havig to grope his way along in it. He took back a grammar, a dictionary, and assorted reading material. By individual concentration and mutual practice, he and Leonce acquired some fluency.

Enough atomic-powered robot-crewed commerce brought enough visitors from overseas that two more obvious foreigners would attract no undue attention. This was the more true because Sancisco was a favorite goal of pilgrimages; there the guru Duago Samito had had his revelation. Nobody believed in miracles. People did believe that, if you stood on the man-sculptured hills and looked down into the chalice which was the Bay, and let yourself become one with heaven and earth and water, you could hope for insight.

Pilgrims needed no credit account in the financial worldmachine. The age was, in its austere fashion, prosperous. A wayside householder could easily spare the food and sleeping room that would earn virtue for him and travelers' tales for his children.

"If you seek the Star Masters—" said the dark, gentle man who housed them one night. "Yes, they keep an outpost nigh. But surely some are in your land."

"We are curious to see if the Star Masters here are like those we know at home," Havig replied. "I have heard they number many kinds."

"Correct. Correct."

"It does not add undue kilometers to our journey."

"You need not walk there. A call will do." Havig's host indicated the holographic communicator which stood in a corner of a room whose proportions were as alien—and as satisfying— to his guests as a Japanese temple would have been to a medieval European or a Gothic church to a Japanese.

"Though I doubt their station is manned at present," he continued. "They do not come often, you know."

"At least we can touch it," Havig said.

The dark man nodded. "Aye. A full-sense savoring...aye, you do well. Go in God, then, and be God, happily."

In the morning, after an hour's chanting and meditation, the family returned to their daily round. Father hand-cultivated his vegetable garden; the reason for that seemed more likely depth-psychological than economic. Mother continued her work upon a paramathematical theorem too esoteric for Havig to grasp. Children immersed themselves in an electronic educational network which might be planetwide and might involve a kind of artificial telepathy. Yet the house was small, unpretentious except for the usual scrimshaw and Oriental sweep of roof, nearly alone in a great tawny hillscape.

Trudging down a dirt road, where dust whoofed around her boots while a many-armed automaton whispered through the sky overhead, Leonce sighed: "You're right. I do not understand these people."

"That could take a lifetime," Havig agreed. "Something new has entered history. It needn't be bad, but it's surely new."

After a space he added: "Has happened before. Could your paleolithic hunter really understand your neolithic farmer? How much alike were a man who lived under the divine right of kings and a man who lived under the welfare state? I don't always follow your mind, Leonce."

"Nor I yours." She caught his hand. "Let's keep tryin'."

"It seems—" Havig said, "I repeat, it seems—these Star Masters occupy the ultra-mechanized, energy-flashing bases and the enormous flying craft and everything else we've glimpsed which contrasts so sharply with the rest of Earth. They come irregularly. Otherwise their outposts lie empty. Does sound like time travelers, hey?"

"But they're kind o', well, good. Aren't they?"

"Therefore they can't be Eyrie? Why not? In origin, anyhow. The grandson of a conquering pirate may be an enlightened king." Havig marshaled his thoughts. "True, the Star Masters act differently from what one would expect. As near as I can make out—remember, I don't follow this modern language any more closely than you do, and besides, there are a million taken-for-granted concepts behind it— as near as I can make out, they come to trade: ideas and knowledge more than material goods. Their influence on Earth is subtle but pervasive. My trips beyond this year suggest their influence will grow, till a new civilization—or post-civilization—has arisen which I cannot fathom."

"Don't the locals describe 'em as bein' sometimes human…an' sometimes not?"

"I have that impression too. Maybe we've garbled a figure of speech."

"You'll make it out," she said.

He glanced at her. The glance lingered. Sunlight lay on her hair and the tiny drops of sweat across her face. He caught the friendly odor of her flesh. The pilgrim's robe molded itself to long limbs. Timeless above a cornfield, a red-winged blackbird whistled.

"We'll see if we can," he said.

She smiled.

Clustered spires and subtly curved domes were deserted when they arrived. An invisible barrier held them off. They moved uptime. When they glimpsed a ship among the shadows, they halted.

At that point, the vessel had made groundfall. The crew were coming down an immaterial ramp. Havig saw men and women in close-fitting garments which sparkled as if with constellations. And he saw shapes which Earth could never have brought forth, not in the age of the dinosaurs nor in the last age when a swollen red sun would burn her barren.

A shellbacked thing which bore claws and nothing identifiable as a head conversed with a man in notes of music. The man was laughing.

Leonce screamed. Havig barely grabbed her before she was gone, fleeing downtime.

"But don't you see?" he told her, over and over. "Don't you realize the marvel of it?"

And at last he got her to seek night. They stood on a high ridge. Uncountable stars gleamed from horizon to zenith to horizon. Often a meteor flashed. The air was cold, their breath smoked wan, she huddled in his embrace. Quietness enclosed them: "the eternal silence of yonder infinite spaces."

"Look up," he said. "Each of those lights is a sun. Did you think ours is the single living planet in the universe?"

She shuddered. "What we saw—"

"What we saw was different. Magnificently different." He searched for words. His whole youth had borne a vision which hers had known only as a legend. The fact that it was not forever lost sang in his blood. "Where else can newness, adventure, rebirth of spirit, where else can they come from except difference? The age beyond the Maurai is not turned inward on itself. No, it's begun to turn further outward than ever men did before!"

"Tell me," she begged. "Help me."

He found himself kissing her. And they sought a place of their own and were one.


But there are no happy endings. There are no endings of any kind. At most, we are given happy moments.

The morning came when Havig awakened beside Leonce. She slept, warm and silky and musky, an arm thrown across his breast. This time his body did not desert her. His thinking did.

"Doc," he was to tell me, his voice harsh with desperation, "I could not stay where we were—in a kind of Renaissance Eden—I couldn't stay there, or anywhere else, and let destiny happen.

"I *believe* the future has taken a hopeful direction. But how can I be sure? Yes, yes, the name is Jack, not Jesus; my responsibility must end somewhere; but exactly where?

"And even if that was a good eon to be alive in, by what route did men arrive there? Maybe you remember, I once gave you my opinion, Napoleon ought to have succeeded in bringing Europe together. This does not mean Hitler ought to have. The chimney stacks of Belsen say different. What about the Eyrie?"

He roused Leonce. She girded herself to fare beside her man.

They might have visited Carelo Keajimu. But he was, in a way, too innocent. Though he lived in a century of disintegration, the Maurai rule had always been mild, had never provoked our organized unpity. Furthermore, he was too prominent, his lifetime too likely to be watched.

It was insignificant me whom Jack Havig and Leonce of Wahorn sought out.

# 14

April 12, 1970. Where I dwelt that was a day of new-springing greenness wet from the night's rain, clouds scudding white before a wind which ruffled the puddles in my driveway, earth cool and thick in my fingers as I knelt and planted bulbs of iris.

Gravel scrunched beneath wheels. A car pulled in, to stop beneath a great old chestnut tree which dominated the lawn. I didn't recognize the vehicle and swore a bit while I rose; it's never pleasant getting rid of salesmen. Then they stepped out, and I knew him and guessed who he must be.

"Doc!" Havig ran to hug me. "God, I'm glad to see you!"

I was not vastly surprised. In the months since last he was here, I had been expecting him back if he lived. But at this minute I realized how much I'd fretted about him.

"How's your wife?" I asked.

The joy died out of his face. "She didn't live. I'll tell you about it...later."

"Oh, Jack, I'm sorry—"

"Well, for me it happened a year and a half ago." When he turned to the rangy redhead approaching us, he could again smile. "Doc, Leonce, you've both heard plenty about each other. Now meet."

Like him, she was careless of my muddy handclasp. I found it at first an unsettling encounter. Never before had I seen someone from out of time; Havig didn't quite count. And, while he hadn't told me much concerning her, enough of the otherness had come through in his narrative. She did not think or act or exist remotely like any woman, any human creature, born into my epoch. Did she?

Yet the huntress, tribal councilor, she-shaman, casual lover and unrepentant killer of—how many?—men, wore an ordinary dress and, yes, nylon stockings and high-heeled shoes, carried a purse, smiled with a deftly lipsticked mouth, and said in English not too different from my own: "How do you do, Dr. Anderson? I have looked forward to this pleasure."

"Come on inside," I said weakly. "Let's get washed and, and I'll make a pot of tea."

Leonce tried hard to stay demure, and failed. While Havig talked she kept leaving her chair, prowling to the windows and peering out at my quiet residential street. "Calm down," he told her at length. "We checked uptime, remember? No Eyrie agents."

"We couldn't check every minute," she answered.

"No, but—well, Doc, about a week hence I'll phone you and ask if we had any trouble, and you'll tell me no."

"They could be readin' somethin'," Leonce said.

"Unlikely." Havig's manner was a bit exasperated; obviously they'd been over this ground before. "We're written off. I'm certain of it."

"I s'pose I got nervous habits when I was a girl."

Havig hesitated before he said, "If they are after us, and onto Doc's being our contact, wouldn't they strike through him? Well, they haven't." To me: "Hard to admit I've knowingly exposed you to a hazard. It's why I avoid my mother."

"That's okay, Jack." I attempted a laugh. "Gives me an interesting hobby in my retirement."

"Well you will be all right," he insisted. "I made sure."

Leonce drew a sharp breath. For a time nothing spoke except the soughing in the branches outside. A cloud shadow came and went.

"You mean," I said at last, "you verified I'll live quietly till I die."

He nodded.

"You know the date of that," I said.

He sat unmoving.

"Well, don't tell me," I finished. "Not that I'm scared. However, I'd just as soon keep on enjoying myself in the old-fashioned mortal style. I don't envy you—that you can lose a friend twice."

My teakettle whistled.


"And so," I said after hours had gone by, "you don't propose to stay passive? You mean to do something about the Eyrie?"

"If we can," Havig said low.

Leonce, seated beside him, gripped his arm. "What, though?" she almost cried. "I been uptime myself—quick-like, but the place is bigger'n ever, an' I saw Cal Wallis step from an aircraft —they got robotic factories built by then—an' he was gettin' old but he was there." Fingers crooked into talons. "Nobody'd killed the bastard, not in that whole while."

I tamped my pipe. We had eaten, and sat among my books and pictures, and I'd declared the sun sufficiently near a nonexistent yardarm that whiskey might be poured. But in those two remained no simple enjoyment of a call paid on an old acquaintance, or for her a new one; this had faded, the underlying grief and anger stood forth like stones.

"You have no complete account of the Eyrie's future career," I said.

"Well, we've read Wallis's book and listened to his words," Havig answered. "We don't believe he's lying. His kind of egotist wouldn't, not on such a topic."

"You miss my point." I wagged my pipestem at them. "The question is, Have you personally made a year-by-year inspection?"

"No," Leonce replied. "Originally no reason to, an' now too dangerous." Her gaze steadied on me. She was a bright lass. "You aimin' at somethin', Doctor?"

"Maybe." I scratched a match and got my tobacco lit. The small hearthfire would be a comfort in my hand. "Jack, I've spent a lot of thought on what you told me on your previous visit. That's natural. I have the leisure to think and study and—You've come back in the hope I might have an idea. True?"

He nodded. Beneath his shirt he quivered.

"I have no grand solution to your problems," I warned them. "What I have done is ponder a remark you made: that our freedom lies in the unknown."

"Go on!" Leonce urged. She sat with fists clenched.

"Well," I said between puffs, "your latest account kind of reinforces my notion. That is, Wallis believes his organization, modified but basically the thing he founded, he believes it will be in essential charge of the post-Maurai world. What you've discovered there doesn't make this seem any too plausible, hey? Ergo, somewhere, somewhen is an inconsistency. And...for what happened in between, you do merely have the word of Caleb Wallis, who is vainglorious and was born more than a hundred years ago."

"What's his birth got to do with the matter?" Havig demanded.

"Quite a bit," I said. "Ours has been a bitter century. Hard lessons have been learned which Wallis's generation never needed, never imagined. He may have heard about concepts like operations analysis, but he doesn't use them, they aren't in his marrow."

Havig tensed.

"Your chronolog gadget is an example of twentieth-century thinking," I continued. "By the way, what became of it?"

"The one I had got left in Pera when...when I was captured," he replied. "I imagine whoever acquired the house later threw it out or broke it apart for junk. Or maybe feared it might be magical and heaved it in the Horn. I've had new ones made."

A thrill passed through me, and I began to understand Leonce the huntress a little. "The men who took you, even a fairly sophisticated man like that Krasicki, did not think to bring it along for examination," he said. "Which illustrates my point nicely. Look, Jack, every time traveler hits the bloody nuisance of targeting on a desired moment. To you, it was a matter of course to consider the problem, decide what would solve it—an instrument—and find a company which was able to accept your commission to invent the thing for you."

I exhaled a blue plume. "It never occurred to Wallis," I finished. "To any of his gang. That approach doesn't come natural to them."

Silence descended anew.

"Well," Havig said, "I am the latest-born traveler they found prior to the Judgment."

"Uh-huh," I nodded. "Take advantage of that. You've made a beginning, in your research beyond the Maurai period. It may seem incredible to you that Wallis's people haven't done the same kind of in-depth study. Remember, though, he's from a time when foresight was at a minimum—a time when everybody assumed logging and strip-mining could go on forever. It was the century of Clerk Maxwell, yes—I'm thinking mainly of his work on what we call cybernetics—and Babbage and Peirce and Ricardo and Clausewitz and a slew of other thinkers whom we're still living off of. But the seeds those minds were planting hadn't begun to sprout and flower. Anyhow, like many time travelers, it seems, Wallis didn't stay around to share the experiences of his birth era. No, he had to skite off and become the almighty superman."

"Jack, from the painfully gathered learning of the race, *you* can profit."

Leonce seemed puzzled. Well, my philosophy was new to her too. The man had grown altogether absorbed. "What do you propose?" he asked low.

"Nothing specifically," I answered. "Everything generally. Concentrate more on strategy than tactics. Don't try to campaign by your lone selves against an organization; no, start a better outfit."

"Where are the members coming from?"

"Everywhere and everywhen. Wallis showed a degree of imagination in his recruiting efforts, but his methods were crude, his outlook parochial. For instance, surely more travelers are present that day in Jerusalem. His agents latched onto those who were obvious, and quit. There must be ways to attract the notice of the rest."

"Well...m-m-m...I had been giving thought to that myself." Havig cupped his chin. "Like maybe passing through the streets, singing lines from the Greek mass—"

"And the Latin. You can't afford grudges." I gripped my pipe hard. "Another point. Why must you stay this secretive? Oh, yes, your 'uncle' self was right, as far as he went. A child revealed to be a time traveler would've been in a fairly horrible bind. But you're not a child any longer.

"Moreover, I gather, Wallis considers ordinary persons a lesser breed. He's labeled them 'commoners,' hasn't he? He keeps them in subordinate positions. All he's accomplished by that has been to wall their brains off from him.

"I've done a little quiet sounding out, at places like Holberg College and Berkeley. There *are* good, responsible scholars at Berkeley! I can name you men and women who'll accept the fact of what you are, and respect your confidence, and help you, same as me."

"For why?" Leonce wondered.

Havig sprang from his chair and stormed back and forth across the room as he gave her the blazing answer which had broken upon him: "To open the world, darlya! Our kind can't be born only in the West. That doesn't make sense. China, Japan, India, Africa, America before the white man came—we've got the whole of humanity to draw on! And we—" he stuttered in his eagerness—"we can leave the bad, take the good, find the young and, dammit, bring them up right. My God! Who cares about a wretched gang of bullies uptime? *We* can make the future!"

It was not that simple, of course. In fact, they spent more than ten years of their lifespans in preparing. True, these included their private concerns. When I saw them next (after his one telephone call), briefly in March, they behaved toward each other like any happily long-married couple. Nonetheless, that was a strenuous, perilous decade.

Even more was it a period which demanded the hardest thought and the subtlest realism. The gathering of Havig's host would have used every year that remained in his body, and still been incomplete, had he not gone about it along the lines I suggested. Through me he met those members of think tanks and faculties I had bespoken. After he convinced them, they in turn introduced him to chosen colleagues, until he had an exceedingly high-powered advisory team. (Several have later quit their careers, to go into different work or retirement. It puzzles their associates.) At intervals I heard about their progress. The methods they developed for making contact—through much of the history of much of the world—would fill a book. Most failed; but enough succeeded.

For example, a searcher looked around, inquired discreetly around, after people who seemed to have whatever kind of unusualness was logical for a traveler residing in the given milieu. A shaman, village witch, local monk with a record of helping those who appealed to him or her by especially practical miracles. A peasant who flourished because somehow he never planted or harvested so as to get caught by bad weather. A merchant who made correspondingly lucky investments in ships, when storms and pirates caused heavy attrition. A warrior who was an uncatchable spy or scout. A boy who was said to counsel his father. Once in a while, persons like these would turn out to be the real thing....Then there were ways of attracting their heed, such as being a wandering fortuneteller of a peculiar sort....

To the greatest extent possible, the earliest traveler recruits were trained into a cadre of recruiters, who wasted no energy in being uptime overlords. Thus the finding of folk could snowball. Here, too, methods were available beyond the purview of a nineteenth-century American who regarded the twentieth as decadent and every other culture as inferior. There are modern ways to get a new language into a mind fast. There are ancient ways, which the West has neglected, for developing body and senses. Under the lash of wars, revolutions, invasions, and occupations, we have learned how to form, discipline, protect, and use a band of brothers—systematically.

Above everything else, perhaps, was today's concept of working together. I don't mean its totalitarian version, for which Jack Havig had total loathing, or that "togetherness," be it in a corporation or a commune, which he despised. I mean an enlightened pragmatism that rejects self-appointed aristocrats, does not believe received doctrine is necessarily true, stands ready to hear and weigh what anyone has to offer, and maintains well-developed channels to carry all ideas to the leadership and back again.

Our age will go down in fire. But it will leave gifts for which a later mankind will be grateful.

Now finding time travelers was a barebones beginning. They had to be organized. How? Why should they want to leave home, accept restrictions, put their lives on the line? What would keep them when they grew tired or bored or fearful or lonesome for remembered loves?

The hope of fellowship with their own kind would draw many, of course. Havig could gain by that, as Wallis had done. It was insufficient, though. Wallis had a variety of further appeals. Given the resources of his group, a man saw the world brought in reach and hardly a limit put on atavistic forms of self-indulgence. To the intelligent, Wallis offered power, grandeur, a chance—a duty, if you let yourself be convinced, which is gruesomely easy to do—to become part of destiny.

Then there were those who wanted to learn, or be at the highest moments of mankind's achievement, or simply and honorably enjoy adventuring. To them Havig could promise a better deal.

But this would still not give motive to wage war on the Eyrie. Monstrous it might be, the average traveler would concede; yet most governments, most institutions have in their own ways been monstrous. What threat was the Sachem?

"Setting up indoctrination courses—" Havig sighed to me. "A nasty word, that, isn't it? Suggests browbeating and incessant propaganda. But honest, we just want to explain. We try to make the facts clear, so our recruits can see for themselves how the Eyrie is by its nature unable to leave them be. It's not easy. You got any ideas on how to show a samurai of the Kamakura Period that the will of anybody to rule the world, anybody whatsoever, is a direct menace to him? I'm here mainly to see what my anthropologists and semanticists have come up with. Meanwhile, well, okay, we've got other pitches too, like primitive loyalty to chief and comrades, or the fun of a good scrap, or...well, yes, the chance to get rich, in permissible ways. And, for the few, a particular dream—"

At that, I envied him the challenge of his task. Imagine: finding, and afterward forging mutuality between a Confucian teacher, a boomerang-wielding kangaroo hunter, a Polish schoolboy, a medieval Mesopotamian peasant, a West African ironsmith, a Mexican vaquero, an Eskimo girl....The very effort to assemble that kaleidoscope may have been his greatest strength. Such people did not need to learn much about the Eyrie before they realized that, for most of them as time travelers, Havig's was the only game in town.

They got this preliminary training in scattered places and eras.

Afterward they were screened for trustworthiness; the means were a weird and wonderful potpourri. The dubious cases—a minor percentage—were brought to their home locations, guided to their home years, paid off, and bidden farewell. They had not received enough information about the enemy to contact it; generally they lived thousands of miles away.

The majority were led to the main base, for further training and for the work of building it and its strength.

This was near where the Eyrie would be, but immensely far downtime, in the middle Pleistocene. That precaution created problems of its own. The temporal passage was lengthy for the traveler, requiring special equipment as well as intermediate resting places. Caches must be established en route, and everything ferried piece by piece, stage by slow stage. But the security was worth this, as was the stronghold itself. It stood on a wooded hill, and through the valley below ran a mighty river which Leonce told me shone in the sunlight like bronze.

The search methods had discovered members of both sexes in roughly equal numbers. Thus a community developed—kept childless, except for its youngest members, nevertheless a community which found an identity, laws and precedences and ceremonies and stories and mysteries, in a mere few years, and was bound together by its squabbles as well as its loves. And this was Havig's real triumph. The Sachem had created an army; the man sworn to cast him down created a tribe.

I heard these things when Havig and Leonce paid me that March visit. They were then in the midst of the work. Not till All Hallows' Eve did I learn the next part of their story.

**15**

The shadows which were time reeled past. They had form and color, weight and distances, only when one emerged for food or sleep or a hurried gulp of air. Season after season blew across the hills; glaciers from the north ground heights to plains and withdrew in a fury of snowstorms, leaving lakes where mastodon drank; the lakes thickened to swamps and finally to soil on whose grass fed horses and camels, whose treetops were grazed by giant sloths, until the glaciers returned; mild weather renewed saw those earlier beasts no more, but instead herds of bison which darkened the prairie and filled it with an earthquake drumroll of hoofs; the pioneers entered, coppery-skinned men who wielded flint-tipped spears; again was a Great Winter, again a Great Springtime, and now the hunters had bows, and in this cycle forest claimed the moraines, first willow and larch and scrub oak, later an endless cathedral magnificence—and suddenly that was gone, in a blink, the conquerors were there, grubbing out a million stumps which the axes had left, plowing and sowing, reaping and threshing, laying down trails of iron from which at night could be heard a rush and a longdrawn wail strangely like mastodon passing by.

Havig's group stopped for a last rest in the house of a young farmer who was no traveler but could be trusted. They needed it for a depot, too. It would have been impossible to go this far through time on this point of Earth's surface without miniature oxygen tanks. Otherwise, they'd more than once have had to stop for air when the country lay drowned, or been unable to because they were under a mile of ice. Those were strong barriers which guarded the secret of their main base from the Eyrie.

The equipment absorbed most of their mass-carrying ability. Here was a chance to get weapons.

Lantern light glowed mellow on an oilcloth-covered kitchen table, polished iron and copper, stove where wood crackled to keep warm a giant pot of coffee. Though the nearest neighbors were half an hour's horseback ride straight across the fields, and screened off by trees, Olav Torstad must always receive his visitors after dark. At that, he was considered odd for the occasional midnight gleam in his windows. But he was otherwise a steady fellow; most likely, the neighbors decided, now and then a bachelor would have trouble sleeping.

"You're already fixing to go again?" he asked.

"Yes," Havig said. "We've ground to cover before dawn, remember."

Torstad stared at Leonce. "Sure don't seem right, a lady bound for war."

"Where else but by her man?" she retorted. With a grin: "Jack couldn't talk me out of it either. Spare your breath."

"Well, different times, different ways," Torstad said, "but I'm glad I was born in 1850." In haste: "Not that I don't appreciate everything you've done for me."

"You've done more for us," Havig answered. "We grubstaked you to this place strictly because we needed something of the kind close to where the Eyrie will be. You assumed the ongoing risk, and the burden of keeping things hidden, and— No matter. Tonight it ends." He constructed a smile. "You can get rid of what stuff we leave behind, marry that girl you're engaged to, and live the rest of your days at peace."

For a few seconds, behind Torstad's eyes, something rattled its chains. "At peace?" Abruptly: "You will come back, won't you? Tell me what happened? Please!"

"If we win," Havig said, and thought how many such promises he had left, how many more his followers must have left, across the breadth and throughout the duration of the spacetime they had roved. He jumped from his chair. "Come on, let's get the military gear for our men. If you'll hitch up a team, we'd like a wagon ride to the site. Let's move!"

Others were moving. They are. They will be.

It was no enormous host; it totaled perhaps three thousand. Some two-thirds were women, the very young, the old, the handicapped: time porters, nurses, whatever kind of noncombatants were required. But this was still too many to gather at one intermediate station, making rumors and traces which an enemy might come upon. Simply bringing them all to America had been an endlessly complex problem in logistics and secrecy.

Beneath huge trees, in a year before Columbus, some took a deer path. The Dakotan who guided them would have become the next medicine man of his tribe, had a patient wanderer not found him. The chronolog he carried, like other leaders elsewhere and elsewhen, would identify an exact place before he set it for an equally precise instant.

Once during the eighteenth century, certain *coureurs de bois* made rendezvous and struck off into the wilderness.

Not quite a hundred years after, the captain of a group explained to what few white people he met that the government in Washington wished a detailed survey prior to establishing a territory.

Later it became common if unofficial knowledge that you saw Negroes hereabouts—briefly—because this was a station on the Underground Railway.

In the 1920's one did not question furtive movements and gatherings. It was common if unofficial knowledge that this was a favorite route for importers of Canadian whiskey.

Later an occasional bus marked CHARTERED passed through the area, setting off passengers and baggage in the middle of the night, then proceeding with its sign changed to NOT IN SERVICE.

Toward the close of the century, a jumbo jet lumbered aloft. The motley lot of humans aboard drew no special attention. "International

Friendship Tours" were an almost everyday thing, as private organizations and subdivisions of practically every government snatched at any imaginable means to help halt the dream-dance down to catastrophe.

Well afterward, a fair-sized band of horsemen trotted through the region. Their faces and accouterments said they were Mong. The invaders never did establish themselves in these parts, so their early scouts were of no importance.

Havig and his half dozen flashed back into normal time.

His chronolog had winked red an hour before sunrise, on New Year's Day in the one hundred and seventy-seventh year of the Eyrie's continuous existence. The sky loomed darkling to the west, where stars and planets stood yet aglow, but icegray in the east. Shadowless light brought forth every brick of walls and keep and towers; it glimmered off window glass and whitened frost upon courtyard paving. Enormous stillness enclosed the world, as if all sound had frozen in that cold which bit lungs and smoked from nostrils.

This band had rehearsed what they must do often enough. Nonetheless his glance swept across them, these his troopers chosen for the heart of the mission.

They were dressed alike, in drab-green parkas, padded trousers tucked into leather boots, helmets and weapons and equipment-loaded belts. He knew their faces better, their very gaits, after lifespan years of comradeship: Leonce, ablaze with eagerness, a stray ruddy lock crossing the brow he had kissed; Chao, Indhlovu, Gutierrez, Bielawski, Maatuk ibn Nahal. For a pulsebeat their hands remained clasped together. Then they let go. He set down his chronolog. They readied their guns ere the sentries at the battlements should spy them and cry out.

The odds favored surprise. The hinterland was firmly controlled, had been for long years, would be for longer. Had not the Sachem verified this on his journeys to his future selves? More and more the Eyrie prospered, not alone in wealth but in recruits to serve the great purpose. So one could be at ease during a holiday. As many agents as possible took their furloughs in winter, to escape its gloom and cold. But the Sachem was always present for a New Year, whose eve began with ceremonies and speeches, ended with revelry. Who could blame a guard if, in the bitterness before dawn, eyes bleared and lids drooped?

"Okay," Havig said, and: "I love you, Leonce," he whispered. Her lips winged across his. The band loped to the door of that tower wherein dwelt Caleb Wallis.

It was immovable. The woman cursed: "—Oktai's tail, I didn' 'spec'—" Maatuk's .45 blasted out the lock. The noise smote eardrums and rang between the sleeping walls. A thought flashed through Havig. *No combat operation goes perfectly. My studies told me, always allow a margin—*

But this was the one part of the whole thing where slippage could most readily throw him off the cliff.

He led their way inside. Behind them, he heard a shout. Was it more puzzled than alarmed, or did he delude himself? Never mind. In the entryroom, up the stairs!

Soles clattered on stone. The impact jarred through Havig's shins, clear to his teeth. Four were at his back, leaping along a dusky skyward spiral. Gutierrez and Bielawski had taken station below, to guard main door and elevator exit. Indhlovu and Chao peeled off on the second and third levels, to capture the apartments of a secretary—Havig didn't know who he currently was—and Austin Caldwell. And here, next landing, brass-bound, here bulked the portal to Wallis.

That wasn't secured. Nobody dared enter uninvited, unless they came armed to bring this whole creation down. Havig flung the door wide.

Again he knew wainscoting, furriness, heavy desk and chairs, photographs of masters and mother. The air lay hot and damp. Frost blinded windowpanes, making twilight within. Maatuk whirled about to keep the entrance. Havig and Leonce burst on into the suite beyond.

Wallis surged from a canopied double bed. Havig was flickeringly shocked at how the past several lifespan years had bitten the man. He was quite gray. The face was less red than netted in broken veinlets, and sagged beneath its weight. Horrible, somehow, because of being funny to see, was his nightshirt. He groped for a pistol on an end table.

"Ya-a-a-ah!" Leonce screamed, and launched herself in a flying leap.

Wallis vanished from sight. Likewise did she, her fingers upon him. They reappeared, rolling over and over across the floor, wrestling, he unable to flee through time while she gripped him and set her will to stay in the now. Their breath rasped through the shrieks of some commoner girl behind the bed draperies. Havig circled about, in search of a way to help. The grapplers were well matched, and desperate. He saw no opening which wasn't gone before he could strike.

Gunfire raged in the anteroom.

Havig pelted to the inner door, flattened himself, peered around the jamb. Maatuk sprawled moveless. Above him Austin Caldwell swayed, dripped blood, wheezed air through torn lungs, while his revolver wavered in search of more foemen. The old Indian fighter must have gotten the drop on Chao, or taken a couple of bullets and slain him anyway, as Maatuk had then been slain—

"You're covered! Surrender!" Havig called.

"Go...to...hell...traitor's hell...." The Colt roared anew.

Across years Havig remembered many kindnesses and much grim swallowing of pain at what had seemed to be horrors inescapable in the service of the Sachem. He recalled his own followers, and Xenia. He slipped a minute uptime while he stepped into the doorway, emerged, and fired. His bullet clove air and shattered the glass on Charlemagne's photograph. Caldwell had crumpled.

Explosions racketed down in the yard, throughout keep and ancillary buildings. Havig hastened back to Leonce. She had gotten legs around Wallis's lower body and thumbs on his carotid arteries. He beat her about the shoulders, but she lowered her head and hung on. His blows turned feeble. They stopped.

"Make him fast," she panted. "Quick."

From a pocket Havig drew the set of manacles and chain which were standard equipment for every person of his. Squatting, he linked Wallis to the bedstead.

"He's not going anywhere," he said. "Unless somebody comes to release him. You stand guard against that."

She bridled. "An' miss the fun?"

"That's an order!" he snapped. She gave him a mutinous look but obeyed. Their whole plan turned on this prisoner. "I'll see about getting somebody to spell you, soon's may be," he said, adding: *When the battle's over.* He left. The concubine had fled, he noticed, and wondered briefly whether she was bereaved or relieved.

On the next level a balcony overlooked the courtyard. Here the Sachem delivered his speeches. Havig stepped forth, into waxing bleak light, and gazed across chaos. Fights ramped between men and knots of men; wounded stirred and groaned, the slain looked shrunken where they lay. Yells and weaponcracks insulted the sky.

There didn't seem to be a pattern to anything which happened, only ugliness. He unshipped a pair of binoculars and studied the scene more closely. They let him identify an occasional combatant. Or corpse...yes, Juan Mendoza yonder, and, O Christ, Jerry Jennings, whom he'd hoped could be saved—

A new squadron of his army blinked into normal time and deployed. And suddenly parachutes bloomed overhead, as those who had leaped out of a twentieth-century airplane, each with his chronolog, entered this day.

The confusion was more in seeming than truth. From the start, Wallis's on-duty garrison, most of them commoners, was nearly matched in numbers by a group of their traveler associates—who had been here for years and had quietly avoided drinking themselves befuddled last night. The fifth column was invented long before Havig was born; but his generation saw the unmerciful peak of its development and use.

Given it, and information carried forth by its members, and that precise timing which the chronolog made possible, and plans hammered out by a team which included professional soldiers, tested and rehearsed over and over on a mockup of the Eyrie itself...given this, Havig's victory was inevitable.

What counted was to minimize the number of agents who, seeing their disaster, would escape before they could be killed or secured. Of secondary importance in theory, but equal in Havig's breast, was to minimize casualties. On both sides.

He let the binoculars dangle loose, took a walkie-talkie radio off his shoulder, and began calling his squadron leaders.

"Between surprise and efficiency," he told me, "we didn't lose many who time-hopped. Some of those we collared 'later.' Knowing from the registers who they were, we could make fairly good guesses at where-when they'd head for. It wouldn't be a random flight, you see. A man would have to seek a milieu where he might survive by himself. That didn't give too wide a choice."

"You didn't net the entire lot?" I fretted.

"No, not quite. We could scarcely hope for that."

"I should think even one, prowling loose, is too many. He can slip back uptime, though pastward of your attack, and warn—"

"That never worried me, Doc. I knew nobody ever has, therefore nobody ever will. Not that that can't be explained in ordinary human terms, quite apart from physics or metaphysics.

"Look, these were none of them supermen. In fact, they were either weaklings who'd been assigned civilian-type jobs, or warriors as ignorant and superstitious as brutal. Aside from what specialized training fitted them for Wallis's purposes, he'd never tried to get them properly educated. If nothing else, that might have led to questioning of his righteousness and infallibility.

"Therefore, those who did escape had their morale pretty well shattered. Their main concern must be to stay hidden from us. And if they thought about the possibility of returning, they'd realize that we'd have agents of our own planted throughout the period of Wallis's reign, just a few but enough to keep a lookout for them and hustle them away before any warning could be delivered." Havig chuckled. "I was surprised myself, when first I learned who some of those people would be. Reuel Orrick, the old carnival charlatan…Boris, the monk who went to Jerusalem…"

He paused for a drink of my Scotch. "No," he finished, "we simply didn't want bandits loose who're able to skip clear of their crimes. And I think—I dare hope—that never happened. How can, say, a, condottiere, penniless, educationless, entirely alone, how can he get along in any era of white America or make his way to Europe? No, really, his best bet is to seek out the Indians. And among them he can do better as a medicine man than a robber. He might actually end his days a useful member of the tribe! That's a single example, of course, but I imagine you get the general idea."

"Regardin' the future," Leonce said, her tone tiger-soft, "we hold that. The Eyrie for the years it has left; the Phase Two complex till it's no longer needed—an' *we* built it. We've learned from our campaign. Nobody will shake us loose."

"Well, in a military sense," her husband was quick to put in. "It can't be done overnight, but we mean to raise the Eyrie's subjects out of peonage, make them into a free yeomanry. Phase Two never will have subjects: instead, nontraveler members of our society. And— goes without saying—our agents behave themselves. They visit the past for nothing except research and recruitment. When they need an economic base for operations, they make it by trade which gives value for value."

Leonce stroked fingers across his cheek. "Jack comes from a sentimental era," she crooned.

I frowned in my effort to understand. "Wait a minute," I protested. "You had one huge problem with spines and fangs, right after you took the Eyrie. Your prisoners. What about them?"

An old trouble crossed Havig's countenance. "There was no good answer," he said tonelessly. "We couldn't release them, nor those we arrested as they came back from furlough or surprised in their fiefs. We couldn't gun them down. I mean that in a literal sense, we couldn't. Our whole force was drawn from people who had a conscience, able to learn humaneness if they hadn't been brought up with it. Nor did we want to keep anybody chained for life in some secret dungeon."

Leonce grimaced. "Worse'n shootin', that," she said.

"Well," Havig plodded on, "you may remember—I think I told you, and the telling is closer to your present than it is to mine—about those psychodrugs they have in the late Maurai era. Do you recall? My friend Carelo Keajimu will be afraid of them, they give such power. Inject a person, talk to him while he's under the influence, and he'll believe whatever you order him to believe. Absolutely. Not fanatically, but in an 'of course' way that's far more deeply rooted. His own mind will supply rationalizations and false memories to explain contradictions. You see what this is? The ultimate brainwash! So complete that the victim never even guesses there ever was anything else."

I whistled. "Good Lord! You mean you converted those crooks and butcher boys to your side, en masse?"

Havig shuddered. "No. If nothing else, I at least could never have stood such a gang of, of zombies. It'd have been necessary to wipe their entire past lives, and—impractical, anyhow. Keajimu had arranged for several of my bright lads to be trained in psychotechnology, but their job was quite big enough already."

He drew breath, as if gathering courage, before he proceeded: "What we destroyed in our prisoners was their belief in time travel. We brought them to their home milieus—that took a lot of effort by itself, you realize—and treated them. They were told they'd had fever, or demonic possession, or whatever was appropriate; they'd imagined uncanny things which, being totally impossible, must never be mentioned and best never thought about; now they were well and should return to their ordinary lives."

"Our men released them and came back for more."

I pondered. "Well," I said, "I admit finding the idea a bit repulsive myself. But not too much. I've been forced to do certain things, tell certain lies, to patients and—"

Leonce stated: "There were two exceptions, Doc."

"Come with me," the mind molder said. His voice was gentle. Drug-numbed, Caleb Wallis clung to his hand as he left.

Havig remained, often toiling twice around the same clock, till he and his lieutenants had properly underway the immense task of making over the Eyrie. But time flowed, time flowed. At last he had no escape from the moment when the psychotechnician told him he could enter that guarded tower.

Perhaps the most appalling thing was how well the Sachem looked, how jauntily he sat behind his desk in an office from which scars and bloodstains were blotted as if they had never been.

"Well" he greeted. "Good day, my boy, good day! Sit down. No, pour for us first. You know what I like."

Havig obeyed. The small eyes peered shrewdly at him. "Turned out to be a mighty long, tough mission, yours, hey?" Wallis said. "You've aged, you have. I'm sure glad you carried it off, though. Haven't read your full report, but I intend to. Meanwhile, let's catch up with each other." His glass lifted. "To the very good health of us both."

Havig forced down a sip and lowered himself to a chair.

"You've doubtless heard already, mine hasn't been the best," Wallis continued. "Down and out for quite a while. Actual brain fever. Some damn germ from past or future, probably. The sawbones claims germs have evolution like animals. I've about decided we should curtail our explorations, partly on that account, partly to concentrate on building up our power in normal time. What d' you think of that?"

"I think it would be wise, sir," Havig whispered.

"Another reason for pulling in our horns is, we lost a lot of our best men while you were away. Run of bad luck for us. Austin Caldwell, have you heard? And Waclaw Krasicki—Hey, you're white's a ghost! What's wrong? Sure you're okay?"

"Yes, sir....Still tired. I did spend a number of years downtime, and—"

—and it had been Leonce who found Krasicki chained, said, "Xenia," drew her pistol and shot him in the head. But it was Havig who could not make himself be sorry this had happened, until Xenia sought him in his sleep and wept because he did not forgive.

Well. "I'll recover, sir."

"Fine. Fine. We need men like you." Wallis rubbed his brow. For a minute his voice came high and puzzled: "So many people here. So many old gone—or are they? I can't tell. I look from my balcony and see strangers, and think I ought to see, oh, somebody named Juan, somebody named Hans...many, many...but I can't place them. Did I dream them while I lay sick?" He hugged himself, as if winter air had seeped through into the tropical warmth around him. "Often, these days, I feel alone, alone in all space and time—"

Havig mustered briskness: "What you need, sir, if I may suggest it, is an extended vacation. I can recommend places."

"Yes, I think you're right. I do." Wallis gulped from his tumbler and fumbled after a cigar.

"When you return, sir," Havig said, "you ought to work less hard. The foundation has been laid. We're functioning smoothly."

"I know. I know." Wallis lost hold of his match.

"What we need, sir, is not your day-by-day instruction any longer. We have plenty of competent men to handle details. We need more your broad overview, the basic direction you foresee—your genius."

Behind the gray whiskers, Wallis simpered. This time he got his cigar lit.

"I've been talking about it with various officers, and thinking a lot, too," Havig proceeded. "They've discussed the matter with you, they said. Sir, let me add my words to theirs. We believe the ideal would be if a kind of schedule was established for your passage through the future. Of course, it'd include those periods your past self will visit, to let you show him how well everything is going. Otherwise, however—uh—we don't think you should spend more than a minimum of your lifespan in any single continuous set of dates. You're too precious to the grand project."

"Yes. I'd about decided the same for myself." Wallis nodded and nodded. "First, like you say, a real good vacation, to straighten out my thoughts and get this fuzziness out of my head. Then, a…a progress through tomorrow, observing, issuing orders, always bound onward…till at the end, when my work is done—Yes. Yes. Yes."

"God!" I exclaimed, a word as close to prayer as I'd come in fifty skeptical years. "If ever there was a revenge—"

"This wasn't," Havig said through lips drawn taut.

"What, well, what'd it feel like, when he came?"

"I've avoided being on hand for most of that. When I had to be, it was naturally always a festive occasion, and nobody cared if I got drunk. Men who regularly deal with him told me—tell me—one gets used to leading the poor apparition through his Potemkin villages, and off to some sybaritic place downtime for one of the long orgiastic celebrations which use up and shorten his lifespan. They're almost fond of him. They go to great lengths to put on a good show. That eases their thought of the end."

"Huh? Isn't he supposed to vanish in his old age?"

Havig's fist knotted on the arm of his chair. "He did. He will. He'll scream in the night, and his room will be empty. He must have thrown himself far in time, because searchers up and down will find nothing reappearing." Havig tossed off his drink. I saw he needed more, and obliged.

Leonce caressed him. "Aw, don't let it gnaw you, darlya," she murmured. "He's not worth that."

"Mostly I don't," he said, rough-throated. "Rather not discuss the business."

"I, I don't see—" I couldn't help stammering.

The big woman turned to me. She smiled in tenderness for her vulnerable man. What she said was, to her, a remark of no importance: "We been told, now an' then as it's dyin' a brain throws off the effect of that drug an' recalls what was real."

# 16

In 1971, October 31 fell on a Sunday. That meant school next day. The little spooks would come thick and fast to my door if they must be early abed. I laid in ample supplies. When I was a boy, Hallowe'en gave license for limited hell-raising, but I'm glad the custom has softened. Seeing them in their costumes brings back my own children at that same age, and Kate. When my doorbell has rung for the last time, I usually make a fire, settle with my favorite pipe and a mug of hot cider, maybe put some music she liked on the record player, look into the flames and remember. In a quiet way I am happy.

But this day called me forth. It was cool, noisy with wind, sunshine spilling through diamond-clear air, and the trees stood scarlet, yellow, bronze, in enormous tossing rustling masses against blueness where white clouds scudded, and from a V passing high overhead drifted down a trumpet song. I went for a hike.

On the sidewalks of Senlac, leaves capered before me, making sounds like laughter at the householders who tried to rake them into neat piles. The fields outside of town stretched bare and dark and waiting; but flocks of crows still gleaned them, until rising in a whirl of wings and raucous merriment. I left the paved county road for an old dirt one which cars don't use much, thanks be to whatever godling loves us enough to wage his rearguard fight against this kind of Progress. In its roundabout fashion it also brought me to Morgan Woods.

I went through that delirium of color till I reached the creek. There I stood a while on the bridge, watching water gurgle above stones, a squirrel assert his dominion over an oak which must be a century old, branches toss, leaves tear loose; I listened to the rush and skirl and deeper tones around me, felt air slide by like chilly liquid, drew in odors of damp and fulfillment; I didn't think about anything in particular, or contemplate, or meditate, I just was there.

At last my bones and thin flesh reminded me they had a goodly ways to go, and I started home. Tea and scones seemed an excellent idea. Afterward I should write Bill and Judy a letter, make specific proposals about my visit to them this winter in California....

I didn't notice the car parked under the chestnut tree before I was almost upon it. Then my pulse jumped inside me. Could this be—? Not the same machine as before, but of course he always rented—I forgot whatever ache was in my legs and trotted forward.

Jack and Leonce Havig sprang forth to greet me. We embraced, the three of us in a ring. "Welcome, welcome!" I babbled. "Why didn't you call ahead? I'd not've kept you waiting."

"That's okay, Doc," he answered. "We've been sitting and enjoying the scene." He was mute for a second or two. "We're taking in as much of Earth as we're able."

I stepped back and considered him. He was leaner than before, deep furrows beside his mouth and between his eyes, the skin sun-touched but leather-dry, the blond hair fading toward gray. Middle forties, I judged; something like a decade had gone through him in the weeks of mine since last we met....I turned to his wife. Erect, lithe, more full-figured than earlier but carrying it well, she showed the passage of those years less than he did. To be sure, I thought, she was younger. Yet I marked crow's-feet wrinkles and the tiny frost-flecks in that red mane.

"You're done?" I asked, and shivered with something else than the weather. "You beat the Eyrie?"

"We did, we did," Leonce jubilated. Havig merely nodded. A starkness had entered the alloy of him. He kept an arm around her waist, however, and I didn't suppose she could stay happy if at heart he were not too.

"Wonderful!" I cried. "Come on in."

"For tea?" she laughed.

"Lord, no! I had that in mind, but—my dear, this calls for Aalborg akvavit and Carlsberg beer, followed by Glenlivet and—Well, I'll phone Swanson's and have 'em deliver gourmet items and we'll fix the right breed of supper and—How long can you stay?"

"Not very long, I'm afraid," Havig said. "A day or two at most. We've a lot to do in the rest of our lifespans."

Their tale was hours in the telling. Sunset flared gold and hot orange across a greenish western heaven, beyond trees and neighbor roofs, when I had been given the skeleton of it. The wind had dropped to a mumble at my threshold. Though the room was warm enough, I felt we could use a fire and bestirred myself to fill the hearth. But Leonce said, "Let me." Her hands had not lost their woodcraft, and she remained a pleasure to watch. Pleasure it was, also, after the terrible things I had heard, to see how his gaze followed her around.

"Too bad you can't forestall the founding of the Eyrie," I said.

"We can't, and that's that," Havig replied. Slowly: "I'm not sure it is too bad, either. Would a person like me ever have had the…determination? I started out hoping for no more than to meet my fellows. Why should I have wanted to organize them for any special purpose, until—" His voice trailed off.

"Xenia," I murmured. "Yes."

Leonce glanced around at us. "Even Xenia doesn't tip the balance," she said in a gentle tone. "The Crusaders would not've spared her. As was, she got rescued and lived nine years onward." She smiled. "Five of them were with Jack. Oh, she had far less than luck's given me, but she did have that."

I thought how Leonce was outwardly changed less than her man, and inwardly more than I had guessed.

While Havig made no remark, I knew his wound must have healed—scarred over, no doubt, but nonetheless healed—as wounds do in every healthy body and spirit.

"Well," I said, trying to break free of somberness, "you did get your kind together, you did overcome the wrong and establish the right— Well, I hardly expected I'd entertain a king and queen!"

"What?" Havig blinked in surprise. "We aren't."

"Eh? You rule the roost uptime, don't you?"

"No. For a while we did, because somebody had to. But we worked together with the wisest people we could find—not exclusively travelers by any means—to end this as soon as might be, and turn the military society into a free republic…and at last into nothing more than a sort of loose guild."

Fire, springing aloft when she worked the bellows, cast gleams from Leonce's eyes. "Into nothin' less than a dream," she said.

"I don't understand," I told them, as frequently this day.

Havig sought words. "Doc," he said after a bit, "once we've left here, you won't see us again."

I sat quite quietly. Sunset in the windows was giving way to dusk.

Leonce sped to me, cast arms around my shoulders, kissed my cheek. Her hair was fragrant, with a touch of smokiness from the little chuckling flames. "No, Doc," she said. "Not 'cause you'll die soon."

"I don't want—" I began.

"Ay-yeh." Barbarian bluntness spoke. "You said you don't want to know the date on your tombstone. An' we're not about to tell you, either. But damn, I will say you're good for a fair while yet!"

"The thing is," Havig explained in his awkward fashion, "we, Leonce and I, we'll be leaving Earth. I doubt we'll come back."

"What was the good of time travel, ever?" he demanded when we could discourse of fundamentals.

"Why, well, uh—" I floundered.

"To control history? You can't believe a handful of travelers would be able to do that. Wallis believed it, but you can't, I'm certain. Nor do you believe they should."

"Well…history, archeology—science—"

"Agreed, almost, that there's no such thing as too much knowledge.

Except that fate ought not to be foreknown. That's the death of hope. And learning is an esthetic experience—or ecstatic—but if we stop there, aren't we being flat-out selfish? Don't you feel knowledge should be *used*?"

"Depends on the end, Jack."

Leonce, seated beside him, stirred in the yellow glow of a single shaded lamp, the shadow-restless many-hued sparkle from my fireplace. "For us," she said, "the end is goin' to the stars. That's what time travel is good for."

Havig smiled. His manner was restrained, but the same eagerness vibrated: "Why did you imagine we went on to build the—Phase Two complex—what we ourselves call Polaris House? I told you we don't care to rule the world. No, Polaris House is for research and development. Its work will be done when the first ships are ready."

"An' they will be," Leonce lilted. "We've seen."

Passion mounted in Havig. He leaned forward, fingers clenched around the glass he had forgotten he grasped, and said:

"I haven't yet mastered the scientific or engineering details. That's one reason we must go back uptime. Physicists talk about a mathematical equivalence between traveling into the past and flying faster than light. They hope to develop a theory which'll show them a method. Maybe they'll succeed, maybe they won't. I know they won't in Polaris House, but maybe at last, in Earth's distant future or on a planet circling another sun. But it doesn't ultimately matter. A ship can go slower than light if people like us are the crew. You follow me? Her voyage might last centuries. But to us, moving uptime while she moves across space, it's hours or minutes.

"Our children can't do the same. But they'll be there. We'll have started man on his way to infinity."

I stared past him. In the windows, the constellations were hidden by flamelight. "I see," I answered softly. "A tremendous vision for sure."

"A necessary one," Havig replied. "And without us—and thus, in the long view, without our great enemy—the thing would never have been done. The Maurai might've gathered the resources to revive space exploration, at the height of their power. But they did not. Their ban on enormous energy outlays was good at first, yes, vital to saving this planet. At last, though, like most good things, it became a fetish....Undoubtedly the culture which followed them would not have gone to space."

"We did," Leonce exulted. "The Star Masters are our people."

"And a lifebringer to Earth," Havig added. "I mean, a civilization which just sat down and stared at its own inwardness —how soon would it become stagnant, caste-ridden, poor, and nasty? You can't think unless you have something to think about. And this has to come from outside. Doesn't it? The universe is immeasurably larger than any mind."

"I've gathered," I said, my words covering awe, "that that future society welcomes the starfarers."

"Oh, yes, oh, yes. More for their ideas than for material goods. Ideas, arts, experience, insights born on a thousand different worlds, out of a thousand different kinds of being—and Earth gives a fair return. It is well to have those mystics and philosophers. They think and feel, they search out meanings, they ask disturbing questions—" Havig's voice lifted. "I don't know where the communion between them and us will lead. Maybe to a higher state of the soul? I do believe the end will be good, and this is the purpose we time travelers are born for."

Leonce brought us partway back to our bodies. "Mainly," she laughed, "we 'spec' to have a hooraw o' fun. Climb down off your prophetic broomstick, Jack, honeybee, an' pay attention to your drink."

"You two intend, then, to be among the early explorers?" I asked redundantly.

"We've earned the right," she said.

"Uh—pardon me, none of my business, but if your children cannot inherit your gift—"

Wistfulness touched her. "Maybe we'll find a New Earth to raise them on. We're not too old." She regarded her man's sharp-edged profile. "Or maybe we'll wander the universe till we die. That'd be enough."

Silence fell. The clock on my mantel ticked aloud and the wind outside flowed past like a river.

The doorbell pealed. I left my chair to open up for a glimpse of Aquila. Three small figures were on the stoop, a clown, a bear, an astronaut. They held out paper bags. "Trick or treat!" they chanted. "Trick or treat!"

A year has fled since Jack Havig and Leonce of Wahorn bade me farewell. I often think about them. Mostly, of course, dailiness fills my days. But I often find an hour to think about them.

At any moment they may be somewhere on our planet, desperate or triumphant in that saga I already know. But we will not meet. The end of their lives reaches untellably far beyond mine.

Well, so does the life of man. Of Earth and the cosmos.

I wish...I wish many things. That they'd felt free to spend part of their stay in this summer which is past. We could have gone sailing. However, they naturally wanted to see Eleanor, his mother, in one of the few intervals they had been able to make sure were safe, and tell her—what? She has not told me.

I wish they or I had thought to raise a question which has lately haunted me.

How did the race of time travelers come to be?

We supposed, the three of us, that we knew the "why." But we did not ask who, or what, felt the need and responded.

Meaningless accidental mutation? Then curious that none like Havig seem to have been born futureward of the Eyrie—of, anyhow, Polaris House. In truth it would probably not be good to have them and their foreknowledge about, once the purpose has been served of freeing man to roam and discover forever. But who decided this? Who shaped the reality?

I have been reading about recent work in experimental genetics. Apparently a virus can be made to carry genes from one host to the next; and the hosts need not be of the same species. Nature may have done this already, may always be doing it. Quite likely we bear in our cells and bequeath to our children bits of heritage from animals which were never among our forebears. That is well, if true. I am glad to think we may be so close to the whole living world.

But could a virus have been made which carried a very strange thing; and could it have been sown through a chosen part of the past by travelers created anew in some unimaginably remote tomorrow?

I walk beyond town, many of these nights, to stand under the high autumnal stars, look upward and wonder.

# ABOUT THE AUTHORS

### CHAD OLIVER

(1928-1993) was born in Ohio. He received his undergraduate education at the University of Texas, and went on to earn his doctorate in anthropology from the University of California at Los Angeles in 1961. He taught anthropology at the University of Texas for most of his professional life, advancing from Instructor to Assistant and the Associate Chairman. He was Research Anthropologist for the National Science Foundation in East Africa from 1961 to 1962, a time which inspired his novel, *The Shores of Another Sea*. He awards were for his historical novels, the Spur Award given by the Western Writers of America for *The Wolf is My Brother*, and the Western Heritage Society Award for *Broken Eagle*. He is survived by his wife Beje and his daughter and son, Kim and Glen.

### WILSON TUCKER

was born in Illinois in 1914. For much of his life he was a motion picture projectionist, and electrician for 20th Century Fox studios. He was an avid science fiction fan, and later a writer of both science fiction and mystery novels. His awards include the 1970 Hugo Award, and the 1976 John W. Campbell Memorial Award for The Year of the Quiet Sun. He was honored as "Author Emeritus" at the 1996 Nebula Awards ceremonies. "I'm a lifelong two-finger typist," he says, "and have never worked on anything except a manual typewriter, a fact that does not fit me for the 21st century; but I can always survive the failure of electricity."

### POUL ANDERSON

is one of science fiction's most beloved authors, whose "enduring explosion" of works has continued without pause since 1948. Born in Pennsylvania in 1926, he grew up to study physics at the University of Minnesota. A multiple Hugo and Nebula Award winning author, and the recipient of the Tolkein Memorial Award, Anderson has produced a body of work that is unequalled for its variety and quality, including countless short stories, novelettes, novellas, and numerous novels. He is married to fellow author Karen Anderson. They have one daughter and two incomparable grandchildren.

# ABOUT THE EDITORS

## JACK DANN

is the author of the highly praised novels *Starhiker, Junction, The Man Who Melted,* and *The Memory Cathedral.* His short fiction includes many Nebula Award finalists; he has also been a finalist for the World Fantasy Award. He is the editor or coeditor of over twenty anthologies, among them the critically acclaimed *Wandering Stars,* a collection of Jewish science fiction and fantasy, and *In the Field of Fire,* a collection of fantasy fiction about the Vietnam war that was hailed by the *New York Times Book Review.*

## PAMELA SARGENT

is the editor of several anthologies, among them the *Women of Wonder* series, *Afterlives* (edited with Ian Watson), *Bio-Futures,* and three volumes of *Nebula Award Stories.* She has won a Nebula Award, a Locus Award, and been a finalist for the Hugo Award; her *Women of Wonder* series was shortlisted for the Retrospective James Tiptree, Jr. Award. Her novels include *Cloned Lives, Watchstar, The Golden Space, Earthseed, The Alien Upstairs, Venus of Dreams, The Shore of Women, Venus of Shadows,* and *Ruler of the Sky.*

## GEORGE ZEBROWSKI

is the author of *Macrolife, The Omega Point Trilogy,* and *Stranger Suns,* which was a New York Times Notable Book of the Year for 1991; his book *The Sunspacers Trilogy* was recently published by White Wolf. With scientist/author Charles Pellegrino, he is also the author of *The Killing Star.* He has also edited several anthologies, including *Faster Than Light* (with Jack Dann) and the *Synergy* series of original anthologies. His short stories have been nominated for the Nebula Award and the Theodore Sturgeon Memorial Award.

**THE ROAD TO SCIENCE FICTION #3**

**EDITED BY JAMES GUNN**

**ISBN 1-56504-821-0 / WW 11089**

**$14.99 US**

**$19. 99 CAN**

VOLUME 3 carries the story of SF forward from 1940 to 1977, through the Golden Age and the New Wave to their reconciliation. It begins with Heinlein's "All You Zombies" and Isaac Asimov's 1941 "Reason" and ends with Joe Haldeman's 1977 Hugo-award winning story "Tricentennial."

VOLUME 4 explores the literary uses of science fiction through a group of engrossing and skillfully written stories ranging from Richard Matheson's 1950 "Born of Man and Woman" to George Alec Effinger's 1988 "Schrödinger's Kitten."

Don't miss out on the "the best exampled history of science fiction" (*Locus* magazine)

LOOK FOR VOLUME 1 IN 1998!

TALES IN TIME:

AN ANTHOLOGY COMPANION TO THREE IN TIME

EDITED BY PETER CROWTHER
INTRODUCTION BY JOHN CLUTE
SCIENCE FICTION
TRADE PAPERBACK ANTHOLOGY
ISBN 1-56504-989-6
WW 10042
$12.99 US/$17.99 CAN
AVAILABLE APRIL 1997

*Tales in Time*, a companion volume to *Three in Time*, rounds up a fantastic lineup of classic short stories of time travel. Beyond space travel, beyond alien contact, *Tales in Time* brings together some of the most respected writers of our time on a topic that man has yet to conquer. Find out just how far we can go...if only our minds could take us.

Brian W. Aldiss, Ray Bradbury, Frederick Brown, Jonathan Carroll, Arthur C. Clarke, L. Sprague de Camp, Philip K. Dick, Charles de Lint ,Harlan Ellison, Jack Finney, Lisa Goldstein, Garry Kilworth, Michael Moorcock, Lewis Padgett, Spider Robinson, Eric Frank Russell, Rod Serling, Bob Shaw, Robert Silverberg, James Tiptree Jr., and John Wyndham.

Introduction by John Clute, co-editor of the popular *The Encyclopedia of Science Fiction*.

FOR EASY ORDERING CALL 1-800-454-WOLF. VISA/MASTERCARD AND DISCOVER ACCEPTED.

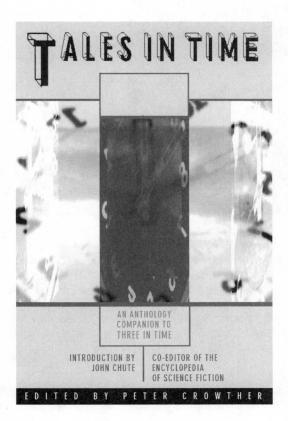

# TALES IN TIME

AN ANTHOLOGY
COMPANION TO
THREE IN TIME

INTRODUCTION BY
JOHN CHUTE

CO-EDITOR OF THE
ENCYCLOPEDIA
OF SCIENCE FICTION

EDITED BY PETER CROWTHER